THE SETTLERS

Set in Palestine from the turn of the century to the Balfour Declaration, *The Settlers* sweeps over a quarter of a century of turbulent events . . . from the strained relationship between the Jews and Arabs, in which the wars of the future were shadowed in the blood feuds and hatreds of an earlier generation, to the vast upheaval of the First World War and the Russian Revolution, to the creation of a Jewish fighting force and the triumphant laying of the foundations for a new land.

"The Israel of today was finally born out of the convulsions, the wars, the betrayals, the valor, the sacrifices, of the men and women who fled Europe to build a new life in the forbidding wastes of the Holy Land. Meyer Levin celebrates those men and women and does them honor. *The Settlers* held me fascinated."

—IRWIN SHAW

"Meyer Levin is one of the two or three best living American writers working in the naturalistic tradition, and *The Settlers* is his *magnum opus*."

—NORMAN MAILER

THE
SETTLERS

by
Meyer Levin

For YITZHAK, *in promise,*
and in remembrance

This low-priced Bantam Book
has been completely reset in a type face
designed for easy reading, and was printed
from new plates. It contains the complete
text of the original hard-cover edition.
NOT ONE WORD HAS BEEN OMITTED.

THE SETTLERS
A Bantam Book/published by arrangement with
Simon and Schuster, Inc.

PRINTING HISTORY
Simon and Schuster edition published April 1972
2nd printing — April 1972
3rd printing — July 1972
Bantam edition / March 1979

ISBN 0-553-12169-3

Published simultaneously in the United States and Canada

Bantam Books are published by Bantam Books, Inc. Its trade-
mark, consisting of the words "Bantam Books" and the por-
trayal of a bantam, is Registered in U.S. Patent and Trademark
Office and in other countries. Marca Registrada. Bantam
Books, Inc., 666 Fifth Avenue, New York, New York 10019.

PRINTED IN THE UNITED STATES OF AMERICA

RETURN

Book I

1

UNDER God's stars, with the younger children lying close on one side and the other side of her, the girls curled against each other on the left and the boys on her right, Feigel truly felt herself like a great mother bird with her brood nestling under her wings.

Not all of them were there. Two had already flown on, nearly a year ago already, to the new-old land to show the way. And of the remainder of her brood not all were nestling here with her. Up ahead by the prow of the ship there was singing, and Feigel could hear her Dvoraleh's voice among the others, mingling with the thrusting voices of the young men.

Perhaps it was good—among so many, a whole group of young men, a girl was safer from some impulse of foolishness that might overwhelm her beneath such a sky of stars on the rocking bed of the sea. For with their revolutionary ideas and their freedom of women, the girls of today were eager to prove themselves in life, even before they felt an ache in their nipples.

Ah, Feigel allowed herself an inward sigh, a rueful yet romantic sigh, over what awaited girls in their lives before them. And perhaps for this new generation life indeed would be different. They felt stronger in themselves. These were strong bold boys, but also with an eager sudden gentleness and bashfulness; these were the upstanding lads from the town of Kostarnitza who had taken up cudgels, even pistols, and driven off the drunken peasants from their pogrom instead of huddling deathly still behind boarded-up windows and doors, waiting, straining ears to hear: would the slaughterers halt at your house or pass on?

Her own man would come presently, stretching out here where she had left part of the floor-throw for him—good she had insisted on carrying it along—here on the farther side of the littlest one, Avramchick, pressed to her as though still part of her flesh. Or sometimes, with the ten-

2

derness that he displayed to the children only in their sleep,
Yankel would lift the infant gently aside so as to make
room beside his wife for himself, then ask her a whispered
"Are you sleeping?" and relate what he had been told in
his long evening's shmoos with the Jerusalemite, the envoy
who was returning from one of his yearly voyages, a shaliach collecting money to sustain the pious Jews of the Holy
City, they whose prayers rose from Yerushalayim straight
up to the Above One for the sake of the Jews scattered all
over the world.

Meanwhile Feigel listened to the songs. First they sang
in Russian, and then the young folk were teaching each
other a song in Hebrew, a new song—

> Who will build
> Galilee?
> We! We!

Some of their voices faltered over the Hebrew words, for
many were from homes where children were no longer
even sent to the cheder but to Russian schools, and on into
the gymnasia. Now a still-boyish voice slipped with a talmudic singsong into the soft, longing melody of "Elijah the
Prophet," Eliyahu HaNavi, calling, calling—

> Come unto us,
> Come in our time.
> Bring Messiah
> Of David's line.

And even though the song was an echo of a pious homey
Sabbath eve, and the revolutionists were godless young
fighters and home-leaving pioneers—chalutzim—after all
they were simply good Jewish children, and they took up
the ancient chant, and the vessel rolled with the refrain,
rolled gently from side to side, come unto us, come in our
time, truly like a mother rocking with a child in her arms.
A mother sways from side to side, a Jew praying sways
from front to back—the thought came to Feigel suddenly,
like one of the amusing thoughts she used to have in her
girlhood, relating them laughingly to her sister Hannah.
But Hannah had gone the different way, to America, Hannah and her three little children, when at last her husband

had been able to send them ship tickets. "Come soon, come soon, O Elijah, come down to us, come bringing us Messiah!" How many times had she herself not sung this song as a lullaby, first to Reuven, now grown up and gone ahead to Eretz Yisroel, "Come, bringing us Messiah, son of David," and then to Gidon, still hovering half-awake at the edge of the singers there, and to Schmulik and even now to her baby Avramchick as he drowsed at her breast. "Come unto us, come in our day, bringing us Messiah ben David!" How was it, Feigel all at once perceived, that she had sung the melody of Mashiach only to her boys and not to her girls? (To the girls a mother sang of dancing at their weddings.)

The children stirred in their sleep and Avramchick huddled closer into her, with at once a frown and a smile on his little face, the way he had. There was a breeze; Feigel spread over them all the father's vast fur-lined coat, the one he had worn when he went forth on his long trips into the Carpathian forests to buy stands of timber. That had been at the beginning of their marriage, before his partner had cheated Yankel out of all he possessed.

Nu! Still they had lived, and brought children into the world and raised them until the eldest was already grown, a man. Was he indeed? Feigel thought with troubled mind of her idealist, Reuven—had he yet known a woman? But how could even a mother ask such a thing, even in modern times?

Under the stars, Feigel permitted herself thoughts that she would never have allowed herself in Cherezinka. In this starry open night with its milky air she felt that her very soul was opening to breathe. As in that remote, sentimental time of girlhood, she asked herself was each star after all a soul in heaven? And was one of those remote and tiny stars the soul of the baby she had lost, the second boy, the one just after Reuven and Leah, the one named Nachman? Only a little while he had stayed with them, and been good as an angel, and then one morning without even being sick he had gone from them. As all the wise ones said, little Nachman had simply decided to return to God's heaven. And was he waiting again to come down, if God should send him?

Perhaps he would even come down into her? It was said

this could happen. Her own grandmother, almost a witch in her divinations, had told such a tale of a mother who had recognized by certain signs, by a birthmark and a tiny cast in the eye, a lost baby come down to her a second time.

And could this be happening even now, within her? Could she be at this moment breathing in his soul? The returning soul of her baby Nachman?

It could be, and it could be that such things were not.

Would she herself ever become a woman of wisdom filled with sagacity? After so many times, ten times if one included the miscarriage after Gidon, and this then was the eleventh time, how was it that she still felt uncertain and abashed within herself, like a maiden unable to be sure of the signs, each time it began? She had believed her body might have had enough and be done with such things, though she was still far from the age of the ancient mother Sarah. She had thought her flow ended, but, as though nature were playing with you, it was also true that the flow ended with each time of conception. And so she had been deceived.

Did her man already know?

"You're not taking anything to eat for yourself—you don't feel well, Feigel?" he had said when she parceled out the hard-boiled eggs, and her surprise had risen and lingered in her, for when did her husband ever notice whether she ate or what she ate? Yankel was not a man to watch over a woman's plate, or even a child's. He was a man driving away in a wagon, or a man standing talking with other men, or a man wrapped into himself in his voluminous tallis, tied with his tfillim into himself, not even with his God—that was how she would think of him when she was angry with him. But tonight Yankel had noticed that she had taken no food. . . . The ship, she had said, and squeezed her lips as with seasickness.

And it could be the ship—it could even be so; she had never ridden on a ship on the sea. Still, sea or no sea, this nausea was known to her. Or could such a voyage also bring a delay in a woman's flow?

There was no one to talk with about womanish things, no older sister Hannah, no woman even of her own folk, though there were a number of goyetes—Greeks, Turks,

Arabesses, who knew?—in long black gowns. Dusty even in the clean sea air, they sat huddled together on the other end of the deck. And so Feigel asked her womanish questions only within herself.

Lying with her face to the stars, Feigel understood now the tales told at home by her grandfather Matityahu the Hasid when she had been a little girl listening at the edge of the circle of men, tales of the vast universe all made of invisible sparks, every leaf, every stone, a spark of the Great Soul of all being. One could not see the sparks because they were within, and they were not really like sparks of fire, but yet invisibly they glowed. One could feel them as life, and as a growing girl she had sometimes felt the spark bursting open and rising in her like yeast in bread. All the sparks, her grandfather Matityahu had explained, yearned to be united with each other and with the whole universe, the Great Soul. For even a stone could yearn. And the sea too, and every drop of water in it was a part of the Great Soul of all being.

For it was so that she felt her children about her as part of her own being, extensions of herself, and within herself Feigel felt the new child in the opening seed, and she also felt drawn, her whole being and even the ship itself, drawn forward by her motherly yearning for the two grown children who had gone ahead before the family to Eretz Yisroel.

Nearly an entire year they had been away from her, Reuven perhaps having fully become a man, and Leah she hoped still a girl, a child, a maiden who did not yet know the meaning of life with a male. Or did Leah already know? Had such a thing perhaps already happened to her young Leah, there in the land? No, it seemed to the mother that in her own being she would have known if this had happened to her daughter; she would have seen it in the writing of her girl's letters.

But it was time, time to go to them. Feigel felt herself pulled—they would not return and they needed her still; how were they living there without a home to live in, wandering from one settlement to another, it seemed, without their own beds to go back to every night. For a man this was perhaps endurable, in his youth, in his time of adventure. But for a girl in her tender years, large and strong though she was—ah, Feigel regretted, she should never have let Leah go there like that!

Gidon came now and lay on the outer edge, and Feigel's brood seemed to have become as one under her wings. She felt Shaindeleh stir, she felt Avramchick's hand in sleep clutching her breast. She was only a small woman, and yet in this milky night Feigel felt herself as large as all this life that had come out of herself.

Her man passed near, pacing slowly with the old Jew from Jerusalem, the shaliach, the envoy whose every step seemed weighted down with the gold he must be carrying back homeward, tied, as Yankel said, in secret pouches all around his body, so fleshly thick that another layer could not be noticed. Her Yankel walked ponderously too, stepping carefully among the clusters of strange passengers, those who had come onto the vessel at Constantinople, and then at Aleppo, and Beirut. Who knew what they were, with their strange tongues, or why they voyaged, all of them, squatting everywhere on the deck, and in the hold below, goyim, with their straw mats and their silent women in black. They did not have to flee pogroms, and no command was on them to return to their Eretz.

Now her Yankel had finished with his shaliach, and came and stooped over her. "Asleep?" And she quietly answered, "No," and already he straightened to take off his coat, removing it carefully, and then bent to undo each shoe, and meanwhile her husband began his recitation of what the pious Jew, the reb from Yerushalayim, had said, all words that had already many times been repeated between them, and examined, turned around, weighed. But in his anxiety her Yankel had to repeat them again, Feigel knew.

Eliza was wakeful, the mother felt it; the girl was ten and could not fall asleep like the little ones; she must surely be wanting to listen, even to get up and linger near the young people singing there at the head of the ship.

"With the Arabs," her husband repeated, "the reb tells me that with the Arabs it is not really the same as with the moujiks. With an Arab you have to keep a sharp eye or he will make off with your horse from under you, but they are not brutal drunkards like the moujiks. They are primitive but they are far from stupid, and they are not drunkards."

Feigel made a sound to let him know she understood the difference. Yet an uneasiness—a fear that was both a premonition and a memory—had been awakened in her. It was like some timeless knowledge, some memory of Amalekites and Jebusites, of violent strangers falling on the Hebrews, of men hacking and cutting at each other, and her arms seemed impelled to extend themselves more firmly all around to protect the forms of the children, still so small. *Where was her husband taking her? to what wilderness?* "They will try to make off with a horse, a cow, even your grain from the field. It is more like a custom with them, they don't look on it as stealing—they do it to each other too, one tribe to another, unless they have a pact between them. It is like in the times of Abraham still, that is their way of life." Her husband spoke with a Jew's patience in his tone, as at home when one talked of the backward ways of the peasants.

"But at least they are not anti-Semites." Feigel repeated her part.

"No. Pogroms they don't have. A czar and priests to send them down on us they don't have. There are rulers from Turkey, officials who have to be bribed at every turn. Like all officials everywhere. But pogroms are not known. The Arabs are not anti-Semiten."

Feigel was quiet. All that Reuven had written about guarding the barns at night, she knew. Even Leah had slept in a hut in the vineyard where Reuven was on watch, and had written in a tone of jest of one time when her screams had frightened away thieves loading clusters of grapes onto their donkeys. So poor they were, Leah said. Yet Feigel's brother Simha's words of only a few weeks ago resounded in her: "Come better with me to America. Surely Yankel can be persuaded. We already have a sister and her husband there in the State of New Jersey. Why go to an old dead land? Come to a new land. Come all of you with us together."

And her brother was now on another sea, gone the other way, from the port of Hamburg. He had gone alone, leaving his wife and children with the old parents—the youngest brother, Simha, gone off to begin a life as a Jew in America. Their sister and brother-in-law would help him and in a year or two he would send for his family.

So too her own eldest son and daughter had gone ahead to another land and now called for them to come to Eretz. Surely it was better to be going together with her man and the children rather than to be left in the old country waiting, another manless woman in Cherezinka? So many women sat waiting, a year, three years, even more; there was Shaina Glickson who was now seven years without her man. And think also of the men far away from home, alone in that strange land, living on tea and bread, and working so hard to save pennies and send ship tickets for their families. Better to stay together and brave the hardships together; she was no longer so young that she had years for waiting.

But who could tell what was best for a Jew?

Feigel tried to bar from her mind the other advice, from her uncle, Heschel the Tanner, who had already been to the Holy Land—twenty years back—and had soon returned, his tail between his legs, half-starved, with dreadful shivering fits of malaria that came over him every three years or so, and with a dark look in back of his eyes. That uncle had been a Bilu, a student idealist of those earlier days, one of a group that had left their university studies to go labor on the earth of the ancient homeland. But the settlements had foundered. Only a few villages had been rescued with help from the "Great Giver," Baron de Rothschild of Paris. Every twenty years it seemed indeed this fever of longing returned on the Jews—like Heschel's returning malaria, he would bitterly declare. But despite the bitter words of her uncle, her own son and daughter had gone.

Still perhaps things were now really different. There was a whole new movement, far greater than what there had been in Heschel's day, for at that time no Herzl had yet appeared. Momentarily Feigel saw the image of Herzl with his broad fine beard and deep eyes, the picture she had brought along in the big trunk from where it had hung on the wall in Cherezinka. Eyes like a Messiah. And even there in Cherezinka, in these last ten years when her children had been growing up, how feverishly everyone had repeated the news of Herzl's doings—now he was being received by the German Kaiser, he was meeting Kaiser Wilhelm in Jerusalem itself! But the Kaiser had not yet handed over the Holy City to him, for it seemed that Jerusalem belonged to the Turkish Sultan. The Turk, everyone explained, was weak and the Germans were his protectors and the Sultan would soon do what the Kaiser asked. And now Herzl was being received by the Turkish Sultan, who for not too much gold would cede the whole of Palestine! In every Jewish kitchen there was a little blue tin box to collect money to buy the land—she and even the children had dropped in their kopecks, the little ones often shaking the box to hear how full it was, in readiness for when the collector came from the Keren Kayemeth. And suddenly Herzl was dead. Already a few years.

But the movement was not dead, her Reuven declared. It was the Jewish people themselves who would be the Messiah, their own Mashiach, and where only a few score Bilu had got up and gone to the Land in the days of her own girlhood—indeed her Yankel himself had dreamed of going in his youth time, this Feigel knew—there were now several thousand young people, good Jewish children, pioneers, chalutzim, like her own son and daughter who had gone up to renew the land.

Indeed Reuven wrote from the land that if his great-uncle Heschel had remained he would even now be handsomely settled in an almond grove, with his own broad vineyards, like a veritable lord! For to aid those of the Bilu who remained the great Baron de Rothschild had stretched out his munificent hand. No, things were not so difficult as in her Uncle Heschel's day; her son Reuven, though an idealist, was sensible, and would not have written that the entire family should come if things were truly so difficult.

Yet who could tell what was best for a Jew? Yankel was mumbling the words, and Feigel moved the child, the little Avramchick, to her other side, saying to her husband, "Lie down."

"Will they go on singing all night?" he grumbled.

They sang on, and he ruminated—To leave had been the right thing, for how could a Jew remain in the land of the Czar after the revolutionaries had lost their revolt and the pogromnicks had again been unloosed! What future was there for the children? There was no life in that land but oppression.

"And with the kind of children we have," Feigel whispered, "who could hold them back from the revolutionary movement? If not Zionists, they would become social revolutionaries. If they didn't go to Eretz Yisroel, they would end in Siberia." It was indeed fortunate that Reuven and Leah had gone away a year ago, for she could see her eldest son in the chained line of prisoners struggling to the desolate far north, and his young sister would have followed him even there. "And if not Siberia, they'd have caught him for the Czar's army."

The younger boys, lying there on her husband's side—how much better to take them in their childhood out of Russia! "If only the Turks allow us to land." Now Yankel had a new source of worry.

But Reuven had written that it was all arranged, she reminded him. Reuven would meet them on the ship's arrival, they would only have to pay a small bribe. They must say they were pilgrims going to pray at the Wailing Wall. Yankel growled. "Another whole night with singing," he complained. "Chalutzim they call themselves. Hooligans!"

She wanted to ask, had he noticed, Dvora was perhaps getting too close to a certain one among the bold young men from Kostarnitza.

Yankel's vast rumble came, his beard rising and falling. She nudged, and he turned heavily, the choked snore subsiding into more peaceful breathing.

Feigel thought about a name for her baby. They had come almost alternately, a boy, a girl, and it was the turn of a girl; still, if this added child should prove to be a boy? She could not risk giving him the name of her lost little Nachman, for then perhaps the Evil One would again snatch him away. There were names for confusing the Evil One—you could call a baby The Old One, Alter, or Abba, the father . . . And if the child should nevertheless be a girl? Girls were much wanted there in Eretz, it seemed.

Perhaps after all things would turn out for the best with them in Eretz Yisroel.

Through his closed lids Yankel felt the presence of the firmament, and the stars were like thousands of prickling reminders. Be watchful of each possession, all sailors are thieves, only goyim are sailors. But even of a fellow Jew you must be watchful; be wary of everyone who offers to help you when you arrive, particularly if it is for nothing, out of his good Jewish heart. Particularly if they want to sell you land. And especially be wary of Litvaks and Roumanians. The redbeard who had tricked him out of the forestry lease had been a Roumanian.

Though Yankel had paid for space in the hold of the ship, young Dvora and his wife too had ended by dragging him up on deck, declaring the air was cleaner and there was no human stench. He had yielded to Feigel because he knew that otherwise, down there in the hold of the ship, she might have begun to have her morning sickness. And why had she done this to him now? Just now precisely in the middle of everything she had had to do it, just when a man faced an upheaval in his life, when he had to uproot himself and take his pack on his back and set off anew to a strange land, a new land, yes, even if it was the old land. The Holy Land should not be strange to a Jew, somewhere that was written. Yet it was new to him, for was his upheaval in any way less than if he were going to America? It was worse than going to America, it would be harder. In the Holy Land there were no diamonds lying in the streets. And he must find a living, while carrying on his back his entire family, so many mouths to feed. And now in this very time, why had she done this to him?

Feigel had not said anything of it, but early though it might be, Yankel knew the signs in her, particularly the avoidance of his eyes because she had not yet made up her mind to tell him.

It seethed in Yankel; but as long as she did not say anything he could not say anything to reproach her.

Still—to be bringing a new soul to be born in Eretz HaKodesh, this was surely a good action, a mitzvah.

As at other times in his life, Yankel obscurely felt that a good deed had been kindled by his wife despite something in himself that might have prevented it had he known. And in his soul he was aware that this was why he sometimes allowed himself to be led by her. Of himself Yankel was not certain. In his idealist years as a yeshiva bocher he had dreamed of a life that could be carried out with perfection. It would be a perfect thing if a man lived an entire life and never transgressed a single one of the six hundred and thirteen regulations, also called mitzvoth. If a man uttered each prayer and each blessing in its proper time each day and each holiday, if he spoke the words of blessing for each act of the day, rising, washing, eating, entering a house, leaving, what perfection that would be! It was not so much that he had dreamed of becoming a tzaddik, but an ideal of perfection had been upon him. But after the excellent

match with a Koslovsky had been made for him, Yankel
had caught the fever of earning, of wanting to prove that he
did not need the patronage of her father, her brothers; he
had gone into the world, buying sugar-beet crops for them
from the peasants. And to make money you squeezed—
how could one help but befuddle a moujik who could not
add seven and nine?—and then he had tried to be a merchant for himself without cheating or twisting or conniving,
and had in his turn been cheated; and then he had turned
himself into a dealer and trader in horses, in cattle. Her
brothers, each time he failed, would tell him how he could
have done well, and though in all this Yankel had stayed
faithfully observant of the mitzvoth, kept, as though secretly within himself the image of a life unblemished by
ritual failings, he knew that beyond the movements of the
lips in the given words, and the perfect binding on of the
tfillim, and all those mitzvoth that a Jew could regularly
follow, a deeper failing was there, simply because he had to
be a man walking and dealing among men. Therefore he
trusted at times to the simplicity of soul that came more
readily in life to a woman; Feigel was a good woman, a
woman of virtue, that he knew, and despite all his sense of
appearing as something of a failure, something of a schle-
miel before her, Yankel sometimes allowed himself to be
led into his decisions, like the decision now to go to Palestine since Reuven and Leah were already there.

A saying of Rabbi Nachman's that the Hasidim were always repeating wafted about behind Yankel's closed eyelids— Wherever a Jew goes, he is on his way to the Holy
Land. But then if a Jew goes to the Holy Land itself, what is
the meaning of this saying? That was a question that would
have sent her Hasidic grandfather running to his rebbe!
No, the Hasidim could wait forever, back there in Medzi-
buz, or they could wander off to America, all the while
crying out for the Mashiach to hurry down from heaven's
Garden of Eden and lead them to Eretz, but meanwhile he,
a simple Jew, was on his way there by himself.

In this moment Yankel's heart swelled and he was
awake. He was really doing it. He was doing it in earnest.
A Jew like himself, without much luck in the world, not
clever like his clever brother-in-law Kalman, the Rich Koslovsky, not particularly powerful in his body, not even a
sage of the Scriptures, and yet where others feared to take

such a step, he, pack and bundle, with his entire family, had heaved himself up and was approaching the land of the fathers! There welled up in Yankel that sense of the miraculous nature of all existence, of the wondrous things that can happen to a simple human being, and the words for this feeling, for this gratitude at living to see the day, the arriving moment of fruition, came to his lips. He must say the Shehechiyanu.

His eyes now open to the full star-misted sky, Yankel moved his lips with the words: Blessed art Thou, O Lord our God, King of the Universe, who hast given us life, and sustained us in life, and brought us to this time.

But again doubts came over him. Was it indeed such a mitzvah to return to this particular land? What of Rabbi Nachman's saying, after all? *Wherever* one goes—so it need not be Palestine at all. Should he rather have gone, should he still go, to America where his wife had kinfolk who would help them? And with a new baby, too.

He was not clever enough to find the inmost meaning of such a saying as Nachman's, Yankel told himself. And it had had to be Feigel's brother Simha who had brought up the troubling quotation. Though Simha had never in his life got through a page of Talmud, he was one of those Jews who could spout you apt sayings from the Tractates or from the Gaon of Bilna, as though he were a scholar of scholars. Everything he had picked up from others. So by that saying of Rabbi Nachman's, Simha had proved himself right in going to America.

Yankel saw again the family gathering in that month of barred windows and doubly barred doors, after the assassination of the "minister of pogroms," Plehve, may his name be erased from eternity and let an eternal fire burn in his entrails in Gehenna! It was Reuven, his own eldest, the book reader, the freethinker, a godless son who since his Bar Mitzvah had never once put on his phylacteries, it was suddenly Reuven who had challenged all his uncles to go to the Holy Land.

Hadn't they been drumming at God's ears four times a day for nineteen centuries, Reuven demanded, with their pleading and their beseeching and their promises and their weeping and their breast-beating, to let them return to the Holy Land? Well, who was stopping them? The Turk? The Turk was nothing. A little baksheesh. Others had gone. A few coins and the doors were open. It wasn't even far. Only halfway down the Mediterranean coast. Why must they drag themselves to the other side of the world, to America, the capitalists' "paradise," with its ghettos and sweatshops as everyone already knew, the Golden Land for those who sweated gold out of the toil of their brothers?

To this, Feigel's clever brother Simha had replied with another maxim: the long way around was the shortest way, and if the streets were not paved with gold, where did the remittances come from on which half of Cherezinka was living? And as for Eretz Yisroel, that was where a Jew went to die, and die they did, even the young, as had the Bilu in their time, as his uncle Heschel could tell them, he who had barely crawled back with breath in his body. From hunger and from fever they died. Besides, Simha reminded them all, Mashiach had not yet appeared to lead the Jews back as it was written. Or did Reuven perhaps believe that the journalist from Vienna, that unbeliever, that apicoiras Theodor Herzl, had been the Messiah? And as for America, it was just as Rabbi Nachman had said, Godliness was everywhere, and whichever way a Jew goes if he is a decent and observant man—

What the saying really meant, Reuven had interrupted, was that a Jew could not *escape* his destiny to reach the Holy Land. And therefore the best solution was to go at once, directly, and an end! "Well said!" Feigel had proudly cried out, and Yankel himself had felt pride at the clever answer his son, despite being an unbeliever, had given his wife's falsely clever brother.

But Feigel's eldest brother, Kalman, who owned the sugar-beet mill, had taken another view altogether. "Why go anywhere? Why flee? Why uproot ourselves? There have been pogroms before and there have been edicts before; the storm blows, you sit quietly in the cellar and the storm blows over. Here in Cherezinka, God be thanked, we are alive and well. A few heads have been cracked but they will mend, the hair will grow back, not even a scar will show." And Kalman blew smoke from the long Turkish cigarette that he held cupped in his hand, while he smiled his prudent wisdom upon Yankel.

A few cracked heads. Might his own head be broken, and every bone in his body, the smiling one, the cigarette smoker, the wealthy gvir with his sugar-beet mill! In Kalman's interest and for his sake, Yankel had stood up to the raging peasants, refusing to pay a kopeck more a pood for their beets, until a drunken Ivan had leaped from his wagon onto the platform, his whip raised. Yankel had spit in the moujik's face, it was true, before the whiphandle came down on his head. So he had been carried home, blood clotting his beard, and all the children had wailed and lamented around their Tateh, Leah hurrying with the kettle from the stove to help her mother with warm water to cleanse the wound. It was then that Feigel had declared: "And end! We must go! We must leave this gehenna! An end!"

Nevertheless at the family council there was Feigel's fine fat brother, the gvir, with his voice as smooth as schmaltz, declaring there was no cause to flee. And there had been the younger generation as well, Kalman's son, one of the intelligentsia from the goyish gymnasia, talking of smuggled pistols and iron staves and the new spirit of self-defense, of Jewish fighters in Homel and Kostarnitza and Odessa who had beaten off pogromists. So declared Kalman's son Tuvia, who was the same age as Reuben, also a free-thinker, a revolutionist—he had even Russified his name—Tolya he now called himself—and he had a fat-lipped smile like his father's. He too announced there was no cause to flee, indeed it would be treason to the social revolution! In the revolutzia everything would be changed, everything would be solved! No, the revolution had not been broken at all, promised Tuvia-Tolya, the mighty stream flowed underground, and when it burst forth again, it would sweep the world clean!

Oh, what a tumult and confusion in the family. They were like a double-span of horses in the forest pulling a heavy half-buried log out of a wallow of mud, Yankel told himself, with the driver's long whip reaching them whichever way they tugged and struggled, and each beast pulling in another direction under the lashes.

And so he had permitted Reuven to leave for Eretz Yisroel. Better Reuven should labor and risk himself for the Jewish cause at least, than for the Russian revolution. Better a Zionist with a plow than a Narodnick with pistols and bombs. That had been Feigel's pleading too. Let Reuven go. If not to Eretz, he will end up in Siberia.

And then came a new confusion. If Reuven went, his

sister Leah stubbornly insisted she too had to go. A girl not yet seventeen, but already a "new woman" with equal rights: if a man can go, a girl can go too! Always Leah had followed Reuven around, more like a younger brother than a sister. Together they had joined the youth movement of the Jewish Workers, laborers of Zion, going to the secret meetings behind the wall of flour sacks in the rear of Mendelovitch's bakery. What was to be done with a girl like Leah who went out beyond the town into the fields and asked the peasants to teach her to plant potatoes?

Regarding his eldest daughter, a feeling had come over Yankel in those days as though the house were bursting with the femaleness of the girl. She had grown like some Russian peasant woman, broad-boned, tall, nearly a head above himself, taller than her brother Reuven, full-bodied, with great red cheeks and strong teeth. Though he was not of the backward over-observant Yidden who forbade themselves even to look at a woman for fear of Satan's temptation, Yankel in those days in the presence of his large energy-charged daughter felt an inkling of the fear of those pious men: It was not so much a horror of some drunken sin happening, as between Lot and his daughters—for one thing Yankel was no drinker, only a schnapps now and then to close a bargain—no, it was the surge of femaleness that he felt with Leah in the house, of an overpowering presence of womankind that he had not even sensed in the deepest of permitted doings with his wife. Nor, thank God, did he sense anything like this now from his younger daughters.

And Feigel too had taken count of this in Leah. In the whole village there was not a Jewish boy of the height and size of Leachka, and in any case could one even hint about matchmaking to a girl of today? But there among the pioneers in Eretz a shortage of girls existed, it was known, and perhaps Leah would find herself a big strong chalutz; so perhaps for her to go with Reuven would after all be a good thing.

"Let her go with Reuven," Feigel had decreed at last. "Leah will keep an eye on her brother; otherwise, idealist that he is, he will forget to put food into his mouth, even a cucumber, the vegetarian!"

For this of late had been an added complication in the house. Reuven the idealist had declared himself against

meat-eating. He and Leah had even started a vegetable garden in the yard, planting cucumbers, tomatoes, carrots, and
cabbages, to the amazement of the shikseh who helped in
the kitchen. Reuven had brought home botanical books,
and Leah had got the peasant girl to bring seeds from her
family's own garden. In their experiments the brother and
sister had, astonishingly, raised a bed of strawberries larger
than any to be found in the market. Only in his vegetarianism did Leah fail to follow her brother—she devoured everything, flesh-food, milk-food, engulfing with lip-smacking
love whatever she put into her mouth.

A whole group was planning to leave for Eretz Yisroel.
But this one went away to a university in Switzerland, and
that one decided to wait a bit, and finally out of their entire
band of Workers of Zion, how many really went to labor in
the fields of Zion? They talked and talked, like the Bilu in
Yankel's own youth time, but who indeed rose up and
went? A Reuven and a Leah. One fine morning they were
ready with their packs all packed, and their comrades escorted them with singing and banners to the train for
Odessa, and unbelievably they were on their way!

Then letters came to Feigel from Leah, with a few words
added at the bottom from Reuven to father and mother.
All, all was good. Difficult but good. No one went hungry,
believe them! And even when there was no work to be had,
because Baron Rothschild's Jewish effendis preferred Arab
serfs to Jewish laborers—What was an effendi? Like an
estate-owner with his moujiks—But despite the hardhearted Jewish effendis, the workers managed, they
clubbed together with their bits of earnings so that no one
went hungry. Believe Leah, such was the spirit!

All was good, and Eretz was a land of such beauty, Leah
said—before her as she wrote there lay an entire field covered with wildflowers like with a great red scarf—such
beauty had the land, that it sang in your very soul! Reuven
too in moments of communication could write such
thoughts. Not true that Eretz was entirely a heap of barren
stones. The hills were stony, alas, because of those devils
of Bedouin with their flocks of black goats. These Bedouin
were not the same kind of Arabs as the fellaheen settled in
the villages; these were wanderers who lived in tents, and
their goats devoured every shoot of green, every sapling
with its roots, and then the despoilers moved onward, leav-

ing hills of bare stone. The fellaheen were a good people but miserably poor, ignorant, and exploited like serfs.

But such a land was Eretz! It needed only tending! All was good, all was going well, except that the settlers from twenty years ago, in Baron Rothschild's paternalistic villages, had become each like a little baron himself, an overlord, a Jewish effendi with his own Arab serfs!

And then would come tirades against these "old" settlers—what were they but exploiters in their turn, as bad as the Russian landowners! Was this a way to build Zion? What had become of their ideals, these pioneers of a generation ago, now sitting with pianos in their houses, while their daughters practiced the scales up and down, and Arab fellaheen toiled in their vineyards! Arabs were even wandering in from Syria and the Lebanon to work for them and new Arab villages sprang up around the Baron's settlements, while Jewish workers begged for a day's employment! Was this the way to build Zion?

A bitter smile lay in Yankel's beard as he read such words. Was his son after all so different from himself, despite Reuven's godlessness? He too at Reuven's age had been touched with the ancient dream to go and settle in Eretz Yisroel. Besides the few students in the Bilu, who went as laborers like the chalutzim of today, there had been small groups of land buyers called Lovers of Zion. But he had not had enough capital to join such a group, and Feigel's family had frowned on the idea.

Now it appeared to Yankel that all was a circle, that he was beginning the voyage he had wanted to make over twenty years ago. Perhaps he had sent ahead his son and daughter because he had meant to be drawn by them, just as Moses had sent forward emissaries into the land. New settlements were being opened, Reuven wrote, good settlements in the Galilee, and this time they would be confined to the principle of self-labor, by Jewish hands alone. Come, come with the whole family, we will all work together, and the young brothers and sisters will grow up on our own soil, with clear eyes and high heads!

There was a change in the sky, a grayish mist, and eastward on the rim of the sea a solidity appeared at the base of the mist. Then a hint, a lessening of density. Yankel drew himself erect. Within him welled up a sense of trembling and even fright, as though the curtains of the Innermost were about to part before him and reveal the Shechina.

No one else was awake.

On his stocking feet, he watched, eastward. A tint appeared behind or within the gray mist, like a warmth of blood returning to the ashen face of the dead. The dead earth. Then, outlined at the base a darker strip was taking form.

Yankel stooped and touched his second son, Gidon. This son, who had only now completed his Bar Mitzvah, was at least not entirely godless. Not as yet—though who knew what would come in the days ahead in the company of his freethinking brother Reuven.

Gidon too had been sleeping lightly, awaiting the presence of the land, and he was instantly on his feet, standing with his father to behold the land before others in the family—who were not men but only women and small children—should arise.

He stood, a stocky lad with square shoulders and long arms, broad hands and large knuckles that were raised just now, child-fashion, to rub sleep from his eyes.

At the prow Gidon noticed a few chalutzim too were rising, standing, speaking softly to each other, pointing, as the darker shape of the earth formed itself out of the mist. The words from Creation came to Gidon, *tohu v'bohu*, out of chaos and emptiness God formed the earth, and God said, "Let there be light"—and so it was at this moment, light was appearing behind the dark form of the earth. Here where their ship rose were the waters, and the waters were gathered in to make the land. It was of the water here, it was of this very water as it reached the land before him, that God had spoken. Gidon felt a lifting of mist within his own mind. For all of this, until now, he had never clearly comprehended.

His father was winding on his tfillim, and motioning to him to make haste so as to properly greet this rising day, this new birth of life, of the world, and of their family's life. Without withdrawing his eyes from the unfolding beauty of the universe, Gidon reached for his velvet tfillim bag, drew out the rolled-up leather strips and wound the coils around his left arm while dimly he followed a thought, a realization—this binding on of the tfillim was a strength. Like a boxer binding leather around his wrist. Was that perhaps why the old men in the shul did it? to remind themselves of the mighty fighters in Israel in the ancient days?

His father had already completed the placing of the front-let on his forehead, strapping between and above his eyes the small receptacle that contained the vow of faith. Gidon knew he was not imaginative but yet today an image came to him: this was like a searing-in, like words of fire burning into your mind—I am a Jew, a Jew bound in with my God.

Now his father touched his lips to the tallis and, with the old circular movement that Gidon had never quite caught, swung himself into the prayer shawl as he swung it about him, so that he was wrapped away in the world beyond. Thus from childhood he had always seemed to Gidon, as to all the children: when at prayer, Tateh was removed from them; the long heavy tallis around him reaching with its fringes to the floor became a magic wall. Tateh, within, was enclosed with the Almighty. Until he emerged, un-wrapped, to shout at them and berate them and command them. This, Gidon recalled, had been his first childish con-ception of his father.

Of course he had grown and heard the disrespectful jest-ing of the older village boys about religion, and heard the views of his older brother Reuven the freethinker, and to his own mind had come the bitter questions about God and the pogroms. And at his Bar Mitzvah, when Gidon had wrapped his own tallis around his shoulders, he had not felt he was like his father enclosed with the Almighty. How-ever, a feeling of being a man among Jewish men had reached him. He had kept up with the daily prayers for a short time, out of a kind of sympathy he now felt for the old Tateh who, he began to see, did not have much luck in his doings, and also for the sake of peace in the house for his mother. He didn't want to give his father more reason to complain about all his sons becoming atheists.

This was the time when Tateh had traded in horses, be-fore he lost half his stable to a plague of horse cholera and had to go back to work as a weighman at the sugar mill for Uncle Kalman. It was a time when Gidon helped in the stable, and he had taken to it, enjoying the careful blowing of the beasts over the pails of water he set before them, and the way they rubbed against you, their smell, their goodness if you were decent to them. He had learned by himself to ride a horse and had become a real shaygetz in his galloping. And a new thing had happened to him. The peasants and the peasant lads began to talk to him in a new way, not like to a Jew, and he had even felt in a kind of vague fear that his Bar Mitzvah came just in time or he would have burst away from it all. So too was this leaving for this new land—it was just in time. For it was said that there in the new land there were Jews like plain peasants, people like he now felt he was made to be, and there he could be such a person and still a Jew. These were people without cleverness, without arguments, people who didn't twist their heads to gain every little advantage but went and did what had to be done with their own hands, and an end.

Yet today somehow in this arrival Gidon found himself listening, harkening to the words he automatically recited in the prayer, his own words as they came from his lips today, and the same words from his father. Today it did not seem, as the clever fellows at home had said, meaningless and foolish to repeat by rote the same words of prayer each morning, any more than it did to rise and wash yourself every day.

So it was with the chalutzim too, he saw, as he glanced toward the bow of the ship: one after another of those splendid fighters from Kostarnitza now reached into his belongings and, freethinkers though they were, each brought out a siddur, and a few even wore the tallis. There was a lanky fellow with a reddish stubble clinging to his cheeks, the one who had sat together so much with Devoraleh—he had an odd expression, half-sheepish, half-defiant, as he wound on his tfillim.

The sky was all at once clear, unflecked, a freshly unrolled canopy of blue, and amazingly close to the ship lay the golden thread, the shore.

Sands. Nothing but sands.

—No, no, the little band of young men assured one another, and they seemed to include, in their reassurance, Reb Yankel with his sons and daughters, no. Everything grew here! they cried as they gazed with feverish eagerness at the yellow, empty shoreline.—Behind the sand dunes was good solid earth, they declared to each other, and everything grew, almonds, grapes, oranges, melons delicious and sweet, sweeter even than the melons of the Crimea, while inland grew wheat and barley and corn. In this climate and in this soil could be grown every fruit, all the produce of the earth!

Now presently a heap of structures could be discerned, a hill from which there emerged several pencil-like minarets, and spires with crosses.

This was Jaffa!

"Yaffa—yaffeh," Yechezkiel announced to Dvora, practicing his Hebrew. "Ir shel yoffi." The city of beauty; the name meant beauty.

"With their crosses and crescents," remarked his dour friend Menahem, the usually silent. "This is what we see to greet us."

"Wait, one day we'll put up the Star of David, higher than all," said Yechezkiel.

"Lighted with electricity, like in America," said Menahem, made loquacious by the wondrous moment, and Dvora uttered a rosy little "Ah." For Menahem, her friend Yechezkiel had told her, had even sailed to America and had seen the new wonder, electricity.

Dvora felt Yechezkiel's arm tighten around her waist, and his lips were brushing her ear whispering, "This is a moment, dear one, we will share through all our lives." Yechezkiel had sensed her inmost thought! And unseen because of the chaverim crowding around them, Dvora slipped her arm, too, around Yechezkiel's waist. At once as they stood there sealed together, the entire length of their clothing in contact, Dvora experienced a revelation. Her arm around his body, and his arm around hers—this was not simply comradeliness, the comradeliness with a spice of flirtation that she had enjoyed during the voyage under the uneasy eyes of her mother and father. Yechezkiel's arm encircled her entire waist and his spread fingers rested on her body as though to hold her very organs, as though sealing to himself what made her a woman. And then against her own hand Dvoraleh felt, through the cloth, the muscle of his loin, and flushing, her senses swollen and vibrating, Dvora knew that this was how a woman held a man's body during the act of love, and she wanted to rush into her mother's arms and weep together with her and murmur Mamaleh, Mamaleh, for in this instant she understood the lot of all women, even to the feeling of a child growing in the womb.

Just then her eyes met Yechezkiel's, turning back from the glowing shore. Their eyes met in complicity, and Yechezkiel swiftly bent his face to hers in a short, burning kiss, the first true kiss of a man and a woman between them, the first such kiss of her life. Then they both gazed outward again with profound seriousness at the homeland where they would lead their joined lives and—they now knew—raise their offspring.

All through the voyage Dvoraleh had gravitated toward Yechezkiel, though warning herself to keep a wary heart, as he was without question the most dashing and handsome of the four chalutzim from the town of Kostarnitza—the famous group that had posted themselves at the corners of the ghetto and fired pistols and driven away a drunken mob of pogromists. Now they too were coming as pioneers to Eretz Yisroel.

The young men from Kostarnitza composed a little circle to themselves during the voyage, and she had, as it were, nestled into their girlless group. More and more she had stayed alongside Yechezkiel, though there was also his friend Menahem, small, wiry, with a dark soul, who kept his eyes on her. Differently. This one had known women, he had even run away from the famous Volozhin yeshiva and been a sailor in the far ports of the world. Late at night after the singing when some of the boys finally stretched out to sleep, Menahem too would move off, and then Yechezkiel always wanted her to linger a bit longer with him alone, but she so far always slipped away.

Yet during the days there had been times for talking alone together, and he had revealed his soul to her. Yechezkiel knew he was not witty just as she knew she was not really beautiful, but Yechezkiel was strong and good. He wanted to hurt no man, wanted not to be devious and take advantage of others, not to bargain and confuse the moujiks—indeed, such twisting took too much troubling of the brain, he told her with the boyish smile that she loved. His father was a seller of household supplies to the peasantry, and Yechezkiel did not want such a life. Nor had he even wanted to hurt the drunken pogromists, some of whom were his father's customers. He wanted to be a new kind of Jew, no longer huddled in a townlet and haggling in the market, but living in nature, in the open, and raising children who could ride horses. He wanted no longer to be told—in Kiev a Jew may not reside, in Moscow a Jew may not live, in this town you need a permit and in that town you may not enter; no longer to have to buy false papers, to employ subterfuges and bribes.

Then how do you imagine we shall land in Palestine? Dvora teased him. But as his face grew dour, she squeezed his hand to show that this of course was a different matter, this would be the last time, and in any case, as her brother Reuven who had the same ideals as Yechezkiel had written, by what right should the Turks tell a Jew whether he could or could not enter Eretz Yisroel?

The vessel was already in an awakened turmoil, with the children running everywhere, climbing the rails, stumbling over the goyish passengers, who shouted at them angrily.

"Feigel! See!" Yankel called to his wife, who had dressed herself in her brocaded gown for this day, and was braiding the hair of little Eliza, the dainty one, the pretty one. Yankel too had prepared himself for the arrival, donning his fine black silk coat, rubbing his black, wide-brimmed round hat to a gloss against his sleeve. Now as his wife came to his side to gaze at the land, there was on Feigel's countenance the glow of her best days, the glow of a good Sabbath eve when he came home from the shul and saw her standing by the window dressed and waiting, perhaps tying a last velvet ribbon in little Eliza's long golden braid.

Wild beasts, nothing else! the Jewish passengers cried, warned though they had been of what to expect when the Arab boatmen came thronging aboard. Without asking whose, what, where, these pirates with their daggers in the sashes of their wide drooping Turkish trousers suddenly seized luggage, bundles, featherquilts, flinging everything over the side without even glancing to see if your possessions fell into the water or into their little boats that jumped like popping blobs of goosefat on the waves.

With their very bodies Yankel, Feigel, Gidon and even the small children tried to block off their belongings from seizure, but the huge shouting bandits pulled things from under them, from out of their hands, all the while keeping up their heathenish screaming and cursing, and where could you turn to, who could protect you? Where was Reu-

ven, Yankel demanded, couldn't he have come out in one
of these rowboats? Others had come aboard, some Jews of
affluence could be seen, and Turkish officials in uniform
had arrived, wearing the red tarboosh; meanwhile from all
sides money was being demanded of him by fierce Arabs in
long white gowns, by fierce Arabs in European clothes,
also wearing the tarboosh, by wilder Arabs in the loose
black cotton trousers that drooped from their behinds—so
much for each head they insisted, small children the same
price—a tax, a bribe, a boat charge, what was it for, who
knew? A fortune they wanted! They didn't even give a Jew
a chance to compute how much it all came to in rubles,
they demanded gold francs, and the pious shaliach, the
fund collector from Yerushalayim who at least could tell
you the value of a bishlik—he was already gone. There he
was below on the sea, with two other Jews in caftans sitting
calmly in one of the tossing little boats, being rowed
ashore—how had he managed to climb down?

Even as Yankel was gazing at the departing Jerusalemite, his wife tugged at him in terror—an Arab had seized
one of the children, little Shaindel, and was about to hurl
her over the rail! Shaindel kicked and screamed, and while
Yankel pulled at the Arab, and Eliza in fright threw her
hands around her father's neck so as to be saved from the
same fate, and while Gidon manfully tried to wrench
Shaindel back, a Turkish official yanked at Yankel's other
arm, demanding something in a harsh angry voice, in some
unknown tongue, Arabic, Turkish, who could tell?

At last Yankel understood—*papieren*, papers, and letting
go of the Arab, he managed to reach for their papers, all
prepared in a bundle, to show to the man. But the official
snatched them from Yankel's hand and was gone!

"Our papers!" Feigel gasped, and hurried after the Turk.
God alone knew what would happen to them without papers! Meanwhile Dvora ran after Feigel to remind her that
Reuven had written that a red card must be obtained for
each passport, Yechezkiel too had said so, a card was given
to religious pilgrims, and they must answer all questions by
saying they were all pilgrims coming to pray at the Wailing
Wall in Jerusalem. They were not settlers. They were here
on a religious journey and would soon go back. Of course,
Feigel agreed, so Reuven had written, but who would have
known that the papers would be snatched out of their

hands? Who knew if they could even land without them? Who could have known even officials would behave like wild beasts?

The young men from Kostarnitza, Gidon saw, were already climbing over the rail and leaping down into the small boats. Each one stood poised until the little vessel was tossed up by the crest of a wave against the side of the steamer, and then in that instant you leaped, to be caught by an Arab boatman standing in the prow of the tossing tender below. Gidon could easily do it, he was sure—but what about Tateh in his long Sabbath coat, and what about his mother? "Don't be afraid, Shaindeleh, I'm coming," he called down to his little sister, already handed into the rowboat by the Arabs. But as Gidon clambered half-over the rail, he heard his father cry out anew, "Help! Bandits! Help!"

A giant Arab had seized his father's fur coat from atop their pile of belongings. Managing to reverse his balance, Gidon jumped back onto the deck where his father was pulling at the tail of his greatcoat. The boy seized hold of a dangling sleeve and pulled with his entire strength, and together father and son managed to yank loose the garment. That was as Reuven had written—you had to be strong with the Arabs, show no fear! Then they respected you.

But even as Yankel clutched his fur coat, he saw his entire household being invaded. Gidon struggled to save the bedding, the girls howled and wailed as the bundles with all their cherished possessions were taken, and Feigel had her arms spread over the cookpots. In the midst of this, a sailor from the boat's crew came howling at them, waving his arms, "Off! Off!" They must at once descend from the ship.

Despite the rising heat, Yankel put on his fur coat over his black silk. One of the heroes of Kostarnitza, Dvora's stalwart boy Yechezkiel, had lingered behind his group and now hurried over to say farewell, he would meet them in Eretz Yisroel. Then above the tumult, thank heaven, a Jewish voice was heard, a strong reassuring voice telling them they would find all their belongings in the port, they need have no fear. But suddenly Feigel let out her most piercing shriek, "Shaindel!" The little vessel below them with Shaindel already in it was being rowed away. The child's shriek echoed her mother's.

Wild visions assailed Yankel as his wife clutched him, distraught with the same terror—little girls carried off and sold into harems, gone for life! Their Shaindeleh! Swallowed into the sands of the desert! Quick, they must follow! Thrusting one leg over the rail, Gidon sat astride it while he took hold of the smaller children one at a time, grasping each around the waist until the moment came to swing them down to the Arab boatmen, who caught them by the legs.

Little Schmuel insisted on climbing over by himself, then came Eliza, half-tumbling, shrieking and laughing, into the arms of the huge laughing boatman, then Dvora managed, furling her skirt below her knees and somehow holding it gracefully with one hand as the grinning Arab reached up for her amidst evil-sounding shouts from the others. Leaning far over, Gidon handed down Avramchick, and then his mother came. With surprising deftness Feigel was already down into the bobbing boat, her girls around her. Since a boy could not offer help of this kind to his father, Gidon now dropped down himself, and waited.

Yankel Chaimovitch was in one more dispute over baksheesh. "Baksheesh! Baksheesh!" the devils shouted from all sides, their open hands thrust out, and then suddenly he saw the little vessel with his entire family, wife and children, pulling away, like the other vessel with Shaindel, chopping and plunging in the sea, and from Feigel and the children a wail arose, "Tateh! Gevald!" Theirs was the last of the rowboats.

Amidst the desperate shrieks and yells from above and below, the savage Arabs down there churned their little vessel around and waited for him. "Leap, leap!" a sailor shouted in Russian as Yankel mounted the rail. The remaining coins were pulled from his hands, and he was pushed. The great fur coat floated about him, the steamer slid away with a sudden lurch, everyone below screamed, and he felt the angry waters already seizing his feet. But he was pulled, the coat half over his head—where was his hat? His head was uncovered before the Almighty!

The hat had fallen into the sea. The salt water stung his face and matted his beard. "My hat!" Yankel howled as he was tumbled into the bottom of the bark.

"I have your hat!" Feigel cried; she snatched it from the water and gave it to him, dripping.

So they were rowed, the Arabs chanting now, and Feigel naming the children one by one to make sure they were all there, little Avramchick with his huge gray-blue eyes, never crying or complaining at anything, and Schmulik to whom it was all a game, but what of Shaindeleh—would they find her? And would they also find all their belongings ashore? And would they meet Leah and Reuven? And if not, where would they go, what would they do? If only the little boat would move more quickly! It seemed to remain in the same place in the water! Would she soon have them all, Feigel worried, all her children, even Reuven and Leah too, with Dvora, Eliza, Gidon, Schmuel, Avramchick, and oy, Shaindeleh, would she have them all safely in her bosom? Soon, soon, on shore.

The father meanwhile touched his fingers against his inner belt to make sure that nothing had been lost in the terrible leap, and all the while he calculated in his mind what it had already cost him to get off that cursed ship, twice what he had allowed it would cost, enough money to feed the family for several days.

The little vessel plunged into the troughs but did not sink; his hat seemed already to be drying in the sun, but the gloss was gone; Yankel put the hat on to cover a Jew's head before the Above One. For a moment there was peace; the family gazed toward the city—houses of stone could be made out now, yellowish in color, and now even a few clusters of green trees, palm trees, standing before them on the hill that bulked into the sea, forming the harbor where Jonah the Prophet had taken ship.

All at once, still in mid-sea, the Arabs stopped rowing. Two of them abandoned their oars and stood up amongst the passengers, hands outstretched. "Baksheesh!" they roared, their great teeth bared under their pirate mustaches. The remaining boatmen rested on their oars—were they growling or laughing?

Five or six other passengers were in the vessel with Yankel and his family; two were ancient Arabs in their long white gowns, curled back amongst the baggage as though they were part of it. On the best seats in the middle were a few men wearing western clothing, perhaps merchants, with the air of experienced travelers, and among them was one who spoke Arabic. Bargaining began. Fists were shaken, a dagger was even pulled out, the chief pirate lifted aloft a suitcase—at least, Yankel saw, it was not one of theirs—and threateningly held it over the water. Now another of the bandits came to Yankel, seizing him by the lapels. First all their possessions would be thrown into the sea, and then they themselves!

Finally the man who spoke Arabic handed over money, and after much shouting, a little more. Though watching closely, Yankel could not tell how much had been extorted. The man was not a Jew or he might have settled a price for them all. Now, having made his bargain, the goy settled back and watched, even smiling, as the Arab bandit tried to seize from Yankel's hand a few coins he had brought out for a start. At last the goy leaned over and showed Yankel what he must pay—a small fortune, a robbery!—while the Arab still growled and threatened and demanded more, and another of the boatmen tried to seize Yankel's watch, pulling it by the chain out of his pocket. But at last they were saved, every passenger had been fleeced, the rowing began again, and in a moment the bandits were singing and laughing as though it was all a friendly game that they played every day.

And where, Yankel suddenly realized, was the great chest? the trunk from the hold of the ship? Would it be put ashore or would the steamer sail off with it?

A group of people could be made out now on the stone jetty; Gidon was the first to recognize their own, Reuven and Leah together! Thank God, Feigel saw, Leah already held Shaindeleh aloft to them! Everyone began to wave, in the tender, on the shore, yet even from this distance Feigel discerned that Reuven didn't look well. Leah was waving energetically, but Reuven only raised his arm once or twice and let it drop.

As the boat pulled to the wharf there was a tumult of embraces and weeping, even Leah's tears flowing on her happy beaming face, and Shaindeleh was relating her adventure, the whole family one cluster of flesh until the mother, having kissed her eldest son all over his face, held him off and studied him worriedly. "You have fever, Reuven, I can feel it on my lips."

"No, no, nothing, Mamaleh," he shrugged. "A touch of

kadahat," he said disparagingly. "I am just up from a little kadahat attack." And they had written that his malaria was finished!

"He shouldn't have got up," Leah shouted over the commotion. "I told him, stay in bed, but he had to come!" At least she herself was glowing, bursting with health, red-cheeked, her arms thick and strong. Leah had grown even taller, a giantess! Only, Reuven was a shadow of himself; at the open collar of his blouse his bones could be seen. His face was all hollow too, and his eyes glowed on the surface; what had at first seemed excitement was surely fever. Yet something of triumph was there too, Feigel saw. A fulfillment. He had got them all here. His brothers and sisters would grow up here, and not in the land of the czars.

Reuven put his arm around young Gidon's shoulders. The boy's eyes were also aglow. They were family eyes; both mother and father had them, as though both sides of the family were one, with the same warm dark Jewish eyes undercast with melancholy. Even in Leah with her beaming energy and joy, that dark look could suddenly peep through. Feigel recognized it from her own self; even in pretty Eliza with her feminine ways the melancholy would appear, masked as a childish wistfulness. And here in the midst of the outpouring of gladness, the sating of hunger for each other, Feigel saw the darkness behind the eyes of her eldest son.

"Nothing, the kadahat attack is over!" he assured her, and turned smiling to his father. "Nu?"

Yankel would indeed have wanted to savor the moment when a Jew at last set his foot on the shores of Eretz Ha-Kodesh, and even in the little rowboat he had prepared a Shehechiyanu to be said as he stepped ashore. But in this tumult the words he spoke were not to God but to Reuven. "So, you made us all come."

He had surely not intended to say these words, but a thousand devils tormented Yankel—how much money those bandits had torn from him on the one boat and the other, and what would he yet have to pay to retrieve their papers? And Feigel pregnant. And here was Reuven scarcely able to stand on his feet from the kadahat, the pioneer hero, and this fever was lurking for them all. Suddenly the land seemed hostile, the voyage a terrible mistake. How would he feed them all when his coins were gone?

"Your hat, Abba!" Leah was laughing. Already he was no longer tateh but abba, in Hebrew. And water still dripped from the brim of his good hat.

Meanwhile Reuven, surveying his father in his great fur-lined coat, his boots, his round velvet hat, the most respectable of Yehudim, cried out with the abruptness of the feverish, "Why wait! We must begin at once to make a new man out of you!" With this, Reuven darted to a stand in a row of stalls crowded against the wall behind them, an open market tumbled with bolts of cloth, earthen pots, tin pots, clocks. There Yankel saw a stand selling headgear, white tropical helmets for Christian pilgrims, red tarbooshes, Arab scarfs, caps. From a pile, Reuven seized a workman's cap, a common cap such as any wagon-driver wore in the old country, and before Yankel knew what was happening to him, his son had swept the fine round hat from his head and planted the work-cap on it. "There! Now you belong here, Father!"

All the children broke into laughter, and the vendor too, a Jew with a little yellow beard and watery eyes. Yankel felt stripped, shamed, his dignity wrenched from him by his eldest son. He had come, it was true, to labor, to pioneer— was he a man who had ever turned away from a task in all his life?—but this, this clownishness on the moment of his arrival in the Holy Land was like insulting a Jew on the Sabbath. Even a moujik wouldn't be so crass. Only his own son, the freethinker.

Nor did Reuven know why he had done it; such prankishness was not usually his way. Seeing the thunderstruck look on his father's face, he had an impulse to apologize, to say it was a touch of the fever; but just then a striking figure appeared before them, a ponderous bearded personality in a dazzling white flowing gown with a colorful sash and a jeweled curved dagger case, yet wearing a light straw Panama hat—perhaps a high Arab effendi? But with such a beard? The personality gazed upon the cluster of children, each a head taller than the next smaller, and with a beneficent smile, as though he were no Arab but Elijah the Prophet himself, the dignitary exclaimed, in good Hebrew, "Now here is a family for Eretz Yisroel!" And beaming on Yankel and Feigel, the Palestinian pronounced the blessing of welcome, "Beruchim haba'im!" Then taking a pinch of snuff, he went on his way.

Leah gazed after him. "Do you know who that was?" Her face was aglow. "It was Ostrov himself, Yehoshua Ostrov the Land-buyer." Ostrov, she explained, was an early settler who had gone up and down the whole of the land until he was known in every Arab village and every bedouin tent. He could tell you what tribe a man came from by his dialect, and he could speak to each in the tongue of his region. He was known also in Damascus and Beirut, he was the friend of every Arab effendi, and he had been the first to urge the purchase of a vast tract, those sands that could be seen stretching away from Jaffa to the north. A whole new Jewish town was to be built there one day, around a great new gymnasia, a modern high school, for the entire yishuv. When Avramchick grew up he would have a gymnasia to go to!

"Even the sands, we have to buy from them?" Yankel mumbled, but his daughter was filled with enthusiastic news of other great plans, especially in the Galilee, and meanwhile Reuven rushed about to complete their papers. A word of Turkish, a word of Arabic, he had learned. "Sit, sit, rest, everything will be in order," and he left them with Leah.

Twice Reuven had to come hurrying back to his father for more money. And why, Reuven demanded, had he changed currency in Constantinople? "How much did they give you?"

"Twenty-four."

"Here you can get twenty-nine." Yankel stared disconcerted at his son—then why had Reuven not written a word of warning? Meanwhile on all sides vendors pressed on them soap, beads, even crosses elaborately encrusted with mother-of-pearl. An Arab boy, chattering excitedly, pushed a whole box of crosses at him. Yankel pulled away, avoiding the contamination, and spat. Even in Eretz Yisroel a Jew couldn't get free of their Yoshka.

A short distance off, Yankel could see Reuven paying out his money to some sleepy-eyed Turk; Reuven was paying too much, he was sure—the socialist had always disdained a bit of honest bargaining.

At last it was done. Reuven had their pilgrim cards. And the big trunk with their belongings was safe, it had been hauled down from the ship, Reuven had seen it with his own eyes in the shed.

Yankel's family started picking up their bundles and va-lises, Gidon driving off a shouting swarm of porters while Leah cheerily called out an Arab word to them that got them to leave off. The family would carry the things them-selves. And with Feigel constantly turning her head to make sure that not a child had been lost, especially Schmu-lik who had already once disappeared at his first sight of a camel, they formed a line and moved on into the narrow crowded lanes of Jaffa.

Moment by moment Yankel's heart was growing heavier with misgivings. Now the stench and filth of the Oriental city was upon him. This was not what he had envisioned. A place of dignity, among lemon trees, a barn with a good cow or two, a goat, green fields, and going out with his sons to their labors. Sabbath at ease beneath his own fig and vine. Of course, once away from this fetid Arab city all might yet become true.

In the swarming passageway they had to string out single file. The stink was in the very stones—urine, garbage, dead fish. Fierce, ugly cats darted from behind the stalls. And the Arab children, some entirely naked, the older ones in a few rags, pressed around them crying "baksheesh." Tots hardly bigger than Avramchick, beggars already! Other children sat apathetic against the hovels, their eyes crowded with flies.

Reuven led the family up the lane. —The Galilee! He was explaining, everyone was leaving for the Galilee! A true Eden! In his last letters he had already written this, declaring he was arranging for a homestead for them. They would go at once, he said now, they would go tomorrow morning to the recently opened Zionist settlement office. They would be received by Dr. Lubin himself, the director. A family, a whole large family like this—whenever had any-one seen such a family arriving!

And even in that crowded lane it was true they were a spectacle, for now they had entered a Jewish part of the street where there were shopwindow signs in Hebrew and Yiddish, and out of doorways shopkeepers and housewives appeared to gaze on the immigrants—so many children! sons and daughters for Eretz Yisroel! A blessing on them!

Smiling, calling a welcome, they asked, "Where does a Jew come from?" It seemed as though the entire Jewish population was embracing the arrival of Yankel Chaimovitch with his family. Many already knew Leah, and cried out cheerily to her, "Your family has arrived! Bless God! Beruchim haba'im!"

But out of nowhere there came a doleful wretch with inflamed sick eyes and a ragged beard, who whispered savagely as he passed close to Yankel, "Fool! Turn around, get back on the ship and go home!"

The moment they entered the hotel, Feigel felt better. A true Jewish house, with an odor of home, an odor of cleanliness and warm bread. This was the Zuckerman place, a home to all the lads of the Poale Zion, Leah told her, while calling out greetings to one and another of the young men who sat over their glasses of tea, immersed in discussions. Mother Zuckerman had already come out of the kitchen and was counting the numerous Chaimovitch children with mounting admiration. She already had heard—Leah and Reuven had told her—the entire family was arriving—but such fine Jewish children! such bright faces! Such a family, arriving after such a journey! They must be hungry! She would make a large omelette for them, they must want to rest, and how did it feel to be in Eretz Yisroel! Like her own, Mother Zuckerman gathered them to her.

The family would best lie on the roof; there were no rooms just now, but in any case in the late wave of heat after the holidays, the roof was better, it would cost the father less, and she had prepared a whole separate corner for them with fresh straw mattresses. It was not luxurious, her hotel, but clean she tried to keep it, and that was not easy in Jaffa. And leading them outside to mount a stone stairway, Mother Zuckerman was already deep in household talk with Feigel, telling her that in a place like this, no sooner was the Arab girl finished sponging the floors than she had to begin all over again.

Throughout the meal there was still no moment for Feigel even to begin to talk to her eldest daughter of those things, she already saw, that had not been written in the letters, and that gave her anxiety. Why was Reuven again suffering from his fever when Leah had cheerfully written that it was cured? He looked somehow another person—

what had happened to him in this year? And in Leah her-self Feigel thought she detected glints of darkness or even embarrassment when their eyes met; something difficult needed to be told, though her big girl was so happy at their coming.

Mother Zuckerman's milk-soup was good, the meal was like at home, but they must try a dish from here, Leah said, something called hommus, and at last it was brought, a white paste in olive oil, to eat with bread. "The chalutzim live on it, like the Arabs," Mama Zuckerman laughed, and explained to Feigel how it was made from crushed chick-peas, and seasoned. Eliza tasted it and made a face, but Gidon scooped it with his bread. "Already a native!"

It was only after the meal when Leah returned to the roof with Feigel to sort things out that the time came to talk. Reuven and Yankel with the young ones had gone back to the port to bring out the big trunk, and Dvora was lingering below, for the lads from the boat had also found their way here to Zuckerman's.

Feigel began with her anxiety for Reuven. The more she learned of his kadahat, the more she feared; would it re-main with him all his life then, coming back in these at-tacks? And what of the younger children she had brought here?—Look at me! Leah said. Not everyone caught it, nor was it everywhere. When you were in the bad places, you had to take quinine every day. Then slowly as they decided who should sleep where, and while they lifted and in-spected the bedding—inside the hotel there were bugs, Leah said, but not here on the roof—bit by bit their year unwound before Feigel. Much, with Leah, was as she had feared. Good she had come. For at last when they sat down on a straw mattress, in a gush her daughter told of the Handsome One she had sometimes mentioned in her let-ters, a "good comrade," though she had always mixed him in with the other "good chaverim," a Dovidl, a Rahel. Only now Feigel came to see how it all had been in their first year in the land, how much had happened to them that was not in the letters, how the deepest things in life, even the edge of death, had been touched in these months, and she shivered—If the worst had happened, she would not even have been here, she would have been so far away. Good she had come, for these torments were still not ended, surely she was needed. For her big Leachkeh, whom she had wanted to believe still a girl, was no longer so. And her Reuven, who she had imagined would pass into manhood here, had remained, his sister sighed, without anyone. To both, much, much had happened.

2

IT WAS here to Zuckerman's that Reuven and Leah had been brought a year before by a gangly, bespectacled Workers of Zion comrade named Avner who attended the arrival of ships. It was the same Avner, Reuven cried excitedly to Leah on seeing him, who had spoken at the secret meeting in Kishinev where he had gone with their cousin Tolya Koslovsky two years ago.

Tolya wore a student cap and was already a member of a social revolutionary cell, but he had condescended to listen to "the other side," the Zionists. The lanky Avner, come back from Eretz at the risk of arrest, was no fiery orator. Like a teacher, he set things forth. Thus and such were the labor conditions. These were the limited possibilities at present. Spadeful by spadeful the land would be built, brick by brick. No use to go begging as Herzl had to the great powers, the British, the Kaiser, the Sultan, for rights in Palestine. Go to the land and work. Solemnly Avner had repeated the ancient saying of Rabbi Hillel, "If I am not for myself, who will be for me? And if not now, then when?"

Tolya was sarcastic. "There he stands, your leader, even a modern fellow who claims to bring socialist ideas into your Zionist movement, and whom does he quote? A rabbi. Reuven, Zionism is a movement that will never rid itself of religion, which means superstition and reaction." And he was off on a flood of quotations from the brilliant young Jewish revolutionist Leon Trotsky, who had led the strikes and headed the soviets in St. Petersburg and was even now on the way to Siberia.

"Forget you are a Jew, immerse yourself in the world revolution!" Tolya exhorted. "Only then will we get rid of the curse on our people! The trouble with you, Reuven, is you are still at heart a yeshiva bocher!"

"You are wrong! I am a freethinker!" Reuven insisted to his cousin. He had left the yeshiva and was reading at home, while working in Tolya's father's sugar-beet mill to help out, for his own father had had another failure. Now he retorted to his cousin from the writings of Joseph Brenner, the Awakener, who had broken with the Jewish Socialist Bund and joined the Zionist camp. "What are our Jewish socialists? They're blown by the wind, trying to ape the goyim, but they are dancers at a stranger's wedding. They rush to lead a strike in the steel mills, yet not one Jew is a steel worker! First we must become ourselves, tear off our masks and face the emptiness of our own lives. Even our leaders, our intelligentsia, are false to themselves—they want nothing but to be acceptable to the goyish intelligentsia, they're simply assimilationists, and so are our social revolutionaries. We will be true social revolutionists when we remove the motive of getting away from our own people, and are revolutionists so as to reconstruct our own Jewish life. And for that we must remove ourselves bodily. Only as workers in Zion—"

That was the way! That was the only way, Reuven decided. The writer, Joseph Brenner, was a vegetarian and he too, after reading a screed against flesh-eating in *The Awakener,* decided no longer to eat meat.

In the last year at home, Reuven and his sister Leah had grown closer and closer. They had planted their vegetable garden. Every scrap of knowledge that Reuven brought from his self-teaching from botanical books drew wondering enthusiasm from Leah. They saved their kopecks and made their plans. And when they arrived in Jaffa, though Reuven had exchanged hardly ten words with the leader at that secret meeting in Kishinev, Avner had remembered him and cried out his welcome. And the boy had brought his big strapping sister, too!

From the harbor, Avner had taken them here to Mother Zuckerman's. Then, too, tea-drinkers had been sitting around the four or five little tables, where you entered from the street—workers who had come to Jaffa from the settlements for a bit of news of the world, for a look around, to find out if jobs were more plentiful in Rishon, in Petach

Tikvah?—or perhaps shamefacedly to inquire for a boat home.

Upstairs were cots, seven or eight to a room, and there were also a few holes off the stairway where a sick chalutz might lie in miserable solitude trying to overcome his fever, his dysentery, his bleak despair over a failed ideal.

On the very day of their arrival, eager to begin at once to labor on the earth of Eretz, the brother and sister, leaving their belongings with the Zuckermans, had set off across the sands to the settlements.

A diligence plied between Jaffa and the little chain of "the Baron's" villages to the south, Rishon le Zion, Nes Ziona, Rehovot—First in Zion, Miracle of Zion, Broad Fields—but Reuven and Leah chose to set out, as befitted laborers, on foot. It was best, Mother Zuckerman advised Reuven, at least to carry a stick.

Suddenly before an endless stretch of dunes the town of Jaffa stopped. Leah sat down on the earth, unbuttoned and pulled off her shoes, her stockings, and Reuven did the same. So now they were barefoots, as the Baron's settlers called the chalutzim. As the thinker Borochov wrote, you must renew your contact, bare feet to the bare earth! How warm, how good it was, under their feet!

At that time in this sleepy impoverished byway of the decaying Turkish empire, there were scattered perhaps three hundred thousand inhabitants in all, less than a tenth of the population supported by the land in the thriving days of the ancient Jewish kingdom. But here along the coast behind the rim of the dunes was a relatively prosperous area, the golden strip bearing the golden fruits, groves of oranges and lemons, almond trees, and vineyards. South of Jaffa were the richest plantations of the Arab effendis, and amongst them in the last quarter of a century several Jewish settlements had grown. To Reuven and Leah and their comrades this growth was on a mistaken basis.

The Jewish planters had started with the best intentions. Even before the Lovers of Zion groups had begun to arrive from Russia and Roumania, the moribund, pious old Jewish community in Jerusalem had caught a spark of the back-to-the-land ideal. A devout textile magnate from England, Moses Montefiore, had visited the Jews in their hovels within the ancient city walls, the pious ones who lived

on a system of dividing donations from abroad. It was
called the sharing out, the chaluka. With the thought of
changing their mendicant mentality, of bringing them out
from their dungeon habitations into the clear air, and of
providing them a means of self-support, Montefiore had
built houses just outside the Old City walls and set up
looms powered by a windmill. This industrial effort had
failed, but a few of the enlightened supervisors sent by
Moses Montefiore had remained. Tolstoyan and Fourierian
ideas of a return to nature were in the air, and there had
also come to Jerusalem a leader from the French Jewish
Society, the Alliance Israélite Universelle, who founded an
agricultural school on the Jerusalem-Jaffa road, calling it
Mikveh Israel, the Well of Israel, and hoping to lure to it
the sons of those same chaluka Jews. From all these impulses together, a small group of Jerusalemites had ventured
down to the coastal area, bought swampland around the
source-springs of the Yarkon River, and founded a village
they called Petach Tikvah, the Door of Hope.

Though Arabs living on a hill some distance away had
warned them against the infested lowlands, the good Jews
built houses and brought down their families. Joyously harvesting their first crop of grain, they carried it triumphantly
to Jerusalem in a garlanded convoy of wagons, like King
David bringing back the Ark of the Law from the Philistines, up the very same road. But that winter many in Petach Tikvah died of yellow fever. One house after another
stood abandoned, until the village was so empty that a settler's body lay for a week undiscovered.

A few years later, with houses built on higher ground, a
new effort was made. In the same years groups of the Lovers of Zion had begun to arrive, founding their colonies
south of Jaffa. Foundering in their first year for lack of
water, they had desperately sent an emissary to Paris, to
the "Great Giver," Baron Edmond de Rothschild, and he,
a pious Jew, influenced by the Chief Rabbi of Paris who
was himself a Lover of Zion, and impressed by the horny,
toil-hardened hands of Reb Feinberg, the emissary, had
given money for well-digging. Gradually the "Great Giver"
had turned the redemption of the soil of Israel into a personal project, founding a score of new settlements in addition to subsidizing earlier ones. The Baron's overseers con-
trolled everything. They even selected bright children for

schooling in France, and the daughters of the pioneers returned home playing Mozart.

Fellaheen in nearby Arab villages found they could earn more in Jewish settlements than they could from their tiny share of the crop on their debt-ridden lands. And so, year by year, the Jewish planters themselves went more rarely into their vineyards. The golden orange was discovered, more profitable than the grape, and their groves expanded. Only a few of the Baron's more isolated settlements in the Galilee kept to "real" farming, growing wheat.

The Baron's private messianic movement seemed to have leveled off after creating but a dozen villages. It was then that a new wave of pogroms stimulated Theodor Herzl's politically messianic vision of a Jewish state. This renewal of the ideal aroused a new wave of young people, imbued with a socialist ideal as well, to "go up" to the land. They were called the second Aliyah—the second "going up." They would go up as toilers, chalutzim!

The first steps of the newcomers, naturally, like those of Reuven and Leah, were directed to the already existing Jewish villages that had been nurtured by the Baron, where they hoped to find work. But there, unhappily, they found themselves regarded as a plague. Arab labor was cheap and subservient.

Trudging across the sands, brother and sister were for quite a time alone. To their left, inland, they had kept in view a fringe of greenery where the citrus groves began; now, as they plunged downward on a dune slope, the groves vanished from sight, and all before them and surrounding them was sand.

This was a moment that neither was to forget. Each pioneer in later years was to be fond of relating something akin to a mystical experience when "Eretz entered into him." So it was now with Reuven and Leah. The skinlike smoothness of the untrodden sand, the absolute cleanliness of all creation, the pure sea-blue of the quiet Mediterranean, the solitude around them and the presence of each other exalted them. We have done it! Brother! Sister! We are here! Leah's and Reuven's eyes said this to each other in a pledge of fervor, joy, dedication, a declaration that what they had known in their souls to be their true course was indeed so.

So they stood still and breathed, smiling happily to each other.

They would not have expected this joy to come to them in an emptiness of untouched sand. They would have thought it would come when they stood amidst the first Jewish fields; yet it had come to them here in the open dune.

After a time they heard a soft clanging and realized these were camel bells. The caravan appeared on the ridge, coming toward them, perhaps from Egypt as the brothers of Joseph must once have come, returning with their beasts laden with grain, swollen sacks on each side of each animal.

Exactly as in Abel Pam's Biblical pictures, a small Arab on a small donkey led the train; alongside the camels walked other long-robed men. Leah stilled her heart and smiled to Reuven. One should not fear the Arabs.

So the two continued walking as though quite familiar with these dunes, and presently as they neared the caravan the Arab on the lead donkey greeted them. "Ma'asaalam," he said. In this moment both Reuven and Leah caught the real meaning of the ancient greeting offered when strangers approach each other.—Peace, they call out, to say "For our part there will be no hostility."

"Shalom!" both cried, and Leah smiled her large, warm, healthy smile.

A tall one in a long striped galabiya made a remark, then laughed, showing gold-studded teeth. They didn't know he had jestingly offered to buy the shoes and the girl together, but Leah laughed a responding laugh, and kept walking. When the camels had passed, she said to her brother, "There is really nothing to fear. They are good friendly people," and Reuven nodded his agreement. All people were at heart good.

So they reached the top of a high dune and beheld square white houses with tiled roofs, not unlike a shtetl. Presently they arrived at the village. There were Jews with beards and Jews without beards, hurrying, or riding donkeys, or sitting on wagons just like peasant carts at home, or buying from the stands and shops in the open square where there also stood a shul. And there was indeed the little fashion shop that satirists of the Baron's settlements had written about, a shop with women's gowns from Paris in the window. It was all true.

A passerby, one of their own kind—a barefoot—and tall, Leah noticed at once, with thick black curly hair—greeted them with an ironic, "Well, does our Little Paris find favor in your eyes, chaverim?"

At the same time Leah saw in his smile a comradely intimacy, welcoming them for having come here just as he had come. True, his eyes also examined Leah with a young man's speculation. And she herself—was she not after all a girl of seventeen looking at each man she encountered with that fateful romantic wonder—would this be He?

Despite all the talk of a new generation and freedom, at home a girl knew there was constant scheming about a match for her. Already seventeen! And her mother's worried eyes. But she had at last truly broken free, to seek her destined one by herself. Sometimes Leah suspected that perhaps this was even a reason her mother had finally permitted her to come with Reuven, so that she should have a chance to follow her own heart when it came to marriage.

"Work?" the young man chortled, talking to Reuven while his eyes still gazed intimately into Leah's. "In this town if you put on a galabiya and a keffiyah you have better luck." Still, he said, if one of the growers took a liking to you, and if you could live on olives and pittah, the generous Jew might provide you with a cabin in his vineyard as a watchman, for the Baron's settlers had finally learned that their Arab watchmen were themselves the biggest pilferers. And what was the news back there? He had caught himself up from saying "back home," Leah sensed. He spoke of "that place" with contempt and yet a kind of eagerness; how was the movement progressing? He meant not just the Poale Zion, she sensed, but the whole revolutionary movement. Naturally he wanted to know. Then, even while lamenting that there was no work, the chaver grumbled: Why didn't more comrades come, especially girls? The movement—and now it was their own movement, of course, that he meant—ought to organize an immigration of girls!

"Here I am!" Leah laughed.

"Yes, a good sign," he said. "We don't have enough girls even to take care of the workers' kitchen."

"The kitchen!" she cried. "I came here to work on the land!"

"O ho!" and she saw that he had teased her. His name was Moshe, and he now led them to a cabin just outside the high cactus fence of a lemon grove. How good it smelled! "This is our kvutsa," Moshe explained.

Reuven and Leah had already encountered the word in the underground paper of the Poale Zion. A kvutsa was a small group living together, each putting whatever he earned into the common fund. It was a communa, like the communa started by some workers in Kiev to carry them through a strike.

Inside the cabin were half a dozen sleeping places made of planks resting on upended orange crates. A curtain of sacking screened off one corner, which Moshe indicated to Leah with a sweeping mock-bow was for the chaveroth. Just now they had but one girl in the kvutsa. She came in from the yard where she had been hanging out washing; older than Leah, perhaps twenty, with short, heavy legs and a bulging bust, Nahama had a pronounced mustache, pearled with sweat. But at once her warmheartedness engulfed you.

Did she belong to the handsome Moshe, Leah wondered, or to either of the two other comrades who wandered in and out of the cabin, tossing a cynical word into the conversation now and again? You could always tell, simply from the special looks a girl gave, which of a group of boys was hers, but here Leah couldn't tell. Perhaps the Handsome Moshe was free? Only one thing was clear, even here in the kvutsa it was again the woman who was doing all the cooking and washing.

"I'll admit to you honestly," Nahama said to her, "For me, I don't mind. I don't especially like to work in the fields. I like to be in the house." She half-giggled in apology for her backwardness.

A kvutsa was the only way they could manage to subsist, Moshe was explaining. Whoever got work for a day or two put in his earnings. And also, sometimes they managed to get jobs as a group, on contract, all six together, for by using a bit of Jewish intelligence they could get things done far more efficiently than under an overseer, and thus they could compete with the price of Arab labor. Right now they were even negotiating with the newly opened Zionist office in Jaffa to go out as a group to work a tract of land recently purchased in the Galilee. Under Turkish law, if the land was not worked it would revert to the government.

"Stay, stay with us a few days and become acclimated," Moshe urged. Reuven and Leah insisted on paying for food, and Leah went off with Nahama to the village market. There Arab women sat on the ground in a row, each with a little pile of chickpeas and a few eggs on a piece of straw, much like the peasant women in the village market in Cherezinka. Admiringly Leah listened to Nahama bargaining in Arabic. "Oh, you'll soon enough learn a few words, it's much like Hebrew." They bought a large round Arab pittah—it was cheaper than Jewish bread—and at supper each tore off a chunk. Nahama had made a good bean soup, they had cheese and olives, and for each an egg—the contribution of the newcomers, Nahama announced.

During the meal a short young man appeared—Dovidl. He had a huge head with bristly hair, and talked so cleverly that at times Leah found herself no longer looking at Moshe. Indeed from the first instant something completely familiar had sprung into existence between her and this Dovidl, and as in the encounter with Moshe, though not involving man-and-womanness, Leah had a feeling that a meeting of importance for her whole life was occurring here. Unfortunately, as to man-and-womanness, this Dovidl was so small it would have looked ridiculous. Yet here was something perhaps even as important as finding a mate—a friendship could come of it.

He was not a part of the kvutsa, it seemed—indeed he made a barbed little joke about Moshe's snatching up new arrivals. "What were you at home, Poale Zion?" he asked of Reuven. "So what are you doing here with these renegades?" This was a camp of independents, they even had an adherent of the rival party, the Poël Hatzaïr. Not the Workers of Zion, but the Young Workers. A fine nerve that crowd had to call themselves a workers' party, they weren't even Marxists!

"So what are you afraid of!" Moshe laughed.

"Beware!" Dovidl went on. "They are super-idealists, they'll make a vegetarian out of you!"

"I am one already," laughed Reuven.

Dovidl turned to Leah. "And you follow your brother?"

"Not in everything," she declared. She had never been able to suppress her love for her mameh's Sabbath eve chicken, she confessed, and at the smell of potted breast of veal, her whole insides would melt.

From his banter Dovidl turned to his big news; bursting with it, he had hurried to the nearest camp of workers, even if they were not Poale Zion. "They gave me a job in the winery!" he announced.

"No! Just like that? Or did you put on a yarmulkeh?"

Well, he had brought a letter to the manager from a rich Jew at home who knew him. And already Dovidl had a clever plan. He was going to organize the grape-treaders in the Baron's winery and pull them out on a strike! The trick was that this was one place where Arabs could not be substituted, for sacramental wine was the product, and to be sacramental it had to be produced by Jewish hands!

"—and feet!" Moshe laughed.

Therefore, Dovidl triumphantly explained, only barely smiling at Moshe's joke, the Baron's managers would have to give in! He had already made it clear to the wine-treaders that they held the upper hand.

"But what good will this do us?" demanded one of the kvutsa, a tight-lipped chalutz named Max Wilner. The wine-treaders were all strictly orthodox Jews from the old world, he pointed out, far away from—even hostile to—the thinking of socialist workers.

—Ah, Dovidl twinkled, he had already done a little work among them. And he was off, quoting Scripture like a yeshiva bocher, citing the socialistic pronouncements of the prophets. Besides, one of the demands of the strike would be for Jewish labor to be used all through the winery, even in sealing the bottles, and in another year the contract could be still further broadened—already this Dovidl talked as if he had a contract!—so that only Jewish hands tended the vines. There must be something in the Talmud to support such a claim! He would find some rabbi in Jerusalem—

Why not, Reuven joined in the game. Just as the truly pious kept a watch over the fields of grain intended for matzoh, to make sure all was pure—matzoh schmira, this was called—so there could be a grape watch for sacramental wine—a yayin schmira!

"Exactly!" cried Dovidl. He would show the rabbis that

they could get all their relatives employed as ritual watchmen, and thus instantly gain their allegiance.

Everybody laughed. "Dovidl, you're not going to make a compact with the rabbis!" said Nahama.

"Why not? Doesn't Plekhanov say, with the devil himself, if it furthers the cause? So why not with the rabbis?"

"There's your Marxist! He brings friendly letters to the Baron's managers, he makes compacts with the rabbis—next, for the sake of his Marxist revolution, he will become a boss!" snapped the dour-looking one called Max, resorting to Yiddish.

"At least I speak Hebrew, not jargon," retorted Dovidl. And now began a back-and-forth discussion of the kind Leah loved to listen to, where ideals whirled like swords in the air, and the deepest subjects were touched upon. Meanwhile each person was becoming clearer to her as she followed their words with the avidity with which one listens in a new group; Reuven too was feeling his way among them, putting in a word here and there, quoting now from Ber Borochov, now from Tolstoy. It was Max Wilner who kept opposing Dovidl, he had a compact head like stone and was humorless, but he had read more than anyone else. Another chaver, besmeared from a day's work in a lime pit, had the remains of a harelip that had been poorly sewn up, and spoke with a slight difficulty; Shimek, he was called, and his eyes followed Nahama though she didn't seem to have even a glance for him. Already in her life Leah had observed that some persons with a defect insist on doing what is hardest for them; so Shimek spoke much, and everyone had to wait for the words to come out though they had already guessed what he would say. He disagreed now with Wilner, now with Dovidl. It was like the old Jewish saying, if you have three Jews coming to a town, two of them will start opposing synagogues and the third will declare, "I go to neither!"

Just so, they all believed in socialist ideas, but Max Wilner accused Dovidl, "You still adhere to the Socialist International! And what will you do when the International turns anti-Zionist?"

"That can't be!" Dovidl cried, "Each member party has full rights!"

"We must achieve our own socialism in our own conditions here."

"Socialism! You don't even believe in the class struggle, in the victory of the proletariat!" Dovidl snorted.

"We believe in the true classless society, by technical progress."—And again they began throwing quotations at each other, ah, it was wonderful to hear.

Presently Leah noticed that another girl had joined them, a comely girl in a nice dress. One of the daughters of the orange growers, Nahama acidly whispered. And not long afterwards Moshe went off to walk the girl home.

Reuven lay down on the floor to sleep, but Nahama insisted that Leah share her cot. "I am so big," Leah laughed, "you'll have no room." They lay in sisterly closeness. The night was permeated with the scent of almonds.

"I saw Handsome Moshe looking at you," Nahama whispered. "Beware of Moshe, Leah, he will break your heart. He is a heartbreaker." Her whisper trembled.

So that was it. Even where there was a shortage of girls, their hearts could be broken.

In the morning Moshe announced with a wink that he had last night found work for the entire kvutsa. Even the newcomer, Reuven, could come along. Moshe had secured a contract with the village girl's father to plant seedlings to enlarge his grove.

"Take me too!" Leah exclaimed. The men were dubious, but Moshe said she could come along at least to keep them company. Ecstatically Leah strode out with the group—already on their first morning she and Reuven were going to the fields!

Entering by a large wrought-iron gate that interrupted the cactus fence wall, they walked between a double lane of cypress trees—windbreaks, Reuven told her. Behind were orange trees. Leah had an impulse to run over and embrace each one.

Now a horseman came toward them and dismounted. He was middle-aged and heavy, wearing riding breeches with boots and an embroidered Russian blouse. This was the grove manager, one of the few Biluim who had remained, Handsome Moshe told Leah; he had married the daughter of a Lover of Zion, a planter with large holdings. "He still has a twinge of idealism so he uses Jewish labor whenever he can prove to his father-in-law that we cost no more than Arabs." Thus the contract had been made for a lump sum.

At the edge of the field where the new section of the grove was laid out, a half-dozen mattocks lay ready; the men picked them up and went to work. There was none left for Leah.

Moshe, doubtless wanting to gauge the newcomer's worth, paired off with Reuven, digging planting-holes. Reuven's mattock struck the earth and almost in a continuation of the movement lifted out a heavy lipful of soil. Moshe smiled and glanced at Leah. Her brother knew how to work! They were already moving ahead of the other pairs.

Though telling herself she was watching her brother, Leah knew her eyes would not leave Handsome Moshe. His long body moved with the mattock in such balance that no effort seemed expended; as the chevreh said, Moshe was truly an artist with the implement. When her brother glanced back and caught her in her entrancement, Leah flushed.

The ex-Bilu was unwrapping burlap from the seedling roots. As he approached a planting-hole, Leah hurried over to him, and held the little tree upright while he pressed soil around the base. Kneeling, she too pressed down the earth. Here she was already planting trees in the earth of Eretz Yisroel! Warm, pliant, like living flesh it felt to her hand!

When the sun was higher, Nahama arrived on a donkey cart laden with food. She had brought a huge canister filled with tea. There was loaf-bread this time, with jam, tomatoes, cheese. Gathering around the cart in that inimitable relaxed comradeship of respite from labor, the chevreh ate and talked, Reuven and Leah included not even as newcomers but as part of the kvutsa. If they completed the planting in three days, Moshe calculated, they would earn enough to keep the kvutsa for two whole weeks.

"On pittah and chickpeas," one of the comrades said. His name was Araleh, and he was blondish, with a skin covered with freckles, and clumps of hair on his knuckles. He had not been there the night before.

"The Arabs live on it and so should we," replied Max Wilner with his teacherish finality.

"What did we come here for, to reduce ourselves to

Arab fellaheen?" Araleh demanded didactically. "To prove we too can become serfs?"

"The Arabs are workers and we are workers, and when it comes to workers, there is no distinction between Arab and Jew," Handsome Moshe declared.

"Why not raise their level instead of lowering ours?" Leah put in, from the discussions of Reuven's circle at home. But Araleh objected. "This is not the way!" he exclaimed, waving his tomato. "To repeat in Eretz all the struggles we have in other lands, there with the peasants, here with the fellaheen."

"How will you not repeat it?" Moshe demanded. "The class struggle is one the world over."

"We must start at their economic level, and as we raise ours, help them raise theirs," Max pronounced. "We will teach them cooperation by example."

"Idealism!" Araleh shrugged. He, for one, was interested simply in building the land. The land itself. This land. Let the Arabs solve their own problems. Large tracts of land were being bought by the Keren Kayemeth in the name of the whole Jewish people. Why should he labor here planting a grove for an effendi—yes, this type of Jewish landowner was just as much an effendi as an Arab. Instead, they must go as a group and cultivate land that belonged to the Jewish people itself. Not to private growers exporting oranges for the tables of the rich. As for the Arab fellaheen, if they wanted to continue to live in the Middle Ages, that was their own affair.

"But it can never work like that!" cried Handsome Moshe, and they were off on the whole argument—which was to come first, the workers' world revolution, or Jewish settlement of this land?

"Together!" Reuven declared.—Everything had to be worked out here at one and the same time, Jewish settlement and socialism together. Were not those the words of Ber Borochov—

In any case they just now had to go on with the planting, Araleh reminded them, for here was the boss approaching, mounted on his steed, back from his second breakfast at the big house.

So they rose and went to their tasks, but somehow stimulated by the argument. They had been called back to themselves as bearers of an idea, they would never be mere clods in the field.

At the far end of the section, cuttings of a different sort were laid out for an intermediate windbreak. Reuven examined the leaves. "Leah, do you know what this is?" he cried. "It's the tamarisk, the same tree that Abraham planted."

Handsome Moshe smiled at the naïve enthusiasm of the newcomers.

The grove had been planted and now only two men of the kvutsa, Shimek and Araleh, went out to their lime-plastering job. Max Wilner went off to Petach Tikvah to see if things were better, but returned to say they were worse. Reuven felt he and Leah should leave so as not to be a burden on the group. But Leah had a thought. Why should they not first plant a vegetable garden around the cabin so the kvutsa would have its own greens? A long discussion ensued. The bit of land was not theirs, it belonged to the village. But who would stop them from planting? Max Wilner elevated use of public land to a principle. The whole kvutsa labored putting in cucumbers and carrots and eggplant. This did not pass unnoticed, but luckily the first town leader to pass by was "a good one," a planter who had himself once labored as a chalutz. Later he had accepted family money to buy land. He employed both Arabs and Jews. A rather thin man with a compassionate face, the pardessan watched them for a while, said, "Why not? A good idea. But perhaps you should first have asked permission," and walked on. His name was Moshe Smilansky, Moshe said, and he was also something of a Hebrew writer.

"I've read his stories!" Reuven cried, as though to run after the man. "They are good."

"Tell him," Moshe laughed. "Maybe he'll give you work."

The second day Leah straightened up to see a young woman standing there, a neat girl wearing glasses. She was in European dress, a girl delicately made, with small hands, and bare feet. At her very first glance Leah wondered, might this be a girl for her brother Reuven? He was shy, and yet she knew he yearned. At home he had found no one for himself.

Already the others had greeted the girl—Rahel. What was she doing here? Where was Avner?—No use, then, thought Leah, if this was Avner's chavera. Avner was in an endless sitting in Jaffa, Rahel said, so she had come here. Already she was squatting, examining the planting. Just what variety of eggplant was this, Rahel wanted to know, and what was the proper planting depth? Two centimeters, it seemed to her she had read—

"I just plant them," Leah said. "At home they grew fine."

"Oh." At once this Rahel became diffident. "I only know from books," and she began to plant under Leah's direction. A curious one. Even when she poured water she seemed to need a measuring glass. She had prepared herself with book-learning, she was half an agronomist, but she nearly cut off her big toe with a mattock. And yet by the end of the row they were good friends. "If I only had the feel in my hands like you," she envied Leah. "But I'll learn to work, you'll see." Leah wanted to hug, to protect, this delicate Rahel. Again there was a premonition in her that a lifelong friendship had begun.

Just as they finished putting in their vegetable garden, Handsome Moshe brought word from Jaffa, once more rescuing the kvutsa. A forest was to be planted in memory of Theodor Herzl on a tract purchased by the Keren Kayemeth in a place called Hulda on the way to Jerusalem.

Before dawn the kvutsa set off, Rahel among them. Beyond the outmost orange grove the earth stretched cracked and dry; every green thing had been devoured by Bedouin goats. After an hour's walk they came to the site; an old stone hut stood in the field, and there they found the overseer, Kramer, a well-known man in the land, an agricultural expert from the Baron's settlements.

"But you're too late!" Kramer gestured—on the field they saw a number of fellaheen working, taking the pine saplings out of their clay pots and setting them into the soil.

"You've brought in Arabs on Keren Kayemeth land to plant the Herzl forest!" Araleh cried out indignantly.

No help for it! The office in Jaffa had sent them too late; they must leave.

It was then that the memorable rage of Reuven Chaimovitch broke forth, all the more startling to the chevreh as already in these few days he had become known as a quiet and dreamy fellow. But it was a rage that Leah knew, a rage that belonged in the family, a rage that she had witnessed at home, breaking out of her father—not often, perhaps once in a year—but who in the town of Cherezinka did not know that one must flee before the rage of Yankel Chaimovitch as before a tornado?

And like a tornado Reuven rushed down the row of young pines, uprooting them, tearing the newly planted trees out of the earth. The startled fellaheen made no move to prevent him, standing back and staring, looking from the mad Jew to the Jewish supervisor.

"In memory of Theodor Herzl!" Reuven roared. "Jewish land! A Jewish forest! And Jewish hands are not wanted to plant it!"

Leah noticed Rahel watching her brother with such a look on her face as when one watches a superb display of nature, a sky of lightning and thunder. Kramer uttered not a word. He glanced at the sullen members of the kvutsa, and walked into the stone hut.

Reuven remained standing among the uprooted trees. His sister went over to him, and in a moment Handsome Moshe joined them.

"You did well, Reuven," Moshe said.

And Rahel spoke also, as though representing the entire Jewish people, "Reuven, you did right."

A few steps away the fellaheen were gathering together. One moved to pick up a sapling and set it back into the earth. "Leave it alone!" Reuven roared in Hebrew. The Arab shrugged and dropped the plant. Then he and his companions simply squatted down on the earth.

After a little time Moshe went over and spoke to them; it seemed he knew some Arabic. Then Kramer came out and spoke to them more fully. They arose and went away. Now Kramer approached the kvutsa.

The fellaheen were from the village of Zayuma nearby, the overseer said, their sheikh had sent them. Standing with his back to Reuven, Kramer declared that he understood what had happened—did he not have the same ideals in this land as they? Else why was he here, wasting his life in a yishuv full of madmen? But he had his problems too, and not always was he understood. The allocation for planting the forest was virtually nil. He had had to combine and contrive, even to beg, so as to obtain the seedlings, which at last had been donated by the agricultural school, Mikveh Israel. As to these Arabs, a small gift, a sheep, had been offered to their sheikh, who had sent them over, for no pay.

"Of course you are right," Kramer recognized, with a side-glance toward Avner's Rahel. "It is only appropriate to have the Herzl forest planted by Jewish hands. But wouldn't it have been better to speak to me first, rather than rush out like wild men and tear trees out of the ground?"

Then they planted the forest, working for token wages, Rahel staying and laboring for a day alongside Leah and Reuven. A few days later, when Kramer swore there was not a copper left, the kvutsa agreed to work on without pay for another week to complete the planting of the memorial forest.

Everywhere people talked of the tree-uprooter. The quiet, shy Reuven had become a David and Samson rolled into one. The forest planted, they were again looking for work, nearly the whole kvutsa stopping into Mother Zuckerman's in Jaffa where Araleh had a long-standing credit, as there was doubtless something between him and the grown daughter, Saraleh of the long braids. From the kitchen much whispering and giggling was heard, and finally it was the younger sister, Esterkeh, hardly ten, who brought in the great bowl of lentil soup so she could stare at Reuven Chaimovitch, the tree-uprooter, before fleeing to a gust of general laughter.

For weeks there was nothing. The men could only present themselves early each morning in the village square at the "slave market"; there, a grove owner who might need an extra hand for the day would drive up on his wagon, looking them over, sometimes even getting down to feel their muscles before he made his choice. Reuven was taken for a day or two of mattock work. Already word had got about that this patriot was also a diligent laborer, a natural hand with the mattock, as deft as Handsome Moshe himself, but if they summoned him onto the wagon, the squires inevitably jested, "Remember, I want trees planted, not uprooted." Then, when one of the writer Smilansky's steady hands fell ill, the planter himself came to the cabin asking for Reuven Chaimovitch, and on Reuven's steady employment the kvutsa managed to survive.

One morning Dovidl the Clever reappeared. "The wine-treaders!" he proclaimed. He had pulled them out on strike! Everyone must come and show solidarity!

A mixed crowd had gathered at the gate before the winery, the largest establishment in Rishon le Zion. The strikers themselves, mostly older men, heavily bearded and wearing the ritual fringed undervest so that the tzitzith dangled out at the waist, now stood together in a group, looking bewildered and uncertain about what they had done, but reassuring each other in Yiddish that no, a Jew could not feed a family on such a pittance, and the pious Baron in Paris could surely afford to pay a pious Jew better wages.

Another group had already formed, a group of planters and villagers, and these called at them with indignation, addressing each by name: Zalman! Have you lost your senses!—What's come over you! Why do you listen to these socialist troublemakers?—Let them go back to Russia! Do you want the Baron to get angry, do you want to ruin the whole yishuv! A shame!

A wagon drawn by a fat-sided Belgian workhorse drove up, and off jumped a heavyset black bearded settler, holding his long whip. A village founder, owner of an enormous vineyard, in his anger he even reminded Leah a little of her own father on that famous day when he had shouted down the peasants who wanted a higher price for their sugar beets.

"I'll tread the grapes myself!" the grower shouted, marching toward the gate, waving to the other villagers to follow. Before the gate stood Dovidl, and instantly there was a scuffle with Dovidl in the center; the whole kvutsa rushed to his aid, and as Leah planted her bulk before the wrought-iron gate, the planter paused. "Shame!" he shouted into her face. "A Jewish girl! Do you want to bring the Turkish police down on us!" And he appealed to the striking wine-treaders themselves. "Jews, come to your senses!"

On the second story a window flew open. The manager, wearing a high stiff collar and a necktie, stuck out his head. "The winepress is shut down!" he shouted in a blend of German and Yiddish, with a French accent. "I have tele-

graphed to Paris." And to the militant vintner he called,
"BenZion, you too better go home."

By evening the cabin of the kvutsa had been inundated
with barefoots. News of the first strike had emptied out the
whole of Mother Zuckerman's hotel in Jaffa, and Araleh's
Saraleh had also come, bringing a sackful of bread. Leah
and the sweaty Nahama were busy over the soup cauldron,
cutting up carrots that had already grown to a good size in
their garden—what a brilliant idea to plant their own vegetables, everyone exclaimed, it should become a *principe!*
Excited talk went on, rumors of victory; lanky Avner arrived and went into a sitting with Dovidl and Handsome
Moshe; for quiet, they used the girls' corner behind the
burlap curtain.

In the dusk, among the gathering crowd there appeared
a figure, half emaciated, in a peasant blouse, and by his
long ragged beard you would have thought it was Tolstoy
himself. This was the "Old One," Reuven knew at once, the
sage, A. D. Gordon—who had not heard of him? Who did
not already know him, from his writings in the *Young
Worker?* A lifelong member of the intelligentsia, who had
been managing an estate for a relative, Baron Ginsberg of
St. Petersburg, the richest of Russian Jews, he had suddenly, at fifty, left all behind, family, home, books, and
come to Eretz as a laborer. Frail, often ill, he would take
no other task than laboring in the fields.

Catching sight of Dovidl, the Old One called out like a
scolding teacher, "You shouldn't have done it!"

"But isn't he with us?" Reuven was puzzled.

"He's with us, he's with us," Moshe laughed, "only he's
against strikes. He believes in passivity."

"No. In patience!" Gordon had heard them. "In endurance."

"Then how will things ever change?" Moshe demanded,
more respectfully.

They would change. Old Gordon was off on a lecture,
just as though he were reading from his writings. The Jew,
restored to his natural self as a toiler on the soil, would
become stronger inwardly. And thus things would
change—not through strife and conflict that would only
sharpen the difference between Jew and Jew in the so-
called class struggle, for what could this achieve? "They

will only strike back at you. They will divide you," he predicted. "All true strength is from within."

Max Wilner had been listening; now he opened his tight-pressed lips. "Our true vegetarian," he remarked. And he told a little incident. Not long ago Gordon had stayed at the kvutsa. "You know on top of everything he is pious. He puts on tfillim. At least until then he did. One morning I said to him, 'Gordon, you are a vegetarian. How can you bind on your arm and forehead these strips of leather cut from the hide of an animal?' And you know what happened?" Max gave them a moment, savoring his coming point. "The next morning he prayed without his tfillim."

It was from that moment perhaps that Reuven felt his first impulse of dislike in Eretz, though Max was so intelligent and hardworking a comrade, and widely read.

Singing had begun. Despite the words of the sage, which troubled few of them since everyone could not after all live up to all the ideals of a tzaddik, there was a happy sense of triumph. At last a blow had been struck at the barons, big and little! A bonfire sprang alight and already the circle of dancers swung around the fire. Leah jumped into the hora ring, Handsome Moshe was on one side of her, his fingers squarely around her waist, and on the other side she could feel under her hand the bony shoulder of Old Gordon. Almost the first into the circle, he danced as one ageless, possessed, with the ecstasy of a Hasid. Even Dovidl, she saw, was pulled into the dance. Whatever would come in her life, with such good comrades, never had she been so happy!

When Leah danced, some said the earth shook. But it was from fervor, not from heaviness. As is often true of large women, when she danced, her fleshiness vanished, she was possessed of a weightless grace. How good, how good it was, and the words stamped out in their song said the same: How good and how pleasant for brothers to dwell together in unity. It was a Psalm of David, it had become a chalutz song.

Reuven too was swept into the hora; in the circle his shyness was suspended—as long as he was one with the others, he did not feel it, but the moment the circle halted, this shyness returned on him and he stood alone. There were few such solitary moments tonight as the end-gasp of each song was drowned in the upsurge of a new one. Now

Araleh called out the favorite refrain, "Im ayn ani li, mi li?" "If I am not for me, who will be?" The words of Rabbi Hillel, stomped into the earth, harder, always faster. "And if not now, then when, then when!"—"Ay ma-tay!" One by one the chevreh lost breath and dropped out; the circle constricted until there were six, Araleh and Saraleh dropped away, then suddenly Moshe and Leah were standing aside, gasping, laughing, and only Avner's Rahel was left with Reuven. She flew faster, Reuven too, he waved his free hand for others to come back, but everyone clapped them on. "If I am not for me, who will be!"—"Mi-li, mi-li," until suddenly he felt the small of her back weighing on his hand, resting there the briefest instant, and then Rahel broke away, breathing rapidly, shaking her head, her eyes sparkling their acknowledgment. Oo-wah! What a dancer was Reuven the Tree-Puller, the longest lasting of all! But Old Gordon sprang back. Now Reuven and Gordon danced on, the fire lighting their faces. "If for myself alone am I, what am I?" They could not let the dance die, it was as though the whole movement would stop, the chalutziut, the redemption of the Jews, the turning earth itself.

Then Leah leaped back, and Moshe, and Araleh and Saraleh, and Nahama and Shimek, and Dovidl, and Avner and Rahel, Max Wilner too, and the circle expanded, grew larger than ever. "Anu banu artsa," they sang, "We have come to our land, To build and have her build us . . ."

The yard all around the hut and the floor inside the hut were covered with them, the sleeping chalutzim, while in the girls' corner Leah had insisted on giving her place to Saraleh Zuckerman, and she herself lay on the mat with Rahel. Too excited to sleep, Rahel talked and talked in a low voice into Leah's ear; the significance of the event, the first strike, the way was now open, in the orange-picking season they would strike the groves. Jewish labor would become a force, did Leah realize how many chalutzim were arriving? Over a thousand had appeared this year in the Poale Zion hut on the shore near Jaffa. And as many more surely had come to Eretz without registering in their labor exchange. Avner could no longer cope with it all. And a journal was needed, a labor paper to offset the only Hebrew paper with its Old City odor—and suddenly Rahel interjected, "Your brother, what a dancer!" and went on—

Handsome Moshe, she had noticed that Leah was attracted to him. No? And dropping to a more intimate whisper she asked was Leah still a virgin? To her chaverteh, Leah answered honestly, and Rahel now embarked on a lecture on sexual freedom as though it were a duty. About Rahel and Avner, Leah was too embarrassed to ask, though everyone took it for granted.

She and Rahel must have drowsed, for before dawn Leah awakened to movement from the other side of their curtain, among the men sleepers on the floor. Dovidl was up and already making off. "Dovidl, wait!" she hurried out to him—at least a mug of tea and a slice of bread. He took the bread but wouldn't wait for the fire to be made for the water to boil.

From a distance as he entered the village Dovidl already saw them, his fine pious strikers, in a little knot in front of the shul, while their leader, Reb Weintraub of the always-narrowed eyes, was off to a side in a discussion with the planter, BenZion.

So, as Dovidl soon related at the kvutsa, his pious wine-treaders had betrayed him. An advance in wages had been received, but other demands, such as for Jewish hands throughout the winery, would await an opinion by the chief rabbi of the Etz Chayim Yeshiva in Jerusalem. Dovidl himself, of course, was no longer wanted in the winery, not because of his radical labor ideas but because he was unobservant, and unkosher—tref.

With this point, a foxy glint had come into Weintraub's eyeslits.

So it was he who had been used, Dovidl realized; the men had got their increase in wages, and behind their beards they were laughing at him.

Big Leah, bringing hot tea in a large canister as she arrived with the chevreh, at once saw from the way Dovidl walked toward them what had happened. Afterward, sitting on a bench outside the cabin when the crowd of barefoots had gone their way, she listened to his analysis of his mistakes. It was not wrong to work with the religious element, as with any element, for to grow strong the maximum of groupings must be drawn in. Though he should have realized that BenZion the planter would approach the pious

workers with his tallis-bag in his hand. The mistake was
that before the strike, he, Dovidl, should himself have obtained some sort of hold over the men.

"Nu," she said, "no use to sit with a let-down nose."
After all he had done something. He had shown that a
strike could be effective even here in Eretz.

But then there was no work at all to be had. The orange-
picking season was slow in starting. And as Old Gordon
had predicted, the growers were striking back in their own
way. Each dawn the chalutzim stood in the "slave market."
The "little barons" would drive up and stop at the Arab
side of the square. Entire families of Arabs they led off to
do their cutting, never a Jew. Even for Arab wages, chalutzim were not wanted.

The little kvutsa was breaking up. Shimek of the twisted
lip had received a letter from home, from his father, saying
his mother would not live through the winter. Though
everyone knew about such letters, he was going back—with
the vow that he would soon return to Eretz. Moshe was
going off to try the Galilee, where it was said hands would
be needed for a big plantation being started for wealthy
English Jews, on the shores of the Kinnereth. "He's running away from his orange-grower's daughter," Nahama
scornfully told Leah. Things had reached the point of tears
and marriage demands. And soon poor Nahama herself
was running after Handsome Moshe to the Galilee.

With the picking season over, even Reuven's days of employment were few. It seemed almost as though their coming here were a failure. Who would have imagined, with all
the difficulties that had been forecast of fevers and of Arab
bandits falling on them, that the greatest hardship would
come from other Jews refusing to give them work?

Mama had scented out the difficulty and was sending
them bits of money—Leah could almost see her unknotting
the kerchief in which she tied away coins, the coins saved
from household money—Mamaleh's kniplach. There could
even be enough for passage home if need be, their mother
hinted.

From Rahel came the thought of Jerusalem. Months in
the land, and they had not even gone up to Yerushalayim!
No, Leah denied to herself, it was not because they might

leave Eretz without seeing the holy city. They had no thought of deserting. In Jerusalem, Rahel said, they might find building work. Chalutzim were learning to become stonecutters. Women must learn this trade as well! So, with Avner and Rahel, she and Reuven set off.

At every turn, Avner gave them historical lectures. That was really where his heart was, in searching out old names of villages and valleys; even the names of Arab villagers he sometimes traced to Biblical days, believing these were descendants of Jews who had in the distant past become Moslems to save themselves. But when would he even find time for this important work?

Here in the low hills was Samson's land, the vale of Sorek where Delilah lived. How empty it all was! The air was quiet and luminous, and sometimes they walked for an hour, two hours, without coming upon a village. A small herd of sheep might be seen grazing on a hillside, and once there suddenly appeared three Arab girls with water-jars on their heads, coming from a spring. In the girls' village they were given hospitality, sleeping on mats in the guest-hut of the sheikh; it was here, Avner told them, that the Ark had rested on its way to Jerusalem.

Then they were making their last ascent, between two ranges of grayish, barren hills, on which one could see traces of terracing. All this had once been covered by fig trees, olives, and vines. Rahel suddenly launched into a discourse on forestry. Conifers would be the best. All these hills could be green again. But the bald mountains stretched as far as the eye could see, like the planet earth before plants were created. Tens of thousand of seedlings would be needed, Leah said, and where would they come from? Even for the Herzl forest, seedlings had been scarce. "Then we must grow them! You and I! That's something we can do!" Rahel cried and began to sing as they climbed. She had taken Leah's hand, and they walked behind Avner and Reuven, the huge girl and the little one, their hands swinging as they sang a wordless Hasidic melody. And there atop a hill as barren as the others was the city.

The massive walls, as they approached, appeared to Leah just as they must always have been, even in David's time. Rising in the center she saw a vast golden dome, and though she knew it belonged to those others, a mosque, it seemed to her it was the Temple. Just so, just there, it must have stood.

Through the covered lanes with their stalls, Rahel and Avner led them into narrower, still more twisted lanes, with glimpses of hovels along dark stone stairways, and suddenly around a double corner they found themselves before the Wall. Why should they—all unbelievers—be drawn to this symbol of fanatic Judaism, of weeping and despair? Yet so it was. They had had to come here first.

Exactly as in the picture that hung in her grandmother's house in Cherezinka, Leah saw the high wall made of great blocks of ancient stones—ah, in those days Jews indeed knew how to hew stones! In the crevices grew bits of grass like tufts of hair on an old woman's face, and swaying in prayer at the base of the wall were the old men of the picture, and also a few weeping old women.

Then came beggars tugging at you and demanding the names of your deceased so they could say a Kaddish, and Reuven wanted to leave.

Against the opposite end of the Old City, in Mea Shearim, Rahel led them into the courtyard of a rectangular building, once a monastery, she said. Even as they approached, Leah heard the stonecutters' hammers tapping away; in one corner of the yard a few chalutzim sat on the ground, their faces gray with stone dust, each with a block before him, chipping away under the eye of a tiny Yemenite with short ear-curls, the master. In another corner, before a huge upended block of stone from which a striding Elijah half-emerged, was a sculptor who turned, gazed on Leah with a broadening grin of appreciation, let out an enormous Oho! and came and walked around her as though she were an object in a museum. Oho! he whistled again, from behind a mufflike mustache, and demanded of Rahel, "Where did you find her?" This was Yosi, Rahel said. "Where will I get a block of stone large enough!" he cried out.

All around the courtyard were tiny workshops, a few with looms, others where sheets of brass were being tapped into ornaments. The deserted building had been obtained by Professor Schatz, the great Jewish painter from Roumania, Rahel explained; he was reviving Jewish culture. There he was in the weaving shop, and Leah saw a bare-headed man with a wild beard, like Yosi's statue of Elijah, except for a large stomach. The professor embraced them all, an enthusiast, a lover of everyone. It would be wonderful to have a chalutza learning stonecutting—Leah was just the one for it. He was building his new Bezalel Art School and Museum on a hill outside the Old City; a great new city of Jerusalem would grow up around his new museum! Reuven too—yes, he needed workers for the walls! "Come tomorrow!" And he beamed on them, and hurried off.

Upstairs, Rahel stuck her head into one door after another, all of them opening onto the balcony, to find places for Reuven and Leah. The building teemed. Meanwhile they rested in Avner's room, where there was the usual bed of planks resting on kerosene tins, an orange crate made into a bookcase, and on the floor a large mat with a water jug.

In the yard a soup cauldron cooked, and in no time Leah was quite at home, helping with the soup. During the day she sat among the chevreh, chipping away at the golden-hued blocks of stone; though the Yemenite, who was called Abadiah, had at first balked at teaching a woman, she had simply taken her place, and now he was her friend. Professor Schatz passed, and beamed on her. Reuven was already at work on the new Bezalel building, carrying stones up to the masons. He was even to receive a wage, as Professor Schatz had just returned from a money-raising trip abroad.

It was like the kvutsa again. In the talkative evenings a circle of chaverim sat on the mat in Rahel's room, next to Avner's; on her mat was a samovar and she poured tea for everyone; after endless discussions and song-singing, Avner would go back to his own room, others would depart, Reuven would silently leave Leah at her own door and go to the chamber he shared with a half dozen chalutzim. He had understood finally about Rahel and Avner—what was there to understand? But Leah saw that he was unable to keep his eyes from the girl.

For herself, Yosi the sculptor had got her to pose for him, in the afternoons when her stonecutting stopped; he was modeling her in clay, a life-size figure with arms bare, and his hands seemed more often on her than on his clay. Though half her size, Yosi was unabashed. Where he got his energy no one knew, but four times a day he would

disappear into his cavelike chamber, and after the door had
been closed for a time, you would see a girl flitting out.
Nurses! he bragged. From the nearby French hospital. He
even hinted at nuns.

A month went by. Professor Schatz again ran out of
money and halted his building operations. There was no
work to be had in Jerusalem, and Reuven was miserable;
what was he doing here in the city—he had come to labor
on the soil! Luckily, a message came from Dovidl in the
Galilee, calling Avner to a meeting. Why not go along?
And there Reuven and Leah found their destiny.

They walked by way of Samaria, and there they saw another land, a land filled with olive groves and flocks on
green hillsides; no Jewish settlements were here, though
Avner halted them at one effendi's house where a Russian
Jew named Shertok had been installed with his family to
manage the estate. Music was heard, they had brought in a
piano, and the youngest boy, called Yehvda, was a genius
on the violin. A real Jewish family, alone among the Arabs.

Two young daughters wanted to go off with them, while
the eldest son—with the name of Moshe—small, slight and
witty, jested with Leah that she must divide herself in two,
and one of her should stay here!

On the third day they came out on the vast flat plain of
Jezreel, with the morning dew rising off the swampland and
the stretches of tangled underbrush. All morning they followed a wagon trail toward the soft-rounded breastlike
mountain of Tabor. Before nightfall they managed to reach
the settlement of Mescha, a walled enclosure of some forty
houses—how far from everyone it seemed! Yet here were
the real Jewish farmers they had heard of; the center lane
of the village was filled with cattle being brought in from
pasture by little boys with sticks and dogs, and as they
watched the cattle turning off each to its barn, Leah heard
her name called. A stocky young laborer with a large
head—Dovidl himself. In these few months he had already
become the real thing, Dovidl declared, a plowman no
less—why torture his head with politics!

Though this was also one of the Baron's settlements,
here there were no Jewish effendi. Dovidl's own employer
labored side by side with him in the fields, a real peasant,

and the farmer even refused to pay land-rent to the Baron's agent!

They ate their supper at a large round table in the farmhouse, the housewife serving a chicken soup such as you would not find in all the rest of Eretz Yisroel, while Dovidl overwhelmed them with talk of yields of barley, of fodder-crops, of mules and oxen, as though he had been here all his life. Reuven was loquacious as never before, not shy, not even refusing when the farmer's wife, exclaiming, "Oh, a vegetarian," insisted on making a special milksoup with dumplings for him.

Of the farmer, Yehuda Shepshovitch, Reuven asked a thousand questions, and Shepshovitch had a way of replying as though each problem were nothing, you found a way to overcome it. Naturally, this settlement flourished. Why? Because they bought virtually nothing from outside, they did not seek to get rich and raise crops for gold, like the orange growers, the pardessanim; here, they grew what they needed, vegetables even four times a year—fodder, wheat, barley, the beans called fuhl; they had geese, chickens—in sum, a true farmer's life.

"What milk!" Reuven cried.

"And what cucumbers!" Leah added. Could she take along some seeds? Though where she would plant them she didn't yet know.

As to the milk, Shepshovitch had journeyed to Holland last year and brought back a prize pair of cattle. Never again for him the scrawny black cows of the land. His yield was three times as high and much richer in fat. His bull was now breeding to the little black Arab cows and in a few years the whole of Mescha would flow with milk. And as for honey—taste it!

Seeing her brother so filled with admiration, Leah asked, could they perhaps find work here in Mescha? Nu— Shepshovitch ticked off the names of the villagers; this one had sons, and that one already had a helper . . . With Dovidl, he discussed various prospects in the nearby villages of Yavniel and Sejera.

Alongside Sejera, a training farm had been started, so farmhands were now plentiful, but Shepshovitch would keep his ears open as far as Yavniel was concerned. If Dovidl said Reuven was a good worker, then a good worker he must be!

They walked out into the open compound. In the Jaffa area the villages had been spread out, but here each house faced the compound, forming a kind of community. Behind each house was its yard and stable, and the rear wall of each stable was connected on each side by the continuous surrounding wall so as to make an enclosure of the entire village, open only at the gate.

Just then an Arab rode up, sitting a slender-legged brown mare. He sat taller than most Arabs and was, oddly, blue-eyed. "Our watchman," Dovidl remarked with an accent of distaste. "They're not even Arabs. Circassians from the Caucasus, that settled here the devil knows why. They have their own village. You find everything, in this mishmash of a country!"

The watchman wore crisscrossed bandoliers and carried a long rifle. "Our protector!" Dovidl spat in the dust, a rural manner he had already picked up in his transformation to a man of the soil. Exchanging greetings with the farmers around the compound, the watchman rode out to circle the village wall, while a couple of grown sons closed and bolted the gate.

Was there trouble in this area, then?

"Trouble?" Dovidl shrugged. "He makes a few rounds and rides home and goes to sleep." The Circassians had been given a watchman's contract for the three or four settlements in this area, but it was all blackmail. True, there was a nasty pair of bandits, sons of a half-Bedouin who called himself the Sheikh of Fuleh, a collection of huts in the middle of the plain inhabited by tribesmen from the time the Turks had built the railway line. They had been brought over from across the Jordan to keep materials from being pilfered. Some had settled there, though yellow fever was bad. Those two sons of Fuleh had good horses; they were known throughout Galilee for preying on travelers or running off with livestock if they caught a few cattle grazing away from their herd. But such raiders never ventured inside the settlements, Dovidl went on. The contract with the Circassian watchmen was nothing but tribute, arranged by the Baron's representatives in their compromising way, and Dovidl for one wanted to see it ended.

Suddenly this diminutive farmhand, in the oversize pair of boots that Shepshovitch had lent him, was the cocky strike-leader again. Could anyone really believe that Dovidl would remain here, a simple plowman? "We'll soon change things!" he declared, with a touch of conspiracy in his tone, to Leah and Reuven. For though these Galilee farmers were better than the planters of the coastal villages, where was the real difference in outlook? Had Jews come here to continue the fearfulness of their old ghetto mentality, paying bribes to goyim so as not to be attacked? The first requirement of manhood, of a people, was to be able to stand up for itself, and this Dovidl declared was the new spirit that must come to the Yishuv before real progress could be made.

He was talking through Leah to Reuven, who began to feel uneasy. This farmer, Shepshovitch, had seemed an admirable man to him. What was there to change?

Just then there came a rattle of wagon-wheels outside the gate; Dovidl himself hurried to open it, hailing four men in a mule-drawn cart. One Reuven and Leah at once recognized—he had been at a workers' conference in Ramla, where they had stopped on the way to Jerusalem, and had spoken often and with fire. Galil, he called himself; the son of an enormously wealthy lumber merchant of Minsk named Gewirtz, he had interrupted his law studies to become a social revolutionary, and then been won over to Zionism. Now he was at the training farm in Sejera, not far from here. Two others on the wagon were brothers; even in the evening light they looked fierce, with mustaches like double-pointed daggers that reached beyond their cheeks. These two were called Zeira—Shabbatai and Aaron, Kurdish Jews from Turkestan. Even there, it seemed, there were Zionists. They now were from Sejera, from the village itself, where they had a homestead. The fourth was quite young, a boy called Herschel from the training farm. The ride had been without incident, Galil said, and the whole lot of them at once went off with Dovidl, who made a motion with his head to Reuven to come along, and shrugged at Leah, excluding her.

So they were up to something, the fine chaverim, and even they, with Dovidl and all their "equality," were excluding women!

What they were up to, she found out quickly enough from the eldest Shepshovitch daughter Genya, a placid, buxom sixteen-year-old who, unfortunately, Leah had seen at first glance, was not the type for Reuven, a vain girl and a gossip. The men were forming a secret society, Genya said; they wanted to replace the Circassians as watchmen, they wanted to ride around on horses, but they didn't even possess a revolver between them, much less a horse. Besides, the village leaders would never agree to give them the contract unless the Baron's supervisor for the whole area, the all-powerful Jacques Samuelson, agreed, and Samuelson wouldn't agree, as he had his own arrangements with the Turkish police chief, the Bimbashi, in Nazareth to keep everything quiet. Her own father, though, might be for it, as he hated everything to do with the Baron and wanted complete independence. And also Dovidl had already stirred up some of the younger lads of Mescha for the scheme. Their secret society called itself Bar Giora after the last defender of Jerusalem against the Romans. They had a fearful secret oath in blood, and not everyone could join—they had tests, and accepted only the bravest.

All this Reuven was learning in Dovidl's room, a lean-to by the barn, in which there was a cot, a table with a water jug, a chair. A few milking stools had been brought in. On the window ledge Dovidl had his books.

Nine men had gathered, a pair of them from the settlement of Yavniel, farmhands like Dovidl, one of them affecting an Arab keffiyah and fancy boots, something of a loudmouth it turned out—Zev the Hotblood he was called, and he interrupted everyone. The main thing was to show no fear, he kept repeating, show you were strong and fearless, and the bandits would give you a wide berth. He had grown up with Arabs, in the north, in Metulla. Theirs was the ancient code, an eye for an eye, a tooth for a tooth, a life for a life. What was the Turkish government to them, they whistled at it. They kept their own laws. Show them you could be strong and determined according to the ancient tribal laws, and they would respect you. A life for a life.

To this, the fierce-looking Zeira brothers cried their approval.

Galil, with a swift, intimate way of talking, interrupted them. "Agreed, we must show strength, and no fear, but even the old laws don't always demand blood for blood. In many cases payments are made. We are not seeking to start blood-feuds. We must stand for law. Sometimes even the law of the land, instead of tribal laws and the feud." Once a blood-feud, a ghoum, was begun there would be no end. Between some of the Arab tribes, where a ghoum existed, men were killed on each side, generation after generation. No, if there was a death, their organization must aim to apprehend the killer and bring him to law. Even with the Turks. Once and for all this land must be brought into the world of today. There were Arabs too, in the cities and among the effendi, who would prefer it. "Nevertheless, as you say, we must quickly make known that we can be strong in the old way too. We must be crack shots, each of us. We must outride their best riders. We must win ourselves a name in the whole of Eretz." He looked to Reuven, as one who already had a name, and Reuven saw that even in the Galilee his angry deed was known. But the thought of turning into a guardsman, riding the rounds at night, did not attract him. —Would they all be guardsmen, he asked, or could they perhaps also make their own settlement?

A thought! Dovidl took this up. A good thought for the future when they were well established. Certain members could stay in the settlement which would be their base, while others went out to guard the villages. Their wives could tend the poultry and the dairy.

"Wait!" Galil brought them back to earth. "We don't even have wives!" This was true, except for the Zeiras, who were married and indeed had their own farm in Sejera. Concretely, now, how were they to obtain their first watchman's contract?

"Why not here in Mescha?" Dovidl suggested.

The local settlers would never agree to dismiss the Circassians.

"We can chase off the Circassians!" Zev the Hotblood offered. But Dovidl had already thought of a plan. The watchman, after putting in his appearance, each night went back to his sleep in Kfar Kana. So then someone had only to let a mule out of a stable through the small gate in the back wall. Dovidl himself would set up a howl, "Thieves!" The settlers would wake, rush to their barns, discover a mule was missing, shout for their watchman—and where would they find him?

"Asleep in Kfar Kana!" The Hotblood laughed, won over.

Whereupon they themselves, the Bar Giora, would offer

their services as their watchmen who would live right in Mescha itself.

So it was agreed. The intimate-voiced Galil, looking at Zev, reminded everyone that all that passed between them was secret. There were some who had been admitted tonight who were here for the first time and had not yet been inducted into the society. If all were ready, the induction would proceed.

Zev was the first; leaping up from his stool, he took his place before the table. Dovidl reached back to his books on the window ledge, drew forth a Bible and placed it on the table within the glow of the kerosene lamp. From somewhere, Reuven saw, a huge pistol had appeared, and Avner placed it now beside the Bible.

In sudden solemnity, Zev put one hand on the Bible, the other on the gun. It was Shabbatai Zeira, standing alongside of Galil, who administered the oath.

"Say after me: In blood and fire, Judea fell, in blood and fire, Judea will arise."

Smacking his lips, Zev almost shouted the words.

In Reuven, dismay was deepening. Now the boy called Herschel from the Sejera training farm repeated the oath, his voice going high at the end.

"Reuven?" Startled, he heard Galil calling his name. Galil looked so young himself, his locks falling across his forehead. In a way it was all like what children did, making vows of blood. Yet something in Reuven held back. A swift rider he was not, and he had never held a gun in his hand. Blood and fire. The words rumbled in his head. No, he could not. In labor, in sweat, Judea must arise. In decency, in love.

"Excuse me," he said. "I—it's a very serious thing. I— I'm not ready."

He felt Dovidl's hand on his shoulder. "We wanted you to know about us. If the time comes, we will speak to each other." Of a sudden Reuven felt Dovidl was something more than he had judged, not only a clever one, but a man who saw into your heart. Half-babbling, Reuven added, "You know, if there is a need, you know you can count on me." Just what he meant, he hardly understood himself.

Early in the morning, as Leah emerged into the yard amidst the chicken-cackling and the smell of compost, an arm went around her waist from behind and a voice laughed, "Don't pull up any trees!" It was Handsome Moshe! What was he doing here? He had come for supplies, the kvutsa was beyond, over the last ridge, on the shore of Kinnereth. The kvutsa? The same, not the same. Maxl the Hardhead was there, and a few new ones.

"Nahama?" she asked.

Moshe grinned. "No."

But Araleh had come, with Sara Zuckerman. The kvutsa had received a contract from the Keren Kayemeth to plant a whole tract of land. "Come back to us"—to him.

And presently Reuven and Leah were aboard Moshe's wagon, Leah sitting next to Moshe on the seat. Suffused with excitement, she hardly heard Moshe's explanation; her hands she had to hold clasped in her lap to keep from reaching for his curly hair. So much had she longed for him, without admitting it to herself.

Araleh and Saraleh had actually been married—hadn't she heard, there in Jerusalem? Married, and by a rabbi, with a great feast in the Zuckerman house in Jaffa. Old Zuckerman, who spent his life in the shul, had complained that he had always known that such would be the result of his wife's harboring every barefoot chalutz in the land. But every hungry mouth had been stuffed with roast goose and kishkes! And now, with nine chalutzim in the kvutsa's new place here, and Saraleh the only woman—she needed help.

"Oho, so that's what you want me for," Leah said.

"No, not only!" Moshe dropped his voice so it was for her alone. She felt a flush in her very limbs.

"What are you planting?" Reuven asked from behind.

"Just now, eucalyptus trees, against malaria."

As the mules labored to the top of the ridge, Moshe pulled the wagon to a halt, for them to behold the land. And just as Eretz had possessed him on the dunes beyond Jaffa, at this moment Kinnereth entered into the heart of Reuven Chaimovitch. The glowing sea, slender and long, with a billowing curve like the gown of a bride, reclined before him. The bride his young manhood longed for, by her side he would pass his life, and she would give him peace.

His sister too beheld the beauty of Kinnereth, the swelling form like the harp of King David that gave it its name;

yet profoundly as Leah felt this moment of beauty, she felt it also through its effect on her brother. Her heart knew what was taking place in Reuven. And a touch of apprehension arose in her, for there is danger in feeling any love so instantly and deeply. As in that moment, in that night of dancing, when she had felt him falling in love with Rahel, who, he knew, was already Avner's.

"Beautiful," declared Handsome Moshe, but there were those who recognized beauty without being possessed by it.

"Beautiful," Leah agreed.

Moshe pointed out to them the lands of the kvutsa, but only a wild, uncultivated area could be seen, with the Jordan River lying there twisted like a great hairpin. It was not until the wagon was winding down near the level part of the rutted lane that they made out a structure, a small abandoned khan with a cubicle atop the roof. This was the kvutsa's abode.

Araleh's Sara ran out to meet the wagon and when she saw another woman she burst into tears.—Oh Leah! She had been so alone here.—Still sniffling, she demanded first of all the quinine Moshe had fetched. They had run short, and two of the chaverim were down with kadahat, she explained to Leah, hurrying with her into the house.

The sick men lay on their boards against the wall in the dim gloomy room lit only by a beam of light from the small square window in the thick wall. With their gaunt stubble-covered faces Leah barely recognized them, but there was Shimek, already returned from Russia—his mother had not been so sick after all. His dulled eyes lighted and he mumbled the blessing for guests, "Beruchim haba'im." The other was a good worker known as Tibor the Jester, who had only stayed with them a few days in the old kvutsa. "Leah is here!" he cried. "With so much flesh it can't be a vision!"

She had picked yellow wildflowers when they stopped, and now at once found a little jug and set the flowers on the sill of the small window, in the light.

It was scarcely a month since the kvutsa had come to this place, but how the members had altered! In their hut near Rehovot they had been close to civilization, among townsfolk, with a coming and going, and several other villages nearby, but here the little group was alone in a wilderness. At night, Saraleh said, not even another lamp could be seen. Saraleh didn't stop chattering.—Ooy! she was so glad to see another girl! She wanted to hear all kinds of things that men never talked about—yet in her eagerness she didn't give Leah a chance to say a word. It was difficult for her and Araleh here, she confided, because they were the only couple. Their happiness—she confessed she was ashamed before the other boys who were so alone. Because of being a couple, she and Araleh had been given the little room on the roof to themselves, while down here all the men were crowded. "You can stay in our room with me, and Araleh will sleep outside on the roof, it's so warm here," she offered, but Leah hastily assured her, no, she would put up the usual curtain in the room below.

Here, Leah's romance with Moshe took place. There were no daughters of grove owners to distract him, and among the other men it seemed stolidly accepted that she was for Moshe. Even Reuven seemed to be waiting for it to happen, as though on his own part he had found his love, the Kinnereth, while she had come to her man.

Struggling with the outdoor cooking fire that smudged her cheeks and smarted her eyes, Leah caught herself worrying about how her hair would look should Moshe come by. And when the whole kvutsa except Saraleh went out to the fields, Leah at first walked between her brother and Moshe, and then, when Reuven got into an argument with Max Wilner about where to plant oats and where to plant wheat, she walked ahead with Moshe alone.

The air at night was a warm balm caressing the skin. One night in a nest of high grass by the shore she lay in his arms, with only their clothes between them, and Leah's thoughts were in turmoil. Just as Rahel was with Avner, should she not become Moshe's complete chavera, his woman? Yet she saw her mother's face, and even her aunts', and would she herself want her younger sister Dvora to do such a thing? Entire generations of behest and condemnation seemed to weigh against the honesty and simplicity that should rule between a man and a woman in their desire, so that, still, she lifted his hand away from her clothing.

One thing Leah happily noticed was how, just now, she no longer felt the largeness and fleshiness of her body but felt feminine and delicate like Saraleh. But then suddenly there would intrude the desolate words of poor stricken Nahama, "Beware, he is a heartbreaker." The words would not go away. And another image assailed Leah, the image of her Moshe making light with that pardessan's daughter in Rehovot, even lying with her—not simply like this, but more completely. It was lewd to imagine such things. Yet a sudden wanton sense of power arose in her; that village girl could not succeed, could not hold Moshe, but she herself could be the woman really to hold this man. Poor Nahama had not been strong enough, either. But might it not truly be that he was destined for herself? And Leah asked herself, how could she know such feelings—she was an ignorant girl, not yet eighteen—though she had read *Anna Karenina*, where there was such a man as Moshe.

And also the greatest curiosity of all now urged her. To know what it really was with a man. But this was unworthy; not merely to satisfy this would she begin!

They were staring into each other's eyes; his eyes were warm, liquid, darkly luminous like the waters of the Kinnereth, and he pressed his mouth on hers again, and turned so his weight lay on her and she felt his manhood, as she called it to herself, it was throbbing, through the cloth. But Araleh had married Saraleh, and in her girlish palavering—womanly now—Saraleh had told Leah, Ooy, she had been such a bourgeoisie, she had not been able like a free woman to bring herself to it before marriage; even though she had felt how Araleh suffered, yet she had made him wait. With this, Saraleh would suck in her lower lip, peering at Leah but not openly asking her whether she had already yielded to Moshe.

No, it must not be a yielding but a meeting of two beings, Leah told herself, and "Not yet, not yet," she groaned, managing to turn so that his body was off her body and the throb against her was gone. Oh, why could she not be a complete companion to him, like Rahel to Avner?

A wagonload of eucalyptus seedlings arrived from Chedera, and at dawn Leah arose to go with the men to plant them along the muddy, flooded Jordan banks. Not only did she feel the hollow urge in her hands to be planting, but now her entire body demanded to cleave alongside Moshe wherever he went. Since a woman could not stand for long in her skirts in the muddy water, Leah took Reuven's other pair of trousers and went behind her curtain. If Tateh should hear of this, brother and sister jested, a woman going forth in men's clothing, a sin of sins! But Leah could not pull Reuven's trousers closed and had to hand them back. Then came a roar of remarks from the men, with Tibor Kalisher declaring that the first test of a chavera must be whether she could wear the trousers of a chaver. Of a brother one did not speak! And another pair of trousers was flung in to her. Leah herself had patched them— Moshe's. In a tumult of confused feelings the big girl drew them on, flushing as she closed the buttons; it was as though what she had not been able to go through by the Kinnereth was by this now foredoomed, consented.

When she came out to Tibor's banter—he was up and working now, but Shimek still lay ill and offered his boots—she didn't dare look at Moshe. At least she had on her own blouse! But while she lifted her arms to tie a kerchief around her hair, Leah felt Moshe's eyes on her as though he too knew it had all been decided. She felt his gaze on her breasts, upraised in the movement, and as her nipples, become stiff and aching, pressed against her shift, she knew with startling clarity that this must be the aching in the stiffness of a man.

—Emancipated and modern as they were, could they really entirely free themselves from those backward ideas of sin, Reuven wondered, as he walked behind Moshe and his sister in the trousers. A love affair was certain now, and to their mother he had promised that he would watch over his young sister, and what did he himself know of love? Work, work to exhaustion was the only way to rid himself of the image of Avner's Rahel that tormented him every night. Even when he lay down, with his body, his very bones, dissolving from exhaustion, still the sexual torment came, as though his sexual organ was not part of that body but a fierce adversary that waited untired for the night, perversely strong when the rest of the body was exhausted, and would not let him sleep.

Moshe—who really knew Moshe? He did not boast of his women among the chevreh, but only gave a wise smile when certain names were mentioned. Yet could one say to

a chaver, stay away from my sister? To speak intimately to
Leah, Reuven knew, was now his duty, but this had become dreadfully difficult, as though she were an older and
not a younger sister. Perhaps—walking ahead of him the
two of them looked so fitting together—perhaps this could
be a good love for her with Moshe? Reuven wanted Leah
to have the joy of love as he knew she wanted it for him;
she was always pointing to girls for him. And also, since
they all believed in the freedom of love, how could he raise
questions when it was his own sister and with their own
chaver?

So as he and Leah were laboring close to one another
planting the slender tree-stalks in the mud under the knee-
deep water, at one movement their eyes met and both began to speak, almost together, "Reuven" she began, flushing, while Reuven said, "Are you in love with him, Leah?"
   "I want terrible to be close to him all the time," she
gasped in a half-wail, sucking in her lower lip, like Saraleh.
   All at once Reuven felt an overwhelming wish for their
mother to be here and take from him this burden, take care
of her daughter. He straightened up and they looked at
each other, and a girlish, somewhat silly smile came over
his sister's large round face. At least there was no estrangement between them, Reuven felt, with some relief. But
what should he now say to her? Forbid her? "Leahleh, you
know all that is said about Moshe. He runs after every
woman he sees."
   "I know," she wailed, and Leah's simple, good face had
a contortion as before tears. "And I know there's no one
else for him to look at here, so even a big horse like me—"
   "No, no!" Reuven declared almost sternly, "Leah, you
are beautiful! You are a big beautiful girl!" His voice
dropped a bit lower. "I have to admit the two of you
looked handsome together." And he felt a pang of guilt. It
was as though he had just given his sanction to his sister.

If it was to happen she would have wanted it to happen
here on their own piece of earth in a beautiful way. But
when the restless urge was on her at night and she felt
Moshe sleepless too, on the other side of the hanging, it
could not happen in that way, for everyone would know

they were slipping out, her brother would know, she would not be able to face them all.

Not yet. It must happen perhaps, but not before the eyes of all.

When their first crop, a stand of fodder, was cut and brought in, and the intoxicating scent from their hillock of fresh hay filled the yard, Saraleh picked up a song she had heard somewhere, about the haystack, the goren.—"In the goren, in the goren"—the song went—in the goren, couples made their nests, and passing by you could not see them but you could hear their twittering.

Once each week on his donkey there came Gedalia the Carrier, a shriveled, parched-looking Sephardi who brought not only the post but messages gathered along his route, and small purchases he had been asked to make such as medicines, or needles and thread. This time he brought a letter from home, from Mameh. Her brother Simha still wanted them all to come to America, she wrote. If things were not well, Mameh knew Reuven would never say so, but Mameh counted on her, Leah, to be sensible and remember that whatever happened, they could always come home to gather new strength. Gidon would soon be Bar Mitzvah; he had grown. He rode horses and was strong. Dvora too had become a young woman and longed for her older sister.

How homesick she was for them! No, not too much for Cherezinka, but for the family, her father too, ununderstanding as he was. Leah longed for the sight of Tateh with his fringes dangling over his trousers.

For Moshe, Gedalia had a note given him in Sejera. On Thursday, when the kvutsa usually sent the wagon to Yaviel for the week's supply of bread and other things, Galil would be there for a meeting. It would be well if Moshe brought along Reuven, too.

"Go, go along with them, Leah," Saraleh urged, "if only for a change of faces." So on Thursday morning she put on her white blouse and mounted the wagon.

It was on that ride, as he handled the mules, that Reuven fell to brooding, while the two of them, Leah and Moshe, sat behind on the wagon-bottom. The certainty came to

Reuven that the whole family must come here, or else his young brothers and sisters would be lost to Eretz, they would surely at some time go to America. But his father, in the middle of life, what could he do here, what use would he be? A thought had been forming. There were rumors that new villages were soon to be established. A combination had been made between the two great Barons who had been settling Jews on land, Baron de Rothschild here in Eretz, and Baron de Hirsch in America and Argentina. Millions had been spent by Baron de Hirsch to transport Russian Jews to Argentina instead of to Eretz. But now these funds would be used in Eretz as well. And in the new combination there would be a different atmosphere. No longer would supervisors peer into every family's pot. The new villages would be for families pledged to work their own parcels of land; the Zionist office was even to have a hand in selecting the candidates. Perhaps in this way the whole family could come. For himself, though Reuven believed in the principle of the kvutsa, in sharing all and not owning anything, there had nevertheless come problems. Each day, he had difficulties with Max. All their ideas for developing the land were divergent. Every idea Reuven wanted to try was "a dream," "needless," "premature," a waste of their scant funds and energies. Though Reuven demanded of himself that he should live by the decisions of the group, he had come to think of Max as short-sighted, domineering, even hateful. It was wrong to feel this way toward a chaver, but what could he do? And besides, was not a family something like a kvutsa? Everyone sharing everything? Even if he had difficulties getting along with Tateh it would be no worse than with Max. Thus, his plan was forming.

The scent from the haystack behind each house enveloped them as they arrived. Those from Sejera were not yet there. Leah sat with the wife and daughters of the mukhtar, Yona Kolodnitzer, in whose house she was to sleep. For a while they sat on the doorstep talking idly, and when the mother and girls went in, Leah sat on, her whole being filled with a kind of intoxication, as though she sensed the breathing of every infant in the village, every calf in the stables, and she knew she would not pass this night without being changed.

In the wagon from Sejera there was also a young woman. Tiny, wearing glasses. Leah at once knew this must be the famous Nadina the Firebrand. She had just returned from a voyage abroad on some mysterious mission, and already one could see that there was something between her and Galil. Nadina too was well-educated, the daughter of a wealthy Jew of Smolensk. A social revolutionist as a young girl, she had led a strike in her father's factory. It was Nadina, people said, who had smuggled in from Germany the pistol used in the assassination of Plehve, the "minister of pogroms." When an informer betrayed her revolutionary cell, she had luckily again been in Berlin, and for her own safety had been lured to Palestine by the pretended sickness of her brother, a Zionist, who was an engineer in Haifa. Then the land itself had made a Zionist of Nadina. It was whispered that she was the one woman accepted as a member of the secret Bar Giora.

As Leah approached, it was Nadina who cried out, as though not she but Leah were the famous one. "At last we meet," she cried.

Much was to be done. From the Bar Giora had come the first watchmen, riding the rounds. They had received the watchman's contract at Mescha and had formed a cooperative called the Shomer. But Galil wanted to organize the whole Yishuv to be able to defend itself. Presently Shabbatai Zeira galloped up in full regalia on the Shomer's magnificent white stallion. Zeira wore a kind of Cossack coat, with not only bandoliers but belts of bullets, and he flourished the longest rifle ever seen.

The steed was the only one owned by the Shomer. It had been purchased with the last dinar each chaver could muster, and even this would not have been half enough but that Shabbatai's wife had produced a small secret hoard of napoleons that her mother had given her on her marriage. Shabbatai Zeira himself had gone to Damascus and bought the mount, and when the farmers of Mescha had seen that the men were equipped with such a fine steed, they had finally broken their contract with the napping Circassians of Kfar Kana, though the dismissed watchman of Kfar Kana grumbled and made threats.

Galil led the discussion. The entire Yishuv must be protected. Isolated points such as the kvutsa at Kinnereth, for example, must be able to defend themselves. Weapons would be needed.

As a start, Nadina had brought back a small sum from her voyage to Europe for purchases. And from a knitting bag she carried Nadina produced a six-chamber revolver, handing it to Moshe. Presently, Galil took Moshe and Reuven aside to teach them the use of the weapon. Despite his principle of pacifism, Reuven agreed that to be able to defend was necessary. For defense, even women should learn.

In the dark, as they emerged from the meeting, everyone was suddenly gone, Galil disappearing with Nadina, Reuven going to sleep at Zev's. And as Leah walked slowly toward the Kolodnitzer house, Moshe came alongside her, making talk for a moment, and presently she walked with him, as one drugged, toward the goren.

It was as though she were explaining to her mother: in your day you walked forward to stand under the wedding canopy; as you said, you had only once before seen Tateh, when the matchmaker brought him to the house, and here I am walking to the goren with a man I have worked with side by side in the fields, a chaver. Is this worse? It is as though my whole life was planned for me to come here and join myself to him on the fodder reaped from our ancient earth.

So her thoughts mounted, and as they fitted themselves into their own little nest in the soft hillock of produce, Leah treasured to herself each small movement in her bridal night as though each movement between them were a picture she would keep in the album of her heart.

But then the sensations were so rapid, sensations like fish darting through cupped hands, she could not hold them, and she still had to sweep away traces of shame in herself. A great inner triumph she felt, too, that she was daring to rise beyond all girlish fears, all ghetto admonitions, and to be a free woman, to be like Nadina, like Rahel, and to love. His mouth was so completely joined to hers that the sensation in her lips was one with the sensation below. It was all one. It was how you saw God, she suddenly felt, their joining, and the way of creation, and the melting together of the universe in a single unity, love, God, one flesh. This is my beloved and I am his. Why was her mind thinking? Let her only feel, only feel. Love.

Then he lay back. She still glowed, and tried to keep out any ignorant questions, and so as not to ask them Leah turned and buried her face on his chest, her lips on the fragrant warm skin. Presently Moshe's arm came around her and stroked her hair, and she heard from him the word that sanctified what she had done. "My beloved."

Moshe was not insincere. He had spilled, to be fair; his very first girl in his student days in Odessa had insisted that he should in this way protect her, and he still considered it the safest way for himself as well. This time the little spell of after-melancholy had hardly made itself felt, submerged in the triumph of a virginity. Perhaps Leah would indeed be the one, the one who would complete and hold him. For until this time, even with a virginity, as for example with the sweaty Nahama and her fears and tears, the after-melancholy had taken seat for long spells.

The largeness of Leah, the strong bones, fitted to his body. He had not felt so good since Katya, a student revolutionist, a real Russian girl who, he later comprehended, had almost commanded him to her because she wanted to feel how it was with a Jew.

Moshe was from Poltava; his father, an estate manager, had sent him to a cousin in Odessa to study medicine. He had not taken to it and had tried to read philosophy, somehow managing a year, but it was life that absorbed him. From childhood he had known he was a favored one, growing tall, with an appealing brightness in his face. All the mothers clucked out the same word, "chenevdik," which meant that something in him sparkled to them. In adolescence the girls turned their heads to look at him and hurried away giggling. Moshe was fine with boys too, a champion hand-wrestler, and he liked everybody. Still he was somewhat uncertain when the fellows turned to him as a leader. In Odessa his cousin, a far better philosophy student than Moshe, let him lead their little circle, but somehow Moshe usually got from his cousin a feeling as to which way he should lead.

In their student-circle discussions, Hegel and Marx were a bore to him, though he could repeat the essentials and was for the revolution.

When they turned into activists, Moshe was given the leadership of a small unit distributing leaflets on the Odessa

docks. In his unit was Katya. Moshe found himself more
and more possessed by the need to be in the company of
girls and one of these, a married woman, took him during
the day to her bed. Despite their free-love philosophy Katya showed jealousy and left him, taking up with his
cousin. The married girl dropped him because her husband
became suspicious, but by then Moshe had learned to detect the already experienced and willing ones from the way
they looked at him. Still, arid spells happened, and a few
times he even went with the lads to prostitutes.

When the dockers' strike came and arrests were made,
Moshe had luckily already left that circle because his
cousin had pulled him to a meeting of the Jewish Self-
defense group. It was after Kishinev. A brilliant young
journalist whose articles they all read, Vladimir Jabotinsky,
had addressed the meeting, stirring up a great fervor, and
Moshe found himself volunteering with his bespectacled
cousin to carry clubs and defend the entry to a Jewish
courtyard. The boys selected him as captain.

It turned out they were all Zionists. Moshe had never
paid much attention to Zionism, but now his cousin converted him, and also one of the Young Zionist girls took to
him. He had never yet known a Jewish girl who would be
completely free. Basheh was quite short, with thick legs,
and it irked him that she always wanted to walk with him
in the street. Alongside him she looked a dwarf. Yet
Basheh had her own room and she would prepare tasty
things for him. And—where she had learned them he did
not know—Basheh sought out all sorts of lewd tricks to
arouse and please him. It was all getting somewhat dangerous, Moshe feared, for how would he have the heart to hurt
her, to break off—and also she did not want him to spill,
she clutched him fiercely to her at the climactic moment,
she might even become pregnant so he would have to
marry her.

Four boys were going to Palestine. His father, and even
his mother, urged him to go, for they still trembled that
Moshe would be arrested. His cousin wanted to go but was
determined first to finish his course in medicine. The girl,
Basheh, just then was acting worried and would not discuss
the reason. So in a way Moshe had fled.

But he told himself he was nevertheless sincere in his
Zionism and Socialism. Once in the land Moshe felt wholly

a chalutz. As to the girls—here it was not so easy; the chalutzoth were few, and like Nahama with her mustache, were
not as attractive as the daughters of the grove-owners who
looked at him with lighted eyes but not with that other
look, the look of the experienced and willing. In his longing
to be in the company of attractive women he wasted many
hours walking with these virtuous daughters, holding hands,
reciting verses of Lermontov. They kissed tenderly, even
passionately. There was that sweet one in Rehovot, daughter of a well-off planter—Moshe had even thought he might
marry that one, but then how could he face the scorn of his
comrades? Marrying a pardessan's daughter! But now, with
Leah, things might turn out quite good.

For Leah there followed many glowing days. Her
brother knew at once, she was certain, and looked more
tenderly at her. Even so, she could not speak to Reuven of
it as she might have to a sister who divined what had happened. Yet because it had happened for her, Leah wished
more and more strongly that it would happen for Reuven,
wished that she could help him find someone, and with
Saraleh she went over and over the names of virtually every chalutza in the land, perhaps to invite this or that one
to visit the kvutsa?

Saraleh had sensed about Leah at once, and with her at
least Leah could now exchange profound womanly insights.
The whole kvutsa too soon understood and accepted the
thing that had happened, accepted it as long expected, and
with true comradely decency—no one made remarks.
When sharing out the food, she had to restrain herself from
giving bigger portions to Moshe, though after all he was a
larger man and needed more nourishment! But Saraleh
confessed that in her turns at serving she felt the same impulse for Araleh, telling herself he was the hardest worker.
And they laughed happily together.

It was strange to Leah that, although younger and a girl,
it was she who came to know physical love before her
brother. But Reuven did not appear unhappy. On the Sabbath he had started the habit of going off by himself seeking for various plants that were mentioned in the Bible. Or
sometimes, climbing to the Arab village, Dja'adi, examining their crops in the field, he even managed to talk a bit
with the fellaheen—Arabic was not far from Hebrew—and
would bring back samples of their wheat, kernels that were

small and poor—he said they suffered from a blight. Reuven collected one strain and another and planted the samples in little squares. From across the Kinnereth, on the heights, the wheat was excellent.

Thus on the Sabbath Reuven would leave Leah with Moshe. Their arms around each other's waist, they strolled along the shore of the Kinnereth; the whole shoreline became their bed, and through the reeds they would gaze out at the little fishing boats that sometimes came down this far from Tiberias. Leah made Moshe see how graceful was the movement of the fishermen when they cast their nets.

It was Araleh who suggested that they too catch fish, at least for their own table, but Max Wilner as usual was opposed, on the calculation that investment in a boat was not justified. The argument raged for two night-sittings and became acrimonious when Saraleh offered the point that they could also use the boat for pleasure. Were they here for pleasures? Max sneered. At this barb Saraleh burst into tears, Araleh got angry, and Leah for the first time felt that a hidden bitterness was in the men, even in Max, for having to live without women.

Somehow Araleh secured a small half-broken boat which he patched and caulked after his working hours; he had traded a pair of Saraleh's hose for it to an Arab fisherman, and one moonlit evening the married couple took the boat out a distance on the water, and sat there quietly. They were still keeping to themselves the knowledge that Saraleh was pregnant; only to Leah had she told the secret, under the strictest promise that not even Reuven, not even Moshe, would be told until Araleh agreed. A woman simply had to confide in another woman, and this her husband understood. But they were perplexed. A baby, in a kvutsa? What problems this would bring! Leah imitated Max Wilner tightening his lips. "You should have first brought it up for discussion. It is not in the plan. We are not yet ready for such luxuries."

Araleh's little vessel meanwhile belonged to all, and on another night Moshe and Leah, lying on its bottom, drifted under the moon. The boat fitted like a seashell around them, Leah whispered, and then it rocked gently with their clasped movement. And this time, this time something happened within herself that came as an overwhelming surprise, as though an enormous wave rose up inside her and carried her on its crest to an infinite pinnacle and then sweetly ebbed her down. She gasped, she was in awe at such joy. Moshe held her fiercely, exultantly, and Leah knew what she felt was at last like what the man felt. And at the same moment Moshe had given his seed in her, let happen whatever might happen. And Moshe did not turn away afterward nor did she feel that instant of strange misery in him; even in his voice to her a change had come. It was not as though, in that mysterious unspoken struggle of mating that went on between a man and woman even in love, Moshe had given in, but as though he had admitted to himself, this was she, he need seek for no other. Leah was content.

Then came the day when Reuven pronounced the wheat ready for cutting. That night he hardly slept, and he was up before the others, stoning his scythe, and one for Leah as well. The entire kvutsa went out to the field, even Saraleh standing in line with the men, though for her a sickle had been provided, as she was not strong enough to hold a scythe and besides everyone understood now that she was pregnant, though the problem had not yet been brought up.

When tall Moshe cried "Now," the whole line swung in unison and made a step forward.

The sweat soon came, and songs came; for a time Reuven restrained his step so as to keep in line with the others, but when Moshe moved ahead Reuven swung faster and kept up with him. Now Araleh stepped ahead and the cutting became a bit of a contest. Leah showed them what a woman could do, and kept up with the foremost.

Toward breakfast time, all were nearly in line again, and turning they saw Saraleh, who had gone back, now bringing their food on the donkey cart across the cut field. All the harvesters drew up straight and gazed back on the expanse of their labor. "Ours." It was an elation. This was not only the grain of the land but the grain of the workers. A new way was being cut across this field, and Max solemnly declared, his face for once shining with pleasure, "Chevreh, we have made history."

That night in a long sitting they went over their calculations; Max had kept the accounts, and even when the crop was estimated at a low price, it was certain that they had covered the entire loan of the Keren Kayemeth for the mules and seed and their food, and could calculate for their labor a wage one-fourth larger than they might have earned on hire. With enthusiasm Max foresaw how a kvutsa such as theirs could settle on a piece of land such as this, and how they, the workers themselves, without owners and without the Baron's experts to tell them what to plant and what not to plant, could develop their cooperativa, with their own cattle, their own fowl, how they could enlarge the farm, and bring farming machines from America, and resettle the land! "Chevreh, do you know what we have done here? Not only have we produced a good crop—we have produced an instrument! No more will the chalutz have to stand in the slave market and depend on the whim of the planter for a day's work. No more do we have to bring ourselves down to the standards of the fellaheen. We can set our own pace, our own development, and the fellaheen can learn from us if they want to. We have shown that the kvutsa is the solution! We don't have to wait for villages to be built and owners to arrive to reclaim the land. We ourselves can go out on land that belongs to the whole Jewish people, and reclaim it!"

Now Shimek slowly repeated the thought. Not private, a farmer on private land, but socialist farming on land that belonged to the Jewish people. This was the way!

Reuven was inspired to still another vision. With socialist farming, experiments could be made such as no private settler could undertake. Not only crops of the usual staples, barley and corn and chickpeas could be grown here. From the Jordan they had ample water for irrigation. With a pumping station, they could develop intensive farming, and support a much larger population.

Araleh too had a plan; to construct a sluice-gate to regulate the waters of the Jordan. Suddenly everyone had a plan . . .

"Wait! Wait! Stick to reality!" Max objected. "All this is in the far distant future—"

"Why?"

—With irrigation, Reuven went on, orange groves could be planted, and bananas as well. In this climate they could grow every fruit and vegetable on earth. A Garden of Eden could be developed here—And higher and higher went their enthusiasm until it burst into song, burst out into a hora in the yard, while Max vainly summoned all to sleep, as the harvest must continue at dawn.

"Never mind! We'll be ready! We'll be ready!"

News of the kvutsa's success spread quickly to the training farm at Sejera, and chalutzim began to arrive to lend a hand and see how it all was done, and by the end of the harvest there came Rahel, sent down by Avner from Jerusalem, to write of their feat for the new journal of the Poale Zion. A long table was set up in the yard, there was a feast; Dovidl and a whole wagonload of chalutzim from Mescha arrived with a few bottles of Zichron wine; Nadina and Galil arrived, and Nadina made a speech. "Chaverim, you have proven here that our new way of life will succeed! Not only will our Jewish movement in Eretz embrace this socialist way of life, but the downtrodden Arabs too will learn from us and throw off the medieval yoke of the effendi! And one day"—she took off her glasses, tears were blinding her—"one day over the vast steppes of Russia, communards will go forward, to harvest as you have harvested, for the benefit of the workers themselves, and one day even in capitalist America it will be the cooperativa that owns what it produces from its own toil on its own soil. Chaverim and chaveroth, you may be proud!"

Such a glow of love embraced them all at that plank table, it was as though they had grown and reaped the first grain known to man, and all their little animosities and grievances were melted in this joy, and Reuven, gazing at Rahel with Avner, felt released from his long secret desire, felt it was indeed true that an overlove existed, a comradely love that was purer than sexual love between men and women, and suddenly from his lips there came the song of Elijah bringing Messiah, but not with the melancholy Diaspora-tone of suffering and longing. The song of Elijah came bursting out in joy.

Leah and Moshe leaped up to dance, the singing rose, and quickly the whole crazed circle of them were stomping on their harvest floor, their bare feet in this way beginning to thresh the grain, all of them roaring and feeling inexhaustible, earth-demons, earth-angels, children of the giants that once walked the earth here in this place, prophets with the word of universal love and truth and plenitude flowing up from their limbs.

Surprisingly, after this triumph, the kvutsa again began to break up. First came a violent dispute over Saraleh's pregnancy, now too visible to be ignored. A remark of Araleh's at a sitting that they could now afford to get a cow to assure their own milk supply unexpectedly brought a sarcastic response from Max—Saraleh could assure her own milk supply. As Araleh leaped up in anger, Max withdrew any offensiveness in his remark; but after all the kvutsa had not been consulted about their having a baby, and the kvutsa was yet in no state to support child-raising. In a communa this too should be planned and consented to by all.

Leah was flushing. She had luckily not become pregnant, but perhaps the boys were wondering whether she too—? And suddenly it came out that the womanless men had indeed been thinking and even talking of this problem amongst themselves, and that several agreed with Max's argument.

After all, he pointed out when the sitting became more calm, in Plato's ideal society the children were raised by the state. In their communa there was no personal property. The idea that a child was the personal property of the parents must be abandoned. All children would belong to the whole kvutsa. Therefore their conception must be planned.

"Shame!" cried Saraleh, and Araleh had to soothe her. It was the theory of it; by nature a child would have ties to the parents, even Max would agree.

Certainly, Max said, but as everyone in the kvutsa would be contributing to the support of the child—of its children, as in time there would of course be others—then such questions as upbringing, education, and the place in the community must be settled by all, not by the parents alone as in bourgeois society.

Araleh balked. Surely the parents would have the deciding word!

They would have their vote like all other members, Max maintained.

The discussion became heated. Leah felt upset, both sides seemed right, and yet—if you had a child. . . .

Saraleh sat mute. Moshe with a rather foolish look rose to remark, really what decision could they make? The child was already well on its way and surely things could be worked out. Perhaps next time they would have time to discuss the *principe*.

"It seems to me the *principe* is clear," Max said. "No one is forced to agree. Ours is a free society. Those who cannot live by our beliefs can always leave."

Only a few days later came another nasty moment between Araleh and Max. The kvutsa's clock had broken down, and as Araleh was the only chaver to possess a watch, a wedding gift from Zuckerman, he had been leaving it lying on the table. But that day, as he was plowing alone far afield, he picked it up to take along. "Leave it here," Max said in a voice more commanding than comradely. "The rest of us will need it."

"But it's my watch."

"Your private property?"

Certain things were personal, not community, property, Araleh retorted. The watch was a gift from his father-in-law.

"So now we have bourgeois sentimentality?"

Araleh burst into a tirade. "My watch is not mine, our child will not be ours, next it will apply to my wife!"

The story was repeated and the chaverim resented it that one of their own number should have stooped to the same slander spread by outsiders against life in a communa. They were going through enough deprivation without having the lucky bastard who had his woman make such remarks.

This time the breach was not easily healed. Araleh and Saraleh stayed up in their room, failing to come to sittings, and mutterings even arose about the privileged ones with their private chamber.

In the meantime another clash came; now it was between Reuven and Max over a question of plowing. Max had received a German catalogue of farm implements in which deep-plowing was declared to yield a doubled harvest. Though it would strain the kvutsa's funds, he insisted they must order the heavy plow—the soil must be deeply turned over to tap its full resources. Reuven, though also given to the most advanced agricultural methods, in this instance argued that the light Arab plow was better adapted to the stony soil of the area. Besides, grain crops did not tap the deep soil. What was really needed first was a pump to raise up water to the fields for irrigation.

Another raging sitting ensued, with half the men siding with Max, half with Reuven; Moshe for the plow, Shimek against, Leah asking if there was no money to buy a cow, how they could afford this expensive plow, Tibor jesting, "A cow or a plow, that is the question." Araleh and Saraleh had returned to the discussions, and Araleh argued that it would take two pair of mules to pull such a plow, something they surely could not afford. The vote came, the sides were even, and Max announced he would therefore cast his deciding vote and order the plow.

Soon after this, Saraleh quietly told Leah she and Araleh had made up their minds to return to Jaffa for her child to be born. And Araleh had a quiet talk with Reuven. Perhaps the kvutsa was not the final way. He had been thinking of another way, a "semi-cooperativa," as it were. All would be owned together; the crops, the livestock, and labor would be shared as here, but each family would live its own life. He had heard of a new settlement being planned not far from here, further along the river, and perhaps if Reuven was interested, he would make inquiries at the Zionist officer in Jaffa.

"No, I don't know, as for me," Reuven said. For a homestead, for one thing, you had to be married.

But the thought came back to him about bringing the family from home.

Then, when they went out to plant another stand of eucalyptus, Reuven fell ill. Leah was the first to notice it, for he made no complaint. But in the evening she saw it in his eyes, his unfocused gaze. She felt his hands; they burned.

Almost, Reuven welcomed it, as the burning brand that Eretz put on you. Only when you had passed through the fever were you truly a part of the movement of redemption. And so he lay on his planks, his eyes glazed, hardly able to lift an arm while his sister sponged sweat from his face, taking kitchen work so as to remain near him.

When the tremors came, Leah grasped him and held him

to her; Reuven's muscles became hard and rigid and the whole body began to thrash not like a human body that belonged to itself, but like a thing, a thing overwound with tight steel springs. Like the kvutsa's old clock when she had wound it too tight, and suddenly felt the whole thing spin backward, loose and lifeless. Reuven's eyes had yellowed like when you turn down a lamp. It seemed to Leah there was no longer the glaze of fever in her brother's eyes, but the glaze of death. "Moshe!" she cried wildly, letting down Reuven's rigid body and running in panic to the field. Moshe was far, everyone was far, the bare field seemed endless, but at last Moshe came running. Reuven was pouring sweat, the tremor was over.

In an hour it began again. Moshe decided to ride for Dr. Rachman in Mescha, but Leah was so fearful of the day of waiting until he brought back the doctor that instead they harnessed the wagon, putting a bed of straw on the bottom. Reuven had become so weak that Moshe had to carry him in his arms to the vehicle.

Dr. Rachman saved him, of this Leah was always certain. Though Reuven was already filled with quinine, the old doctor got more into him. With Leah he stayed by her brother's side all through the night. Twice more the wrenching tremors came, and the second time Reuven was in a delirium, trying to rise and go to work, crying "I must get up! I must get up!"

"Help him to stand up," the doctor said. Leah helped him. Reuven stood, tottering, his teeth knocking from the tremor, while she held onto his burning hand to steady him. Oh, how she then wanted to engulf him and give him her strength. "Beloved, my loved one," Reuven plaintively repeated, "appear to me, appear." It was as though he awaited the Shechina. Tears ran down Leah's face.

Moshe had been dozing fitfully in the wagon; now he stood in the doorway, workless, sorrowful. Then the seizure was over and Reuven lay on the cot.

The doctor patted her hand. Oh, what a good man he was, to have come here with the earliest settlers, to have remained here through the years, riding to Sejera and Yavniel when needed. Now he told her to try to rest. He had a leather couch there, an old leather couch he had long ago brought all the way here from "home." She lay down. The doctor went to the other part of the house, to his wife.

In the morning Reuven awoke with the sweetest smile. "Now I have the land in my blood," he said to Leah and Moshe. He had crossed over to the side of those who had engulfed the kadahat.

Though he had passed the crisis, Reuven's face was hollow and his limbs were reeds. As the mules were needed at the kvutsa, Moshe had to return while Leah remained with Reuven. Her brother's strength did not seem to return; she could barely coax him to forgo his vegetarianism and sip a bit of chicken broth. A month of convalescence was needed, Dr. Rachman said; Reuven must not go back to the deadly heat of the Jordon valley. He had best be taken to the convalescent home in Zichron Yaacov, and the doctor wrote a note for her. Luckily a villager was driving as far as Chedera, and could take Leah and Reuven in his wagon. From Chedera, Zichron was but a few hours away and they would manage to find another ride. Once in Zichron, Leah was determined to get work, so as not to burden the kvutsa with keeping her brother in the convalescent home.

Zichron Yaacov sat on a hill from which the salt marshes of the Mediterranean shoreland could be seen and the sweep of the sea. Just as they arrived, the western vista was under such a sunset sky, with such purple clouds undershot with fire, that Reuven breathed in the beauty of the world once again and Leah felt heartened. He would get well here. On the horizon they made out ruins, a Crusader's castle called Athlit; they must one day go there, Reuven said.

This village was one of the Baron's best, with a large winepress and a street of goodly houses, and in a wooded nest on the crown of the hill was the rest home kept by the kadahat expert, Dr. Hillel Jaffe, who at once put Reuven into a whitewashed room on a bed with sheets.

But how would she find work here? The settlers of Zichron were known for their avoidance of Jewish labor; they had an entire village of Arabs at the bottom of their hill, and even when it came to housework and the kitchen, the Arab women had long ago learned the laws of kashruth as well as the fine points of Roumanian cooking. "Don't worry, don't worry, my girl, I am not worried, so why should you worry? In time you will pay me," the doctor told Leah. But as she would not rest, and went from house to house, he put in a word with a leading family, the Aaronsons, and told her to try there.

It fell out well. This was clearly one of the most substantial places in Zichron, Leah saw, with two dwellings, one quite large, on either side of the courtyard. In the center stood an enormous shade tree, and behind, you looked out over a rich valley called Faradis, or Paradise, so named, Reuven had already told her, by the Crusaders.

Mother Aaronson reminded her of her Aunt Minna, wife of her mother's rich brother Kalman; she wore a fine ruffled shirtwaist over a high-boned corset, with an elaborate ritual wig topped by a lace cap, as though she were living in the city. As it happened, her Arab woman had chosen Erev Shabbat to have a baby, Mother Aaronson declared, not as one who complains so much but as one who is patient with the foibles of the simpler folk. The Arab woman had sent up her twelve-year-old daughter, a primitive who had never held a dish in her hand and had already broken a French porcelain bowl. As to her own daughter, Mother Aaronson complained with a touch of pride, her Sara was a modern girl who didn't even know how to light a fire in the kitchen stove.

Leah soon saw the daughter—plumpish, a few years younger than herself—as she crossed the yard from the smaller house, eyed her and at once announced that Leah must never go into the cottage—as though Leah had any thought of it—for that house was the laboratorium of her eldest brother Aaron, the famous agronomist, and he was away in the United States of America on an important mission, and above all his books were not to be touched!

Leah could scarcely feel offended, for the girl babbled on in evident adoration of that brother who even as a young boy had been selected by the Baron's agent, Jacques Samuelson, and sent to the best academy in France, in Grenoble; he had returned and made important discoveries which soon would be announced to the world. He was now in Chicago where, Leah must know, the most advanced agricultural machinery was made, and Aaron intended to bring back such machinery to Zichron.

—Fine and good! Leah thought of the chaverim having

to decide between a cow and a plow, and of Reuven with his dreams of agricultural experiments, and his self-taught agronomy learned from a book seized here and there, and pored over by candlelight after twelve hours of labor in the fields. And yet she could not feel envious, and even found herself telling this girl that she too had an older brother interested in agronomy—he was recovering just now at Dr. Jaffe's, a chalutz.

—Oh, a barefoot, the girl said, but with interest, so that, unable to suppress her matchmaking instincts, Leah even glanced again at Sara Aaronson—in a year at most she would bloom. "If he is convalescing," young Sara offered of her own volition, "and is so interested in agronomy, I might lend him some books if he will be careful. Can he read French?"

"No," Leah said.

"Or German or English?" Sara Aaronson's own brother of course read them all.

"A little German, but the best is Russian." All there was in Hebrew he had read, and Yiddish was no longer mentioned.

"Oh," Sara said. There were a few works in Russian, but the best were in French. She would see what she could find.

There was also a younger sister named Rifka, who aroused in Leah a longing for little Eliza, and there was another brother who dashed off on his horse every morning. The father she liked; he went off early to his vineyards and labored there himself side by side with his Arabs.

In the second week, when the Arab woman returned to the kitchen and Leah saw she was no longer needed, and when Reuven, though discharged from the convalescent home, was advised still to rest in this hill climate, it was Father Aaronson who bethought himself of a place for them, the watchman's hut in his vineyard.

The hut was raised on posts so that one could look out from it over the rows of vines that flowed down the slope, and one could look out to the vista of the sea. The grapes were already fat, clusters hanging like full goats' udders from under the vines. Reuven hoped to be strong enough by the time the gathering began to be employed in the cutting; perhaps Aaronson would employ both of them, among his Arabs. For though Dovidl had sent word from Jerusalem that Reuven was not to worry about money, that the sick fund would pay for his care, he did not want to draw a copper from the fledgling fund. Reuven was worried, too, that they were needed back in the kvutsa, and shyly he let Leah understand that he realized he was keeping her from her Moshe; perhaps now that he was well enough to manage, she should go back.

How hard it was to be away from Moshe she herself had not expected. What if meanwhile some other girl should appear and attach herself to him? No, Leah told herself, for then it would not have been real love with Moshe, and it was best to know this sooner rather than later. But if that which they had felt together was not real love, then what could be real in life?

Suddenly Moshe himself appeared in Zichron. At the sight of his form, glimpsed from the perched-up hut, a kind of glad shame added itself to her wave of joy, partly sexual shame and partly the shame of having doubted him.

But her Moshe had come with news to which he tried to give, as he told it to her, a regretful tone, even while Leah saw how it excited him.

The movement had chosen Moshe for a mission back home; he was to establish training farms and show young Zionists the kvutsa way of life, then bring back to Eretz with him the first such group of new chalutzim.

"And chalutzoth," Leah bravely jested. For why had they picked the Handsome Moshe if not to deal with the shortage of girls?

"Yes, girls for the others," Moshe laughed. For example he would keep a sharp eye out for the right girl for Reuven. "After all, I myself am satisfied!"

Yet it came to her, lying at last again in his arms, under the vines, it came with the contentful sigh ending their first lovemaking, that even of this a human soul had to remain wary. How could life show anything more certain than in this joining that a man and woman felt together? Yet even in this, there crept into Leah's soul a bitterness of doubt that she did not want to acknowledge, no, she had no bitterness. Only, after that time in the little boat on the Kinnereth, a peculiar understanding had come to her: things that seemed fated to be, and that even seemed accomplished, could also turn out untrue. There in the vessel when the new ecstatic convulsion had arrived within her body she had felt that what she had now experienced was conception. Yet a few days later her period had come. Perplexedly, even blushingly, Leah had drawn Saraleh into a discussion of womanly things, until Saraleh, comprehending, had revealed to her the knowledge she had received from her own mother on the eve of her marriage. Only in certain weeks of her month could a woman conceive. And what Leah had felt, like a wondrous discharge of love joining the disharge of the man, was not necessarily conception. It was, Saraleh said, simply the full joy of love.

So she had not conceived. Though tonight she did not know what to feel. To have his child in her would be the old, indeed the unworthy way of a woman's keeping a man. Yet even without reference to keeping him, even if her Moshe should stray away from her—to have and keep his child, their child, would that not have been what the life-urge intended? And here too something puzzled and disturbed Leah, for she had always trusted in the purity of her life-urge, her inmost feeling, and here she saw that nature too could deceive. For again tonight, even had she so decided and dared it, it was not her time to conceive. Oddly, the maxim of Theodor Herzl drifted through her mind. "If you will it, then it need not remain but a dream." And on this trust in human will, all they were doing here was being done. Yet a dim sense pervaded Leah of some possible flaw in the working of the universe, so that despite the most pure, the most deserving and innocent effort of will that God could expect of man, even in the truest love, the end could be barren.

No, she was only sad because Moshe was going away.

It was but for a limited time, for a few months, and Leah told herself she must banish the overshadowing of melancholy. They thrust themselves together as though to hold forever joined, their bodies sealed, as at the instant of all creation.

To help them earn a bit, Mother Aaronson contrived still to give Leah a day's housework now and again, especially the heavier cleaning for Sabbath Eve, as her Arab woman had still not regained her full strength. On one such afternoon, when Leah was at the Aaronson house, a young girl climbed up the ladder to the hut; Reuven knew it must be Sara. She had brought two huge books, wondrous French botanical volumes filled with delicate engravings of all the plants of the Levant. "I believe my brother himself would have lent them to you," she said, as she placed the volumes carefully on the table. "That is why I decided to bring them. He likes to find people seriously interested in studying." And then she simply gazed at him. Reuven in his eagerness was about to open the books, but on impulse first hurried to the basin in the corner and carefully washed his hands. A smile, an illumination, came over the girl's face and their eyes met. Why he didn't know, but she reminded him of Leah when she had not yet grown so tall, and was somewhat plump like this. He realized the girl had come out of curiosity to have a look at him, nothing more. Now he carefully opened a volume, leafing back the tissue paper over a magnificent, detailed engraving of a papyrus plant such as grew in the Huleh.

Could he read the Latin name? she wanted to know.

Yes, he had taught himself Latin nomenclature.

She smiled again. Her brother had discovered many plants that were not even in the books, she said. Sometimes her brother took her with him on his excursions, they rode on horseback, they had explored the whole of Galilee and even the Hauran . . .

And on and on she talked of her brother, and then all at once, abruptly, she bade him a farewell Shalom and was gone.

Nor did she return. It was as though she had satisfied herself in seeing the chalutz, and that was enough. As for Reuven, the image of the girl remained with him as something fresh, something good that had happened, but surely nothing more.

Now there were pastoral days on the Zichron hillside when the long-bearded, patriarchal Aaronson walked among the rows of vines where the Arab girls and women in their many-colored gowns knelt at the cutting, and Aaronson made certain no stem was injured.

In the evenings Leah would watch her brother, his head bent in the lamplight, his thick hair wild around his ascetic face; he was using a Russian-French dictionary that she had found for him—in Zichron there was even a bookshop.

It was at this time that Leah talked of her longing to have the family here; she too had thought of it. She worried about Dvoraleh, who was of the age when she needed a big sister to confide in, and she ached for their baby brother Avramchick; in each letter Mama had told new wonders of him—of how, even so tiny, he showed consideration for others, not like an infant, but like a person! And Gidon and Schmulik—Leah expressed Reuven's own thoughts—what would become of them if they remained in Russia? Another tradesman? another fur worker?

Reuven admitted that he too sometimes longed for their own place where there would be no bickering over each thing he wanted to do, where he wouldn't have to hear Max's constant refrain, "No, Reuven, you can't volunteer to find your own time. Your time, chaver, the same as for the rest of us, belongs to the kvutsa." Sometimes he envied a simple farmer like Kolodnitzer who could bring his own cattle from Holland if he could manage it, and develop a new breed. If Tateh would agree to come with all the children, perhaps indeed they would receive a homestead—surely they would be put at the head of the list. The new settlement being planned would be quite close to the kvutsa, and Reuven had even wondered—he and Leah might stay on at the kvutsa, but with the family farm so close by, he could keep a corner of land there for himself and carry out some of his ideas, on his Sabbaths.

"And what does Tateh have there in Cherezinka? Nothing but a life of insults and falling into debt each time he tries to break away from our Koslovsky and his sugar-beet mill." On a farm even in bad years a family could manage to live on a cow and their own produce. And think of the boys growing up straight, riding horses, plowing the fields.

"Oh, if we could only get them to come," Leah agreed.

And so they wrote long letters home, describing to their father the comforts and good life of the settlers in such a village as Zichron, and telling him of the new settlements waiting for families such as theirs.

3

IN HIS first night on the Zuckerman roof in Eretz Yisroel, Yankel Chaimovitch did not sleep well. Bad dreams sifted through his mind; he stood in a ship made of reeds like a basket, and water poured in through the cracks; the ship was going down, and small birds with sharp open beaks pecked at his shamefully uncovered head; he stood in the synagogue, called up to read the weekly portion, and his son Reuven the eldest snatched the tallis from around him and he was naked.

Before dawn Yankel arose, took his tfillim bag, carefully brushed and put on his round hat, and crept down the out-side stairs with the thought of finding in the narrow lane a little shul they had passed the day before. Hardly had he stepped from the hotel when there in the grayish light stood a pious Jew with a small, pointed red beard and red-rimmed eyes, a prayer bag under his elbow, offering to guide a Jew to a shul.—A newcomer in the land? He spoke with a Litvak intonation. Beware of red-beards and of Lit-vaks, Yankel reminded himself, but already this Yidl had found out how many were the children in his family, had blessed each child by name, and remarked understandingly what a problem it would be to provide for such a huge family, and the children nearly all of them still small ones, may they thrive each and every one! Out of interest for a fellow pious Jew with such problems, there occurred to the red-beard a timely opportunity—a full-bearing orange grove requiring only the smallest cash investment, and providing a good living—a bargin to be snatched up, since land was leaping every day higher in value.

The Litvak kept nudging closer, as though he had di-vined the moneybelt and wanted to get a heft of it. He himself, praised be the Name, had seven mouths to feed and so he could understand a Jew's problems. To settle in a new colony? In the Galilee? There came a shrewd smile and an inspection from his blinking eyes.—Why be dragged

away to the ends of the earth and wait seven years until a
tree grew and bore fruit? And the heat! It was a gehenna
there in the valley. And the fevers! Three out of four died.
Here in Jaffa even if a Jew did not possess enough capital
to finance a full-bearing grove, he could make a decent living
in the town itself. There was an excellent little shop—
implements and building materials—that could be bought
just now from a Jew leaving to join his wealthy brother in
America.

They were already inside the little shul, and without
leaving Yankel's elbow, the red-beard, Reb Nussbaum,
whispered to him about this one and that one in the minyan, influential Jews in Jaffa, some wealthy, some with
good connections, and while racing through the prayers, he
threw in a few words under his breath. After the Kaddish
they would take a droshke, he would pay half out of his
own pocket, and they would visit the widow who owned the
orange grove—God grant her grove was not yet sold, it
was only partway to Petach Tikvah, no distance at all, it
would be just like living in Jaffa itself.

—No, he was not taken in by this Nussbaum, Yankel
told himself—A luftmench, here in Eretz Yisroel too they
were to be found. If you wanted a king's palace, he had it
for sale in his pocket. A husband for your daughter?—
behold, he was a bit of a matchmaker too. But still even
from such a type, if a man was careful, he could at least get
an idea of how things stood in this land. Yankel was not
yet ready, he told himself, to be led around by the nose by
his son, to be dragged off God knows where to a wilderness of fever and heat.

If only he had come here in his youth as he had
dreamed, he too would now be the possessor of a fine
house such as he now beheld, with fig trees in the yard,
and a bower of vines, and with his daughters sitting in the
house practicing on the piano while matchmakers came to
propose excellent suitors descended from the Gaon of
Vilna. Instead, here he was a homeless man with a flock of
children and only a few gold pieces sewn away.

There was indeed a widow, though she greeted Reb
Nussbaum rather icily—a woman's humors. Stiffly
corseted in a black gown, she squeezed out a smile for the
newcomer, and led them to a parlor with red velvet chairs

with tassels, brought, she said, all the way from Berdichev. An Arab woman at once appeared with almond cakes and a pitcher of a cool milky drink with a wonderfully refreshing taste—lebeniyah, she called it. Ah, the widow said, everything looked fine and easy now; her husband might-he-rest-in-peace had been a Lover of Zion, and she told the whole tale of how this pestilential swamp had become a paradise. Three children they had lost. Only one daughter had survived; she was married and lived in Paris. There the widow wanted to end her days, close to her grandchildren. "Enough, enough have we suffered in our lives, enough we have given to this land of our heart's blood—"

Feeling somehow an imposter, when the price was mentioned, Yankel still tried to maintain the air of a man of means. But the widow surely had sniffed him out; her eyes narrowed and her voice was harsh as she said something quickly to the red-beard. She did not offer to accompany them to inspect the grove, nor did Yankel even get to see it, for at the gate there stood his son Reuven.

"What are you doing here! I had to come looking for you!" Reuven cried. "We are expected in Dr. Lubin's office!" He had arranged for the chief of the settlement bureau to see them, the entire family, "And you, you run off with this parasite, listening to his grandmother's tales! Bobeh meises! A ready-made estate! A little baron with Arab serfs, is that what you came here to be?"

Luckily, at the shul, Zuckerman the hotelkeeper had overheard the conversation and sent Reuven after the red-beard, one of the most notorious swindlers of Jaffa, just now swarming with their kind.

And on the way back Reuven continued: Did his father know what troubles there were in Petach Tikvah? And around that very widow's grove! Yes, bitter strife in which Turkish police had been called by Jewish landowners to club and beat up Jewish workers who asked for nothing but a day's work! Did Yankel know that before taking back a single Jewish worker the Baron's little barons had forced them to sign a paper that they would not smoke on the Sabbath?

At this Yankel had to hide a smile in his beard. Perhaps indeed he should live in Petach Tikvah. But his son raged on. What sort of homeland would be built, what sort of human freedom—

In one thing Yankel agreed. He too did not want to have serfs, Russian or Arab. He wanted to work his fields with his own hands, his sons laboring beside him, his daughters milking cows in the shed. Only, Reuven need not imagine that Yankel Chaimovitch was about to appear before the head of the Zionist office in Jaffa wearing that wagon-driver's cap!

Now they had to wait for Leah who had vanished.

Seizing the hour, she had hurried to the Poale Zion office and there luckily found Avner, talking to yesterday's newly arrived chalutzim. One thing at least Avner was able to tell her—Moshe had got to Constantinople and stayed there a few nights; then he had taken ship for Odessa. All this was in a letter that had just been brought from a good Turkish Jew whose house served as a way-station. But none of the new arrivals had seen or heard of Moshe in Odessa. This was worrisome, certainly. Avner was never one to be-little a situation, yet he was not one to panic. These new arrivals were not actually Odessans, they had only passed through. It could be that for certain reasons Moshe was keeping out of sight. At least no bad news had come.

But couldn't he send an inquiry?

"Leachkeh—" only the tall, gangling Avner seemed able to sense how feminine and helpless she often felt— "Leahleh, you don't imagine we haven't already done it?" The instant there was news, good or bad, he promised it would be brought to her even if he had to walk himself from Jerusalem.

The family was waiting, and her mother saw something in her face. "No, no, I can't explain to you," Leah told her as Reuven hurried them through the lanes, but her mother even asked, "You heard something? Of the one you told me about last night? Moshe? What has happened?" Leah shook her head mulishly, and Feigel felt stricken. With the first one, her first daughter, she had already failed. She had not been able to protect the girl.

The stairway was crowded. Here in this little office, then, was the compound result of all the orations, the journeyings and the gatherings, the World Congresses, the fervid discussions in Vilna and Bratislava and on New York's

East Side, the bribes and the subterfuges, bringing Jews into the land wearing white helmets as travelers, or even garbed as monks and nuns, or, some said, carried in as sacks of potatoes—building the Land brick by brick.

Up the stairway clattered the Chaimovitch family, the girls with their shining hair, neatly braided, smelling a bit of licekilling kerosene, the boys, as Yankel had insisted, with the dust cleaned from their shoes. Even on the stairway, settlers and chalutzim made way for the family—they stood pressed against the wall to watch the troop move upward, led by the father in his fine capote and round hat, followed by Big Leah whom everybody knew and greeted, and a whole flock of younger brothers and sisters and at last the mother, wearing her finest gown and a crocheted shawl, still a noble-looking wife.

So they entered the inner office. A neat, small man, stoutish, clean-shaven, and cultured one could see at a glance, a Jew who addressed them in German instead of Yiddish, he already knew of Reuven. "Your son is an outstanding worker, known in the settlement," he told Yankel, beaming, "and your daughter too! Ah, if we had ten thousand like them!" And he related with relish the tale of Reuven and the Herzl trees replanted by Jewish hands.

Then, still beaming, Dr. Lubin placed his hand on each smaller child's head in turn. "Altogether how many sons and daughters? Seven, eight?"

"Nine," Dvoraleh whispered to Leah, having divined her mother's condition, and Leah, even in this tumultuous moment, oddly felt a kind of jealousy—the same jealously she had felt when she heard that Saraleh was pregnant.

—Not every day did such a family arrive! the official went on. For such a family special efforts should and would be made!

And even before Yankel could put in a word, things had been arranged as Reuven wanted; they would leave with the first wagon, tomorrow, for the Galilee, for the new settlement being built by the Jordan.

The official scribbled a few words on a bit of paper, a folded note—a pitkah—the whole country, Reuven smiled as he put it in his pocket, was being built by pitkah. And still with a thousand questions to ask—What about a shul? What of a cheder for the boys?—Yankel found himself moved benignly out of the office without the German's even pronouncing a blessing for the journey.

There were two wagons going with supplies to the Galilee; in one of the wagons, implements and tins of kerosene and even, underneath all this—Reuven caught sight of it—Max Wilner's huge iron plow from Germany, marked for the kvutsa. That stubborn Max with his deep-plowing obsession! Reuven was so furious he could have thrown it off the wagon, but Leah calmed him; the chevreh had after all voted on it. A waste! he fumed all the more angrily because he was curious as to what the results would be. They didn't even have the animals to pull it! A steam pump was far more necessary!

The other wagon was entirely for the family, laden with the large trunk from the port, and all their bundles. Young Gidon sat up with the driver, the pockmarked Kalman the drayman, wearing his old Russian cap, the kind Reuven had bought for Tateh. Already Gidon assessed the mules correctly, remarking that the right pulled more strongly. And Kalman promised to let him try the reins along the way.

So they rode out. How would they manage to live until crops came, Yankel worried. The loan that had been mentioned in the Zionist office would hardly be enough for many months, but Reuven had at once agreed to it, before Yankel could put in a word.

Meanwhile the children were excited beyond measure by Leah's description of the Sea of Kinnereth with fishing boats and with flocks of wild geese coming down to sit on the water. Shaindeleh—Reuven and Leah had already changed her name to Yaffaleh—wanted to know whether they could raise white geese on their farm, and Schmuel wanted to know the size of the fish caught in the lake.

And Jerusalem? Was a Jew, Yankel muttered to Feigel, not even going to see Yerushalayim? Not even going to utter a prayer at the Wall? Jews journeyed all the way to Eretz only to shed a tear before the Wall and here, having come this far at such great cost and with such hardship, to what wilderness was his unbeliever of a son dragging him without even a sight of Yerushalayim?

"It's only another ghetto full of beggars," Reuven responded. "And Yerushalayim won't run away, it has stood there for some time."

"We'll go, we'll go to Yerushalayim, but better first to get settled so we can go with a peaceful mind," Feigel calmed Yankel. And counting in his mind the money it would have cost to take the whole family first to Jerusalem—and truly what did it mean to his children, atheists the lot of them—Yankel subsided. He would make his own voyage, he promised himself; perhaps he would take Gidon if Reuven meanwhile didn't succeed in making an atheist out of him as well.

Beyond Petach Tikvah there was only a narrow, lonely wagon road. When, after stretches of wilderness, of high briars and weeds, they passed an Arab village with bits of cultivation around it, and saw a few women walking with jars on their heads like Rebecca in the Bible, all the girls excitedly asked Leah if she had learned to do it. "It makes you graceful," Dvoraleh cried and, before anyone knew what was happening, she had jumped off the wagon and was walking along trying to balance a teapot on her head.

Yankel frowned, and Feigel said "Stop your foolishness," while Leah began to lecture them all on the dreadful backward state of Arab womanhood. It was nothing to laugh at, she told Dvoraleh and little Eliza; a woman was a mere chattel, a slave. A girl of ten could be sold by her father to a toothless old man of sixty. Some Arabs owned two or three wives and made them do all the work in the fields, while the Arab himself sat in a cafe smoking his narghileh.

For long stretches they saw no one. Then out of the emptiness there appeared two horsemen, thundering alongside, daggers in their belts. The girls huddled together, but Leah and Reuven cheerily called out an Arab word, *Marhaba,* while Kalman the drayman even held a conversation with the two. One of the riders stooped down, received a cigarette, and said something to Yankel laughingly, before they thundered off.

"What was he laughing at?" Yankel demanded. "What did he say?"

"The weather is good, the rains will come soon if it please Allah."

"Then why was he laughing at me?"

"Oh, he said you are a rich man, you have so many girls."

"A rich man! With four dowries to pay!"

"With them it is the other way around," explained Kalman. "A daughter is a good investment. A pretty one is worth ten camels."

And so the sun shone on them. Reuven pointed out wild bushes that he said were the castor plant from which castor oil could be made; the children made faces because he said the plant grew everywhere and perhaps it could be useful. Experiments should be made. Then he pointed out places with Biblical names, and Yankel was nevertheless pleased that despite his godlessness his son spoke so much of the Bible. How then could he be an atheist?

Then the wagons halted while Feigel spread their meal and they shelled and salted their eggs. Even Yankel was in good humor.

Before they reached Chedera, at dusk, a somber weariness had come over them all. Feigel, with their youngest, Avramchick, asleep sprawled across her lap, felt that the weight of the child somehow protected the new one unborn within her from the jolting of the wagon. No, she would not lose this one, he would cling to her womb waiting to be born in Eretz Yisroel.

A silence had fallen. Where, how much further, would they be going? How did people live, alone so far away in this emptiness, a whole day's distance from other Jews?

One room in the khan was for women, and there a few cots could be had for the girls; Gidon and Schmulik declared they would sleep on the ground in an open shed in the yard with Reuven and some chalutzim gathered there.

Halfway into the night, the barefoots, as Feigel had learned they were called, were still chanting their songs in the yard, Leah and Dvoraleh among them. The same songs as on the ship:

> Who will build Galilee?
> We will build Galilee!
> We! We!

Perhaps, Feigel hoped, Leah would dance out of herself whatever was troubling her.

Then, going to the outhouse, Feigel passed a tiny room without even a door; here too, as in the lodging in Jaffa, a young man lay ill on a pallet. As she passed, a sound come from him. She went in. Even in the dark she could see the water jug near his pallet, but he was too weak to reach it. Feigel held the jug to his lips, and he babbled, "Thank you, Mama."

"What is your name, my son, where are you from?" she said, brushing the damp hair from his forehead and putting her hand there. How it burned!

"Mati, from Grodno," he managed.

Matityahu, the name she had been thinking of, the name of her father's father. From the sunken eyes a dark flicker seemed to float out toward her, and Feigel had to exorcise what came to her mind. Nay, she had already chosen this name in memory of her grandfather. "Live," she said, "live and be well." Let it not be drawn from this boy.

When they emerged from the valley to the opening onto the great plain, Reuven told the boys this was where Saul and Jonathan fell to the Philistines, and when they crossed the plain he told of the Ten Tribes taken away; in the afternoon, the wagons rounded the bend at the foot of Mount Tabor, and Leah told Dvora of her namesake, the prophetess who had preached on this hill. As they neared the village of Mescha, also called Tabor, Leah began to call everyone they passed—everyone knew her. Yankel saw there were householders no younger than himself coming from the fields with implements over their shoulders. Perhaps his son had not misled him after all.

At the gate of the village, housewives, children, the whole town gathered around the two wagons; what news in Jaffa? The drivers handed out packages—a roll of oilcloth for one woman, spices for another. For this one, Kalman the drayman remembered a message, for that one he had brought a pitkah. More men were arriving from the fields, some astride their mules, one with his little girl, the age of Shaindel-Yaffaleh, who had run out a distance to greet him, sitting delightedly before him on his large Belgian farmhorse.

There, pumping water into a trough, Leah caught sight of Dovidl. He was wearing high boots far too large for him, and even a bandolier—Dovidl a shomer! Something about him always gave her the impulse to laugh, though one couldn't laugh at Dovidl, he was too clever. She ran toward her good friend—had he heard anything of Moshe?

"How would I have heard anything you haven't heard of Moshe," he asked, "when you are just coming from Jaffa?"

Still, if something had happened and no one else would tell her—?

Solemnly, Dovidl shook his head. There were no secrets from her among the chaverim.

"My whole family has come!" Leah cried. "To settle!"

He beamed. Then sighed. "Leah, they have called me to Jerusalem."

"To Jerusalem?"

"Yes," Dovidl declared resignedly. Avner was over-worked. He needed help with the new journal, *Unity*.

"But that will be wonderful!" Leah cried. "Someone like you is needed more there than here."

Dovidl sighed again as though he saw his true life flowing away, the good life of the fields, of productiveness and gratification. "You really think I should go?"

Just then a young woman hurried toward them calling, "Dovidl, the boots!" It was Bracha, the wife of Shabbatai Zeira, the Kurdish watchman. While pulling off the shomer's only pair of boots, Dovidl continued his speculations: could he really be of more use in the headquarters than on the land? Must he enter a life of organizational work and politics? "You know, Leah, the Shomer is making progress, we already have two horses," he said, handing the boots to Bracha. Unlike the boots, he said, a shomer's horse could not be used both day and night, so for the night-watch they had borrowed money and bought a second steed. And in a moment the boots appeared on Zeira as the dark Cossack figure rode out, erect and fierce.

Gidon was staring, mouth agape, at the mounted shomer, and Dvoraleh too could not take her eyes from the horseman.

"Then if the riders need the boots day and night, perhaps you should leave them here and go to Jerusalem," Leah said to Dovidl. He always made her feel brighter.

"Nu, Leah, perhaps you have just settled my whole life," Dovidl laughed.

Over the last part of the way, Zeira warned, the wagons must stay together, and he would ride with them until beyond Kfar Kana. Last week even Dr. Rachman had been waylaid on the road to Sejera, and his horse had been seized from under him.

"No!" But Dr. Rachman was known in every Arab village, he always went when they called him, even across the Jordan!

The mukhtar, the mayor, of Kfar Kana himself had brought back the horse when he learned from Galil of the affair, Zeira related. Half the children of that village owed their eyesight to old Rachman. Still, the glimpse of a good horse made the bandits forget themselves. They would seize the steed of the Messiah himself!

The village was passed without incident; in midafternoon the wagon mounted the last ridge of Mount Yavniel, and Reuven felt the old exaltation rising up in him. "Look!" he cried as the lake was revealed below them, his Kinnereth, his shining bride, as beautiful as the first time his eyes had beheld her. "See how it is shaped like a harp," he repeated to the young ones. "From that, it gets its name."

Leah saw how her brother's eyes were glittering. She began to sing, and though Reuven rarely sang except when he stomped the hora, now he joined her. The younger children picked up the tune "Yahalili" and, as the wagons creaked downward, even Yankel hummed in his beard.

This, all of them understood, even to little Schmulik, was a moment of joy and unity they might not reach again in their entire lives, a moment each must cherish forever. Indeed even two-year-old Avramchick sensed everyone's joy and began jumping restlessly on Feigel's knee.

Catching their excitement, Kalman the drayman looked back on them, smiling, on Eliza the beautiful little girl, on Dvora with her breasts already high, on Yaffaleh, on Schmuel, on Avramchick, on Big Leah the chalutza.

Deep into her soul Mama Feigel breathed this moment, telling her son yet to be born that she had carried him from Cherezinka to Eretz Yisroel, to his destined birthplace here beside the lake of song, the harp-shaped Kinnereth.

But was this all? The wagons halted in a yard before a small old khan of black stones—was this the vaunted kvutsa of Leah and Reuven? And not a soul to meet the wagons, Kalman grumbled, after plaguing him to haul the big iron plow! Had they all been butchered? Were they all dead in there?

Leah had already hurried inside. Max Wilner lay with his face to the wall; he did not even turn. On another pallet lay a chaver she had never before seen, the lad who must have wandered in during the last few days; he too was in fever. Then Max muttered, "Shimek went for help."

"I've brought your German plow," Kalman announced. "I've got to get on while there's light."

At the mention of the plow, the shivering Max sat up. "Can you," and somewhat shamefacedly he included Reuven who was in the doorway, "Can you bring it in here? It will be safer."

It was so that Max could lie there gazing at it, Reuven knew. The hardhead! The stiff-neck!—As stiff-necked as I am, Reuven thought, and went out to the wagon. With Gidon and the driver Kalman, he dragged the clumsy iron structure through the doorway. "Yallah! Behold thy beloved!" He forgave Max, though it still rankled that Max had used his own vote. Yet, for planting bananas, deep plowing might show results.

"I'll make tea," Leah said. She would have to remain here with the sick chaverim. The family could continue on to the new settlement; it was less than an hour away, Kalman said, if the ford across the twist in the Jordan was not too high just now.

"When did Shimek go?" Leah asked. They should have encountered him on their way from Yavniel.

"This morning, to Sejera," Max replied.

"Sejera?"

"He's coming back with a whole new kvutsa. Seven fellows from the training farm."

"A new kvutsa?" Reuven stared at him.

"What else was there to do? Call in Arab workers? Give up the place? Desert?"

"But—for such a decision—"

"Moshe goes off! Areleh and Saraleh leave! You and Leah are away for months at a time!" In feverish anger all Max's old resentments poured out.

Bleakly, Reuven felt, was it still his place? His kvutsa? Where he had dreamed of a Garden of Eden for his comrades? After all that their group had gone through here, and after the first crop and their triumph together—to give the place over to a whole new group of strangers?

From the wagon his father called testily that night would catch them on the way. "I must stay here with them," Leah repeated, her eyes telling her brother she understood all he felt, but that he must not yet decide.

Reuven went out and mounted the wagon.

Beyond the kvutsa there was scarcely a set of ruts. Desolation, rock-strewn soil reaching as far back as the high ridge they had crossed. On the opposite side of the Jordan, the late afternoon sun began to color the sheer wall of rock in its purplish red; beyond, up there, lay the plain of Golan. With each day's passing, Reuven had been in the habit of gazing across on this glowing rock wall, in never-failing awe at the beauty of creation. But on this day the cliff seemed harsh, oppressive; all earth was estrangement. All the elation of the family's first view of the valley from the Yavniel heights had departed, except in the boys; the parents' apprehension and anxiety had returned.

"Caves!" Gidon cried out, pointing up the Yavniel ridge, and little Schmulik demanded to know who had lived there. The fighters of Bar Kochba?

"Christian monks once lived in them," Reuven answered distractedly. "Around this sea their religion began." Even this remark heightened the tension in the wagon. His father's face grew livid. Was this the moment for Reuven to discourse about *them!*

But at last the wagon rumbled onto a bypath: in a moment they would reach the new settlement, their home.

On a flat area halfway up the hillside the wagons halted. A few men in long saffron robes, Sephardim they must be, sat on the ground, tapping on blocks of black stone. There was a wooden cabin, such as one saw on construction sites, and a shed for work-animals. But where were the houses, the barns of the settlers?

From the cabin the overseer emerged, in riding breeches and clean boots—Kramer again! He glanced at the wagons, at Reuven. "There are no trees planted here as yet for you to pull out," he remarked, but without hostility.

Reuven cursed himself for not having come before to inspect the site. But when could he have done it, sick as he was, and with only four men left in the kvutsa? And he had not even known Dr. Lubin would really send them here. Reuven handed Kramer the note from the Jaffa office.

"I'm sending you the Chaimovitch family," Kramer read out aloud. And then he gazed at the wagonload of immigrants. "What family? Who family? Are they out of their heads there in Jaffa?"

"To join the settlement," Reuven repeated, as though the settlement would materialize simply by his speaking of it.

Kramer extended an arm in a broad gesture. "Do you see a settlement?"

Yankel was staring grimly at his son.

"But I heard even before I went to Zichron to the hospital that permits had been granted for the houses here," Reuven began. "They said that Dr. Lubin himself went all the way to Constantinople and bribed everyone up to the valet of the Sultan's bedchamber to get the building permits."

"Maybe he greased them in Constantinople, but he didn't grease them in Tiberias," Kramer snapped, "or in Damascus either." And did Reuven know there was a whole turmoil in Constantinople, that the Young Turks were rising, and that meanwhile a new governor had come to Damascus?

Who didn't know this? The entire yishuv was arguing whether the Young Turks might not change everything if they came to power. Surely they would open the doors to progress!

But as a man who is not obliged to explain himself to every passerby, Kramer shrugged, and in his habitual way turned his back, marching to his hut.

On the site Reuven now saw the outlines for several houses had been laid out, with one or two courses of stone. "But nevertheless you are building!" he cried. "How long will it be until a house is ready?"

Kramer paused before his door. "Stones we are permitted to cut," he said. "To build a house with windows and a roof is another matter." And he pointed with his chin to a tent. Emerging and staring at them was a Turkish policeman, planted by the Kaymakam of Tiberias to make sure that no roof was laid until an order came from Damascus. Again baksheesh, for the new governor there.

"In any case," Kramer remarked, "all these houses are already bespoken; the owners are coming from Roumania."

And waving to Kalman the drayman to unload the materials, he entered his hut, closing the door behind him.

Where would they even spend the night? It was now that Yankel broke out at his son with every bitter disappointment of the voyage. "Where have you brought me! Where have you brought us with small children to a wilderness of murderous Arabs, infested with deathly disease! You, my son full of enlightened knowledge and wisom! Come, he writes his father, come, bring the children, everything is ready, all is prepared!"

Yankel was shouting so that all the workmen heard. His face was livid, and there was spittle on his beard. Reuven, as an equal rage rose up in his own self, clenched his fists until his nails cut into his palms. However unjust the accusation, he would not raise his arm against his father. . . . If only Leah were here!

"A curse on you and your lies!" the father shouted. Feigel stood, her face showing her great distress; the children had fallen back. "A curse on this place!"

They gasped. Yankel lowered his eyes. Kalman the drayman stepped toward him. "Shah, shah, Reb Chaimovitch. It is only a mistake such as we have here in the land every day—" but as Yankel turned his face of bitterness on him, Kalman went back to his unloading.

Gidon had walked off a small distance so as not to look at his father in his rage; little Schmuel was halfway to his mother and the girls, his cheeks red and his eyes furtive as though he did not know where to run.

The mother waited, a woman who knew the way of her husband. This bitter anger of Yankel's, did she not know it? His curse was not a true curse, it was a cry to God to witness that it was not he, Yankel, but others who were at fault for his misfortunes. This was the rage that came after each partner deceived him in business, it was the rage against her brother who had used him to draw the anger of the peasants, and now it was against his own son, so that whatever went wrong, Yankel would not be to blame.

In her soul she did not despise him, for in her soul Feigel knew Yankel was a good man who wanted only to provide a decent life for his family, and who labored without end. But he was not a clever man, and also he was honest in his heart and by religious training; thus, when he had disappointments and failures, he always needed someone to blame for his victimization. Then, when before the Above One he had called out his rage and laid the blame elsewhere, he would turn to overcome his misfortunes with some remaining unknown strength, and somehow he always managed.

Kramer had opened his door. "The men sleep down there," the overseer said, motioning toward the riverbank, where they saw two square stone huts. "Tomorrow we'll see what can be done."

Reuven had already started downward, with Gidon behind him. From the wagon Kalman called: What was he to do with the huge trunk? Should he drop it off here?

"In a deep hole in the earth!" Yankel cursed, and then said, more quietly, "Bring everything down there."

Near the river, some hundred paces apart, stood two hovels made of the local black stone, abandoned since who knew when. Atop the first, Reuven saw, rushes had been laid to form a roof; inside that one, the stonemasons had their pallets.

The second hut was doorless and roofless except for a few dried rushes over one corner; within hung a stale odor of ancient dung and accumulated filth. Still, there remained a shred of daylight and it could be cleaned. He kicked at the rubbish. Gidon, stepping inside onto the earthen floor, also kicked at the rubbish. "Along the shore there are plenty of reeds." Reuven said, "Do you have a knife?" Gidon pulled out an enormous clasp knife, opened it, and started off.

Feigel came in. At the base, the walls jutted out to form benches, and on these, bedding could be placed. "Dvoraleh," she said as Dvoraleh sniffed, "perhaps in the other hut they have a broom and a pail?"

Now Yankel entered and gazed around. "Tomorrow we will see what to do," he declared. "Tonight there is no choice but to lie here."

Together with Dvora, there returned a middle-aged man wearing the long yellow-striped gown of the Sephardim and carrying a pail of water and a home-tied broom; he was from Tiberias, a stonemason; Dvora was laughingly trying to understand his words, spoken in Ladino, the Spanish Yiddish of the Sephardim.

Yankel engaged him in the holy tongue, loshen koidesh,

using the Ashkenazi pronunciation as in his prayers, though here in Eretz, as he already knew, it was the Sephardic that was spoken. The mason managed to understand Yankel's Biblical Hebrew. Soon they were immersed in a pietistic discussion, while the family made the hut habitable.

—A worthy ideal, the Sephardi said, to come and revive the soil, though as for inhabiting the Holy Land, his own family had lived here in Tiberias for many generations. So the land was not uninhabited. In Tiberias there were several thousands of Jews, even Ashkenazim as well, latecomers from only a generation ago. The city was not far distant, less than two hours with a donkey, if it was not a lazy one. For his Sabbaths he went home.

Reuven and Kalman carried in the large trunk from the wagon, and Feigel had them set it in the center of the hut. Opening the lid, she at once found her red velvet spread with the tassels, and arranged it over the trunk—a table. Presently the Sephardi brought over his own kerosene lamp, insisting the family make use of it—there was another one among the men. Feigel gave him a thousand thanks, and set it on the "table." In a moment he had returned again, carrying a large circular pittah such as they had seen in Jaffa transported on wooden platters atop the heads of young girls. It was soft and thick, and kept edible longer than the small rounds that quickly became dry. And in a twist of newspaper, their friend had also brought a pinch of coarse salt; it came, he said, from the Salt Sea.

Uncountable blessings Yankel poured on him and on his children forever. Feigel was near to weeping.—On Sabbath, said the Sephardi, who bore the distinguished name of Abulafia, Yankel must come to Tiberias to their synagogue, which was near the tomb of Maimonides.

And so they were home.

Feather quilts and bedding were unfolded on the stone beaches, making a long line of sleeping places around the walls. Already Feigel had settled Avramchick for the night. Gidon, with Schmulik jumping up to hand him the withes, had soon lightly roofed over the hut; in slivers between the reeds, the night sky could be seen. Dvora's spirits had risen. It was romantic, she said, and she and Eliza made secret wishes on a star glowing between Gidon's rushes, disputing who had seen it first. Shaindeleh-Yaffaleh was asleep, wearing an expression of contentment.

Yankel went out and stood before the doorway, gazing at the opposite hills, now a black wall. Edom, was it? Of Reuven he would not inquire.

Yankel felt as thought God's will had manifested itself. Thus he had been brought here to this corner of the beginning of the world. As it was written, In the beginning, so it was for him now a beginning, even if in the middle of his life.

Feigel too had emerged. Because they had arrived here, and the trunk was safely in the house, and there were beds around the walls, Yankel quietly said to her, so that she would know that he knew, "Feigel, you are carrying?"

"It happened," Feigel said.

"If it was ordained," Yankel said, "then it is well that it will be in Eretz Yisroel." To bring a new life in this land would be a mitzvah.

"Let it be with God's blessing," Yankel said.

Just so, perhaps, it had been with Abraham and Sara late in life, after the angels appeared at the door of their dwelling and told of a coming birth.

As for Reuven, when the best that could be done had been done in the hovel, he would not stay, not under the same roof or pretense of a roof, for the angry words his father had hurled at him still boiled in him with their injustice. Reuven walked up the hillside to where the fields would have to be cleared, and he sat on a stone under the stars and gazed out over the mirror of lake in the distance to his left, a black mirror. A black day it had been. He did not know if he should return there at all to the kvutsa, as, with the new chevreh arriving, he would not be urgently needed. Nor could he simply walk away from here and leave his father with the whole family to struggle in all this uncertainty.

He stretched out with his head on the stone. How could he demand of the kvutsa that the decision should always go his way? It was true that with Moshe and Araleh they had often left Max and Shimek defeated. If he accepted the communa as a principle, a *principe*, and he did accept it, then he must learn to be one with all the chaverim, and not place the judgment of some, or worse, of himself, above

any others. It was hard, hard to learn a just way of life.
Perhaps he was meant to live alone.

In the hills the jackals howled.

Leah's tea strengthened Max and also the new young
chaver; perhaps they had only felt miserably alone and dis-
couraged. The new one had indeed come as a wanderer,
having heard so much of their kvutsa; it was a way of life
that appealed to him, he said. Ephraim was his name, and
he came from the village of Motol, near Pinsk, the very
village of a new Zionist leader who had sprung up since
Herzl's death, Chaim Weizmann, hadn't they heard of him?
Never mind. From young Weizmann he, as a boy, had
learned, "Build, build, don't wait for others to do it for
you," so he had come to build, and here instead he found
himself a burden, a sick man.

"Don't worry," Leah encouraged the enthusiast, "now
you have had your kadahat, the land has entered into
you—that's what my brother says."

—Had she had any news of Moshe? Max Wilner asked.
Then from a corner he brought a half-broken straw coffer.
It was Moshe's, he said, he had found it under the bed-
boards; perhaps it should be in her care.

Carrying it up to her little chamber on the roof, Leah
opened the lid. Inside were personal oddments, even the
photograph of his mother and father that Moshe had once
shown her—would he have left these things if he had any
thought of not returning? A pair of old leather gloves, the
fingers torn. She would sew them. Would that be foolishness? And then a scattering of papers, letters, a Hebrew
exercise book, all disordered, a man's way. She would
really not have begun on the letters, except that the first
sheet that caught her eye under the lamplight said "Beloved Son." So Leah read on, her heart storming. So much
like the letters Mameh had written to Reuven. Admonitions always to wear a hat on his head since it was said that
the sun was so hot in Eretz, people died of their brains set
a-boil. And Misheleh—she knew how her Misheleh was
with the girls, a mother was happy her son was so fine-
looking and attractive, but still he must have a care. Even
though it was said that the chalutzoth in Eretz were so modern and free, at least let her son not bring her the shame of
getting a Jewish girl into trouble—

Further, there was family news of uncles and aunts and cousins, and then of a certain Katya who had written, asking for news of him. . . . Instantly Leah sensed, this was the one. Could Moshe perhaps even have gone back for her? But no, everything she knew in her body denied it. Moshe had not gone away to leave her.

. . . They longed for their son at home, he had been away nearly two years. Gladly his father would pay the cost of the voyage if Moshe would but come for a visit. . . .

Suddenly Leah's heart felt illuminated. Surely this was what had happened. Why had she tormented herself, casting up every imaginable fear, seeing him in dungeons? Moshe had slipped home for a visit.

On one of the envelopes she found the address. To surprise him and write to him there? But instead she wrote a friendly letter to his mother, and so as not to frighten her in case something after all should have gone wrong, Leah said she was an acquaintance of Moshe's from Odessa and had just arrived here in Eretz Yisroel, and perhaps his mother could tell her where she might get in touch with Moshe? That way, if he had appeared at home, his mother would surely say so. Leah gave the Zuckerman address in Jaffa. And feeling all this was of a deviousness far beyond her, Leah laughed at herself, and lay down to sleep, making his name silently with her lips, Moshe, come to me, dear one, come!

Reuven opened his eyes to the sun rising directly over the heights of Golan. He watched the mist lifting like a bride's veil from the sleeping lake, and told himself he must make certain that their house would be built in such a way that if he were one day to live in it after all, that each morning of his life as he awakened he should open his eyes to this sight. He would never tire of it.

Lying there, gazing over the water, Reuven recalled a tale of his first employer, Smilansky, that the writer and planter had heard from an Arab teller of tales, about the birth of the Kinnereth:

> In the far-off days when Allah created the heavens and earth, he created a lovely pool, Kinnereth, in the form of a woman lying still, with her limbs tucked under her, and nothing moving but the slow ripple of her smooth blue hair.

In the same day he created Jordan, a rushing stream, noisy and bold. Allah looked on what he had created, and the clear innocent Kinnereth found favor in his eyes, he loved Kinnereth, but Jordan he saw as a creature of evil. Already, Jordan was winding about Kinnereth and, jealous for the gentle pool, Allah commanded his ministering angels to imprison Jordan in a cave at the foot of the King of Mountains, the Hermon. But Kinnereth they set down in a broad valley, engirdled by protective heights, and fed by springs that break forth from the Golan and the Bashan and the mouths of the valleys.

Then it came to pass in a day of thunders and terrors when the upper powers contended with the lower, that Jordan broke out from his imprisonment, thrusting aside a great stone and bursting forth. Twining and darting down clefts and along ravines, escaping notice, he reached the broad plain and made his way to the heart of Kinnereth.

Then Allah was told, "Jordan is come to Kinnereth!"

Allah's anger burst forth. At his fury, the whole world was terrified; the earth trembled and the heavens wept, the mountains quivered and the valleys quaked.

Then Allah opened a way southward from the broad plain, and rolled Jordan down, ever downward to the gates of death. "For what you have done, O headstrong one," Allah chastised Jordan, "unresting shall be your days. From the mouth of the cave you shall tumble down, downward you must ever go, bearing your toil unto death. Into Kinnereth you have come, and from her you shall go forth, nor shall you remain in her even for an instant, for Kinnereth you shall not know."

And to Kinnereth, also, Allah spoke. "Since you have allowed Jordan thus to encompass and beguile you, without turning away, you shall forever be bound to your place, crouching at the foot of the rocks, licking their dust, never to emerge."

Thousands of years have gone by, so goes the tale, yet the word of Allah is not changed. Jordan incessantly runs on, knowing no rest, leaping from stone to stone, slipping from crevice to crevice; into Kinnereth he enters, but must not stay; forth he goes, bearing all his vigor unto death.

And Kinnereth? There she crouches at the foot of the rocks, licking their dust, bound hand and foot.

Yet sometimes Kinnereth bestirs herself of a sudden, and storms and rages. She cries out, waves come riding one on another, flinging themselves against the flanks of the rocks which they smother with white foam. Her cries cleave the heavens. Kinnereth lashes herself like a dreadful beast; her blue locks turn white and scatter far and wide in a fury, while a sameful roar bursts from her, the roar of tempestuous desire.

But the rocks stand closed about her as though dead, without moving.

The waves scatter in all directions, break into fragments, and fall back powerless into Kinnereth. Cruel is the silence of heaven.

Kinnereth at last also becomes still. Little by little she subsides into her repose. She is silent and crouches submissively at the feet of the rocks. Again her waters grow smooth and blue and deep. Innocence and modesty are within her, a light mist of sweet breath rises from her soul. Jordan flings himself ever downward without repose.

But he could not lie here dreaming. Jumping up, Reuven began to carry stones off the earth, placing them in line where it seemed to him the field should end. First he carried over the very stone his head had lain on. He could not be certain this segment of the settlement would be theirs, yet he began to clear the field where he had lain, as though, in some vague echo of Jacob's dream, the field had become sanctified to him.

Then the sun was visible and movement began among the building workers. He saw his father climbing up from the riverside. As Yankel neared, something eased in Reuven, and he even smiled to his father. The old man had put on the working cap.

"What will I do with you?" Kramer grumbled when Yankel stood before him outside his cabin, a ghetto Jew with his tzitzith dangling from under his blouse. Then Kramer decided. "You are in a hurry for a house?" he repeated, including Reuven with Yankel. "Here you have stones already cut. If you know how to build, you can put up walls." He would even pay the regular wages.

On his father's wages alone, Reuven saw, the whole family could not possibly be fed. And within an hour Kramer would have seen that Yankel Chaimovitch was no stonemason. "To lay stones, I know how," Reuvon said; had he not labored on the new Bezalel house for Professor Schatz in Jerusalem? And he would show his father how it was done. Kramer shrugged. It could even be seen that the overseer was not displeased, as it would be told in Jaffa that he had already settled a whole large family on the new site.

Below the very area where Reuven had begun to clear the field, a first course of stone had been laid out, making the outline of a house. "If the Turk interferes, tell him it is a stable," Kramer said. Shelters for animals needed no permit.

Yankel seized hold of a barrow. He would fetch the stone blocks from the Sephardi. Yes, the Above One had made day and night, so that each day could be a renewal.

At the end of the new day, when Reuven and Yankel, without having quarreled the whole time, came down from their labor, there was Leah arrived from the kvutsa, and the entire family was thus together. Leah had brought seeds, and with Dvora and Eliza, she was already planting her carrots and tomatoes on a patch that Gidon had cleared behind the hut. The new young men, she said, had arrived from Sejera—Shimek had fetched them in the wagon—they were good lads, she told Reuven, and Max had asked for him to come and plan the new crops. Though if he were needed here, he could stay on . . .

"So that Max can do all the planning himself?"

No, no, Reuven must not be angry. They had had a long sitting with the newcomers. It would be a good kvutsa again. And could he imagine who had appeared? Nahama had come back. She had taken over the kitchen at once, and that was why Leah had been able to come here to help the family settle. And did he know that Shimek and Nahama were now together?

That was why the harelip had been visiting every Sabbath in Sejara. Nahama was thinner, Leah said, her skin was clear, apparently a steady chaver was good for her. And Leah gave out a sour little laugh, unlike herself. Reuven remembered about Nahama and Moshe.

But quickly Leah returned to her truer nature. Nahama and Shimek seemed now really in love, she declared. She was happy for them, especially poor Shimek with his lip. And they were naturally being given the upstairs room. She herself had insisted.

Leah's face remained cheerful, but her eyes turned away. As she stooped there on the ground, poking in a seed with her finger—her way of planting—Reuven put his hand on his sister's shoulder. "When Moshe returns," he said, "the kvutsa ought to begin putting up a few dwellings for couples."

She turned her face up to her brother. "Reuven—maybe I shouldn't have—I found some old letters from his family, in his box, and so I wrote to them. Only like a friend asking if they knew where I could reach him."

Reuven nodded. If only in some way he could help—but what did he know of these things, of girls and of love?

Hadn't she learned to trim blocks of stone in Jerusalem? When Yankel and Reuven went up to work, Leah came with them, but Kramer frowned. A woman. The stonecutters would not accept it.

"But the stones are for our own house!" she protested.

Who could deny Big Leah? She sat by the foundations of the house and began to tailor the stones that had to fit around the window opeings. Hearing the tapping of the hammer, the Sephardi, Abulafia, came over and stood watching. Smiling up at him, Leah showed him a squared edge and asked if he thought it smooth enough. He ran his fingers over it, half-smiled, half-sighed. To Yankel he remarked, "You have a big strong girl. She works as well as a man." Then he admonished her, "Best you should get married." And half-smiling, half-sighing again, the Sephardi went off to his own labor.

Still, the big girl was restless. The family hut by the river was crowded. Planks were laid over boxes so as to widen the stone benches, and Leah slept with Dvora, who snuggled in and chattered about the boy she had met on the boat, Yechezkiel—where could he be now? He had sworn he would come to find her! Then she tried to worm the truth from Leah. "And you, Leah, didn't you have a someone, there in the kvutsa? They say that here a chavera if she really loves a chaver—"

"Dvoraleh," Leah said, "it isn't the way it seems from what people say. Our girls are very serious."

"I know, Leah. Oh, I know. But if a chaver and a chavera really love each other—"

"Then with us it is the same as a marriage," Leah said. "A marriage is only a formality." Somehow she could not say what her little sister was really aching to know. That it had been. That to her it was like a marriage. Perhaps best that Dvoraleh should not fall into such an uncertainty. "We mostly have regular marriages." And she told how Araleh and Saraleh got married and now had a baby.

Her mother she could not deceive. There came a moment when they were alone in the hut, and Feigel half-hesitated before bending to lift up a full pail of water for scrubbing the benches. "You're carrying, Mameleh?" Leah blurted out. Her mother met her eyes a bit sheepishly, and then, fully as woman to woman, she said, "It happened. And you, Leah—you are no longer a maiden?" There was only an uncertain shred of questioning left in her tone.

At last release came, and Leah blubbered out the whole story, begging, "What do you think, what do you think, Mameleh? I know there are such men, men who feel trapped to remain for always with the same woman. And perhaps that is why—perhaps Moshe felt he had to run away from me?"

Feigel nodded and nodded, trying to bring her daughter's trouble into her own heart, casting over, though she had had only her Yankel in her life, all the events between men and women that she knew of. She thought of those men who had gone to America and postponed sending for their wives year after year, until it somehow became known that they had secretly taken new wives in America. And there were men also who had in them a compelling need to be conquerors of women, whose entire nature seemed given over to leading astray young girls and young wives, and perhaps each time such men really believed they loved. Yet also as Feigel was trying to find some word to help her daughter, she herself experienced a wave of relief, for there might have been a pregnancy—at least this had not happened. Then too there came to her a puzzlement at herself, that she was not ashamed of Leah, or even greatly shocked. Had it happened at home in Cherezinka, she would surely have been distraught with fear that her daughter's shame would become known in all the village, but here, surprisingly, even a kind of curiosity rose up in her, as though she were the one who was still a girl finding out things about life. And also there rose up a faint, a shocking sense of envy, for Leah had known how it was to lie nakedly with a man in pure love. (For surely, something within Feigel told her, they had been naked, and not, as throughout all of her own life with a husband, thrusting and receiving darkly among night-clothes under the covers.) Within all of her troubled pain for her daughter, she flushed, seeing this large vibrant girl, this woman her daughter, and imagining the man, even larger, a man so handsome that every girl—and Feigel believed this was as Leah said—wanted to fling herself at him.

What a fine couple they must have made. Feigel could see it, through Leah's longing words—at last a man who was seemly for her. So it should be, so it should be on earth. Feigel could not find it in herself to utter a word of blame to her daughter, or to think, as Yankel would think in anger should he come to know, that the man's desertion was God's punishment for Leah's wantonness.

"But Mama, what should I do?" The poor girl knelt and put her head in Feigel's lap, her sorrow of a hugeness with her body. Then raising her eyes, Leah said in the timorous voice of a little child, "I sometimes think—if I should just go and search for him?"

The idea had only now declared itself in her, but seemed to have long been present.

"Wait, wait," Feigel said. "Wait." Was this the only word given to womankind? "From what you tell me, if he is such a one that cannot remain with one woman, what good would it do to run after him?"

"Then at least I would know. . . . And perhaps he is in trouble, Mama, perhaps he has been arrested—"

"Then it surely would be known to your chaverim," her mother said.

So they went over and over all the tormenting thoughts that Leah had already examined again and again, and still the only answer was to wait, at least until she perhaps heard something in answer to the letter she had sent his parents. She must wait.

Nevertheless the talk with her mother had relieved her heart, and, the hut being so crowded, Leah decided to return for a time to the kvutsa, where Nahama needed help, and where perhaps they would hear something.

All at once, and despite new baksheesh, the Turkish inspector halted the stone-laying on their walls. They should not have been so foolish, Kramer said, as to arch over the door and window openings; they should have filled the walls in solid, and opened the apertures later on. How could he pretend this was a stable? Even the horses of the Sultan had no such stables. For the present they had better stop their construction work. A new effort was being made in Constantinople itself for actual building permits.

But at least the fields were being laid out. A gnomish, self-important personage, Chaikin the surveyor, originally from Bialystok, with a diploma from Berlin, as he let you know at once, quickly made it clear to Yankel that he had come only as a favor to Jacques Samuelson, the representative of the Baron himself; he had laid out all of the settlements. He was now very busy laying out an entire Jewish city on the sands north of Jaffa. But he had come all the way here, for how could there rise up a new settlement in the land but that it was first marked out by Berel Chaikin?

By dint of flattery, and with Gidon running and carrying his instruments for him, Reuven managed so that the area in the chart on Kramer's wall, penciled Chaimovitch, was the first to be measured off. Yankel and even little Schmulik, trudged out into the field, and small heaps of stones were set up as Chaikin measured the corners. At once, while the surveyor was still writing notations on his map, all the Chaimovitches set themselves to clearing rocks from their land, piling them where Reuven that first night had begun a fence. His stones proved almost exactly in the right line, they had to be moved only a bit.

The next morning there was the entire family, girls and all. It was a sight to see, and even Kramer rode out to behold it. Reuven, bare to the waist, was carrying a huge rock against his chest, and the father with a pickax was prying out another; the sturdy Gidon and his sister Dvora and the smaller girls and the little boy Schmuel, all were swarming over the field, each trying to carry larger and larger stones, clearing their land, and as the mother brought up breakfast for them with the toddler Avramchick at her skirts, the child began imitating his brothers and sisters, wobbling toward the fence with stones in his two hands. They would hardly leave off work to eat, Reuven hurrying back onto the field with a chunk of bread still in his hand. They wanted to plant before the heavy rains.

There they all were again at dawn, an hour before Kramer's own men began on their jobs, Reuven and Gidon together prying away with a long iron bar at an enormous boulder. It was a bar they had borrowed from the settlement site, but though they should have asked his permission, Kramer let the matter go, watching them exert themselves until their forehead veins bulged out. But the rock was still unbudged. Then there came the father, Yankel, approaching with a mule harnessed to a drag. No—this could not be permitted—without so much as a by-your-leave!—

"Reb Yankel!" Kramer shouted.

Indeed, catching sight of the overseer whom he had not expected so early, Yankel showed his uncertainty. "I will take him back in a moment," Yankel called, "in time for your workers. You promised us a loan to buy our own pair of mules."

The whole family was staring anxiously at the overseer. Strict as he was known to be, Kramer could not show himself hardhearted. "See that you do," he snapped. "And next time you had better ask me." He rode off.

They managed, all of them pulling and pushing, along with the mule. Looking back, Kramer saw them yelling and slapping at the animal, the older brothers prying at the rock until it finally budged and was torn from the soil. They all let out a scream of triumph, the little girl and boy, Yaffaleh and Schmulik, and the toddler Avramchick, dancing around the stone as it was dragged away. Kramer even waved.

Gidon led back the mule. He took a handful of oats and fed the animal from his hand, pleased with the feel of the careful large lips against his palm.

Only a few days later, the manager called Yankel into his office in the cabin. "What was my part I have done," Kramer said, and handed Chaimovitch a large document to read and sign. This was his allocation in the settlement that was to be known as Mishkan Yaacov. Yes, a name had been given. For here perhaps was the very site where Jacob had rested after his flight from Laban.

The overseer was beaming. A proud man—after all, he had been raised in the Baron's colonies where every Jew thought himself a little Rothschild—he too wanted to build the Yishuv. He had kept pressing for their papers, he said—here they were. A loan for a pair of mules, a cow and seed.

Should he go to Damascus to buy the animals? Yankel wondered. Better in Mescha, Kramer advised; he had heard that Shlomo Idelson had a good pair of mules to sell.

On work animals Yankel considered himself an expert. That very day Kalman the drayman, who had appeared with a wagonload of floor tiles, could take him to Mescha on his way back. The next day, there came Tateh, driving his own wagon behind a high standing pair of work animals, and tied to the tail of the wagon was a black ewe with milk-filled udders nearly touching the ground, that Idelson had given him into the bargain! More! In a wicker crate in the wagon, Yankel had two fat hens, and at once Dvora took them in her charge.

As for the mules, they might have been the finest steeds in Arabia, the way Gidon was already currying them. Nor could even Reuven find any fault in the animals or in the price Abba had paid.

In the morning the procession went out to the cleared field. Though Yankel had dealt in horses and mules, he had never thrust a plow into the soil and was somewhat uncertain of himself before Reuven, who had plowed and sown.

From all the land around it, their section stood out, flat and clean, with the stones they had carried off lining the edges. Soon the soil would shine, open and black, the only portion that was plowed.

At the corner of the field, Yankel halted. Mameh too had come, and the whole family grouped behind the plow. This time even Reuven did not show impatience with his father as Yankel raised his beard to heaven and asked a blessing upon their field.

Who first would put his hands to the plow? Yankel hesitated. Perhaps it would be better if Reuven, who knew how—

"You begin, Abba," Reuven said. "It isn't difficult. Only hold on, and if you strike a stone, pull back." On his own shoulder Reuven slung the small leather pouch of seed.

"Nu, God willing," Yankel said, and took hold of the handles. He had forgotten the reins. He stooped, then put them around his neck as he had seen peasants do. Gidon begged, "Let me hold the reins." It was such a fine morning. There were clouds but the air did not yet smell of rain. There was a breeze, and even from here one could see that the Kinnereth was rippled. Already birds were circling; the

girls were there to shoo them off the seed. Yankel felt
kindly, and let the boy take the reins. So they began.

It was indeed an odd feeling to follow the plow, different
from what a man had felt at anything else in his life. It
pulled you, and yet you were the master. So in the middle
of his life he was transforming himself to a man of the soil.

Gripping the handles more tightly than need be, Yankel
strode firmly, but almost at once the plow swerved. He
could feel Reuven behind him, watching critically. With an
effort of his shoulders, Yankel tried to straighten the implement, but the point stuck in the earth and the handles were
wrenched from him as the plow stood on its end. Gidon
pulled the beasts to a halt. "Slowly, slowly." Reuven came
up and with his mattock dug out a rock. At once the beasts
pulled ahead and Yankel stumbled as the plow lurched forward. But then for a stretch it went smoothly and even in a
straight furrow; he felt his son behind him, spreading the
grain, and turned once and saw with what an expert movement of the wrist Reuven flung the seed so that it fell
evenly as raindrops on the opened soil. Feigel and the girls
stood behind in a cluster. Tears came to Yankel's eyes, and
this time too he whispered the Shehechiyanu. To have
come to this moment!

But meanwhile his furrow had gone crooked.

4

WHEN green shoots peep out in the garden plot behind
the house in orderly little rows, and when washing is hung
out to dry, and when hens scratch away in the yard and
peck at the earth, and a pair of mules crunch fodder in the
lean-to, all that a good Jewish household needs for the Sabbath Eve is gefulte fish and a sweet warm chaleh. Gidon
already had caught fish in the sea, and though it was not
carp, it had scales and so might be eaten.

As for an oven, there was an aged Arab from the village
on the ridge, who called himself Sheikh Ibrim, though it
was said he was not really a sheikh, and who spent most of
his days on his horse, riding here and there and gossiping.

His mount was an excellent small bay that Gidon loved to watch for its highstepping movement, and this horse was the only possession left to him, Sheikh Ibrim constantly repeated, since he had sold his lands to buy brides for his five sons, one of whom was now mukhtar of their village, Dja'adi. All this land along the Jordan had been his, he would say, though long ago because of pestilence the village had moved up onto the ridge. Indeed it seemed, according to Kramer, that Ibrim had been paid something as a quitclaim, though the land had for decades gone to swamp with the yearly overflow of the Jordan.

When Reuven and the kvutsa had labored planting eucalyptus in the mud, Ibrim would ride near and watch them, warning them the place was pestilential. One day Reuven had tried to explain to him how the pestilence, it had been discovered, came from the sting of a mosquito, and how these trees, absorbing the water, would clear the swamp where mosquitoes bred.

Sheikh Ibrim had listened to all this, and then told the tale in the village of how the mad Jews believed the pestilence came from the sting of a mosquito, making a swift jab against his leathery old skin and laughing with the rest, for the mad Jews were all lying sick to death down there, with glazed eyes, in the abandoned pestilential khan. Seven men and two women were living there together, the women belonging to all!

In another abandoned half-ruin near the river there was now a whole family. Riding by and observing them, Sheikh Ibrim was touched by their ineptitude. They let their women cook over an open fire, like Bedouin; the big rains were coming, and the Jewish family had only open reeds for a roof. First, he sent down two of his grandsons to show them how to weave a tight roof of withes; the boys were of the age of Gidon, and while they worked, they did not take their eyes off the graceful little sister with the long swinging golden braids, Eliza, moving in and out of the house as she helped her mother at her tasks.

When Sheikh Ibrim came down, to be thanked and thanked again for his kindness, and to be given ribbons for his womenfolk, he studied the primitive cooking arrangements of the Jews, who in their curious way had brought many new tools and machines to this land, and yet did not know how to build a simple earthen oven. And so he came down again with his grandson Fawzi and supervised the construction of a taboon. Gidon quickly understood how to heat it up and showed Feigel how to use it for baking, and Feigel herself discovered that it was excellent for the Sabbath cholent.

Early that Friday, Yankel found himself sent by Kramer with his wagon to Tiberias to fetch ironwork from the smith. It fell well. Since his arrival here, each Friday the longing had come over Yankel to stand in a shul amidst the murmur of prayer from fellow Jews; alone, as each Sabbath eve approached, he had made his way along the riverbank to a little cove he had found for himself, to bathe for the Shabbat, remembering the steam bath in Cherezinka and the Jews good and bad, the friends and the swindlers gathered there, the bits of news and wisdom and also of stupid womanlike gossip that drifted through the steam, and occasionally the chance that came of a good business stroke; remembering all this, Yankel felt his loneliness.

Here also, on the road before one came to Tiberias, there were baths, he had been told, the ancient natural baths with hot water coming out of the earth; in the winter season, Jews from Jerusalem journeyed here to cure their bones of rheumatism and other ills. In Tiberias itself were synagogues, both Ashkenazic and Sephardic. Although he had to return home before the Sabbath fell and therefore would not be able to remain in a shul for the prayers, still he might find a few men lingering about the study house for a shmoos. He had labored well and felt he deserved this day.

The wagon road passed directly before the steam baths as one approached the city, and also, higher on the hillside, one saw a domed structure, the tomb, Abulafia had told him, of Rabbi Meir Baal Ness. But Yankel drove by the baths so as first to finish his business for Kramer. The town itself, with its single dusty street and the open market with its stalls for meat and fish and bolts of cloth somehow was homelike to him. The half-ruined, thick, surrounding wall of black stone made him think with a pang of sin that he had not yet gone to Yerushalayim.

Arabs and Jews were mingled in the market like peasants and Yidden at home, and what with the Sephardim in their long striped gowns, he could hardly tell a Jew from an Arab in his galabiya. Bethinking himself of Abulafia, who no longer came out to cut stone, Yankel spoke the name questioningly in a Sephardi spice shop where he bought items that Feigel had written down, cinnamon, and saffron; the shopkeeper knew the family, but Yankel had a certain shyness—he did not want to impose hospitality, especially just before the Sabbath when every household was busy, so he asked rather where the Abulafias' shul might be found, and there, in a courtyard and up a flight of outer stairs, was a long chamber with whitewashed walls, scarred old benches and an elaborately embroidered silk curtain hung before the Ark. Now, in the middle of the day, the shul was empty. But simply to stand there a bit made him feel easier.

Last hour purchasers still stirred about the market. Yankel passed a row of Jewish butcher stalls. It was long since they had had meat; they would all become vegetarians like his son. But he was again spending from the small capital brought from Cherezinka, since he now worked mostly on his own land, and crops were yet distant. Still, Yankel thought of the faces of the children—Gidon, a meat-lover—the boy worked hard alongside him. Yankel approached a stall. Fowl was costly, and of good cattle flesh such as they ate at home, there was none. Feigel would have known what was best to put into her pots. Finally he bought scraps of sheep meat.

Then before he reached his wagon an impulse overcame him. Fine white geese sat in wicker cages. Yankel thought of Shaindeleh, jealous of her sister when he had given Dvora charge of the chickens. In Yankel there was a tenderness of his daughters, rarely shown. Feigel would relate all their doings to him and speak of the nature of each, knowing how much this meant to him, yet little passed between himself and the growing girls except that the pretty Eliza knew she could always wheedle her tateh. But lately she no longer came and sat on his lap to twist her fingers in his beard. With the youngest, Shaindel, there was another feeling in him altogether, and Yankel knew this was in Feigel too, a curious hovering sense of worry, though nothing was wrong. She was not lovely as Eliza had been even as a baby. For that matter, neither had Dvora shown particular beauty as a child; yet she had grown now into an appealing girl, roundfaced, with a short neck, but

warmhearted-looking and womanly, resembling her
mother, and recalling to him his first sight of Feigel. When
she was proposed as his bride, his first reaction had been
that the maiden was no beauty such as he had dreamed of,
but then he had a slowly growing feeling that she looked
very nice, and even, when she flushed and her eyes came
alight, beautiful. Of Leah he only thought now in a kind of
bewilderment; when she had grown so tall and strong, towering over him even at home, she had seemed a force beyond him, though he felt her love perhaps more powerfully
than that of any other of the children. Only—something
had happened in Leah with this chaver who had gone off
on one of their mysterious missions; Yankel did not permit
himself to envision his daughter lying with a man, and Feigel was silent, receding as into the realm of womanish
things. His thoughts returned to Shaindel, Yaffaleh as she
was called here. She was too small, too young, for judgment of her appearance to be made, and yet Yankel knew
in his heart that the little girl would be ugly. Her body was
lumpy, fattish, and though all the girls except Eliza were
like Feigel, short-necked, little Shaindel seemed to have no
throat at all, her head sitting heavily on her shoulders, and
her face with heavy jaws. She simply was not favored. It
was foolish to worry about a little girl of six, Feigel said—
no matter how she looked, she could turn into a beauty.
And her nature was sweetest of all. When Shaindeleh came
and took his hand to walk with him sometimes, there was
nothing, nothing she wanted from him—as it would be
with Eliza. Shaindel wanted only to walk with her tateh.

So, suddenly, Yankel bought two white geese in their
wicker cage to bring home to Shaindeleh. Nor could this be
counted as an extravagance, as it would be the beginning of
a flock.

Then, starting homeward, Yankel gave himself leave on
the outskirts of Tiberias to spend a few coins for the bath.
There was still time if he did not linger. The bathhouse was
a vaulted stone chamber—who could tell how long it had
been standing here—perhaps since the times of the great
rabbis who had come to purify themselves in the mikveh
here. And as he put off his clothes onto a stone bench, and
took the towel handed him by an elderly Jew in a yarmulkeh, Yankel experienced in that dim chamber, where he
stood naked, something that he had in a way been expect-

ing all through this day, the first day when he went about
by himself a bit freely in the land.

What came to Yankel was, though in a different way,
what had come to Reuven and Leah, when they found
themselves alone in the hollow of a sand-dune beyond Jaffa.
Yankel for some moments experienced a surpassing sense
of returned peace, of having overcome all his fears of the
world, of being a good father, a good Jew, a decent man.
The odor of wet stone with a tartness in it came into him
with a kind of returning familiarity, though at home in
Cherezinka the benches had been of wood. He breathed in
the close warm air.

Advancing to the square pool of water, Yankel dipped in
his foot. The water was indeed warm and of a peculiarly
penetrating quality. It was known there were curative min-
erals in this Tiberias water that dissolved away the weariness from inside your bones. Slowly Yankel let himself
down into the small pool, and stood on the bottom, his
neck above the surface, his beard wet. His whole body felt
engulfed by something good; it was a feeling akin to a stirring in his very soul. "A mechayah," he said, half-aloud. A
perfect pleasure!

"Your first time?" a voice asked in Yiddish, and Yankel
made out the head of another man of about his own age in
the further corner. Then began between them the thing
Yankel had really most longed for all these weeks, a
shmoos. A talking. A feeling-out and talking-out with
someone of his own sort. A father of sons and daughters
too, of children of various ages, and in such a meeting,
there is always in men as well as among women the
thought of a possible shidach—a match. A Russian Jew
too, it seemed; his family came from Vinnitsa, the seat of a
Hasidic tzaddik. But like Yankel, Reb Bagelmacher was
himself from a family of anti-Hasidim, Mitnagdim; his forefathers had been bakers, bagel-bakers to be sure, his
grandfather, a Talmud chacham, had opened an inn, and
Yankel even believed that in his forest-buying days he had
one night stayed there, in Vinnitsa. No—or at least it could
not have been with the Bagelmachers, his new friend said,
since the family had come here to Eretz over thirty years
before, moving their inn to Tiberias. Nu, one made a living, though the season was brief. The season was just
barely beginning. In winter Jews came for the warm baths,

excellent for rheumatism and liver trouble. On Fridays, with a turmoil of Sabbath preparation in the pension, Bagelmacher took refuge here for his midday rest.

As for Yankel, he too told his story, perhaps exaggerating a bit his status as a merchant from Cherezinka who had liquidated his capital and come to Eretz to redeem the land. Until the new settlement would fill up he was alone, the first to come, he said, and what he missed there was a shul.

—Whenever he was in Tiberias, he was welcome, declared Reb Bagelmacher; they had their own little synagogue, Russian Jews like himself, and Yankel felt refreshed and made his way home.

It was truly a good Shabbes. Yaffaleh, overjoyed with her white geese, climbed on him in his chair and kissed her tateh all over his cheeks. The meat was in time to be cooked, though it proved not of the best. Still, Feigel kept some in the oven and on Shabbes itself the meat melted in your mouth.

At sunrise each day, the little girl went off with her geese, down to the waterside, paddling with them, sitting dreamily, not so much watching them as being with them. She gave each a name, and would question and admonish them, "Estherkeh, when are you going to lay eggs for me?" One day Estherkeh swam off, pulling into a thick stand of reeds. Yaffa followed, wading carefully in the mud bank, breathless. And soon she came running up to the house, the trophy in her hand, telling how Esterkeh had led her a clever chase, pretending to stop, paddling further, and how at last Estherkeh had wiggled into the mud, making a small hollow, and—

To eat one single goose-egg—the first? Queen Esther might become angry and lay no more, Yaffaleh pleaded. Then let her grow a flock, Feigel decided, in time there would be plenty of eggs, and geese too, for feasting. At Passover they would have a Seder with their own roast goose! But to this Yaffaleh wouldn't even listen; she was already running back with the egg.

One morning Yaffaleh saw her white mother goose emerging from her thicket, and there, paddling to one side of her, came her brood; the child counted—seven of them, still shaped like eggs, seven goose-eggs with tiny heads. The mother turned her queenly head to make sure of them—could she count? No, a goose couldn't count, that was why you were called a goose if you couldn't add numbers; yet Yaffaleh felt the mother goose knew perfectly well how many goslings there should be.

Now Yaffaleh had a great desire to rush back to the house to tell Schmulik, to tell Avramchick, to bring them, the whole family must come running to gaze on this wonder. But how could she leave even for an instant? She stood transfixed. And watching, the perfection of the universe was revealed to her. How cunning, how divine was the way in which the creature floated out slowly, and her young followed, the glowing forms moving as stars moved across the Milky Way in the sky!

But how far was the foolish mother going to swim with her goslings? Suppose she swam out to the Kinnereth and a storm arose? The sea rippled in soft strokes like when Dvora combed her long flowing hair. But how foolish to worry—hadn't she already noticed that her geese sensed, even sooner than the fishermen, any change coming over the water? Hadn't Gidon told her that fishermen watched the wild geese on the Kinnereth so as to know when to head homeward?

Still further her Queen Esther moved with her brood; Yaffaleh waded a few steps into the water, she began to cluck, to call them back. At last Estherkeh circled; her shoe-button eyes looked directly into Yaffa's, and she lifted her head proudly so her neck was a tower of David. Her babies were a fan of pearls behind her. Yaffaleh waded a few steps further, then, in an outburst of love, she plunged, dress and all, into the water and swam out, hugging her mother goose while the smooth beak pecked a kiss on her mouth.

Just as Dvora fed the chickens and Yaffaleh had taken charge of the geese, so Gidon was master of the mules. They were kept for the time being along with Kramer's; he had named them Habib and Baksheesh, because Habib, the beloved, was the friendlier, and Baksheesh was always demanding an extra mouthful before he would stir. Baksheesh was a thief, too, Gidon related, but a clever one. When fodder was placed in the cribs, Baksheesh would steal from his neighbor, but not from the neighbor on his left, his partner Habib—no, he stole from Kramer's company mules—after all, the Rothschilds could afford it!

Gidon's bragging about this cleverness soon got to Kramer's ears. The overseer was not one to tolerate such matters; Baksheesh must be placed in the end stall, he ordered. But there the wind blew in, and rain too when it rained. One morning Gidon went off with their ax to a small island in the middle of the Jordon, where scrub pines grew. Bringing back several slender poles, he built a lend-to against the hut. In any case Kramer had charged them too much for the feed; now they would keep their beasts at home.

Dvora received word of Yechezkiel. The young man from the ship had not forgotten her, oh no! It was Leah who brought the news, coming from Yavniel. Only a few days ago, having heard there was a sitting of the Shomer at Yavniel, she had walked there, the whole way. For she had had a thought. Perhaps Moshe had been given an additional mission, a secret one, to bring back arms, and through this had fallen into trouble? Galil would be sure to come to this meeting, at which young men were to be examined as candidates for the Shomer, which now guarded virtually all the settlements as far as Rosh Pina.

Before their closed sitting she drew Galil aside. In his direct way he answered her. Even in a secret matter she had a right to know, he agreed, and he was sure he could trust her. And it spoke well for Moshe that he had not told her; Moshe indeed was to have brought back arms for the Shomer, but this part of his mission would have been carried out only on his way back. It was known that he had left Constantinople, but from there, nothing was known. In Odessa he had not appeared, not at the Poale Zion and not at the Zionist office. Those who had to do with such matters had been notified and were still at work on the question. Yes, the vessel on which he had sailed was known, a tramp Greek lumber ship; it was now somewhere on the seas, but one day it must return to Constantinople or to Odessa. "Leah, he is important to us, not of course in the same way as to you, but believe me everything is being done. Be patient yet a while."

Then she had tried to persuade Galil, "Let me go and

find out." At last he had promised that, if the present inquiries were futile, her plea would be considered.

While there, she had begun to talk to a likable youth, one of the applicants who were being voted on, trying to ease her nervousness. And when he learned she was Leah Chaimovitch, and that her sister was right here on the other side of the heights of Yavniel, the boy almost forgot about the Shomer!

"You know," Leah teased Dvora, "at that moment I think he even forgot they were voting on him. He wanted to come straight here with me! He's in the training farm at Sejera and said he would come on Sabbath Eve to visit you," she ended.

"No! Tonight! And they accepted him into the Shomer?" Dvora fell on her big sister's breast, weeping with shameless girlish joy, and then she began to fly about the hut, the yard, putting up washing, taking down washing, beginning to sweep the stoop, running inside, exclaming, "Oh, what a pigpen, a hegdesh!" and covering the beds, and suddenly demanding of her mother whether there would be raisins in the noodle kugel.

"What's happened, what's come over you?" Feigel demanded, seizing Dvora's wrists. "Not the kadahat? Your face is flushed."

"Her friend from the ship—he's here at Sejera. He's coming for Sabbath Eve!" It hardly needed Leah to explain.

A guest, even a suitor, and how could there be a Sabbath meal for such a one without a fowl? From the two hens Dvora had raised a small flock. But here it was already noon. And where was there a slaughterer? There was no longer time to go to Tiberias or even to Yavniel and return. And to slaughter a chicken without a shochet—this, Tateh would never allow.

"It doesn't matter, he's coming to see Dvora, not to eat chicken," Leah laughed at her mother, yet Feigel was dismayed. Somehow the whole worth of her life seemed to totter at this moment on the ability to provide a proper Sabbath meal for a guest. And in her worry she hurried out to find Yankel. Perhaps if Gidon took the mule he could still ride to the shochet in Yavniel and come back in time? Or, Feigel was even ready to ask Kramer for the loan of his horse!

"Who is coming, the Messiah himself?" Yankel gasped. "Whatever we ourselves will eat for the Sabbath, this shomer will eat, and enough!"

But Gidon had heard, and a few moments after Feigel had returned to the hut she saw him in the yard, stalking one of the chickens. "Gidon, what are you doing?

"Have no fear, it will be a true shochet!"

Dvora, Schmulik, Eliza, even little Avramchick had joined the chase as the terrified birds flapped out of their very hands, squeaking *gevald!* To these doings Feigel shut her eyes. It was Schmulik who caught one of the young chickens, holding her feet while Dvora tied them. "But Gidon," she whispered, "where are you taking her?"

Gidon winked. "To the Yemenites. They have a shochet, don't they?"

"But from Yemenites Tateh won't accept it."

"A shochet is a shochet." He shrugged. "They're religious, aren't they? They're Jews, aren't they?"

With a grimace Gidon babbled an abracadabra in imitation of a shochet's blessing, as he made the motion of slitting the chicken's throat. Then he imitated the bird's final flapping, a stagger, a shivery collapse, and little Avramchick laughed, though a bit doubtfully. The Yemenites Gidon had thought of because one of them, a stonecutter, had appeared when Abulafia the Sephardi had ceased to come. At first glance, the slender dark-skinned worker had seemed an Arab, but there were ringlets before his ears. In any case it turned out that Kramer had got him to labor for Arab wages.

In an odd nasal Hebrew, the Yemenite had explained to Gidon that he was from the little settlement by the Kinnereth. Indeed Gidon had noticed their poor straw huts at the edge of the lake, made of nothing but reed matting. It was a man of Yavniel who had journeyed down the Red Sea to the land of Yemen a few years before, and brought back a number of these families; they were like Arabs, but they were religious Jews—their tribes had lived there in Yemen since the days of the Queen of Sheba, they said. In this way, before the new wave of chalutzim came, the farmers of Yavniel had thought of bringing themselves a supply of Jewish labor. Diligent workers the Yemenites were known to be, and undemanding; they lived on very little, like the fellaheen. Only, many of them had sickened and died.

Under a pepper tree the Yemenite shochet squatted, his feet in a little pool of feathers clotted with chicken blood. He had already finished. Behind him in the hut with its straw-mat flooring, his wife was completing the last scrub-up for the Sabbath, and through the open doorway, the place shone with the many-colored covers of the pillows and bolsters on their sleeping mats.

Gidon held out the chicken. In his singsong Hebrew the shochet asked what the boy wanted. "Slaughter her, what do you think!" And Gidon held out a coin.

"Your father sent you to me?" the Yemenite asked, turning his own head on its scrawny neck with a birdlike, questioning air.

"A guest is coming for Shabbat. We didn't have time to go to Yavniel, so quick, slaughter it."

"A guest for Shabbat?" the shochet temporized.

"My sister's suitor. It's a mitzvah." This was a touch, Gidon knew, that would fetch the man. With the religious, everything connected with a marriage was already a mitzvah.

The wizened little slaughterer had indeed begun to glow at the word. He hummed a little as he took hold of the fowl and felt it. Aha, a meaty young bird, might the children of the marriage be strong and live long! He began to intone the blessing and the knife moved so swiftly you could hardly tell what happened. The line between life and death was nothing.

The coin the Yemenite waved off. Let it be with his blessings, he said. "Are we not all descended from Solomon the King? And may the family increase. Good Sabbath."

And running all the way back, Gidon presented the bird to his mother. "A real kosher shochet," he insisted. "He said the same blessing as the shochet in Cherezinka." And he repeated a few words, almighty this and almighty that, in a Yemenite singsong. Feigel gave a dubious sigh. Who knew—with Gidon, Yankel still got along, so perhaps Yankel would let it pass. Dvoraleh took her brother's face between her hands and bestowed a kiss on his forehead. Still somewhat worried, Feigel turned the bird this way and that, inspecting it. "The Yemenites aren't pious enough for you?" Leah cried. Taking hold of the dead chicken, she began to pull off the feathers. "They're a thousand times more pious even than the Jews of Mea Shearim in Jerusalem!"

"People say they are half Arabs," Feigel worried.

"They are more Jews than we are."

"That wouldn't be so much," her mother replied tartly. Even while she hesitated on the final decision, Feigel rushed about, filled the large water pot. How small the bird looked, and how many mouths were they? At least Reuven, who had come from their kvutsa for the Sabbath, need not be counted, the vegetarian. She herself, Feigel calculated, need take only half a wing to make a semblance. Meanwhile she instructed Dvora to take a few raisins, a few almonds, some bread crumbs for the stuffing. Ach, how little she had taught her daughters! Nu, what would be would be. If Tateh said no, then the bird could be given to the Yemenites. With them it would be kosher, let them make a feast of it!

"In this wilderness," Leah protested, "who is there to peer into your pot to know whether it's supremely kosher or not? Do you think you are still in Cherezinka?"

"God can see into the pot," Gidon quoted, but without levity, as though in all fairness offering his father's argument. His mother looked at him with a look intended to be scolding, but it failed. "It is enough for your father to know," she said. "Your father you must respect."

The father had ended his labor early and gone down to his waterside mikveh. A Jew in the Holy Land alone with his God, he would recite the words of welcome for the arrival of the Sabbath bride. Then he would walk home as the sun disappeared over the ridge, come home like a Jew from shul, saying "Good Shabbes" as he entered the house.

The afternoon waned. The aroma of roasting chicken spread over the yard. Surely it could be smelled as far as Sejera itself, Eliza teasingly declared to Dvora, and if her shomer had not really made up his mind whether or not to come on his visit, the aroma would fetch him.

The afternoon was all but gone, and the suitor had not yet appeared. Dvora tried not to show her worry, but riding from Sejera he might have come by way of the Three Rocks, where many were waylaid.

No, Leah cried, he'd come straight over the ridge, by the short cut, and besides they wouldn't dare waylay a shomer!

Feigel, watching the sun, had another worry. If the young man should come riding after the Sabbath fell, would Yankel even allow him into the house?

In a moment Yankel would be coming home from his prayers by the river, poor man without a shul to go to. The best would be to explain about the shochet to him even before he reached the house—for surely the aroma would reach him. And the best one to explain would be Dvora herself—no, even better, Eliza. For Eliza he had a special softness.

Three times Eliza had re-done her braids, ending by tying a broad white bow atop her head. The vain one! Her mother always related that the first object she had seized in her baby fingers had been a tiny hand-mirror, and she had never since left off admiring herself. "Go, go, Elizaleh, explain it to Tateh, that with the Yemenites, a shochet does it exactly like the High Priest in King Solomon's Temple."

Eliza walked out across the yard to meet her father. She had put on her white dress with the billowy sleeves, and with the crowning white bow, the slender girl in the twilight haze appeared to Yankel taller, she appeared like a young Sabbath Queen herself, his daughter approaching to meet him. Words from the Song of Songs, still on his lips from the Sabbath prayer, hummed in Yankel's ears, and in this moment, as he recognized his sweet young Eliza, with the broad curve of the river in the last sunglow behind her, a hand-mirror for her loveliness, his heart stood still. In this moment all was as it should ever be, a perfection reigned in the Above One's universe, and for this moment he had come here, and brought his Feigel and their children here through such heavy difficulties.

Eliza twined her arm in his.

"So? Has the young man come?"

"No, not yet, Tateh, they are a little worried."

Yankel glanced up at the ridge. There was still time for a rider, but not more than a few monents. Still, suppose a Jew were to consider that instead of gazing up from below, he was watching the setting sun from the top of the ridge?

"Dvora is afraid, if he might have taken the way of the Three Rocks—" Eliza said.

Just then Yankel caught the scent from the house. "What is your mother cooking, then?" he demanded.

"Father, you know there is a shochet here!"

"What? He fell from heaven? Elijah himself, perhaps?"

"No, Tateh. Right here nearby. A perfectly kosher shochet, and we never knew it."

"He has been hiding in a cave?"

"The Yemenites have a shochet," Eliza said.

Yankel stopped in his tracks. "The Yemenites have a shochet. This I understand. For the Yemenites, the Yemenites have a shochet. And so what is that to us?"

"So—we have chicken for the Sabbath, for Dvora's shomer."

And at this moment, before Yankel could declare himself, the thunder of hooves came to them, and with his keffiyah flying in the wind, Yechezkiel clattered down the hill, streaking to outride the last rays of the setting sun, or indeed as though he were borne upon them. Already the boys were running from the yard to greet him as he reined up, the steed of the guardsman triumphantly pawing the air.

"Baruch haba," Yankel offered nevertheless, as the rider's boots struck the ground. The boy seemed larger than he had been on the ship, more a man, that much had to be admitted. And glancing at the departing sun with a sternly measuring look, Yankel declared, "You arrived in time. Shabbat shalom."

The young man laughed self-consciously. "Our mare can outrace the sun itself!"

Gidon was already stroking her flank, while she flaired the water-pail he had brought.

"Careful, don't let her drink too swiftly," Yankel admonished.

"I know."

Feigel was standing in the doorway. "Shalom, gveret," Yechezkiel greeted her respectfully. "I come to pay your family a visit. With your permission." He included the father.

"Welcome! The guest is welcome! Come in!"

—In the old days at home, Yankel was thinking to himself, this was not how it would have happened. First there would have been a go-between to feel out the situation, then discussions of the yiches of the groom—of his lineage, of his scholarly attainments—then friendly bargaining over what the bride might bring on her side of a match—but what did his daughter have to bring in this world? He could provide no dowry for her. And besides, here in the Land it seemed that—aside from the old religious communities—things weren't done like that any more. Two young people saw each other, took to each other, and the parents would be lucky if the couple even took the trouble to go before a rabbi and stand under a canopy, instead of throwing themselves together on the haystack as no doubt Leah had done, though Feigel and all of them were keeping it a secret from him, and the fellow who had done it with her had vanished. . . . And this prospective groom, what did he have to show except his horse—and the horse wasn't his, for that matter—among the members of the Shomer everything was owned in common: the horse belonged to the whole troop of them, even the boy's boots.

This Yechezkiel—even from the ship Yankel had felt it—the way the boy liked to preen himself. Look at him with the tassels on his keffiyah. But for that matter they all were like that, dressing up like Cossacks or like Arab sheikhs—that was part of their way.

Another question—and he could already hear Feigel fretting over it as soon as they would be alone in their bed. How could they allow a younger daughter to become betrothed, even perhaps to be married, while the eldest, Leah, was as yet unwed?

Still . . . this was Shabbat, not the time for worrying. And Yankel entered the house, pronouncing the Sabbath peace.

Feigel had retreated to her pots in the corner; sniffing, though he already knew, Yankel demanded, "What have you cooked here?"

Schmulik and Yaffaleh were at the other end of the room pretending to know nothing, but their eyes betrayed their complicity. Would their father's rage burst forth now? Would he allow the chicken to be eaten?

Yankel went closer and gazed at the fowl lying on its back on Feigel's largest plate, the head to one side with one eye staring as though in defiance. From one to the other of the family Yankel gazed, as though to settle in his mind which of them had done this thing. Schmulik tensed, ready to rush out the door if the anger should fall his way. But his brother Gidon, he saw, stood quiet without flinching under Tateh's questioning gaze.

Now Yankel turned his eyes on his wife. With her lace

shawl over her sheitl, and her gown of dark brown silk with its lace insets, she was dressed as though this were already the wedding. The stone hut shone.

And this doubting moment Feigel seized upon to light the silver candlesticks they had carried from Cherezinka and to say the prayer of the wife. The chaleh lay on the table glistening in the candlelight. Truly his Feigel was a housewife of highest merit, a beryeh, in his heart Yankel admitted it, and yet this could not alter what was kosher and what was tref.

Having completed the candle-blessing, Feigel turned to him and said calmly, "The bird is kosher. I saw myself. Everything was properly done."

Now, with finality, Yankel turned his eyes on Gidon, while his wife continued, "I myself sent him to the shochet. Imagine, how we didn't think of it until now I don't know, but among the Yemenites there is a shochet!"

So with this they had thought to get around him.

It was the guest himself who saved the moment. Yechezkiel had stepped outside, and from his saddlebag he fetched back a bottle of wine, holding it aloft as he returned, his face shining. Good sweet wine from Zichron Yaacov. "For the Kiddush," he said, like a decent Jewish boy, and Yankel could not refuse to open the wine and lift his glass as he chanted the blessing. Even the elder children, Reuven and Leah, the unbelievers, to his surprise, joined with an "Omeyn."

Somehow Feigel had managed seats for everyone around the big trunk that was covered with the white Sabbath cloth; there was a bench that Gidon had made, and two old chairs had been acquired, and a plank on boxes made a bench on the other side. There they sat, a family with a suitor for a guest! Tearing off the end of the warm chaleh, Yankel spoke the blessing for bread. The chaleh was soft and sweet to the tongue.

He recited the "eshet chayil," the "woman of valor" passage of Proverbs to his wife.

All was good. Feigel served out portions of the gefulte fish, made, as had to be, of two kinds of fish—fish that Schmulik had brought out of the Kinnereth, and with large servings of the fish, she hoped that small portions of the fowl would suffice.

Perhaps because the girls were all nervous at the pres-

ence of the suitor, they didn't chatter as much as usual.
And suddenly the guest himself became loquacious. Yechezkiel told how worried he had been as to whether the
Shomer would accept him. He and his friend Menahem—
the little dark one from the boat, surely they remembered?—they had trained themselves together, or rather
Menahem had trained him, as this friend knew everything,
he had been around the world as a sailor and he had
learned to ride as a cowboy in America! So they had gone
off together for a whole week with no provender, to live off
the land. They had gone to the Huleh swamp.

"Ah!" Reuven cried. "The Huleh!" Every plant, every
bird was said to be found wild there. And Gidon too grew
excited. Had they seen herds of water buffalo?

"Plenty!" cried Yechezkiel. "Even wild boar—" He
caught himself up, but Yankel already understood; this
would-be son-in-law, to whom the boys were listening as
though he were the Maggid of Dubnow himself, was
simply another young atheist who would not even have
stopped at eating the flesh of the wild pig of the Huleh.
Yankel wanted to spit. He was not all that stupid, he told
himself, he knew what went on in their world of chalutzim
and chalutzoth. His eye fell on Dvora, her face glistening,
her lips parted. Would it ever occur to a daughter of his
after she was married to keep a kosher house? Why had he
troubled so, to bring them here to the Holy Land? What
was God's land to them?

The suitor was recounting tales now of wondrous fields
on the other side, beyond the lakes and swamps of the Huleh, of rich, black earth. One day they would settle there,
far up in the north in the foothills of the Hermon, as far as
the lands of Dan; they would form their own kvutsa of men
of the Shomer, and from their settlement they would send
guardsmen all over the yishuv. He was speaking more and
more to Reuven and Leah as though they were the heads of
the family, and Dvora too looked to her big brother and
sister, and not to her father and mother.

Feigel brought the fowl to the table.

—Let them have their chicken, whether it was really kosher or tref only a rabbi could judge, and what did it matter to these godless ones? For himself, Yankel waved aside
his portion. This way also there would be more for the
guest, surely as big a gobbler as he was a boaster.

The young couple sat late by the waterside.

The older brother and sister too were by the river, strolling along the bank.—The boy was certainly not profound, was Reuven's judgment, but a good, brave lad, good material.

"And Dvora, is she profound?" Leah asked. Yet she sometimes wondered at thoughts that came from her younger sister, and even in this moment had an intuition that Dvora might have more capacity than this boy Yechezkiel. But then wasn't the woman usually deeper than the man? Hadn't she felt something of this with Moshe?

The pang struck and Leah fell silent, walking on. Her brother knew she was thinking of Moshe; yes, it was true that there was a touch in Yechezkiel that was like Leah's Moshe, something adventuresome, romantically handsome . . . Reuven peered at Leah's face in the half moonlight but could not bring himself to speak of Moshe; it might be more pain than comfort. For an instant he pressed her hand.

In the morning the entire family strolled into their fields, Yechezkiel among them. Across the stepping stones where the Jordan, in the bend, flowed shallow, their first stretch of planted earth could be seen, the grain already rising out of the ground. How quickly this had happened! They all hurried to cross, Yechezkiel giving his hand to Dvora, and then also to Mameh. But just as Feigel, the last in the procession, reached the other side, a wail arose from behind. It was Avramchick. "And me? And me?" the toddler called, standing to his knees in the stream. He made a sight at once so pathetic and so comical, so sweet, standing there, that all of them burst out laughing together. Only Feigel, who could tell why, by what vagary, wiped a sudden tear from her eyes, while Gidon hurried back and fetched Avramchick on his shoulders.

Eliza knelt, brushing her cheek against the blades of green, her long golden braids touching the ground. How lovely was this little sister in her vanity, Reuven said to himself, and her eyes glanced up and caught his thought. "Everything grows more quickly here," she said.

Yes, the eucalyptus trees that the kvutsa had planted had already leaped up a full two meters, he said.—Did she know that the eucalyptus was not from Eretz, but had been brought from Australia? Every plant adapted itself here, no matter how far away it came from—

"Like our Jews," she mocked him, and Reuven felt confused among his younger sisters, even before this child of eleven, and before Dvora already walking with her boy, and Leah already made a woman, and his mother surely wondering and pitying his aloneness. Calling to Gidon, he began to climb; he wanted to show Gidon a certain place he had found.

Through brambles and high thistles they came to the clutter of stones, almost covered by the tangled wild growth. Here were the remains of a stone door-frame, the lintel still resting on the half-buried supports. Here was a large black rock, hollowed out for pounding grain. From long, long ago, who knew how long! Still further above were caves in the face of a sheer wall; to climb there would be a problem.

"Even before Abraham. Even before the Canaanites," Reuven said in curious awe, as though all who had lived here, even the cave dwellers, were in some way their kin.

From up here, one saw every twist and wandering of the Jordan, and even on the far side, the paths up into the stony hills to the heights of Golan. A vantage point, Gidon said.

Reuven pulled some stalks from among the rocks and stripped a few small dried kernels into his hand. He rubbed off the husks and idly put the few grains under his nose, then between his teeth, and then spat them out. The kernels were hard as though petrified. Some windblown seeds probably, that had taken root and then deteriorated in the thin soil, choked among the ruins. Still, he stripped another stalk and dropped the grains into his pocket.

Risen from his Sabbath nap, Yankel went out late in the afternoon by himself as far as is permitted in a Sabbath stroll; in Cherezinka it had been to the end of the town by the stream, and how was he to measure it here? The shore of the Kinnereth? A little further along the shore were the huts of the Yemenites. From one of them a nasal singsong came. The door was open and he could see them, a scant minyan, squatting along the wall while their elder stood at a reading-stand they had made from a crate and placed in the center of the hut. On the side toward Yerushalayim, on a table against the reed wall, stood an ornamented Torah ark, doubtless carried by them from home.

As Yankel hovered in the doorway, one of them came to him. Yankel knew the man, the one with the wispy goat-like beard, the stonecutter. "Shalom, a good Sabbath to you," Yankel said. "A good week to you and yours," the Yemenite responded.

To them, it suddenly occurred to Yankel, he was perhaps himself to be doubted in his worship, for had he not heard somewhere that the Yemenites frowned on the ways of the Jews from the west, the "Franks," for might not Judaism have been polluted in being dragged all over the roads of Europe? Though these Yemenites did not even know what it was to wear shoes, or to lie on a bed instead of the ground, one thing was certain—their daughters they did not give over to apicoiresim!

"If I may be permitted, it is a long while since I have prayed with a minyan," he found himself saying. "Though our ways are not exactly the same as yours—"

"Is there not one Torah for all Jews?"

After that Sabbath, Yankel went now and again to pray with the Yemenites, even returning home to remark to Feigel that there were men of remarkable Torah knowledge among them; and whenever a chicken had to be prepared for the table of a Sabbath eve—and who knows, when Passover came, even a goose might be slaughtered—here was a shochet, just at hand.

Still the family remained alone. The settlement was being built, and it was not being built. The walls of several houses could be seen standing, though of course unroofed. There came Jacques Samuelson himself, the Baron's manager for the entire north, a man of fine bearing who always put his hand over his heart when he said "Believe me." In Constantinople, he explained, the Young Turks had at last toppled the ancient monster, the Sultan Hamid, but whether their new government would prove good or bad for the Yishuv was uncertain; certain it was that among their first acts had been the closing of the gates to Jewish immigration into Palestine, but uncertain it was whether these measures would endure. Another few months and

things would arrange themselves, he was convinced; the
settlers from Roumania would come, somehow they would
be admitted to the land, and the village would take on life.
Patience.

Reuven and Leah nevertheless grumbled at home about
the lack of schooling for Schmulik and the girls. Leah tried
to make them study Hebrew with her in the afternoons,
and Yankel insisted that Shmulik read his Chumash every
morning, but the boy raced through the passages Yankel set
for him and then ran wild outdoors like a young Arab,
or brought back fish from the sea. Let it be, Yankel said to
Feigel. He had not wrenched himself away from Russia
to make intellectuals out of his sons. He had come here to
return to the soil, to make farmers of them, for all the ills
of the Jews had come from their bookishness. Fortunately
Gidon was not a bookish lad—he had finished cheder and
that was enough—and as for the girls, Eliza and Dvora had
learned at home to read, let them addle their heads reading
romances. By next season the settlement would surely be
inhabited, with a school and a shul. If Schmulik learned his
numbers a year later, what did it matter? The thirty families from Transylvania were bringing their own teacher, a
fine melamed, Samuelson had assured him.

One day a forerunner appeared from Roumania, a stout
merchant named Issachar Bronescu. He arrived on Kalman's wagon from Jaffa, wearing a heavy woolen suit,
though he carried with him a German book containing
complete statistics on the climate of Palestine, tropical Tiberias included. But, after all, it was still winter, he declared to Yankel, and in winter a man wore winter clothing.

Though of Yankel's own age, Bronescu seemed younger;
his cheeks were clean-shaven down to a stylish square-cut
chinbeard of curly black hair. "Naturally we are all prepared to undergo hardships," he proclaimed. Yet it was
only sensible to made the best preparations; therefore he
had come in advance. And he made lists of implements,
provisions, and furnishings for the settlers to bring with
them, even inquiring delicately of Feigel, with apologies,
about women's intimate needs, and then of Yankel about
what stock of merchandise he should import, for Issachar
Bronescu himself planned to open a store.

At least he was observant, for when he came down to

their hut, he kissed the mezuzah Yankel had fixed on the doorway. "Truly pioneers," he complimented the family. "And such fine healthy children!" Feigel offered him Yankel's chair, and said she would bring tea. But no, she must not trouble herself, he insisted, for she was now noticeably heavy with child. He sat himself down on a box. But then, as she brought tea and sesame-seed cookies, for her sake, so a guest could be properly received, he moved to the comfortable chair. His own wife could never be so brave, Bronescu declared. He would ship an entire household of furniture here. And as for Yankel, might one ask what occupation he had followed in Russia?

—A merchant, Yankel said.

—And in what merchandise had he dealt?

—Timber. Sugar.

Aha. Aha. The visitor's eyes still calculated the contents of the hut.

"Roumanians," Yankel growled, when he had gone.

"At least—people," Feigel said.

It was altogether a winter of misery. In a torrential rain the taboon melted away and Feigel had nowhere to bake her bread. The river flooded its banks, and the earthen floor was mud. A disease caught Dvoraleh's chickens; half the flock staggered about with their heads askew, it tore your heart out to watch the poor creatures as they struggled to live, and strangled. Nor could the flesh be eaten.

From the kvutsa, Reuven sent Leah with a book in German, and they made out that this was a well-known disease, an epidemic. In the Arab village too flocks were dying; Dvoraleh had gone up there when Sheikh Ibrom insisted they use his own oven to bake their bread, and she blamed herself for having perhaps carried back the chicken disease. Leah was fearful of bringing the contamination to the kvutsa, and scrubbed herself with yellow soap and even changed all her clothes before returning there. But in the kvutsa her own disaster awaited her. Just that day the mail had come, with a letter for her from Russia. From Moshe's mother. Despite the roundabout way Leah had made her inquiry, the mother had understood all. For had not her Moshe written to her, the mother said, of his Leah? Of his wonderful chavera who was dear to him as no other girl he had known, and with whom he at last felt that a real life was opening before him?

Why would this same Leah be writing to her for news of the whereabouts of Moshe? Moshe must have gone away somewhere, the mother understood, and he had disappeared. For neither had they been receiving any letters from their son. The blow of his disappearance had stunned them. She and his father had puzzled and reasoned. Moshe could no longer be in Eretz Yisroel, for whatever might have befallen him there, God forbid, his comrades would have known. And now the mother understood why his Leah had written to them, believing he might have gone homeward.

Each day, the mother wrote, she had expected the sight of her Moshe approaching the house. She spent whole days at the window. And Moshe's father had at last gone to Odessa to make inquiries. And then the real blow had fallen, and Leah must prepare herself.

Moshe had been sent to Siberia.

Leah sat stunned, unable to speak to the chevreh, even to Reuven. She let Reuven take the letter from her hand to read the rest that she had barely absorbed from the lines that quivered before her eyes. Not as a member of Poale Zion had Moshe been seized, but for his old revolutionary activities. As a mere boy handing out revolutionary leaflets in the port. Even before Moshe had gotten off the ship, the Okhrana had seized him. They had held him in secret, and only now had the sentence become known. Ten years, ten years in Siberia! Even to what place in Siberia could not yet be discovered.

She would go, Leah blurted. She would go, she would find Moshe, she would be with him until together they could escape.

And then she rushed out into the rain.

To be alone. The chevreh understood; let her be alone. They looked from one to another, and to Nahama, the only other chavera. Nahama also—only the earlier members, such as Max and Reuven, recalled it—had had her troubles over Handsome Moshe, but now she was come to an understanding with Shimek. "Let her be by herself," Nahama repeated.

When Leah had not returned after a time, Reuven went

out and found her sitting by the river. He sat down beside her. She turned her head, bending it down to reach his shoulder, and he raised up his arm to put it around his sister's shoulders. The huge bulk of her body began to shake with a tremendous sobbing, heaving in enormous waves, so that his arm could hardly hold her. Yet it was the anguish of a girl, a poor girl feeling weak, helpless, small, needing desperately the comfort of a man.

The betrothed, Dvora, was the first to come down with the fever. It came over her one afternoon while she was helping her mother with the washing, bent over the tub in the yard, for since her suitor had come, Dvoraleh had taken to helping with every household task.

Dvora felt a tremor, her eyes saw strangely, the tub shimmered. At first Feigel, as in all things with the girls, thought of womanish matters, but she knew it was not Dvoraleh's time of the month. Or could it even be that she had, like her sister—? No, not Dvoraleh. Feigel felt the girl's hands, her forehead, and took her into the house to lie down. It could only be the kadahat. Schmulik ran for Gidon, who mounted the mule and rode to the kvutsa, bringing Leah back with him, and a supply of quinine, a large chunk wrapped in a page from an old journal. By the time they reached the hut, Dvora, her damp hair pasted to her face and neck, was having hallucinations. All night Leah sat with her, and Feigel kept rising, though Leah begged her, "Mameleh, sleep."

The worst time had come, they all knew it, the time when every evil befalls.

Schmulik came down with the fever the very next day. Should they send to Mescha for Dr. Rachman? But he would only do as they were doing; had not Leah nursed Reuven and half their kvutsa through the kadahat? Still, the presence of the doctor—if anything should happen, God forbid, and they had not gone for the doctor?

Before evening Yankel himself, though he had struggled all day to remain on his feet, gave way to the pestilence. The hovel was like the kvutsa on that first day when the family had passed by, a dark heap of misery. Feigel moved from her stricken children to her sick husband, wiping their faces, begging them to swallow a little soup, praying to the Above One that, if one must be taken, it should be herself, but only after she had brought into the world the soul she carried within her.

And when Dvora seemed to have passed her crisis, sitting up weakly and asking for food, it was the turn of Gidon, and then as though some stern angel were marking each off on his list, it was the time of the little one, Avramchick.

The child was stricken worst of all. On the second day, as the mother held him, rocked him, his flesh was afire as though the little body were passing through Gehenna itself. "The doctor, the doctor," she begged. Who would ride? Gidon lay sick, and Yankel too. But Reuven had now come from the kvutsa, and borrowing Kramer's mare, he galloped to Mescha.

Avramchick was not as the other boys had been when little; he was like a happy angel from the sky, and Feigel had always trembled for him, picturing him to herself as a soul not yet entirely fast within the body. Gidon and Schmulik she recalled on their sturdy small legs, and the way Reuven too had been as a child—all the boys had tugged away from her, marching into every doorway and thrusting their noses into every man's workshop in Cherezinka, from the moment they could move about. But Avramchick still clung to her skirts. His large pale eyes were gray like some tranquil sky and looked on everything with pleasure but without surprise. Nor did he try to seize hold of everything he laid eyes on, the way boys did who were strong in themselves.

This was not to think that he was like the girls. The girls even as toddlers were as they were now, Leah busily trying to do all that she saw her mother or her brothers doing, Dvora passive but willing and even in her first years like a sweet flower, freely ready to give off her perfume, and Eliza vain and decided in her ways, saying yes to this and no to that, and Yaffaleh with her large head and thick limbs, goodness itself, hugging every living creature, a dog, a cat, a wounded bird, her geese. Yet all the girls were in some way the same, they were true in their essence, in their fate as women, just as the boys were manly.

Only Avramchick was not like any one of them. Feigel did not let herself think of the little Nachman she had lost. And she was haunted now by an image that came back from a while ago, the image of Avramchick on that

Sabbath when they had crossed to the fields, left alone on the other side of the river crying, "And me!"

He had never quite reached his strength in his body, so that now in his fever Feigel was terrified that his soul might decide to return above. He it was who had almost at once on arrival in Eretz Yisroel caught the eye-sickness, so that his pale gray eyes were rimmed with red, like sometimes the moon when strange things are to happen on earth. The child had not complained of the irritation, only come and buried his face in her skirts when the eyelids burned, just as he had done now when his whole body began to burn. She had laved his eyes in diluted boric acid. She had sniffed the odor of a poultice brought down by Adafa, the Arabess who brought down goat-cheese from Dja'adi and had shown her how to make the cheese after Yankel had bought their own goat. The poultice smelled of urine, it was like the remedies of the moujik wives in the old country, and though sometimes Feigel had followed their advice—as when Reuven had the whooping cough and she had made him breathe in the odor of burning dried dung, and it had helped him—an instinct this time held her back from applying the poultice to Avramchick's eyes; too many Arab children were half blind. Leah had continued the laving with boric acid, and this had brought down the inflammation. But now even quinine did not bring down the fever. Avramchick retched. It was as though the poor child was not himself doing this, for he did not wail, but rather as though his little body produced the ugly mucus while his eyes looked steadily at her to say this was not he, so that she pressed him close in her terror as though by her own strength to hold his undecided soul within this world. Avremeleh, Avremeleh, she crooned, and when the chills shook him, Feigel wanted to take him back within her body and keep him safe until he was well. It was as though he were even less certainly in this world than the unborn child within her, now nearly come to term; the thrusts were determined and sturdy, to tell her he was already like the other boys, his brothers. But Avramchick lay on her distended body, his small arms around her sides, and his head in the cave between her heavy breasts.

In that hut of misery Big Leah moved from one to the other, bringing broth, bringing tea, her eyes in their dark hollows hardly closed all week, her voice sometimes hoarse and whispery from weariness. One good thing, the anguish for Moshe was for the time covered up in her, though with all her life she would have preferred to have her family in health and let the anguish burn. "Rest, rest," she kept urging her mother, "or you too will fall sick with the fever, and then what will become of the children?" And on her side Feigel kept repeating the same to Leah. It was Leah more than her mother who hovered over the stricken Tateh, mopping Yankel's brow all night long in the worst night of all, and holding him down when he struggled with the wild strength of the enfevered to rise to go to the fields.

Gidon was the first to rise, tottering out, declaring he was well, it was finished; he fed the mules and watered them. The others still lay stretched toe to head on their pallets around the walls.

And it was Leah who, before Dr. Rachman arrived, quietly lifted the limp body of Avramchick away from the breast of his mother, who did not yet know that the fever had at last burned through the final fragile hold of the flesh on his uncertain soul, which had risen away.

With this first sacrifice a legend arose about the soul of Avramchick and the plight of his brother Reuven.

For when Reuven borrowed the swift mare from the supervisor, Kramer, his ride was known, as everything is known that happens in the land. Among the Arabs of Dja'adi it was known that a Yahud was galloping to Mescha on the famous swift mare of the tawny mane. The Arabs of Dja'adi wouldn't touch what belonged to Hawadja Kramer, for he had long established friendship with their mukhtar, and old Ibrim had received money for long-abandoned land. And though Kramer did not employ any villagers in the construction of the houses, there were greens and eggs bought from them, cheese and olives as well, and soon more Yehudim would arrive with money.

But across another twist of the Jordon was the village of the Zbeh, a bitter, marauding clan who had a long-standing feud with Dja'adi, a ghoum that had endured for twelve years and claimed some thirty dead from each tribe. Despite this or because of it, what was known in one village was instantly known on the other side; a few horsemen of the Zbeh were constantly circling around, and nothing escaped their eyes.

Nor would the Zbeh have dared to try for the steed while Kramer himself rode her; he stood too well with the Turks, and the bastinado was a certainty. Yet here was an opportunity to waylay the mare.

Since it was certain dark would fall before they could reach the settlement, Dr. Rachman had at first urged Reuven to wait overnight; he would come in the early morning—he was the one doctor who never had it in his heart to refuse, though what could he do? he said. "Quinine you have, and they all have taken quinine. Reuven, you went through a bad kadahat yourself, you know there is nothing much I can do."

But his baggy unhappy eyes acknowledged that there was the one thing: to be there. For the doctor to be there. This one added remedy, could it be denied that it sometimes made the difference? For the eyes of the sick, particularly a sick child, to fix themselves on the face of a doctor?

And so they rode out, hoping to pass the dangerous place atop the ridge still during daylight, and they reached the ridge in time, but nevertheless four of the Zbeh stormed out from behind a rock shelter, blocking the way.

Though he could not recognize each man by name, nevertheless Dr. Rachman knew the Zbeth and the tribe knew him, for had he ever refused to come to tend a daughter of the tribe bleeding in childbirth? "Yours you can keep, Hawadja Doctor," the first marauder called, "but the tawny mare we must have."

In Yiddish Reuven shouted to Dr. Rachman, "I'll hold them off, go, on to my family. Send help!" And in the same moment Reuven jumped down, pulling Kramer's horse with him into a crevice, while he fired off the revolver that Kramer had insisted he carry. Dr. Rachman's horse reared but moved on. Perhaps Zev the Hotblood, the shomer in nearby Yavniel, might hear the shooting and come galloping.

How it was Reuven never understood, but in that single moment he had slipped like some experienced warrior into the best position. The crevice was like a trench, and a verge of rocks gave him a protected firing point. Kramer's mare stood strangely quiet, like some heroine—it even came to Reuven's mind—in an opera when men fight over a woman, and she waits to be led away by the victor.

The Zbeh fired at his rocks and he fired with his pistol,

still not aiming, only hoping to keep them off, and even in this moment tormenting himself with the thought that he did not want to kill. They wheeled before him for position; doubtless they did not want to injure the steed. Ceaselessly they screamed blood-curdling curses at him, obscenities in Arabic, filth against a man's mother.

The sun was behind him, directly in their eyes. Would they rush at him to seize the horse?

And then there happened something that Reuven did not understand. Their shouting suddenly ceased. They drew together on their mounts. He saw them in a cluster, one huge dark menacing form. And instead of charging upon him, they wheeled and thundered away.

What became widely talked of afterward was learned from a very old shepherd of Dja'adi, who sometimes talked with a very old shepherd of the Zbeh.

The Zbeh tribesmen related that they had beheld a golden circlet coursing around the head of the Yahud, a live, golden circle of light that was protecting him. An angel hovered over the Yahud, they saw, and so they had departed.

Some said the mare had tossed her tawny mane, and with the sunlight coming through it directly into their eyes, the Arabs had seen a golden vision.

But when Feigel had passed beyond the stony silence of her first grief, and when she heard the story told, she said it was the soul of Avramchick that had paused on the way to heaven and hovered over the head of Reuven his brother, protecting him from the murderers.

The little white bundle with the body of Avramchick was placed in the ground high up at the far edge of the fields, just beneath the tumbled stone ruins of the village of ancient times. It was Reuven who chose this place that was to become the cemetery of Mishkan Yaacov, and in his choice was the thought that this was where his own body would lie one day.

And so, as they repeated to each other—the family, and the chaverim from the kvutsa, and the Chevrah Kadushah, the sanctified burial men who came from Yavniel, and the elders of the Yemenites as well, and Kramer and his workers—this little body in a shroud was the first sacrifice here.

It seemed to Reuven as though some blind, compelling

perpetuation was in process, and they were bound forever, as in the most remote of times, to place their sacrifice in the earth when coming to dwell in the land. The thought terrified him, he wanted to wrench himself away from it— even Abraham had been freed of that gruesome demand. He must banish, banish this thought; who could free him of it? His eyes caught sight of Leah, but in all her sorrow he would not add to her burden this dread fantasy that had come to his mind. To this haunting vestige of an ancient superstition, there now joined itself the legend people had already begun to tell of how the soul of Avramchick had saved him. Was he then after all not even a rational man? Was it not reason and will that had brought him back to this land, this earth? Was all that a self-delusion and a pretense, and was modern man even more ironically the slave of unremitting determined commands? Yet meanwhile his lips were moving automatically, and then with intention, in the Kaddish of his father and brothers.

Yankel's eyes were downcast; he could not look into the face of his wife. It was not that he feared an accusation, but because he, a man, did not know how to reach to, even to acknowledge, the suffering of a woman, of his wife. —"Praised and extolled," he repeated, "exalted and glorified, lauded be the Name . . ." A man could affirm, but in all these days and months of hard life since they had come here, he had time and again wanted to touch his wife with words of understanding, words she must need, just as he himself had so dreadfully felt the need for a talk with a man like himself. Just so, Yankel knew, his Feigel must also feel the need for a woman, a woman to whom there could be an outpouring of her womanly heart. Even with all the sons and daughters of her flesh to sustain her, Yankel knew her need, how in Cherezinka she would sit for long hours with her sister Hannah and be assuaged; here, she had not even a neighbor-woman. The thought of leaving this place, of perhaps going on to America or even returning to Cherezinka, prevented Yankel from looking up into the face of his eldest son; yet words prepared themselves in his mind. "For the sake of your mother, we must go. This is too much to ask of a woman—see what this land is doing to her." And he would also be impelled to break out, "You wanted your young brothers to be brought here so they would have a new life in their own land, but instead of life, it is bringing them death."

Then also to Yankel at this moment came that Sabbath image, when all his sons and daughters had walked onto the field with him, and little Avramchick had cried from the other side of the river not to be left behind; Yankel seemed to feel the child's hand slipping into his, after Gidon brought him across the stream and set him down. Yankel turned away his head, but everyone saw the tears come onto the father's face.

—Perhaps then, Leah told herself, it was all too much to ask for, from the older generation, from her mother and father. She would take them back to Cherezinka, and then go on as far as Siberia to meek Moshe, one faraway day to return with him to Eretz, to the kvutsa.

Yet as they all turned from the little area of fresh earth, where Leah promised herself she would come and plant a tree, her eyes were assaulted by the sun-drenched blaze of the valley, yellow and red, quilted with wildflowers, sparkling with dew, "exalted and glorified," offering an anguish of over-exuberant life.

It was the mother who released the final thought that they all felt within them. "Now we are bound to this land," Fiegel said. "We could never leave our Avremeleh to lie here alone."

During the days of sitting in mourning, Gedalia the letter carrier came on his weekly round and brought Feigel an envelope that had been two months on its way from her sister Hannah in America. Then surely Hannah must have had a premonition.

While the rest all clustered to hear Hannah's words, Leah, who also had received a letter, seized the moment to be alone with it. Moshe's mother had written again. —Our dearest Leah—she wrote, and there was important news. They had received the name of the Siberian village where almost certainly Moshe was living. It was in the region of Irkutsk. Moshe's father had traveled to St. Petersburg and engaged the eminent lawyer Igor Rabinovitch, a specialist in defending social revolutionaries, a lawyer with the highest connections in government circles, and thus Moshe's place of exile was known—the village of Tarakusta—and the moment further word was received, Moshe's dear Leah would be the first to be told.

She could not contain herself. "Tarakusta!" she cried. Did her father know of the place? Had Reuven perhaps heard of such a place? Surely Dovidl would know, or certainly Avner. Didn't someone in the kvutsa have a book with a map of Siberia? "Tarakusta, in the region of Irkutsk." How did one arrive there? How long would such a journey take?

There still remained two days to sit in mourning, and though her mother told her it was not an obligation of women to sit the whole seven days, and that her father would not think ill of her if she went to the kvutsa to try to find out more, Leah contained her impatience; she could not cut short this farewell to her little brother.

That very afternoon Dvora's young shomer, Yechezkiel, appeared from Sejera. Riding over to the kvutsa, he came back with a Russian geography schoolbook that one of the chalutzim had carried with him to Eretz. There was a large map spread over two pages, a map of the whole of Russia, but the part that showed Siberia was empty and white as the snow itself. Here and there appeared a speck of a name; Irkutsk they found, but there was no Tarakusta. Then, as they raised their heads from the book that was spread under the lamp, Yechezkiel struck his brow for not having thought of it before—in Sejera there was someone who would surely know! A new chalutz had appeared, only recently escaped from Siberia with false papers he had made for himself. He knew everyone among the exiles! The stories he told!

It was to Leah as though she were already on the way to Tarakusta—only how could she let the family remain here like this in all this misery—her mother heavy of heart and a month before her time? Even with Dvora to help in the house, should anything happen there was no midwife nearer than Yavniel, and the doctor was still further, in Mescha. Suddenly a plan came to Leah. The entire family must move for a time up to Sejera. There, at least, there were people, a whole village of older settlers, besides the training farm. Mameh would not feel so lonely there, she could talk out her grief to other women like herself who had also suffered in their lives, also lost children. And

Schmulik and Yaffaleh could go to school in Sejera. As for leaving the farm for a time, the animals they could take along with them. Reuven could come over occasionally to keep an eye on the crops—in winter little care was needed, the grain would grow—and when the houses on the hillside were completed and the Roumanian settlers arrived, then they could all return and live like human beings!

Feigel did not disagree. Yankel was still weak from his fever, she said, and away from here he would perhaps not feel he must be up and laboring from morning to night. A midwife was to be had in the village of Sejera, and besides, the thought came to her, in the state Leah was in, it was best to go with her, or the girl might even try to leave for Siberia!

Only Gidon refused to fall in with the plan. "I'll stay and take care of everything," he said. But who would take care of him? Feigel worried. —He himself! her son laughed, and even patted her. "Mameleh, go!" There were a few workers in the other hut, he would manage very well.

The chickens that had survived in Dvora's flock they took with them. Yaffaleh wept at parting from her geese, though Gidon promised he would watch over them: "I won't eat even one!"

A sprawling one-time caravanserie only a few minutes' walk outside the Sejera settlement was being used as the farm training center, and the director, Yud Eichelberg, by moving a few chalutzim about, cleared two rooms together for the Chaimovitches; though narrow, the rooms were whitewashed and even had tiled floors. In the same structure, Nadina too was housed, and Galil, and at the long table in the cheder ochel—the eating hall—Nadina pointed out to Leah the young comrade from Siberia, a husky lad with a clever glint in his eyes. Tarakusta? Moshe? Who hadn't heard of Handsome Moshe! Lustily, he told the story. "That one! Imagine Tarakusta—you know what it is? In the furthest wastes, whole days by sledge from the railway, ten huts, maybe twelve. The Siberians there fish through holes in the ice. Besides our Zionists, we had in Irkutsk a little band of social revolutionists, already a few years they were there, and to one of them, his girl came out from Odessa. Very comfortable. One day this couple hears that this same Moshe is in Tarakusta—a long time ago a comrade in their cell. Fifty versts on a sledge they travel to greet him. Piff-paff, the social revolutionist comes back alone, the girl has remained there in Tarakusta and is living with Moshe! For Handsome Moshe you don't have to worry, even in the furthest wastes of Siberia!"

In her torment Leah did not know what to do with herself, where to hide, where to go with her foolishness. Not back to the kvutsa. Though no one would taunt her, no one would laugh behind her back, how would her eyes in her shame meet Nahama's? So Leah told herself she could not leave her mother here, she must at least remain until after the birthing. At Mama's age, who knew what might happen, God forbid.

Everywhere on the training farm, Big Leah was to be found at some task, wearing hobnailed men's shoes as she clumped through the barn to help with the milking, or even with shoveling out manure. Or one encountered her constantly in the yard, fetching this or that for her mother.

To her sister Dvoraleh in the clouds of her love for her shomer, Leah surely could not talk of what had happened to her; let Dvoraleh dream. Her mother had somehow heard the tale, and Leah was thankful that Feigel did not speak of it. But a great sweetness had come between them in these weeks. Feigel at last let herself be tended, and when the time came the big girl lifted up her mother from the bed and carried her in her arms to the birthing stool that the midwife had brought to the room.

Eliza and Yaffaleh were sent away, but Dvora, soon to be married, was allowed to take part in the preparations, spreading out linen, and fetching hot water from the big kitchen. Only after the pains came rapidly did Chaye-Pesya, Sejera's midwife, thrust her out.

It was Leah's hands that received him, the throbbing new flesh on her broad palms, as though this little brother were in a way her own child that she had missed creating, when she had let her moment pass by. It was as though her mother out of her boundless goodness and understanding had even brought this child for her.

Leah turned him on her hands, and then the cry of life

was heard, so powerful a cry that it resounded from the stone walls of the old caravanserie, the round little face fiercely red—the cry of anger, the cry of Chaimovitch rage! "A true Chaimovitch!" Leah laughed, for all at once her healthy, cheerful laughter had returned.

"Give me him," and Leah let her mother feel the black hair on his head—not fuzz but hair—and the thrusting limbs. "Avramchick," Feigel whispered. "Nachman." The soul had returned again, but this time in a sturdier body.

Schmulik, in the yard, was sent to call Yankel from his post as stablemaster. "Tell him a briss, a briss!"

Yankel walked in with dignity, nodded and nodded over the newborn, and said to his wife, "Nu, Feigel, a fine boy. Rest, sleep." And as the women shooed him out along with Schmulik, he added, "To give birth in Eretz Yisroel, truly a mitzvah."

5

IN SEJERA there was life—families with children, and a cheder, so that Schmulik had to go back to study, and Yaffaleh and Eliza too sat and studied there. The village had a mohel—a circumciser—as well, Chaye-Pesya's husband the carpenter, so there were many jests about Mottel the Mohel and his shavings, while Mottel himself insisted that his one desire was to give up carpentry and till the soil; for what other purpose had he come to Eretz?

A joyous briss was held in the cheder ochel of the training school. Reuven and Gidon arrived from the Kinnereth, and it was the chief of the Shomer himself, Galil, who bore the babe on the pillow to the circumcision, while Dvora's betrothed, the young shomer Yechezkiel, exuberant after a single schnapps, cried out as a drop of blood was seen, "That makes him one of us already! A shomer, born in the land!"

Leah remained on in Sejera; she could not tear herself away from her baby brother, nor could she yet return to the kvusta where all with Moshe had happened; Reuven assured her that Nahama was managing well enough at the kvutsa, and besides, a second girl had appeared there.

The infant had been named Mati, Matityahu after all, for if he were named after Avramchick or Nachman, might-their-souls-rest-in-peace, why then—Feigel had confided her worry to Chaye-Pesya and Chaye-Pesya had fully agreed—the Evil One, reminded by the name, might come to seize him. "I know it is foolishness," Feigel admitted to Leah. But still, her grandfather Matityahu had lived past the age of eighty. Faintly, there came to Feigel the burning eyes of the poor feverish chalutz, also named Matityahu, whom she had seen the night when they had stayed in the khan in Chedera, and the eyes seemed thankful.

Yankel had assumed a new stature. Even the chalutzim in the training farm showed a jovial respect for the bearded old tateh with his tzitzith, father of a new son, and the head of the establishment, Yud Eichelberg, now assigned him a wage for his supervision of the stable.

Then a kitchen crisis arose, and the whole of the Sejera center was on the verge of collapse, and it was Abba Yankel who now with a display of an unsuspected modern spirit saved the situation. It was for this that the young people gave him their final accolade, declaring that the old Chaimovitch was "a real chevrehman."

The crisis began when Nadina the Firebrand raised a revolt over Yud Eichelberg's apportionment of labor. "Why must women always be assigned to the kitchen and the laundry?" she set up the old cry, and, organizing Leah and Dvora and two chalutzoth into a committee, Nadina marched with them to Eichelberg's little office in the stone hut by the gate from which he was able to keep an eye on the yard and the whole caravanserie. You could never hold his eyes with yours, since his eyes darted everywhere, yet he listened well and replied to every point.

To their astonishment, the training director at once agreed with them. "You are right in principle," Yud Eichelberg stated. "All tasks should be equally shared by men and women. But nature herself is unequal. What do you want, to plow?"

"Why not!" Nadina seized on it. "You must teach women to plow and men to cook! Every task must be interchangeable!"

"Nadina," he said patiently, "after all, certain tasks require physical strength, and men are the stronger."

"In plowing, it is the mule that supplies the strength, not the man!" she snapped, and even her opponent had to smile at the Firebrand's clever retort. Thus, plowing became the issue. Women, Nadina firmly insisted, must be taught to plow.

On principle, Eichelberg again conceded, he had nothing against it; if a woman wanted to plow, let her go out and plow—and his eyes rested for a moment on Leah—why not? "Some women are stronger than some men." But who would instruct the girls? Every man in the place was busily occupied. Indeed some of the watchmen of the Shomer were working the soil by day and going on guard at night. And besides—his eyes wandered, worriedly—"We urgently need people to handle the new chicken incubator." The first in the land, it had just been brought from Jaffa, sent on a ship from America, the donation of Jews from the state of New Jersey.

"Why, I have an uncle there. In New Jersey!" Leah burst out.

"We have much to learn from them in America," Yud Eichelberg happily picked up her remark. Did the chavera, for instance, know that the Baron de Hirsch had established a whole settlement and a school for Jewish farmers, there in New Jersey? "Is your uncle perhaps one of the farmers?" As far as Leah knew, no, he was not a farmer but a merchant. "We could multiply our poultry tenfold," the overseer said enthusiastically. The incubator was a revolutionary invention, and it required special study and care. The regulation of the temperature, the turning of the eggs at the precise moment—it was like a factory, pouring out chicks by the hundreds. His eye lighted on someone hurrying across the yard, and he called out a message.

Nadina sternly brought him back to the subject. Women demanded the right to plow, not to tend incubators as in a factory.

"Chavera Nadina, you must understand my difficulties—" Besides, in plowing, there were times when a certain agility was required. A woman's skirts—

"We will wear trousers," Nadina proclaimed.

Though his every argument had been countered, and Eichelberg had even agreed to look about for an instructor, days passed. True, he was having problems in setting up the incubator. But, as though to increase the provocation, the men came in from the fields talking about nothing but how many furrows they had plowed, and how the mules and oxen had behaved. If the subject of women plowing was mentioned, they grinned. Perhaps the girls would like to ride out at night with them too, on guard duty?

Nadina flared. Hadn't she taken her full part in the 1905 revolution in Russia? Since when were men braver than women? And calling together her committee, the Firebrand proposed that the kitchen would go on strike the next morning unless plowing instruction began.

Yud Eichelberg was leading a team of mules from the stable when Nadina brought him the ultimatum. "Take us right now to the fields, or the girls walk out of the kitchen."

"Be careful, Nadina! Don't come close to them!" a chalutz called out. "Those mules are in heat, and it is dangerous for any female, including a human female, to come close to them!"

Involuntarily Nadina jumped back, her pince-nez flying off her nose and swinging on its cord. And a vast howl of male laughter arose, spreading all over the yard, while Eichelberg with a solemn air of concern pulled aside the mules.

Worse, Nadina didn't even understand the cause of their laughter, and, running back to the kitchen, she exclaimed indignantly to Leah, "Now they have another excuse—the mules are in heat so a woman can't go near them!"

Leah stared at Nadina, and then herself burst out laughing. She laughed, shaking so hard that the pot in her hand spilled over. "Nadina, a mule—a mule—you mean you really don't even know—?" And by now all the other girls were in convulsions, though Dvoraleh was flushing at the same time she laughed.

The revolutionary Firebrand, child of a factory-owner, really did not know what a mule was, and when Leah explained to her, Nadina became doubly furious at "having been taken advantage of."

"Leave the dishes!" she commanded. "We are going out on strike right now!"

The field workers had already finished their early bread and tea and gone off to their labor, to return in a few hours for their full breakfast. It was on returning, ravenous, that they beheld all five of the girls standing outside the kitchen door, arms folded.

In general the men took the strike in good humor, themselves firing up the big stove, cooking the kasha, cutting up tomatoes and onions, and then—back to the fields, leaving the eating hall a shambles. All day the strike was a source of jest and half-serious argument. By evening, with bits of eggshells all over the tables and the floor, and every plate and cup twice-filthy, the strike had become a burning issue.

Ostentatiously, the girls had prepared a warm, savory soup for themselves alone, though two of them—not Galil's Nadina—were caught sneaking plates out, each to her chaver.

Dvoraleh was torn. She listened to the young wife of a shomer, "Be happy you are a woman. Do you want to ride all night in the darkness and have your bones maybe broken by the club of some bandit—if you are lucky enough not to get shot from behind a rock? We women have the best of it—we stay in the house, sew, cook, and have our children near us." And then the young wife added, with a touch of cunning, "If we are foolish enough to learn to plow, next thing they'll be sending us out to do all the work in the fields, like the Arab women, while the men sit in the cafe with their domino boards and play shesh-besh."

Presently Nadina emerged from a conference with Yud Eichelberg in which Galil had acted as intermediary. On her part Nadina had conceded that not every woman wanted to plow—but those who wanted to learn, she insisted, must be taught. And Eichelberg had pleaded that he had already asked one man after another to undertake to teach them, but a strange reluctance had appeared. On this one thing, the men begged off. They said they would feel foolish. Let the women find themselves an instructor, Eichelberg temporized, and he was ready to assign them a pair of mules and a plow.

It was Leah who, without knowing why, thought of her father. Somehow it seemed to her that it was not certain Tateh would refuse. But how to put it to him?

The kitchen strike had not really reached Yankel except as one of the strange antics of the chalutzim and chalutzoth, for when it came to the family's meals, Feigel scorned the cheder ochel and prepared their food in her own little corner.

"Tateh," Leah asked, "is there anything in the Torah that says a woman should not plow?"

Indeed, not an uninteresting question. That the Torah said you should not plow with an ox and an ass yoked together, anyone could tell you, but as to a woman plowing—a Talmud sage he was not. Yet if women worked in the fields, if they worked the earth in a vegetable garden, what then was the difference? If a man should die and leave no sons, and his widow was strong enough to guide the plow, would it be a transgression?

"Then maybe you will instruct us?" Leah asked.

For a moment Yankel was taken aback. But all these chalutzim with their modern ways, like his own son Reuven who thought of him as an alter kaker, let them see, these revolutionists with their vaunted ideas, whether a plain, pious Jew could not be as modern in his ideas as they!

And so Yankel announced for the sake of peace in Sejera, that he was prepared to go out with the girls to the fields.

Leah and Dvora, together with Nadina the Firebrand, and a laughing-faced girl named Miriam who openly declared that she was doing this because she liked to be among men, were to be the first group. The plowwomen were up early, making themselves ready for the historic occasion, while several other chaveroth now returned to work in the kitchen, even putting raisins into the porridge as a recompense for the discomfort they had imposed on the men with their strike.

Nadina already possessed a pair of trousers, having disguised herself as a young Hasid in her escape from the Okhrana, and Dvora wore trousers of Gidon's that Mameh had brought along for mending, while for Leah, there was found a patched pair belonging to Tateh, who was portly

enough so that she could pull them on, though they were
short in the leg. Inevitably as she pulled the garment over
her hips, there came to Leah the recollection of that other
time—the time when they were all going out to plant eucalyptus trees—how, as she pulled on the trousers of
Moshe—No, such memories were forbidden.

Shoes too. In the yard the girls had gone barefoot or in
sandals. Only Leah possessed a pair of heavy workshoes.
But somehow with scurrying and laughter and borrowing,
in boots and in huge oversize clodhoppers, the girls were
accoutered, and presented themselves at the stable.

Yankel took one look at them and turned his back.

The whole plan was impossible. For does not the Torah
declare that a woman shall not put on the garments of a
man?

However, on an inspiration from Dvoraleh, this crisis
too was solved. The girls returned to their rooms, and each
put on a long skirt under which the trousers could not be
seen. Yankel was dubious, but talmudically concluded that
what a man did not see, he need not know.

And so at last they went out behind the mules. Leah
took to the work at once; the beasts obeyed her, and her
very first furrow was straight. "Like a man's!" declared
Galil, coming over with a few chaverim from the next field.

"Why a man's? A straight furrow is a straight furrow,"
Nadina bridled, and all at once to everyone's astonishment
Galil lifted her straight into the air, and with a burst of
open laughter that was rare for him, set her back down
between the handles of the plow. And he remained on the
field, watching.

By sheer will power the tiny Nadina managed to cling to
the handles, though the mules kept swinging their heads
around and thrashing their tails as at a bee. Several times
when the animals lurched, Yankel had to lunge for the
plow, almost wrenched out of Nadina's hands. Nor could it
be said that her furrow was straight—indeed, when she
managed to glance back, she was startled by the snaky
path. "Never mind," the diplomatic Galil said, "it reminds
me of when I tried to sew a seam."

As for Dvora, when she pointed the plow into the earth
and felt the soil parting, that same blushing sensation came
over her as when she drew on Gidon's trousers, the secret

and exciting touch of shame, the confused feeling that there
was something perversely daring yet inappropriate in what
she was doing. Nor could she feel herself in command of
the tall beasts, as was Leah. The mules knew this too, and
kept halting as though to remind and to tease her. Yet
Dvoraleh kept smiling and declaring to her big sister who
walked alongside her that there was nothing like plowing to
make you feel you were indeed part of the renewal of this
land.

But to herself, she told herself it was, after all, good to
have tried to plow, for now at last she understood something about men. She understood why of all the toil on the
land they liked best to go out and work the soil. She would
whisper this to Yechezkiel. Perhaps tonight in his room in
the hour before he went out on his rounds, and when his
chaver, Menahem, understandingly absented himself. But
no, perhaps it would be unfair to say such a thing and
excite her Yechezkiel. How close, how close she had been
to giving way lately in their embraces, not only because of
the melting in her body, but also she had wanted to prove
to herself that hers was not a love that withheld itself so as
to lead a man into marriage. Only, what had happened to
Leah with her Moshe intervened and held Dvoraleh back.
Her Yechezkiel was good, he loved her with all his soul, he
would never—and yet, like an old-fashioned girl, she could
not. When the danger in her grew, she would always get
Yechezkiel to call Menahem back to the room, pretending
she wanted to hear more of his adventures from the time he
had run away from the yeshiva.

The mules had completely halted, Dvoraleh realized, and
she was just standing there.

At the noon meal Yankel was the center of much questioning and genial laughter. Oh, he attested, the girls had
done well enough, he had not minded instructing them at
all, he would instruct any chavera who desired it! This
brought even more laughter. —Oh, this old pious Yankel
who had just fathered a new child—there was more to
him than anyone had thought! And Yankel now enjoyed a
sort of fame—Reb Yid who taught women to plow!

Only Leah took regular turns with the actual plowing.
The work tired her into the very depths of her being and in
some way left her, at night, with less longing. As for

Dvora, she became more and more absorbed in the chick incubator. The first batch of eggs had failed, filling the barn with a dreadful stench, and it was she who discovered for Yud Eichelberg that too much heat had been applied in the ambition to hatch chicks even more swiftly than in America.

Every ten minutes she ran to look at the thermometer, and, as hatching time neared, Dvoraleh could not be brought to leave the closed, stifling room. It was she who first heard the tiny sound of a cracking shell and then a cheeping, and Dvoraleh rushed out into the yard with the news, crying unbelievingly, "They're alive!"

Soon now, in a few weeks, she and Yechezkiel would be married.

It was to be a double wedding, and something of a royal wedding, for suddenly Galil and Nadina too had decided to be married. Their wedding, it seemed, was in some way a legal necessity for the revolutionary Nadina's safety in the land, so the marriage was not really a betrayal of the principle of free love.

Besides, this double wedding in the Shomer would really be a celebration of the spring harvest, which fell at Passover. It was the cutting of the winter grain, Nadina explained, that was really the origin of Pesach, and hence, as the renewal of an ancient agricultural festival, Passover could be celebrated without their bowing to religious observance.

From all over the land delegates were coming, many of them on foot all the way from Judea, for, in addition to the weddings and the harvest festival, there was to be a meeting at Sejera of the new united agricultural workers' union that Dovidl and Avner had at last succeded in organizing. During the whole of Passover week, things would be happening. A wild-riding fantasia was promised: the settlers of Mescha and Yavniel and Sejera were lending their steeds so that every Shomer could be mounted at the same time, galloping in the celebration.

The year was good, the valley a golden cup of grain, cattle were fat, the mules brayed exuberantly in the fields, the whole Galilee sang.

And the younger girls were learning a dance. It was Leah who devised it; where she got the idea from she did not herself know, but it came to her, a dance of the harvest. First there would be a row of boys in white blouses tied with blue cords, then a row of girls in white gowns with blue sashes. Before them, three men would go forward with their scythes, the first reapers, cutting a square open space in the field, and then in this space the dancers would appear, the rows of boys with a reaping sweep, the upward swing carrying them leaping into the air, and behind them the row of girls first bending with downstretched arms in a gesture of gathering, then raising their arms palms upward, as for an offering. The boys would circle them, and the inner circle of girls would move counterwise to the boys, and in the end boys and girls would skip in high leapings together.

She had found among the Sejera villagers a lad who played the halil in unison with his father who played the accordion; Mama Feigel was sewing costumes, and little Eliza, though younger than all the other girl dancers, had pleaded so much that Leah had placed her among them.

There was to be a real Seder, too, after the harvest ceremony. It was Yankel whom Yud Eichelberg had asked to arrange a Seder for the forty young men and women of the farm training center; godless though they were, the chalutzim and chalutzoth came from good Jewish homes and surely would feel their homelessness at Pesach.

And so Chaver Reb Yankel, as the young people now called him with wry affection, went down with a wagon to Tiberias and brought back matzoth and horseradish and the kosher-for-Passover wine of Zichron and all else that was needed. Meanwhile, busy as she was with her dancers, Leah, with Dvora and a few chalutzoth to help her, transformed the upstairs floor of the caravanserie with olive branches and flowers and barley sheaves. "What have you done here! It's Pesach, not Succoth!" Yankel objected when he returned, but he let it be.

Stopping in to inspect Dvorlaleh's decorations, Yechezkiel and his friend Menahem decided one more touch was needed, and they brought a scythe and a rifle, fixing them crossed to the wall; the farmer and guardsman together, Yechezkiel explained to Dvora, while Menahem adjusted the rifle in such a way that it could be easily seized if needed.

Below, at home by the Jordan, Gidon had gone out manfully all week in his reaping, taking his bread and a jarra of water, intending to surprise them all when the family came back after Passover to help him in the harvest. For the barley was ready, the first to spring out of this earth since who knew how far back.

The wheat too was nearly ready. He waded into the green mass high as his waist and stripped a handful of stalks, rubbing his palms together and blowing away the chaff as he had seen Reuven do when he went over to the kvutsa. The grains remaining on his palm were small, and it seemed to him they were a bit pulpy. In another part of the field it was not the same, the grains were harder. Was this perhaps the blight that Reuvan had worried about when Tateh had bought the seed in Dja'adi?

On the Sabbath, his brother came over from the kvutsa, marveling at the extent Gidon had cut, all by himself, in the barley field, and then they waded together in the wheat, taking samples here and there. It was the blight, Reuven was certain, affecting perhaps a tenth of the crop; it was not disastrous, but yet he was angry. No one had listened to him, not Tateh, not even the chevreh at the kvutsa, for Max Wilner had planted the same local seed.

Then, in his sudden way, Reuven crammed a handful of the blighted grains into his pocket and rushed off at a half-run toward the fields of the kvutsa, leaving Gidon standing there.

In their outermost wheatfield, almost bordering on Mishkan Yaacov, Reuven plunged from one corner to the other, taking samples. The grains were everywhere firm and good. From the same seed. In the same soil. What could have happened here? Was it mere chance, a good batch, a bad batch, as old Sheikh Ibrim believed? And then as Reuven stood there puzzling, the one difference came to him. These were the fields that had been plowed with Max Wilner's new deep-cutting plow.

But why? A different nourishment from the earth?

What was the cause of blight? A germ of some kind, an infection, he had read somewhere. Who would know? If he had a microscope, perhaps he could see; he could compare the grain, the blighted and the whole. Pondering, he made his way back to the yard of the kvutsa.

There was Max, with a few of his faithful, studying pictures of agricultural machines in a booklet Max had received from Chicago, America. One machine had huge whirling blades that reaped the grain while horses drew it across the field. Nahama and her Shimek were excitedly discussing with Max: might not a mechanic be able to build such a machine here from the picture?

In general, Reuven and Max had ended their rift this season, partly because they were among the few "old ones" left from last year's kvutsa, and partly because with more chalutzim on the place, things were expanding, and Reuven had even been allotted a special plot, and a certain amount of time for his agricultural experiments, so he kept much to himself. Still there were flareups.

"Max," Reuven said, "we need a microscope."

"A microsope?" What had got into him now! Did Comrade Reuven have any idea what a microscope cost? There were a thousand other things that were more important! This reaping machine, for instance. For the price of a microscope you could import a reaping machine!

—But if they could find out the cause of blight, Reuven said, in the long run it would pay the price of a dozen reaping machines! And he pulled out the two samples of grain.

"Then ours is good! So what are you worrying about!" Max grinned at him, and several of the younger lads laughed. "What do we need a microscope for?—here we see the results! It's the deep plowing that did it, you yourself now admit! So you see I was right."

"Yes, Max, you were right. But why is it? Why does deeper plowing make a difference?"

"Ach, Reuven! When we can build a laboratorium, we'll put you at the head! Another Aaron Aaronson we have among us."

To avoid exploding in anger, Reuven went off. But the mention of Aaronson gave him a thought. Perhaps go to Zichron and consult him?

Sitting atop a wagonload of barley sacks to be dropped off on the way at the merchants' in Tiberias, Reuven, with Gidon too, and a number of the chevreh, set out for Dvoraleh's wedding and the great doings in Sejera.

Such gladness was in the air, simply that all were arriving, the whole group of the previous day, and this day a flood, a force of workers in the land, and nearly all talking Hebrew! Each greeting held the incredulous—"What, you're here!"—Here, not only from Petach Tikvah and Chedera and Beer Tuvia in the south, and Metulla in the north, but here really from Vilna in the north and Odessa in the south, from Poland, from Roumania, from God knows where; that was the incredible—to have reached this farmyard in Sejera, despite the dangers of secret meetings in Kishinev behind the baker's flour sacks, to have come here despite the cell walls of the dungeon in Kiev—Here I am!—Mendeleh, you came!—Yehoshua, you too!—Leah! Rahel!

So busy she had hardly a moment to embrace Rahel as the whole Jerusalem group arrived in the caravanserie yard, "Rahel! you haven't seen my baby!" Leah cried. No, her mother's baby naturally! Her new little brother Mati, born here! And over the cradle, amidst Rahel's cluckings and exclamations, she went on: "You'll sleep here with us, we'll find room."

But where was Avner? Avner was to meet her here, Rahel said, he had been to Constantinople to study the political situation, now that the Young Turks were in power; he would deliver his report at the conclave.

"Ah, what a strong baby!" and their intimacy swept back on them. And now little Dvora was getting married! Not a word was said between them of Moshe; Leah was grateful. She had to hurry back to her dancers, the procession was starting to the fields, the entire village was coming out to watch.

"But, Leah, where did you learn this!" Rahel cried when the dance was completed. The steps, the movements, it was as though Leah had witnessed this in the days of King Solomon, Rahel kept repeating. Here before their eyes the true Hebrew culture was being brought back to life. How had Leah come to imagine it so clearly? Had she found pictures—in history books perhaps? "It just came to me," Leah said happily. "I asked myself how it must have been done in those days, and it came to me." How pleased everyone was! And little Eliza, so slim, with the grace of a princess!

With the new baby, with the joy here, Leah felt certain now she had found her life again—she did not need Moshe, just as surely as with his shikseh in Siberia he did not need her.

Then Avner arrived, and with him a notable guest. On the way back from Constantinople, in Damascus, Avner had met Ostrov the Landbuyer who was hurrying home for Passover with exciting news. Here in Sejera they were the first to know. Ostrov had at last bought the Fuleh!—a large section of the great plain, Emek Yisroel, the Vale of Israel, long owned by Syrian bankers living in Damascus.

Beaming, still wearing his flowing Arab robes with the broad ornamental belt over his enormous girth, the pasha-like Landbuyer sat in the courtyard among a circle of chalutzim, painting a glowing picture of the fertile fields that would be drained from the bog, of the Jewish villages that would flower on the great plain, the heartland of Palestine.

Dvora's Yechezkiel and others of the Shomer were aflame with the words. At once, Shabbatai Zeira cried, they should go out and send a plow across the area. Here in the heartland, in Emek Yisroel, the quick-minded Galil proposed, they should establish the Shomer's own cooperative. And at once they fell to making lists: how many mules, how many cows—while Dvoraleh pleaded, "And an egg incubator from America!"

More and more the yard was crowded with arrivals: Wagonloads came; chaverim from the other side of Tabor could be heard singing "Yahalili"; the wagon from the kvutsa, with Reuven and Gidon, arrived. "Ah, you missed Leah's dancers," Rahel cried to Reuven. "Your sister found the authentic movements from the past, exactly as I saw in the library in St. Petersburg in pictures of excavations!"

He too had found something from the far past, Reuven wanted to tell Rahel, for he had brought with him the curious wheat grains from below the caves. But being near her brought back his shyness on him. Meanwhile, little Eliza—in her costume and with her hair in ringlets, he had not at first glance even recognized his own sister—was insisting she would dance the whole dance over for them. While she ran off to fetch the boy who played the halil, Reuven hurried to Yud Eichelberg's office where there was a shelf of agricultural works.

It was not only the blighted grain he wanted to look up; he recalled that when he had been convalescing in Zichron, the Aaronson girl, Sara, had brought him her brother's French encyclopedia of plants, and there—it stood perfectly before his eyes now—he had seen a drawing of ancient wheat stalks as they were found in an Egyptian tomb: "The mother of wheat." Luckily, here on Eichelberg's shelf, he found a copy of the same encyclopedia and turned to the drawing, but what the French text said, he was not certain.

Leah came and dragged him out—Eliza was ready to repeat the dance for him and Rahel. "Already he has his nose in a book!" She pulled him into the yard, book in hand. The boy began on his halil, and Eliza in her long white grown swooped like a gleaner. Meanwhile Reuven, finding he stood next to Rahel, showed her the page— didn't she read French?

"Reuven, not now!" she said, but after they had applauded Eliza, she translated a few lines for him. " 'An ancient type of wheat shown on ritual sculptures in Eygpt, also in Greece and Persia, indicating a common origin from some original wild plant, the mother of wheat, as yet undiscovered.' Oy, Reuven, why all this now?" she said.

"Then to find this mother of wheat would be important? a discovery?" Reuven mumbled, and brought out in half-trembling hands the dry grains from his pocket. Rahel glanced down and then burst into a laugh. "Ay, Reuven!" Didn't he know that Aaron Aaronson had already made this discovery, four years ago, on the slopes of Mount Hermon? Didn't he know even that? And she turned back with more praise for his little sister Eliza.

At least, within his shock of disappointment, Reuven felt free of his dream of Rahel.

Only Leah had caught his humiliation. After all, without any knowledge of Aaronson's work, Reuven had found the ancient wheat himself, she was reminding Rahel; but he didn't want her to say this, he ran off, and in any case, just then came a commotion.

Half-stumbling into the compound, gasping, his shirt in tatters, there appeared a bald, short man, Pechter the photographer; coming from Haifa to record the historic farmworkers' meeting and also the double wedding, he had been waylaid. His puffy face smeared in dust and sweat, his high-pitched voice hardly understandable, Pechter gabbled out his story backwards, as though everyone must already know what had befallen him. From the bushes—his valuable apparatus and the donkey—his coat and money torn away—he was sure he had shot one of them—in his shirt he always carried a pistol . . .

At last Galil made a coherent story of it. Pechter had come on the train from Haifa to the stop at Fuleh. There he had hired a donkey and loaded his apparatus on it. Halfway to Sejera, assailants had attacked him, ripped off his coat, knocked him to the ground. They had made off with the animal, the photographic apparatus, everything! But he had fired his revolver, he believed one had fallen and been dragged away by the others—

"One fell? You are sure?"

He had seen him dragged away.

"How many were there?"

Three, perhaps four, they had all assailed him—

Mounted?

Mounted, mounted. The bandits had surely followed him from Fuleh.

—The one who had fallen—could he be dead?

Pechter gulped down water.

—Had the fallen one moved by himself, or had they carried him?

Pechter could not tell. He had been beaten, robbed, blood was in his eyes—

Zev the Hotblood was already mounted, shouting that once and for all they must finish with the marauders of Fuleh. It was surely the same two bandit brothers, there—

"But he says there were more," Galil pointed out, "and those two always go alone."

Never mind how many! A raid, and finish with the whole rotten village.

"Zev, get down," Galil ordered. Startled, Zev looked around, as though everyone should cry out.

"I'll go myself," Galil said, and as this was no longer a rebuke, the Hotblood dismounted. Just then Menahem, having completed a patrol of the fields where the first grain lay cut, rode up to the gate; Galil motioned and they galloped off together.

Pechter, proud of knowing every byway in the land, had taken a donkey path instead of the wagon road. Menahem and Galil followed it, high along the slope. An extraordinary quiet lay over the valley. At this time of day a few fellaheen could usually be seen in the fields below, or a woman or two passing with a headload of brambles for firewood. But today everything below them lay vacant as on the day of creation, and the air was still.

Every Arab had vanished.

There was not one who sat at the long plank tables, even to the young Schmulik, who did not feel that on this night in this place the Pesach was as it must have been the very first time. Listening, the way the Hebrews had listened for the pursuing Egyptians. The men's ears were strained for the sounds of attackers, or, on the favorable side, of Galil and Menahem returning.

At each neighing—was it only from animals already tethered in the yard?—Zev the Hotblood and young Aaron Zeira started up, only to sit back slowly as Shabbatai Zeira and Avner unmoving remained in their places. Dvora's Yechezkiel was rigid; he had kept a seat beside him on the bench for Menahem. On his other side, Dvora whispered to Leah, "He is listening more for hoofbeats than to the Haggadah."

It was Yankel Chaimovitch who intoned the Passover Haggadah, sitting enthroned at the head table, against a velvet-covered pillow that Feigel had brought along. On one side of him sat Yud Eichelberg, and on the other side the guest, Yehoshua Ostrov, appearing in his splendid robe like Elijah himself, come from heaven a little early—before the moment in the Seder when the door is opened for the Prophet. Avner and Rahel too sat at the head table, and Nadina, with an open place beside her for Galil.

Turning to the guest, Reb Yankel with fine dignity offered him the saying of the holiday blessing. Ostrov, who sat against a vast embroidered goose-feather pillow supplied by Chaye-Pesya, which seemed to increase even his imposing girth, now raised the Kiddush cup and sang the blessing like a veritable cantor. The whole room was affected. A deep quietude fell, then Yankel raised aloft the matzoh plate and recited the Aramaic words. By their very close-

ness to, yet difference from, Hebrew the words made everyone feel carried back to an archaic timelessness.

"This is the bread of affliction that our forefathers ate in
Egypt. All who are hungry, come and eat—"

The words were of today. To have arrived here after
walking all the way from Jaffa with only a few olives and
dry pittah in the shoulder-bag, to have arrived here
amongst the chevreh with their kitchen open—come and
eat!

Now Schmuel was embarked on the Four Questions, but
as he began to singsong the words in the dutiful rapid way
he had recited them in previous years at home, he suddenly
heard these words in their meaning, and spoke more
slowly. From the long table of chalutzim and chalutzoth, a
tense awareness reached to Schmulik. This was no longer a
rigmarole like in Cherezinka, where he had once had to do
it in the house of his rich uncle; now Schmulik heard himself asking: what makes this night different from all other
nights, and halted as though expecting to be given a new
real answer, here in Sejera. Then he recited the rest, about
the bitter herbs, and the dipping of the greens, and the sitting and leaning, and the singsong came back into his
voice, and his father embarked on the readings.

Through the long passages, Yankel felt an inattentive-
ness. From the back tables some were slipping out into the
yard. The recitation of the Haggadah became like a separate matter for himself alone and for Ostrov, with Eichelberg also picking up a line here and there.

Didn't these godless fools understand that every word of
the long recitation was as sanctified as the vows in Aramaic
that had moved them at the beginning? Why could they not
see that they were desecrating the very past that drew them
here? One day, because of their failings, everything that
was good in what they were doing in this land might be
cursed and destroyed. And suddenly Yankel heard the crucial words on his lips.

"Therefore let each man look upon himself as though he,
in his own person, went forth out of Egypt—"

The words came hurtling out of the night of the past like
the shots they had been expecting from the dark fields.
Reuven, Dovidl, each chaver, had been hearing the long,
life-long familiar recitation in the back of his mind, some of
them following the rabbinical passages, some not; then in

this moment each, as though wrenched out of slavery to assume the burden of a freeman's life, was struck with the words. First, a few arose from their benches, then others stood up—was it an old custom returning or a demand that had come from within? But all were standing, and thus they drank the second cup, each man as though "in his own person going forth."

Leah hurried to the kitchen to help serve the feast; it was a chance to ask for news, but nothing had been heard, not a cry, not a shot, all was peaceful. Galil was no hothead, nothing would have happened to him, he was surely inquiring cautiously whether the Arab had died. Perhaps he had even ridden to the convent in Kfar Kana to which Arabs sometimes brought their wounded.

From the hall came Yankel's reading:

"These were the plagues that the Almighty our Lord brought down upon them—"

A number of voices joined in the enumeration of the plagues—Frogs, Lice, Locusts—but Rahel and others did not move their lips, and with each horror, voices fell away.

Yankel continued. As he named each plague, he dipped his finger in his wine and flecked off a drop onto the floor. They need not think, these chalutzim, that the older generations had no pity. From far back this sign had been ordained, to spill the wine of rejoicing. Yet the plagues had been the way of the Above One to free His people.

Reuven, Yankel saw, was silent, and Gidon's lips had ceased moving. How could his own sons, how could any Jewish son, fail to understand? The plagues were God's punishment; let God's punishment fall on all who had tormented, murdered, enslaved and brutalized the Jews since that dread time in Egypt. Behind his own lips, Yankel added the names of all those tormentors, Czar Alexander and his minister Plehve who had ordered the pogroms, the Christians and their popes, with the burnings and tortures they had inflicted on the Jews, the wild Bedouin and the thieves and marauders who waylaid you on the highways, all, all, let God's rage fall on them!

"Darkness!" he pronounced, his voice sounding loud and alone except for half-murmurs among the guests, and an echo from Ostrov and Yud Eichelberg. Let God sink every enemy in blackness as He did the Egyptians! And then

Yankel's lips came to the final plague, the slaying of the first-born. His own tongue hesitated.

What father could utter this in hatred?—Pity us all, forgive, have pity, a far-distant voice within him seemed to be calling, as though an Abraham sat within the soul of every Jew calling to God in unceasing bewilderment, as at the command for the sacrifice of Isaac. Yankel moved away his eyes from Reuven—not you, not you, was ever meant, despite all our angers.

But all that the Almighty in His justice deemed necessary was necessary.

Still, far back, even in the age of the great sages in Eretz Yisroel, there had been Rabbi Judah who surely must have felt the same hesitation to repeat the ten horrors, for he had solved the command to recall them by using instead only the initial letter of each word. Yankel intoned the awful words of the final dread affliction, and then read out the acrostic of Rabbi Judah, *Detsach Ab'ash B'Ahab*. In this, more voices joined.

It was during the call to open the door for Elijah, though the door had in fact remained open throughout, that the hooves were heard. Hurrying in, Galil went straight up to Avner and Yehoshua Ostrov, and the three of them put their heads together. Menahem waited by the door among a cluster of chalutzim. But all around the tables the men and women already understood the news; the marauder had died.

From one to another the dread word was dropped. The ghoum. The blood feud. Now it must come. Who could tell on whom it would fall? Somewhere in a field, on a road, a Jew would be shot down. Around Pechter the photographer, who had seemed more upset over the loss of his apparatus and at not being able to take the historic pictures he had come for, than over his shooting affray, a dead silence now formed. He cried out, "What did I do? I only defended myself!" but no one turned to him. Didn't they all know that he, more than anyone else, might fall to the avengers? That as soon as he left this place he might be hunted down? In the silence toward him, it was as though he already were no longer here in this world.

Among the women too a strangeness had fallen, as though they could no longer speak to one another. In each woman, the soul shrank from the forbidden wish that some other man, not hers, might fall, if one must fall.

Unheard, Yankel read the closing lines before the feasting. Only once did there come a response. When he came to the cry, "Pour out the heat of your anger upon the goyim who do not heed your ways!" the voice of Zev the Hotblood rose shouting, "Destroy them!"

After the third cup, there were no voices starting up in song, nor did the children merrily hunt the Afikomen. In the place of Elijah who would one day bring Messiah, evil news had been brought, and for these godless chalutzim, it could only appear as further proof that all creation was devoid of justice, that there was no Above One looking on. Just so, in the old country, the unbelievers had cried out, "An end! See what it brings us!" when, for the devotion of Pesach, the Jews were visited with the accusation of blood in the matzoh. There was the Kishinev libel that had led to the terrible pogrom. And from his youthtime Yankel remembered a tale of a terrible blood accusation from a priest against the leading Jews of Damascus; the whole world had cried out over it. Several had died or gone mad in prison. And the cynical "enlightened" unbelievers had sneered, Where is your God to reward you thus for your devotion?

Ignorant and blind the "enlightened" had been, just as tonight they were ignorant and blind. Precisely because a catastrophe was caused to happen during the Pesach—was that not proof that God was there, that the transgression of the unbelievers was intolerable? For when else should He give His sign, that His people should know His anger?

What then was today's transgression? Was it something beyond the falling away of this whole generation? Was it not God's anger that they had had the chutzpah to bring their godlessness even here to Eretz HaKodesh? And was the Above One not telling them that therefore He would not accept their Pesach?

But with whom among the chalutzim could he even talk of these things? Yankel would rather have been sitting at a table with some family in the village than here with his own unbelieving sons and their comrades. The Landbuyer, Yehoshua Ostrov, had sung a beautiful Kiddush, it was true, but now he was so busily conferring with the rest of them—who knew if he would even raise his cup to call out, "Next Year in Jerusalem!"

By Arab tribal custom, Ostrov pointed out to Galil, what had happened did not inexorably demand a blood vengeance. It had been a death in a fight, and since it had happened in the course of a highway robbery which even the Turks were sometimes wont to punish, he believed an intervention from one of the Arab notables might arrange things. Still, as Galil knew, a peace payment would have to be made.

"The death is unfortunate, and we may even have to make such a concession to their ways," Galil said, "but the highway robbery is something else. This we cannot allow to go by. We have to live here." He proposed that a notable be found to act as an intermediary and that a peace payment be agreed to over the accidental killing, but only on condition that the marauders be turned over to the Turkish police and their robbery dealt with by law. "Even if they only lock them up for a few months, it will make clear that the Shomer will not let such attacks go by."

It seemed a possible plan by which the Shomer might avoid a blood feud and yet emerge from a bad situation with respect, and it was a stroke of good fortune that the Landbuyer, who was on good terms with every notable in Nazareth, should be present. Early in the morning, Yehoshua Ostrov and Galil would set out.

They raised their glasses for the last cup.

"Next Year in Jerusalem" rang out firmly then, by all in unison, with solemnity.

Carrying her armload of plates into the kitchen, Leah found Rahel and Nadina leaning, each on the sill of a rear window, peering into the dark. Each held a large revolver, resting it on the sill. And Nadina was talking of a resolution to be placed on the agenda for tomorrow: women as well as men must be accepted as active members into the Shomer because—

She broke off. Was there a movement out there in the dark? A small distance away was the cemetery of Sejera, with a dozen or more gravestones, deaths mostly from kadahat. Behind the headstones, whose rounded tops could barely be made out, attackers could lurk, slipping from one stone to another as they came closer. They could fire and flee amongst the stones.

From the kitchen doorway a cry broke in on the girls. It was Avner. "What are you doing here? You could be shot at from the cemetery!"

"Exactly," Nadina said in her caustic tone. "And as you left the windows unguarded, we are here."

That year Chaye-Pesya's husband, Mottel the carpenter and mohel, had at long last fulfilled his dream and planted a field of grain. On the holiday Mottel could not resist strolling out to see his crop. Yechezkiel, on an early round, rode past him, and Mottel chattered, "I wasted my life breathing sawdust! Enough, enough! Now I'll become a man of the soil!" Chortling, Yechezkiel rode on.

At the far end of the fields he noticed something odd. On a small heap of stones such as marked the border of a field something fluttered—a white keffiyah it seemed. As he neared, he saw it was so; the top stone held the cloth from blowing away. What did this mean? It made Yechezkiel uneasy; he swooped low, snatched up the keffiyah, and hurriedly completed his rounds.

At a high point stood an oak where Menahem was to meet him. His friend's face darkened. "It's their sign!" Somehow Menahem already knew such things; this was the mark of the ghoum.

Yechezkiel, youngest member of the Shomer, stared at the keffiyah lying so lightly on his palm, as though he too ought to be able to read its message. "Stay out of sight, be careful." Menahem took the headcloth; he was already galloping back to the compound.

From all but the forward table, the feasting boards had been dismounted, the benches were swung over to make rows, and the front table was now the presidium. There Avner stood, ready to make his report on Constantinople, while Dovidl rose up for a moment beside him, calling earnestly to the chaverim who were chattering in the aisles to take their places, as much had to be accomplished this morning. The sight of the two of them standing together, the diminutive Dovidl and Avner the "langotch," always drove Leah to mirth, and, despite the general tension, this rose in her, but Dovidl, catching her expression, gave her a stern look. He was wearing a broad, low-slung revolver-belt that could be seen under the table hanging almost to his knees, with a pistol-handle protruding from the hoster.

At last the chalutzim were attentive as Avner in his low even voice read his report like a classroom dissertation. Nadina, wearing her pince-nez and taking secretarial notes, often requested him to repeat a statistic.

There was in Constantinople no significant labor or socialist movement to which they could look for understanding or support. It was an error to look on the Young Turks' revolt as a people's revolution. It was a movement basically imbedded in national pride, and the triumvirate of leaders, though determined to introduce modernization, had no socialist background or leaning. Since they were intensely Ottoman in their outlook, they were not likely to support or even to tolerate a movement of Hebrew awakening, even in this small part of their empire. He feared the tendency would go in the opposite direction—toward a stress on Ottoman culture, even outside of Turkey proper. However, the basic democratic framework of a parliament existed, and perhaps, because of the vast illiteracy and backwardness of the odd assortment of peoples and tribes that made up the Ottoman Empire, the Kurds, the Armenians, the Persians, the Ethiopians, the Syrians and assorted Arab tribes even as far as Yemen, it was possible that a highly developed sector such as their own, even though a tiny minority, might gain a strong progressive influence.

"The fate of our movement here in the foreseeable future is bound up with the Turkish regime. We are part of the Ottoman Empire, with all its illness and corruption. We must work within that framework."

What did this mean, then? It meant political work in addition to their pioneering. It meant making an effort to elect as members of the Turkish parliament at least one or two of their own labor party delegates, who could then strive within that parliament for a general broadening of democratic methods that would help every group in the Ottoman Empire, Jews included. It might be possible to make alliances with parliamentary delegates from some of the more developed communities, such as the Armenians. If their party could secure even one representative in parliament, perhaps from the Sanjak of Jerusalem, where Jews, if you counted the religious body, were after all the majority, then their representative could work to begin with for liberalization of the immigration laws. They might also succeed in altering the absurd restrictions on the building of houses. All this was a long slow way around, but it was the only way in sight.

And to do this, Avner went on, even to embark on the long way around, required certain preparations. "Who among us in our own movement can read and write freely in Turkish? What do we know of Turkish customs and of Ottoman law?"

The idea came as a shock. The chaverim looked one to another. This, too? A new load to be borne? Yet Avner carried on his exposition, and it seemed incontrovertible. They must move their eyes from Europe to the Levant. They must turn from European culture and absorb Ottoman culture before they could hope to introduce European ideas. They must start at the very beginning, literally to learn the ABC's of the Turkish alphabet. While some of the older communities here, the Sephardim particularly, had cultivated a knowledge of Turkish, the leadership of those groups could hardly be counted on to further the socialist workers' movement. Therefore competent chaverim must be detached from their labors here, and sent for one or two years to Constantinople to study intensely and to prepare to enter politics. Only then could a real beginning be made. Only then could they hope to cease depending on the fragile system of bribes and connivances, on connections and influence with petty government officials and with notables, a system not only abhorrent and immoral, but also precarious in the extreme. Only through entering politics and pressing forward on the democratic front could they broaden their base, and build the Yishuv as of right, rather than through quixotic spurts of tolerance from one kaymakam or another.

At each point Reuven nodded his head in agreement, and Leah sat erect, feeling awakened, feeling brought back from her wanderings in personal, selfish problems, love problems and the desires of her body. She felt recalled to the task, now looming greater than ever before. Under the Sublime Porte one had seen no opportunity for change; now with the Young Turks one could see an opportunity. It was as though all of the chaverim listening to Avner here were like the Jews come out of Egypt, free of the Pharaoh,

listening to a Moshe, to Moshe Rabenu, Moses our teacher
—and momentarily the name did not awaken a pang in
her—telling them what they must do along the hard but yet
hopeful course that lay before them.

A gaunt, complaining woman, yet one who always made
them laugh with her unabashed frankness, Bracha Zeira,
wife of Shabbatai, was holding forth in the kitchen on the
sorrows of being the spouse of a shomer. As always, no
matter where one encountered her, her babies hung about
Bracha, dangling from her breast, or tucked under an arm,
or hanging onto her skirt, while she went ferociously about
her tasks.

Now Dvora felt herself included in the wives' talk as
though she were already married; some of the remarks addressed to the whole kitchen even seemed directed at her.

—To be the wife of a shomer, Bracha grumbled—a great
honor and distinction indeed! In Mescha, now called Tabor, where her Shabbatai had been assigned after Zev the
Hotblood was moved to Yavniel, the farmers provided you
with a hut attached to the stable, large enough to serve as a
privy and smelling the same, and in their generosity—for
who could feed a family on a shomer's wage?—they
brought you a few turnips and cabbages that even a Christian Arab would feed only to his pigs. But since these fine
Yehudim in Tabor didn't have pigs, they gave their garbage
to the watchmen! "As for your man," she grumbled on, "at
night he rides the rounds, so what use is he to you! You
might as well take a cucumber to bed!"

A shocked hoot arose from the chaveroth, while Bracha
gazed pityingly at Dvoraleh who was washing cucumbers at
that moment and held a large specimen in her hand.

"From cucumbers you got all those babies, Bracha?" one
of the women cried out, and the hoots turned to shrieks.
Dvora was grateful that their attention had been diverted
from herself; her hands were burning so from embarrassment that she held them in the dishpan to cool them. In
these last days, she felt a ripeness as though she were indeed a plant; her insides ached and cried out for the swollen male part of Yechezkiel, and indeed Bracha must have
understood what was taking place in her, and have spoken
not in offense but in a kind of sympathy. No matter where

or how they lived, whatever time of night or dawn her Yechezkiel returned, she would be stirring, waiting for him.

They seemed two notables of the same station, sitting together on a European sofa that snugly held their double girth, their coffee cups before them on a table of intricate mother-of-pearl Damascus work. Galil sat opposite on a lavishly inlaid Damascus chair, letting Ostrov the Land-buyer carry forward the conversation with Saïd Hourani, his good friend. The cool, arched chamber gave upon a gardened courtyard; the house was the finest in Nazareth, sitting high above the cluttered market. Two rounds of ceremonial coffee had already been consumed, and all the inquiries for the health and well-being of fathers, brothers, and sons had been answered on both sides with proper showings of concern; also, Hourani had complimented Ostrov on his successful land transaction in Damascus, already known in Nazareth.

For there was, as Galil had learned, though not in such ramified detail as Ostrov, a relationship between the Hourani clan and the Sursuk banking family by various intermarriages, though the Houranis were newer in the land. They went back only a few generations to the time of Mohammed Ali, the conquering adventurer from Egypt—originally a mere Albanian mercenary—who had for a time taken Palestine from the Turks. Bedouin fighting tribes as well as all sorts of hangers-on had swept in with Mohammed Ali; some had taken lands and established themselves, intermarrying with daughters of the regional sheikhs. In this way, and through loans made on crops, the Houranis had grown rich and powerful, owning a dozen villages in the area of Tabor. From Saïd Hourani himself, Ostrov had purchased, on behalf of Baron Rothschild, the land on which the settlement of Mescha arose, and this sumptuous Nazareth house had been built with that money. Vast olive groves, the most extensive in all Palestine, stretching unbroken for a half-day's ride, belonged to the Hourani family, and the Houranis were also clever in trade, operating an olive-oil soap factory in which, Galil gathered, Ostrov himself had an interest when it came to export. Though Moslems, they owned a hotel frequented by Christian pilgrims to Nazareth, and a Hourani was mukhtar of the city.

It was to this point that Ostrov now applied himself, sympathizing over the troubles that had recently been experienced when a party of Christian pilgrims from America had been waylaid and robbed on their journey to Capernaum. Undoubtedly it was the work of the bandits of Fuleh.

Saïd Hourani agreed. He himself had been much upset by the incident, and considered it was high time for the Christians to make themselves felt with the Turkish gendarmerie. He was in a position to inform his good friend Ostrov that the police chief, the Bimbashi Achmed Bey, had indeed received a sharp reprimand from Damascus. The American consulate had made itself felt, and no matter what gifts Achmed Bey might have received from the bandits in the past, no more depredations would be tolerated on Christian pilgrims in this area.

"Nor on Moslems and Jews, I trust," Galil put in smilingly.

At last then the Landbuyer opened the specific issue. Only last night an incident had taken place, and even though Jewish guardsmen could well take care of matters in their own way——

"Indeed this is true." Hourani voiced his respect for the Shomer.

——Still, for the sake of peace in the region, the Jews preferred to prevent a ghoum before it began.

——The matter would not be entirely simple, Hourani said, reflectively. Clearly he already knew some details. Though he would do his best, and if called upon to act as an intermediary . . .

Ostrov expressed his appreciation.

——But as fate would have it, the boy who had been killed was the younger brother of the two notorious bandits of Fuleh, and to restrain them from a personal revenge according to their code in such an instance——

Galil and Ostrov exchanged quick glances; this, of its being the young brother, they had not yet known. At the door of the Christian hospital, from a nun, Galil had only been able to learn that a young Arab with a gunshot wound had been brought there and had died.

Apprehensive, Galil felt he should perhaps hurry back to Sejera with this ominous news, leaving the rest, here, to Ostrov. But fresh coffee was brought.

The young shomer sat on his steed, a large dappled workhorse not really suitable for a watchman; it belonged to the training farm. As instructed, Yechezkiel remained under the tree, peering out between the branches; the air danced a little in his eyes. He was undressing his bride. Perhaps even tonight, still before their marriage, they would slip away to the goren, go somewhere away from all the others, and Dvoraleh would truly become his chavera, his mate, his bride. This would be their own secret marriage. And then in a few days there would be the wedding before her family and all the chevreh. But first they would mate in pure love, slowly they would uncover and reveal their whole bodies to each other, just as Adam and Eve . . .

The keffiyah grasped in his hand, Menahem was entering the meeting hall, uncertain as to whether to interrupt Avner, when he distinctly heard the shot. But for his abrupt whirling around, the others might not at once have recognized the sound, but now several men jumped from their benches. Zev, catching sight of the scarf in Menahem's hand, shouted "I told you! I told you it would happen!" adding a stream of the foulest Arab curses. Avner broke off and turned to Dovidl, who had leaped to his feet at the same time pulling at the huge pistol in his holster.

Menahem snatched his rifle from the wall decoration. Others were already running toward the field, picking up rocks and staves, some of them even pitchforks. One of the lads was mounting Menahem's horse; pulling him down, Menahem galloped off after Shabbatai Zeira who was already beyond the gate. In the field he passed the Chaimovitches running, Reuven, Leah, and Gidon, who carried a dagger. "The oak," he shouted, "Yechezkiel."

Yechezkiel too had heard the shot and charged down in its direction, into a barley field. He already knew; there, but a few moments ago, Mottel the mohel had taken his stroll, so pleased with himself for growing a crop at last. What sort of shomer was he, Yechezkiel reproached himself, to have left the man alone in the field at such a time, why hadn't he sent him off homeward! Thinking he saw a movement in the grain—or was it the air dancing?—the young shomer wheeled his clumsy horse, managed to raise his rifle and fire at the spot, but already he himself was

struck, his body swaying backward, while an echo from
how many sittings, how many protests, in his own voice, in
Menahem's, rose in Yechezkiel, "They all of them have
good fast horses, while we——"

The pursuit, the wild shooting, the shouting led to nothing, and stillness returned over Mottel's field; all was motionless where the people stood assembled over the two
bodies, that of the crinkle-skinned carpenter, and that of
the smooth-faced young shomer, the bridegroom. The first
cries of revenge, of "Fight fire with fire," had dwindled
away, and even the fiercest stood as though overwhelmed.
Only a muttered "Savages!" could be heard from within the
crowd, sometimes in a man's bitterness, sometimes in a
woman's tone of anguish.

Nadina had taken on herself the task of telling Chaye-
Pesya in the village. But Dvoraleh, running into the field
with Bracha Zeira, was met halfway, and knew. She
stopped stock still. Then there came out of her throat a
sound she had never made before. It came out of the throat
of Bracha too and the other women gathering around them.
The ululation rose and spread over the hills, the shriek of
mourning women awakened in their throats from long,
long ago, as it had been heard in this same land.

Then, walking between Leah and Bracha, Dvora came
and stood over her Yechezkiel. He did not appear hurt. He
looked as she had imagined he would look after they had
loved and drowsed, and she alone half-awakened and
looked at him sleeping.

One ear was to the ground and the wound was there,
some said. Dvora knew she had not yet understood he was
gone and that therefore she was not weeping. She stood as
in some tale in which a girl, still a virgin yet already a
widow, vows to become a nun—but those were Christian
tales. What was the way for her she could not know.

Fitfully, in different corners of the yard, little groups debated what should be done.

"For one, the Arabs have killed two!" Zev cried. "Then
for two, kill four!"

"No, track down the actual murderers, be it to the ends
of the earth," cried Aaron Zeira.

"Burn down their entire village, that will teach them," another shomer demanded.

Some said it was for Reuven to decide, as he would have been Yechezkiel's nearest of kin, his brother-in-law.

With Reuven there could be no question about adopting the blood feud like the bandits themselves. It was not because he was a man of fear, the chevreh recognized—after all, Reuven alone had once held off four assailants. But what else was to be done, with honor?

In a closed sitting with Shabbatai Zeira, Avner and Dovidl, Reuven was included. Presently Galil returned from Nazareth, heard in the yard all that had happened, spoke for a moment with Menahem, then entered the sitting. Since it was clear that the ghoum came from the brothers from Fuleh, Zeira said, why wait further? Let the Shomer pass sentence on them and select a man to carry out the sentence. He turned to Reuven.

"If this is an affair of the Shomer," Reuven said, "it is not for me to take part in your decision."

What should he make of himself? Was he a coward, avoiding the dread decisions that life sometimes imposes on a man? Was he truly following his inner beliefs, or was he merely leaving to others the abhorrent tasks of life? Dvoraleh's bewildered face, the stretched-out boy, the body of poor Mottel in the field of his first crop—how could he dare call for more murders in their name? Had he not already once before, when the question was posed to him without the immediate distortion of emotion, gone away from their slogan of fire and blood?

Galil himself argued for the way of the law. The Fuleh brothers should be seized, but then turned over to the police. "That will show our strength." And demanding a murder trial and the death penalty would show that they of the Shomer intended to have civilization and justice in this land. Thus the new regime of the Young Turks would be called to the test.

Angrily, Shabbatai Zeira shouted, "Our men die, and you want to use their deaths to test Turkish courts!"

Even Avner and Dovidl were divided. Dovidl believed a far-reaching moment had come. The Zbeh were widely hated among the more settled tribes of villagers, and the esteem of these Arab villagers would be gained by removing the marauders. "We may try to change their ways later and bring law into the land, but first we must win esteem in their own light."

Then Dovidl too was talking of execution by the Shomer.

Avner hestitated. Did the Shomer even have the strength to face a ghoum? He tended to side with Galil. To capture the murderers would show strength. Everyone would realize this was more difficult than killing them from ambush. And then they could be turned over to the law. That need not perpetuate the ghoum.

In the end, Avner and Galil persuaded the others to the way of the law, but matters did not fall out as they planned. The Bimbashi of Nazareth, Achmed Bey, quickly appeared in the village of Fuleh with four gendarmes. As expected, the brothers were not found, but Achmed Bey carried off the father, giving notice that the brothers must surrender themselves for their father to be freed. In his Nazareth garrison, it was well known, Achmed Bey had the services of a drunken army physician who skillfully kept torture-victims alive as long as was necessary. Let the brothers hasten to give themselves up, and spare their father.

The bandits surrendered the following day, galloping openly on the highway to Nazareth with wild outcries, as in a fantasia. Charged with the murder of two Jews, they were lodged in the fortress where they would be quite safe from the reach of the Hotblood and others of the Shomer, and where there was a constant supply of arak and kif.

Before Passover was ended, a pair of Achmed Bey's gendarmes clattered into the yard of the caravanserie. From across his saddle, one of them set down Pechter's photographic apparatus on its three legs, carefully, with a grin of achievement. It would never have been pilfered, he explained, had the photographer agreed to take pictures of the two bandits and their young brother, when they stopped him in Fuleh. At his refusal, they had felt offended. The younger brother, a bright lad, had felt sure he could learn to use the apparatus himself, so his brothers had decided to borrow it for him. It was a great pity that Pechter, who didn't understand Arabic, had started to shoot and had killed the youngest brother, thus starting the ghoum. However, a trial would be held.

And on the last day of Pesach, the wedding took place of Nadina and Galil. The ceremony was solemn. Two rows of mounted men of the Shomer faced each other with their muskets forming a pointed archway, and through this the couple walked to the chupah. Finally they had decided not to have a rabbi. As every former yeshiva bocher knew, a pronouncement by the groom before witnesses sufficed, and so, to Avner and Dovidl, Galil and Nadina equally declared they took each other for wife, for husband. Some of the girls whispered—why didn't Avner and Rahel also already go through with it?

Then still another marriage custom was observed by the unobservant. A wineglass was placed on the ground, and, amidst jesting at keeping the old custom, Galil lifted his foot and crushed it.

"But why then should the Jewish groom be a destroyer?" Reuven reflected; "why was it done?" It was said to be a reminder, even in time of rejoicing, of the Temple and its destruction, but perhaps it was intended to remind man of the fragility of the best in life; or again perhaps it symbolized the dominance of man in a marriage—but in that case why should Nadina have accepted it? Some said it showed that though the Temple was destroyed, the Jewish stream, through marriages, defied destruction and would continue. But emancipated scholars declared it was altogether a foreign custom, even a pagan one, that Jews had taken over after the dispersion, perhaps in Germany.

As his thoughts wandered thus, Reuven heard the assembly in the courtyard with one voice shouting aloud the oath of the Shomer, taken from the Bar Giora and no longer secret;

> In blood and fire Judea fell,
> In blood and fire Judea will arise.

He still refrained from repeating it.

Dvoraleh had insisted she wanted to attend, and standing with Leah and Reuven, she watched the ceremony with glowing eyes as though taking the whole of it into herself, for what she herself would have experienced. When her turn came to embrace the bride, it was Nadina the hardened revolutionary rather than the bereaved Dvoraleh who broke into tears.

6

NOW came several good years.

Scarcely had Yankel returned with Gidon to their farm to complete the harvest, when the head of the administration of settlements for the whole of the Galilee, the Baron's overseer, Jacques Samuelson himself, arrived in a carriage with the new kaymakam of Tiberias, a Young Turk hardly young, and so enormously fat that the carriage body leaped up on its springs when he heaved himself out. But after the visit of the Belly, as Azmani Bey was promptly dubbed, the long-established lone gendarme folded up his tent and decamped. In a blaze of effort, Kramer brought in more workers and set every man to completing the roofs; tiles went up in a chain from hand to hand, and, aside from a lock on the door and glass in the windows, the Chaimovitch house, the first, was ready to be lived in even before the High Holy Days. From the hut by the river Yankel and Gidon brought up the huge trunk, the bedding, the pots. And then Yankel rode up to Sejera to fetch the family.

Different enough from a year ago. His own wagon, his own mules, and now he was bringing the family to his own house.

They kept running in and out of the house, the front door, the back door—as though there was more to be discovered, as though they had not themselves placed each stone rising on the walls. Still, a person entered, and there was a room on one side and a room on the other. In the rear of the right-hand room was an innovation, for, as water was ample here, a well had been dug for each house, and in addition to the pump in the yard, there was in the back corner of this room, a sink with a smaller hand-pump. Schmulik had to be stopped from continuously demonstrating the inside pump or the whole house would have been flooded.

This would be the room of the parents with the new

196

baby, Mati. In the front part would stand a real table with chairs. Expansively, Yankel consented to the purchase of the table and as many as six chairs—very well, even eight—in Tiberias, with the very last, he swore, of the gold napoleons he had brought with him. There might be just enough money for a bed also; let Feigel once more have a real bed to lie on, he said, though his grown daughters snorted that he too would share in this luxury.

For the other room a mirror was needed, little Eliza insisted, and she wheedled and whimpered until Feigel brought out a few coins knotted away in one of her kniplach, the last one, she said. But then Yankel declared no, let her keep her coins, he would find money himself somewhere to pay for a mirror for his daughters.

Now Eliza demanded that a curtain should divide this second room; she had had enough, she declared, of telling her brothers to turn around when she was dressing and undressing. At this, a hoot and a howl burst from Gidon and Schmulik, the younger one running wildly behind her and ruffling up her skirts, while she shrieked and chased him, with Dvora and Leah still convulsed over her airs. The brother and sister rolled on the new tile floor, pummeling each other until Eliza suddenly leaped up, demanding with haughty dignity, "Don't touch me! Leave me alone!" and Schmulik, somehow intimidated, backed off, though with a final growl, "Girls stink," that made Feigel give him a light slap across the mouth. It was all due to the excitement of the new house. Ordinarily, thank the Above One, her children were decent.

The great trunk was put into this room. While Leah stayed on to help arrange the house, the room was indeed crowded, so a bed was made every night for Yaffaleh on two chairs in the parents' room. As soon as they were settled, Leah said, she would return to the Kvutsa, but first she would put in a large vegetable garden. And each morning she clumped out to her labor.

Not only did she plant early-ripening tomatoes and carrots, peas, cucumbers, cabbages, radishes, lettuce and her faithful eggplant, but also, in front of the house as well as in window-pots and even in an ancient hollowed-out black stone that Reuven brought down one Sabbath from his place of ruins, Leah planted an endless assortment of flowers, so that there would always be some in bloom. From everywhere she brought seeds and bulbs and cuttings; even when Yankel drove with the whole family to Tiberias to buy the furniture, Leah managed to encounter an eccentric Englishwoman who had come to live in Christ's Galilee and was delighted to give the big Jewish girl plants and seeds from her heavenly garden of roses and lilies.

Little Yaffaleh caught her sister's flower-planting fever, and together the giantess and the chunky small girl would wander the shore of the Kinnereth for rare wildflowers to transplant, or, while alone, watching her growing flock of geese, Yaffaleh would suddenly perceive a blossom half-hidden beneath a rock and carefully dig it out to take home to Leah. Once in the middle of a burning hot day Yaffaleh even left her geese, to rush breathless to her big sister, her hands cupped around a wild orchid of such hues that Leah seized her and hugged and kissed her. By every law of horticulture the plant should not have lived, but twenty times a day the big and little sister knelt over it and petted the earth around it, and Schmulik even jeered that he saw Yaffaleh kissing the flower and whispering to it, until the fragile roots took hold.

A grape arbor too was put in, and from Yavneh, Kalman the Drayman brought a young fig tree, the gift of Yona Kolodnitzer from whom Yankel had bought, at last, a true Holland calf. Then Gidon carried down from the Arab village the seedling of a carob tree, that in a future year would spread wide branches to give them shade, and sweet pods to chew on.

Meanwhile Feigel herself made a demand and even declared that, like the chalutzoth of Sejera, she would stop cooking and conduct a strike, unless once and for all, now that Yankel's first crop was in and the grain was sold and they had a house, she was provided with a true oven to bake in, instead of an earthen taboon that choked her with smoke, and in a strong winter rain melted away in the yard.

There was in Mescha a settler who had built for himself a true Russian oven inside his house, the sort that one slept atop of, in the old country. No use to tell her that in the heat of this place the entire house would become a sweat bath. Good, then Tateh would have his sweat bath! Feigel retorted.

In the end, Josef Idelson, brother of Shlomo Idelson

from whom Yankel had bought his mules, came from Mescha with a wagonload of tiles, and remained with them for a week while Gidon helped him build the oven. Half of the back wall was removed and the room extended outward to accommodate the structure. The oven was even given a facing of decorative tiles made in Nazareth, that glowed with yellow and green intricacies. And the cholent that issued from this real stove on a Sabbath, when they sat on their real chairs around a proper table, a cholent made with sweet carrots already from their own garden, eaten with chaleh baked from the grain of their own fields, made Feigel declare, "Now we have become human beings again."

But a change of some kind was coming over her Big Leah, the mother saw. Though the girl was cheerful and full of song as ever, Feigel sensed that Leah in some way was letting go of herself as a young woman. She had always eaten with good appetite, but now she ate enormously; she was always clumping back into the house and was even careless about dirtying the floor while she took herself a thick slice of bread and butter, like some growing boy, like Schmulik before going out to help Gidon in the field.

The waistbands on Leah's skirts had to be let out, and the tiecords on her petticoats were hardly long enough now, so that the knotted ends were hard to undo, and sometimes, because of her thick fingers, Leah had to ask Eliza to unfasten her. She was still such a young girl, hardly twenty, so lively with her comrades—it pained Feigel to watch Leah sitting in the evenings with Schmulik over the endless games of dominoes that the boy liked to play until he was half-asleep at the table.

Surely it would be livelier for her at the kvutsa: the communa was growing in numbers and there were still three men for every girl. Another communa was starting too, farther along by the lake. But Leah lingered at home.

For Dvoraleh, Feigel would still not have thought about a man—a length of time had first to pass; yet the bereaved girl from day to day seemed in better equilibrium than her sister. It was Dvora rather than Leah now who tended to little Mati, with his weaning and his diapers, though Big Leah at every free moment would fondle him and cluck over him. Dvora also was seriously learning to cook, to bake bread and strudel, for with the new oven baking was a pleasure. From Sejera she had brought chicks hatched in the incubator, and already she had a fine new flock, which she was feeding according to a book from America; she had actually, by herself, puzzled out how to read English. Between all these tasks with which she occupied herself, Dvora seemed to Feigel much like a young housewife in the old country whose husband has gone to America, and who tends her baby and her home, waiting; it would be unseemly as yet, Feigel felt, for Dvora to be exposed to young men, to go visiting the kvutsoth. But Feigel did not fear for the girl. The time would come when a man would take his place in her life. Only for Leah was she troubled, and one evening, when Schmulik had fallen asleep over their game, and Leah had gone out into the yard to breathe in the night for a moment, as she said, Feigel went out to her.

"Leahleh," she asked softly, "are you still longing for that one?" Let his name be erased from eternity, let him set there in Siberia until ice froze over him!

"No, Mama," Leah said.

It was the truth and not the truth. If he were to appear, perhaps despite everything she would go to him. But what she truly feared was that somehow the femaleness in her might make her give way to another, since not to him. Some nights, and sometimes even in the midst of the day, there came over her body such a longing, such a hunger for a counterpart, that she feared if she were among men, she would become like a certain chavera who was talked of, who went about lying with one man or another, no matter who—to give the chaverim surcease she pretended, but perhaps really to give herself surcease.

"Why don't you go sometimes on a Friday evening to the kvutsa?" Feigel said. "On Erev Shabbat they have liveliness there, it would be good for you."

"You needn't worry so for me, Mama," Leah said. "Perhaps I'll soon go back to the kvutsa." And then she added, "A family is a little kvutsa too."

Then the settlement itself became livelier. One fine day, a whole group of Roumanian settlers arrived, with their leader, the same Issachar Bronescu who had last winter inspected the site. Leading a long caravan, he brought three wagonloads of possessions of his own, topped by his richly dressed plump wife, and four children, the eldest a boy of thirteen—who could tell, perhaps even a prospective groom for Eliza!

Behind the three wagons of Issachar Bronescu came a dozen others, each loaded high with bedding, trunks, and articles of furniture, truly an exciting sight. All Jaffa was empty of wagons, declared Kalman the Drayman; never before in the land had such a huge caravan been organized.

At the entrance to the settlement stood Kramer with Jacques Samuelson himself to welcome the newcomers, but it was Yankel Chaimovitch who had been designated to come forward with bread and salt, and Feigel and her daughters had laden a long outdoor table with a veritable feast, offering milk to the children, and cool, refreshing le-beniyah to everyone, while the men were offered a l'chayim; on the table were herrings and cheeses, including the salty goat-cheese that Feigel had learned to make from the Arabs, and pickles and radishes, sliced onions, slabs of her own butter, loaves of fresh bread, and plates of sesame cookies that she and Dvoraleh had baked in the oven.

These were the first ten families: others were coming in a week, in time for the holidays. All the householders were of a younger age than Yankel and Feigel, with children ranging up to fourteen, but most of them only just ready to begin cheder. They had indeed brought their own me-lamed, a youngish one with a clipped beard, and he was a shochet too. Before a week was over, Issachar Bronescu had got the melamed to start the cheder going, and had also opened his general shop with household supplies, hav-ing fetched more wagonloads of goods from Tiberias—pails and farming tools and whole kegs of nails, oil lamps and extra glass chimneys, kerosene, and all manner of things that a settler or his wife might have forgotten to bring from Roumania.

The settlers were mainly from the region of Kluj; some had been merchants of the smaller variety, no better off than Yankel himself, as he reasoned it; one had dealt in hides, another had helped his father who sold spirits to the peasants—decent Jews, each with enough savings to get him through the first year, and perhaps even the second. Everything had been carefully planned and prepared, but none of them had ever been a farmer. A hundred times a day the men came to Yankel with their questions, put as though in truth they really knew quite a bit but were only inquiring about local conditions: what was best to plant first, and was it advisable to buy a calf or a cow, and how much should a farmhand be paid—a chalutz, naturally, not an Arab—though if an Arab was hired to do a little additional labor, how much for example? And their women flew in and out of Feigel's kitchen from morning to night, with half of them borrowing the use of her oven to bake in.

Yet, except for all such contacts as these, in which the older family of the community was glad to help the newcomers, there soon came a separateness between the Chaimovitches and the Roumanians. Yankel had always distrusted Roumanians, and here it was his fate to have fallen among them. They borrowed implements which they did not return until four times reminded. The women, Feigel said, ran in to borrow a cup of flour, a few onions, and to bring anything back seemed unknown to them. How could you ask back a cup of flour? Some of the householders came to Yankel for advice and then went off and did the opposite. So why did they have to bother him? Also the newcomers would stroll around his parcel of land and study his house as though he had stolen in before them and seized all that was best. Or else it was as though they, having organized the entire affair of the settlement and applied for the land and arranged with the Baron's office and the Zionist office for everything, had done him a favor in letting him slip in and benefit from all their efforts!

Of the malaria that the whole Chaimovitch family had got into their blood here, of the year of kadahat and death they had suffered while planting eucalyptus trees to protect the whole settlement, these fine Roumanians seemed to understand nothing. Besides, devotedly observant Jews though they professed to be, Yankel caught sight of one and another of them smoking on the Sabbath. "Let the kadahat take the lot of them!" Yankel grumbled.

"Nu, nu," Feigel soothed him, "They have just arrived. It is hard for them, even though they have it so much easier than it was for us. And here they see that you already have a fine meshek and harvested fields, while their land is covered with stones. So it is only natural for them to be envious. Still, for the children, for all of us, it is better now, it is livelier to be living among people. You have a shul to go to, and the children a school."

It was true; he had long ago fallen off from praying with the Yemenites; that had been only a curiosity, for their ways were too strange for him, and now the synagogue at the end of the open street, with the schoolroom attached to it, made a man feel at home, even if there was a Roumanian twang in the prayers. For the children too it was better, though Schmulik, while there was no cheder to go to, had done many things around the farm.

It *was* better, though Schmulik did not agree, having now to be shut up every day again, like in Cherezinka. Not only boys were in the schoolroom, but girls as well, since the melamed considered himself "enlightened," and the Roumanians too had an "enlightened" outlook. So Yaffaleh had to pen up her geese every morning while she went off with Schmulik and Eliza to the study-house. The melamed would teach not only the Torah, Issachar Bronescu had declared, but such emancipated subjects as geography and arithmetic and even physiology. And he would teach in Hebrew, certainly in Hebrew, for were they not true Zionists!

Before a week had passed, Leah caught sight of Schmulik one morning running toward the river. She called to him; he ran faster, but at last halted for her to reach him. In a rage, he held out his palm for her to see the rising welt. The melamed!—But for what?

For what? In a sputtering mockery, Schmulik imitated a singsong recitation in their foreign-sounding Ashkenazic Hebrew. "That's how we are supposed to learn. He doesn't even know how to talk our own Hebrew here in Eretz!"

True, the accent was the old-country Hebrew such as Tateh used in his prayers. That could soon change. But the rod was something else! Leah marched back with Schmuel to the school. Already she had been upset to find that the girls were sent home two hours earlier than the boys. Girls needed less education, it appeared, according to this enlightened instructor who used the rod of the old-country cheder! Somehow Leah's irritation increased on the way, as they passed yard after yard, and she saw that not a spade had been turned, though she had urged the Roumanian women to start to raise their own vegetables. Since Arab women came down every day with their baskets of eggs and greens, this seemed enough for the newcomers. Leah could already see that it was not a new life they would make here, but the old one, with peasant women coming to the door to sell all that was needed. As she neared the school, she could hear the singsong recitation. What Schmulik said was true—it sounded just like in the cheder in Cherezinka.

Pulling open the door, Leah cried, "Here we speak the Sephardic Hebrew."

The melamed turned and saw her form filling the doorway. Reb Hirsch was an immaculate man; he wore a silken yarmulkeh and, even in the heat, his long alpaca coat. With his clipped beard uptilted, he had an air of self-esteem.

"Do you want to teach them yourself, Miss Chaimovitch?" He held out his pointer to her, the same one surely that had come down on Schmulik's palm.

"This is exactly what we don't need!" she cried. "We in Eretz don't teach by beating!"

"Nor do I," melamed replied quite calmly, still using the odd Ashkenazi diction. He turned to the class. The room was quite orderly, the boys sitting in the front rows, the girls in back. Most of the children had been his pupils in the old country; they were looking on with enjoyment. "Nor do I," Reb Hirsch repeated, "except when it comes to savages who unfortunately don't understand anything else." Now came a burst of laughter from the class.

All at once, it came over Leah that Schmulik had indeed been running wild. His only friends had been two Arab boys from Dja'adi, who tended a small flock of goats, and with them he swam, wrestled, climbed, explored caves.

"A quiet word, perhaps?" Reb Hirsch approached, and feeling herself awkward in the doorway, Leah retreated to give him room; in the entry, the teacher revealed to her that Schmulik had mocked him, and hurled a book at his back. As to the melamed's brand of Hebrew, "I am aware, gveret, that the Sephardic accent has been adopted in Eretz; as in all things, it will take a little time to change our ways. I am, as you see, attached to tradition, but also somewhat emancipated; I have not come here to impose the old ways on the new."

He really was not bad at all. Indeed he had cultural ideas. A great event was coming to their village at the end of the holidays, with the visit of the poet Chaim Nachman

Bialik to the new settlement—could she not do something cultural, perhaps with a group of girls? the melamed asked. Somehow Reb Hirsch had heard of her harvest dance at Sejera.

Though Leah had barely more than a week to prepare, she enlisted six of the Roumanian girls, besides Eliza, and in secrecy rehearsed a surprise. The idea had come to her from watching Yaffaleh with her geese. Eliza would be the proud mother floating with her neck arched, and the other girls her brood. All in white. And then at the end they would all chant a famous poem by Chaim Nachman Bialik, "To a Bird," and there would be a presentation of flowers.

The girls were as excited indeed as a flock of birds, but when the movements had already been learned, it was clear that Eliza was too small to represent the mother-goose. Eliza herself saw it—she would look ridiculous, she declared to Leah. And as by a single thought, all the girls together cried out that Leah herself must be the mother. Leah demurred. How would she look, a big fat cow among the slender little girls? People would laugh. But the girls clung to her and insisted; she looked so beautiful when she showed them the movements, they said. After Leah had tried to get Dvora to do it, and Dvora had proven absolutely unable to manage the little stretching movements with the neck, she at last gave in and took the role.

Arriving with a whole party of dignitaries in a fleet of three carriages, the poet, a portly man of serious appearance, with a large imposing head, apologized that he had only a brief time to spend at their settlement, as he had yet to move onward to the kvutsoth. Then as Issachar Bronescu's welcoming speech went on and on, it seemed there would be no time for the "cultural program." Except for the diasppointment this would be to her girls, Leah was almost glad. But the speech ended in time after all, and Bronescu's eldest son, Tsutsig, who played Mendelssohn on the harmonica, began their accompaniment.

Leah, in a full white robe made from an abaya, which she feared would bring laughter, moved forward, with the little girls in their floating white tulle costumes moving behind her.

No one had yet laughed. Then when Leah turned her head this way and that, stretching it in the movements that were meant to make them laugh, the laughter came. She could have hugged the whole crowd! Now moving sedately, she chanted the poem's first line, and the soft voices of the girls rose behind her in response.

> Singing, singing, O my birdling,
> Sing the wonders of the land
> Where spring forever dwells . . .
>
> Falls the dew like pearls on Hermon
> From the snowy heights descending
> Tearlike, does it fall?

Leah, the girls, and then everyone turned their heads toward the snow-topped Hermon. Like a prophecy was the poem, heard here!

> How fare Jordan's shining waters
> How the hills and how the hillocks
> And the mountains all?
>
> And the laborers my brothers,
> Have not those who sowed with weeping
> Reaped with song and psalm?
>
> Oh that I had wings to fly with,
> Fly unto the land where flourish
> Almond tree and palm!

At the end, as the goslings all clustered close around her as though under her broad wings, there was a great burst of applause, and she was sure she heard the voice of Bialik himself crying "Bravo!"

The poet came forward and took her hand in both of his. He asked her name. Then he declared, "Leah, you are a living poem, and each of your girls is a verse of song!"

It was more wonderful than the harvest dance in Sejera. But all was not yet over; the gift was yet to be presented. The flock of girls floated to one side, and Yaffaleh Chaimovitch stepped forward. On this day, with white bows in her long braids, and in a pink dress with ruffles that Feigel had made for her, Yaffaleh looked only as awkward as other little girls look in their clumsy stage. Her face alight, she carried a huge bouquet and presented it to the poet with the words, "Twenty-seven different kinds of flowers grown in our own gardens."

The beaming poet was so affected that many said they saw him brush tears from his eyes. "Twenty-seven blessings," he said, "on the daughters of Mishkan Yaacov, who have garlanded my visit with beauty."

Feigel, holding Mati in her arms, and with Yankel beside her, heaved such a proud sigh of nachess that the poet recognized her as the mother and came over, offering his felicitations, even declaring yes, yes, he had already heard of the Chaimovitch family, heard great things, and he was sure much more would be heard of them!

It was indeed the day of the Chaimovitches, everyone declared!

On a Thursday, toward sundown, a visitor rode up to the Chaimovitch yard. Dvora was the first to see him, but she did not on the instant recognize Menahem. He was even darker, his eyes were more impenetrable than ever, though when he spoke his Shalom to her, they glimmered with a golden touch of warmth, like a kerosene flame in a dark corner.

Menahem had come for her, Dvora felt at once, but she gave herself no recognition or response to this feeling. "Shalom, Menahem," she said. "It's a long time since we saw you."

Nearly a year, he reminded her.

"You have been away?" Nothing had been heard of him, she had just realized.

He had gone to live with a tribe of Bedouin in the south, he said, so as to learn something of their ways, as well as to learn to speak Arabic.

Gidon and Tateh were just coming in from the fields; it seemed to Dvora that Menahem must have calculated to arrive at this hour, and as they all went into the house, the entire family greeted him warmly. Yet Feigel had to persuade him to stay for the meal, for he was really on the way to the kvutsa, Menahem said. "But at least you must take something in your mouth," and so he sat down with them.

There was an important meeting at the kvutsa, Menahem said, for at last the men of the Shomer were going to establish their own settlement, and it was from Reuven's

kvutsa, now called HaKeren, that they planned to set forth.
All the chaverim and chaveroth would be coming, a whole
crowd, to help the Shomer's settlement get started in its
first days. Suddenly he declared to Dvora and Leah—not
to Dvora alone—"You must come too!" And then—to
Dvora—"We are even bringing an incubator!"

For the rest of the meal, Menahem talked more to Gidon than to anyone else, relating things he had learned
among the Bedouin. For example, he explained how, by
examining a camel's track, they could tell you the age of
the beast and with what he was laden. He told how by their
tribal laws the test of fire on the tongue was still used to
know if a man was telling the truth; he had himself seen it
administered, and there was a degree of effectiveness in it,
perhaps because a guilty man's mouth became dry out of
fear. And other such things he talked of. Then he had to
leave; he took messages for Reuven, and repeated that
Dvora and Leah should come to the founding, Galil and
Nadina had sent their greetings and wanted the girls to
come.

"He is a strange one," Leah remarked, as though to begin a discussion, but Dvora felt no need to talk of him.

There were over thirty chaverim now at HaKeren and several new cabins had been built. The old stone relic was
used only as an eating and meeting place.

In the compound just now, there were a number of wagons, and several tents had been put up, for the whole of
Sejera seemed to have arrived, preparing to go out and
found the new settlement of the Shomer at the foot of
Mount Gilboa.

When Dvora and Leah reached the kvutsa, most of the
chevreh were inside at a sitting which it appeared had been
going on all day and night. Up at the front table sat Galil
and Nadina, and there also was Reuven, who for the moment was chairman, while Max Wilner was secretary. An
expert, a Professor Bodenheimer from Berlin, Leah already
had heard, had been brought by the Zionist office to help
with the formation of the new cooperative settlements.
There he stood, wearing a suit with a collar and necktie,
answering questions about his "plan." But each question
was a long rambling speech, and Reuven didn't feel he
should cut short a chaver, so that when slow-speaking Shim-

ek began one of his dissertations, repeating what everyone already knew, it was Nadina who broke in, asking him first to wait for the Professor's replies.

It seemed that the expert had devised an entire cooperative system, more perfect than what had been learned in the experiences of the first kvutsa. The new system was to be a complex structure in which each member shared equally up to a certain point, but beyond that there were special rewards for excellence in production. But all this applied only to the men, and Nadina was outraged. "What about women?" the Firebrand raised her eternal outcry. "Are we chattels?"

For the women the professor proposed a separate cooperative of their own which would undertake, on contract with the watchmen's cooperative, to operate the kitchen and laundry, the poultry run and perhaps the dairy.

In the midst of the dispute over this, someone interjected, "What about the members with aged or sick parents in need of aid? Shouldn't such chaverim receive special allowances? Shouldn't the principle be 'To each according to his needs'?" And the hubbub became so great that Reuven put his hands to both ears, while Max Wilner took the gavel from him and banged on the table.

Going outside, Dvora caught a glimpse of Menahem; he was sitting on a bench with the weary air of one who had heard it all and knew the outcome and would re-enter only when the palaver was over, and things needed to be done. He was telling a newly arrived chalutz about the Bedouin, and Dvora had a feeling that Menahem even raised his voice for her to hear. "They wanted me to remain," he was saying. "The sheikh offered me one of his daughters for a bride and even without bride money." Isn't it an offense to refuse? "I told him my choice was already made among my own people, and that with us a man has only one wife."

Dvora wandered away.

They marched out from HaKeren on Sunday morning, a whole column of them, singing. Ahead rode Galil and both of the Zeira brothers in full regalia, with crossed bandoliers and streaming head-cloths. Some forty chaverim marched along, and a dozen chaveroth, the men and many of the girls with mattocks over their shoulders. Then came wagons carrying plows, fodder, tents, large milk-canisters filled with tea, sacks of bread, huge baskets of cucumbers and tomatoes, pails and washtubs and a helter-skelter of axes, saws and building materials Rahel had appeared from Jerusalem—would she miss such an occasion—though Avner could not come. She strode along with Leah and Dvora, singing and chattering. Menahem, among the mounted, rode by, back and forth along the column; each time he smiled down to them and waved, but he seemed preoccupied. When a stop was made for a meal, he appeared and sat with them amidst a group of chaverim, yet paying Dvora no particular attention. It was as though everything that would happen must happen, but as yet he still left her free.

Before sundown they reached the site, above a rill water at the foot of Mount Gilboa; Ain Harod, the spring was called, and each began to repeat to the others that this was the historic spring where Gideon had tested his warriors, watching as they knelt to drink, discarding those who knelt with their mouths to the stream, vulnerable to attack, and taking only those who raised the water in their cupped hands, while eyeing the plain warily.

The eyes of the settlers too were on the plain. Their apprehension was for fever and swamp. But how open, how vast was the flatland. And what a sky! This they repeated to each other while some put up tents, and others began to chop away the tangle of high brambles from the ground where the yard would be; still others, with the eager explanation that no one ever knew what the Turks might get into their wooden heads to claim against you, hitched mules to four plows and went out to make long furrows in every direction.

Menahem had a special task. With Galil he rode across the neck of the plain toward a mound that rose up from the flatness, a tel—some said these hillocks were places where ancient villagers for centuries had dumped their offal, since Arabs did not make use of it as manure. Others said they were the sites of the ancient villages themselves, covered with the dust of the ages. Near the tel, the riders came to a cluster of black tents belonging to Bedouin who encamped here every spring. It was Menahem's task now to conduct the greeting of peace.

It was for this, after the troubles in Sejera last year, that he had been sent off on his mission, following a sitting at which he himself, in anguish over the death of Yechezkiel, his closest friend, had cried out, "To be strong—good; to take revenge—we must be ready when necessary. But we have come here to live, not to kill and be killed. And what do we know of these people? Why don't we learn their ways, and their language, and how to live in the same land with them?"

Galil had backed Menahem's view, pointing out that although a few such attempts had haphazardly been made and a few adventurers had gone out among the Bedouin, an orderly approach to the problem was now a necessity. And so Menahem had been assigned to the task. It was not so much the settled villagers as the Bedouin who were the raiders and attackers—that must be understood; even the bandits of Fuleh were only a generation away from the life of the tents, Ostrov the Landbuyer pointed out, and with Ostrov himself, Menahem had journeyed down to Gaza, to the house of a notable who welcomed the Landbuyer as a brother. From there, after a few days of hospitality, Menahem had ridden off alongside a son of the notable to a mud-hut village near Beersheba, linked to the same family. After a time there, he had gone into the Negev region to herdsmen in their tents, living with the sheikh, also of the same clan. All this had been slow, and, Menahem would admit to Galil and some others, mostly tedious. Though as to tedium, he had found himself drifting back into a state of tranquillity that he had learned to attain in long voyages as a seaman.

He had gone out with the herds and learned something of sheep and goats, he had sat through hours of small talk about weathersigns, and accounts of remarkable feats of horsemanship, he had smoked the narghileh and in long silences punctuated by remarks of wisdom, sometimes sayings from the Koran, or even tales of the Patriarch Abraham, he had come to feel almost as one of them. He had nodded at the right time, and smoked kif, and after he had picked up enough of the language to speak, he had told of some of the wonders he had seen in the outside world. It was mostly of America they wanted to hear, of the riches and wonders.

Of long-standing feuds he had also learned, unending tribal feuds over the use of a well, or over a violated daughter, or an insult that had to be avenged. Of the small

signal flag on a tent that told of a marriageable daughter he
also knew, as he knew the unceasing copulation-jokes
among the young men who had no bride money, no
woman to lie with, and also he was laughingly shown the
sport of using a sheep. All this was as the bestiality he had
touched time and again in the bleak life of a sailor and
wandering laborer; to be a man among men, one had to
share in their contaminations, though, in the seven years of
his world-wandering from adolescence to manhood, all this
had passed through him much as a gonorrheal dripping
and fiery injections that finally cleaned it out. So after
those years, when a voyage had carried him back to
Odessa, Menahem had remained among the Jews, taken up
with the good lads of Kostarnitza, told them his tales of
adventure, and joined them to come to Eretz. The bed-
bugged cribs of any seaport became, for his tales, mysterious seraglios in Barcelona, a veiled Princess Fatima beckoned from the hidden rear door to a walled garden in
Alexandria, the flea-ridden filthy cot of a grimy Bowery
hotel became a room with a private bath and the miracle of
electric light, and a voyage on a train of cattlecars, watering the doomed beasts and shoveling out the steaming
droppings, became a cowboy's odyssey over the vast spaces
of the American wild west.

So now, as Menahem lived his season with the Bedouin,
absorbing the tales on their side of some legendary invader
of harems, or of the faithful love of a steed for its master,
he became meanwhile as agile on a horse as any of the tribe,
and learned the rhythms of coffee-pounding, and the contemptuous epithets of the tent dweller for the settled villager
whose soul was soft as donkey shit; he heard tales of long
ago and not so long ago, tales of herds of sheep and of cattle, but best, of horses cleanly driven off from the possession
of the plodding tillers of the soil, the spineless fellaheen.
But these were not habitual raiders, the Beni Aghil; such
things happened when they happened. Sometimes, too, on
the mat of the skeikh, there would unwind probing discussions with him, touching on the forefathers of long ago, the
cleverness of Jacob in winning all the striped sheep from
his father-in-law, though some said this was no longer true
of the marking of sheep; others told tales of Ishmael, the
true first son of Abraham.

And so now among the Bedouin near Gilboa, when the

greetings of peace had been exchanged, and Menahem and Galil had been welcomed into the guest tent, and while the coffee was being pounded, and as Menahem passed excellent Turkish cigarettes to the half-dozen men who had gathered, he was able to acquit himself well. He spoke of the Beni Aghil, where he was as a son, and the tribe was favorably known to the meager little sheikh with whom they sat, who stemmed from below Beit She'an. Delicately Menahem probed as to their numbers, and their habits of movement, and let it be known that he and Galil were of the Shomer. Of them indeed the sheikh said he had heard much, as excellent horsemen and men of honor. Many more compliments were exchanged, with probings on each side, until at last the time came to make clear that the men of the Shomer would be dwelling nearby, and that they wished to dwell in harmony together, for were not all of them sons of Abraham? The sheikh and his sons would be eagerly awaited in the settlement, so that the men of the Shomer would have the honor of offering them hospitality. And if medicine was needed for the eyes of their children, or if there was any other such need, the house of the Shomer was their house.

So, with a last ceremonial coffee, and a last distribution of cigarettes, the visit was ended, and Menahem and Galil rode back, agreeing in their assessment that good relations could be established; the lands of the kvutsa were well outside the seasonal grazing area of these Bedouin.

The chaverim were gathered around the campfire. A kettle steamed on the rocks to be picked up now and again for replenishing a mug of tea. Leah's voice joined in the workless Hasidic melody that someone had launched into the air, and other voices joined. Menahem squatted down beside Dvora.

The tales of Menahem's voyages she had heard in the evenings when he had sat with her and Yechezkiel; he would draw from his wanderings and adventures until you wondered what to believe, and just when you decided it was all imaginings, something would be proven true, not that Menahem cared to offer proof. But someone else on another day might mention an event, a person who had figured in Menahem's tale. Thus, he had taken part in a revolutionary plot to assassinate the Czar and his ministers; Nadina the

Firebrand, as everyone knew, had escaped capture in these events only by a hair. Once Menahem told of having received a pistol in St. Petersburg from a certain Lutek. And from Nadina, Dvora had at some other time heard how she had delivered a pistol to a certain Lutek. There could be no doubt that Menahem had done something there, escaping "in his own way." And he would simply go on to relate the adventures in Africa, in Brazil—he could speak Portuguese and English too, and yet he seemed to take none of this as of any consequence.

How much and how little need a man reveal of himself for a woman to join her life to his? With Yechezkiel there had been nothing that needed revealing—a great stalwart boy, goodhearted through and through, cheerful when his body was active, when he rode, when he worked in the field, a great eater, and she had simply felt love. All year Dvora had tried to think about that love. Not only to feel, but to think. Around her she could see husbands and wives, her own mother and father, with no flush of tenderness ever between them, and yet in their late years they had produced a child. It seemed that, when the time came, something had to happen in a woman, and in the life that continued from then onward, a man and a woman always managed to find things to talk about together; they talked of each thing needed and wanted in the house, and then of their children, their neighbors, their relatives, so that all this together must take the place of that first romantic time of overwhelming love.

When she thought of Yechezkiel now, she felt a love and sorrow that was oddly very much like the love and sorrow over dear little Avramchick. And the thought came to Dvora that Menahem was aware of this change in her grieving and that it was for this Menahem had waited— that in his being near her in the last days and yet making no advances, no claim on her, Menahem had in some wonderfully considerate way been sensing out all this that she now recognized in herself. He had been sensing out whether he could not come nearer and enter her life.

For the first time, though so little had been said between them, she experienced a sweep of endearment toward him, for the delicacy of his thoughts for her. And in this she could not know that all through the time of his absence Menahem in the subterranean way that was part of his being had known what was taking place with her. At intervals he had come with his Bedouin "brother," the sheikh's eldest son, for pleasure in Gaza, and passing through Beer Tuvia had managed to pick up a word of the doings of the Chaimovitch girls; once Galil and Nadina together had come down to the Negev in a horseback journey they had taken to study the whole of the land, and brought him news of all that was happening in Sejera and all Galilee, about the Chaimovitches and about the Roumanians arriving in Mishkan Yaacov, and thus he had known that Dvora was there at home.

The circle around the blackened teakettle had dwindled, and Dvora realized that Menahem was speaking to her alone, as though continuing a long conversation they had been having about his visit with Galil to the Bedouin over there across the plain. "You know, Dvora, they sit there in their tents, and here we have come in our tents, perhaps like Abraham coming among the Canaanites—" It was a thought that many had vaguely felt tonight. But Menahem jumped to something else. "When I was a boy, I went once with my stepfather to a Russian village where there were no Jews—"

But she had never known Menahem had a stepfather. The way he talked to her now was different from the way he had talked when he told his adventures. With one ear she heard him tell of his stepfather who bought pelts from the peasant hunters and bragged of tricking the thickheads who were even unable to add, but with the other ear, Dvora caught the story of his childhood, the household of stepbrothers and stepsisters, his sense that they were all in league against him, of his labor of carrying piles of pelts and drying them, of his mother who was always groaning and waiting for calamities. He talked on and on. The singing had died out with the fire; at one moment, Leah passed by on her way to the large tent for chaveroth, and Dvora said, "I'll come later." His words glinting with irony and bitterness, Menahem talked on, of his cheder and of how, before his Bar Mitzvah, he had organized a plot to beat up the melamed, and how his stepfather had given the beating back to him with a broad leather strap, and then shipped him off to the strictest of yeshivot, in Volozhin. Could she imagine that for a time he had been intensely religious? Night and day he had devoured the Talmud. The Cabbala had attracted him, though it was forbidden to study its mysteries before the age of forty. Meanwhile he had organized a revolutzia for the students to be allowed to read books of mathematical science. The yeshiva had cut off their food, the other boys had given in, and he, expelled, had gone not home, but to Odessa. . . .

It had grown chilly. Another would have put his arm around her, drawn her close. All at once, Menahem stood and gave her his hand, raising her up, It was the first contact of the flesh with him, a hand not aflame but holding a dry heat as of the sun. Dvora left her hand in his. They walked in silence and her blood made her dizzy. They came to a small tent, and it was Menahem's alone, though all the other chevrehmen shared three and four in a shelter. Menahem was one of those, Yechezkiel had told her admiringly, who in his own way, without asking special favors or taking advantage, always managed to arrange himself.

He drew her inside, and, stooping to kneel on the rush mat, she came into his arms.

Menahem would know just what to do; he was a man. With her innocent Yechezkiel, would either of them have known what gesture to make next? Menahem's kiss was solemn, and then, his voice half-strangled, he said, "Dvora, long before, already on the boat—"

A distracting, almost frightening perception came to her. Could she even then have been seeking him, through the other? Was it Menahem to whom she had been going all the time? Or was some powerful law of life working within her, telling her this had to be so from the beginning, to make it possible for her still to believe that there is in life only one profound love? "Yes, on the boat, I knew," she said.

Some things, Menahem said, he had retained from his period of intense faith and belief. The idea of the destined one, the besherteh. Only the idea of destiny could explain the cruelty and tragedy he had seen in the world. Destiny had to be ruthless. And yet he also believed in the human will. Did she understand?

Dvora half smiled in the darkness.

And in that moment she felt entirely at ease. She raised her arms and unpinned her hair. Within the tent was black dark, but a sound came from Menahem at this movement of hers, a sound of such immeasurable relief that she was

carried back to the time of their ship's approach to Jaffa,
after the long voyage they had undertaken with such fear
of its perils, and their worry—would their loved brother
and sister truly be waiting there on the shore? And then
came the blessed moment of crying out. "They're here!
They're waiting for us!"

Both were kneeling; Dvora undid her dress, and knew he
too was casting off his clothing. Then they lay down together
on the mat; Menahem was trembling.

7

The settlement of Gilboa itself soon became a mother of
settlements, as chalutzim went out from it just as the men of
the Shomer and their friends had gone out from HaKeren
in a line of wagons. They went out now to found another
and another kvutsa in the Emek.

Dvora's marriage ceremony was held when she became
pregnant; indeed four couples in succession were married
that day in Gilboa, and as a concession to certain leaders in
the Zionist movement who gave ear to all sorts of silly
gossip about the kvutsoth, a rabbi was brought from Chedera to perform the rites.

The feast was marked by a great triumph for Reuven
Chaimovitch. For nearly two years Reuven had been trying
to grow potatoes. In Yavniel, in Sejera, even in Rishon he
had been told by those who had tried before him that the
matter was hopeless. Potatoes simply would not grow in
Eretz Yisroel. Planted, they rotted in the ground. If by some
miracle they sprouted, the result looked like a crumpled
worm covered with blight.

Again and again, in HaKeren, Reuven had planted potatoes brought, after much correspondence, by chalutzim
arriving from Russia. And his spoiled potatoes had become
such a jest with Max Wilner and other chaverim that he
dared experiment no further.

Then in a Russian agricultural magazine he chanced
upon an account of a potato blight in the Don region that

had ended when seed potatoes were imported from Ireland, where only the hardiest plants had survived the terrible blight of a decade before, when much of the population had starved to death.

And so, virtually in secret, Reuven had gone about procuring seed potatoes of the Irish variety. Not daring to have Max find out what he was up to, he had had the samples sent to Mishkan Yaacov and had planted them in the garden at home. Leah had cared for them.

And behold, just before the family was to leave for Dvora's marriage, he and Leah had dug up their first potatoes, firm, unblemished, and succulent even raw.

There was a touch of slyness in Reuven. Everyone, every Zionist notable from Jerusalem and the new Jewish town of Tel Aviv, and from Sejera, and also those from his own kvutsa who had sneered at his failed experiments, would be at the festivities in Gilboa. And so, with stealth, not even letting the rest of the family know, he and Leah had packed a sack of these very first potatoes in the wagon beneath all the good things Feigel was taking to her second daughter.

And while all the others were busy with a thousand greetings, Leah found a grater, and in the shanty that had been put up for an extra kitchen, she set to work grating her potatoes. The first to discover her secret was Rahel, who put a finger into the batter. "Real potatoes?" she asked, surprised, and Leah announced, "The first in Eretz. Reuven grew them."

"No! But it's been proven impossible! They rot!"

"Reuven grew them."

Despite the rapid expansion of the Gilboa kvutsa, the cooking was still being done as it had been in the beginning, over an outdoor fire on a tin grate resting on stones. As the odor of the first potato pancakes rose into the air, Tibor the Comical from HaKeren, walking by, suddenly halted in his tracks. He sniffed, and cried out, "Latkes? Real latkes?" and with one swoop of his hand snatched the first browned potato pancake that Leah was sliding onto a plate, crushing fully half of it into his mouth.

Gasping with the pain of the burn, he nevertheless devoured the second half, only blowing on it a bit, with impatience, while Leah and Rahel doubled over with laughter.

"Nu, it was worth it!" Tibor gasped and reached for another. "May my tongue burn out if it isn't ambrosia!"

From then on it was a stampede. Vainly Leah pleaded that they let her set aside a pile for the feast. Vainly the sated Tibor stationed himself by her as a pancake guard, proclaiming that he was the Shomer Latkes. Could he refuse a sample to Dovidl? And Avner? And after their leaders, why, the chaverim demanded, should there be such favoritism for the privileged? Around, and behind, and under, the chevrehmen darted, teasing, pleading, snatching. Leah hit at their hands, shouted epithets in Yiddish and Arabic, choked on her own laughter and the smoke from the griddle, while they kept calling out, "Leah! Beloved! One latke!" "My soul perisheth for a latke!"

As she scraped up the last of the batter, Leah called out, "Chevreh, have mercy! It was Reuven who at last grew potaotes in Eretz, and he wasn't even had a taste."

At this a roar arose for Reuven, who was hovering at the edge of the crowd, grinning almost guiltily. Ceremoniously, the chalutzim opened a circle and drew him in. As the last pancake was lifted from the griddle, Rahel took it on a plate and offered it to him. "Our own Aaron Aaronson!" she cried.

Reuven loved her again. He loved her with the purest of comradely love. He forgave her in his heart for what she had said about his wild wheat at Sejera. If he ever succeeded in getting a good strain of date palms, she would be the first to taste the fruit.

As for Leah, in this moment her entire being overflowed with love, her love embraced all the chalutzim, all, all, and the whole Emek stretching before them, and all the fields growing green, and the whole Eretz, she could embrace the whole of the land and hug it to her body, and be appeased.

The big girl was restive. For a time she stayed in the new kvutsa, working one day in the kitchen, another day with the field crew, or even the construction crew, or suddenly, she would ask for a pair of mules so she could plow up a plot for vegetables. She kept changing her sleeping place. When the extra crowd of helpers who had come for the founding moved on, Leah remained the only one in the girls' tent; the few others had coupled off. At once Zev the

Hotblood, posted here on guard, began annoying her. He seemed to take it for granted that he could enter the tent in the middle of the night for "a little visit," in accordance with a legend he had already made for himself when he had been the night watchman in Mescha and again in Yavniel. It was said he would slip in through the bedroom windows of grown daughters and even of young wives whose husbands were away, for "little visits" between his rounds. Indeed he had been sent away from Mescha after he had been seen climbing out of a back window one night from a house where the husband was absent; he had only been having a glass of tea to warm himself, Zev said. In this case the husband happened to be disliked by the whole of the village as an ill-tempered brute who wouldn't share the flame of a match with a neighbor, so to spare the wife the complaint had been against Zev's repeated absence from duty. But wherever he went there was scandal.

Oddly, in Gilboa the chaverim seemed to take it almost as a joke that Zev was pestering Leah. Surely a girl her size need not worry about being overpowered! And when she complained, Nadina even delivered her a piece of intimate womanly advice about deprivation, and psychologia, and normal life in the atmosphere of a close community, concluding with a strong hint about comrades helping each other in their natural needs.

Though everyone in the new kvutsa urged her to stay, it suddenly came to Leah how much Mameh must need her at home now that Dvora was no longer there to help. And her group of girls there in Mishkan Yaacov—after the dance for the poet Bialik, they had kept together around her, and she was teaching them vegetable gardening—her girls also were in need of her. Besides, Leah was overcome with longing for her baby brother Mati and the clever questions he had begun to ask about the sun and the stars and the universe, when Tateh, as soon as the little one could talk, tried to teach him, "In the Beginning . . ."

Coming home, Leah was startled at the way little Eliza in these few weeks had turned into a whole new young person! There was a new touch of decisiveness in her voice, yet this was softened by an appealing touch of girlish womanly complicity in her glance. It took a look from Mameh to make Leah realize what had happened—Eliza's first menstruation had come, and now the pisherkeh comported herself as a full equal, or even more, as a young woman who would know better than they had how to manage her life.

When Leah, coming in from field work, pulled off her hobnailed shoes, Eliza would pointedly lift them at finger-edge and set them outside the door. As for herself, Eliza had always been dainty. In the market stalls of Tiberias she had bargained in Arabic through three separate visits for a pair of red harem slippers embroidered with glittering slivers of mica, until the beset vendor cried Allah save him! this girl would make her husband rich and all merhcants poor! And he gave in to her price.

These slippers Eliza wore about the house, and strangely, while everyone else's things lost luster or became bedraggled, Eliza's dainty footwear lasted quite well, the embroidery never losing its glitter.

In that great trunk brought from the old country she had found some shirtwaists of their mother's, blouses with lace cuffs and frills down the front, and with a little needlework Eliza had arranged them so that even on a weekday, should a visitor come to the door, the young lady looked dressed for Sabbath. Unlike Leah or Dvora, she loved to sew and crochet, and from an Arab woman in Dja'adi who still came down with eggs and cheese to sell to the Roumanians, Eliza had learned how to weave straw, so that the house was now adorned with her bright-colored mats.

Though little Mati always rushed into Leah's arms for her great hug when she came home from field work, the elder sister saw that he was quite happy to tag all day after Eliza, and if he tripped, it was to Eliza that he would present his bumped nose for the kiss that made it well.

Nor were Leah's village girls so constantly around her. While a few kept up their gardens, they were now in the age of intimate whispery friendships, like Eliza with Bronescu's daughter Malka, spending much of their time visiting each other back and forth.

The worst was that Zev the Hotblood, from whom she had fled, now appeared in Mishkan Yaacov on duty as shomer. No other than Zev had Galil found for them! A treat for the Roumanian wives! Quartered in a shed behind Bronescu's store, Zev never passed Leah without a leer and a vulgar invitation. "Nu, Leah, you know where to find me! Better than Zev you won't find anywhere!" Or, with a heavily-brushing palm too low on her back, "Ah, what a waste of good woman-flesh!"

One moonlit night Zev managed to get at her. A cow whose labor was delayed had to be watched during the night, and on the second night Leah insisted that Gidon must get his rest while she took his place in the stable, sleeping on the hay.

It was not the poor troubled beast that awakened her, but deep in the night Leah started awake to a presence. Zev was stretched out on the hay, his large hand hovering over her breast, and his face raised above hers so that were she to cry out his mouth would stop her. Even in the bluish darkness Leah saw his expression, the eyes intent as though everything was already understood and happening between them and he was watching on a woman's face her passion rising and overcoming her. And his own features usually so heavy, with the full lips so repulsive to her, now were changed, drawn into harmony in a man's glowing power.

She had to force herself to pull away to the other side, deeper into the straw, but Zev's hand followed and clamped down upon her breast. Like some obscurely admitted rule of the night-game between men and women, a rigidity came over her that forbade her simply to throw off the hand. For then, if her movement aroused him further, it would become a matter of struggle between bodies alone.

"Zev, let me be," she said. "You have nothing to do here."

"I came because you summoned me." Leah had not expected him to speak with such inner knowledge of women, but only crudely. Ah, he was experienced. The hand exerted a slight pressure as though of its own weight; already he was showing her that he could be skilled and delicate in his caress.

"Zev, I don't want to have trouble with you. You've come to the wrong place. There's no tea here."

"Milk is even better." With a knowing, testing look in the corner of his eye, his head with the lips parted was moving downward to her breast, and this time she wrenched herself free. "Go about your watch!"

"I was far on the other side when I felt your call," he said, without stirring. "I felt you were lying here on the hay, alone, longing for a man. That's true, isn't it? This you cannot deny. So, in answer to your longing, and to my own desire for you, I was drawn and I came."

"Your own desire for me or for any other female flesh! Get out!" And with this Leah sat erect. Zev stirred, and gazed at her as though there was no need for him to rise, since she must soon lie down again alongside him.

"Leah," he said with a different tone, the easy intimate tone used by a man to a woman he has already lain with, and with whom he can be frank and comradely, "Leah, with each other you and I don't have to have pretenses. You are a passionate woman who has far too long been deprived of her man, and I have a great lust for you. One superior article deserves another. I know that between you and me it would be something extraordinary."

At least he had reverted to his own crude self. Over her distaste there nevertheless rose a dismaying wonder—could it be that Moshe had talked loosely about her even to one such as Zev, that he had boastingly described her most abandoned ecstasies the way one man does to another? Were Moshe and this Zev not after all the same sort, hunters of women?

And even this dismay in her, the brute also caught. A boor endowed with delicate sensitivity about women. "Why be angry? If a man praises a woman to another man, it's the best compliment. After all, most of the women a man lies with are nothing but holes—"

"Zev, enough of your foul mouth. Get out of here." This time she jumped to her feet. At least she was fully dressed, having lain down in her clothes, thinking she might have to fetch help during the night.

"Leah, there are so few women a man can talk to without pretenses. Believe me, if there was even a chance that your man would be coming back one of these days, I wouldn't approach you. But why should we both suffer such strong need—"

"Go satisfy your need with the nearest she-goat," Leah found herself blurting coarsely. "I'm not an animal."

"Nor entirely am I." He too had at last risen from the hay, and Zev was facing her with the air of a man who, having been insulted, has a certain right of response. "I am not so much an animal as you would like me to be. Because in that case you wouldn't feel in danger of wanting me."

"All right, you are an idealist, a benefactor of womankind. I still don't want you. Can you believe it?"

He stood without moving closer, a man fully aware of his potency. There was no denying this about Zev. It was not a potency such as had emanated cleanly and insistently from Moshe, for from Zev it reeked. The stable was the place for it, it was part of the animal odor, and to Leah's angered shame, she felt herself as though steeped in the after-odor of cohabitation, of two bodies in bed when the seed has already been spent and a wallowing lust is again awakening.

"Don't play the delicate maiden with me," Zev said, with his eyes deliberately denuding her. "I know the things women tell each other about men, the same way men tell each other about women when there's a partner that's something special. The women that are real women—they tell each other about me—isn't it true? I've even had some women admit they couldn't rest until they tried me, to find out if all they had heard could really be true." He laughed grossly.

There was such a childish sexual pride in the lout bragging of his prowess that Leah was able to laugh. Poor foolish Zev, he had himself released her. And with this Leah became fully awake, all her startled night-feelings, her half-immersion in a seductive drowsiness, were fallen away and she even found herself, in a partly amused clarity, with a certain sympathy for the lout. For what else was Zev but the most bumptious of all men of the Shomer—a braggart, a liar, a troublemaker!

Yet in spite of everything, some quality held people to him. There was a force, a self-belief, a power around him as though he were not merely a watchman on a horse but a creature of an important destiny who was meanwhile filling in with ordinary tasks, awaiting his time.

"Yes, Zev," she said, "you are famous among women. All the wives in Mishkan Yaacov confide in each other. Each morning they count up between themselves how many you visited the night before, and describe to each other the fantastic things you did to them! They come and tempt me with their revelations until my whole body burns for you! Ay, ay, Zev, do you want to know what we really say about you? We say that in spite of being such a braggart and a nuisance, you're a courageous shomer and an excellent horseman, only you're sure to make trouble if you stay long in one place, because there are always a few miserable unhappy women who desperately try to get a little pleasure, so they let you in. Everyone agrees the best thing for you, and even for the Shomer, would be to get you married, but what girl would want to risk herself with such a lout? That's what we say."

A whole series of attitudes had come over him. At first Zev had listened with a broad smile as though to say: Go on, make fun of me, you'll be like all the rest and lie down with me in the end; then he seemed a bit uncertain whether he should not after all show offense. A woman could refuse him, but there was no need for her to make fun of him! In the end he was like a cheating butcher who laughs when you catch him with a heavy finger on the scales. Ah, he laughs, other women are stupid, so he fools them and enjoys cheating them a bit, but you are different, with you he won't try any tricks, he will always be honest.

Then a fortunate thing happened. The cow began to go into labor. Hurriedly, Leah lighted the storm lamp; the forelegs of the calf emerged and then the birthing halted. The animal got to her feet and stood in the stall with the calf partly out; she didn't seem to feel anything at all, and began chewing fodder. After they had waited for what seemed a long while, watching with increasing anxiety, Zev, without further ado, took hold of the protruding forelegs and began a careful steady pull. The calf emerged undamaged and at once tried to rise to its wobbly legs. The mother turned her head and began to lick.

Now, on Leah's compliment on his work, Zev began to talk of his experience as a boy on his uncle's farm in the northernmost of the Baron's settlements, Metulla, on the lower slope of Mount Hermon.

Like everyone, Leah knew that Zev was an orphan of the Kishinev pogrom, and that he had been brought by an uncle to Palestine, but she knew little more. The settlers up there in Metulla were not much heard about; life there was said to be barren and poor.

His uncle had made him work without end, Zev said, and had beat him without end. Once for losing a calf—just like this it had half-emerged, he had pulled too hard and it had come out choked and dead. After the beating he had run away and lived among the Druze on the mountain ridge. There among them he had learned to ride and shoot.

—An independent boy, a bit like Gidon, she thought. But now he was bragging again about how even the Druze lads made him their leader, saying his eyes could detect animal tracks where only a shadow had passed. And "by my life" he swore, telling about the slim, smooth-skinned Arab girls who had stolen to him in the fields where he tended the sheep, and taught him their special ways of making love. No—seriously! It was unimaginable! He was ready—and now at least he made his offer half-comically— to show her these secrets at any time.

What a liar, Leah laughed to herself. The Druze were known to be the most watchful of all over their daughters. Still, she let Zev brag and tell of his adventures: Of how the sheikh himself had offered him a daughter without bride-money (just like Menahem's tales!) and how he had even been initiated into the secret rites of the Druze religion. Oh, he could not reveal a single detail, it was truly secret, but every year, as she knew, their tribes gathered not far from here, on the other end of the Kinnereth, on the rock ledge known as the Horns of Hittim, and if she wished, he would take her, though women of course had to remain outside the secret conclave.

"Exactly like the yearly meeting of the Shomer," Leah snorted. "That's what you are in the Shomer—no more advanced than those superstitious tribes with their secrets for males only."

In the end Zev had come away to the Galilee and become a shomer. "Something called me to my own people," he said. "Leah, you will laugh at me. Everyone thinks of me as a yold. An ignoramus. I am. I admit it, I am not proud of it. When Galil and Nadina and the rest of them start with their theories from books and their arguments, who am I to give an opinion? I let them talk and I walk out. But I can tell you that after talking all night and breaking their heads, howling 'Borochov said this' and 'Gordon wrote that,' they come out of their sitting and do exactly what I decided we would have to do in the first place. Yes, they could all have become members of the Duma or professors in the university, they made great sacrifices to come here and ride the rounds on the fields, no better than an ignorant yold like Zev from Metulla. They

sleep with each other's chavera only after quoting Bialik to
her, but I can tell you the same hot little bitch rolls in the
goren with Zev without waiting for even a word of poetry.
All of our fine intelligentsia want to return to the soil, to
labor with their hands, to produce a new people, to remake
the Jews. It's people like me who will be produced out of
the earth of Eretz; here I am already, half a Jew, half an
Arab, and maybe this is not exactly what they are writing
about in all their literature."

What had brought him to this outburst? Did he think
that in some way she too felt herself above him? On his
lone rounds in the night, were these the forces and angers
boiling in Zev, and was it this also that drove him to seek
some woman, some haven, some way to discharge the fury
in him? Leah again felt a powerful intuition that in some
way Zev would be singled out, that an event waited for
him, and she could not be sure whether it would be something dreadful or of high worth.

Light was beginning to come, and the newborn animal
turned toward it, while the mother's tongue followed on the
still-matted skin. "Nu, I'll make us some tea after all!"
Leah said. "You can tell everyone you spent the night having tea with me!"

After that time Zev appeared more than once, coming to
the kitchen at the pre-dawn hour, for Leah had taken over
from Mama the task of rising before everyone else to prepare tea for the men. Despite all his vulgarity and loudness,
and her real dislike of much in his character, there remained between them almost the same kind of special link
there is between a man and a woman who once spent a
night in physical intimacy, a night which left them feeling
they knew the truth about each other, but which the
woman does not feel called upon to repeat.

Nevertheless Leah was restless and even a little afraid
that in some foolish moment she might give way, and make
another great mistake in her life. At times she would run
off to HaKeren for a visit with Reuven. Staying over one
Sabbath when Old Gordon held a literary meeting, she
asked Max Wilner to put her on the work sheet and stayed
on, telling herself that Eliza was now enough of a help for
Mama in the house. But not a month had passed before she
was telling her old chavera Nahama, with whom she was

now on better terms, that she was thinking of trying life in Jerusalem.

"Leah, you run around like your tail was on fire," Nahama observed. The kvutsa had voted to begin having children; she was pregnant and had taken to knitting. "Take my advice, chavera. Handsomeness is not the most important thing in a man, just as beauty is not the most important thing in a woman. . . ." All at once Leah's former irritation with sweaty Nahama came back over her.

When Leah asked leave of the kvutsa to go for a few months to Jerusalem to help Avner's Rahel start a tree nursery, even Reuven chided her. "Leah, perhaps next time the kvutsa won't accept you back."

But in Jerusalem she did feel better. With Rahel, Avner, Dovidl, she settled into what seemed a little kvutsa of their own. The courtyard where Leah had learned stonecutting was now taken over for rows of clay pots containing Rahel's seedings. Except only for Yosi the sculptor, who kept his corner, Professor Schatz had at last moved the artists and artisans to his new Bezalel building, the one on which Reuven once had labored.

Leah had arrived just in time, Rahel said, for she was eager to expand her tree nursery and also to train young girls, as Leah had done in Mishkan Yaacov. To train girls in the city of Jerusalem itself for agriculture was most important. Already Rahel had several young chalutzoth busy with watering cans over her seedlings, but she hoped even to lure daughters of the Hasidim from Mea Shearim to the work and to teach them to become women of the soil.

Somehow here Leah no longer felt that persistent inner harassment, as though she were uncertain she was in her proper place for what life must bring her. To their courtyard came the movement's every question and problem. Chalutzim would appear from all over the land to have a word with Avner, and newly arrived young men came here too; Leah could always fill an extra plate of soup and find room on the floor of someone's room for another sleeper, and all evening they would sit around the samovar that Rahel had now moved into Avner's room, holding discussions.

Just as Avner and Dovidl were a pair in their political work, so Leah and Rahel were a balanced combination. Nor did the cross-weave of the four of them feel unbalanced to her, even though Rahel and Avner were a man-and-woman pair; with herself and Dovidl there was a bond, too, almost the better for being untrammeled by sexual matters.

As to that side of life, Dovidl did not seem troubled. From time to time, one young chalutza or another would be seen about with him. Magnetic and finely made in his small-boned way, who could say that he was not handsome? But Dovidl seemed to brush sentimental matters aside as not of great consequence against the pressing and constant accumulation of "problemoth." These "problemoth" were the shared fare of their intimacy, and here Leah was made to feel that her thoughts, her advice, represented the healthy wisdom of a good devoted worker without complications or outside motives, and therefore Dovidl in the end always turned to her with his "Nu, Leah, and what do you have to say?"

But then a sum of money at last arrived for the two leaders to fulfill the plans agreed on, already a few years ago, at that fateful conference in Sejera, for Dovidl and Avner to go to Turkey to study and prepare to enter Ottoman politics, perhaps eventually to seek election to represent Palestine in the Young Turk parliament. From the Labor Zionists among the needle trades in America there came a collection to be used especially for this purpose.

Two Arab notables from Jerusalem held seats there in Constantinople, and were even proposing resolutions against the sale of land to Jews—while their own families went on selling. It was only to drive up the prices, Ostrov the Landbuyer said. But as there were more Jews than Arabs in Jerusalem, if the religious ones could be got to vote, surely at least one seat could be gained.

Soon after Dovidl and Avner had gone off, Rahel took it into her head to go and study agronomy in France; somehow she would support herself by giving lessons. And despite Yosi the sculptor whistling at his work in the yard, and despite all the chevreh who came and went, Leah felt alone in Jerusalem.

8

ONLY a few years. And from the slope of Gilboa you could see, instead of a jungled marshland, long slices of cultivated soil, patterns of red and yellow and green, not only of the Shomer's kvutsa, but of a new settlement behind it, a larger one, calling itself a kibbutz. And there was a third, edging down the flat expanse of the Emek. But all this was not to come without loss.

Still another cooperative settlement was about to be founded on a large central tract alongside the railway, near the stop at Fuleh. For months there had been delays, for in the midst of the area was a cluster of huts, an Arab village now dwindled to a dozen families. They had hardly been spoken of when Yehoshua Ostrov bought the land from a mortgage holder in Beirut. "They will move off, they will clear out, they have nothing there anyway, most of their sons have gone off to Nablus and they will go to their sons," the mortgage banker had assured him. "When your people are ready, they will go. You will perhaps pay them a little something for their dwellings, though in any case they no longer own them, they have nothing, nothing."

The dwellings were of mud and straw, of the poorest kind, low huts without windows, Shabbatai Zeira said after he had gone to have a look at the place; each was a single room, where in the rains the family's few goats crowded in as well. Who inhabited the village was even hard to say. Once it had been a better place, but as it became impoverished, some of the families had moved elsewhere, and there was a mingling now of squatters—a few cousins, he believed, of the Zbeh who had settled around the railway stop in Fuleh, where some of them worked a bit as porters.

But the inhabitants of the huts had not moved off even after the deed for the lands was received. Menahem rode out with Shabbatai and Galil. The land was overgrown with thickets, except for here and there a cultivated patch of barley, barely enough for a family's own use. Or a melon

230

patch. In the little village, small children ran naked or with a few rags around them. The mukhtar's guest-hut was barren, except for a straw mat. He came to greet them, a small, oldish man with only one good eye; a dour-looking son appeared, and also sat with them, after calling back into the near hut, from which a boy after some time came, carrying a battered finjan of coffee with yellowed little porcelain cups on a tray. Meanwhile the old sheikh had not waited to tell his woes.

No, for several years now they had not troubled to make crops, for what use was it? Each year the portion of the crops taken away by the moneylenders from Beirut had grown greater. When the grain was ready to cut, the moneylenders even sent a man to sit on the fields to watch that not a sheaf was hidden away. First the fellaheen had had to borrow money on their grain to pay the taxes imposed by the Turks, and each year the taxes grew, and then the moneylenders took their share, greater each year, until there was nothing left.

It was true, the sons had gone away, entire families had gone away, for after the land had gone back to a wilderness there was more sickness. When the Kishon River flooded in winter, the fever came. Now they had been told that nothing was their own and they must leave, but where should they go? This was where he himself had been born, and his father before him, and generations before; this had always been their place. True, the land itself had long been owned by others, in Beirut, who never came here, and to whom they had paid the first half of the crop, and from whom they had received loans in time of need. And in the last years, nothing. A few goats remained. But as they always had lived here and had cultivated this land, how could they be made to leave?

"Because for many years you have not cultivated it at all," Shabbatai Zeira said. "This is the law, as everyone knows."

—If the Jews would come, and the land would be worked again, the old mukhtar said, perhaps there would be work for his people as well, and they could stay here and things would be better. Thus it had fallen out in the valley of Faradis, when the Jews came.

He looked at them in the quiet manner of a man old enough so that it is not for himself he is concerned.

"It is not our way," Galil explained, "to have others do our labor for us. We are Jews of a different kind."

"You have new machines, and money," the son said.

"We have not come to make things worse for you. The land was bought in good faith. But we must think what to do so that you will not be the worse for it."

The discussion dragged on, and turned to questions of crops, and weather, and circled back to the question of their houses, while Zeira smiled wryly as if to say: what worth could these hovels have? Still, the three cups of coffee were consumed, and though the son became more sullen, the greeting of peace was exchanged on parting.

Even Dr. Lubin himself came from Jaffa for the sitting. The villagers, Zeira cried, were demanding inordinate prices for their hovels, as though they were palaces of marble. And they demanded also to be paid for considerable areas of land which they claimed they still cultivated.

"We've already paid for the land, hovels and all! How many times do we have to buy it!" Shabbatai was for showing strength and simply moving them off; otherwise there would be no end! If an Arab grew a single melon on a piece of land, he would claim an enormous field forever.

On the other side, one of the young chalutzim of the new kvutsa that was to go out and settle the land said, "Why not let them stay there?" He, and his chaverim too, he was sure, had not come to Eretz to drive the Arabs from their homes. The tract of land was large enough—why not let the Arab village remain, and let the fellaheen keep the patches of land they were cultivating, while the kvutsa redeemed the rest?

Over this, a debate arose. —It would never work!—Had it ever been tried? Why shouldn't it work? —Were there not Jewish and Arab villages side by side near Jaffa? —But the land was bought and paid for, why should it be given back?

—The policy of the Settlement Office on this problem, Dr. Lubin interposed, was clear. If people had to be moved from land that was acquired, then substitute land must be bought for them. Obviously, it was impossible to settle large areas without disturbing a single inhabitant, but it was better to be over-generous, even to pay both the owner and the tenant, rather than cause hatred and strife. Indeed, Yehoshua Ostrov had already spoken with the Houranis in

Nazareth, and it was possible to acquire a hillside tract from them, quite suitable for the dozen families that had to be moved.

"So we have to pay not once or twice but three times!" Zeira muttered, pulling at his fierce mustache, first one end, then the other.

"Not if we leave then some land and let them stay where they are," said the young idealist.

Now Galil rose to speak. In his eager, almost sputtering, way of talking, he poured the whole future before the newcomers. What they must think about was not only this immediate problem of moving a dozen families some twenty kilometers to a site that would in any case be healthier for them, but they must think about the whole relationship of the two peoples in this land. Not long ago he and Nadina had ridden the entire length of it. It was a land sparsely populated, but it was not uninhabited. True, in ancient times this land had supported ten times the present population and more. Now much of the land was gone to ruin, and all those sitting here had come to redeem it. Wasn't that the first object? What had he and Nadina seen? They had seen entire areas that were waste, like the shorelands, like the Emek before them where only patches were still cultivated, like the hills of upper Galilee, like the Beersheba region in the south. They had also seen areas that were well-tended and blooming, as in the region of Samaria. For what had happened in the recent past? The Arab population in the lowlands had thinned out because of poverty and disease. They had left the lowlands where swamps came in the rainy season, and it was therefore in these areas that redemption was taking place. Chedera was an example of it, Petach Tikvah was an example of it, and here before them was the whole Emek of Jezreel.

What should be the future course? They must redeem areas and make them Jewish areas. Thus in a concentration of population, a culture could grow, a people could grow, their institutions could grow. With his whole heart, Galil declared, he believed that Jews and Arabs would live on good terms is this land, side by side, but he did not see that they would intermingle as one. "Our ways of life are different. Our ways of thinking are different. We can complement each other, but each wants to remains what he is—and to try to become a single, combined people would destroy the very ideal that brought us here, to redeem and rebuild ourselves as Jews, while we redeem and rebuild the land." Therefore, as he saw it, even in this immediate example that faced them, the policy should be to encourage two lines of development, Jews with Jews, Arabs with Arabs. He did not mean estrangement or a principle of separation. In the towns and cities Arabs and Jews would do business together, have constant contact. But here, for the small group of Arabs themselves, how would they feel eventually in a whole area of Jewish settlement? Wouldn't there always be the danger, as in the Baron's early villages, of the Arabs becoming the economic dependents of the Jews, becoming the toilers of the lowest order, even alongside a communa? Therefore he was in favor of resettling these few families among Arabs near Nazareth, though it meant paying three times over.

Still, not all the Arabs agreed to move, and the negotiations dragged on. It was Shabbatai Zeira who found a way to put an end to it. With Achmed Bey, the Bimbashi in Nazareth, things could be arranged. It would cost far less than the exorbitant prices the Arabs were demanding for their huts. And there would be no accusation that Jews drove them out.

One day Achmed Bey and a troop of gendarmes appeared in the village, threatening to seize the houses and all that was in them for non-payment of taxes. Goats and sheep would also be seized. He left his two gendarmes in the village and gave the mukhtar twenty-four hours to pay the taxes, or move everyone out.

That night, at the house of Saïd Hourani in Nazareth, the whole affair was settled, at a reasonable price, with part of the money even applied to back taxes. The next day the villagers loaded their few clay jars and cooking utensils and straw mats and small belongings onto their donkeys and, driving their meager flocks, started for the hills below Nazareth.

Not long after the new kvutsa, Emek Yisroel, had moved onto the land, the younger Zeira, Aaron, while fetching them a cartful of sacks of oats from Sejera, found himself suddenly attacked by two mounted Arabs. Beside him was a young chaver of the kvutsa, Yitzhak. Flinging him the reins, Aaron lay prone on the sacks and returned fire. The cart arrived in the new settlement with Aaron Zeira dead, his blood soaking the seed.

Whan Aaron's body was brought home to their farm in Sejera, the first outcry from the mother of the Zeiras was, "Did he shoot back?" Aaron had kept firing as long as he lived, Yitzhak declared. Then the mother asked, "Did he kill any of them?" It was she with her spare hard flesh on strong bones who had brought her two grown boys in a wagon all the way from Turkestan after their father's death, and taken up a farm in Sejera.

If any of their assailants had been hit, he did not know, Yitzhak said. They had been fired on from ambush. The enemy had not come out.

"Then one must be killed," the mother demanded.

She came to the emergency sitting of the Shomer, at Gilboa, standing with her surviving son Shabbatai before Galil himself, and made the demand. One must be killed.

"Not one, but two!" roared Zev. "We didn't avenge Yechezkiel, and this is the result. They spit on us!" It had been the same pair of bandits from Fuleh, he was sure, for only recently they had been released from the Turkish prison. "We will never be respected until we have finished with them!"

No decision was taken. It was for Menahem first to try to find out who had done the thing.

Shabbatai spoke little those days—they knew where he stood. But Zev would not let up. He cornered every shomer who came in for the Sabbath. At every sitting he cried out, "All they can understand is strength! An eye for an eye, or better, two!"

"Strength, but also the strength of restraint," Galil still argued. "They will really respect us only when they know we have the power, but do not kill indiscriminately." It was as yet far from clear who had made the attack; Menahem had consumed innumerable coffees with the neighboring Bedouin who might have heard something, and with the Houranis in Nazareth, and even with Sheikh Ibrim in Dja'adi, but whether it was the bandit brothers of Fuleh, or one of the villagers moved from the land, was still uncertain. He could bring back only words of commiseration for the brother of the fallen shomer and his mother and his young wife. Both Zeiras were respected in all Galilee for their honorable ways and their skilled horsemanship. "Like one of ourselves," he was always told. Yet, again and again, hints were dropped to Menahem about the evil let loose in the region when the notorious bandits of Fuleh had been let out of prison.

Now Shabbatai Zeira was convinced from his own explorations that it was the brothers of Fuleh who had killed Aaron, and he threatened that if no decision was made he would take matters into his own hands. Before the decisive sitting of the inner command, Menahem found himself going through one of his darkest times, brooding and silent with Dvora, and laconic with the chaverim. He took extra night duty, preferring to be alone. He believed in the way of Galil, and yet in his own soul this time Menahem was swayed toward the view of the avengers.

Then came another killing, unprovoked, brutal. In the kibbutz of Kennereth, just beyond HaKeren, a young chaver, going from their new pumping station to fetch back a pot of tea from the cheder-ochel, failed to return. Hours later, searchers stumbled on his body, on the field he had had to cross, the skull crushed, his throat cut. In the morning, tracks of two horses, side by side, were picked up, but lost along the river.

One night it was known that the commanders were meeting; they sat until dawn. The next day Shimshoni, known as "The Practical," went with a wagon to Damascus, returning with five pistols and eight rifles hidden in sacks of grain, one of the guns so ancient that it must have come from the army of Napoleon. Some said all this was only to increase the Shomer's show of strength, but Zev talked so much of "an action" that many believed the lot had fallen to him.

It had, however, fallen to Shabbatai Zeira, as of his right, and with him, Menahem. The two bandits of Fuleh must be finished with, destroyed. Yet the action must be carried out in a particular way. It must be understood, yet not clearly known as an action of the Shomer—just as the murder of Aaron Zeira was now everywhere understood as the deed of those two, urged on by some of the villagers who had been discontent with the price paid for their removal.

The best would be that the two bandits of Fuleh should vanish. Of their many victims among the Arab villages they had raided, and among the pilgrim guides they were again waylaying, any could be said to have done the deed. Yet those who needed to understand and respect the Shomer would understand.

Shabbatai Zeira was for a direct attack, for waiting for them on one of the paths they often used out of Fuleh, and leaving their bodies for the wild dogs and hyenas. Who would retaliate for those two? They were hated by all.

"Still, they are of the Zbeh," Menahem cautioned.

"An offshoot, despised for their father's having settled in a house and gone to work for the Turkish railway," Zeira countered.

—Perhaps, Menahem said, but the sons had returned to the old marauding ways, they were admired for their bold feats, they had cousins on the other side of the Jordan. If their bodies were left to the wild dogs, it would be the worst of dishonors. But if they were to disappear without a trace, though the count was not yet even, the act would be well understood and yet not seem to be aggravated by insult.

Thus it was to be done.

The thought of the sea came to Menahem just after another carriage was waylaid at the Three Rocks. The brothers of Fuleh would surely return there again, since it was a favorite trick of theirs to wait at the rocks after a train had stopped at Samekh, and goods had been loaded onto wagons for Tiberias.

It came to Menahem that from a small boat hidden in the reeds the rocks could be watched. And afterwards the bodies, weighted with stones, would lie deep in the water, for there were places in the Kinnereth that had never been fathomed.

The plan appeared whole in his mind one Friday, in the middle of the night, just after he had rested in silence for a time beside Dvora and then slipped back from her cot to his own. The plan came whole, and he was somewhat ashamed that the vision came there in the same room with her. And on a Sabbath eve.

Though he had long ago, even in the yeshiva, become an unbeliever, yet, as many of the chevreh admitted, one could not after all completely rid oneself of all vestiges of superstition. But then, if this plan for the execution had come to him with the Sabbath, and if his task was still an act of justice for the killing of Yechezkiel whom he had loved as a brother, and whom Dvoraleh had purely loved, then was this not from God?

In his mind's eye Menahem saw the whole of the coming action repeated and repeated. During his wanderings in America, one of the wonders Menahem had beheld was a moving picture in which a train robber raced on his horse alongside a steam engine, and like many other spectators, Menahem had sat twice, three times, watching the film, as though the next time perhaps things would happen differently and the train would race safely away.

So in his mind the scene of what would take place at the Kinnereth now repeated itself, as though to assure him that it would indeed unalterably happen precisely in the way he envisioned, and that a different outcome was impossible.

And exactly as he had seen it, and made preparations with Shabbatai Zeira for doing it, the thing took place, so that in the doing Menahem felt himself little more than a spectator.

The boat required for the task would be the little bark that lay in the cove once used by Tateh Yankel Chaimovitch as his mikveh. The vessel had been left there by Araleh and was occasionally used by the boys for fishing.

A few times, in preparation, Menahem took Dvora and the baby on Sabbath visits to the grandparents, though the first time Nadina made such a fuss about their removing little Yechezkiel from the Infants' House for a night, that a whole meeting had to be held to discuss the *principe* of the matter. The cause was finally won on the double argument that on Sabbath a child was to be with the parents, and also that from earliest infancy a child born in Eretz should feel the whole of the land as his home.

Once at the Chaimovitches', Menahem would leave the women in the house enjoying the infant Yechezkiel and endlessly comparing his traits with those of his little uncle Mati when at the same age. Meanwhile, with Gidon, Menahem would go off to fish. Thus the sight of him in the Chaimovitch boat would become familiar.

Perhaps Gidon understood the intention. In another few years, when Shmulik would be able to take over his work on the farm, Gidon thought of joining the Shomer, and already he was as good as accepted.

On the second fishing trip, Gidon came out with a question. If he were to become a shomer, he said, there was one thing he wondered whether he would be able to do if it fell to his lot to do it.

"And what is that?" Menahem asked.

Gidon wondered if he would be able to hunt down a man. Then all at once he asked directly, "Did you ever shoot down a man? Doesn't a shomer have to do that sometimes?"

"I have shot and they have shot!" Menahem said. "But it has never yet happened to me that I took aim and shot and saw a man fall dead."

Around Fuleh the brothers showed themselves boldly, and it was quite simple for Menahem to learn the hoof-marks of their mounts, as the Bedouin had taught him. The brothers rode most often side by side rather than in file, so that he came to recognize their tracks at a glance. Exactly as after the murder at Kinnereth.

Early on a Sabbath, Menahem caught sight of their tracks where they had galloped along the ridge of Mount Yavniel and then gone down the slope. Let it be so. On a Sabbath it would less likely to be thought of as a Jewish affair. Perhaps it was pilgrims they were after, pilgrims on their way to spend Sunday at the Christian sites.

Before Menahem picked up Shabbatai Zeira at Sejera, much of the morning had passed. The aged Turkestan mother, coming to the gate to watch them ride off, muttered a blessing in her home language; Menahem caught the name of Aaron alev hasholem. She understood.

Separately, he and Shabbatai made their way over Jewish fields, meeting at the boat. The coil of rope had already weeks before been placed in the bark, and good-sized field-stones lay nearby in readiness. Now Shabbatai lifted the stones to Menahem who placed them evenly.

The sun was already downward though not far enough to come into their eyes as they moved out onto the water. With satisfaction Menahem saw that the entire southern portion of the Kinnereth was empty of fishermen; he had counted on this likelihood, since those of Tiberias seldom came this far.

Everything happened exactly as in the moving picture he had watched in his mind. When the vessel slid among the reeds, he saw at once that the Fuleh brothers were still

there at the rocks, dismounted, smoking, waiting. A swath
of sunlight came between the boulders and gleamed on the
gilded circlet each wore with his white keffiyah. The target
must be sited directly below this headband, at the ear. Fortunately too, the horses were not in the way; they stood
nose to nose in the shade.

Since the troubles had resumed, few carriages or wagons
chanced the road alone when passing the Three Rocks. The
bandits were waiting, surely, for the sound of perhaps only
two carriages together. The brother who sat closest to the
road drew on his cupped cigarette and let out his smoke
carefully, dispersing it with his hand, reminding Menahem
startlingly of how he had gone with Yechezkiel once on a
Sabbath to visit Dvora, and they had had a smoke in the
yard, and Yechezkiel had kept making the same dispersal
movement with his hand, fearing to offend old Yankel
Chaimovitch with his smoking on the Sabbath.

There was just time; the nearer horse had already
pricked up his ears and would turn his head. Shabbatai had
already raised his rifle; he would shoot first, they had
agreed. Menahem watched Zeira's aim, on the target on the
left, and took the other one. He heard Zeira utter his brother's name, "Aaron, achi," before he heard the shot, and as
he too fired, Menahem silently moved his lips to form
"Yechezkiel." In that very instant, the head he had fired on
turned toward him so that the bullet entered slightly forward
of the ear, toward the eye.

The horses, long trained to gunfire, in the first reaction
showed only a muscular ripple. Then their necks arched;
they moved sidewards as though to be mounted. In the
stream of light, how perfect they were! Together they
swung their heads down and gazed on their fallen masters,
their nostrils flaring. Their heads turned now toward the
parting reeds, toward the hunters coming ashore, and in the
eyes of the nearer animal, Menahem believed he saw the
widened pupils, here greatly magnified, of a woman who
gazes in total comprehension, in accusation, in fatedness,
on a conqueror approaching. Then, with a single movement,
the two beasts, uttering a dreadful neighing, strangely like
a woman's ululation, bolted through the passage between the
huge rocks.

He had not foreseen the horses bolting. Clearly he had
left this out because neither he nor Zeira would have

dreamed of taking them; that would be signing their action.

The mounts would be caught and traced back to this place, so much was certain—but how quickly? The shots too might draw someone in this direction, though, just as likely, imagining it was the bandits at work, a chance hearer would choose to ignore the echoes.

The rest of the picture resumed its movement the way he had envisioned it; Shabbatai was with him in every movement as though he too was repeating what he had seen many times. Leaping from the boat, Menahem remembered to raise away the seatboard, which simply rested on two slots in the gunwales so as to simplify the removal of a catch of fish.

Grasping the nearer body by armpits and feet, Shabbatai and Menahem swung it into the vessel. Then the other. They picked up the rifles. Together they pushed the bark away from the mudbank, then vaulted in, one on each end so as not to touch their feet to the cargo. Menahem fitted the seat back into the slots. When they sat to row, each carefully cramped his feet up the side so as not to touch what lay in the bottom.

Only with their rowing did the moment of the shooting return to Menahem. He saw now the Arab's eyes for that fraction of an instant meeting his own, with a total hatred, and yet with a comprehension and even an acceptance of his death. It was as though in that fleeting measureless encounter, Menahem was accepted by the Arab as a man who lived and killed according to their own ways.

Now Menahem met the gaze of Shabbatai. Whatever had haunted him before had vanished. The eyes were intense and quiet, and looked into his own as though they expected the same quietude to come back in response. "It went off well," Shabbatai said. And Menahem said, "Thus far."

While Shabbatai rowed, Menahem set to work binding rocks onto the bodies. This proved more awkward than he had foreseen, for the two lay as one in the curve of the bottom, and the slight rolling of the vessel gave them movement so that in sudden gruesome moments an arm would be flung alive against him. He found himself avoiding any touch of the flesh, grappling and binding only where there was clothing. Around each pair of ankles he managed a tight knot, with a section of rope looped around a large stone. But something in him preferred not to bind a weight around the neck.

At last Shabbatai left off his rowing, stood, and again lifted away the seat so they could manipulate the bodies more readily. Placing them face to face with the heaviest rock in the middle between them, the avengers laced them together firmly as one entity. As he worked with Shabbatai, Menahem's momentary abhorrence dropped away, and he and his partner handled the bodies in the same way as the stones, as parts of a task.

Once the binding was done, they replaced the seat and rowed together, further out to where the color of the sea was a shade darker with depth. Dusk now enwrapped the vessel. With the seat once more removed, Shabbatai stood up as one who throws a net, while Menahem crouched and lifted one end of the longish object against the side; then together they quickly rolled what was firmly bound into the sea. The bark righted itself and swayed while the men regained their balance. The Kinnereth had become choppy. But soon they regained Yankel Chaimovitch's mikveh, and taking out all the rifles, those of the bandits added to their own, they turned the boat on its side and cleaned it well. Casting a final glance around to make sure that no sign remained of their work, the two walked away.

9

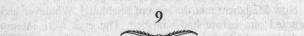

THE RENOWN of the Shomer had become so great that villages as far away as Rehovot signed contracts with the guardsmen, while young lads were so eager to be accepted into the Shomer that they trained for a year in advance before applying for the annual examination. One unfortunate boy from a well-known Jerusalem family who stood before the committee and was refused because he appeared unstable in temperament, it was told, went out and killed himself.

In Gilboa, the wave of new guarding contracts brought a wave of new babies. Now the construction of a new Infants'

House could be added to the budget. Much debate was given to the details to make it perfect. It would be built of cement blocks; each room would hold a "generation" of six. It was Nadina who argued for the figure of six as the correct number to occupy one chavera on infant-care duty, as well as making a good-sized group to grow up together.

Several meetings had to be held on the subject of infant care. The question was even raised by Shimshoni the Practical, who was also an ideologue: whether it was right, since they were building a new and just society, that the care of infants should always be by a woman. Should there not, for the effect on the child, be a rotation with men?

Impulsively Dvoraleh cried out, "Then there should also be a rotation in childbearing!" Dvoraleh didn't often open her mouth at meetings, but when she did, everyone agreed, she was priceless.

Nevertheless the question of child care was a difficult one. The first crop of babies—four of them, born at irregular intervals—had been a great strain on the resources of the kvutsa, Nadina pointed out. As they all knew, the couples had made their own decisions on the subject of having a child, or even in some cases, she feared, the chaver and chavera had made no decision, but in so vital a matter had let matters happen by impulse or accident. The consequent babies, though loved by all, had been intensely cared for by their mothers in the first months, and in each case the chavera's work time had been lost to the kvutsa. Besides, on principle it was doubtful whether such old-fashioned individual care was the proper thing for a child who was to be raised in a communa. She and her chaver, Galil, had as yet refrained from parenthood precisely because they felt that the settlement was not firmly established economically, and also because the subject of group child care deserved more study and planning. But now she and Galil were ready to enter the prospective parent group of six—or really twelve, Nadina corrected herself with one of her rare outbreaks of laughter that made her suddenly look girlish.

During Nadina's recital, Dvora had experienced a moment of guilt, for she and Menahem had been among the selfish ones. But she still could not bring herself to discuss at an open meeting whether and when she should have a child; she wished she could be as modern as Nadina.

Already, Nadina pointed out, even with the unplanned

infants, certain important things had been learned. Instead of giving the mothers alternating periods of duty in the infant-room, the kvutsa had learned to avoid emotional charges of favoritism and bitter scenes by assigning the care of the babies to a non-mother. They had improvised also such simple devices as the bell-call which permitted nursing mothers to work anywhere in the settlement, as each could now come to the baby-house when her signal rang out.

Dvora's signal had been three rings, as she was the third to become a mother. Before her own baby Yechezkiel came, she had been amused with the rest of the chevreh to hear the strokes of the bell and see the chavera flying across the yard to feed her infant, but when her own time came, a different feeling developed. Hurrying across from the poultry house, Dvora had each time experienced a curious embarrassment. Why was it? The whole kvutsa was proud of her little Yechezkiel, the first boy born in Gilboa—though of course in a communa there was as much pride for a girl as for a boy. Yet when she ran to suckle the child, she felt self-conscious. Even her own mameh had shown no embarrassment in suckling a baby before whoever happened to be in the room; with newborn Mati at Sejera there had been a constant coming and going of Leah's friends and her own. And here in the baby-house there was even no question of being watched as she bared her breast, since strict rules of sanitation kept the chevreh out of the room. There was only the embarrassment of being seen running to the bell. Perhaps she was backward, not equal to the new ways.

The worst had come after the first month, when it had been decided to follow the example of Reuven's kvutsa, the earliest, and keep the infants even at night in the nursery room instead of with their parents. In that way the sleep of several sets of parents would be undisturbed, they would be fresh for their work, and also, Nadina had explained, they would develop no resentments against their own babies for waking them up with their howling. While Nadina now reviewed all this at the sitting before coming to her point—everyone knew it was useless to try to get her to skip a single step—Dvora recalled how, the first nights after her baby was not there beside her bed, she had lain half-awake listening for his cries from the infants' room across the yard. She was certain she would recognize them, a boy's,

not a girl's, though twice, running through the mud barefoot in her nightgown, she found herself wrong. The time
that it was indeed Yechezkiel who howled, Nadina herself
was on night duty.

"Don't pick him up!" she snapped when Dvora rushed
into the room.

Dvora halted. Suddenly tears gushed. "I can't! I can't!"

"Chavera Dvoraleh, it's only way. It's for the children
themselves."—Did they want a generation of strong, self-
reliant young men and women to grow up in the land? or
even here, children on apron strings?

"I know, I know, but maybe something really hurts
him—"

"He must cry himself out." Instead, the two other babies
awoke and joined in the howling. "Chavera!" Nadina
sternly commanded, "go back to your room. I am busy
here."

"Can't I help you, Nadina?"

"It's not necessary. You've done your day's work with
the chicks."

The next day Dvora had discussed the question with the
two other mothers and found that already they did not feel
as strongly as she did.

"You'll see, in a few weeks you'll stop listening at night.
My chaver is thankful he no longer has to be awakened
every time a baby cries. He's always in a good mood now."

But the chaverim of those two were on duty at the farm,
while just now her Menaham was away all week. It would
have been less lonely for her with little Yechezkiel in the
room. And Dvora didn't know what tormented her most,
the feeling that her baby really was crying for *her*, that he
knew by instinct, perhaps by the odor of her breast, which
one was his own mother and cried for *her* to be near, or
the dreadful thought that once he was picked up by no
matter whom, the infant quieted.

"I know I am suffering from a primitive instinct," she
would say to Menaham when he returned, "and that we are
making a new kind of life here . . ." "But why," she
would sometimes sigh when Leah visited, "why did it have
to fall on us!"

She was not as strong in revolutionary ideas and matters
of *principe* as Leah and Reuven the vegetarian. They were
the ones who lived for ideals. Often she wished that Leah

would remain here at Gilboa to guide her. At other times it came to Dvora that in her womanly life she had already gone beyond what Leah had ever experienced; she was a mother.

—It would be best, Nadina was explaining, to plan for the new group of infants to be born all in the same season, preferably in fall. And she began to read out the names of the comrade couples who had signified to Shimshoni, just now secretary of the kvutsa, that they wanted to become parents.

Again, and even though she herself was not involved, Dvora found herself flushing. "Pnina and Josef. Gavriel and Aviva. Ruthie and Yoshka. David and Shoshana." After each pair of names it was almost as though Nadina waited for applause. And indeed heads turned toward those named, and smiles of many sorts broke out, some knowing, some joyous, some questioning, with laughing jibes, too. "Yoshka, you really think you can do it?"

"Chevreh!" Nadina sternly put a stop to such levity. With herself and chaver Galil, she summed up, that made five couples already in the group, and as six would be the optimum number . . .

"Suppose Ruthie and I have twins?" called out Yoshka, the irrepressible. Nadina ignored him. For a sixth she proposed that a couple who were already parents should take part, as this would add another dimension to the question of a brother or sister relationship—something they must inevitably approach. It would be the first opportunity to raise children so that all were as brothers and sisters, no different from those who were biologically so.

And before Dvora could think, she heard her own name and Menahem's spoken by Nadina. Would they like to undertake the sixth? And a wave of approval was felt in the room, expecially toward Menahem, she sensed, for everyone seemed to know that he had carried out some very difficult and secret mission, and was deserving of respect.

No matter how it had been decided, the prospect of becoming pregnant again was welcome to her. For Dvora understood now her own mother's numerous pregnancies; despite everything, this brought a period of peace in a woman. She would gladly enter such a period again, for lately she was troubled for Menahem. His silences were heavier. True, even in their silences they communicated.

When she had first become pregannt, Dvora had held back from telling him, yet before anything showed, it was he who had one night suddenly declared, "If it is a boy, we will call him Yechezkiel." In that moment she had gratefully known that it was this same wish, already in her own thoughts about the baby, that had kept her from speaking of the pregnancy to Menahem. How she had loved him for relieving her. It was as though in the times of silence that came over them they were wandering each through some dark tunnel, but, by the miracle that was the proof they belonged to each other, they always came out together, in the same place. The fear in her was that some time it would not be so. On that night, so relieved had she felt that they had made love unceasingly and irrepressedly, as though to conceive their Yechezkiel all over again.

But lately Dvoraleh felt a bewilderment; she did not know where Menahem would come out from these new silences. He had done something that was needed, she knew, all knew, he and Shabbatai together, though no one must talk of it. Secret duties sometimes came to men of the Shomer.

If she became pregnant, she would feel Menahem's absences less strongly. He had been sent down for a time to the furthest guarding place, near Gedera, and he came home to Gilboa only every second Sabbath.

But to have the prospect called out in this way, as though it were about eggs for her incubator! To feel that all the chaverim were watching, and that when she and Menahem went to their room, it would seem as though the watching continued through the cabin walls.

Shimshoni's half-bald head was glowing as he bent over the sheet of paper, adding their names.

For weeks after the meeting jests were endless. When those of the selected fathers-to-be who were on guard duty at far-off villages left at the end of the Sabbath for their posts, chaverim and even chaveroth never tired of demanding, "Have you accomplished your home duty?" And endless were the jests over the distribution of articles for personal use, as Motkeh, in charge of such supplies, promptly struck the six future fathers off his list for preventatives.

"What will a man do when on duty away from home, if he is called in for the Shomer's night time tea?" was a favorite jest. Ever since the scandals about Zev the Hotblood, the "Shomer's tea" in the middle of the night had become a byword.

"We'll father a crop of little shomrim all over the land!" boasted Ruthie's bright-tongued Yoshka.

To which Motkeh, the supply-man, would declare, "That's my whole scheme."

In Gilboa, following another pattern that had been started at HaKeren, the cabins were built with four chambers side by side, opening onto a common front porch, and in each room were two cots—sometimes three. When a chaver and chavera paired off, Shimshoni would manage to move people about so that they could have their two cots in the same room, without a third if they were lucky. A marriage bed such as parents used in the old country was unsuitable, for on separate cots a man and woman did not disturb each other with their different hours of rising for their tasks.

It had become a habit when Menahem was home that they would go to their beds separately, and then Menahem would come over to hers. Almost always, in that same reassuring sense that they emerged out of their tunnels to discover themselves together, he knew when she lay wanting him, and came over to her. And then, when it was done, he would return to his own cot. At times during her first pregnancy, Dvora had experienced a different kind of longing, so she would go over to him and sleep almost the whole night pressed against his back. They had discovered for themselves the pleasure of lying naked under the sheet, and when her abdomen grew round, a peaceful sleep, such as neither had ever known before, come to them when they fitted together, this time with his front against her back while his hand rested on the curve of her pregnancy.

Such a time now came again. A rotation was made of the guardsmen for the more distant settlements, and Menahem received farm duty for a time in Gilboa.

But one night, as he lay against his wife in this way, and she turned to him in her sleep as she sometimes did, and cast an arm around his shoulder, a dreadful sweep of terror came over Menahem. He lay rigid, awake but as though immovably sleepbound in his nightmare. The child within her was a heavy stone pressed against his belly.

After a long while, he was able to lift Dvoraleh's arm away and turn her so that they were in their old position.

Against his embracing hand, her abdomen was highly resilient like a breast and in her sleep his wife pressed her back still closer against him, with a sweet sigh.

But Menahem could not sleep again; he felt his forehead sweating. Without waking Dvoraleh, he slid from his cot and went to rest on hers, across the room. At last his terror receded.

He did not speak of it to her. Of what troubled him he could speak to no one, not to Shabbatai Zeira, who was made differently, not even to Galil. Once, when Shabbatai rode in from his farm in Sejera for a sitting, there came a moment of comradeliness when Menahem had an impulse to ask . . . But how should he ask? Should he ask how Shabbatai slept?

Those two horses, Shabbatai remarked, had been seen near Hittim, ridden by tribesmen of the Zbeh. Oh, how Zeira wished they could have kept that pair of steeds! And they talked of horses and guns.

The nightmare did not come again, though each night, if Dvora moved to his bed, Menahem found himself waiting for it. When she grew big so that there was no longer room on one cot, and it was natural for them to sleep apart, he felt relieved.

Then in the final months Menahem accepted another turn away from home. And on watch in Benyamina, the anxiety came over him once more, not this time as a nightmare, but with persistent imaginings that came on him during his rounds. The child would be born a lifeless lump. Or else a fear for Dvoraleh would come over him. With the first baby he had experienced not the slightest worry, but now before each Sabbath Menahem rode home in apprehension.

Yet nothing whatever happened. A second boy was born, perfectly formed and lively. Dr. Rachman had trained one of the girls, Guta Krakauer, in nursing and midwifery, and all went off without incident. When Menahem returned for his Sabbath, the three-day-old was lying in the new Infants' House. Again a boy, and the first of "the six." Indeed, one of the six chaveroth had not even become pregnant, and there was talk of that couple losing their turn. But Nadina was so enormous that Yoshka's joke about twins seemed about to come true, so there might be a class of six babies after all.

Dvora and Menahem were hailed as the champions. Only, Dvora complained to him that, by the newest decision, babies had to remain in the Infants' House from birth; the mothers were not to keep them even for the first month, and all night she had a dreadful emptiness in her, she felt hollow.

In Menahem the weight lifted. It was as though by staying away in these last weeks he had kept a curse from falling on his wife and child. If there had to be pain, it was better that he should carry it always silently within himself.

The boy would be called Giora, after the last defender of Jerusalem, for whom the earlier secret group, the one before the Shomer, had been named.

Already her second daughter was twice a mother, while what was to become of her eldest? It was for Leah that Feigel worried, even though the big independent girl had shown herself cheerful and singing when she last came to the meshek, at Passover. Between the lines in a letter from Jerusalem, now, Feigel was certain she detected a new emptiness and loneliness, for Leah's good friends had scattered, to Turkey, to France—what was ever to become of her big girl? Still longing year after year in her foolishness for that mamser in Siberia! Therefore as the High Holidays approached, Feigel dropped into her husband's ear the thought that surely the time was at last come for him to make his journey to Jerusalem. The wheat crop was bountiful and entirely without blight, since they had done as Reuven said and used the deep plow borrowed from the kvutsa. To wait longer to go to the Holy City would be a failing. And in Jerusalem she could see how Leah lived, and what was doing with her daughter.

Yankel could well take his ease for a few weeks, leaving the farm in Gidon's care. Two cows had calved, and Yaffaleh's geese were the fattest in Galilee. The keeper of the best pension in Tiberias, Reb Bagelmacher, with whom Yankel had struck up a friendship in the hot baths, now regularly came out in his wagon to buy geese for the Sabbaths and holidays. The poet Bialik himself had slept at Bagelmacher's pension during his famous visit, and had praised the roast goose. But the real gold mine for Yankel had proved to be Reuven's potatoes. Though Reuven's kvutsa was now also producing a crop, and Reuven had not stinted in handing out seed potatoes even to the Roumanians, the potato hunger of the yishuv seemed insatiable, prices remained high, and the money for the first two crops alone had bought Yankel four cows now giving milk.

So wide was Reuven's renown for the feat of the potatoes that the noted agronomist from Zichron, Aaron Aaronson, had himself arrived to inspect the second planting at the Chaimovitch farm, and Reuven had come from the kvutsa to meet him, for to the kvutsa itself Aaronson would not go because of some old, bitter dispute with the chalutzim over Arab labor in Zichron. Finely dressed in American clothes, the agronomist had just returned from a visit to that land, where the richest Jews had acclaimed him for his discoveries. Tramping with Reuven over the potato field, Dr. Aaronson had taken samples, and then invited him to come to Zichron to visit a whole new center of agronomy that he was building with money provided by the American Jews.

Sitting at the table with the whole family for tea, Dr. Aaronson had complimented Feigel on her preserves—even better, he said, than his own mother's, and his mother's were renowned in all Zichron. A fine, polite, polished person. It came out in the talk that Reuven and Leah had held watch in Aaronson's father's vineyards, when Reuven was recovering there in Zichron from kadahat, and Reuven told Aaronson he had even studied agricultural books from Dr. Aaronson's library!

"How is that?" Dr. Aaronson said, a trifle sharply, though with a smile of curiosity. "I never let my books go out!"

"Your sister took pity on me and loaned them to me," Reuven said. "Though I couldn't understand the French, I studied the drawings."

"Ah, it must have been when I was in America to publish my wild wheat discovery."

At this Reuven in his modest way mentioned that he also—though of course a few years after Aaronson's discovery, had found some wild wheat growing, not far from here. (That he had not then known of Aaronson's discovery he did not say.) At once the two men were deep in discussion again. Though Feigel could not follow their talk, it was wonderful to see how such a highly educated agronomist respected her son as an equal. She brought three more kinds of jam. Reuven even took out from a yellowing enevelope in his pocket the grains of ancient wheat that he had found on the mountainside. It was for just such a discovery that Dr. Aaronson had become famous all over the world, and here her own Reuven, without ever having been sent for years of study in France by the Baron, had made the same discovery! Had Reuven found these seeds only a few years earlier, Feigel grasped, it would have been her son who became world famous!

Yet for Dr. Aaronson it had to be said that he complimented Reuven with all his heart, like a true gentleman. Taking from a special leather case in his coat-pocket an eyeglass such as watchmakers use, he studied Reuven's seeds and declared that though he himself had found eight different varieties on the Hermon, Reuven's was still different and a ninth. "We will call it the Chaimovitch strain," he announced, "Chita Chaimovitch!" And he carefully folded the grains into a clean paper sachet from another little case that he carried, saying he would make further examinations in his laboratory with a microscope. At this, Reuven said there was something else that he had long wanted to put under a microscope. And he told of the wheat with the fungus he had found a few years before, and of the disappearance of the fungus when the same strain had been planted in a field that had been deeply plowed. On the Arab fields the fungus was still to be found.

Dr. Aaronson became excited, asked many questions and then said Reuven was welcome to come and use his laboratory whenever he wished. But as to the fungus, he believed he knew the answer. The tiny parasite that spoiled the wheat-kernels dropped its eggs on the ground for reproduction. In ordinary shallow plowing the microscopic worms born from the eggs could crawl out, but in deep plowing, they were surely buried so far that they died.

—That must be it!

Hardly ever had Feigel seen Reuven so happy. You would have thought the Schechina had been revealed to him. Here he had puzzled his head for years, and Dr. Aaronson had found the answer in one moment.

"Ah, no, but it was you who found the answer, empirically," Dr. Aaronson said. "What you did, plowing them under, must be taught in the whole land!"

"It wasn't even I," Reuven said, with his usual modesty

and honesty. "It was a chaver in the kvutsa who insisted on deep plowing, and I was even against it!"

They laughed together over the tale. By such accidents, Dr. Aaronson said, many great discoveries were made—not in the laboratory, but by people like Reuven in the field, who observed things.

"A fine man," Feigel said when the agronomist had left; "A real scientist such as we need in Eretz," Reuven declared. And though Feigel caught the tiny flicker of envy in her son's eyes, and though there was a sigh in her that it had not fallen to him to receive the high education of which his mind had surely been worthy—yet she was not truly worried for Reuven so far as his work went. He was satisfied in his work at the kvutsa; they had even installed for him a huge engine that pumped water, such as he had long dreamed of, and he was showing that not one but two main crops a year could be grown. All through the region Reuven was becoming known as an expert under whose hands even a stone would bear fruit.

Yet he continued among the unmated men of his kibbutz, and surely in this he could not be happy. Though Feigel did not worry about him as much as about Leah—an unmarried son of twenty-five was not as serious a matter as a lone girl of twenty-three, and no longer a maiden, even if in their world of chalutzim this did not appear such a dreadful blemish.

And so Feigel persuaded Yankel, and he harnessed a mule, and Feigel, having cooked and baked for two whole days, packed the wagon with roast goose and chicken, with chopped liver and sesame cookies and strudel, with gefulte fish and cheeses and jellies and all manner of good things for her big daughter in Yerushalayim, as well as with boiled eggs for the journey.

The first glance told Feigel she had done well to come here. Though Leah rushed to them across the courtyard, glowing and joyous in their arrival, and instantly started distributing Feigel's good baking and cooking to hollow-chested chevrehmen who kept appearing from a bewilderment of crevices and doors, and though the yard was covered with Leah's pots of seedlings and flowers, and though a few young girls at work among the pots came hovering adoringly near their teacher, and though Leah's room into which she led them had jugs of flowers covering the window sill and all over the table and on the floor, still Feigel sensed an inner desolation, and her daughter's talk was to her a tumult of emptiness.

Leah had a thousand activities, a thousand plans, though to Feigel it seemed that even the few coins needed for tea and sugar must be scarce. Hundreds of her seedlings, Leah enthusiastically explained, were going to a new kvutsa near the ancient tomb of Mother Rachel; the chevreh there were waiting for their loan from the Zionist office, but the planting could not wait; perhaps she would even join this new kvutsa; and also she was helping every morning in a children's nursery that a friend of hers had started here in the quarter—it was a chance to learn an amazing new teaching method that her friend Clara had brought from Italy—it was called Montessori; they had Jewish and Arab children together in their kindergarten, called a gan, Moslems, Christians, Jews, all sitting together, each a darling, four-and five-year-olds. Of course few of the children had parents who could pay, and also she and Clara served them crackers and milk, which was all that some of the poorer ones had to eat all day long. Then also she was thinking of going down to plant gardens for the new city of Tel Aviv—it was a desolation of sand, gardens were needed on Rothschild Boulevard and she had been asked to put them in; also she wanted desperately to come to Gilboa to see Dvora's new baby, but she was so busy here—how she loved her Yerushalayim. Tateh must come with her at once, she would show him Jerusalem!

Yankel would have wanted to find his way to the Wall by himself, or perhaps with a crony; perhaps he should have made the journey with a good Jew like Binyamin Bagelmacher from Tiberias, whose season had not really yet begun. It irritated Yankel that his women lingered along every stall, fingering the silks, gawking at the trinkets. Past shopwindows overladen with crucifixes and beads and medallions of their Yoshka, he fled. Surely there was some other way to the Wall, so one could walk only among Jews and avoid these horrors! Separating himself by several paces from the women, pushing on through dark, arched-over lanes, among the Arabs with their donkeys and among pithhelmeted Christian pilgrims, he inwardly fumed. What did all these goyim have to do here in Yerushalayim, the city of David, of Solomon, of Jeremiah! At last Leah called to him to turn into a side-lane, and there he saw others like himself, decent Yehudim with prayer bags. Following them down hollowed stone steps, Yankel stood all at once in the passageway so familiar to him from the picture on the wall at home in Cherezinka.

Before the immense stone blocks that reached upward like some barrier to the Other World, Jews stood intoning their prayers, some standing by themselves, others a few together, and at a distance from the men there prayed a few aged, beshawled women.

He had long delayed, true, but in these years it was as though he had been earning his full right to come here; he had made another man of himself. Or, it was as though he had in these years shredded away from himself the false flesh of the dispersion, and here he now stood, a farmer who had succeeded in feeding his family from the soil, in making a whole life in Galilee, and who was now come from there with produce in his wagon as to the Temple itself for the High Holidays. It was almost as though he had brought a sheep and would now go up to the great court-yard at the top of this high wall, with his offering.

No impulse to moan or wail at the Wall came to him. From his prayer-bag Yankel drew out his tfillim, and wound them on. He swung himself into his long tallis. Within his tallis he was away from all the wrong in the world. Standing before the ancient blocks of stone, Yankel at long last felt his life justified. All his errors and all his unworthy past slipped into nothingness. If his eldest daughter had thrown away her virtue and was now deep in unhappiness, then Feigel would help her somehow. Perhaps Leah had suffered enough. If his sons did not follow him, then they themselves must answer for their ways. Adonai, Adonai, Yankel's lips spoke, I have come, I am here.

Feigel and Leah watched him standing there, heavy-shouldered, another Jew among a line of tallis-wrapped Jews, swaying with a cradle-rock, close against the high wall of great stones. Feigel herself moved close. In the crevices, moss grew. She put her lips to a stone, and asked the Above One to bless her children and give them a good life. When she drew back, she sniffled and was not surprised to

feel tears in her eyes. Leah was reminding her of the custom of writing a prayer, a wish, and placing it between the
stones, and Feigel found a bit of paper and wrote in Yiddish, "Gottenyu, bless my children and grandchildren, and
give them a good life." She began to fold the paper, then,
turning from Leah, she added, "Send a tall man, a good
husband for my eldest daughter Leah." Leah played for a
moment at snatching the bit of paper so as to read Mameh's prayer, but Feigel pressed it deep into a fissure and
sealed a kiss over it.

Her man, her Yankel, said a Kaddish for his own father,
and for the first little lost son Nachman, so long ago in
Cherezinka, and for Avramchick, and for Dvora's murdered bridegroom, Yechezkiel. Then he embarked on
Psalms.

So as not to disturb Tateh, the women had withdrawn.
Finally he came out to them. Leah wanted to show him
more; through a lane where Arab dragomen in broad-
sashed white abayas were leading a party of pilgrims, they
came to an awesome set of wide stone stairs. A few Arabs
standing there half-barred the way, muttering "Yahud," but
quite cheerfully Leah gave them a good-day in Arabic,
while she handed over a coin. "Don't worry, we can go
inside," she said lightly, but the feeling of abomination had
come overpoweringly upon Yankel. Above, at the top of
the broad stairway, he could see in the center of the vast
open place the edifice with the glowing golden dome. For a
confused instant it had been, to him, the Temple. Within
that confusion, his daughter's words babbled to him about
Abraham's sacred stone, the rock altar that had been made
ready for Isaac. The stone was here, they claimed; it could
be seen inside there, in the very center—she had seen it.
For another few coins, inside there, in their golden-domed
mosque—

Violently, Yankel pulled back.—But it is ours, our stone,
our place, not theirs! the tumult shouted within him. And
the dreadful mistakenness, the hopelessly inverted wrongness of the world of man swept back upon him, swept away
all of God's tenderness and rightness that he had felt when
he stood before the Wall. Look how insane, how wrong and
perverted it all was and forever would be! How could this
ever, until Eternity, be set right? Over the rock of Abraham, instead of the Temple stood a heathen mosque. No,

he did not want to enter under their golden dome, to set
foot in their place of abomination! The entire history of the
Jews was churning within him; how could he explain if
they didn't understand in themselves? What was all this to
his own daughter, what could it mean for his own sons,
that in this land, in Yerushalayim itself, on the holiest of
sites, they were mere sightseers! They thought nothing of
giving a few coins to a Jew-cursing Moslem guide to slip
them into the Holy Place—the Jewish Holy Place that
these heathens had forbidden to Jews! Here where the
Temple had stood! Plowed under by the Romans, dese-
crated by the Christians, owned by the Moslems—tfoo!
Sightseers! Buying postcard pictures of the mosque!

Yankel turned away into the crowded lane, and his wife
and daughter followed at a distance behind him.

Preparing the evening meal with her daughter in the narrow room, the moment seemed good to Feigel for what was
needed, and she began roundabout by speaking of Dvoraleh and Menahem, and how well things had turned out between them. And Leah herself inadvertently led to the
point, "I sometimes wonder at Dvoraleh," Leah said, "if
she doesn't even think of Yechezkiel." There was no criti-
cism in her voice but only a questioning touch of bewilderment. Her tone, Feigel recalled, was exactly like that of a
little daughter who asks about childbirth, "But Mama, if it
hurts so much, then—to have another baby—aren't you
afraid?"

"You know she does think of Yechezkiel," Feigel said.
"Even if they had not named their first child after him, she
would still think of him all through her life. But, Leah,
Dvora has become a woman."

Leah's face turned heavy. Then Feigel began from another direction, speaking of little Mati, what a little mensch
he was becoming, the love of the whole village, running,
climbing everywhere on his stout short legs—

Her daughter's face livened up. "Oh, how my heart longs
for him," Leah said. "Why didn't you bring him, Mama?"

Now Feigel brought out of herself for her daughter
something that she had never thought she would share.
"You remember, Leah, how before he was born, I believed
it could be the soul of Avrameleh returning?" Leah smiled,
wondering whether her mother still held with such supersti-

tion, and Feigel smiled as well, for now all was becoming more intimate between them. "It's a few years now since a small thing happened," Feigel said. "It struck me so deeply at the time that I didn't speak of it to anyone." First she recalled to Leah the time when their little Avramchick alev hasholem was still alive, and the day when Tateh and the whole family had waded across the river to go into their field, and Avramchick had lagged behind, and they had all turned around to see him standing there on the other side of the water afraid to cross, calling "And me? And me?"

Mother and daughter sighed over the memory, yet Feigel still held a pensive smile. She turned over a blintze on the pan, remarking that Yankel liked them crisp, and continued, "When Mati was exactly the same age of Avramchick was on that day—you were already here in Jerusalem, Leah—a thing much the same took place. We all went over to the field, forgetting him, he must have run off to look at something on the way. Then suddenly when we were on the other side, what do you think? That baby came marching through the water by himself. 'I'm here too!' he announced to us!"

They treated it with a touch of laughter, though their eyes communicated something else—a seeking of meaning, and of awe. "Ah, my poor sweet Avramchick," Feigel sighed. "But you see, my fears were wrong, what happens to us is not always the same." And then she said, "Come home for a while, Mati longs for you."

Perhaps, after all, she could begin again, Leah felt, simply as a girl still learning from her mother.

It was only this that Gidon had needed! With his giantess of an older sister again in the room, a female effluvium pervaded the place—like in a cow stable at times, he could swear. Even before Leah came back, he had felt uncomfortable because of Eliza. The smaller sister, Yaffaleh, didn't trouble him, although on her chunky body the breasts were already larger than Eliza's. But all at once in the last months with Eliza the room seemed unlivable to him. Suddenly it was decreed that if he came from outside and the door of the room was shut, he must knock. And even after knocking, he couldn't simply walk into the room—after all, it was his room too!—but must first wait until the lady said yes, he might enter! No longer was it enough for him to turn his head when she undressed; half the time now Eliza would ask him to step out of the room altogether. The little pisherkeh! How long was it since she had stopped wetting her bed! And if by chance coming in hot and sweaty from the fields he started to change his pants, she would let out a shriek.

Let be, he knew what it all came from, though no one had ever bothered to explain it to him, with their female secrets. Already from far back—he didn't exactly recall how he had made the discovery—Gidon knew that women leaked blood every month. Perhaps it had even been way back in Cherezinka, when the melamed didn't want to explain what the passage meant in Chumash, the laws about the time of the month for women, and one of the boys afterward had told him about the bloody rags, and it was nauseating what was under their dresses. And in all her pretended daintiness Eliza was just as filthy as the others too, for one evening when she was away at the Bronescus' visiting her friend, their daughter Malka, he had come upon a stiffly clotted rag among some petticoats she had left lying around for Mameh to wash. The time of the month was supposed to start with girls at her age.

And if she was not at Malka's, Malka was here, endlessly babbling, the two of them, and then for a different reason he would stay out of the room, because already Malka upset him with that look he had heard his mother say the Roumanian women had in their eyes, a sidewise look.

The worst part about sleeping in the same room wasn't even from the girls, it was because of himself. He couldn't always stop himself. No matter how still he lay, he was afraid they would know, they would even smell what came out. Almost every night he fought it, in torture. He wondered how his brother Reuven the idealist could endure it all these years, since he still didn't have a chavera. Perhaps it was true that if you were a vegetarian it was easier and that was one reason Reuven was a vegetarian. Or perhaps it was even true that in a kvutsa the girls in a friendly way helped the men by releasing their torture even if there was nothing between them. After all, it was only natural. On a farm with animals you saw how natural. He wanted to talk to Reuven but could never bring himself to begin talking about such things; they liked each other, but they were not the same.

Sometimes Gidon wanted to howl like an animal calling a mate.

Some nights, though he tried to keep from rubbing himself or even tried to squeeze it to choke back the seed, the stuff came out over his hand, and some of it stained the sheet. His mother surely had noticed but said nothing, it was a thing that boys could not help, it was nature just like the leaking of the girls. But now Leah would do the washing and she would notice. With Leah he had always felt more understanding than with any of the others; with her he might even bring himself to talk about the things of nature, but what could she tell him that he didn't already know? A man had to suffer through it, that was all, until he found a modern understanding chavera, or even until he got married. The jokes about doing it with sheep, and about men with boys, he already knew from long ago; this too was in Chumash where they forbade things, and this too the melamed had not explained. Or the zonoth—he had picked up such talk from Arab boys and from some of the workers on the Roumanian farms, but these chalutzim only talked, they didn't go. You could get diseased, the chalutzim said, and later in life become insane, or blind. It was even said there was a certain house in Tiberias. But it was better simply to spill in the hand or in a rag. Even when the time would come when he earned money—no, he must find a true chavera and they would love each other in free love, as Leah had, everyone said. Yet he was angry and could kill such a fellow as that Moshe, look how miserable he had made poor Leah, ruining her life.

One day it came to Gidon that exactly because of Leah and the room's being now so crowded, he could do something he had long wished but had not dared propose. He could leave the whole room to the girls and poor Schmulik, and go and live by himself. Often, passing the stone hut where they had lived before the house was built, he had thought of this. It stood empty, and had become as dilapidated as before, with the roof half decayed and the door fallen off and the floor covered with clots of dried offal. But there, with a little work, he could arrange a wonderful abode for himself. And if he were lucky enough to find a chavera, she could even slip in there to visit him. He didn't think of exactly who. Not Malka—she was like Eliza who would never do such a thing—they considered themselves superior to boys and in any case, aside from the disturbance her presence gave him, he really disliked Malka Bronescu and had no longing for her. At times a vision came of a little Yemenite girl, slim and swift, who had a few times caught his eye, there by the Kinnereth—but they were very strict with their daughters, and with Arab girls it was dangerous to meddle—no.

The first visitor to appear in his hut came as Gidon rose the first time from the fresh straw mattress that Mama had stuffed for him—for unexpectedly she had made hardly any objection to his move except for worries about scorpions, and had come down with Leah to thoroughly clean the hut, which Leah had then supplied with a water jarra and pots of flowers.

It was Fawzi, who appeared, laughing, shouting joyously as he neared, "I have her! She is mine!" and Gidon saw him crossing the stream, leading a colt of almost unbearable beauty, the color of honey, with her tail fastidiously arched as though she were holding up her skirts as she stepped with the finest articulation from stone to stone. Gidon rushed out and gazed at the young mare who now moved up closer behind Fawzi and placed her head over his shoulder, like a girl when she wants to make clear to everyone which boy is hers. It was unbearable. She had Roumanian eyes. Gidon leaped at Fawzi, laughing and pummeling, and they rolled on the ground. How had he got her? Surely he had begotten her off her own mother!— And you! Fawzi retorted. The best you would be able to beget is with a field mouse! Throwing Gidon off, he dodged into the hut and examined each thing, picking up Gidon's shaving cup, his razor, his mirror, taking a sesame cookie from a dishful Mama had left there, and then through a full mouth Fawzi divulged the secret of his possession. Did not Gidon remember how in this very place, when he, Fawzi, first came down with his grandfather Sheikh Ibrim to build them a taboon, a pledge was made?

Seizing a pencil that lay on the table, looking around for a bit of paper and finding none, Fawzi proceeded to write on the freshly whitewashed wall. Laughing all the time, he wrote in large flowing Arabic script, and with a flourish whirled around. He had learned to write!

Now Gidon recalled how the ancient Ibrim had fingered some books of Reuven's and asked, "Who here can read?" And the astonishment, Gidon recalled, on old Ibrim's face when he learned that not only the boys, but also Leah and Dvora and little Eliza could read and write! Even the girls! It was then that Ibrim had turned to his grandson in a flow of Arabic which they had not understood.

"He promised me my own horse when I could read and write as well as you!" Fawzi cried. And at last the imam up there in Dja'adi had taken pity and taught him. "Can you read this, you son of an inkpot?" Fawzi wrote more on the wall. Arabic Gidon could not read, though Menahem had learned quite a bit, and even Reuven had taught himself their alphabet. "May Allah watch over this house!" Fawzi rattled off, giving him a teasing look, and they burst out laughing together, Gidon poking at him and calling him a mamser, which Fawzi well understood, calling Gidon in turn a puny outcast from a rabbit hole, suckled by a jackal. Then they went out like brothers to examine each point of the colt, whom Fawzi had named Ayesha. With her first foal, he already planned, he would buy himself a bride!

Gidon did not conceal his envy, for it increased Fawzi's pleasure and pride. "For a horse such as this, all my own," Gidon declared, "I would learn to read and write in five languages!" Fawzi gazed at him. "Her first foal is yours," he suddenly said.

That was far off, nor could he accept such a gift, so impulsively offered. With the Arabs, it was a gesture that spoke of great friendship in the heart, but it naturally had to be refused. Meanwhile Gidon could think of nothing else except how to get himself his own steed. He thought so intensely about it at night that sometimes even his sexual troubles subsided. A thousand plans for earning money by extra labor for some of the Roumanians he discarded; even if he could spare a few hours a week, it would take over a year to gather the money. That his father should pay him a wage he kept putting out of his head. But now every little incident with his father came to shouting. Gidon went to the house only for meals and rushed out when he had eaten, returning to his own place to brood. Once he rushed out in the midst of the evening meal because something the old man said angered him; it was Leah who came after him to the hut.

Gidon was sitting in the dark and his big sister sat down by him without lighting the kerosene lamp. He was going through a difficult age for a young man, she said, nature was in some ways cruelly perverse and had placed in man these terribly powerful sexual urges that were badly timed; they began too early and tormented a man years before they could be released in the right way with the woman he loved. Or perhaps it was not nature but civilization that was to blame, for, in earlier times, as could be read in the Bible, and even in the time of their own mother and father, their own people too had recognized the need for younger marriages. And she believed, Leah said, it was this natural sexual need that made him so short-tempered these days, especially with his father.

"He doesn't have to order me, tomorrow do this, do that—I know what needs to be done, I know better than he."

Leah grasped his hand. "I read in a book that Rahel gave me in Jerusalem—it is a book of psychology—a Jewish scientist in Vienna says it is normal for young men to have such feelings against their fathers, even to want to kill them," she half-laughed. "It comes from primitive urges."

"Psychology!" Gidon repeated. "A scientist had to discover such things? This scientist should have known Tateh!"

"And Gidon, don't think it is only men that suffer. Women too suffer from terrible needs when they do not have their man . . ."

He squeezed back on her hand. He was grateful that Leah had offered these words from her own inmost pain, it was like a kiss of peace from his sister on his forehead.

"Nu, Gidon," she said with a quick-drawn breath, "the only help we can have is sometimes to talk it out. Tell me—maybe just to me you can tell it—is there some special girl perhaps that you keep dreaming of and wanting?"

"No, no," he blurted out. "It's not even that so much— You know what I dream and want—you'll laugh, Leah— it's a horse."

And they both broke out laughing. Leah laughed like a roll of thunder. She would finally manage to get control of herself and begin to say something to him, and then the thunder would roll forth again from her mouth and inundate the room as though it would break through the walls. Her body shook like an earthquake. "A horse! A horse! And I thought it was Malka Bronescu!" This time she did seize him in an embrace that engulfed Gidon entirely, while her mouth, oddly fresh and cool, blessed his forehead.

In a rush of words Gidon explained it all—how, even if he were working as a hired hand, he could manage to buy a foal, paying it off while he raised it. But when he had only hinted at this idea to Tateh, the old man had grumbled, what did they need with a riding horse that would stand eating its head off all day without working!

Calmly now, Leah lighted the lamp. "You are right, Tateh is exploiting you," she declared.

After that it did not take long. From all sides arguments fell on poor Yankel. With a swift steed of their own, Feigel pointed out, they could more quickly fetch a doctor or medicine in case of need. Eliza kept repeating how pleasant things were for Malka Bronescu whose father kept a horse and often took Malka riding with him in their little brougham.—Never mind the Roumanians, Leah pointed out—a new family had just come from Russia, from Bobrusk, and even they owned a riding horse. Besides, on any homestead in the land an excellent young laborer like Gidon could command a good wage in addition to his keep, and buy himself a horse if he wanted to.

It was Shabbatai Zeira, the horse-expert of the Shomer, who on his very next journey to the market in Damascus selected a yearling of the finest desert breed, a young black stallion who, the dealer promised, would outrace the swiftest bullet. And even the price and the time of payment was no problem. "Take him, take him with you," said the Syrian. "I know you of the Shomer!" and he grasped Zeira's hand in termination of the transaction, both understanding full well where the price stood.

Part of the money Gidon had already sent with Zeira, for though a son does not work for wages, he now received from Yankel a monthly sum for personal expenditures. As to Shabbatai's choice, where could an equal be found? Gidon named his horse Yadid, and slept with a long rope from Yadid's halter tied to his wrist, in case marauders should try to steal his beloved friend.

On Sabbaths now he galloped with Fawzi, going as far as the Huleh, where they hunted quail and wild geese, which Fawzi knew where to sell in Tiberias. Often they raced their mounts. On the level stretches by the shores of the Kinnereth, the mare was likely to be swifter, while on the climb toward Rosh Pina, it was Yadid who was more likely to win.

Reaching the upper lake, a vast swamp as large as the Kinnereth, they would break off wild sugarcane stalks to suck, and feed pieces to their horses.

In the swamp they had to proceed cautiously, as tales were told of hunters who had vanished in the quagmires. Set your foot on soft ground, and soon you would find yourself unable to pull out, and sink down slowly to your knees, your waist, your neck, your mouth, your eyes, and no one would ever find you. Such were the tales Fawzi related. The pursuit of the wild boar was most dangerous, as the cunning animal would lead you to the most dangerous parts of the swamp.

Yet one Saturday a wild boar broke from a clump of high papyrus reeds not far before them, and they could not stop themselves from hunting it. Twice they lost the animal, and each time it was Fawzi who again caught his movement, the second time leaping in his eagerness onto a muddy stretch, so that he had to lie flat and extend his rifle to Gidon who, seizing the end from firm ground, pulled him out.

But they had the pig backed against the open water, his long snout vibrating as though from some long lost reptilian time, as though even now it would shoot a stream of poison at them. The boar would charge; Yadid and Ayesha had followed close to the hunters, and as the wild boar's tiny, evil eye sought out the horses, the boys knew it was there he would charge, to rip the underbelly. The hunters fired together and seemed to have struck each into a burning, hating small swine's eye.

With the greatest caution they worked their way, this time Gidon before Fawzi, who held to firm ground, until finally they could pull the enormous carcass out of the slime. It lay before them. What a repulsive animal it was, and each said, no wonder it was forbidden to eat it.

Not for its ugliness, Gidon said—it was because the meat rotted quickly and in the old days had brought disease.

Just as much that it was repulsive and ugly, a beast of Satan, Fawzi said. But the Bedouin in these parts killed the pig for skin and bristles. Some said the meat could even be sold to the Christians in their monasteries.

The wicked, challenging idea came to both at the same moment; their eyes met and they laughed. Fawzi already had his knife free to cut a souvenir. "You don't believe in the kashrut, like your father who prays," Fawzi said, testingly.

"I don't believe in all these things, all those rules," Gidon said. "Do you believe like your father?"

They fell to talking in this vein. How much should a person believe? In God, Gidon said, yes, he believed. Not exactly in everything the way it was written, and not in all the rules, but he believed in God.

Fawzi too said he believed in God, and he believed in Mohammed the Prophet. Now that he could read, he was reading the Koran, and it was different from only hearing it read in small pieces by the mullah.

But many things in the Koran were the same as in the Bible, Gidon had heard from Reuven. Not only such things as everyone knew, that Moslems also were forbidden to eat pig. But Abraham—wasn't he too in the Koran?

"Yes," Fawzi said, with his odd touch of merriment that came when he spoke of serious matters. "Abraham is the father of us all."

—Did they have in their Koran the story of when Abraham was ready to sacrifice his son Isaac? Gidon asked.

—It was Ishmael, Fawzi said. Abraham was ready to sacrifice Ishmael on the altar, and was stopped at the last moment, when God sent him a sheep instead.

And he laughed.

"In your Koran, is it Ishmael, not Isaac?"

"Yes, it was Ishmael." And they both laughed.

All at once, Fawzi cut away a section of hide from the haunch of the pig. The flesh lay exposed, firm and darkly pink. They looked at each other, and the odd, soft laugh was repeated.

"Would you eat it?" Fawzi said.

"Why not?" said Gidon. "It is only meat, and it hasn't had time to spoil. It is not such rules that are important."

"To eat pig is the worst," Fawzi said. His eyes rested on the meat, in fascination.

"Do you want to taste it?" Gidon asked.

"Have you ever tasted it?"

"No." Where would he have tasted it? Suppose it had been offered to Reuven, would he have tasted it? But Reuven was a vegetarian. But before, when he was away from home, that summer among the Russians?

Fawzi was cutting off a slice of the meat. He held it out on his dagger. Something turned Gidon's stomach—perhaps from the sight of the dead boar's ugly snout.

"Not raw," he said.

"We will make a fire." Still with his mischievous gleam, Fawzi set about picking up twigs. Flies had been attracted, and now, up above, a few buzzards began to circle. Next, hyenas would come near. With a growing sense of disgust, of vileness here, Gidon wanted to shrug and declare they should start home. But Fawzi held the meat over the little fire, that flared up each time fat dripped on to it. Meanwhile, somehow Fawzi had got to talking of women again. He described how, on your wedding night, you could test if you had married a virgin. His older brother had told him how to test with your finger. With his free hand, he demonstrated to Gidon how to make sure. —But in a kvutsa, Fawzi said, his eyes alight, was it true the girls did it with all the men?

No, Gidon said, it was not true. Each had her own, the same as a marriage.

Was this really so? Fawzi asked, as though surprised. Was Gidon certain?

"Yes," Gidon said. His brother lived in the kvutsa, and his sister Leah also had lived in one, and his sister Dvora was married in a kvutsa and had a child. So he knew for certain.

Fawzi seemed disappointed. The meat was ready and he held it out on his knife. Gidon shrugged, blew on it, waited till it had cooled a bit, and then took a bite. It tasted much like calf's meat, a little sweeter perhaps.

He held the knife with the bit of meat toward Fawzi.

His friend hesitated, laughed, took the dagger by the handle, touched his tongue to the meat, then bit off a small piece, chewed once, spit it out, and laughed again, handing the knife back to Gidon.

Gidon flung away the remainder. They got up. A pity to

waste such a carcass—perhaps they should tell some Bedouin when they passed their cane huts down below?

"They'll find it," Fawzi said. "Or let there be a feast for the hyenas."

The hunters departed. Every once in a while on the way back, they looked at each other, somewhat abashedly, somewhat defiantly; perhaps, it occurred to Gidon, like two men who had been to a house of shame together.

10

FOR EACH settlement it seemed there had to come a time that was to form its legend, a time of testing, of fever, or hunger, or of blood; so it had been in Sejera on that tragic Passover of two deaths, Dvora's Yechezkiel and Mottel the Carpenter, and so it had been with the shooting of a Jewish watchman and two Arabs in what began as a squabble in Rehovot, and so it had been when Aaron Zeira was killed in the founding days of the Kvutsa Emek Yisroel, and now the legend of Mishkan Yaacov was to be formed.

Some would say it was only because of the misunderstandings between the ways of one people and another. Others would say it was because of hatreds being stirred up against the Jews, of late, in two Arab newspapers that had started, *Falastin* in Jaffa and *El Carmel* in Haifa. They had even tried to accuse Moshe Smilansky, Reuven's first employer, of the shootings in Rehovot, though he had not been anywhere near. With false witnesses they had tried to get him hanged by the Turks. Menahem managed to read what they wrote to stir up the villagers, but Shabbatai Zeira sneered—how many fellaheen could read? Galil and Nadina said religious hatred was behind it all, the imam would read the papers to the villagers to stir them up. But these papers were owned by Christians, not Moslems, Menahem said, and though the Moslems disdained all unbelievers, they did not have the hatred of pogromists. The fellaheen were not moujiks. It was wrong to sneer at them. To this, Reuven hotly agreed. Each trouble had its own cause.

There were feuds, killings among the Arabs themselves, much came from pride and hot-bloodedness. In the cities there might be some highly placed Arabs who did not like the coming of the Jews, while others saw advantages; but in the villages, the fellaheen were indifferent. And after each trouble, did they not settle down to peace with their neighbors?

Leah found herself staying on at home, not that there was any man to be seen in prospect for her there, but at least she was no longer subjected to annoyances by Zev the Hotblood, for the shomer had married the daughter of one of the Roumanians, Lula Janovici—he had already got her with child, it was said—and now, as everyone jested, the shomer had to take his midnight tea at home. Even though gossips had it that Zev managed a second snack through a certain bedroom window at the other end of the settlement, he at least no longer went about putting his hands where they were not wanted.

In the Chaimovitch yard, Leah had started a nursery school, a gan, using the new Montessori method she had brought from Jerusalem, and while this absorbed her energy, there was also a new friendship that gave her a sense of appeasement here.

The Roumanians next to the Chaimovitch farmyard had lost heart and returned to Kluj, and in their place had appeared an American—not altogether an American, since he was originally from Bialystok, but Joe Kleinman had spent fifteen years in America in a place called Nebraska in the west, where the philanthropic Baron de Hirsch had tried to establish Jews as farmers. The colony had fallen apart, Kleinman related, for sooner or later every Jewish farmer had put a pack on his back and gone off to peddle needles and buttons and eventually to open a store in some crossroads town, until Joe found himself the only farmer left. And since for some unfathomable reason he liked to live amongst Jews, maybe because they made him laugh, he had found himself lonesome out there in Nebraska and had decided—if with Jews he had to be, then why not in the Jewish land itself? So he had picked himself up one day, as he said, and come here to Eretz with his ever-willing wife and their two girls, the ages of Schmulik and Mati, though the boys would have nothing to do with them. Kleinman was given to jokes—his very name was a joke, he pointed out, as he was not a little man, but huge. This would have been a man for Leah! Even though he was eleven years older! But, alas, Joe, or Yosef as he now called himself, was well married. He and Leah laughed frequently over her predicament as to the size of men, and he offered, if she found a fellow whom she otherwise liked, to stretch him up for her. But at least Joe Kleinman's presence served as a constant reassurance to Leah, for see, there were indeed some tall Jews in the world!

Now, if she would only accept a goy, Kleinman would jest, he could import her one from the American west, where none was less than eight feet tall; he would have a sample shipped along with the farm machinery he kept bringing over. Not that he had so much money as to pay for all these machines, he would say, but his wife had brothers who owned stores.

Kleinman had brought with him catalogues with pictures of all sorts of American machinery, even newer things than Max Wilner knew about, and Reuven would come from the kvutsa and study the pages, while Yosef translated the particulars. What things there were! Machines to plant, machines to pick, machines to bale hay, and the biggest wonder of all, a wooden box as large as a small house—a threshing machine. The stalks went in at one end and pure clean grain poured out into a sack at the other end! Next year, Kleinman vowed, he would import one. Already he had brought a reaper, the first in the land. Kleinman sat perched on a high seat while a huge wheel with protruding blades whirled through the grain; not only the Roumanians, but Arabs from as far as Kfar Kana came and stared in awe as he reaped an entire field in a single day. Mansour, the mukhtar of Dja'adi, came down himself and after some urging took Kleinman's perch on the machine. But if such machines were to be brought here, the mukhtar questioned reflectively, what would be left for the fellaheen to do?

In Kleinman's house there was a large canister in which cream was turned into a sweet ice. Yosef's wife, Clara, now called Chava, let the children turn the handle, producing ice cream for them all, and even for Leah's Montessori children as well. Ah, America!

The village cattle grazed as a herd under the eyes of Alter Pincus, a venerable sage with a wispy white beard like a chinaman; he was the patriarch of one of the Roumanian families. Alter's great-grandson Shaikeh was that summer already big enough to do his running for him, while the patriarch sat on a stone, looking like a prophet except that his beard might have been thicker. Shaikeh was Mati's age, and their companionship was one long wrestling match in which, as in the races between Gidon's horse and Fawzi's, neither consistently triumphed.

Mati kept his eye on his own family's cattle, knowing the grazing preferences of each one—Schorah the black, mother of Bathsheba the beauty, and Malka the queen, who liked to stray near the riverbank and who gave the most milk; also there was Klugah the Clever, who would obey neither Shaikeh nor Alter Pincus when Mati was anywhere near, and finally Zipporah the Stupid, who would always take the wrong turn and had to be kept from entering other people's barns to be milked.

On this morning Mati took his herd somewhat apart, to the end of the family's fields, where the barley was being cut, and they grazed steadily on the stubble. His next older brother Schmulik, already big enough this year to swing a scythe, was deep in the field, but not able to keep up with Gidon who mowed at the far end. When their neighbor Kleinman was finished with his machine on his own fields, he would lend it to Gidon, he had promised, and what remained on the field would be mowed as by the wind. By the time Mati himself was grown up, Yosef Kleinman told him, machines would do all the work for everyone. Yet in a way Mati wanted the whole process to hold back until he had shown how well he could swing a scythe.

Just now Mati was sharpening a goad, using a flintstone he had picked up in the riverbed. The stone fitted well into his palm, and though the edge was not as sharp as a knife, he was managing to take off shavings from the stick. Thus he was a man of long ago, as Reuven had explained to him. These stones were washed down by the winter rains that made fresh crevices among the rocks below the caves; among the tumbled stones that had fallen into the stream and been slowly washed along, one could espy such flinty ones, sharp tools that had been shaped by the hands of cave dwellers long before even the time of Abraham.

Down by the river he saw a boy from Dja'adi, Abdul, with his flock of black goats. Abdul was older than himself, but younger than Schmulik, and he had a brother the age of Gidon, Gidon's friend Fawzi, who raced his Ayesha against Gidon's Yadid, and went hunting with Gidon as far as the Huleh.

Abdul's goats moved in on the stubble, feeding not far from Mati's cattle, but this was permitted, Mati knew. It had been discussed by several of the Roumanians standing in the yard with his father, and they had all agreed, very well, let the Arab sheep and goats come onto the cut fields, it was a good thing to be friends, and though there was no lack of grass up there among the rocks, let their flocks also graze on the stubble. Later, Fawzi's father had come down, riding into their yard; as with so many of the Arabs, one of his eyes was unfocused, and he was one of those who sat all day up there in their cafe, complaining that his sons were lazy. Abba himself had told Fawzi's father that it would be permitted for their flocks to graze on the mown fields, but not in the grain.

The green stick was hard to cut and Mati concentrated on his work. After a time the goad was finished, and he looked up, but he no longer saw Abdul or his black goats. Mati moved his gaze then along to the standing, uncut grain. To God it must look like golden hair on earth, if there was really a God. And deep in the smooth field he saw a slight movement. Abdul's goats were in there devouring the grain itself.

Shouting a foul Arab word that he was forbidden to utter within hearing of his mother and sisters, Mati rushed to drive the goats out from his barley, but Abdul rose up from where he had been lying, and shouted back the filthiest of mother-curses. Brandishing his goad, Mati tried to chase the animals out; Abdul placed himself in the way, and Mati charged him. They tumbled together, rolling, scuffling, with a sudden shriek from Abdul as the pointed stick tore into his cheek. "I'll put your eyes out!" he spat, his face close to Mati's, his breath a stink, and his thumbs thrusting. Mati tore at the hands. Abdul's sinews were like vulture talons. Already Mati's eyeballs pained as though bursting from their sockets. With the flintstone still in one hand, Mati slashed, and a talon gave way. One eye was free. But from under Abdul's other thumb, Mati felt a doubled pain, and then terror of an eye destroyed as in the face of Abdul's father; with a heave that was beyond his own strength, he wrenched himself around on top of his enemy, in the same movement pulling his head backward, free of the grinding finger.

But with his bloodied hand, the Arab boy had reached for his dagger, and now Mati felt a burning streak along his back. Wildly he kept striking with his sharp stone, feeling blows on his head, smelling their bodies together, and in a maddening way, sensing the goats all around them continuing to feed.

Then Schmulik's voice was on top of them, but as though from afar, commanding through a thickness of wild curses, "Leave off!" With such violence had Schmulik torn away Abdul's knife-arm that the break of the bone was heard.

The howling and shrieked pain of the boys had already brought men running from nearby fields, Arabs and Jews arriving simultaneously and falling upon each other, the grown cousins and half-brothers of Abdul rushing with their staves at Schmuel. From above and below men came as to a tocsin, some on foot, some on mules, some on horses, and presently the entire field was alive with shouting and fighting men. A few for the first instant only stood calling out for everyone to stop—then they too started flinging accusations and insults at each other like gobs of dripping dung. Suddenly one would ride down on an adversary, who would strike back with a stave, and there would be an additional melee, men rolling on the ground, others trying to strike into the heap, still others arriving and trying to pull the fighters apart until they too were fighting.

The first boys were already separated and held away from each other, Abdul with his arm limp and face bloodied, and Mati doubled over on the ground, face down, while Gidon, who had arrived at a gallop, tried with a cloth torn from his shirt to staunch the flow of blood from the open lips of the dagger-gash in his little brother's back. Maledictions and accusations reverberated in the sultry air.

The men, somewhat subdued by the sight of the wide-open gash, stood now in two lines, gesticulating and shouting still, but at least separated from one another. Yet suddenly at one end or the other, with a thrown stone, or an insult hurled, bodies would come together, and others add onto them, and the melee was resumed.

Already it had been cried out in the settlement that marauders in a multitude were carrying off grain from the fields, and that little Mati Chaimovitch had been cut to pieces. Barely up from his early morning sleep, Zev the Shomer came charging into the battle. It was a confused moment. A melee had started again, and from Dja'adi, Abdul's brother Fawzi also came galloping, charging into the fight, swinging a rake. Without pause, Zev raised up his rifle and fired.

Every movement in the field was suspended in midair. Until that moment it had been a squabble, a fight with blows, with sticks, but no more—except for Mati's flintstone and Abdul's dagger, no weapons had appeared.

None but Zev had come onto the field with firearms.

All stared at Fawzi as though waiting for his body to topple. Then, unlimited battle would be released.

But Fawzi sat unhurt.

It was the mount, Gidon saw, not the man who had been hit. Ayesha wildly flung up her neck, and something like a bloodchoked outcry, more human than animal, came from the wounded beautiful mare as her legs stiffened. Over Gidon's first sense of relief that no human was slain there spread an engulfing dismay, grief for the beautiful animal, then anger. That stupid Hotblood with his shooting!

"It was not meant! It was not meant!" Gidon cried out as Fawzi slid off his wounded horse. "Fawzi! Take mine!" And even while his heart died in him for the loss it would be, Gidon's hand reached out the halter.

But his friend only spat on the ground between them. "Take care of your brother, Yahud," Fawzi said, his tone flat.

Mati, half-raised up, had again slipped to the ground, his limbs trembling, blood oozing from under the bandage.

Together with the sick-eyed father of Fawzi and Abdul, their uncle the mukhtar had appeared. Sitting his horse, Mansour listened to several of the angry fellaheen, glanced down at Mati, looked sharply at the wounded mare, then glared at Zev, who still held his rifle crosswise on his saddle. With an angry gesture, the mukhtar motioned his people from the field; clearly this was not the end. Dark-faced and muttering, the Arabs of Dja'adi turned and followed

Fawzi as he slowly led his Ayesha. The head of the mare hung low, the tawny neck clotted with gouts of dark-brown blood.

Already most of the women of Mishkan Yaacov were worriedly coming out into the open, and several began to shriek when they saw, in the wagon coming from the fields, the bloodied Mati, face down on the bed of straw. But it was not Feigel's way to wail at the sign of calamity. Running forward with a basin of water, while Leah climbed onto the wagon with white cloths, Feigel with one quick look at the wound sucked in her cries and directed her husband: he must drive straight to Tiberias.

Lately there had been, anew, a few instances of trouble at the Three Rocks. Stamp out vermin, and more rise from under the earth. Should not Gidon ride alongside to protect the wagon? But he might be needed here; the very air was oppressive. From the fields the Roumanians were pulling homeward, gathering their implements and turning their wagons toward the village. Some said a shot had been heard from Dja'adi—surely the wounded horse was now dead. Would there be a revenge? They discussed and disputed. A dead horse is not a dead Arab. To an Arab his horse is worth more than a human life. They could kill for a horse. Who knew what really went on in their heads? Though with Dja'adi there had never been real trouble. What was it the fellaheen had kept shouting?

—That they had the right to graze, Gidon repeated.

"But only on the stubble! Not in an uncut field!"

A triple watch must be mounted. That hot-headed Zev must not go out alone.

Zev defended himself angrily. He had done right to shoot, or Fawzi would have split Gidon's head with the rake he was wielding.

Gidon decided to escort the wagon past the Three Rocks and then hurry back to the troubled village. It was best, also, that Leah, on the wagon, should carry a pistol.

Kneeling over the child on the straw, as the wagon bounced off a large stone in the road, Feigel saw the bandage slowly staining anew, and in anguish watched Mati's blood seeping from under the edges. Leah bent with her over the wound, and in helpless terror, they gazed at each other. "Yankel, the stones," Feigel begged, yet what could the poor man do? To avoid them he would have to go slowly. Cautiously Leah undid the cloth, and the gash lay there before them, partly clotted, but with blood seeping up through a break in the crust. Little Mati raised up his head a bit and complained, "Ima, it hurts." Desperately Feigel held the flesh together with her fingers, her child's blood slippery, then sticky on her hand, the wagon lurching— "Yankel!" —but still everything within her cried "Hurry— quickly," and meanwhile Leah worried that the dust from the road could infect the wound.

So at last in this drawn-out agony they came to the pharmacy in Tiberias. As the boy was lifted on Yankel's arms from the wagon, women in the marketplace were already wailing, each as though the child were her own, and there even arose from somewhere the frightened beginning of a death-ululation.

Yankel laid the child face-downward on a bench as the apothecary, called from behind, hurried to them. A short-bearded Jew in a yarmulkeh, half a doctor he was—and at a glance, Gottgetrei said, "This must be sewn up at the hospital. It is not for me." Meanwhile he carefully cleaned around the wound; with the burn of the peroxide, Mati let out a howl, and this at least relieved Feigel's heart, for in the bravery of boys, the protesting howl was permitted and meant all was yet well.

In the crowd at the door of the pharmacy, Leah noticed their neighbor Joe Kleinman—he had recognized their wagon. "What happened, Leah?" In a word she told of the fight. Was Mati all right?

"He'll live," she was now confident.

—Good, said Joe Kleinman—he would gallop back, he might be needed in the village. Still he lingered watching as the pharmacist, calling his apprentice to mind the shop, moved to lead them to the hospital.

Yankel again picked up the child across his arms. Was God once more demanding the offering, it came to him, again the bringing of the sacrifice to the altar, again the akeda? Had he been brought to Eretz so that a Jew might over and over be tested with the brutal sacrifice? Wasn't one dead child—his Avramchick—wasn't one enough?

Then, as Yankel stepped with his burden outside the

door, it was as though all the embittering perversion of history were suddenly revealed to him. There before him indeed loomed the heathen altar! The cross above the large wrought-iron gate of the Christian mission confronted him from the end of the street, just as the golden-domed heathen mosque had confronted him in Yerushalayim, replacing the Temple over the rock of Abraham.

A sacrifice to their idols!

Yankel stood rigid. "I cannot."

"But, my fine Jew, where would you take him?" Gottgetrei demanded. "This is the only hospital in Tiberias. As far as Safed—on the hilly road—the wound is sure to open again."

Several Sephardim had gathered, and a whole talmudic dispute rang in Yankel's ears. It is forbidden, it is permitted, was not Gottgetrei himself a good pious Jew? But as Yankel stood dazed, uncertain—was it the body of Avramchick on his arms? —there suddenly returned over him an anger at Reuven for bringing them all to this gehenna. Was the fellaheen slaughter with knives any different than the moujik's pogrom with hatchets? Adonai! what do you want of a Jew?

While Yankel stood rigid, frozen, Leah cried, "Give him to me!" Yankel's head was shaking to say no, while inwardly he cried to himself, Spit on their cross but enter the hospital! At that moment, Joe Kleinman broke through the circle and lifted Mati from Yankel's arms. Yankel saw them walking under the cross, Feigel and Leah together with Kleinman. He could not follow; his legs were stone.

In the mission yard a number of Arab women squatted, holding their sore-infested babies, but already the door opened as someone white-clad—a priest, a doctor, who knew?—beckoned to them. Leah took Mati over from Yosef Kleinman. "Go home," she said, feeling his anxiety about his family, and he was a good man to have just now in the village; he would calm them all with his American humor. "Tell Gidon and the children Mati's all right," she said. Then she recalled that Yosef always went unarmed and insisted that he take her pistol—he would be riding alone, and trouble was in the air. "That's what makes the trouble," he said with his wide grin, and refused.

When another white-clad one, in broad robes, drew close, Feigel was not without apprehension. Might they even try to sprinkle water on her son before they treated him? From far back in the old country such tales came to her; this she knew was the terror Yankel had felt, and as the priest took the boy from Leah, the mother stayed close, holding onto Mati's hand.

But they did not carry him into a church. It was a white-washed room, though with a picture of their Yoshke on the wall, a sad Sephardic face with fine eyes, not unlike those of Gottgetrei, the pharmacist; Feigel kept her gaze averted from that wall.

They had placed Mati on a high white-painted table. speaking their own language to each other—it was English, Leah whispered to Feigel, this was an English Christian place—the priests or doctors probed the wound. Several times Mati sucked in his breath, but now he would not cry, and one of them patted his head.

The doctor-priests were asking something of Feigel, then of Leah. Leah could only shake her head to show she did not understand English; she tried a few words of Hebrew, but they shook their heads. Anxiously, Feigel tried to ask them what they wanted, in Russian, in a half-Yiddish German, and at last between a mingling of words in Hebrew and Arabic, and a gesture of sewing, she understood and nodded vigorously. Indeed they must sew it up. But that wasn't quite it. Leah caught the meaning—brave? was the boy brave? Then one of them, the one in the broad gown, bent his cheek against his hand, meaning sleep, and shook his finger—he meant they would not or could not put Mati to sleep. Was he brave?

Leah began to explain to Mati, but he had understood their Arabic better than she. It would hurt; if it hurt too much, they would put him to sleep, but if he was brave, it was only a little sewing, sewing your skin like when you tear your shirt. "Sew," he said. The child turned his head away and waited.

The mother must now leave the room, the priest insisted, and Feigel slowly went out to where Yankel stood. At least Leah remained with Mati.

Watching the priests put the needle through the candle flame, Mati clutched Leah's hand tight. The needle came now. He did not cry out. In Arabic a doctor said, "A man."

It seemed unending. Again the needle stabbed, the small

body stiffened, but not a sound came. Again. Again. Twenty times. Then it was finished, the wound was dressed, The Christians made compliments to the little son, and they lifted him from the table, a bandage tightly swathed around him just below the armpits. Carefully, carefully, Mati could stand. He could walk, but not run, they cautioned him. Brave, a man!

Leah asked what was owed, and they smiled and pointed to a small box; it was oddly like the blue and white collection boxes of the Keren Kayemeth Le Israel, only a cross was on it. "Don't ever tell Tateh!" Leah enjoined Mati, as she hurriedly put in a whole Turkish pound in silver.

On the way back the boy fell asleep in his mother's lap. Under his bronzed face, the yellow tinge was still there from the loss of blood. "You know what," Leah said, "we'll ask Chava Kleinman to make him some ice cream."

The whole afternoon a stillness had lain on the fields. Gidon rode the rounds in one direction, Zev in the other— he was after all the shomer. The Arab fields too, they saw, were deserted. Though this made Gidon apprehensive, Zev, as they exchanged a few words when they completed their circles and met, insisted it was not a bad sign. "It is they who are afraid of us," he said. "They are afraid if your brother should die, we will take revenge."

Zev's thought was a vileness to Gidon. "He isn't dead and he won't die!" he snapped, and what did Zev really understand of the Arabs? Perhaps the best would be, Gidon speculated, if he were to ride up right now to Dja'adi and talk to Fawzi, and ask after Abdul's arm that Schmulik had badly wrenched, and tell them Mati would be well. Though Fawzi's spat out "Yahud!" still burned in his bowels, coming just after he had offered his own horse, his own Yadid. No, the whole affair would have to be straightened out in some other way. Perhaps Reuven should go up and talk to their mukhtar—in such matters Bronescu was useless. Though not yet. Tomorrow or the next day, after tempers had cooled.

So Gidon reflected as he rode his rounds, but underneath it all a profound dismay grew heavier. That "Yahud!" It must always have lain there even in Fawzi. Just as the whole hateful outbreak this morning had lain in Dja'adi.

Late in the afternoon Gidon had an urgent feeling that the wagon was returning, and encountering Zev at the end of his round, he said, "I'll miss the next circle, I'm going to meet them."

He galloped as far as the Three Rocks; the wagon was just coming, all was quiet, and Gidon rode alongside listening to the account of Mati's bravery under the stitches. The boy was awake and grinning at their praise. She was going to borrow the American machine and make ice cream, Leah declared, and then added, "But didn't Joe Kleinman tell you that Mati was all right? He was in Tiberias and rode home ahead of us."

No, Gidon had not seen Joe Kleinman.

"He was worried about the trouble, and in such a hurry to get home."

As the crop fire had started on the far side of the fields where Gidon would have been circling, it was not detected at once.

Only at the end of Zev's own round, when he reached the high point, did Zev see the rim of the blaze. At first glance it was like a sunset reflection that sometimes came from that direction, but what was he dreaming of?—over the low streak of crimson there was black smoke.

As he galloped, the widening blaze unfolded before him, and Zev realized he could do nothing by himself to halt it. And by now he would catch no one there, unless it was an ambush as well, with the dirty cowards waiting to shoot him down. Firing off his rifle as an alarm, he now wheeled toward the settlement, cursing Gidon and the Chaimovitches, the whole lot of them, even though he had agreed that Gidon should go meet the returning wagon.

Hearing Zev's shot, Gidon cut across the fields, galloping, leaving the wagon to enter the settlement. On the rise he saw the blaze and doubled back, yelling "Fire! Fire!"

In the first confusion some of the villagers leaped on their horses, their mules, with anything they could seize, a rake, a mattock. Zev met them midway, reviling, commanding, "Sacking! Wet sacks! Do you think you can put it out with your hands?"

"Whose fields?" each settler demanded, begged, while Zev thundered from one house to the next, and Gidon on the other side charged them, "Bring mattocks, sacks, wet sacks," and in every yard a racing in circles began, some pumping water, some women even running out with brooms to beat off the fire, others screeching at their children to get inside the house. Bronescu had flung open his shed and was handing out empty burlap sacks from a pile there. People snatched them and ran and had to be called back to wet them, wet them! A wagonful of fire fighters galloped off. Whose field? Whose field? "Yosef Kleinman's!" Zev shouted. Yet where was Yosef? A fire-break must be plowed; Kleinman must bring his reaping machine and cut a wide swath across the grain—

"He hasn't come home," his wife cried out.

"But he left before us, at least by two hours!" Leah exclaimed. And on top of the conflagration a new horror-fear blazed up in them.

Not a sign of Joe had been seen on the road. At the Three Rocks all had been quiet. No, he must surely have been delayed, stopping to buy something more in Tiberias, or perhaps he had stopped at one of the kvutsoth. Yes, that was it. He must be at HaKeren. None could be spared to go there now, everyone was running to fight the fire, and Chava Kleinman distractedly ran with all the others, to Joe's fields, then turned back and started the other way, toward the kvutsa.

Yankel had already lifted a plow onto the wagon. Eliza was emptying sacks of grain and wetting the burlap in the washtub by the pump. Yaffaleh was pumping while Schmulik lifted an empty barrel to his father on the wagon and then handed up pailfuls of water for Yankel to dump in. The entire family was starting for the fields; Leah had to seize hold of Mati, "Stay here!" To Eliza she called, "Stay with him. Don't let him move."

Mishkan Yaacov was all at once empty, the bit of street quiet and deserted in the waning sun, as though Sabbath had fallen.

And this was the moment chosen by the Zbeh. It was the time of waning light when the ancient Jew led the herd home, his great-grandson driving the animals from behind.

When the fighting had started in the morning, Alter Pincus had moved the herd, the Chaimovitch cows among them, somewhat closer to the village, where they could readily be moved inside the village walls, and there he had kept them grazing all day. But now, just as the herd was beginning its movement homeward, horsemen swept in from nowhere. They were in front, behind, on all sides, pounding around the startled beasts that pressed together in panic. And when Alter, too bewildered to be terrified, seized the rope of his own cow, protesting she was his, a Bedouin simply rode him down, smashing the old Jew's head with his rifle butt.

The boy Shaikeh, darting sideward to run away, to run for help, found himself chased by a laughing tribesman who cornered him as he crouched against a rock, and, still laughing, took aim. The shot made a hole all the way through the boy's head.

The Jews would be too busy with their burning fields now to turn back over a stray rifleshot.

Only Chava Kleinman heard it, from the path where she was hurrying to the kvutsa; in her panic it struck her as though she were hearing Joe shot dead. For a moment she stood stock still, straining for the death to pass, then she managed to make herself take shelter behind a rock, and she saw the cattle herded by the riders, white ghost waves of robes floating across the twilight haze, and patches of white from the sides of the cattle, and after this was gone from sight, she stumbled through brambles in the direction the shot had come from. There was still enough light for her to make out the thin-spun white hair and beard of Alter Pincus, and then, though she was not a brave girl like Leah Chaimovitch, she nevertheless pursued the horror and found the little boy, too; he was lying, a clump of contracted limbs against the rock, the way a child gathers itself together in a chilly bed.

Chava sat on the ground and her grief for the murdered old man and the boy was her grief for her husband, whose death she knew but would not yet admit into herself.

The fire was not yet to be readily conquered. Though there was no wind, the midsummer heat in the Jordan valley was like the inside of an earthen baking oven. Some even said the fire could have started of itself or sprung in this heat from a cigarette spark, since a donkey path went through the field. But with blackened, sweat-running faces most of them turned and looked toward Dja'adi. They must be standing up there on their hill and gloating! To take such a revenge! Let the Arab fields be set aflame in return!

In their fury the farmers smote their sacks harder on the ground, a close line of them like a line of demons making an inroad on the line of flame. But beyond the end of their line the fire moved forward with a hissing devouring sound, like some exultant beast. A hundred paces inward, their arms and heads lit up by the approaching flames, Yankel Chaimovitch and the young Mikosh Janovici and still another plowman stumbled after their mules through the dark, while boys shouted and goaded to keep the animals from shying away from the oncoming scorching heat.

Already by the time the fire fighters had reached the scene, Kleinman's fields were cindered, and the flames had now eaten half across the sector of Yasha Janovici, the father-in-law of Zev. At least with Zev now, no fault could be found; he commanded with skill and presence of mind, he was everywhere, flailing with two sacks at a time where a spear of flame suddenly shot forward, riding ahead of the plowmen to trample a path for them, galloping where new sparks could be seen. Early, he had thought to send Gidon back for Kleinman's American reaper, and Gidon was now slashing a secondary firebreak beyond the plowline, should the flames leap across.

In the sweat and fury of their labor the entire village worked as one, the Roumanians and the two Russian families; even the melamed, his torso bare, swung shovelfuls of earth against the smoldering edges of the fire. A number of women worked by the water-barrels that had been hauled to the field, wetting the sacks and passing them forward, the younger girls running with them to the fire-line, the larger girls and boys standing with Leah and flailing at the flames.

Slowly, slowly, the blaze was conquered, leaping up again in one corner to jump the plowlines, or stealing out from a patch of smoldering cinders only to be smothered again. Two entire holdings had been lost, Kleinman's crop and Janovici's.

Wiping their smarting eyes even though each fire fighter told the others not to, snorting, spitting and half-vomiting to retch out the acrid smell that crawled through the nostrils and throat down into the very intestines, the settlers

were already saying to each other that all must bear a
share of the loss.

As they slowly drew into a group, casting a final look for
spots of flame over the dead fields, curses and mutterings
of vengeance sparked up again out of their weariness.
Young Gidon did not join in this. Once he remarked to
young Mikosh Janovici, "If it came from Dja'adi, they
would not have done it here, they would have done it on
the same field where the boys stopped them from grazing."

Mikosh gave him a puzzled half-angry look, but did not
reply.

Then Gidon suddenly realized that, Zev being married to
a Janovici, it could have been a revenge.

Only when, limp and stretched exhausted in their wagons,
they dragged themselves toward the village, did the night's
full catastrophe come to them. A few of the older people
who had remained at home stood half inside the gate
around Chava Kleinman. She had made her way back.
Even in the dark it could be seen that her face was
haunted.

From all those standing there around her, in Roumanian, in Yiddish, the same words came like bird shrieks;
Alter Pincus and Shaikeh murdered, the Zbeh, the cattle,
the entire herd, Alter and Shaikeh . . .

So it was the Zbeh after all, Gidon realized. The fire to
draw away the whole village. And then the herd, and
blood. The Zbeh from over there, from the heights of Golan. Something came to him from far back, from cheder
memory. This was Cain, this was Esau, this was embittered
Ishmael.

────⌁────

Chava Kleinman could not be left by herself, and Leah
went over to spend the night in the house with the wife and
daughters of the missing Yosef. The little girls went quietly
and obediently to their room; the first time the mother
looked in, they feigned sleep—but then as she stood in the
partly opened doorway holding the lamp, an intake of
breath, less than a sob, came from the smaller girl, and the
brave pretenses were ended. Chava went in to them.

Leah heard them weeping together, the three of them,

and waited for them to cry themselves out. Sitting alone by the table, she struggled against the feeling that her nearness to anyone brought misfortune and tragedy. Moshe, Dvoraleh's Yechezkiel, Avramaleh. It was she who had begged Mameh to come to Eretz and bring little Avramaleh here. No, she would not yield to such a way of thinking.

If only there were noises, animal calls, voices, hooves! Even the jackels were silent tonight. As though the cindered fields lay on a dead world.

11

THE SITTING was in the rear of Bronescu's store, deep into the night. With the cattle stolen and the fields burned, an old man and a child murdered, it seemed impossible that all this was retaliation from Dja'adi for the shooting of a horse.

Reuven had come from the kvutsa; from Yavniel there was Shimshoni the Practical, just now stationed there for a turn as shomer. Back and forth the men puzzled. Shimshoni upheld Zev's view—the fight in the field, even though a shot had been fired, could not have been a provocation for such disasters.

—If it was the Zbeh taking advantage of the fight in the field, to make a raid?

—Perhaps it was both the Zbeh and Dja'adi together?

—From Dja'adi they hate the Zbeh. They have a ghoum.

—It's between two families. Otherwise, they have dealings.

—But what could have become of Yosef Kleinman?

Bronescu was for calling in the Turkish authorities.

Not yet. Either Galil or Menahem or perhaps Shabbatai Zeira must surely be on the way from Gilboa.

Shimshoni spoke what some were thinking. "If Yosef Kleinman rode in on the Zbeh while they were taking the cattle, he must have tried to stop them. They could have killed him and taken his horse."

"Then why didn't we find his body in the field with the others?"

"Perhaps he pursued them and got killed on the other side?"

"Sometimes they hide the body," said Zev. "That's one of their ways."

In Reuven, something deeper wove, drawing back to the old troubles in Fuleh, to the Arab boy killed there in a theft. And then two Jews in retaliation, Dvora's Yechezkiel and the carpenter from Sejera. With Galil, he had pressed for the way of law and justice, the jailing of the murderers. And then a third, young Aaron Zeira. And the assassination at Dagania. For all this everyone knew that the Shomer had at last made an end of the Fuleh bandits. They had vanished and never been found; the Three Rocks had been their haunt, and there it was rumored to have happened. And there it could have been Kleinman had vanished.

And now two more Jews had been added, Alter Pincus and Shaikeh. Was it to be an endless alternation of deaths, a ghoum without end? He kept seeing little Mati, the long raw seam on his back when Leah had rebandaged him just now. The deeply puzzled look in his little brother's eyes, even there the dark look of Chaimovitch melancholy, of a profound sense of an absolute failing in the universe, felt by a child. What could a man do, what could even a whole society do of itself, when the others were moved by a totally different morality, as from some other universe?

With the earliest thread of light, Gidon rode out to the Three Rocks. There was nothing. Not the mark of an ambush, a scuffle, nothing.

He was leading Yadid in the muddy area behind the rocks when a Arab boy approached. Gidon knew him. He was not from Dja'adi but from a fisherman's brood—the children loitered around the area and would come up to you asking for a cigarette. Now the boy carried something under his arm. Nearing, he brought it forward with an uncertain smile. It was Joe Kleinman's cowboy hat.

His throat half-choked up, Gidon tried to keep his questions unexcited. "Where did you come by this hat, Jamal?"

—Oh, he had found it.

"Where?"

"In a field."

"A field? Not here by the Three Rocks?"

"No, a field," he swore. "Over there." He would show.

Had the boy been sent, Gidon wondered? "You know whose hat this is?"

"Cowboy. American." A fleeting shy smile. Perhaps he really had found it.

"Jamal, you saw the cowboy?"

A tick of the tongue. No. Gidon brought out two cigarettes and gave one to the boy. Had he not seen the man? Or his horse? A black mare?

—Ah, Jamal knew the mare well.

—Had he seen her yesterday?

The tongue ticked, no.

At last, after receiving the second cigarette, Jamal led Gidon to the field where, he said, he had found the hat.

Not far off the road. Nothing. Not even a hoof mark. A stony field of scattered wildflowers.

Perhaps the cowboy hat had been thrown there as a marker? By Joe Kleinman himself? By the Zbeh? Perhaps it had not been Jamal who had found it, perhaps it had been entrusted to him as a beginning of some sort of bargaining?

The boy asked if Gidon wanted to buy the cowboy hat.

Then Kleinman was surely killed. Was this the beginning of bargaining for the body?

—He had indeed seen nothing? And the cowboy himself?

Nothing! The boy swore vehemently, by his future in paradise. Let his tongue be cut out, let his eyes be taken from his head, he had seen nothing! And in the absolute candor of those eyes, Gidon knew that whatever this Jamal had seen, for now he had seen nothing.

—Did he perhaps have more to sell?

No. Was there a glint of mischief? Even of contempt?

Compressing his bitterness, Gidon gave the boy a coin, letting him grumble about the price. There would be more, Gidon said, if he brought word of the cowboy himself, or his horse.

Now the boy looked a bit frightened. As Gidon took the hat, he knew that he took this thing on himself. In some of his pronouncements Zev was right; only in their own ways could you deal with them. Otherwise how was one to live with them in this land?

Gidon rode back slowly. Whom should he tell of this? When the Kleinmans had first arrived, the cowboy hat, in constant fun, had gone from one head to another. Eliza had perched it above her long braids, Leah had tried it on, and Yaffaleh, and the boys, and he himself. Once when Tateh was in a good mood, Eliza had even perched it over his yarmulkeh.

Entering through the small stable gate in the back wall, Gidon just had time to conceal the hat in the hay when Chava Kleinman appeared—she must have been anxiously watching for him. Already the woman seemed shrunken, her American clothes too large. Chava Kleinman was always giving clothes to his sisters, frilly shirtwaists and even gloves—Eliza could not resist them.

No, no word of her Yosef, Gidon shook his head as Chava followed him about the yard, no, but perhaps that was a good sign. Mama and Leah came out to her, insisting there was still hope; she must eat something, take something into her mouth, Feigel kept repeating, she must have strength for the sake of her daughters at least.

It was a time before he could manage to show the hat to Leah alone. And then Gidon saw the dark look come into his sister's eyes; she held the cowboy hat against herself and stroked it, and behind the surface of her eyes was that darkness as when the world was a void of darkness.

At last Leah sighed. "He wouldn't even carry a pistol. What did they want of him?"

"His horse," Gidon said. The further thought, he couldn't yet bring out.

All morning men came riding from Yavniel, from Gilboa. Wild rumors had spread of a pitched battle. The Chaimovitch yard became the gathering place—twenty, forty men milled about; some said the Zbeh would yet attack in force, to wipe out the whole of Mishkan Yaacov.

Menahem and Galil arrived; behind Bronescu's store the sitting resumed. —A delegation must go to Damascus, even to Constantinople, Bronescu kept proposing, while Zev shouted—Mount a full attack and ride after the ma-

rauders! With an entire herd of cattle, they could not have
got far. Not to lose another moment!

Galil cut him short. In his quick, breathy voice he asked
of Gidon exactly what happened. Gidon told of the fight,
"Zev shot."

"Until then no one used firearms?"

The Hotblood was glaring at Gidon. "No."

"Was it necessary to fire?"

"It must have looked bad to Zev when he rode up. I am
not the one to say if shooting was necessary."

"Aha." This would be for the Shomer to decide amongst
themselves.

And the burned fields, the cattle, the two dead, and Joe
Kleinman—where was the connection? As Galil understood it, the Arabs of Dja'adi were not even on good terms
with the Zbeh.

"Some take wives among the Zbeh, they cost less," Menahem said. A queasy smile went around the table. —There
were threads from one tribe to another, Menahem went on,
and the family feud had long been quiescent, but in his
view it would be wrong to conclude they had done all this
together.

"And Joe Kleinman?" Zev broke in. "Joe Kleinman
wasn't murdered from Dja'adi in revenge for their damn
horse?"

"Have you gone crazy!" Menahem burst out. "It's not
their way! You don't know them!"

"They're all alike!" Zev spat on the floor. "I was raised
with Arabs, what have you to tell me about their ways!
We're wasting time! They'll get beyond reach with the cattle. Come on!" He rushed out.

Mikosh Janovici jumped on his feet to follow Zev, who
was already mounting. Galil shouted, "I command you,
Zev! Get down!"

In the uproar, Gidon found a moment to tell Menahem
quietly of the hat. His brother-in-law gripped his wrist.
"Don't bring it up now."

Within Menahem, remotely yet powerfully, as when you
strain two hooks together and they don't quite link, Gidon's words reached toward that other, deeply submerged
event. Profoundly, Menahem knew that what had happened to Kleinman at the Three Rocks was not connected

with the fire, the cattle. A coincidence. And yet more deeply, all, all was connected, just as roots all reach into the same earth.

And to Gidon, as he watched the clouded face of Menahem, there also came a sense of connection, but to a different source. It was as though he were an Arab looking at the coming of the Jews. With their fat cattle from Europe. With their newly invented machines from America. It was not a thing of reason that arose. "Yahud!" he recalled Fawzi's outburst.

"And who set fire to the fields?" Zev was shouting, though he had obeyed and dismounted. "Go, go find out a little about their fine mukhtar Mansour up there. You think he didn't call in the Zbeh? You can be sure he'll get his share for our cattle! Go, let their goats gobble up the crops! Next, they'll lay claim on the land for grazing rights forever! Go! Blame me for protecting the fields!"

All morning the tension remained. Added guards rode the rounds, but not a man of Dja'adi was seen anywhere.

In the Chaimovitch yard, Feigel was feeding everyone— she would be eaten out of house and home, but let that be the worst, Mati was saved.

A volunteer from Yavniel said a few Arabs of Dja'adi had come out on their height and looked down on the burned fields. Mikosh Janovici still urged, "We should go and burn theirs!"

All at once word spread that two of the Roumanian families were packing to leave Mishkan Yaacov altogether and would sell what was left at a bargain.

Then came a distraction. A single cow walked slowly into the center of the village, from the direction of the river crossing. All ran toward the animal and onward beyond her as though the remainder of the herd must be following. "They can't be far!" Zev shouted and galloped to the crossing. But even the Hotblood would not rashly clamber alone to the heights on the other side.

Schmulik had run to the cow, excitedly seizing her halter. "It's Klugeh," he cried out, the wise one. He himself had given her this name, the cleverest of the cattle, and here she had proved herself, for somehow Klugeh had broken from the marauders and found her way home.

But already the whole Zeidenschneur family from the other end of the village was pushing and dragging at the cow, claiming she belonged in their barn, she was theirs, black with a white star!

Half the stolen cattle were black with a white star, from the same strain, but Klugeh was Klugeh, Schmulik cried, everyone knew her!

Yet, as it became clear that no other cattle were returning, more claimants began to say the cow was theirs, pushing and dragging at the bewildered animal who planted her hooves in the dirt and urinated.

"God in heaven!" Eliza cried out with a rage unknown in her, here was one cow left in the entire village on this day of disaster with two people lying dead waiting to be put into the ground, and the Roumanians would tear apart the single remaining cow with their quarreling over her!

Suddenly Yankel Chaimovitch stormed into the center of the street. "Let her go!" Klugeh knew her home. Let everyone stand aside and the cow would go where she belonged.

The cow waited, gazing around her as though she were judging mankind. Deliberately she now dropped a steaming turd. Then she went directly into the Chaimovitch yard.

Presently another odd thing happened. In the Kleinman barn was a young calf that had been kept back yesterday to have a sore tended. Now the bleating calf hurried across toward Klugeh. The cow had never let any but her own approach, she would kick away the offspring of others, but as though she comprehended all that had happened, Klugeh remained still while the orphan calf approached and suckled.

The story spread in the village. "It will yet be like that among all of us." Hanna Zeidenschneur predicted. "Only orphans will remain."

In the midst of all came the Turks—the Kaymakam himself, the fat Azmani Bey of Tiberias, with his entire force of eight mounted gendarmes headed by their Bimbashi.

As they were seen approaching, a command hastily went out, "Hide all weapons!" Even the watchmen could not be certain but what the Turks would seize their arms, and as for the numerous settlers from Yavniel who had come to help—let them scatter into various houses as visitors, as relatives come for the funeral.

Hurriedly, Leah collected rifles and pistols and ran with them to the stable where Gidon had long ago made a false bottom in a manger. From Bronescu's shop, word came flying that the Kaymakam was demanding Zev the shomer. Of the killing of Alter Pincus and Shaikeh, the disappearance of Yosef Kleinman, the theft of the herd, the burning of the fields, the stabbing of Mati—later, later he would hear their complaints, the Belly declared, as he sipped a syrup, but first he must have the shomer, Zev the Hotblood. Oh, he knew the name.

Despite her antipathy for the Hotblood, Feigel, when his young wife came running distraught, proved her mettle. "Into the oven with him!" Feigel cried, and she was only sorry the oven had cooled down since the last baking. Might he roast and bake in Gehenna with the trouble he had brought, she declared, though not where his wife could hear her. And somehow, with pushing from behind, Zev crawled through the oven door, howling that he would stifle.

Already the Bimbashi's gendarmes were thrusting into people's houses, searching for arms, while the Bimbashi himself stood with his curved sword unsheathed in the open center of the village, surveying all.

A step ahead of the Turks, Yankel hurried a dozen of the Yavniel men into the synagogue to say Kaddish for the slain, while Malka Bronescu and Eliza took away the men's pistols under their dresses. "Into bed!" Feigel now cried to Leah as the last of the revolvers and rifles were pushed under the mattress. Who would dare search the bed of a woman in her time of the month?

Two of the Bimbashi's men strode into the house, real Turks where before there had been mostly Arabs in the police. These were squat, swarthy men with stiff end-pointed mustaches that reached out, Yaffaleh even in her terror could not help whispering to Eliza, like the feelers of the giant cockroaches, the djukim. Eliza giggled nervously, bringing glares from the gendarmes. She moved behind her mother, who was already pouring cool lebeniya from a pitcher for these djukim.

Mati stood still, staring at the gendarmes. All that was happening burned like the wound in his back. In the midst of his fight to drive out the goats from the barley, there had been the knife cutting his flesh, and when his friend Shaikeh had tried to save the herd, he was left lying there with a hole shot through his forehead.

Mati had seen the dead Shaikeh, even though he was not to have seen him. He had seen Shaikeh lying with Alter Pincus in their house; there had been much talk among the fathers and mothers; some said let the children see, let them see what a world we live in, here in Eretz; others said no, it is not for them to see. Though Mati had been told to remain at home, he had gone and been inside Shaikeh's house before he had been noticed and taken out. Shaikeh and Alter Pincus had been dressed to look as though they lay asleep in their Sabbath clothes.

Even though Schmulik all day had been bringing news that Zev was about to lead forth all the men and capture back the cattle, Mati knew the cattle were gone, just as he knew Shaikeh and Alter Pincus lay dead, just as everyone could see the fields were black and the crops burned.

Now the Turks were poking around his house with their swords out, lifting the corners of the feather quilts on the beds. They would find nothing. This was the first part, to fool these stupid Turks was only the beginning of getting back at all the enemies, all those who were against the Jews, who tried to devour your crops, to take your cattle, to kill you.

One of the Turks opened the door to the second room, and Leah let out a female shriek. The Turk with his sword jumped back as though stung by a scorpion.

Now he began rooting into every corner, the cupboards, the shelves, picking up each thing that might look valuable. He took up the Sabbath spicebox made of silver. Would he try to pocket it? The Turk's eyes moved sidewise, they met Mati's, then Ima's, and the cockroach put the spicebox back on the shelf. Mati looked to his mother and she smiled.

Gidon came in then, with the Bimbashi himself just behind him. "Where have you hidden your guns?" the Turk demanded. "I know you shoot well, you are an excellent hunter."

"Schnapps," Gidon said to Feigel, and, as she brought the Rishon brandy, Gidon began a conversation in words of Turkish he had picked up, about hunting in the Huleh marshes, for this Bimbashi was renowned as a killer of wild boar.

But the Bimbashi would not be distracted. "Where is your great killer the Hotblood?" he now asked, though in better humor, indeed like a good-natured man beginning to bargain. "What trouble you give me by hiding him! If we had not to hunt for your Hotblood, we could hunt for those who took your cattle."

Two lay dead and they did nothing, but over a horse they were capable of hanging a man. "Zev is worthless, he only makes trouble for your women," the Turk laughed, and stared with open lust at Eliza. A child. They had no shame.

"Zev is gone. Do you think he would wait for you?" Gidon said.

"May that devil roast in a thousand fires!" the Bimbashi blurted, and at this, though tragedy was around them, Eliza had to rush behind the great oven to stifle her unwanted laughter.

There was another of the gendarmes poking in the yard, even in the latrine—might he tumble in head first!—and now in the stable, might he receive a pair of hooves in his belly! But he had moved past the manger, Feigel saw, and was now pushing the bayonet of his rifle into the hay, let him swallow needles in his bread!

Then the Turk leaned in, searching for something with his hands. What could he have found there? The gendarme straightened. From the hay he pulled out Yosef Kleinman's cowboy hat! Ponderously shaking the straw from it, he marched into the yard with a look both cunning and uncertain.

"That's mine!" Gidon rushed out and seized it. "I slept there!" But already Chava Kleinman was running from her house as though the finding had communicated itself through the very walls. Seizing the hat from the Turk, she stood trembling, while from her mouth came, as from Dvora's that time in Sejera, the woman's howl over death, the ululation that emerged of itself as though not from the body but from some primordial cave. Gidon tried to explain to her—by the Kennereth, the Arab boy—and he had put the hat away here, for he was not yet certain, he didn't want to alarm her.

The unearthly howling continued to issue from within her, and wives came running as to some call that belonged to womanhood alone, the way each animal knows its call. Mameh supported Chava on one side, and Golda Janovici on the other, while her two little daughters buried their heads against her and wept.

Throughout the village hysteria and panic spread; some women gathered their children into their homes, and other women ran outside and in, some of them distractedly pulling washing from their clotheslines, calling, seeking their husbands, crying out that now they too for certain would depart from this murderous land, nothing remained here but death, they would take their children and leave!

In all this, the burial of Shaikeh and Alter Pincus was being made ready. Yankel Chaimovitch had gathered with the small band of elders who constituted the Chevrah Kadushah, the burial society of sanctification, and they were about to carry the young and the ancient body, each in its white shroud, to the wagon to be taken up the hill. Just then, even in the house of the dead, a pair of Turkish gendarmes appeared to make their search. Obtusely they crowded into the room, using their rifles to push aside the crowd.

In blind rage Yankel hurled himself against the two of them, with each arm yanking a rifle free, forcing back the startled soldiers, driving them out of the house, shouting hoarsely, "Defilers! Vermin! Can't you see there is a burial here! May you be buried under the flaming mountain of God's wrath!"

Behind Yankel the entire house of mourners now let out their rage. The two gendarmes, having at last comprehended, stood grumbling with a kind of half-shame and yet bluster. The Bimbashi galloped up, to be met with a flood of complaining voices in three languages, none of which he understood. Yankel flung the two rifles at the feet of his mount. With but a few harsh words at Yankel, the Turk waved his sword for the funeral to proceed.

In a way this had a quieting effect, as the entire village followed the wagon up the hill.

Several headstones were now to be seen alongside Avramchick's in the cemetery cleared amongst the rubble of some ancient village here, and each mourner from to-day's village knew each grave—normal deaths from malaria, from heat prostration, even from bodily failings. In the six years of the settlement, these were the first deaths of blood.

With the bereaved family, Yankel ranged himself by the double grave; he stood here, a father saying Kaddish for a young son, but to have to say Kaddish for your son and your grandfather together, that was at least a demand the Above One had not made of him. Marcu recited the words tonelessly in hardly more than a whisper. He was a slender youngish householder who had come here really because of Alter Pincus; in Roumania the entire family had lived on rents, and when Marcu's own father had died, Alter Pincus had sold his properties and brought everyone to Eretz. In place of Marcu's Shaikeh, Yankel could not forget, it might have been his own Mati who was sacrificed yesterday. Marcu had never been a part of the minyan in the shul, and indeed was a shadowy person in the village, while his wife was little seen. They had two younger children, a boy and a baby girl. It was already understood that the family would leave.

When the villagers returned from the burial, the Turks were waiting in the square. Now the Bimbashi commanded all the men to assemble in the center of the street; they must form two groups, those of Mishkan Yaacov to be separated from the outsiders.

What did he want of them? Everyone turned to Bronescu, to Galil, who had been sitting with Azmani Bey—had the Turk come to help here or to make things worse? If not to search for Kleinman, if not to help find the herd, let the Belly with his Bimbashi and the gendarmes together go back to Tiberias and leave them to their troubles!

The Bimbashi, a buttoned-up lump of a man with a huge deeply pitted nose and black hairs sprouting from everywhere, from his nostrils, from his ears, had a way of disregarding the person he was talking to and pursuing his own murky intention; one could never tell whether it was for good or bad until the last moment when he would utter his command. Perhaps he would yet march them all off to prison in his black fortress in Tiberias.

Bronescu appealed to the Kaymakam, who sat nibbling in his carriage, watching his Bimbashi, with a faint glitter

of amused anticipation on his melon-round face. Azmani
Bey only waved the mukhtar aside.

The settlers moved hesitantly, with words between them
in Yiddish—who should go to one side and who to the
other? Occasionally from the carriage Azmani Bey tapped
with his whip handle and pointed otherwise. Though he
scarcely moved out from Tiberias, it was astonishing how
knowing was that fat brain; the men of the Shomer he
knew, each one, and now when Menahem remained with
the Chaimovitches, the Kaymakam instantly pointed his
whip for him to go over to the outsiders' group.

"But I am their son-in-law," Menahem stated.

"You are a shomer. From Gilboa."

Menahem moved to the outsiders. "As in the days of
Ashur!" Reuven muttered, his lips pressed together, as even
he was ordered over to that side. Not only Ashur and the
Assyrians, but in how many other times, under the Romans, the Persians, the Saracens, had Hebrew men in this
land been made to stand with their hands bereft of weapons
while strangers, foreign soldiers, walked commandingly
among them, each step treading on their manhood!

Standing with the younger boys just outside the line of
men but apart from the women, Schmulik edged closer to
where Gidon stood, as though from him rather than from
his father he would know what to do.

Now the Belly spoke. "There has been killing here.
Blood and fire, as you proclaim. And in the water, too," he
added, with a mysterious knowing chortle. "Do you imagine the Turk is so ignorant?" He gazed with self-satisfaction
toward Galil. "Now they have killed yours in return. And
your hotbloods want to kill theirs. Let it stop! In my sanjak it is I who decide who shall die because he has killed."

What was the Kaymakam's meaning? Blood in the water?
One man looked to another, puzzled, yet between Galil and
Menahem something else passed. Was it then not because of
yesterday's troubles that the Turk had arrived here? Was it
not over the shooting of the horse that he was searching for
Zev? And in Menahem the two straining hook-ends now
touched each other, all but snapped together around his
burden.

For Zev had never been satisfied at being left out of the
secret deed. With prodding hinting he had gone about making remarks about the vanished bandit brothers of Fuleh.

He must have guessed something, perhaps from Shabbataï Zeira, for Zev had even once knowingly joked to Menahem about the bandits having vanished from the earth, but who knew about the sea? The tale had reached Azmani Bey, perhaps it was for this the Turks had come to seize Hotblood. The Turks could be taking Zev at his word, believing it was he who had done the deed.

Or was there something more? Could something even have been cast up from the sea? From those unfathomed depths of the Kinnereth, to enrage the Zbeh?

The men from Yavniel, and all others who did not belong here, except for Galil, the Kaymakam commanded, must leave at once.

After a moment's hesitation, Galil nodded and the Yavniel volunteers began to move to their mounts and depart. Menahem too had to depart, though he managed to pass close to Gidon and remark, "Remind your mother that what's cooking in her oven may burn." For now he was deeply perturbed not only that Zev might be caught and blamed for the deed, but that something might be beaten out of him. Zev had only made a guess like everyone else, but Menahem felt a tragic heartsickness now, felt an enchainment from that deed that had had to be carried out, to the innocent Joe Kleinman, and onward to some unknown consequences that still might lie beyond.

Gidon managed to repeat Menahem's message to Schmulik, who slipped over to Feigel. She hurried back to the house. It was unwatched. Cramped, gasping in a caul of sweat, his always red skin now appearing afire, Zev had to be pulled like an enormous roast out of the oven. Gulping a whole pitcher of water, he listened as she told him of the Kaymakam's orders, even the Belly's strange outcry about blood in the sea. At this Zev became upset. He gave hasty instructions for his family; he himself must get far from the village. And through the back gate he was gone.

Azmani Bey had turned to the remaining Jews, the villagers. There was still danger of bloodshed in this area, he declared. Their mukhtar must come with him to Tiberias until all could be clarified. And he beckoned to the bewildered Bronescu who, still clinging to his dignity, advanced as though it were by friendly invitation to the carriage. Now, announced the Belly, his lips broad with satisfaction at the surprise he was about to produce, the entire settlement must be evacuated until safety was restored in the area. His men would remain to guard their homes and possessions.

An astonished gasp arose. Then came outcries. The crops! The houses! All would be looted! The poultry, the bit of livestock that remained! And what of the herd? The stolen herd? Why should the victims be punished instead of the vandals! The marauders would surely return and sack the entire settlement!

As to the herd, Azmani Bey replied, their cattle had evidently been taken off across the river to another sanjak, where he had no authority. He would make the proper inquiries, he declared, reverting to the tone of an administrator. But for their own safety, the evacuation must proceed at once.

In the end, again in conference with Bronescu and Galil, the Kaymakam agreed that two men from the neighboring kvutsa could come each day to inspect the houses against pillage. The kvutsa could also send men to harvest the remaining grain.

Quietly, Galil spoke to several of the householders and the younger men, Gidon among them. It was best to obey. The Belly knew of something. A raid in force, he had hinted, to finish off the whole village.

Already, Galil reasoned, in the panic that had taken hold of the women after yesterday's disasters, several of the Roumanian families had decided to leave. Rather than have the settlers infecting each other, it was perhaps better that the Turk should order them out. If there really was to be a raid, let the Turks be responsible here. They could prevent a slaughter. In a few weeks, the Belly had promised, all would be clarified and the settlers could return. No, he had his informants, the Belly, and it should not be assumed he was against the yishuv. Besides, from HaKeren, their shomer would be watching. The village would not be destroyed.

Everywhere women were hurrying with bundles of linen and baskets of silverware, youngsters chased after squawking hens, men piled pieces of furniture, implements, crockery, they hardly knew what, onto their wagons. In the Chaimovitch yard Yaffeleh tried hurriedly to bind her geese foot to foot, but there was no room to take even half the flock. She wanted to walk to Yavniel driving her geese before her, but Gidon promised that Reuven's kvutsa would take care of them.

Suddenly Leah declared she would not leave at all, she would stay. Next door Chava Kleinman was refusing to leave—perhaps Joe would yet appear, perhaps he had thrown his hat as a sign for her and then escaped somewhere, and he would send a message or all at once return. Only Leah was able to talk to her—for the sake of her girls she must go. When Chava Kleinman at last agreed, it was on condition that Leah come with her.

They tied Klugeh to the wagon; the orphan calf stayed at her side. Feigel carried out the Shabbes candlesticks, the spicebox that the Turk had eyed; the wagon was piled as high as when they first arrived, with bedding, even with the old trunk from Cherezinka, but the new furniture had to be left in the house. At the last moment Leah rushed back for the framed picture by Abel Pan of Shulamit from the Song of Songs that she had brought from the Bezalel in Jerusalem.

"Nu?" Feigel said as Yankel hesitated to mount.

"The Evil One take them all!" Yankel spat. Let it be Russia, let it be Eretz Yisroel, where was a Jew safe from pogroms?

And thus the long procession of wagons left Mishkan Yaacov and strung itself up the hillside. At the head rode Galil, and it was Gidon who guarded the tail end. As the Chaimovitch wagon ascended the hill, Mati, sitting backward, tried to keep his eyes still on their house. The wound throbbed in his back, and on the front side, his heart seemed to pulse with the same pain. Why were they leaving? Was it all because of him, because of his fight with Abdul? Something was wrong in this world of people, and something was wrong in the place where they lived, if Turks could come and tell them they must leave; yet it was hurtful to leave this place, even if Reuven was still close by in the kvutsa, and Leah and Gidon kept saying they would all soon return to their house. Mati could no longer ask anyone why they were going away because they answered him only with the lies they had for children. And besides Mati sensed that even the big ones themselves didn't know.

The Turkish masters were ordering them, just as they, the big ones, ordered him.

At the top of the ridge Menahem waited to meet the wagons. They moved past him downward into the valley of Yavniel where all was relatively safe, and behind the last wagon there came Gidon. But as the last wagon started its descent, Gidon no longer followed. He remained on the ridge, looking down on Mishkan Yaacov, deserted except for the Turkish Bimbashi and his men.

Menahem called to him.

"I'm staying here," Gidon said. "I'm staying on watch."

Menahem did not need an explanation. "I'll come right back to you as soon as they've reached Yavniel," he said. "Gidon, take no risk. This is not for you alone."

Not far to the left were the caves. Did he have water? Gidon patted his gourd. Still Menahem hesitated, but a rear guard was needed on the wagons, and this young ox would not be budged. "Don't worry, you'll find me here," Gidon said, and Menahem rode off.

Only two hours passed before Gidon saw movement on the far side of the river's loop where the crossing was to Golan. He placed his rifle firmly, steadied on the rock. His position was a small fortress. How perfectly he saw them, a group of five horsemen, sent to reconnoiter. Two remained on their side, while three crossed in file. They would bring back word whether to attack and plunder the deserted settlement.

The excitement in his blood now, the slight beating in his head, was not of the hunt. It was more, he knew, and other. A kind of grief was in him that the world was so ordered, yet he felt nothing of the blind killing hatred he had expected. He was part of the order of the world as he lay here watching the approach of murderers.

Then the first rider was at the maximum point from where he would turn to slip toward the village. The fading light was on him perfectly, he was as though picked out, with all else fading away.

Gidon fired and, as he was inserting another cartridge, the Zbeh doubled like a broken branch from his mount. The second rider plunged forward, and it took two shots to destroy him; the third had turned back and already half-

way across the stream before Gidon stopped firing. Wild
shots were coming toward him, but the riders would not
attack. He had done his deed.

Something was relieved in him, for Joe Kleinman, for
Alter Pincus and Shaikeh, but the deeper dismal weight in
his heart, the sorrow and sickness for the way the world
was had only become heavier. Here he had done for the
first time what he had wondered about and feared he must
one day do: kill man. An impulse to clamber down, to
gaze at the kill, touch, know, quickly vanished. And an
impulse of weeping within himself, as though a piece of his
own being, his human faith, had been shot to death, remained. Not on your Bar Mitzvah do you become a man, a
son of the commands of doing what is right, but to become
a man there is perhaps another day, a bar mavet, when you
must become also a son of evil and of killing.

Gathering everything, the ejected cartridges as well,
leaving no sign, though they would nevertheless know the
place, Gidon mounted, riding toward Yavniel.

Menahem met him on the way. "They came? How
many?"

"Two fell." And he told the details.

After a moment, Menahem said, "So you have hunted
man."

Gidon nodded and their eyes met in gloom.

12

THE SETTLERS of Yavniel were understanding and generous. For a fortnight the families of Mishkan Yaacov were
with them, only a few going on to Mescha. Every kitchen
was crowded with women, every barn with sleepers, and
talk, rumors, plans filled the time. Menahem and two more
of the Shomer went off each day to reconnoiter. The abandoned settlement stood untouched.

Perhaps in their own way the Zbeh had counted up that
in their ghoum a sufficient revenge had been reached. If
Kleinman was to be counted, and he was certainly no

longer living, then it was still they who had killed the more, even counting the last two who had fallen. And they had the herd.

One day a sheikh of the Tabor region, related to the Houranis of Nazareth where Menahem had lately visited, and himself a notable long friendly with the settlers of Yavniel, rode in for a visit with their mukhtar, the elder Kolodnitzer, reputed to be a sage. When coffee had been sipped, and remarks made about the weather, the crops, the health of each and his family, the sheikh remarked on the great value of friendly relationships and peace among neighbors, and the sage replied that nothing on earth was to be more highly desired or cherished, recalling how Father Abraham had been a man of peace, and quoting the psalm, What is so good and so pleasant as brothers dwelling together. Peaceful friendship was worth gold and more than gold, the sheikh remarked, and Kolodnitzer concurred, adding that life too was worth more than gold. The sheikh said, so was honor.

A few men of Mishkan Yaacov were summoned to take coffee and join in the conversation, which centered on the value of honor, friendship, of a fine horse, and on tales of enemies who had settled their differences and become as brothers.

In the end it was said that a dead horse was nevertheless not like a dead man, though a good horse is better than an evil man. Yet a horse can be replaced. Though the sheikh told a touching tale of a tribesman who so loved his mount that when the faithful animal was wounded in a fight and had to be destroyed, the master turned his pistol against his own heart and died as well. Horse and master were buried together and their burial place became a shrine. But better than a feast of mourning is a feast of friendship. A feast, a sulha, erases bad memories and replaces them with memories of enjoyment. Indeed the sulha should be one that would be long remembered, a true feast of peace and friendship with provisions of twenty whole sheep. This became reduced to twelve, since the finest geese and poultry would be added without number, and all else without measure, for who can set a measure on love among good neighbors living together in peace?

As to the vanished farmer Kleinman, the sheikh took a

vow on the heads of his own sons and grandsons that not a glimpse of the American's steed had been seen in all Galilee, and when word was known of the man or of his horse, it would instantly be brought to them.

And so wagons were loaded again and the people of Mishkan Yaacov, all but five families, returned over the heights of Yavniel toward their village. From the ridge they saw it—still only half believing, they saw the entire settlement lying intact before them, neither burnt nor demolished, and perhaps not even too badly despoiled.

In each house small things had been looted, surely by the Turkish gendarmes; here an entire iron cookstove and there a set of curtains that should not have been left behind, and in one house, even a chamberpot! Still, much worse had been expected. Also, Issachar Bronescu had returned from Tiberias where, he said, Azmani Bey had treated him respectfully, keeping him in no prison but as a guest in his own house! They had had many talks. About the ways of the Shomer, the Kaymakam had great curiosity, but of course Bronescu knew nothing of their secrets and could tell him nothing. The brothers of Fuleh, Azmani Bey related, had been great heroes to their cousins across the Jordan. Their sisters, renowned beauties, were married to powerful families in the Zbeh. Yet, Azmani's friend, the Kaymakam of Amman, had made strong inquiries for the missing herd, and had had interesting talks with the elders of the tribe. Perhaps things would now remain quiet. There need be no more blood—though the herd had best be forgotten. To search for it would be of no use, and would only bring more trouble. Let it be a price of peace. Too many on both sides had been killed. And indeed the Zbeh with their flocks had used, at times of scant rain in their region, to come over to this side of the river, and now complained that old grazing grounds were gone.

To Azmani Bey's house had come Jacques Samuelson, the Baron's highest representative, and he had given assurance that loans for new cattle would be quickly provided.

"Loans!" cried Yasha Janovici. "And my burned crops?" But others quieted him. "Who tells you to be in a hurry to pay off the Baron's loans?"

Meanwhile Arab women began coming down from

Dja'adi selling goat's milk, lebeniya and eggs, and life resumed.

Menahem himself came for a time as shomer, and to Leah he related how Zev had been summoned to Gilboa and judged. Not only had he used firearms with needless and unwarranted haste in the scuffle with Dja'adi, but it was his loose tongue that had set the Zbeh to searching the sea for the two bandits of Fuleh, who were kinsmen. Something, it was said, had been found in the Kinnereth; though what they had found was not yet known. Zev's loose talk had brought all this disaster. For the Zbeh had watched, and picked the moment for their revenge.

Angrily Zev had raged at them all; cowards and compromisers, they would yet learn that his was the way, the only way to deal with Arabs, blood for blood. Only then would Jews be respected. The judgment: Zev was brave but temperamentally unstable and unsuited for the Shomer. Expelled, he had gone off to the south. It was said he was forming a watchman's group in the outermost settlements, near Beersheba.

"But his wife and child are here."

Menahem supposed that in time Zev would send for them.

Of Gidon, Menahem said, it was thought best that he should leave the area for some time, as it was dangerous for him to remain. Though the Zbeh could not be certain who had stopped their raid when the village was empty, still such things had an uncanny way of becoming known.

—But if Gidon went off, Yankel growled, what of the farm? How was he to manage the work, all alone?

Schmulik was nearly of the strength of a man, and Leah would stay on and help, and as the stable was nearly empty, things could be managed.

Where should Gidon go? Should he join the Shomer, then?

Though he had proven himself, he was still young, Menahem said. But if he wanted to become a watchman, doubtless in a year he would be accepted.

It was Reuven, coming over on the Sabbath, who made another suggestion. Gidon had a natural way with horses and mules; why should he not apprentice himself to a veterinary for a year or two and learn the profession. Even if he later joined the Shomer, this knowledge would make him doubly valuable. This appealed to Gidon. Inquiries would be made of a veterinary in Jaffa.

At the end of that week, only a few days before the sulha was to take place, an Arab boy spoke to Schmulik when he came down to the river to water the mules. For gold, he would show where the cowboy's body could be found.

Schmulik rushed to Gidon in the fields with the news, and Gidon at once came and questioned the boy. He was not the one who had found the hat, nor was he from Dja'adi but from one of the stray Bedouin tents on the way to Tiberias.

La, he did not know who had done the killing of the cowboy.

—But he had seen?

"Nothing."

"Nothing?"

"Perhaps horsemen." "Horsemen? Who?" Gidon demanded.

In sudden terror the boy cried out—Not of his own people! Not they!

It took a coin to start him again. Not from his own tents, that was certain, but then of what people?

—La, he did not know.

—Strangers? Just what had he seen? How many?

—Two. They had leaped at the horse and dragged off the Yahud.

—Had there been a fight?

—Yes, a fight.

—And then?

He was silent. Gidon refrained from seizing him, shaking him. "Hear me. No harm will come to you. No one will know what you have told. Only I."

The boy gazed at him uncertainly. "It is worth gold."

"Gold. I have said it."

The words came in a tumble. With knives they had killed the cowboy and thrown the body in the river.

"Where in the river?"

That he knew. He could point out the place to them. And the little teasing smile appeared, and the eyes looked away. First the gold.

Hurrying back to the village, Gidon sought out Mena-

hem.—From those few tents on the way to Tiberias. Menahem knew them.

—Perhaps after all the lad's own father was mixed up in
it? Gidon wondered.

Menahem doubted it. "The ones in those tents—they live
on what they get from Jews. Their women clean in the hot
baths." Let the boy be paid a few coins to begin with, and
more only if he disclosed the body.

Returning with Gidon to where the boy waited, Schmulik beside him, Menahem showed in his hand a whole
golden napoleon. The boy led them to the banks, where the
Jordan flowed from the Kinnereth. "There," he pointed to
a clump of willows. "There they threw his body into the
water. I swear by my mother, I saw it with my own eyes."
And he made as though he would take an eye out, were he
not speaking the truth. "You can burn my tongue with
fire."

It was by the secluded cove that Yankel had used as his
mikveh. Within his head Manahem felt a thudding, a pulsing, as though the dark secret of the universe were about to
be revealed before him, and yet he would not understand
it. He himself was as nothing, a scrap in the world, and his
hands had touched some awful mystery. All was secret and
unknowable unless by some revelation, for here he stood
and Gidon stood beside him seeing what he saw, yet to him
something unutterable, a balance of evils in the depths of
creation, was being half-revealed, while Gidon could not
know.

Schmulik had shed his shirt and trousers; diving into the
water, he swam along the bottom but saw nothing. At last
he rose and climbed out, shaking his head.

Vowing still more passionately, the Arab boy even offered back the first coppers that he held in his hand. The
body could not have drifted, no, he had seen them tie rocks
to it.

"Rocks?" Menahem echoed.

"Heavy rocks."

"Then why do you say so only now?" Gidon demanded.
"Each time you speak, you saw more. Perhaps you were
close enough to see who tied the rocks?"

No, no, he had been afraid to come closer.

"Show us exactly where."

"Here, here." He stood by the water's edge.

Mati had appeared. When Gidon had come for Menahem, he had known. At once, without a word from them, he understood all that was happening and would have dived into the water but Gidon forbade him. Schmulik went in again, exactly at the point the Arab boy showed. Among mud and smooth stones on the bottom he suddenly touched the edge of a rough feeling rock, and scooping with his fingers around it, felt that it was large, and sunken in. Then alongside it, partly under the mud and as though one with the mud, his fingers touched another substance and instantly withdrew. Even he, who had been taught by Gidon to clean out the entrails of a slaughtered animal, now drew back, and quickly emerged.

Both Menahem and Gidon returned with him into the water, there where he led them. When Menahem put his hand to the substance, it was as though something locked itself tight in his breast; the two groping and striving ends that had touched were at last locked together, and he was sealed within himself. To what purpose he did not know, but a design was being carried out in him that was not as in the lives of others.

Laboring together, going several times up for breath and down again, they at last freed the body and brought it to the surface. Where the large rocks had been tied at the neck and at the feet, the ropes were imbedded in the decay, and in the water Gidon cut them away from the bluish bloated form. The corpse rose and floated of itself between Gidon and Menahem, while Schmulik climbed out onto the bank and with a broken-off eucalyptus branch drew it near.

Gidon, himself sickened, caught the long solemn gaze of Mati, a gaze bewildered yet comprehending. "Take Mati home," he said to Schmulik.

"Say nothing yet," Menahem instructed the boy.

Schmulik was reluctant to go, for had he not discovered the body? And here was a matter of full manhood. Though his insides churned, though the taste of worse than bile was in his throat and mouth, he would not take his eyes off the corpse as the men turned it and counted the knife-gashes where the flesh still held, rotted, formless. Even in the hands—Kleinman must have seized at their daggers with his bare fingers. And the front side of the head, what had been the face—one could not look.

"Go away!" Gidon cried angrily to Mati to cover his sobs, and Mati retreated a small distance.

So they covered the form as much as they could with Manahem's dark shirt, and the Bedouin boy stood before Gidon with outheld hand for his money. "I have told you the truth." Menahem laid the gold coin on the boy's palm and he fled.

She was strong, Chava Kleinman insisted, strong, strong. If Joe could die such a death, then she could bear to see it, and who could tell what would haunt her more, the sight of it or the guilt of an ultimate desertion? At last in Leah's company she saw. She looked and looked until her eyelids slowly closed of themselves. Then the shroud was placed. The chevrah kadushah came, and the whole village followed.

After the seven days of mourning, Chava closed up her house, asking Leah to take the chickens and the goat. Issachar Bronescu's daughter Malka was soon to be married; he would arrange for his son-in-law to take over the Kleinman meshek.

The American reaping machine Chava gave to Gidon. Then she returned with her daughters to her sister in Omaha, Nebraska.

Yankel never again bathed in his mikveh. It was contaminated.

The feast was held. Mansour the mukhtar and several elders of Dja'adi, together with Sheikh Ibrim, the father and grandfather of many, expressed their anger at the ugly deed that had been uncovered. It was surely the new bandits of the Three Rocks that had done it, they kept repeating, and they surely had taken Hawadja Kleinman's fine mare.

The ancient Ibrim fell into talk with Menahem and spoke of that first pair of bandits who had made an evil place of the Three Rocks—the sons of Faud of Fuleh, whom he had known in former times, a worthless one, a hyena. He was no longer in Fuleh? Ah, then Faud had surely gone back to the Zbeh with his remaining sons, or his grandsons, who must now be grown. It could well be that the same bad hyena blood was in them, and that, hearing there was trouble, they had come racing to pick off what could be picked off. And it was the fate of the American to have run into their path.

His yellowed eyes peeped into Menahem's.

—So it must have been, the men of Dja'adi repeated all around them, to Reuven, to Menahem again, to all who would listen, and who could say otherwise?

It was indeed a big sulha, with notables from as far as Nazareth, even Saïd Hourani himself on the Arab side, to show how good was the peacemaking, for should not the sons of Abraham, cousins and brothers, dwell side by side in peace? The Kaymakam from Tiberias also arrived, Azmani Bey in his fez, and for the Jews, Yehoshua Ostrov could be seen in his flowing Arab robes, and the smiling Jacques Samuelson as well; and Galil arrived at the head of a delegation of the Shomer, their bandoliers resplendent, their rifles highly polished, their steeds caparisoned with tassels.

The Chaimovitch family walked up through the fields together with other families of the village, while the young men, Gidon among them, formed a galloping troop, wearing Arab keffiyahs, pulling up with their steeds pawing the air. Then suddenly a group of mounted Arabs galloped out to greet them, the mukhtar's son in the lead, howling as they sped, whirling and also pulling up short, their mounts pawing the air; then the two groups of horsemen charged abreast in a race over the hill to the open field before the village.

Here the feast was spread. To begin with, platters of fine goat cheese, olives, pomegranates, grapes, jugs of cool lebeniyah, baked eggs, and piles of warm pittah. From the Jewish side, heaps of gefulte fish and potato pancakes and preserves and Feigel's thin-flaked strudels alongside the thin-crusted honeycakes of Dja'adi.

Over smoldering live embers the spitted sheep were crackling, and in the center, the mukhtar's own contribution, tended by a specialist from Kfar Kana—a whole calf, inside of which there was a roast lamb, inside of which was a dove.

The notables of both sides greeted each arrival with embraces, pledges of eternal friendship: Are we not all sons of Abraham!

From behind the crowd now came Schmulik, leading a

finely caparisoned mount. Though his every sinew throbbed to ride her, Gidon took over the halter and led the noble animal to the center of the open circle, presenting her to Fawzi.

The young men fell on each other's necks, embracing in brotherhood.

Among all the men who were there, who could not recognize at once that this was the most perfect, the swiftest, mare to be found in the souk of Damascus, white, with an arched tail and lean withers, a steed of the sort that was bound to become legendary.

Fawzi mounted. In the very first race he was ahead of the whole field, like a flying banner.

Mati found himself alongside Abdul, with whom, that day in the barley field, he had begun the scuffle that ended in bloodletting. On Mati's back was the scar which Abdul now touched and examined, running his fingers along it, and then showing on his own body various wounds and scars from that day and from other times. Watching the horsemanship games, they laughed together when an awkward rider lost his balance and half tumbled from his saddle. After many riders had missed, it was Gidon whose lance pierced the tiny red handkerchief that hung from the branch of an oak. Great cries arose from both sides at his perfect horsemanship.

The women of Dja'adi appeared, carrying large circular trays of lamb and rice. With great forethought, the animals had been brought to Yavniel for slaughtering, and all had been prepared the Jewish way. "Kasher, kasher," the mukhtar assured the guests, and many, even of the older ones, though Yankel smilingly refrained, tore off pieces of meat with their fingers and dipped hunks of pittah to scoop up rice, all smacking their lips and exclaiming over the excellence of the feast. Then to Issachar Bronescu was given the honor of slicing open the roasted calf, and after him the Arab mukhtar, Mansour, ceremoniously cut open the lamb within the calf, and held aloft the dove.

Eyes were already puffed with overeating, but the feast was renewed with great compliments. Young lads of Dja'adi formed a line with Fawzi at the head. A drumbeat began; straight-backed with arms straight down at their sides, clasped hand to hand, they began to stamp out the debka, Fawzi's free hand waving a kerchief, as he whirled up in sudden leapings, with high calls of song. At one moment Fawzi swept Gidon into their line, into the leader's place, handing him the kerchief to whirl. Straight as young trees, their feet moving ever more swiftly in perfect unison, the young men danced.

Leah, flushed, happy, could scarcely keep her feet on the ground. Reuven's whole kvutsa was there, Old Gordon as well, and chaverim from Kinnereth and Gilboa. Standing with Leah, Reuven's feet too began the movement, brother and sister caught into the Arab ululation with a Yahalili! and already they were in a hora circle, their feet stamping the ground. Old Gordon was on Leah's other side—it was like the early days. "Yahalili!" A chaver had brought an accordion along, and he picked up the beat. Several young Arab lads were drawn into the hora, stomping in the circle while the Arab girls moved closer and laughed more freely. Songs rose, in Arabic, in Hebrew, and of the elders all wore beatific smiles, as to say at heart we are all alike, all friendly. People passed food to each other insistently— fruits, delicacies—and those who drank filled each other's cups with wine, and all declared and truly felt they were as one, that each people was good, that they were good neighbors and true friends.

Yet, beyond the warmth of a pledged friendship, of knowledge of healed wounds on both sides, beyond exclamations of good will, what could each group say to the other? They stood in little circles, Jews, Arabs, with ready smiles on their faces, all nodding, all smacking their lips and putting their hands over their hearts to vow they could not eat a morsel more, and beaming and exclaiming at the excellence of the feast.

So, on the eve of the first world war, the two villages above the Jordan made peace.

CHOICE

Book II

13

THROUGHOUT all the Galilee, and as far as Gedera in the South, there had spread the tale of the battle of Mishkan Yaacov, the tale of how the Chaimovitch boy, Gidon, alone on the ridge, had saved the evacuated village from total destruction. A young man like that was made for the Shomer, that was certain.

But Gidon was not certain he wanted the life of a shomer. One sundown he had a serious talk with his brother-in-law Menahem who, after the disaster, had been sent by the Shomer to take over the night rounds from Zev the Hotblood. During his free hours in the day, Menahem had come over to help the family cut a last field of forage. It was a brazen day, the heat not even lifting in the late afternoon, and when the rest of the family drove homeward, collapsed on the high-piled hay wagon, Gidon chose to go down and dip himself in the river.

Menahem walked along with him, not only because it was still unwise for Gidon to move about alone, but because the time had come to talk out Gidon's plans. Of his being welcome in the Shomer there would be no question, and besides the Shomer could send him out of the area, at least for a time, and this was desirable. So after their first life-reviving plunge in the stream, Menahem brought up the subject. "Have you given some thought, Gidon, to life as a shomer?"

Gidon stood still, letting the feeling of the water's freshness seep all through his body. His brother-in-law's sinews were like strips of dried meat; Menahem brushed off the clinging droplets of water, a thing done. Sometimes Gidon wondered whether Menahem savored anything in life.

Everyone, Gidon knew, expected him to join the Shomer. And how could he say to Menahem, himself a watchman, what he thought of such a life, spent riding the rounds on the lookout for thieves in the fields? The riding itself, if the mount was good, and in the freedom of the night, could doubtless bring times of wondrous satisfaction. But where was the accomplishment in catching some miserable thief loading sheaves onto a donkey? Or even in firing at some marauder sneaking toward a stable? In order to have the satisfaction of planting and working the land, Menahem himself gave the free hours of his afternoons to · labor in the field. "I've thought about it," Gidon said to Menahem. "The Shomer is important. But to me—I like to work in the stable, in the fields . . ."

With his dark penetrating glance, Menahem seemed to have read Gidon's unspoken thought. "True, riding the rounds doesn't give a man the satisfaction of direct productivity," he said. "That is why the Shomer has built its own settlement at Gilboa, so that we can alternate our duties, and take part in productivity as well."

"I know," said Gidon. But this aspect too, the cooperativa, did not strongly attract him. "One has to be that kind of a person," he said, "and I don't think I am that kind of a person. I am not so much an idealist as Reuven and you others. I want to have my own place."

"I am not so much an idealist myself," Menahem shrugged, with that shadowy tight-lipped smile of his. "For me, the kvutsa is a practical way." But there were also members of the Shomer who kept up their own farms, he reminded Gidon—like Shabbatai Zeira in Sejera. Gidon nodded; that was true—and yet . . .

Menahem was still studying him, measuring him, as though deciding how much more to say to him. Dipping under the water, Gidon let himself soak until the freshness penetrated all through him, and when he came up, he saw that Menahem too had dipped under and was aglitter, even smiling with freshness and well-being. "And then," Menahem continued, "you know that riding watch is not all there is to it."

Gidon knew. He knew there was something more, something mysterious, secret . . . he even felt he understood what it was, though he would not have been able to explain it. So he nodded seriously, sensing that now his brother-in-law would speak of these important things.

Menahem did, and he didn't. First he repeated what everyone took for granted; yet by naming these matters, man to man in nakedness, there was a trustful acceptance of Gidon as one who had earned his initiation into manly

responsibility. —The Yishuv was growing at last, Menahem reminded Gidon. The workers were becoming
stronger even though they were still seriously split amongst
themselves. One day, who knew how it would come about,
the Jews would become a nation here. The whole world
was on the brink of an explosion, perhaps war, perhaps
revolution, and in this upheaval an opportunity might come
and the Jews must be ready to seize it.

Here in the land the best men, the most determined men,
must stand banded together, alert and disciplined. And
wise. For this reason some of the most able chaverim had
been sent to study in Constantinople. This was why a brilliant and educated man like Galil, who was a doctor of
jurisprudence, had become a shomer, and why Galil and
an educated woman like Nadina remained as simple members of the cooperativa—to be part of the movement. And
Gidon must remember that a network of watchmen spread
out and working all over the land was an ideal instrument
for keeping in touch with all that was happening everywhere, so that when the time came it would be they who
were prepared and could take control.

Gidon nodded automatically; naturally, this was something he had always understood. Only a second later, from
the sheen in Menahem's eyes, it came to him that this was
the whole secret.

It was like what had happened when he was still in
cheder in the old country, and the melamed had one day
started talking about the hidden meaning of the words of
the Bible, the code of gematria which used the number-
value of each letter in a word to make other words. Every
boy knew that there was a cabbala and that skinny half-
starved talmudists went about hinting that the power of the
universe was secretly known to them. But if they were masters of such power, why did they live such miserable lives?

Something of this, Gidon felt toward Menahem, who
when in the mood could weave fantastic tales of his adventures all over the world, always with those glowing eyes of
vision. How could a handful of watchmen one day seize
control of the whole land? From whom? From the Turks?

"—and remember," Menahem added, as they emerged
now from the water, and pulled on their clothes, "it is not
as though we are unopposed even in the Yishuv itself."
Others too were planning to be the leaders of a future Jew-

ish nation, and the entire, all-important question of what kind of Jewish nation would some day be built in the land was perhaps to be decided now, in the beginning. Around Zichron, doubtless Gidon had heard, the sons of the Baron's settlers had organized a secret society, meeting in a cave. The young brothers of Aaron Aaronson, the famous agronomist, together with Avshalom Feinberg the poet and a few more do-nothings, were setting up their own patrols, they galloped around on Arab steeds to protect the flower of Jewish maidenhood, it seemed—

"The Sons of Nimrod!" Gidon laughed. He had heard.

"It is not entirely so simple," Menahem said. Their element, the sons of the well-to-do planters, imagined it was their natural right to become the leaders of the Yishuv. These offspring of the Jewish effendi, the Aaronsons, the Feinbergs, and their cousins and their friends, they would establish a capitalist, landowner class and make joint cause with the rich Arab effendi to keep the land in a state of medieval feudalism. This was really what was at stake.

But then Menahem's whole cabbala, Gidon reflected, was simply the ancient quarrel between the old and the new elements in the Yishuv, between the grove owners and the chalutzim. Had he not heard this argument ever since he came to Palestine? From Reuven and Leah, unceasingly: What kind of land will we build here? Still, his brother-in-law spoke as though tomorrow or the next day a whole nation was ready to rise into being. Gidon had never thought of the problems in such an actual way. But it could be true—things did have a beginning, and the thinkers and planners who caught hold at the beginning could guide the way that things would be. Now he was ready to take his place in life, he must perhaps choose and become part of a movement, as Menahem said, to create one kind of land or another. There was more, there was so much more to a man's life than raising his crops.

"I'll tell you, Menahem, I am not such a thinker as you and Reuven and Galil—I don't so much like to read and discuss. I know, if it comes to matters like what kind of country this will be, I know I am with you. But for myself—" he stood still, and gazed beyond Menahem over the fields. Was he the sort of fellow to be participating in secret, far-reaching plans and therefore in the responsibility of guiding the fate of a whole people? "For myself, maybe I

will just stay here." Already Abba was consulting with him
about the plantings, the stable, as though to say one day
the meshek would be his. "I feel the best for me," Gidon
repeated, as he and Menahem walked soberly, their bodies
cool and comfortable now, over the stubble, "the best is to
stay a farmer."

—Yes, perhaps, Menahem agreed, that was the best.
Such young men, solidly grown to the soil, were the ideal.
Only just now for a time it was not quite safe for Gidon to
remain here; the Mukhtar of Dja'adi had himself hinted at
it. There had been too much talk of Gidon's remaining behind alone. Even though the Zbeh had made off with the
entire herd, and had their blood revenge, they could still be
murderous. Moving freely about, Gidon could be a tempting target. In the opinion of the Shomer, he should go elsewhere for a time. During the winter months, at least.

Leah too had been prodding him. The village was moribund, especially since the troubles. And in Jaffa, in Rehovot, he might meet a girl.

—He could learn something of orange growing, Menahem suggested, for here too, with irrigation, as Reuven insisted, there might be crops of gold.

—Perhaps, Gidon laughed, but he couldn't really see
himself as a wealthy pardessan! But he had indeed been
thinking he might go off to learn something, perhaps to
learn about animal diseases as Reuven had suggested. He
had been thinking of working for a time for a veterinary.

As Gidon and Menahem reached the farmyard, with a
feeling of richer understanding between them, a figure appeared, riding on a horse Gidon recognized from a distance. It was a tired mare that Reuven's kvutsa had used
for years to haul the water-barrel wagon; now that a pump
had been installed, it was everybody's riding horse. But the
rider was neither Reuven nor any of their chevreh. Wearing breeches, boots, and a Russian cap, he sat erect as if on
the finest mount. Though Gidon saw him for the first time,
he was sure who this must be, and indeed Menahem called
at once, "It's Trumpeldor."

Who did not know of Trumpeldor! The soldier-hero who
had once and for all shown the Russians what Jews were
made of, demanding to go back and fight even after he had
lost his arm in battle, at Port Arthur. The first Jew to be

made an officer in the Russian army. And then, despite the invitation of the Czar himself to remain in the army and rise higher, he had refused, so as to come as a chalutz to Eretz Yisroel. One heard of Josef Trumpeldor laboring at Migdal, attending Zionist congresses, appearing at workers' assemblies to call for labor unity—and lately he had been staying and working at Reuven's kvutsa, HaKeren.

Even in the sound of his "Shalom," Trumpeldor's heavy Russian accent could be heard. It was to have a look at this very young man, Gidon Chaimovitch, that he had come, Trumpeldor declared, and he sat stiff-backed, gazing on Gidon, looking him over from head to foot, like a general reviewing troops. But on his long, serious face there was a small self-permitted smile—it even had a certain sweetness.

Already the entire family stood in a fringe by the gate, and Feigel was bustling the girls back into the house to make tea, to prepare the table—see what a guest! Eliza and Yaffaleh went inside, but Leah stayed a while with the men.

He had not particularly looked at her. In the talk, naturally, Trumpeldor included her, a chavera.

As every unwed woman toward every unwed man, Leah had instantly made the additions and subtractions—could she help it? That he stood fully as tall as she, as soon as he dismounted she had measured with her eye. Moreover, she had already known he was tall, she had read descriptions of the hero, she had heard talk of him among the chaveroth. How was it that although he had already been in the land more than a year she had not yet encountered Josef Trumpeldor? First, he had been with his own kvutsa, the group that had come together with him from Russia, and there, as everyone knew, Trumpeldor had his loved one, from his university days after the Russo-Japanese War, a doctoress who had joined him in St. Petersburg. But the kvutsa had not endured—there had even been a suicide among them—and the love affair too had died; the doctoress had gone back to Russia.

Despite, or perhaps even because of, his lost arm, many girls were said to be in love with Trumpeldor. He was indeed handsome, a noble-looking man. Once, Rahel had encountered him at a meeting and she had spoken about him to Leah—Josef Trumpeldor could be of great use to their movement, Rahel had remarked. Out of normal curiosity

Leah had guided Rahel's talk to the personal side, about
his arm. One quickly forgot about it, Rahel said, while
Leah was thinking: of course if a woman loved a man such
a thing wouldn't matter. But even to Rahel she hadn't
dared utter her real wonderings, about whether at night,
with an artificial arm—was it taken off or was it kept attached? She was ashamed of her speculation.

With his single arm he did the hardest work in the field,
the chevreh said. He was a vegetarian too, she had heard—
just like her brother. Purposely Leah had refrained from
going to HaKeren lately. Let fate arrange it, if anything
was to be.

In every smallest detail, the hero now questioned Gidon
about the attack; as Gidon was modest, there were moments when others in the family put in the answers for
him, but Trumpeldor would hold up his hand for them to
allow Gidon himself to explain. The military man's questions were so precise that Gidon became very lively, talking
more freely than ever before, even drawing lines with a
stick on the ground to show exactly what had happened;
they were like a pair of good workmen discussing a piece
of construction. It was gladdening to watch and hear them.
And presently, straightening up from the map on the
ground, Trumpeldor declared to Gidon, "You did well. Excellent."

It was a final judgment. The whole family glowed.

Leah had moved closer, and as Trumpeldor straightened,
she saw for certain that he was even a touch taller than
she, but of course he was in boots and she was barefoot. He
spoke directly to her now, declaring, "Such are the young
men we need." And yet in the same moment her heaviness
came upon her. He hadn't seen her. He had made his remark the way one does to anyone nearby in a meeting, and
as they moved toward the house he continued to speak in
phrases one heard over and over at meetings, only it was as
though these thoughts had just come to him. He discoursed
on the need for self-defense, on the need for personal labor
on the soil; he declared that while a laboring family was an
excellent unit, he himself preferred a cooperativa. He had
reflected much about the principles of communism and the
principles of nationalism, and had concluded they were not
in contradiction; they went together, for just as each communa could become a unit in a nation, so each nation

could be a unit in a world of nations. Hence the ideal of
internationalism, of a unified world, could come only
through the perfection of nations. But the first task here in
the Yishuv was to create unity, unity among the workers'
organizations.

And as they sat down to the table, Leah sorrowfully concluded within herself that the spark was not there between
them. Despite all that would have been right, despite their
belief in the same ideas, and his tallness, she must not expect anything to happen. He was a man closed from others.
Women had loved him, it was true, but perhaps this re-
moteness was why he was still by himself. Perhaps it was
indeed because of the severed arm, for while he made a
point of doing with his one arm all that everyone did with
two, Trumpeldor became offended, she had heard, should
anyone attempt even in the most natural way to give him a
hand—as by putting a dish within reach of his good side.

While Menahem and Trumpeldor carried on the discussion, and while she herself even put in an occasional remark, such as a comment about the role of the woman in
the Yishuv, and while Trumpeldor praised Mama's
blintzes—Leah suddenly perceived there was one who was
indeed falling in love, totally, touchingly and absurdly, with
the Captain.

It was little Yaffaleh.

Though everyone at the table hung on his words, Yaffaleh turned with his turning, breathed with his breathing,
her every movement an echo of his every movement, as
though she were in some way part of him. And when she
was still, she watched him, transfixed, as are all creatures
when the spell comes upon them.

Leah saw it, and because of the fantasies she had allowed
to run so far within herself, what she saw in Yaffaleh gave
her a pang of anguish, for even the most grotesque attachment was something real. How pitiable it was, not to be an
ordinary, pretty girl like Eliza! Eliza would never have to
worry whether she could attract the man who moved her.
But to be too large or to be an ungainly lump—oh, what a
stupid trouble the body was in a woman's life!

Though Yaffaleh was to everyone still the little goose-girl
absorbed in her flock and her flower garden, she had
grown to a woman's form, with heavy breasts unbalancing
her short body. She had the full lower jowls, nearly without

a neck, of her mother. At times, when she led her flock down to the river, Yaffaleh's solid, firm body with its stocky legs, appeared to Leah to have its own beauty of movement, but she knew that her little sister thought of herself as ugly. And just now Leah saw that their mother too recognized what was suddenly taking place in the child. A glance went between them, a flash of consternation yet of tenderness and even amusement, for this was still a child. Why then did Leah feel a stabbing premonition for Yaffaleh? She knew the girl's poesy, and precisely because of her secluded nature, because of her unattractiveness, even from so premature a dream, pain might come.

From the stove, Feigel called to the child and gave her more blintzes for the visitor, and Yaffaleh served him, quietly, without trembling. When he looked up to thank her, in his well-mannered way, Leah saw an illumination come into Yaffaleh's face that dispelled all heaviness and made her momentarily even beautiful.

Now the conversation among the men turned to mules and horses, and as they spoke the Captain kept looking to Gidon for his opinion. Clearly, Trumpeldor was drawing Gidon out, and Gidon's love for animals, his knowledge of their ways, showed at once. With relish he told the tale of Klugeh, the clever cow who had fed the orphan calf.

"You know what I think?" the Captain remarked to Tateh. "Your son should study for a year with a veterinary."

"But that was just what we were talking of, only today," Menahem interposed.

"I myself studied veterinary medicine in Russia, in preparation for coming here," Trumpeldor went on. What had he not studied! First dentistry, then jurisprudence, it was known, and now it became clear that he was also an accomplished veterinary! More easily now, more humanly, he spoke, and so deftly did he manage his blintzes and his tea that all at once you noticed that you had no longer been noticing. Also, he was the sort of man who, once an idea came to him, went on to think of every detail connected with it. There was an excellent horse-doctor in Jaffa whom he knew, a Dr. Gustav Mintz, and he would send Gidon to his friend with strong recommendations. In that way Gidon would be out of reach of a stupid reprisal here, and at the same time he would be developing his natural inclination and learning something that would always be of great use, whether or not he chose to follow it as a profession.

Then, at once, the hero turned to a consequent problem. Could they manage the farm without Gidon? He gazed around the table and his eyes stopped on Leah. At last he was really looking at her. "I hear you are equal to any man in the field," he said.

Even so she flushed. He knew of her.

Schmulik intervened. "I'm already bigger than Gidon was when he started to help Abba, and I can do everything. I can plow, I can keep up in the reaping." Now even the youngest, Mati, announced, as though the Captain had taken command here, that as for Schmulik's work around the barn, he could do all of it.

"School will be starting," Eliza reminded Mati.

"Then what? What is school, what do we learn there?"

"You'll go to school!" the Captain decreed, and as Mati's mouth opened to protest and suddenly closed, everyone laughed. "But every morning before school," Trumpeldor consoled him, "you will water the animals, and after school you can help in the fields."

Mati looked from the man to Leah and then back to the man again, as though it was between these two that things were decided. How tantalizingly the world was made, Leah felt—so as sometimes to give you a glimpse of how good and right things could be! The voice of a man to a child, a family in warm agreement around a table—But only because it could be good, you must not let yourself believe that things would fall out that way. Yet you must not believe that they couldn't.

Menahem had the news first, from a fellow-shomer who passed, riding north; the war had broken out, there in Europe. An Austrian archduke had been assassinated somewhere. Austria had declared war on Serbia, Russia had declared war on Austria, Germany on Russia, France on Germany: the whole applecart was upset, armies were spilling forth in all directions.

Now least of all could Leah remain tied to the homestead. In this remote village, torpid under the oppressive heat of the summer's end, her entire being strained to catch some hint of fate from the outer world. It was like the women waiting outside the cabin at the yearly secret meeting of the Shomer, for some hint of what was being decided among the men behind the closed door. And how would it affect each woman's fate? And wanting to burst in and take part. So it was with the great nations there in Europe; surely the Jewish fate too was being decided.

All day now she worked in her vegetable garden near the house so she could see any wagon that drove into the village. Sometimes a driver even had a recent newspaper. But how to interpret the news? Menahem had gone to Gilboa for discussions. Even if she picked up a scrap of news here, with whom could she weigh its meaning? With her mother, only such items as might have a direct bearing on the family. First, the sons. A blessing from the Above One that they had left the Czar's land! For otherwise Reuven and Gidon too would now be conscripted! And then Feigel worried over her brother Kalman who had remained in Cherezinka, and for his son Tuvia, who would surely now be seized for the Czar's army.

How could Leah discuss with Mameh the thoughts that kept pounding, not so much in her mind as in her heart? Surely this was the revolution! The war would bring the Russian revolution. In some fated and mysterious way it would be the end of czardom. The revolutionists exiled in Siberia would rise up and from Siberia the revolution would spread! She did not dare name him in her thoughts or relate it all to her own fate, for this was too great a thing, too momentous for the entire world. A secret, inspired belief was in her that once the revolutzia had swept through Russia, it would inundate all Europe, and in some way it would also reach to this land. The Jews, Jews like her own Moshe—for in this new turn of events she could allow herself to think so of him—it was such as they who would bring the revolution here, so that in some way when the upheaval was over, there would be Palestine, a socialist land, open and shining and free, the chevreh like some great perpetual committee sitting in Jerusalem, a sanhedrin of chalutzim, and even the fellaheen would enjoy their entire harvest from their own fields, without landlords, without moneylenders seizing the largest part of their crops, and the Arab children, clear-eyed, free of trachoma, would go to schools in their villages, and Arab villagers would live alongside their Jewish neighbors as in a perpetual sulha.

Toward the end of the day, when the men brought in their oxen and mules from the fields, there was more of a lingering now on the town's single street. But the Roumanians asked each other only for word of Roumania, turned to Leah to ask only if there was news of Roumania, sighing with relief that their homeland was still out of the battle. It would soon all be over: the Kaiser was strong, they declared. With whom could she talk seriously? If only she could hear the views of Dovidl, of Avner.

When her father finished his stubborn solitary evening prayer and came to sit down at the meal, there was little to be said, for Yankel Chaimovitch had only one declaration: to him all the goyim were equally evil, let them kill each other off, and let every Jew stay out of their war as best he could.

"In each country Jewish sons have to go into the army," the mother sighed. "In the battles it is Jew against Jew."

—Yes, Yankel admitted, that was a bitter thing, but still the French and English Jews were hardly Jews to him, or the Germans either, for that matter; it was only the Polish and Russian Jews who were really Yehudim, and for them he suffered, and yet, if they had had sense and followed God's command and taken themselves up and come here to build up the land—

"But, Tateh, the war can also bring great changes for the Russian Jews," Leah offered. "Out of the war may come the revolution."

"The revolutzia! What revolutzia? The czars and the kaisers will send all your fine revolutionists to the war and kill them off!" It had always been left as though Tateh knew nothing about her Moshe, and Leah even believed that what he said now was without thought of Moshe or the pain this might still give her. —And what good was their revolutzia to the Jews? Yankel went on. It served only to make them forget they were Jews, and become godless. He spat on them all, with their wars—Czar Nicholas, Wilhelm the Kaiser, and all the revolutionists— "May the cholera overtake the lot of them!" It was the time of Babel again! Any Jew who ran to take part in their wars was a fool. "Look at your fine hero Captain Trumpeldor!" he cried. "He ran to fight the Japanese for the Czar. What for? To show that a Jew could fight. A patriot. What did he get?

An arm cut off. And are there any fewer pogroms in Russia because of Trumpeldor?"

Leah caught a quick glance from her mother—let it pass, Tateh would soon stop his ranting. And on Yaffaleh's face she saw a trembling.

On Shabbat at last she could go over to HaKeren to hear an intelligent word. Lately the discussions there were livelier, as three young men from the first graduating class of the Herzlia Gymnasia in Tel Aviv had come to HaKeren to have a taste of working in the fields and of communal life. They were a bit too young for her, but to hear them argue with Max Wilner and Josef Trumpeldor was a pleasure. They were the brightest, at the head of their class, and they had organized a club to devote themselves to the future of the Yishuv. Each had been assigned his life task. One was being sent, like Dovidl and Avner, to study Turkish law in Damascus—he was the son of Shertok, the Jewish manager of that Arab farm where she and Rahel had once stopped on the way to Galilee. Another, a solid youth named Eli, was among the three sent to learn life in a kvutsa. He was in love with Shertok's sister. They were bright Tel Aviv youth who were not Marxists, but who had visions of building "the just society" here in Eretz. Old Gordon often agreed with them, and Reuven too, but Trumpeldor said the youngsters of the Yishuv didn't understand world politics.

As it was the week of the High Holy Days, Leah put on the long white abaya-dress that she had made for herself at the time Bialik came to visit Mishkan Yaacov. The chevreh, also in their Sabbath clothes, were sitting on the patch of grass that Reuven had grown in front of the cheder ochel, and, remarkably, as she approached, Trumpeldor was discoursing about some of the very things that were on her mind. Leah squatted down beside Reuven. In his clumsy, half-Russian Hebrew, Trumpeldor was declaring that without question in Russia the war would lead to the revolution. Either with victory or defeat, the revolutzia must come. "First of all, Siberia will be emptied."

And with that word, her foolish heart leaped away. It was as though she saw Moshe coming toward her on the wagon-road. She was a hopeless case. Leah heard Trumpeldor's voice and saw him sitting there simply as any other speaker at a meeting, an interesting man, but with no personal call to her. Still wrapped in the fantasy of the returning Moshe, she heard Reuven saying that the quickest way to socialism was for all workers everywhere to declare a peace strike. As he spoke, his face had that impractical, idealistic look that made her feel toward her brother as a mother must feel toward a little boy.

Josef Trumpeldor answered that unfortunately the masses of workers were still too backward to realize they should refuse to fight. Therefore all true revolutionists must go into the war alongside the toilers, making ready for the proper moment to turn them from the war to revolution. Only if the revolutionist fought alongside Ivan would Ivan trust him. And this was particularly true for the Jewish revolutionary leaders and therefore eventually for the Jewish cause. For after all the heart of the revolution was in Russia, and the heart of Jewry is in Russia, and there the movements must join—

"Then we should all lift up our feet and run to join the Russian army, which we came here to escape," declared Tibor the Comical, and, leaping up with a mock flourish, he cried, "Lead on, Josef, I follow!"

An odd expression passed swiftly over Trumpeldor's face —an expression of anger, of uncertainty—he didn't understand such humor. He had not come to Eretz to escape military service, he declared. Actually, in the final analysis, he counted himself a pacifist—

"Except in times of war," the irrepressible Tibor taunted, and there was a burst of laughter. Trumpeldor reddened, but meanwhile a stern voice broke in, "Chaver, about fighting, about war, men should not make jests!" It was Old Gordon who frowned on Tibor, while he lectured all of them like a teacher before forgetful pupils. "What have we here to do with violence, with slaughter, with conquests and wars? The only revolution we seek is within ourselves. We have come here, renouncing their civilization of murder and massacre and Moloch. Only when man returns to his true relationship with God in the world of nature in which God has placed him, only when man restores the balance . . ."

To listen to the words of the sage was always entrancing, and Reuven, Leah saw, sat in smiling enjoyment, while Old Gordon's thin shoulders swayed back and forth as though he were praying in a shul. But from Max Wilner under his breath she heard a scoffing word to Tibor, "Our vegetarians." And then Max began in his hard-headed manner. All this was well and good, but what were the factors that applied here and now? In his mathematical way he recited: the Turks, even though not officially at war, had already closed the Dardanelles, so the gateway out of Russia was locked. Last year's flood of chalutzim was shut off. Whatever was to happen here would have to be faced by those who were already here.

"Exactly!" broke in the youthful Eli from Tel Aviv.

And before revolutions and before wars of the great powers, Max went on, came the basic need of the Yishuv to survive. The movement here would have to survive on its own strength alone, and this was the problem—

On all sides arguments broke out. Nahama's Shimek declared, "Wait. As workers and socialists our fate is bound up with the revolution—"

"Our fate is bound up with our land," cried young Eli.

"But in the end we must join hands with all our brothers—"

"But chaverim, if Turkey enters the war tomorrow, what measures should we take here and now?" Eli persisted.

The talk spread into confusion. Some said Turkey would never conscript Jews. "No, first they'll slaughter us!" Others said conscription was certain, and even if not, the men should volunteer.—But then they might find themselves fighting their own brothers from Russia! Nahama declared it was already known that Jews would be conscripted into labor battalions. Reuven said that this would be better than having to go and kill people. Another chaver argued that the Turks might yet even join the British rather than the Germans.

A chavera said it was wrong to take the attitude that there was no difference between one side and the other: The British and the French were more democratic.

A young newcomer scoffed, "Excuse me, chavera, but the social democratic móvement is a thousand times further advanced in Germany than in England."

Side-arguments broke out. Trumpeldor had become silent.

Leah had a longing for the voice of Avner, of Dovidl— they would know what to think. Where were they? And

Rahel? Scattered in France, in Constantinople. Would they even be able to come home? What would become of them?

How could Leah sit still by the Jordan? The very next day she took herself up, boarding a wagon that had suddenly appeared from Jaffa—Kalman the Drayman had come to buy wheat, Jaffa's warehouses were already empty. And banks were already without currency, he recounted. Merchants were accepting only gold, and there wasn't a napoleon to be had anywhere. Ships were ceasing to sail.

Running back into the yard where Eliza was hanging out the washing, Leah said, "Tell Mama I have been called to an urgent meeting of the Women Workers." For even as a full grown woman Leah was unable to deceive Feigel to her face. It was not that she was such a moralist—to avoid hurting a person's feelings, she was ready to tell a small lie—but in her mother there was such an intuition that Leah would blush like a child if she tried even the most innocent deception. "Tell Mama I'll bring back Gidon from Jaffa for Succoth," Leah added.

In Jaffa it was as though she had been summoned. For even as the wagon neared the town, Leah could see a vessel arriving in the port, with the little Arab boats going out to meet it. On impulse—there might be news—she hurried directly to the harbor, and so it appeared as though she had come expressly to greet Rahel, who leaped out of the first skiff into her arms.

"Have you heard anything of Dovidl? of Avner?" each blurted to the other, and then Rahel cried, "How did you know I was coming on this ship—not a soul knows! I didn't even telegraph my family. Have you seen them?"

"I went to Gilboa last week especially to ask for news of you. Everyone is well."

"But, Leachka, how did you know I was coming on this ship?"

"You see I knew!" Leah laughed. "In my heart something told me!"

And they hugged each other, and in blurts and both talking at the same time, each told and asked what had happened, what would happen, would the war be short or long.

Rahel had not forgotten to bring a gift for Leah, and then and there she opened her valise to find it, a most wonderful book of drawings of the dancer Isadora Duncan,

"She reminded me of you!" And in the midst of the port, as Leah studied the pictures, oblivious to pushing and jostling, Rahel gave her an account of the dancer's recital she had seen in Paris. "Oh, Paris, such theater, such culture, such art!" And the socialist spirit! On their Fourteenth-of-July holiday, Rahel had followed the great Socialist leader Jaurès, and in the vast mass of people she had heard him call out for the workers of the world to stage a universal strike for peace!

"This is exactly what Reuven was saying!" Leah cried.

But Rahel went on, "And now Jaurès is assassinated, and they have started their war!" Rahel clutched Leah's arm. "Leah, it's a world of assassins we live in!"

Rahel had to go at once to Jerusalem, perhaps there was word there from Avner. Her thesis was accepted, and she now held a degree in agronomy, but she was still ignorant, she confided—she still couldn't grow a tomato.

"We will have to begin to grow things, in time of war it is necessary. Leah, I thought it all out on the boat: If the war comes here, we women must grow vegetables—you will have to take charge and show everyone how!"

She would go to Jerusalem by the first train—she had just enough money left for a ticket, for Leah as well—Leah must come with her to Jerusalem.

Just as they were climbing the stone stairway to the abode of Misha, the party secretary, over by the Old City wall, Leah heard the news shouted by Misha to a chaver who was just starting down: a telegram at last from Avner and Dovidl! The pair of them were on the way back from Constantinople. In a few days they should arrive.

But a week went by without a sign. German submarines, it was said, were already sinking ships in the Mediterranean. Rumors came that, although the Turks had not yet declared war, in Constantinople they were arresting Russian subjects. Who first? Russian Jews. In Jerusalem flour was to be had only in secret, and sugar was ten times its former price. Then one afternoon, when Rahel and Leah had gone to Misha's place to help him put out an emergency issue of the paper, there, climbing the outside stairway, the pair of lost travelers suddenly appeared, carrying huge roped-up suitcases. For once Rahel fell so completely into Avner's arms that Leah's heart choked up. As though her own Moshe had walked in from Siberia. After all, between Rahel and Avner too perhaps something had gone wrong—they had been separated for nearly two years. But see—once in each other's presence, everything was swept away.

In the midst of the first rush of questions, Leah and Dovidl paused to share a good laugh at the "unsentimental" reunited couple. Then Dovidl was demanding: How bad was unemployment? What was the situation in the grape harvest? How quickly could a sitting be called? And in Galilee, Leah? What was the situation in Galilee? But he looked so haggard and half-starved, she rushed first to Misha's larder to fix him some food. Two weeks the pair had been on the sea, for a three-day journey. Only by half-words could the events be dragged out of them.

"Nu, what does it matter what happened, we got here!" Dovidl said. It had been a Russian ship, and first it had made a stop in Smyrna. "Listen, we must hold a unity conference. At once, of all the workers' parties. Try to get Max Wilner to come to Jerusalem—"

"A Russian ship?" Rahel repeated, alarmed. "But Germany is sinking Russian ships!"

"We sailed the day they declared war," Avner remarked. "It was also the Ninth of Ab."

"We had two hundred Hasidim from Bessarabia, and from their howling you would have thought the Temple had fallen for a third time!" Dovidl said.

His plan was to establish a massive united workers' organization while allowing each group to retain its own membership; because of the crisis, even the stubborn Max and his followers might now join. But before the unity conference, they must hold a caucus of their own leaders to decide how far such autonomy should go. What he had in mind was an overall central committee with two from each party and perhaps one independent, perhaps Josef Trumpeldor—

"He is at HaKeren," Leah offered. "But then, from Smyrna why did it take you so long to get here? What happened?"

"The Russian captain refused to move out from the Smyrna harbor—there were two German battleships running around there somewhere—"

"We heard, even on my boat we heard about them, the

Goeben and the *Breslin,* oh, they were terribly dangerous!"
Rahel cried as though the men were still in danger.

"Ach!" Dovidl made his contemptuous little lip movement, like someone who would spit except that it is beneath him. So their terrified Russian captain, nothing but a
drunken Ivan, had locked himself into his cabin with a
whole wicker basket of vodka bottles, and the ship lay at
anchor in Smyrna. At night the vessel was black as the sea,
not a match could be struck. The Hasidim in the hold kept
crying out their lamentation like at the Wailing Wall.

"I told them, Yidden, why do you need to go to Jerusalem? You carry your own wall with you!"

And in another human heap in the hold were Moslems
from Turkestan on their way to pray at their black stone in
Mecca, and all they did night and day was to repeat "Ya
Allah Il Allah." Finally Dovidl and Avner had got together
with a few Syrian students who were hurrying home from
Constantinople to Beirut. One of them had a revolver—a
nationalist, with this he was going to raise a revolt against
Turkish rule—but meanwhile they had used it to persuade
their Captain Ivan Ivanovitch that the Smyrna harbor was
the most dangerous place of all for a Russian ship, since
the Turks were entering the war against the Czar and
would therefore at any moment come and seize his vessel.
"Nu—" as if that was the whole of it—"on the third day
we got him to sail on."

"But why did it take so long from Beirut, then?"

Oh, the captain hadn't at once put in at Beirut. They had
given the simpleton such a scare that he was afraid he
would be seized in the Beirut harbor as well, and so he had
sailed straight down to Port Said. There, with the Czar's
allies, the Royal British Navy, all around him, Ivan felt his
ship was safe, and he went back to his vodka.

"Then how did you get home?"

Making his little shrugging movement, Dovidl absorbed
himself in the printer's proofs for the emergency issue they
were getting out. The leading article must be changed,
there should be a unity proclamation . . .

But Leah knew Dovidl, he would tell his story, it amused
him to tell it this way. How good she felt here with her old
friends again, in Misha's room, the headquarters. How she
loved them all, how much better was such love than the

tormenting love that was *liebe*. "So what did you do then, Dovidl?"

"Do?" They held a unity conference on the ship, the pair of them with an orange grower from Rishon Le Zion who was also on the boat. "That bandit Zukofsky, he never hired a Jewish worker in his life, he used to bring in Arabs even from Syria." And there were still the Syrian students who had to get back to Beirut. Everyone gave up his last grosh for bribe money, and with a considerable sum they had managed to rouse the captain from his drunken stupor. "He went around the port and found us a small Greek cargo ship." It flew a Persian flag and seemed safe from German attack, so the Russian had chartered it and crowded everyone aboard, Hasidim and all. Since it was only a short trip from Port Said to Jaffa, he had taken on no food or water, and having no money left, they themselves had made no provision, either. But the moujik of a captain had not forgotten his basket of vodka bottles, and thus he had lingered for three days along the Sinai shore, while they starved. The Russian was in terror that if he approached the Jaffa port, the Turks would take him prisoner. Suddenly he had decided to sail them back to Egypt.

To make the story shorter than the trip, Dovidl concluded, he and Avner, together with the Syrian students, had staged a little revolutzia, and at pistol point the captain had finally brought the ship to Beirut.

"But Jaffa is on the way . . ."

"The Syrians had the pistol. Let that be a lesson to us."

The Arab students disembarked; they were home. But as for the Jews, being Russian subjects none were permitted to land.

Just then, Avner interrupted with a whole discussion about the Arab students. The two nationalists were intelligent young men, from his own law classes in Constantinople. Their movement was small and secret, but serious. They saw the war as their opportunity to win Syrian autonomy from the Turks—

"But we had one on our boat as well!" Rahel broke in. "From Damascus. A doctor who had studied in Paris, from one of the high Arab families, Nuri el Khouri was his name. We can work with them, in the end I am convinced they will understand our movement. The Arabs will have all of Arabia. The first thing is for all of us to work together against the Turks, to win autonomy."

—But how could this be done? asked Misha, with the blinking puzzled look he had when anything was not in order. When Turkey entered the war—all of them here were surely not about to become traitors?

"Ach! We are speaking as socialists! In the long run—"

"But you just said *the first thing*," Misha repeated.

"It is a historic necessity," Rahel explained impatiently.

"But then how did you get here from Beirut?" Leah persisted.

"What does a Jew do? He looks for another Jew," said Avner. Zukofsky the pardessan—even such a bandit can have his uses—paid an Arab to get a message to the leader of Beirut's Jewish community, a wealthy importer belonging to an ancient family there, and this Jew had found a French vessel in the port and got them transferred to it, Hasidim and all, and thus, on the twelfth day of their voyage, they had come to Jaffa. The Beirut Jew through his connections with the Turks had already opened the way so that they were allowed to debark.

Already, word of the arrival of Avner and Dovidl had spread, and the door kept opening every second. Soon Misha left it open altogether, and chevreh halfway down the stairs were calling up greetings and relaying questions. Constantinople, Avner said, was swarming with German officers; Turkey would unquestionably enter the war at any moment now on the German side. And at that moment, every Russian Jew here in the Yishuv would be regarded as an enemy. "They will round us up. They may deport us. Who can tell what the Turk will do?"

There was only one solution that would enable them to stay in the land and protect what had been built up. "All those who still hold Russian nationality—" and this meant the great majority of the chalutzim—"must at once become Ottoman subjects." There was not a day to lose. The announcement must be proclaimed in this very issue of the paper.

A tumult began. Why—then a man could be conscripted to fight for the Turks! Was there no other way?

"That is exactly the point," Dovidl called out. "We should not even wait to be conscripted. We should volunteer. We should begin at once to organize a Jewish volunteer corps."

Had he gone mad on that ship? Did he perhaps want to become another Shabbatai Zevi and turn himself into a Moslem as well?

But on the boat the pair of them had thought it all out and come to this decision. Even before leaving Constantinople, they had examined the possibilities with the head of the Zionist bureau there. The reasoning was plain. Not Turkey but Germany was the power. Through Syria and down through Palestine was the way for Kaiser Wilhelm to Suez. Already his generals were planning to strike down, through the Sinai. The chances of victory in the war were with the Germans; if the Jews in Palestine supported their side, the Zionist position would be strengthened. After all, wasn't the World Zionist headquarters just now in Berlin?

Murmurs and doubts arose. The Germans had already been halted, they had not reached Paris, and if their first thrust failed, they might not succeed at all. And what of the British fleet? And Russia's unlimited manpower? Suppose Germany and Turkey should lose the war? Why let the Zionist fate hinge on the victory of one side or the other? There must be a full discussion. There must be instructions from abroad—

"Chevreh, we have no choice!" The moment Turkey entered the war, Avner pointed out, they became either enemies or patriots. What the Jews in the rest of the world did, did not matter so much. "Even if the Kaiser should lose the war, the Russians and the British and French could not blame us for having fought on the side of the country we live in, just as their own Jews will fight on their side. But if we hold back from fighting, both sides will despise us. And meanwhile the Turks would be capable of destroying the entire Yishuv."

There was not a day to lose. Dovidl caught hold of Leah. "Leahleh, it's a good thing you're here. You must go back at once to Gilboa and explain the program." She must go to Nadina and Galil—best that Galil himself should come at once to Jerusalem, or even better—they should all meet in Tel Aviv for a sitting, in the little house on the sand; she must leave word also in Yavniel.

And what about Josef Trumpeldor? Shouldn't Josef be asked to come? Leah suggested.

The Russian war hero, to join the Turks? In Dovidl's shrewd eyes she could almost read the lightning of his reasoning. Trumpeldor to head an all-Jewish fighting unit for the Turks! What a stroke it would be! But wait, Dovidl decided, first there must be a conference only for the party leaders. Then—

To become an Ottoman. There was something absurd in it. To be a Russian Jew seemed natural; even here in Eretz as part of the Yishuv, Leah had thought of herself as Russian. Tolstoy and Dostoievsky and Chekhov were somehow like Jewish writers, and the Russian revolutionary movement also was like something Jewish. But the Turks—with their indolence and cruelty—she felt a kind of revulsion in her flesh, as though pressed to lie down with a man who was repulsive to her. And suddenly the notion came, if she should one day have a child—a little Turk with a tarboosh on his head! And then it even came to Leah that in taking the Turkish nationality she would in some peculiar way be still further separated from Moshe.

But as Avner explained, it would not really be the Turks but the Germans they would be joining, and even in Herzl's time, Avner pointed out, this same German Kaiser had been in favor of Zionism. On a diplomatic visit to Palestine, Kaiser Wilhelm had met Herzl in Mikveh Israel and spoken good words for the Zionist movement, though at the time nothing had come of it.

Still, Leah felt, the Jewish masses were in Russia—no, it was all like some complicated chess game, and she had never had a head for chess, there were too many things to take into account, and at least one of the possible moves you were sure not to see. A world of brotherhood . . . perhaps it would indeed come after the war, and then it wouldn't matter what the government was named, so long as you lived your life. Just as here, even with the Turks, they had managed to restore Hebrew and build their own way of life in spite of all.

Turkey entered the war. Already there was a proclamation: enemy nationals must become Ottomans or face deportation. From Rahel in Jerusalem, Leah received a heavy package of forms that the chevreh had at once printed up. Though who knew what sort of papers the Turks would require, these forms were to be signed at once to show the desire for Ottomanization. Leah was to go to every house in Mishkan Yaacov and also in Tiberias. Every man must sign an application.

Her Roumanian neighbors balked. Roumania was still neutral, why should they sign? Once Ottomans, their sons would be taken for the army. Bronescu himself spread the word, don't sign any papers. Wait. There is always time to sign. Nor were the two other Russian Jewish families in the village in a hurry to sign; they accepted the papers and said they would see—none had sons of military age.

In Tiberias, Leah even penetrated the narrow byways to the courtyards of the pious, who had thin, pallid sons with long payess, as in Mea Shearim in Jerusalem. Never had she been in these houses. With his head turned so as not to be looking at a strange woman, a Talmud sage explained to her—already he knew every twist. The best was to arrange for Austrian nationality; with a small payment it could be arranged with the Austrian consul in Safed, and then your son was safe. Others said a conscript could be bought out for a thousand francs, a vast sum, but money must be found; rather than go about with papers to sign, she must go about collecting funds. Leah even found herself at the gate of a yeshiva where the master, unusually young-looking, again keeping his eyes turned away, rapidly inundated her with examples from the Talmud and the commentaries; at the end of his dissertation, she realized that, although he pronounced himself in agreement with her, he had proved that while Jews must everywhere follow the law of the land, even the Ottomans could not seize rabbinical students as conscripts. He snatched a bundle of her applications, as though to throw them away, yet carried them inside.

In the south, trouble had already begun. On the Sabbath, the chief shomer of the region, Motke, brought back tales to Gilboa: a new Kaymakam had appeared in Jaffa and at once issued a ukase forbidding Jews to be watchmen. No Jew could carry arms. Some of the planters were listing their Jewish watchmen under Arab names. Turks were commandeering horses, mules, wagons from the settlements. Sometimes they took drivers with their carts, saying they would be paid a day-rate—shukra, it was called. It appeared that all sorts of supplies were being hauled to Beersheba, surely for an assault on the British canal. In Rehovot, a German and a Turkish commander had appeared together in an automobile, stopping only to order the mukhtar to deliver ten thousand sacks in twenty-four hours! Sacks? Of what? Of nothing! Empty sacks! At least, a blessing from heaven, it was only empty sacks they demanded! They intended to fill them with sand in the desert and throw them into the canal, to block it up! A clever plan of a Turkish general! Where would you find ten thousand empty sacks overnight? Galloping from barn to barn, the mukhtar of Rehovot had made everyone empty out their sacks. He had sent a wagon to Jaffa to buy up all that were available. In the town hall children were set to counting; they became befuddled, but in the end it didn't matter, as the Turks never returned to collect the sacks, but instead, Motke the shomer told them bitterly, a band of Arab laborers came and began to tear away irrigation pipes, hauling them off on camels toward Beersheba—for a water-supply into the Sinai, it was said, though later the pipes were seen rusting alongside a camel-track.

Returning home with all the news from Gilboa, Leah, with Schmuel and Mati, helped Tateh dig a large pit under the barn, where they hid all the grain that remained. And then she was on the way again, to Jerusalem. There, Rahel had a whole new stack of naturalization forms; this time they were official, and Leah must go back and have them filled out. But now there was a tax on each head, and each day the price was being raised. If not—deportation!

Dovidl and Avner already had fifty volunteers for a special Jewish militia in the Turkish Army, and for this too Leah must find candidates in Galilee, pointing out to them that in this way the Jews would fight as a unit. That was of greatest importance. Already the plan was being proposed to Djemal Pasha, the new commander in Damascus—a whole Jewish brigade in the Turkish Army.

But also from Rahel, Leah heard a terrifying story. When Rahel had gone with the papers into the Old City, where the narrow lanes of the Jewish quarter were twisted up with the lanes of the Armenian quarter, she had been told of frightful whispers among the Armenians. How the

news came one hardly knew—there were no letters any
more—some said that word had been brought by a priest.
But in the Armenian area that lay between Russia and Turkey, ghastly massacres were taking place. The Turks had
always hated the Armenians, Moslems hating Christians.
Now they were destroying entire villages. Worse than pogroms. They took away all the men except the old ones—
who knew where to? nothing was heard—then they hanged
the elders, burned and looted the houses, raped the women,
and finally drove women and children out onto the roads
to the desert to die. It was a barbarity not to be believed. If
this was what was meant by deportation, then at once, every Jew must sign and become Ottomanized!

In Tel Aviv an emergency council had been formed by
the mayor and other town notables; they had taken over all
the stocks of flour, they were printing a kind of scrip to be
guaranteed by the banks, they had sent cables to important
American Jews for emergency help. By good fortune the
American Ambassador to Turkey was a Jew, a millionaire
named Morgenthau who had only a few months before
himself visited the Yishuv; he had even been in HaKeren
and had complimented Reuven on his Garden of Eden.
This American Jew would intervene with the Turks not to
deal harshly with the Jews.

14

TO STAY by himself in peace, Gidon would have been
satisfied to fix a bed in a corner of the stable, near the
soft-eyed, silver-coated mare that was boarded there by a
Tel Aviv merchant; he almost envied the Arab stableboy
who slept untroubled in the hayloft. But Frau Doktor
Mintz, as she called herself—she spoke of her husband as
Herr Doktor—did not consider the stable fitting for a Jewish "assistant." Nor, luckily, Gidon thought, did the woman
find room for him in her house. She spoke only German;
on the very first day she had made Gidon an angry speech
about the striking teachers who insisted on introducing He-

brew into the Realschule in Haifa—fanatics! There were
not even any Hebrew words for what was studied there!
Her husband, who had studied in Heidelberg, ought to
know!

With the husband, fortunately, Gidon felt at ease, even
though Mintz wore a high collar and tie, and rode out in a
fine carriage with a doctor's bag. Doubtless all this was
because of his wife. For at work Herr Doktor Mintz would
take off his collar and roll up his sleeves. When he had to
deal with a bad-tempered animal, Gustav Mintz poured
forth choice curses in German and Arabic. With Gidon he
conversed in a sort of Hebrew; with the fine riding horses
he boarded, it could be reconized by his cluckings and
nose noises that Mintz knew the language of animals as
well.

As for a sleeping place, Leah had taken Gidon over to
the Zuckermans' hotel where they had all stayed on the
first night of their arrival. Here Leah was embraced by the
early members of her kvutsa, Araleh and Saraleh, the
Zuckermans' daughter. On every visit Leah twitted them,
"Well, haven't you had enough of city life? When are you
coming back to the kvutsa?" Araleh always said he longed
for nothing better, only just now he was building a new
pension for the Zuckermans on the sands of Tel Aviv. A
builder he had become!

There at the Zuckermans', Gidon indeed felt at home,
though Saraleh—probably on Leah's instructions—was
constantly trying to find a chavera for him. Her younger
sister Aviva was already "taken," she sighed. In the evenings the pension was lively with the comings and goings of
chalutzim from the settlements, bringing bits of news. And
what with their constant discussions, he hardly had time to
sit in his room and study the large book on cattle diseases
that Mintz had loaned him. Besides, it was in German.

Not all the chalutzim were eager to become Ottomanized. The Poale Zion were mostly for it, as their party demanded, but among the non-party chalutzim there was
considerable doubt. Some were even slipping out from the
land, trying to reach America. All sorts of rumors were
exchanged about ships that might be sailing to Spain or
Egypt. And when it came to the Jewish Brigade proposed
by Avner and Dovidl to fight for the Turks, terrible disputes broke out. Naturally if the Poale Zion was for it, the

members of the Poël Hatzaïr were against it, some were
pacifists, and several times the arguments became so violent that they fell to blows, pacifists leaping in rage on their
taunters, who quoted bitter, angry verses from Bialik's
"The City of Slaughter" at them and mocked them as being
no better than the timid yeshiva bocher of old whom the
poet excoriated. Mama Zuckerman would scream Shame!
and Araleh and Gidon had all they could do to pull the
fellows apart.

Gidon himself, when it came to signing the Ottomanization papers, felt something holding back his hand. He
would wait until Leah came again. As to the Jewish Brigade—if one could fight simply as a Jew, not for the Germans, the Turks, or even as some wild ones wanted to do,
for the British or the Russians—ah! . . .Nevertheless, when
he read the arguments for the Brigade in the Poale Zion's
Achdut, the plan seemed sensible. If Jews fought here under the Turks, it would give them a claim to the land. Suppose the British should try to invade from the sea—if the
Jewish fighters held the land, that would count for something! All the graduates and the students in the last class in
the Herzlia Gymnasia were ready to join the Turks as a
body, it was said.

"And you think the Turks will let us fight as a unit, after
they forbade Jewish watchmen to carry arms?"

Things were different now. They had even sent an enlistment officer to the Herzlia Gymnasia to find men who
knew Turkish, to train as officers. "They desperately need
men who can read and write."

"Exactly. A few officers here and there. They'd scatter
us. They'd never let us have our own unit."

The new Kaymakam appeared in the streets of Jaffa. Gidon caught sight of him clattering past in his carriage, inspecting everything. A dark wooden face with a hawked
beak and button eyes, a Turk of Turks, Bahad-ad-Din he
was called, and leaning half-out, he gleamed at every
woman, as though making notes for future use. Before
noon, Herschel the Newspaper, an out-of-work chalutz who
came to pass time at the stable, had much to tell. The Kaymakam came straight from the Armenian region, it was
said. In Jaffa too there was a small Armenian colony, and

the dread whispers of what Bahad-ad-Din had done to their people had already been heard.

No sooner had Bahad-ad-Dim turned into Herzl Street to acquaint himself with freshly built Tel Aviv, than he halted his carriage, leaped out, summoned two military police who rode behind him, and ordered them to tear down the Hebrew street sign. A crowd gathered, watching in silence. All down the street the Kaymakam continued, stopping before each sign to watch it torn down. That same night, Mayor Dizingoff was summoned to the Kaymakam's fortress in Jaffa. The Jews were trying to set up a nation within a nation—this must end! Street signs would be only in Turkish! Nor must the blue and white flag be shown!

Each day, new edicts. On the backs of letters the postal authorities suddenly discovered extra stamps, with Hebrew writing. What was this! A postal system of their own? a nation within a nation? At once, police appeared in the offices of the Keren Kayemeth and seized all the sheets of stamps. Go explain to the Turk that for years such donation-stamps had been sold to raise money to buy land! Whoever was henceforth found with such stamps in his possession, decreed Bahad-ad-Din, would be subject to arrest and even hanging. Go, laugh at the thick-headed Turk!

Next, letters written in Hebrew were forbidden altogether. The military censors could not read them. And now the postal services through foreign consulates were ended. The Young Turks suddenly decreed void the "capitulations" of the old regime, which, because of vast debts, had made a whole system of concessions to European governments allowing their subjects to conduct their own affairs through their consulates. No longer could foreigners hold their own courts in Ottoman lands, no longer were foreigners immune from Turkish demands. Finished! The Ottoman Empire must be restored to glory. Teaching in all schools must be conducted in Turkish.

Very well, one put in a few more classes in Turkish, in any case useful to know. But the jokes about the Turk's stupidity turned more and more to gall.

It began to seem as though the whole effort of the Yishuv would be erased. And the people as well. Starvation loomed; there was hardly a week's supply of flour in the warehouses. Then a miraculous sight appeared. Frau Doktor Mintz herself came running into the stable one day to call her husband, he must come and behold the sight! Without rolling down his sleeves, the veterinary hurried out behind her, and Gidon too, and there in the Jaffa harbor they saw an enormous battleship, and from its bow waved an American flag. Tons of wheat were being unloaded for the Jewish community—sent by American Jews. Fifty thousand dollars too, it was said, had been sent by the banker Jacob Schiff and other rich American Jews. After all, many were originally from Germany, and so they still had influence with the master-ally of Turkey.

And there also were packets of letters from America. One of these reached the Chaimovitch farm, for Feigel's sister had read in the Yiddish press of the dreadful fate, who even knew what, deportation, starvation, that hung over the Jews of Palestine. The whole family must come at once to America, she said. Her husband would provide ship tickets. At the very least Feigel must send the young girls!

Though most of the wheat sent for Jewish relief had promptly been seized by Bahad-ad-Din for the Turkish Army, a new aura, almost of respect, was visible among the Turkish officialdom. For the time one heard no more threats of Jews being driven out like the Armenians; new "rapid" forms for Ottomanization were distributed, though with a still higher tax on each head . . . As yet it seemed the rulers had not decided just what to do about the Jews. One day the entire population of Rehovot was commanded to present itself at a government office in Jaffa with applications filled in for immediate Ottomanization. The elders hurried all night from house to house, and before dawn the whole of Rehovot, on donkeys, in droshkies, on foot, hanging from crowded diligences, poured down to Jaffa. Until noon they waited in the street before closed doors. At last a functionary arrived and opened the building. After an hour he closed it, sending everyone home. The usual jokes were made. The way of the Turk. But uneasiness grew.

Then on a drizzly December day a troop of militiamen, emerging from the fort, suddenly began arresting Jews on the streets of Jaffa, while others with lists in their hands went into the houses.

Herr Doktor Mintz had ridden off to attend to an outbreak of hoof-and-mouth disease in Rishon- le Zion, brought by diseased cattle the Bedouin had driven in for slaughter for the army. Gidon was alone in the white-washed stable at the rear of the courtyard, when two soldiers appeared carrying long bayoneted rifles. "Russki! Russki!" they shouted, amidst a stream of filth as they poked at him, and then, with a burst of joyous laughter, one of them stood his rifle against the wall—the bayonet reached higher than his head—while he ran to the stall of the silvery mare and unloosed her. "Not Russki!" Gidon burst out, and at this the Turk doubled over with laughter, even slapping him on the back as he repeated Gidon's cry and pointed to the horse, "No Russki? Turki!"

But as Gidon tried to pull the mare back, the other soldier instantly leveled his bayonet at his face.

From the house, hysterically repeating "Deutsch! Allemand!" as she pointed to herself, Frau Doktor Mintz came running, with her two little boys bravely trying to push themselves between their mother and the soldiers. A third Turk, with some sort of officer's marking, perhaps a sergeant, appeared from the street. In Arabic, in bits of Turkish, in a flow of German, Frau Doktor Mintz was trying to explain that her husband had already paid for Ottomanization papers, the papers were coming any day, her husband the professor was educated in Germany and had high connections. Without listening to her, the sergeant gleefully leaped onto the silver mare. She reared, but the fellow knew how to sit a horse. His two soldiers were repeating the great joke to him—not Russki, the horse, Turki. And he shouted out, "Ho, ho, now she is Turkish for sure!" and galloped into the street, with Gidon and Frau Mintz and her children flocking in despair behind him.

There Gidon beheld a stream of bewildered, terrified Yehudim, the bearded long-coated ones, amidst flocks of women and children, some with hastily tied bundles, some with large valises, as though they had kept them packed and ready. A few he recognized—a watchmaker, the keeper of a little grocery—the numbers growing as Jews were hustled out of their homes, the new victims crying out to those in the street: What do they want of us? What is happening?—Is this the deportation?—Gottenu, where are they taking us!—and calling messages to Arab shopkeepers in their doorways: Tell Sosya, tell my brother, send for Dizingoff, they pillaged everything!

Already with soldierly stoicism, Gidon held his rage.

This was not the moment when anything could be done. To Frau Doktor Mintz, who had sometimes treated him as a stableboy but who was now tearfully appealing to him, he kept repeating assurance: her husband would soon be back, they were lucky he had not been at home to be seized, as this way he could be free to find help for them. The words *gerush*, deportation, was now echoing along the street, while everywhere the militiamen shouted "Russki, Yahud —Out! out!"

As the procession descended toward the port, from doorways and windows sympathy and encouragement was shouted out to them in Yiddish, in Hebrew. Cables were already being sent, the world would be alerted, the American ambassador in Constantinople would at once intervene—as though he would appear at the bottom of the street to save them by the time they got there. Here and there a figure darted alongside the procession, gold was passed, someone was slipped away.

Then as they drew up before the gates of the ancient stone structure, a fresh wailing arose—this was the Armenian monastery! As though Bahad-ad-Din in one of his vicious jests was telling them of their fate.

The hallways were already crammed, alcoves were jealously guarded by mothers commanding their children not to move out of reach. Up and down, names echoed—anxious, desperate calls— "Yosele, where are you?" "Batya and Misha! Batya!" while rumors swept through, "It's for ransom, Meir Dizingoff is coming with gold!" And between the airless walls, a crowd-stench was settling and making them all into one flesh.

In the incredible way of some women—as it would have been with his own mother—there were those who had already established their family circle on the floor around a primus stove and were unknotting some large kerchief in which they had hurriedly bound up a supply of food.

Was it only in Jaffa that this was taking place, or would the seizure reach out to Jerusalem and even to Galilee? If it was to be a death march into the wilderness, wouldn't it be better to draw together some of the chevreh at once, and even tonight overcome a few of the guards and break out? Or perhaps he should himself try to break out in some way, catch hold of a Turk in the night in the yard and strangle him for his uniform, then make his way to Gilboa to tell what was happening, let the Shomer decide what to do? No, these were foolish imaginings, impractical. But Gidon couldn't remain inactive, just standing here squeezed against the wall. Squirming his way through the solidly filled corridor, he found himself in the courtyard, which was filling up with those who couldn't press their way into the building. You had to step carefully over legs and bundles. The rain at least had stopped, but the stone pavement was mud-streaked and slippery. At the rear, before the single cubby-hole of a latrine, a line waited.

Here in the yard the shouting and wailing and the anxious calling of names was even worse. In the midst of this, Gidon heard the solid, authoritative voice of Herr Doktor Mintz, as though commanding a halt to a cattle stampede. Pushing toward it through the multitude, he found the veterinary just inside the gate, talking to the Turkish guard in that imposing manner that made everyone call him Professor. "They're here! they're here!" Gidon shouted, and the Turk himself opened a path for Mintz, all the way through the yard and into the hallway, to his wife and children.

Brandishing some official-looking document, the Herr Doktor gathered them to him; Gidon saw palms meet and the Turk's hand gliding into his ballooning trousers, as he now made a path outward for the entire Mintz family. But before Gidon, the Turk stretched out a forbidding arm; even the all-powerful Mintz could do nothing, though he cried out "My student!" Stubbornly and knowingly, the Turk repeated "Russki," and Mrs. Mintz, Gidon saw, was becoming terrified that they would all be held back because of him.

"I promise you, I promise you!" Mintz declared in parting. Gidon had only a moment to scribble a note to his family. "Don't worry about me. Try to stay together and be well. Whatever awaits me, I shall try to meet it as a man. Your son and brother, Gidon." In the last moment, as he gave Mintz the paper, he bethought himself that he should have put in a word of love.

With the gradual sorting out of the families, of children to their parents, the shrieking had ended. Now a squad of militiamen was working through the yard and the hall, taking the Jews, a dozen, twenty at a time, into a long, high-ceilinged room. Portraits of the Christians' Yoshke and other holy pictures hung against the stone walls. Behind a long table sat the Kaymakam himself, his reddish eyes gleaming in his scimitar face. Already a warning whisper had spread amongst the people, so that only a few coins, a few women's baubles were placed on the table when the guards commanded, "Everything! money, jewels, everything! For safekeeping for the journey!"

What journey? Out there in the harbor of Jonah the Prophet stood one vessel; she was neutral, flying the Spanish flag. It was a ruse, some said—the Turks would carry them all to some desolate North African coast and set them ashore to be murdered by the bandits, the Berbers. Or to perish of thirst and starvation. Others said the voyage would be in the opposite direction, to somewhere on the wild Turkish coastline, and they would be driven into the desolation where the Armenians had perished.

In his turn, just inside the doorway, Gidon found himself in a group of long-bearded pious old men, wearing tzitzith, talking only in Yiddish, their faces in terror, but their eyes ceaselessly roving, exploring for a chink, a hole, a crack, a way out— Which one can be bribed? How much?—and whispering avidly amongst themselves. No, his father would not be like these.

And presently Gidon stood before the Kaymakam. Money, valuables, he had none; he received a kick, a soldier's boot like a mule's hoof, and he was through another door into a vast swarming room, among those to be deported. Herscheleh the Newspaper caught him, steadying him from the kick, keeping him from whirling around to return the blow, and informing him authoritatively that the Kaymakam's plan was to have them all sunk and drowned at sea by a waiting German submarine, as though accidentally.

"Idiocies!" There stood Araleh, and not at all downcast. It was to be Alexandria, he declared with certainty. And he was trying every way he could to have Saraleh and the baby brought here. While others wanted to bribe their way out, Araleh wanted to bribe a way in for his wife and child. "It's the best!" he cried to Gidon. "Under British protection, we'll be safe."

"Alexandria?" the Newspaper scoffed. Even the Turks were not so stupid as to send hundreds of young men to the enemy side, where they could join the fight.

"Alexandria," Araleh insisted. "To them, as fighters Jews are nothing."

A burly, short man appeared, Dizingoff himself, the mayor of Tel Aviv. He came into the long chamber, warding off the clamorers that swept around him. Mounting on a bench, the mayor, in an exhausted, croaking voice, declared that all possible was being done they need not despair. Cables had already been sent to the American ambassador in Constantinople, the noted Morgenthau had intervened before, he would intervene again. In any case a postponement had positively been secured and the ship would not sail this night.

A new wave of pleading arose, and the mayor managed to listen to each one, taking messages, promising to try; even Araleh spoke to him—and he promised to inform the Zuckermans. Moreover, there would be food, blankets for everyone, there was no reason to despair.

Already, Arab vendors were squeezing through the back door with piles of warm pittah.

Not long afterwards Araleh heard Saraleh's call and there she was in the doorway, the baby in her arms, her father and mother behind her, carrying bedding, suitcases, bundles, even cooking pots. To Gidon it was almost as though he saw his own family arrive.

With a thousand admonitions and lamentations they made their parting at the door, Sara's mother unable to leave off kissing her grandchild, yet repeating "It's better, it's safer, Araleh is right," the father pressing still another gold coin, even some old Russian currency on Saraleh, and Mama Zuckerman, even in the midst of the turmoil remembering to ask Gidon, could she do anything? had he sent word to his family already? Again they kissed the baby, and old Zuckerman, as the guard was pushing them away, called out to Araleh a last name of some Jew in Alexandria with whom he had done business, "Judah Musara, go to him!"

While Araleh brought in the suitcases and the baby's pot and a huge wurst, Gidon helped with their enormous bundles of bedding. He must stay alongside them, Saraleh insisted.

As night fell, the encampment in the huge room had already become a kind of entity, one vast organism breathing and sighing and heaving in the dark.

Pushed, hurled with their bundles and bags into the tenders, with the Arab boatmen, fierce as always, shouting and cursing above the wails of the women, the barks ramming and twisting together alongside the Spanish vessel, the bandit boatmen seizing blankets, pots, satchels, featherquilts, pulling all they could lay their hands on away from the frantic refugees, shouting Baksheesh!—thus, in a madness just as wild as on that day Gidon had arrived here with the family, he was departing.

Content that he had no baggage in this world, nothing at all to be taken away, Gidon in his turn clambered aboard. Good also that he had no one, such as a wife, from whom he might have had to be separated. In such a time as this it was best.

And there, as Gidon looked down from the deck, there on the water, standing erect in one of the last tenders, he saw his captain. Three Turkish militiamen and an officer were in the bark, surely as a mark of the captain's importance. Yet Trumpeldor stood as though in command, and mounted the ship's ladder as though to take command. Adroitly catching rung above rung with his single arm, he swung cleanly on deck, in his polished boots, in his Russian uniform, wearing all his war medals.

Already his name was being passed among the chevreh, with surprise and awe. Many of them the hero himself recognized, calling greetings to one and another, and to Gidon too, "Shalom, Gidon!" just as though he had quite expected him to be there. And looking around at the young men who were gathering toward him, Trumpeldor declared, "Good. We will go to fight."

Still, it was strange to have been delivered onto a ship to be carried away who knew to what fate. Already, as terrified Yidden repeated Herscheleh's latest rumor, that the ship would nevertheless turn in another direction than Alexandria once it was out to sea, Trumpeldor said quietly to the young men around him, "We must prepare. If they try any tricks instead of heading for Alexandria, we will seize the ship."

The ship was moving out of the harbor. Along the sands as far as the Herzlia Gymnasia of Tel Aviv—it did not look so large from out here—one could see clusters of figures;

they had hurried along the beach to prolong their farewell, to stretch the parting as far as they might. You no longer could discern if they were waving their arms. It seemed to Gidon that he could see deep into the land behind them; his gaze seemed to go as far as the Emek and beyond to the meshek itself. He worried about the good pair of mules, Oved and Hazak; would Schmulik and Tateh have sense enough to hide them somewhere before the Turks came and seized them? Would Leah at least be at home when his note arrived, so as to reassure Mameh? Ay, and little Mati. Suddenly he felt a longing in his limbs for a mock wrestle with the boy, for Mati's supple muscles wriggling out of his grasp and the boy laughing out a good Arab curse. In a broad swing, the ship carried them away from the shore.

Until it was out to sea, until the last desolate cries from those on the land had become like bird cries, there was tumult among the deportees, but now this too faded into a low monotonous complaint of the Yidden and their Yidde- nehs. And in the movement on the great water there was a sense of being carried on the bosom of destiny.

At the prow, the young men squatted around Trumpel- dor. He had neither been picked up in the raid nor ar- rested, Josef related, but had come of his own choice, de- manding to be placed on the deportation ship. For when the decision to Ottomanize had appeared, he had reflected on it and become convinced that it was a mistake. Al- ready in the kvutsa he had presented his reasoning. All hope lay with the West and with the revolution which would come in Russia. But the kvutsa was divided, many following Old Gordon, the pure pacifist. So he had put on his boots and his old military jacket and come to Jaffa, intend- ing to leave the land. The Turks were merely providing him with free passage. An army of Jewish fighters must indeed be formed, but not on the Turkish side as the party leaders proposed. They must fight on the side of Britain, France and Russia.

If the German-Turkish alliance should win the war, Pal- estine would remain in the Ottoman Empire. Could it be imagined that the victors would turn over Eretz to the Jews? However, on the other side, should the French- British-Russian alliance be victorious, then the vast, rotting old Ottoman Empire would surely be broken up. New nations would arise in those huge territories, and there was at least a chance that if the Jews fought on the side of the Allies, they would be rewarded in the breakup. Indeed they must seek to fight in Palestine itself, to help drive out the Turks, and then they could claim Eretz for their own!

It was as though Trumpeldor had given clarity to the tumultuous thoughts in Gidon's own mind. Perhaps the roundup had been a stroke of fortune, even the hand of God, if one believed in God, saving him from fighting on the wrong side.

Araleh had joined the group and was squatting beside him. As Araleh nodded agreement with Trumpeldor's reasoning, Gidon felt even more strongly that this was the view that would prove correct. The one-armed one's voice, speaking matter-of-factly as though in a field report, had already gone far into a sweeping strategy, far beyond anything Gidon could himself have imagined. Why should they remain a handful? Why shouldn't a vast Jewish army be formed? Jews from all over the world would join them! One day soon they would debark from British battleships onto the Palestine coast and seize the land, driving out the Turk, slicing the Ottoman Empire in two! It could even be the decisive stroke of the Great War, for was it not over the empires of the East that the powers were fighting? Thus after two thousand years Eretz would be won back by Jewish soldiers themselves!

Had it not already been shown that the homeland could not be attained the way Rothschild had tried, by money, by land-buying and bribes, nor even as Herzl had tried, by political maneuvering with the Sultan, the Kaiser, the Czar? No, the homeland must be won back by Jewish soldiers.

"But," Herscheleh asked the question foremost in their minds, "if we Jews fight alongside the enemy—"

"The Allies," Trumpeldor corrected him.

"All right, but if we join the other side, then what of all the Jews remaining in the Yishuv? The Turks will slaughter them in revenge."

Therefore the attack must be a surprise, and swift, the Captain said. A vast British armada would land the Jewish army all along the shore, and there would be no time for the fleeing Turks to take revenge.

And here before them lay that vast armada! The hours had passed, and Gidon raised his head and saw a harbor filled with ships, a tremendous vision entirely new to his eyes, of vast steel structures crowded together until they covered the sea, an expanse of high turrets bristling with cannon, like enormous lances, the entire armada forming one immeasurable engine constructed by man. What could withstand such a force!

Standing at the prow, Trumpeldor gazed as though the armada had already been assembled to carry out his plan; within a few short hours these ships could steam up to Jaffa, it would take no longer than their own voyage here just now. The whole Yishuv would rise to support their Jewish army, another Jewish army from Russia would come down and attack the Turks from the rear, the British and French would meanwhile seize Constantinople from the sea, the war would be quickly ended, and Jews would come streaming from all ends of the earth to build up Eretz Yisroel.

Here were the British, clean men in khaki knee-trousers, with impatience and boredom and contempt in their voices, crying out short commands to the Egyptian port-workers, "Yallah, Imshi!" Not only from the sight of their armada, but from the first sight of the British—though he had not doubted Trumpeldor's assessment—Gidon knew who would win the war. These people would win. Except for an officer or two, he had not yet seen the Germans. Even though everyone said they were formidable, organized, modern, strong, nevertheless these unperturbed British would win.

Quickly enough the deported Russian Jews found themselves led to a long structure, a quarantine building in the port, formerly used, some said, for pilgrims to Mecca. Already there were Jews from Eretz in the barracks. Many had come in the last weeks, on any ship they could find. Among them were numbers of young men who had been fearful of Turkish conscription.

At once the newcomers were fallen upon with questions about relatives at home, and there were reunions, and already various combinations were being made for the best corners in the barrack rooms, and already the newcomers were being aided by finely dressed Jewish women of Alex-

andria who were followed by black Arab porters in long
galabiyas with red sashes, carrying baskets of food.

The pious Jews quickly found themselves with other caf-
tan-wearers who had already organized a cheder for their
children. The better-off Jews of Jaffa went forth to hotels.

No sooner had their group of future fighters got hold of
a barrack-room and set down their blankets than Trumpeldor, appropriating a small table that was the sole piece of
furniture, set himself up in a corner, with a sheet of paper
in front of him, to write out his Jewish army plan to present to the British.

As was his way, he could think or speak of nothing else.
How many able-bodied men were already here before their
arrival? A good hundred. And perhaps the Turks would
expel still more, in any case hundreds more would surely
flee here from Palestine. And among the Egyptian Jews?
Surely at least a few thousand would volunteer. Without
question, a regiment could be gathered.

The next morning, Josef had opened his recruitment,
taking down names on a sheet torn from his notebook. He
would not present an empty plan to the British. As the
sheet was passed around their circle, Gidon was the seventh to sign. Some were writing their names in Hebrew,
some in Russian. He wrote in Hebrew. At once he felt a
pure sense of relief. This was his own deed, not like the
signing of the Ottomanization application. This time he felt
clean.

After some thirty names, Trumpeldor's list lay on his table, unadded to. From the religious ones there was even
grumbling at him. What was he up to—dragging their sons
into the war? They recited passages and proverbs about the
wars of the goyim; when Trumpeldor passed through their
section of the barracks, a few even spat at his heels. As for
the merchants and others who had been caught up in the
Jaffa raid, they rushed in and out of the Mafrousi barracks,
trying to get visas to America. "It doesn't matter," the Captain growled. "If we have thirty we will go, and if we have
ten we will go, and if we have ten thousand we will go."

In the morning he called his men into the courtyard,
divided them into squads of eight, and began to teach them
to march.

The whole refugee population poured out, watching.
Some made jokes, some glowered, a few young men after

watching for a time sidled up to Josef Trumpeldor and added their names to his list. Araleh watched for a while, then left. That evening Saraleh confided in Gidon. "I know it eats in him, not to be with you, to stand idly by. But it's because of me and the baby. What should I do, Gidon?"

He loved her; it was a woman like Saraleh he would want one day to find to love. And Gidon was moved, that for all his being younger, she should ask him for such serious advice. "Who knows, this may all come to nothing," Gidon said. "If it really becomes something serious, then Araleh can decide."

But immediately things took a turn. In a carriage with one of the finely scented aristocratic young Jewesses of Alexandria, who came every day to help refugee mothers take care of their babies, there appeared a short, energetic, youngish man, a journalist. Quickly, he was in and out of every barrack room, talking to everyone. Wearing glasses, with a scowling yet sympathetic face, he talked rapidly in Russian, in Yiddish, writing down a word, a name here and there, sweeping through the crowded building, seeing everything at one glance. Much later when they read what the journalist wrote, they marveled how he could repeat every detail: the samovar an old bobeh had set up in a corner, the color of a scarf on a girl's head, the shtetl a family had come from. Meanwhile his own name had spread; this was the well-known correspondent from Odessa, Vladimir Jabotinsky, and in no time he was in the courtyard watching Trumpeldor drill his men, who by now marched with straight backs, in step. Good, bravo—the reporter even clapped his hands. With Josef he was at once as a brother; the hero was of course known to him, though they had not met before. Instantly the journalist was involved with the plan for a Jewish army. As soon as he had heard there were Jewish refugees from Palestine here in Alexandria, he had rushed over from Europe, he said, with just such an idea in back of his own mind. What Josef was doing was exactly what should be done. Snapping out his questions, the journalist was oddly like a prime minister receiving information from his military chief. Right. Correct. Tak. Tak. Understood. Jabotinsky himself had been one of the self-defense organizers in the Odessa pogrom-year of 1905. And presently the two of them were in Trumpeldor's "office" with their heads together, as Jabotinsky studied Josef's memorandum to the British.

—It has not yet been presented?

—No. Josef had made a few inquiries of a British lieutenant who came here to the barracks—and first of all, the plan must be presented in English.

—Just as well. Before it was presented, there must be more volunteers.

Exactly as Josef himself had thought. Yet if volunteers were not forthcoming, perhaps recognition of the plan by the British would bring them out?

"We'll bring them out ourselves."

That very afternoon, with everyone packed into a huge unused stable to hear the journalist's report on the war in Europe, and on things at home in Russia, they also heard his oration calling upon every able-bodied man to follow the lead of Captain Josef Trumpeldor. Too long had Jews fought for other nations, too long had they expected others to fight for them, and whoever failed to grasp this was like a slave who preferred to remain in Egypt rather than follow the call of Moses. They here would become the new troops of a new Joshua, to free the Land of Israel. They would wear the Star of David on their uniforms, and the world would know again that the Jew was a warrior, a man!

Saraleh saw in Araleh's face that he could bear it no longer. "Go, go and join them. We will be cared for here like all the others —don't worry," she said.

At the end of the meeting a dozen men came up to sign, but before the day was over, fifty more had made up their minds and joined. In the morning the journalist himself moved into the Mafrousi barracks. He was everywhere, usually with two fine Alexandrian ladies on his arm, while he argued even with religious young men about joining the Jewish force, matching their quotations from rabbinical commentaries with equally strong Talmudic quotations on the other side. When his fine ladies were gone to their charitable duties, he was in the company of a handsome young woman from among the refugees who had volunteered to become a secretary. The journalist had even managed to commandeer a small room near the barrack entrance that now served as a headquarters for the Captain and himself; he hurried forth from there in a droshky, sending cablegrams, his secretary divulged, to England, to France, to Russia, to America. The names of high persons fell from his lips. And there came answers to his cables, praise, support, encouragement; he read the messages aloud at the meetings, translating from English, French, Italian.

Now they must win recruits from amongst Egyptian Jewry. To the scented lady's palatial villa, Jabotinsky brought Trumpeldor as a dinner guest. Fascinated that the one-armed warrior hero was a vegetarian, the lady had special dishes prepared for him. Among her guests, a young Alexandrian physician declared himself, even that first evening, ready to accompany the Jewish army. And several young men of the city's ancient Sephardic families appeared a few days later at the barracks—all of them seemed to be named Nissim—declaring they were ready to enroll, though hinting that perhaps they should be enrolled as officers.

New refugees arrived, swelling the ranks. Jews arrived on every sort of vessel—some on fishing boats, all with tales of how they had been fleeced of passage money. In the Yishuv, they related, the Turk was imposing tax upon tax. Food was gold. If it were not for the American vessels bringing wheat, there would already be widespread starvation. And ruin was everywhere. The orange crop remained on the trees, the entire crop, since no ships came to Jaffa to carry the fruit to be marketed in Europe.

Young men, sons of the orange growers, even arrived from across the Sinai desert in camel caravans led by Bedouin hasheesh smugglers. At home the Turks were arresting everyone; old, respected Jewish notables were seized for possession of a Zionist pamphlet. News of the labor leaders? Nadina was arrested. Dovidl and Avner had been seized, and the Poale Zion's journal was forbidden, because of an article describing the raid in Jaffa. —And Galilee? Gidon asked anxiously. Of Galilee they had little news. The food situation was said to be better there.

Enough! the newcomers swore, they were finished with the Turks, they were even ready to fight them.

At last came the conference with a high British officer, a general, and from it Trumpeldor and Jabotinsky returned looking solemn, instantly locking themselves away in the small headquarters room. Gidon stood outside the door so that they would not be disturbed.

How long can a secret be kept from a barrack full of Jews?

Volunteers were welcome, the colonel—not a general after all—had told them. He was the officer in charge of refugee camps, and carried on his face the tight look of having to deal with a smelly situation. The colonel had even promised that the Hebrew volunteers could be kept together as a unit "as there would doubtless be problems of diet." Such, he said, was the practice with other homogeneous groups such as the troops from India, for example. Why, yes—with a little intrigued smile—the Jewish volunteers might even aspire to their own distinctive insignia. But as to being sent to conquer Palestine—in the first place, as everyone knew, soldiers could not choose their battle-area but were dispatched as the high command saw fit. What kind of war would you have, Captain, if every unit could choose its front? He gave Trumpeldor a brief chuckle. And in any case the colonel was quite certain that there was no plan for, or even the contemplation of, a campaign in Palestine.

—What did that matter! Trumpeldor was arguing. At the other end of the world, at Port Arthur against the Japanese, hadn't he nevertheless fought as a Jew and made the Russians, despite anti-Semitism bred in their blood, see a Jew as a man?

—But it would be a great military and historic opportunity lost! the journalist insisted. Here were the ships standing idle. In one single day the landing could be accomplished. No, the mistake on their part had been to talk to a subordinate. With underlings you got nowhere. One must always go to the men at the top, the High Command. Meanwhile their lads could already be told that in principle a Jewish unit would be accepted, with its own insignia, the Star of David.

Yet clearly some great plan was under way, for the harbor that had seemed so overwhelming a concentration of ships and power to Gidon when he arrived was every day even more formidable. And on the land, like overnight crops, vast fields of tents sprang up. It was Herscheleh who brought the secret. An enormous expedition was to sail up the Adriatic to attack the Balkans.

The journalist too had heard the plan. What a stroke! The Russians could push through from the other side and meet the British in Vienna. But still, why shouldn't the British fleet, on the way, so to speak, drop off troops to conquer Palestine, and thus draw attention away from their real objective?

This time a conference was secured at staff headquarters itself. The general had that other look of theirs, the level gaze of keen shrewdness in the narrowed eyes, and also the small tolerant smile around the mouth, a smile of gameness, of readiness to listen even to crackpots, in a determination to be fair and show no prejudice. Yes, the offer of Captain Trumpeldor had been considered. There was indeed the possibility of accepting a token force of Jews. How many could they muster? A thousand?

"If it was to fight in Palestine, we could bring fifty thousand!" the journalist declared.

The general smiled that aside. The fact was that in the coming campaign, no more fighting ranks were needed. Particularly—though he did not question the valor of their men—was there little need for ranks whose training was unfortunately minimal, and whose tradition in combat was unestablished. However, there was an urgent need for transport men. The terrain might be—ah—rugged. What he could suggest to them was a special Hebrew unit wearing their own insignia, to be sure, and serving in transport.

Transport?

Yes. Mules.

The journalist went rigid. Was this a bad joke or a plain insult?

Trumpeldor's face had turned dark.

Their task would be equivalent to combat, the general assured them, since their men would be carrying munitions and rations to the troops in the front lines.

After a moment, Trumpeldor asked heavily, would they be armed?

The small, tolerant smile appeared again; men had their curious pride—after all war was a game, one encountered amusing moments. Yes, indeed, in the British forces every man must undergo rifle training and carry arms.

Mules, porters, haulers of water—it was a sly British insult, the journalist fumed yet Trumpeldor remained silent. "God above, you're not actually considering it, Josef?"

—Mules, transport troops, it didn't matter, Trumpeldor insisted stonily. In the midst of battle all were the same. An opportunity would arise to join the fight, and the world would see what Jews are made of.

Each to his way. The journalist wasn't giving up his vision. Not here by the military underdogs would the issue be decided. He would go to the summit, to London, for it was as a political matter that this must be seen, a worldwide cause, a Jewish army—such a vision could inspire the Jews of Russia, even of America, and to settle for a mule transport risked destroying it.

15

IN EVERY squad, since the mule-corps decision, half were missing; doggedly Trumpeldor re-formed the units. One by one, he explained to the doubters that in an army all were the same, there were cooks, there were messengers, there were artillery men who were far in the rear, and also sudden changes came about so that sometimes a transport unit turned into front-line troops. Certain of the recruits, he saw, even seemed pleased, believing that their chances of being killed would be less. Shrugging, Josef let them believe it.

The journalist received a cable and was gone, first urging them all not to lose heart, he would fight up to the highest in London, for the Jewish army as a combat force!

Among those who left the ranks was Araleh. To go and fight as a soldier, yes, he would leave Saraleh and their Dudu here—but not for the sake of an army mule would he leave his wife and child!

Yet presently there appeared a handsome British officer in a handsomely tailored uniform; he watched their drilling, went away, and next day returned, and made them a speech, translated by one of the Nissims. Just as they were proud Jews, he was a proud Irishman, and he considered it an honor to be assigned to be their commander. Indeed, to be the commander of the first Jewish troops since the time of Bar Kochba would be the greatest honor of his career, the greatest honor that any soldier could ask for!

Josef would of course remain as their Captain, but, since he scarcely knew a word of English, this regular army officer was assigned to link them to the service. And wasn't that proof that the British took them seriously? And what had this Irishman not done? He had led troops in Africa and India, he had fought lions barehanded; if such an Irish warrior was ready to command a troop of mule transport, what was there to be ashamed of!

Soon the men received their uniforms and good strong shoes, and the women from Eretz sewed Stars of David on their caps.

Araleh and Saraleh had found Papa Zuckerman's business friend, a Levantine Jew with a small pointed beard and a perennial smile; Judah Musara had moved them into a two-room apartment, and there Gidon carried his insignia, watching Saraleh's smoothly combed head, bent over the sewing, and the flash of her teeth as she bit off the thread.

The Turks had indeed made a wild attack on the canal and been torn to pieces by waiting cannon. In headlong flight the survivors had flung away their rifles, and here now stood the Irishman over a cartload of weapons, declaring again that he felt like Moses about to lead the Jews from Egypt—imagine, an Irish Moses, he jested—and to each man he handed his gun. Gidon knew the weapon well, a heavy long-barreled musket such as Shabbatai Zeira used to buy for the Shomer in Damascus, paying the price of a camel for each one. And into his fingers, as he held the musket, the very moment returned when he had brought down two enemies. A slow solid determination now settled into Gidon that he was doing what needed to be done.

In full uniform with packs they marched, one blazing day, through the streets of Alexandria, the Shield of David on their caps, and their ancient rifles against their shoulders with bayonets to the sky. A full three miles they marched while little boys, Jewish and Egyptian too, ran along and cheered, and in the doorways of Jewish-owned shops stood their owners, paunchy men like Jewish shop-keepers anywhere in the world, and Gidon saw more than one of them wiping his knuckles across his eyes; on the balconies were women and girls, and even behind the ha-rem grilles of Arab houses, one glimpsed the faces of women.

They marched to the great synagogue built like a Moor-ish mosque, and were blessed in Sephardic Hebrew by the chief rabbi who had a beard almost as long as his tallis. The next morning Araleh came running, he could not after all endure to stay behind. A whole flood of dandy young Nissims also appeared, with their red-sashed ser-vants carrying their boxes of luggage, and one of them, after he had received his uniform, even placed his foot on his box for his servant to lace his boots. The Irishman watched, with that British smile of amusement; he let it be, and even solemnly dropped a wink to Gidon.

To the new recruits, Gidon explained their weapon. It was each time a thing of wonder to watch the look that came over the face of a man as he took his rifle like his own fate into his hands. The first feel of a weapon, declared Herscheleh the Newspaper, was like the first time with a woman—for some it was a joyous union of love, and for some it was a simple need of which they were half-ashamed. At times Herscheleh would produce such re-marks, as from a wisdom-book of his own making.

For Gidon the matter of womankind was still a half-hated need. Even in Jaffa he had known which was the lane of the houses of shame, and many times had wandered through it, half-decided to enter and once and for all rid himself of the need. What had kept him back was a kind of fear of what it would be one day to lie with his loved one and have such memories intervening. All might be spoiled. And also there were diseases. Long ago Reuven had told him that most of the blindness one saw among the Arabs was caused by syphilis. Children were born with it, from the disease of their fathers.

And so he still suffered.

Here in Alexandria, Herscheleh would lead Gidon and a whole flock of the lads through the lanes of cribs, expertly evaluating each whore as from wide experience. But the waiting lines of British soldiers made a man's heart mourn for himself and for all humanity. How man had defiled what was good in life, not only with killing but with whoring. These thoughts Gidon kept to himself while he joined with the others in filthy manly jesting.

Yet what was before him? His twenty-first birthday was approaching, it would come a few days before Pesach, and soon he was going into battle. He might be killed without ever having known what it felt like to enter a woman's flesh.

One thing the British had taken care of. Soliders were issued with little rolled-up sheaths of rubber to protect them against disease; in Eretz he had never actually seen such a thing. One night under his blanket Gidon used one and found that every sensation was felt through the thin covering. Now he remembered remarks of certain young men at home; this thing, then, was also used, even in free love, to make sure that the chavera did not conceive. Rising before reveille, careful not to have it seen, he dropped the little sack into the latrine.

In the evenings what was there to do? Watch the cardplayers? Roam the streets a bit with the Arab boys tugging at your jacket, offering zigzig with their sisters, themselves, or simply begging? With Herscheleh and Tuvia, a hairy-nosed maker of cement blocks from Tel Aviv, Gidon had formed a trio. Tuvia was open with his desires; they would be moving off in a few days now, that was clear from the sudden burst of activity in the harbor. A hole was a hole, he said, what did a hairy-nose like himself have to expect in life? All his life he had gone to whores, and a good whore was as good as some babbling chavera who made a great affair of it and led you on and you had to tell her you loved her—pah, a good whore was the best, but it had to be a decent show, not a line in a crib. Whereupon Herschel declared he could lead them to the real thing, real French girls—he had made the acquaintance of someone who knew.

Gidon did not tell his chums it was his twenty-first birthday. To have them know would have demeaned the occasion even further. Let it be only between him and himself.

At home, birthdays were celebrated only because of Leah. She never forgot. They were not big celebrations such as you read about if you read Tolstoy and Pushkin and all such, stories about nobility and birthday balls and sumptuous nameday gifts—something that was done among the goyim. But in the family there would be little gifts, a magnifying glass Leah had once bought him, and for the girls he always bought ribbons, and for Eliza even scents, in Tiberias.

Gidon had saved his pay and now told himself with a jeer at the world, if it happened tonight, let it happen, his birthday present to himself, a man of twenty-one.

Herschel led them first to a belly-dance cafe where they saw the usual fat women rolling their bare stomachs; there, an oily-haired young man sat down with them. Greek, even half-Jewish, he claimed—who knew what. The place to which he would now take them was not open to all comers. Indeed it was the secret dwelling of a pair of exquisite young French girls who were maintained in luxury by two of the wealthiest pashas of Alexandria. Since such men were fat and old and not free every night from their families, he winked, the French girls were eager for company . . . No, not expensive—indeed, if the girls took a liking to you—

And so they went.

It proved not precisely as the pimp had said, though at least it was no cribhouse with a waiting line. In a walled lane, behind the whoring district, a Senegalese opened the door, recognized their guest, and admitted them to a carpeted salon smelling thickly of incense. Presently a woman entered, her huge bosom half-bursting out of her spangled gown, her face heavily powdered. With inward resignation Gidon recognized her as what life offered to him—a madam, this must be—and after she had extracted orders for champagne from them all—the while Gidon calculated his funds—she spoke a few words into the hallway, in French, and then several scantily-dressed girls came into the salon. One was in a filmy chemise such as he had once secretly fingered among Eliza's things, and another wore a loose open robe showing her black lace underwear, while a third wore a spangled ball gown cut so low that you could see the inner sides of her breasts, though not quite the nipples. At once, Tuvia put his hairy arm around this one and went off with her down the hallway. Herschel sat down with the first, the one that wore the filmy chemise, and the one in the open robe came and sat on Gidon's knee. At least she smelled clean and looked young. She called him *chéri,* and half in gestures, half in French words, conveyed that she came from Marseilles, even singing the refrain of the French anthem, laughing happily when he understood. And he? Palestina? "Yahud?" she cried, and deftly unbuttoning his fly, she took his member out, touching the circumcised tip and laughing triumphantly at her divination. Somehow, though still in the open salon with Herscheleh, he did not even feel embarrassed.

After a moment Gidon followed the girl to a small chamber containing a divan and pillows. She peered closely at his member, gave it a quick squeeze for disease, he guessed, and then lay down, motioning to him. It did not really matter that they kept their clothes on, for he could not have held back, even to undress. The sensation, the relief as he plunged into her was like the balm of the plunge into the Kinnereth when your body and head were at the end of endurance, suffocating and dazed with the pulsing heat of an endless hamseen.

The girl's eyes were open and her face seemed to him to be dreamy. The pleasure—it was truly something entirely unlike what he had ever felt when ashamedly doing it to himself. But he could not prolong the pleasure and she laughed with a girlish knowingness, and rose. Then he saw her going behind a screen of arabesques; she must be washing her parts, and he had a moment of depressed bitterness, even a sense of filth. It came to Gidon's mind that he had already brought down two men in death, before he entered a woman. And had those two died without knowing what this was? He had not even seen their faces, to know whether they were young or older.

And what was this after all? It was like when some men drank so as to make themselves feel less miserable, except— as Herscheleh might jest—instead of taking something into yourself, you let something out. Gidon did not want to think of it as like a poison that you let out, like the stuff of a boil that was burst. No, no, there must still be joy to be found in it, when it was different, when it was with a girl you cared for. Yet this relief, this was why, despite all, men went to prostitutes. Something in him mourned that such had been the first time for him, and also that he alone knew.

In spite of all, he was trying already to recapture the

pleasure of it. The girl emerged; Gidon noticed she was carrying a basin, with a little towel; approaching, she bent and laved his penis with lukewarm water, smiling, it seemed to him, really naturally. Perhaps, as it was said, such girls really liked what they did. At least she was pleasant, and young, and careful of cleanliness. He experienced a lightening of heart; she looked at him and said, "Bon? Good?" as she dried him with the little towel. Instantly his member was erect and throbbing, and she laughed her girlish laugh as though this was a compliment to her. On impulse Gidon said, practicing his new-learned English, "It's my birthday."

"Birt-day? Oh, yes—birsday! You? Today? How many?"

"Twenty-one," he said.

She repeated it on her fingers, twice, both hands, then a single finger, laughing. She gazed quietly into his face. Pointing to herself, the girl said, "I—twenty." Again she put up both hands, twice. Then, setting aside the basin, she came to him and with one movement pulled the black lace chemise over her head and was naked. It was the first time Gidon had seen the whole nakedness, and this somehow affected him more than his blind thrust into her. Now she began to tug away his clothing.

Gidon flushed. "I—no more money." He made a gesture of turned-out pockets.

"Birs-day present!" the girl laughed. And touching her finger between her breasts, "I—Nicole."

He repeated her name. "Nicole."

This time he did not discharge so soon, he continued carefully to make it last, and she made sounds of rapture and breathed heavily, and let out a great happy sigh at his climax.

When she was leading him from the room, Gidon gave her the few coins left in his pocket, and the girl said, "You come back. Ask for me. Nicole. Yes?" At the door she tipped up on her toes and gave him a quick kiss on the mouth. It was like the swift innocent kiss of a schoolmate, Miraleh, long ago in Cherezinka when he became Bar Mitzvah.

No, it wasn't so bad with a whore. Gidon felt almost as though he had won to himself a woman's affection. He wondered, could she have known it was not only his birthday but his first time? With a girl, a man could know for certain, Fawzi had told him, and even tried to show him with his fingers. If he got a wife, he would do that at once, Fawzi said, and if she was not a virgin, he would kill her, it was allowed! How could a man do that, put his fingers there, with a girl he had just taken to wife, and whom he loved? But of course with them it was different, they had tribal customs. Then Gidon wondered, could a woman also know it, of a man? If he ever found his true woman—and almost certainly, for the kind of girl with whom he would fall in love, it would be her first time—would he let her believe that he too came as a virgin? Perhaps tonight something had been spoiled for him. What of Reuven? Could it really be that Reuven still kept himself pure? Now came a whole confusion of feelings, of thoughts, Gidon even thought of Saraleh, and if Araleh were killed, and should she come to love him, with a widow it would not be the first time, and yet in this, a man was not supposed to feel it mattered. Why was that so?

Herschel was waiting for him, smirking. Almost angry because Herschel seemed to know it was his first time, Gidon only grunted at the Newspaper's eager "How was it? Did you know what to do?"

"All right. She was clean," Gidon said, and wondered in himself if he would ever tell of this to a loved one, even his wife. Fortunately Herschel went on to give all the details, true or fancied, of his own whoring, and left Gidon to his silence.

Mules were brought in ships from Corfu, and again the men became certain it was in Palestine they would land, for these mules were particularly used to such rocky, hilly terrain; the rumors about the Adriatic were only a ruse. All day Gidon labored in the corrals at the call of the Irishman, sorting the animals, examining donkeys brought for sale by Egyptian fellaheen. Speaking Arabic, he haunted the souk with the commander for bridles, for saddles; he searched out carpenters to make frames for the water-tins to be loaded onto the mules. The time for sailing was near, the great enterprise had enfevered the entire city. Then oddly at their moment of going forth came Pesach.

Araleh and Saraleh would go to the Musaras, and offered to take him along, but Gidon found himself appor-

tioned with Herschel and Tuvia and several other of the
chevreh to the home of one of the Nissims.

A splendid, tall, red-sashed Senegalese—the brother,
Herschel jestingly whispered to Gidon, of the servant in
their French whorehouse—led them into a dining hall that
combined Arabian and European splendors. Huge Vene-
tian chandeliers hung from a ceiling of Moorish arches;
along the sides of the room were little bays with nests of
divans covered with striped silken sofa pillows, and a vast
Persian carpet that Herschel assessed offhand at a thousand pounds sterling was spread over the tiled floor. There
were carved high-backed chairs, and the table was a long
white field planted with silver goblets and ancient silver
candlesticks encrusted with rubies. There were Arab servants in a multitude, with soft bare feet and murmuring
respectful voices.

Their host and hostess, parents of the Nissim, wore European dress, the woman in a gray silken gown with pearls
everywhere, her hand smooth and soft as though it had no
bones in it. A grandfather presided, wearing the long white
robe that was traditional for the leader of the Seder, though
his beard was fashionably trimmed and he spoke French
with his family. There were small children too, a petulant-
looking boy of Mati's age who would say the four questions
and who gazed on their uniforms with a curious sullen
stare, as though he was not certain whether to resent them
or be pleased. But it was the daughter who made Gidon
sick at heart.

The mother he had seen before—was it with Jabotinsky?—coming to the barracks with baskets of good things,
even brandy-filled chocolates for the brave Jewish volunteers. But now he saw the daughter, with her round sweet
face echoing the mother's, and inevitably the words from
the Song of Songs resounded in his head—"dove's eyes,
thou hast dove's eyes, and two breasts like roes in the
field"—and such was not ever for him, the pure daughter
of a fine house of aristocratic Egyptian Jews who were performing the mitzvah, as his father would say, of entertain-
ing Jewish soldiers for the Seder.

"If these are the fleshpots of Egypt," Herschel whispered, "no wonder so many of the followers of Moshe Rabenu wanted to return."

As they were seated, with a servant behind each chair,

Gidon suddenly felt as though he were already describing all this to his little brother Mati. What an upside down world it was, he would tell Mati: "There in Egypt, Jews now have Egyptians for their slaves."

Ensconced among pillows of orange and green and saffron and purple on a throne-chair, the grandfather remarked to the guests, in a fluent Sephardic Hebrew, though to his family he spoke French, that although his descendants were only half-believers, he himself had had the good fortune of having been raised in a pious house. His ancestors, he mentioned, were Spanish Jews who had established themselves here in Alexandria long before the expulsion from Spain.

The Seder was long and meticulously carried out; the sullen boy, with just the proper degree of formal respect underlaid by a superiority to the ways of the past, rattled off the four questions. But what struck Gidon, with a secret feeling of shame as well as an impulse to share the jest with Herschel, was the moment when the beauteous daughter of the household arose from her seat to pass with a silver ewer and a little towel along the table for the hand-washing ritual. As his own turn came and she bent over so that the musk of her breasts reached him, the similarity with that laving ritual on his birthday night made him flush.

What sort of person was he being turned into? At home he had never had such cynical thoughts.

The mules were already being hoisted onto their transport vessel, kicking savagely in midair, their screams intermingled with shrill piping from the troopships, with steam whistles and braying boat-horns and military auto-horns in the port and with hoarsely shouted curses and commands. Araleh, checking a long list in his hand, called out "The saddles!" Trumpeldor himself hurried over to the Irishman, shouting above all the noise; the special saddles for the muleteers had not arrived from Cairo.

The commander seized hold of Gidon: "You come with me." A translator might be needed—and they stormed up and down the railroad yard from one Arab dispatcher to another.

But it was Trumpeldor, galloping among the sidings, who suddenly caught sight of a carload of saddles being shunted from one train to another. Atop the heap sat a

Sudanese guard, his rifle across his knees. "Ours!" Trumpeldor shouted, swinging himself by his one arm onto the moving train.

Letting out a jumble of shouts, the guard raised his rifle. Gidon caught a few words as he ran toward them.

"He says they're for the British Desert Lancers."

In the commotion, the engine had now been halted, while an immaculate Lancer captain sauntered up. "Saddles for the bloody Jewish muletenders?" he said to Trumpeldor. "My dear fellow, I'm requisitioning them for my Lancers. Your Jews can ride on their fat Jewish behinds."

Josef's face became stone. By now he understood English well enough. It was as though his entire body was about to explode from within. Leaping over the tracks, the Irishman was beside them, shouting. "Bloody Jewish muletenders, are they? You'll be begging them on your bloody knees for a drop of water. I command you, give over my saddles!" Though the Irishman's was the higher rank, the Lancer captain drew his pistol. "Go command your rear-line sheenies. You've no command over me!"

Gidon was transfixed. Was this then how it was to be? Away from Russia, living in Eretz, he had indeed forgotten. Was it a great stupid mistake to believe that when Jews acted like other men, the Cossacks of the world would be changed?

The Irishman and the Lancer had faced each other down. Suddenly a staff officer hurried over, and settled the affair. The muleteers were to have their saddles.

As they returned to their transport, the Irishman seemed to feel he had to say something. Jews, Chinamen, golliwogs or bloody British dukes, all were soliders to him, the the bloody Desert Lancers or the King's Guard itself had no more right—

"It doesn't matter," Trumpeldor said stolidly, and at last Gidon felt he understood this habitual expression of Josef's. "It doesn't matter."

Never had there been such a armada. As far as the eye could see, stretching like a metallic covering over the water, were the ships of their expedition. Surely, each man repeated in awe that he himself was here, that he was part of something so overwhelming, surely this was a day of historical fate.

Despite their direction out to sea, the old conviction again swept over the men of Zion—they were headed for a landing on the Palestine coast. Naturally there would be a deceptive sweep outward. No, really they were for Palestine.

And what of his brothers and sisters? Gidon wondered. Could they in some way sense his nearness?

At home, it was somehow known that a Jewish army was gathering in Alexandria. From messages written in minuscule script under postage stamps and sent through Switzerland, word had arrived in the Yishuv. Surely Gidon would not sit idly by, Gidon would join the fighters. And Mati was seized by a doomlike fear for his brothers. When the girls had lain down on their side of the room, Mati turned to Schmulik with the fear that tormented him. He saw them, on one side Reuven, who had somehow become a Turk in a tarboosh, and on the British side Gidon; they lay behind rocks, each shooting at his enemy, and suddenly Gidon leaped up in a wild charge and Reuven—Reuven must recognize Gidon at once, Reuven must stop shooting—

Schmulik laughed. Idiot. First, who knew for certain whether Gidon had joined the British, and second, the Turks anyway didn't want Jews fighting in their army and Reuven was still at his kvutsa.

"Then who do we want to win?" This was Mati's unending puzzlement. Even in cheder the melamed talked and talked about it, pretending that they were in the days of Zedekiah deciding whether the Jews should join the Egyptians against the Babylonians. "Remember the warning of Jeremiah! If you join the Egyptians, you bring Babylon down upon you!" And hadn't Jeremiah proved to be right? Today it was the Turks and the British—

"They can all go to hell," Schmulik said. "I'll take the mules up to Gidon's cave and hide them."

And Eliza crossly demanded, "Keep quiet and let me sleep."

They had become Ottomans. The Kaymakam made the men come to Tiberias to receive their papers, and rather than go by wagon and risk having the Turks seize his mules, Yankel set out by boat, together with a group from the kvutsa, Reuven among them. Each day, from Samekh, a boat sailed to Tiberias.

"So behold, a Turk already!" Tibor lifted the sweat-rimmed tarboosh from the head of the ancient Arab at the tiller and planted it on Reuven's head. One more moment and the jester would have swept off Yankel's hat as well—it was his Sabbath hat that Feigel had rescued from the sea—but Reuven intervened. "Tibor, let be."

A Turk, a Russian, what could they change in a Jew? To Yankel it was as one. Perhaps the Ottomanization might at least make his landholding more secure.

Entering the black-stone compound, Yankel was seized by the same aversion that had always taken hold of him in Russia when he had to approach a government official. In the one-time fortress, the group of Jews waited. As the door opened to an inner room, they caught a few words in German, and two officers in finely tailored uniforms emerged. The few words were enough for Yankel: ". . . . we need at least fifty pair at once." Let cholera seize them! Instead of sitting here, he ought to rush home and hide his good pair of mules; Oved and Chazak were famous throughout the whole valley.

The Jews were called in. By some whim, the Belly wanted to hand them their Ottoman papers himself. The Kaymakam's carpet Yankel estimated at the price of an entire harvest; no doubt his own taxes had gone into it, and part of the stolen flock had gone into the Belly as well. To the last inquiry submitted by the fawning Bronescu, there had not even been a reply.

While an Arab boy carried out the coffee-tray from the visit of the German officers, Azmani Bey peered at the group of prospective Ottoman citizens, his fat-pouched eyes like raisins in a round of Feigel's dough.

"So it takes a war to make you want to become Otto-man," he squeaked, but in good humor. "You Jews are indeed cousins of the Bedouin. You know what the Bedouin say, When the foreigners fight amongst themselves, first see who will win. Then join them." He chortled. "So I suppose you Jews are now giving us a sign of confidence." Lifting up a ready packet of documents, he remarked directly to Yankel, "As an Ottoman, who knows but what you might have had a better claim for your lost herd of cattle?" The mamser, he would stick a needle into his mother's heart. And to the men from the kvutsa, showing he knew their thoughts as well, the Kaymakam remarked with amused malice, "When we defeat the Russians and your Czar falls, then everyone says you will have a revolution and socialism. But have you taken thought, chaverim, if you meanwhile have become Ottoman subjects, how will you go back to join your revolution?" His little eyes glittered and there was a giggle in his voice.

"Our life is in this land, no matter who rules Russia," Max Wilner declared.

"—and your aim is to rule here yourselves!" The voice squeaked up to a higher pitch, but still with a tone of knowing jest.

"Haven't we all requested to join your army?"

"Even your pacifists?" Oh, he knew them, he knew them every one. Then the Belly added, "But we have declared this war is a jihad. Only the faithful are called on to fight! So do you also want to become Moslems so as to join our army?" He chortled again. "But never fear, we will perhaps call on you for other services, now that you have become loyal Ottomani." And he handed them the packet of documents, to sort out amongst themselves.

Soon enough the Kaymakam paid his visit to the area, arriving with an entourage of mounted officers, a few militiamen, and a pair of Germans whose polished boots remained miraculously immaculate in the dust.

When they really wanted to, everyone agreed, the Turks could suddenly emerge out of their indolence and disorder into fits of energetic activity, descending on you, as at tax collection time, with complete lists of men and beasts, plantings and reapings, with inflexible decisions where no baksheesh helped, at least at the start.

So it was now. In each village, Jewish and Arab, the commandancy made its halt. First they were in Dja'adi, and without even waiting for the second coffee-cup, Azmani Bey produced his list. Every son of the village was written down, those who were married, those who were unmarried, those married ones whose wives had no brothers to support them, and so through each category. Three militiamen started the rounds to gather the conscripts. Meanwhile a Turkish officer with a German at his side searched through the town requisitioning horses. Not the most heartrending plea, nor the cleverest guile, could turn them aside. As luck would have it, young Fawzi, Gidon's friend, just then came clattering into the village with clusters of partridge dangling on both sides of his saddle, and at the sight of his spirited steed the German officer's eyes opened in delight. Fawzi was simple and proud enough to praise her. The German even offered a good price rather than requisitioning, but Fawzi turned away with a gush of tears. His uncle Mansour the mukhtar, and also the ancient Ibrim, indeed every man of the village spoke at once for Fawzi, trying to save him his steed; then, though by the regulations he might have avoided conscription, Fawzi declared if they took his horse, let them take him too, if he could but stay with his steed. Here was the true love of the Arab for his horse! the German cried out, and took Fawzi along to care for the mount.

At the first glimpse of the dust cloud raised by the Kaymakam's requisitioning party, Schmulik had made off from the fields with Oved and Chazak.

"Two pair! two pair!" the Turkish officer howled in the Chaimovitch yard, striking the list in his hand. But one pair had been sold off, Yankel protested, explaining that since his son Gidon had gone to Jaffa he had no need of the added work animals.

Leaning from his carriage, the Belly, his eyes now like chips of basalt, screeched, "Oved and Chazak! You would sell your daughters first!" And then with his giggle, "Produce them, or my boys will take your daughters instead! . . . Where's that big girl of yours, the she-ox, she's enough to take care of a whole platoon!"

Choosing to ignore the vulgar taunting, Yankel repeated, "Look for yourself, all is open to you! The animals were sold in Jaffa!" Feigel came hurrying from the house with chopped liver for the Belly, and for the time being, Yankel managed to get out of the situation with only a command to report with his remaining mules and wagon to the station at Samekh to haul war materials.

To the triumph of Issachar Bronescu, who had advised against hasty Ottomanization, not a son of a Roumanian was conscripted for the labor battalions; only a few settlers with their mules were called to "work shukrah" at Samekh.

In the kvutsa, too, it was first the mules and horses that were commandeered, but then the Kaymakam demanded three labor conscripts to start with. They could choose the three themselves, he added, with his sly glint.

At once, Reuven stepped out of the assembled circle to volunteer. There had already been considerable discussion about what to do should this situation arise. A sum had even been set aside, enough to buy off two labor conscripts. And certain members had been agreed upon as indispensable to the kvutsa—if called, they must be bought out. Max as secretary was essential. Nahama's Shimek, in charge of the dairy, also could not be spared. Reuven had been on that list as well, but nevertheless he now stepped forward.

A general cry of protest arose. "No!" And Max even cried out to Reuven, "It has been decided! No!" For a moment, Reuven was torn by the thought that the decision of the group was above his own. On the other hand, if the kvutsa itself had to pick those who must go, bad feeling was inevitable, there would be charges of revenge over old quarrels, of favored ones who were protected. And perhaps he was even being selfishly cunning, for who knew but that as the war progressed the Turks might decide to take Jews as fighters? Better to be in a labor battalion.

Old Gordon gazed on him, with the eyes that saw one's inner motive, and came over and gripped his arm, muttering the traditional words of encouragement, "Chazak v' amotz"—"Be strong and courageous."

A hesitation could be seen around the circle. Several of the newer lads who had arrived during the year from Russia eyed each other questioningly. "Two more! Choose!" The Kaymakam was enjoying himself. Max turned his head. The will of the whole group seemed to point to a notorious lazy one named Feivel, who complained no matter what work he was assigned to. It was even doubtful if at the end of his year of trial, he would be voted a full member.

Before Max could speak his name, he cried out, "Not me! You can't order me! I'm not a full member! I'm leaving the kvutsa"

In the momentary confusion, the Kaymakam's smile blossomed. The fat finger pointed. This young man would come, and as he was not even a member, he would not be counted in the quota. Two more please!

"Chaverim! Don't give him the satisfaction of a dispute between us!" Shimek passed the word. A pair of excellent boys who had arrived together and bunked together now went over voluntarily, alongside Reuven. A pity to lose such hands. It was always the most decent, Nahama remarked loudly, who took the worst on themselves.

In the compound in Tiberias, Reuven found himself separated from the boys, and then sent with a rabble of road-builders up toward Nazareth. Encamped in winter misery on a field of mud and stones on the spur of the range, the conscripts were led out by mounted guards to be placed all along the roadbed, which mostly followed the old carriage track. In swarms so thick there was hardly room for them to squat side by side in the stone-breaking area, and without hammers for each, so that most used rock on rock, amidst quarrels, outbreaks of fighting, with the overseer galloping among them, his knout lashing down, and men tumbling over each other to escape the hooves and the lash, the mass of laborers, Bedouin prisoners, Christian Arabs, village Arabs, sullen, brutalized, were driven as though by sheer numbers alone they would instantly lay down a road here for the use of the huge motor cars of the German commander who had decided on a headquarters at Nazareth. The road was also quickly needed, Reuven saw, for the haulage of heavy, ancient Turkish cannon waiting to be placed on the heights, to destroy an enemy advance should British warships land an army to cut across the plain toward Damascus.

In one heaving pandemonium, beasts and slaves were already dragging up the artillery pieces. Frantic hands were barely given time to put down a bed of stones in front of the cannon wheels. To clear the way, others labored ahead with mules and drag ropes and wild outcries, pulling down trees from the wooded hillside. Only, Reuven saw, with the trees gone, the roadbed would soon slide away.

His own task, in this turmoil, was to chip stones. The food ration was a handful of rough-ground flour, with a few dried dates, each day, and the conscript laborer had to find some way to bake his flour. At mealtimes, Reuven got together with a few Christian Arabs, one a schoolmaster from Kfar Kana named Issa, and they made a small fire, to bake their flour into pittah. Inevitably he thought of the slavery in Egypt under the knout of the taskmaster, and in some remote way was satisfied that he was undergoing this too, though hardly another Jew was to be found here. The Jews had all bought their way out, the Arabs remarked, not without a touch of admiration.—And why hadn't he?

At night they lay on the ground, their little group all together, the Arabs wrapped in their abayas; fortunately Shimek's Nahama had run for a blanket and pressed it on him before he was marched off.

In only a few days, most of the fellaheen dripped with dysentery; the Turks whipped them, befouled, to their labor. Reuven had trained his body to need little, to withstand much, and now he did his utmost to keep clear of infection. In the labor too, he must save the strength of his arms, and he followed the wisdom of the fellaheen, minimizing his effort the moment the overseer had gone by. Yet how long could a man endure? In other times of hardship, as when they had first arrived at the Kinnereth, and all had gone through the fever, Reuven had noticed that there came a rock-bottom time when you either succumbed, or knew you had become rock and would endure. He felt this moment coming once more.

One day he recognized, by the mud-streaked remnants of a good shirt and trousers on a new arrival, another Jew. But —he saw—it was the youngest of the Aaronsons, from Zichron! The young brother of the famous agronomist! How did he come here? Despite all the past hostility over labor disputes in Zichron, Reuven could not deny in himself the bond to another Jew. Young Aaronson approached. He was barefoot—thieves had on the first night stolen the boots off his feet. Wanting to show the Turks the mettle of a Jew, he had volunteered to fight, but it had been his bad luck, the lad spat out, to fall under the authority of the mukhtar of Nablus, a bandit who had always made trouble for Zichron, and who had promptly thrown him into the labor battalion. If he could but get word to his family—his brother Aaron had high influence, even with Djemal Pasha himself—he would be saved. The next day, already sick with dysentery, young Aaronson came begging Reuven to escape with him—he had a plan, but it needed two.

The thought of escape had come to Reuven; if escape meant the preservation of life, it would be right, for this was a foolish and wasteful way to die. But stubbornly something required him to remain to the utmost with the wretched. Besides, of all the Aaronsons, this one was the most unendurable to him; the older brother, despite his wrong views on Jewish labor, was a man who justified his life with his researches for the development of the land. This one had never put his hand to toil, and it was almost an act of justice that they had sent him here.

As to joining in the escape, Reuven was spared a decision. That very afternoon, Aaron Aaronson himself appeared to ransom his young brother. On seeing Reuven, he called out, "But what are you doing in this?"

"Like everyone else," Reuven said.

"You'd better get out while you still have your health."

"When the fellaheen see a Jew caught here, no better off than themselves, they lose all respect for us," the young brother remarked.

The retort that rose to Reuven's lips he held back: "When they see every Jew buying himself out, they'll have only hatred for us."

Several more days he endured, until at last the feeling arose that even to this his body was becoming accustomed. With Issa and a few others Reuven had maanged to form that simple camaraderie of men who even in the worst condition watch out for each other. An overseer, noticing that if given a portion of work to themselves they labored well together, and thus eased his own responsibility, kept much out of their way.

On the day of Reuven's fate, their portion on the roadbed came as far as a certain tree, before which Reuven straightened up in awe. It was one of those ancient trees of Abraham, a tamarisk grown to an unusually broad trunk and spreading splendor, jutting out of the steep hillside overlooking the Emek, its roots partly arching out of the soil like great gnarled fingers gripping the earth. Standing just at the edge of the new roadbed, the tree was doomed. Already a noose lay around the upper trunk and a whole flock of conscripts labored to pull the tree down.

Involuntarily Reuven shouted to them, "Let it stand!"

Issa came up beside him and instantly concurred. This was a tree of legend, the schoolmaster declared; it was said to be from Abraham the father of us all, who from this very spot had gazed out upon the land that his seed would inherit. And Abraham himself was said to have planted this tree to celebrate the pledge.

—It could not really be that old, Reuven reflected, but no matter. It would be a simple matter to deflect the road a bit and let the tree remain. Besides, to pull it out would open the way to erosion; already the soil around its bared upper roots had been washed away.

Oddly, the impulse to save the tree had spread amongst the whole crowd of conscripts, even those who were now bringing mules to haul it down. They hesitated, and he heard remarks among them, in awe, in superstition: this ancient tree was not meant to be brought down.

"No need!" Reuven called, and fell to work deflecting the roadbed, his mattock flashing in swift strokes, singing against the stones. A dozen men fell in with him; for half an hour and more they all worked together. Outbreaks of laughter were heard and bits of song. None noticed the approach of a mounted officer with a scimitar nose, brandishing a saber. Where they had swerved the roadbed, the officer reined up abruptly, mastering his rearing steed.

"What is this?" He was in the midst of them, roaring. On a swerve like this a speeding motor car could overturn! Straight! The road must run straight! "Who did this? On whose orders?" Then he noticed the tree, the ropes still around its trunk. Glaring as though he would push it down by the force of his own anger, he shouted, "If you can't pull it down, bring axes! Where is the engineer? Who is responsible for this?"

"It's the tree of Abraham, sir," Reuven said, stepping toward the officer. "We wanted to save it."

The same annihilating glare was now turned on Reuven. Tree of Abraham! Tree of the Jewish devil! A foul Jewish trick was here! A speeding army motor car could smash right into that cursed tree!

It was Reuven's fate that he again tried to reason. —If the tree were to be pulled out, the roadbed could wash away into gully, he said, pointing.

"Who are you? The engineer?" The Turk spat.

And again—sealing his fate—Reuven began to importune him. Worriedly the schoolmaster, Issa, edged up to the stubborn Jew—didn't Reuven realize who this officer was? "Bahad" he whispered. Bahad-ad-Din, the notorious. But in Reuven, an uncontrollable urge was alight—the

tree! It could never reach him that men might exist who
were not moved by such a work of God; his heart still was
filled with the joy of the way in which the simplest, the most
wretched of labor conscripts had set to work to save the
giant tamarisk. "But why kill such a tree needlessly?" he
cried out. "We can save it!"

"Bring stones!" the Turk commanded. "Out with this
damned tree, and block up the gully with rocks." As for
the Jew—he turned again on Reuven, and there lighted in
his eyes that peculiar gleam that was known to all—the
gleam that came when Bahad-ad-Din was inspired to some
new cruelty. The Jew was so fond of Abraham's tree, was
he? Let him embrace it. Put his arms around it—at once!
Bahad-ad-Din pointed his saber toward a pair of Bedouin
in whose eyes he had already recognized an answering
gleam to his own, and hardly knowing what was happening, Reuven found himself seized by this pair and pushed
against the tree, his arms wrenched as far as they would
reach to embrace the enormous trunk. He could scarcely
keep his hold, his fingers searching for a grip in the ancient
wrinkled bark. "Tie him!" the Turk commanded, now with
amused satisfaction in his tone, as though he felt well disposed toward the victim who was helping carry out his
clever thought.

If they tied him with the loop that bound the tree, then
as they pulled it down Reuven would almost surely be cut
in two. From the crowd of conscripts who watched now
with almost sporting interest, only Issa's eyes reached to
Reuven, intense and strong, as though to support him
through his last trouble. Then quickly, as the two Bedouin
fumbled to loosen the noose around the tree, Issa threw
them a second rope. Only this, Reuven felt, might save
him. They were tying him under the Turk's instructions, a
knot around his left wrist, and around the entire tree trunk
and then one around his right wrist, so tight that the skin
was already torn. Then his ankles, then a length around his
waist, pressing him into the tree, so that he had to turn his
head, the cheek against the bark. "Tighter, tighter!" Bahad-
ad-Din called. "Closer! Like love!" This brought a gust of
obscene approbation. Some of the men took up the sport,
"Find the hole, Jew! Stick it in! Up the ass hole of your
Abraham the Jew!"

Dazedly, weepingly, his soul protested over what came

upon mankind. And just before, they had cried out for Father Abraham as their own, too. And still something within Reuven calculated for survival—if the tree's branches should break the fall, he might not be crushed. And if he should live, if his skull did not strike on a rock when the tree was brought down, oh then, he could even see these same devils helping him to climb out and bringing him a gulp of arak to share the great jest with them. No, this could not be his death. His entire life was not calculated for this. This could not be his death.

Already a lusty roaring came, a cracked whip over the mules, a tremendous straining from below, and it seemed to Reuven that the ancient trunk shuddered against his flesh, and that something indeed from far back, from the birthplace of time itself, and onward through aeons of godhoods imprisoned in trees, something still imbedded in the upward urge of the sap, a secret, an almost-revelation that could yet come to him before he was engulfed in the timeless stream of the hereafter, made him one with the tamarisk.

With utter joy, with enthusiasm now, Reuven's tormentor waved his saber, "Pull!" And then the entire episode halted. Bahad-ad-Din moved briskly out of Reuven's field of vision. The circle of men, too, faded rearward, even Issa, the shouts from below halted, and Reuven remained there alone in his suspended limbo, feeling the pulse of the air, the pulse of the tree, and a rivulet of sweat that coursed down his armpit.

All at once, like some new act in a theater, a whole group of people strode into view—a tall, helmeted German, and with him a figure recognized from photographs, Djemal Pasha himself, with his oiled, curled, Assyrian-looking beard and his flashing eyes. From others not yet in sight, something was being called to them, and the Pasha suddenly became electrified, flinging out commands, rushing at first out of Reuven's range of sight and then back in again, this time with sword drawn, coming directly toward the tree. Was this the death?

With one slash the commander-in-chief cut the ropes away from Reuven's body. Blood had already gone from his feet, and his legs collapsed under him as he tried to stand on the earth; in his wrists, too, there came the needle pain of the returning circulation of his blood, and he heard a blur of half-explanations and commands all around him. Then Reuven saw, behind the Pasha, and as though not unexpectedly, the firm, round countenance of Aaron Aaronson.

"Joseph out of the pit," kept echoing in Reuven's mind, while he heard the agronomist, as one vaunting the accomplishments of a valuable slave, heaping praises on him: this Reuven had a gifted and expert hand with plants, such as was unequaled in the whole land; it was this Reuven who had cultivated the Garden of Eden that Djemal Pasha himself had only this morning inspected at the Jewish settlement called HaKeren, and this man's only sin here had been that he was trying to save an ancient and beautiful tree—gaze on it!

The Pasha gazed. Now, in the way things seemed to happen with Reuven, it so happened that Djemal Pasha, too, was one of those men who have a particular response to trees. Perhaps there remains in them the response that caused men in ancient times to feel that certain trees, certain groves, were God-inhabited. Though this feeling would not prevent the Pasha from ordering entire forests cut down to provide fuel for his locomotives, he nonetheless was moved when he stood before a remarkable specimen of a tree. In a spurt of poetic language, Djemal Pasha declared that he was a lover of nature, of beauty, and that before them was the noblest of trees. Damascus itself had in ancient days been a city famed for its lanes of trees, its majestic gardens, and he would make it again the seventh wonder of the world; this gardener must come with him to plant the true Garden of Eden in Damascus! This man would plant him lanes of trees leading to the palace, and in the palace grounds there must be fountains, flowerbeds, far exceeding in beauty and luxury what he had beheld in the Jewish settlement.

Then Reuven listened as Aaronson explained to the Pasha how the entire valley that lay below them, the greatest part of it still a jungled marshland, could be cultivated to match the few patches that he saw at the foot of Gilboa. The entire army could be fed from the wheat of this valley! And when the road-inspection proceeded, Reuven found himself in the third motor vehicle, between Turkish and German officers, being carried off to his new fate in Damascus.

Removed from his post as Kaymakam of Jaffa after the international outcries over his deportation ship, Bahad-ad-Din had been made a special officer on the staff of Djemal Pasha himself, with the Jewish question as his province. First to be seized had been Nadina. Descending on Gilboa, Bahad-ad-Din had arrested this dangerous Russian woman. A few weeks later, Galil was seized and taken to Damascus. Meanwhile it was not known whether Nadina remained in prison in Nazareth or had also been taken to Damascus. At last her brother, Lev Bushinsky, the wealthy Haifa engineer, was called to an important task by Djemal Pasha, and thus was able to find out that Nadina was now imprisoned in Jerusalem. There Leah was sent.

At the top of the stone stairway, the door to Misha's lodging and secretariat was sealed. Fruit vendors in the lane only shrugged; they knew nothing. Hurrying to the courtyard where Rahel still kept a room, Leah met her friend just returning home, dispirited. Avner and Dovidl too had been arrested; they were in the Old City prison, but she couldn't get permission to see them, she had had to hand over a whole napoleon just to learn where they were held. The party journal had been closed down because of the article describing the deportations, and Misha was in hiding with the party records.

"Nadina, here in Jerusalem?" she repeated. This, even Rahel had not known.

After gifts of money and good Rosh Pina tobacco, they were at last admitted down a dungeon stairway, beneath the Old City wall, downward and downward until they stumbled into a tiny chamber that smelled of damp stone and centuries of urine. There Nadina was, her face thinner, undaunted. While Rahel recited all the news, Nadina carried Leah's canister of soup to her cellmate; the poor Arab woman must eat of it first, she was pregnant. "She's tubercular, something must be done for her, look at her eyes—" they were reddish under circles of kohl. Of Avner, of Dovidl, she was certain they would be deported, but who would act in their place? The cellmate was a prostitute, incarcerated for stealing a German officer's watch—the woman didn't even belong in this prison in the first place, Nadina indignantly declared—she belonged in an ordinary jail, and in any case she must be hospitalized, they must see to it.

Noting down the woman's name, Rahel meanwhile kept

talking of all their problems, of the paper's being closed down. "It must be started again underground," Nadina declared. Perhaps—she had a thought—a place the Turks would never suspect—there was a printer in the religious community in Safed. Avner would know. They must get to see Avner.

But how? Rahel had pleaded with Bahad-ad-Din himself for permission to visit Avner as his wife. The cunning devil had demanded if they were legally married, knowing they were not, and then had refused the visit. Suddenly Nadina changed to Russian. "I think she understands Hebrew," she said of her cellmate, "and who knows why they put her in here? Leahleh—" and at last she asked after her child.

Sitting closer to Nadina, and glowing because of the surprise she had brought, Leah uncovered from the depths of her basket a small clay pot, in which there grew a red geranium. "Buba watered it herself before I left."

"See what my little daughter has sent me!" Nadina jumped up, holding the pot before the Arab woman, who touched it with a longing smile. "Attiya too has a child," Nadina said. And passionately, "You see now how wise it is, Leah, that the children belong to the whole kvutsa? If they should send me and Galil also into exile, she won't feel so deprived of her mother and father."

A lawyer with connections in Damascus had been hired by her brother and was doing his utmost to arrange that Nadina and Galil should be exiled together, Leah told her. "Then you can take Buba with you."

"Leah, have you lost your senses! To take the poor child away from her home, from the kvutsa! I would never make such a selfish decision!" Her tone had gone back to the other voice, the voice of discussions in the movement.

Of herself, Leah knew she could never be so disciplined. That was why Nadina was a leader. In these last times the yearning for a child had come upon Leah, even in the midst of these dreadful troubles, the war, and the arrests, the danger that the whole movement would be utterly destroyed and even the whole Yishuv. At odd moments, at the mere sight of a baby clinging to a mother, this yearning came upon her. In one way this longing relieved her: somehow, strangely, it had replaced the longing for a man. She would return to Gilboa, Leah just then decided, and ask to work in the Infants' House. The decision eased her. "Don't worry, I'll look after Buba myself. Perhaps the war will be over soon, it will be only a short separation for you."

To Dovidl and Avner, too, with a whole succession of bribes, Leah and Rahel at last managed a visit. Already the two labor leaders were judged: it was to be deportation, but not to the interior of Turkey as with Galil; these two were to be expelled from the Ottoman realm. Gone was their new Ottoman citizenship, and their application to form a Jewish fighting unit had been flung in their faces.

In the underground warrens of the citadel, beneath what was called David's Tower, there they sat, both pallid, the color of the stone walls, but in good spirits. While Rahel talked with Avner, Leah drew Dovidl to the other corner. Though as always she had an amused desire simply to hug him—the way he held up that large head of his—she started to impart all the latest news. But Dovidl knew everything already, it must have reached him through the stone walls, and he began a whole analysis of the entire world. Perhaps more account should be taken of the French influence in the Levant. Still, he felt that the party's Ottomanization decision had been correct; what did she think? And he gave her telegrams to send to the Poale Zion leaders in America; urgent efforts must be made to secure ship passage for Avner and himself. Among the Jewish workers in the American needle trades the Poale Zion was strong, despite the opposition of the anti-Zionist socialist Bund, though among the furriers it was said, the Bund was entrenched. Still, everything could be changed once he and Avner reached America. Besides, a quick German-Turkish victory was not at all as certain as it had appeared a few months ago. With the possiblity of a stalemate or even a negotiated peace, the status of Palestine might very well become an open question. The British had thrown back the Turks from the canal, and to protect their canal they might very well, if it came to a negotiated peace, work for a special status for Palestine as a buffer area. And then, in such a situation, Zionism might come in as a solution acceptable to both sides. What did she think? Or even in the event of a possible Allied victory—

Leah listened, agreed, put in a question, all the while wondering what would happen to Dovidl in America, where he would sleep, whether he would find himself a romance—

Suddenly the jailer was ordering her and Rahel to leave. "Yallah! Yallah!" One more coin. One more moment. Now Avner and Dovidl were enjoining the two of them. Should there be no more opportunity to meet, this was the program for the movement: two points. First, arms. Jews must prepare to fight for the land. Arm themselves, however possible. In the final resort rely on no one. "Only ourselves. Be ready to fight." Under no condition should the Shomer or any settlement give up arms, as the sons of Zichron had already done, to their eternal shame! "But Bahad-ad-Din gave them one day, or he would seize their sisters." "Ach, threats! Even if they try to seize our women, better to use the arms than to give them up!"

The second point, Avner said, was pioneering. Redemption of the land must continue, wars or no wars. Whichever side won, the land must be redeemed. As for himself and Dovidl, wherever they were sent they would work to train pioneers. They would enroll young people.

A whole new training movement must be started—in Russia, in America, wherever there were Jews. A Legion of Workers. Arms and labor! The girls must relay this to all the chevreh. This was the two-point program!

"Yallah!" cried the jailer.

Was it the parting? Rahel and Avner gave each other a hug.

Dovidl came to the iron door. "Nu, Leah. Shalom." Impulsively she leaned down and seized his face, planting a kiss on his cheek. They laughed. "Take care of yourself," she admonished. "Shalom, shalom." How she loved him. This was pure, good love.

The next morning Misha the secretary came running. "Quick, quick, to the station—"

Somehow Leah and Rahel pushed their way through to the side of the train just as it began to move, Leah pressing a path through the clutter of vendors, of Arab women, of urchins crying baksheesh, Rahel darting forward and almost reaching the window where Avner's head stuck out. They ran alongside, losing ground. The train had already passed the end of the platform and they still ran, keeping their eyes on the window; suddenly Leah collided full tilt with a Turkish soldier who nearly tumbled over, cursed, then regained his balance. His glare turned into a lewd grin as he called to a comrade, "The big one for me, the little one for you—their men are gone!" And in clumsy Hebrew he shouted after the girls great boasts of his prowess.

16

AS HE felt daylight coming, the world around Gidon began to reveal itself in stages. First, it moved in immense shadowy forms of blackness in which the man-made forms of the vessels were hardly distinguishable from the forms of nature; then the landmass came away from the sky, detaching itself as a great blotch. A mountain was before them, higher than Mount Carmel; the shape rose like an enormous prow massively emerging from the graying dark of the sea. As luminosity came, the heights receded somewhat, and in the foreground appeared crags and ravines and boulders below the unapproachable mountain. But also with the light came the full sense of man-made power gathered on the sea before it.

What he had seen in the harbor of Alexandria that had so overwhelmed him had only been a segregated section of the immeasurably enormous engine here brought together into its wholeness. Spanning the narrowing sea from Europe to Asia, the armada began to glitter, to shine in the rising sunlight; it became one single, extended structure, from tugboat to the most towering of battleships, the new Queen. Even Herschel, who had started enumerating the vessels, the dreadnaughts, the destroyers, the minesweepers, left off and fell silent, for it was a sight each man had to draw into his own self.

Until this dawn they had been uncertain. They were far from the Palestine shore, but neither were they in the Adriatic. Now they saw they were at the mouth of the Dardanelles.

And from the whole of the armada, a massive burst of sound emerged, a battle roar. It came out of the vessels, it came out of the men, it came from Gidon himself, it came from the mules in the bowels of the vessel, and it culminated in a shuddering, concerted burst of cannon fire that must shatter even the mountain that they faced. From all around him Gidon saw streaks of red fire and bursts of smoke, and augmenting all this, in an ultimate wave of thunder, came something he had never seen before, a man-made cloud of airplanes.

In this moment Gidon felt a climax of joy. Simply to be part of this effort, this power, this vast conjoined construction made by man, was a fulfillment of life. And the joy was the greater because their own vessel had almost failed to arrive here to be part of this movement; but despite all they were here. What they had gone through—their first transport stranded on a mudbank, their frantic Irishman finding another vessel and, his frenzy infectious, wildly urging them on as they reloaded the mules in the dark, they must not miss the great attack, and overcoming every sly trick and accident of nature, here they were, they had arrived!

And for this moment it no longer mattered that the strange mountainous point before them was not Mount Carmel but was called Gallipoli; it did not matter that this was no attack to free Eretz, that they would plunge into battle alongside Australians, Scottish troops, small men from India, and who knew what, to unlock a gate for this armada to proceed up the straits to Constantinople. During this high moment, Gidon forgot or perhaps surmounted his fate as a Jew, or even as a member of one side or the other in the Great War. He sensed himself only as a man satisfied to be included in an immeasurable effort that was in some way to turn the very direction of history, of that unknowable design, if it was a design, of which each man must be a part; and even if he were to die in what was happening here, even if the other side could by some incredible accident withstand all this accumulated power, or even more incredibly, destroy it and triumph, even then, Gidon felt, and he knew that all the men on all the ships and all the men in their fortifications in those rocks felt, as he did, a fulfillment of life in being here, and being ready.

Now he understood what Josef had meant when he said that even in fighting for the Czar at the other end of the world against the Japanese, he had known he was fighting for the Jews. And now Gidon was certain that Josef had been right to declare that they must enroll even if only as mule drivers, rather than, as Jabotinsky had urged, to refuse to go. How he would write home of this, how he would tell it to Leah, to little Mati, to Schmulik—if his letters could but find a way to reach them!

And then, in a first lull, the mountain stood before them unaltered. Smoke blotched it here and there but drifted clear. And fire-points flared—ah, they were firing back. But just as the mountain stood intact, the armada lay intact. At the prow of their own vessel the Irishman and Trumpeldor stood, each with field glasses to his eyes. One dared not yet ask for a look.

Araleh had come up. Already in the embarkment of the mules in Alexandria, and last night again in the transfer to this vessel, he had been marked by the Irishman; when the Irishman couldn't decide the best way to stack the watertins, Araleh knew; he knew how to place the mules so their manure could be cleaned out most easily, and everywhere in the pandemonium, he was at hand.

Now with that clear head of his and the quick eyes that were always learning something that "could one day be useful to us at home," Araleh discerned the strategy of the great powers. For all that it was so vast, it was as simple as two dogs fighting. "What do they do?" he reminded Gidon. "They go for each other's throat." So the Turks had tried to make their kill at the Suez Canal and, shaking them off, the British in turn were striking at the straits to Constantinople. After seizing these overlooking heights so that their ships would be safe from bombardment, they would pierce through. They would thus meet their Russian allies coming from the Black Sea, Constantinople would fall, then with their joined might they could send armies sweeping downward through the heart of Turkey to Syria, while another British force came up from Egypt, trapping Djemal Pasha's armies between them. Where? In Eretz itself, there to be ground to nothingness, and Eretz would be free!

Gidon saw it really happening. In this incomprehensible war—as each man sees destiny revolving around his own life—it seemed that the entire design was centered around the farm on the Jordon, where the liberating forces from north and south must meet, and where he with the rest of Trumpeldor's men of Zion, no longer muleteers but soldiers now, rushing down as part of this very force, would chase the last Turks from the yard of the Chaimovitch meshek!

He wrested himself from the daydream. Though still in the outermost circle, their ship was edging closer to the land. In the clear morning light now, they could see the forward rim of their armada at the tongue's edge of the peninsula, but from the heights directly above, from a massive ancient fortress, came a thousand points of fire, and from the mountain behind came puff-clouds of artillery; there were fire-streaks like streaked blood, and shells sending up geysers in the water, and now from the opposite side of the narrows came more blood-streaked cloudlets—German artillery, Herschel said, hurling shells over the neck of water onto the landing beach. The enemy had been ready for them.

In that neck of water the British armada was choked, the naval guns firing back at the fortifications on either side of the water, on the European and on the Asian shore, while all through the mouth of the narrows more ships rode the sea—transports, supply ships, vessels of every description, waiting their turn to approach the shell-splattered beach.

The Irishman had passed his fieldglasses to Araleh, and now they came to Gidon. As though instantly carried among them, he saw men leaping from a bark, clutching high their rifles, staggering to wade ashore, saw one of them contorting in midair like some acrobat and then floating face-down on the water, another soldier leaping over him, saw several men on the sand crawling like landcrabs, some with desperate speed scooping sand with their hands to make a barrier. Then, raising the binoculars somewhat, he saw a beautiful green apricot grove, still and peaceful in the morning sun, and still a bit higher, he saw wide fields of red poppies like those at home. Herschel took the glasses from him. Their ship was once more churning forward, and glancing over the side, Gidon saw a body floating by, and English soldier, face up, still clutching his rifle in his dead hand.

Then he saw Herschel's face; Herschel was on the point of vomiting. And rising up in his own self, Gidon recognized the same fear as Herschel's before the coming death-leap, and then secondly a more shameful fear, that his body would refuse the command, that perhaps it was all true that in Jews there lurked an absence of courage—that before this entire armada of British and Gurkhas and Somalis and men from every stock on earth, and under the wrath of the Irishman, Jews alone would falter, and a roar of mankind's derision would arise to be echoed from the high mountain fortress where the Turk himself was watching them with his binoculars. Despite a kind of gratitude that they were still in the outer ranks of the armada, there came an impatience to try, life or death, and have it done with.

The exultant shouting from that early-dawn sight of their own vast assembled power, and then the cries of anger at the sudden fire opened against them had both been engulfed now in the indistinguishable uproar. Yet in that narrow segment of sky churning with crisscrossed streams of shells, bullets, shards and fragments, there even seemed to be single shells that knew their destination: see that landing barge filled with men—and the missile fell directly among them, so that even if one man lived below the heap of his torn comrades, he was carried down by their tangled weight to create his own death in the sea.

From the mountainhead—Achi Baba it was called—the fire came as though some ancient god need only spit at them. To the soldiers up there, it must be like the time he had waited behind his rocks by the cave and watched his enemy coming, holding their approach in his gunsight.

There were no barges for the mules. From the rail, the Irishman shouted down to every passing landing-vessel to come back for his mules, keeping up his pleading, his cajoling, as he ran along his shipside—they must get him ashore with his supplies. "I've got their water! Those men have no water!" But hardly a craft slowed, and when one did, it was only for an exchange of insults. Already the lighters returning from the beach had their bottoms covered with maimed and wounded, men who lay strangely motionless, with their eyes wide open to tell something, and it was after looking down into their eyes, as a barge passed close enough to scrape the side of their ship, that Gidon saw Herschel choke his mouth with his hand, and hurry to the opposite rail so as not to vomit on the dying.

In this slaughter that was to become a byword in history, a toehold had been secured on the sliver of beach, and at last came the debarkation of the transport unit, the mules and the men of Zion. A long series of lighters, lashed together, had by now been extended from the beachhead with a gangway of planks across them. From the beach itself they could hear men clamoring for water, and the Irishman charged the Zion men into a line across the planks, to hand on the tins, hurrying them so urgently that each hardly knew when he took his place under fire. And now each was fearfully watching his brothers, anxious that all the other Jews should stand well, and amazingly, they stood. Swinging the heavy tins from the man behind to the man before him, Gidon knew this elation. How had he ever doubted? Yet from all the derision in the training camps, the doubt had arisen in himself as to how they might withstand this moment.

The receiving arms ahead of him suddenly were not there. One of the Nissim had been suddenly taken by an uncontrollable trembling. A shell had hit the edge of the lighter on which he stood; it pitched, and he let his heavy water-tin drop.

Gidon caught and steadied him. Already Josef was there, nearly tumbling them all into the sea as he picked up the tin with a curse. Already the Irishman was calling from the beach. "Keep them moving! Don't piss out on me!" Did he still doubt the Jews? They would be able to do it as well as anyone else.

But when the mules were led off, under the incessant shelling, lighters broke under their weight, animals plunged into the water, yanking their handlers with them, some of the boys still hanging onto the halters. Gidon found himself swimming, grasping the rope of a floundering beast.

It was bad enough for the soldiers to get ashore with their packs under that concentrated fire, but to manage with the mules as well seemed beyond possibility, what with the animals' wrenching, biting, kicking, the screaming protests of the beasts rising above the scream of the shells. Laughable this would be, in the telling, after the war.

Dark came. One man was lost, drowned; Tuvia had seen him hit, going down drowning—a Moroccan Jew from their quarter in Alexandria, and Gidon could not help his reaction, "Not one of ours from Eretz."

Then an hour later the Moroccan was there on the beach; only wounded in the thigh, he had managed to swim. It became a great joke that their first dead was not dead, a good omen—at once Moshe the Moroccan was a man beloved.

As after some storm of creation, crates, tins, ammunition boxes lay flung about on the sand. A pair of Zion men had been dragooned into piling up stacks of explosives, only to have a shell fall as with a wild laugh, and mingle them with the wreckage—these dead were dead, a beginning. Again, Egyptian Jews, poor devils from the slums, not men from Eretz, not yet.

More boxes were being unloaded, and Araleh was running from one dumped disarray to another, trying to set order in the chaos; the mules had been led forward to a safer area that the Irishman had scouted out, behind a sheltering mound. There was even grass behind the sands, and the beasts fell to nibbling. But the rope coils for lengthening their tethers could not be found. Josef appeared, already mounted; he had led off his own steed first of all. Galloping away, he somewhere found a storemaster who had managed to set up his supplies, and in a burst of Russian-English, commandeered an enormous coil of rope. Only as Josef shouldered it did the Scottish storemaster notice that the strange-talking captain had a wooden arm. "What in blazes—who are you, man?" he roared, and the legend of Josef Trumpeldor was begun on Galipoli.

Like the Irishman, he was everywhere at once, tethering mules, hammering tent stakes, and when a shell fell, provided it was close enough, he blasted out a Russian "pshak-reff!"

A thought came to Gidon, and he remarked on it to Herscheleh. "He's happy!"

"The vegetarian and pacifist," said Herschel.

They had not yet even completed the debarkation when the first train of pack animals had to be loaded with water-tins and rations and led off into the pathless dark toward an exhausted fighting unit pinned along a gorge; the runner had just managed to fumble his way back through torn barbed-wire hillsides.

"The whole bloody mountain is covered with barbed wire and sniper dugouts," he told them in a ghost of a voice, as he guided them uncertainly. "Oh, these Turkish devils knew exactly where we were going to land."

"They knew, but we didn't," Herscheleh muttered with bravado. "Maybe they even know where we're going to now, since we don't."

The Irishman himself had come along to lead their first mission. After a laborious hour they clambered down behind the runner into a dry wady, like those at home, the mules' hooves unavoidably creating a rumble of cascading stones. How easily they could be picked off! Presently, something happened up front. "Halt" was passed in whispers along the lane. Then another order, "Turn back." Gidon recognized the tread of the Irishman's mount, then heard his blasphemy. That bloody fool messenger ought to be shot. What was urgently wanted was not rations but munitions. Return all the way back, offload, then reload.

And that was not the end of their first task in the war. In a blundering night that seemed to presage the whole campaign, this great campaign on which, in the words of the Admiral's orders-of-the-day that the Irishman read out to them, the fate of the civilized world hinged, in this endless night, as they were again feeling their way through the gorge, there once more came a countermand. The heavy ammunition boxes must be taken down. "Leave them here." And eerily there came a stumbling line of haunted-looking soldiers, Australians, carrying wounded. Loading the wounded onto the mules, the Zion men picked their way back, only to be dispatched once more, dazed, after but a gulp of tea. They must keep working, night was the safest time. This trip was through still another wady, with shells crossing both ways over their heads. As they neared the guns at last, several mules stampeded in terror. One man fell, kicked in the belly by his own beast, a casualty to be derided, and another cried in Yiddish in a startled, indignant voice, "I am shot!" There he stood, still clutching the lead-rope of his mule. A piece of shrapnel had cut through Yitzik's upper arm—he was one of those about whose bravery Gidon had worried, a yeshiva bocher from Jerusalem. In astonishment at himself, Yitzik kept repeating, "Nu? It didn't kill me!" The blood came slowly: it was a flesh wound. Gidon bandaged it. "Your lad never let go of the rope!" the Irishman cried. He would report the lad for a medal, if someone would only spell his name.

So they went on until dawn, their strained eyes itching and red, at last falling on the earth, to sleep without hearing the shells exploding a dozen yards away.

In Gidon's own squad, the deaths began on the third day, for with the incessant calls they had to go out in day-

light too. As they passed under the leafage of an abandoned
olive grove, a shell struck in the middle of the line; as
though the tròop itself were an exploded shell, the men
burst away in all directions, letting go their mules—"They
don't care about medals already," Herschel grunted. The
beasts milled about, their side-boxes bumping the trees,
they screamed, their teeth naked as in bleached dead skulls.
On the path lay two muleteers, again from among the luck-
less Alexandrian boys who had been swept up in the enthusiasm around the Jewish unit and had volunteered. Some
had soon regretted their action, and remained always close
together, each accusing the other of having led him into
this madness. The first casualty had been sheared across
the neck by a flying fragment, and, instantly dead, lay,
head askew. The other was pinned under his mule, his
shrieks mingled with those of the animal that was sprawled
with spilled entrails, its tail fouled, its legs still thrashing in
spasms as it struggled to rise. Frantically Gidon strove to
heave up the hindquarters of the beast so as to free the
man. Where was help? He cast his eyes about—Herschel
stood there but was rigid, terrified; then Tuvia hurried over
with a broken-off branch of a tree that he used as a pry.
But even as they worked the boy's shrieking gurgled downward and became a death rattle.

Josef now galloped in among them, roaring after the
scattering men, "Hold onto the mules!" and swooping
down to catch an abandoned lead-rope. The wounded mule
he ended with a revolver shot in the head. Another shell
meanwhile crashed among the trees, and again the men began to run. "Stand here!" he shouted in Russian. "Idiots!
Where the first one fell is the safest place to stand." In a
burst of blasphemy he reminded them that after each shot
the cannoneer moved his trajectory. The Turk couldn't see
them under the trees. Stand in the shellholes, misbegotten
idiots!

The pattern of falling shells moved on, away from them.
Slowly the men recovered their mules, and gathered near
the fatal spot, most of them after one quick glance keeping
their eyes elsewhere.

Josef mounted; they must move on and deliver their supplies. And now perhaps they would obey and keep their
distance from each other. If those two boys had not
bunched together, only one would have been hit.

Trumpeldor watched the line move past him, then followed, leaving Gidon and Herschel to load onto their mules from the packs of the slaughtered animals whatever water-tins had remained intact.

Finally they were ready. "Come on," Gidon said, but Herschel stood as though paralyzed, even to his tongue. "Come on!"

But Herschel's face contorted, oddly like that of a constipated man in a latrine, making a supreme effort. "I—I can't do it," burst out of him. "I can't go on." There was in his voice something of confoundment, of pleading, even an appeal to their comradeship. And as Gidon approached, Herschel burst out, his tongue completely loosened, "I'm afraid! I'm a coward. A Yiddle from Okup, a coward." Now scathing snatches from Bialik's poem came out of Herscheleh. "A cringing yeshiva bocher, that's all I am! I can't walk into fire, I can't look at blood, I'm no hero from Port Arthur! When the pogromnicks came into the ghetto, I ran and hid in the cellar, I hid under my mother's skirts—I can't do all this, I tell you!" he ended in a sob.

"Herschel, are you finished? Now come on."

The eyes looked into Gidon's earnestly, shamefully. "I tell you I want to. I can't make my body do it. I'm a shitty Jewish coward and that's all."

"This happens to goyim too. We've already seen it."

That was true. Had they not themselves seen Englishmen driven at pistol-point to jump out of the landing-boats onto the beach? "Come on, Herschel, you've already been through it. Come with me."

Herschel made another effort, even a half-step, but then froze rigid, with a feeble smile, as though to say "You see, I tried."

Just then Josef came back to find out what had happened to them. At a glance he understood. "Herschel," he began with a voice of reason and even of compassion.

"I—I'm ashamed. I try. I can't," Herschel repeated with a wild look to Gidon as his witness.

In one movement their leader was off his horse and had collared him. "Zhid! Scum of the ghetto!" And he booted Herschel forward, the blast of his curses as powerful as his heel. Stumbling, recovering his balance, uttering a strange bleat as though some childhood devil were coming out of him, Herschel yanked at his mule and they moved on.

Remounting, Trumpeldor glanced at Gidon but said nothing. His face was still fixed in fury.

They had reached the front-line dugouts of the Australians and were unloading when a new bombardment began. With the others, Gidon and Herschel tumbled into the trench. Trumpeldor sat his horse, unmoving. "Get down! You! Take shelter!" a lieutenant screamed at him.

Josef turned his head. "A man can at least be as brave as his horse," he replied.

The shells came from the dominating height, the great fortification called Achi Baba, never to be taken. A ferocious young Turkish commander was there, it was said, one called Mustafa Kemal, who led out his men directly into volleys of rifle fire whenever the British troops attempted to assault the approaches to his mountaintop. Behind bulwarks made of their own piled-up dead, Mustafa Kemal's men would stop each attack.

From the fort itself the gunners could look down on the whole area, on every movement; only the narrowest ravines were comparatively safe.

Even the beach was bad, as bad as anywhere, open to the heavy guns on the heights; since the failure of the first waves of assault, still heavier German cannon had been added, making the mountain fortress impregnable. Weeks passed, with sallies, retreats, entrenchments. On the beaches the encampments were moved up closer under the cliffs, safer from the Turkish artillery. Making themselves shelters like troglodytes in caves and under rock ledges, burrowing deep into the ground, those who had survived the first assaults felt they knew now how best to manage. And the forward units, in a vast arc beneath the mountain, were also dug in; they would creep a bit further, a bit further upward on the wild slopes of the sub-mountains, digging holes and trenches, while from the fortress above them their enemies also crept a bit further, downward, extending the area of their fortifications, digging holes and trenches, stringing barbed wire on the rocky slopes.

On some days the Turks would suddenly come pouring out of their creases in the hillside, with bayonets fixed, and storm down upon those who besieged them, only to fall in heaps to their machine guns, and on other days the Senegalese, the Australians and New Zealanders, the Irish and

Welsh—and Gidon learned to know each unit—would in turn hurl themselves upward to dislodge the Turks, and leave their bodies on the slopes, corpses that sometimes rolled heavily, lumpily downward until they caught on some shredded tree-stump, or fell back into their own trenches.

To all the forward positions of the Australians, the Gurkhas, the Londoners, the Jewish muleteers now made their regular rounds. They too had learned the skills of survival, and casualties were not as in the first days. The groves and fields, churned incessantly by shellfire, now bore only blackened remnants of trees, pieces of boots, and sometimes segments of men and beasts, left uncollected, in later years to give a golden harvest from this soil. All was bestenched in a heatening atmosphere of acrid gunpowder and putrid decay, and bottle flies thickened and swarmed from the dead upon the living, man and beast, bloated insects settling at messtime on each morsel of food to follow it into a man's mouth.

The locked armies had reached a balance. It would take vast new forces on either side, as any soldier could see, to change this balance so that the defender might be overwhelmed, or the besieger driven back into the sea. Yet neither side would quite wait for this overwhelming force to accumulate; as fresh troops arrived, they were thrown, in some commander's impatience for a victory, directly into an attack, they withered, and then the entrenchments were dug even deeper. From the trenches the men even dug tunnels reaching toward the enemy, crawling forward to explode him from below. Thus an enemy's outpost line would be first gained, then lost to a counterattack.

On some nights, either the Turk or the attacker would crowd men into a forward trench, and at dawn hundreds of bayonet-points would rise to glitter like new grass, and suddenly the men would crawl out screaming their war cries, the Turks their *Allah il Allah*, and the Allies a multiple shriek, and the charge would carry itself sometimes even as far as a second or third trench, until machine guns ground it down; and again after the countercharge all would be restored, except that heaps of dead carpeted the few hundred yards between or lay before the lip of a trench, so that the machine guns had to be mounted up somewhere higher in order to get a free range toward the enemy.

Below, on the narrow shore, the carnage was less, though the Zion Mule Corps was halved now by wounds, by dysentery, by malaria. Yet, though exposed when they went on their delivery routes, the men were well settled in their dugouts by now, with capacious underground shelters for their mules, and in some locations connecting trenches wide enough to ride in.

Some of the troops they served were tireless diggers; the Gurkhas loved to dig wide and deep, and in their sector a man could ride atop his mule from one outpost to another without exposing his head above ground. When a lull came in the fighting, the muleteers would even begin singing as they rode their daily rounds, singing "Tipperary," or teaching the Australians to sing "Yahalili."

One Australian, using his shaving mirror, had fashioned himself a periscope, so that he did not have to lift his head up to aim his rifle, and now every soldier wanted one. This gave Araleh a thought. Herschel, it turned out, had once worked in an optometrist's shop, and with him, Araleh set up the manufacture of an improved model, trading twenty of these to the Gurkhas in exchange for the digging of an entire underground shelter, comparatively clean and comfortable.

A cove had been found, supposedly out of reach of the enemy guns, and each day the men went down in small groups to bathe. It was not like bathing in the Kinnereth, but more like the sand beaches of Tel Aviv. And in the evenings, under a remaining olive tree that was somehow protected by the conformation of the mountain, tale-telling and singing would begin. Some distance away, under the "officers' tree," the Irishman with a few cronies could be seen playing cards and drinking. Among the muleteers, little groups had naturally formed, the Palestinians together, the Nissims in their own circle, the poor Jews of the mellah by themselves. But at times a whole mixture would happen, usually around an argument over strategy, or about the incredible blunders of the commander who guided the war from his island. Why had the mass of troops been landed here at the fingerpoint, to climb head on into annihilating fire, when any Jew could see that the main force, if landed at a northerly cove, could have circled behind Achi Baba and easily opened the road to Constantinople?—Or what was needed, Herscheleh declared, was what the Greeks had used in their great battle to capture Troy, not far from here on the Asian side of the bay, on those blue-green fields they had themselves seen when approaching Gallipoli. An enormous wooden horse the Greeks had left as a parting salute on the shore, then pretended to give up their siege and sail away homeward. But the horse was filled with soldiers.

One day, instead of the wooden horse, an iron fish was used, but it was the Germans who had taken to heart the ancient tale of these waters, for the iron fish was theirs. The huge British warships still sat arrogantly in the mouth of the Dardanelles, and even the Jewish muleteers heard echoes of the sudden, startling explosions, then watched with the unbelief of the entire Gallipoli expedition as two of their mighty protectors, the newest and greatest of naval structures, sank traceless in the sea of ancient military adventure.

The next day the fleet that had remained, reassuringly watchful, in an impregnable circle behind them, had vanished, and the troops on land were alone.

What was to happen? Were they to remain here without end, clinging to the lip of soil?

Slowly Gidon saw himself being drawn into this soldier's life until he understood how men could even of their own accord live their entire lives in an army, comrades together—were it not for the rotten flies and the mosquitoes.

Not all men would be suited to such a life, nor would he choose it for himself, yet with a kind of fright of something foredoomed he saw that, at need, he could endure it well enough. Herschel, though he had gained hold of himself and went out regularly without showing his fear, Gidon saw, suffered ever more deeply, instead of becoming inured. Herschel was not suited. And in Araleh he saw growing another kind of trouble. It grew slowly. First it was seen only on mail-days if he had no letter. Because his wife was in Alexandria and he could therefore receive letters from her, even frequently, Araleh had at first seemed the lucky one. Gidon, with the rest of the men from Eretz, was inured to receiving nothing, except that Saraleh occasionally wrote to him too, so that he would get a piece of mail. But the letters for Araleh in each mail delivery, Gidon saw, now only made him increasingly homesick, and if by chance a mail was skipped, he was even sicker. He would become taciturn; generally Araleh was a man who naturally said yes when asked for anything he could lay his hands on for you, but now he began to say no, for no reason. He wouldn't trouble. Useless to remind him, "But, Araleh, today no one got letters from Alexandria, only the British home mail arrived." He began to voice suspicions that the bloody anti-Semites in the British command in Alexandria were deliberately holding back mail for the Zion Mule Corps. Just as they had even tried to steal the saddles.

For a whole week he had received no mail, and he now was unapproachable. Araleh was certain something was wrong with Saraleh, or if not, then with their little Dudu. Gidon could not think what to say to this. Once, when he began to say that a week was nothing, that he hadn't even heard a single word from home and didn't dare write to them even in roundabout ways, Araleh broke out tersely, "You're not married. You don't have a child."

That was so. But was it so entirely different? Often the terrible longing came over Gidon and he wrote letters in his head, to Mati, to Schmulik, about the comical moments of the war, about the ways of different kinds of men. And even as to Araleh's terrible longing for Saraleh, Gidon sometimes found himself on the verge of saying that he understood, he understood what it was to long to have her near.

Then a letter did come, three letters together for Araleh, and things were only worse. For one letter said the child was fretful, Saraleh was sure it was the heat, but if it didn't pass in a few days, she would take Dudu to the doctor. Saraleh had not put the days or the dates on her letters and Araleh could not tell which was written first. Perhaps the sickness letter was first and if she did not mention it in the others it was all nothing, all past. But also another letter said she had not yet received her allotment from the British. Not even the first allotment. She had not wanted to mention it to him, but she did not like to borrow more money from her father's friend Musara.

Araleh was in a rage. He went directly to the Irishman, who declared he would at once see about the matter, there must be some bloody balls-up at headquarters and there was no excuse for it.

And then came the hardest period. Day after day, once more, a whole week and then into a second week, no mail came for Araleh. And meanwhile others received letters, even packages, from Alexandria. Could it even be revenge for his raising a row over the allotment? Or perhaps the worst had happened. If the child had died, Saraleh couldn't bring herself to tell him. That was the only thing that would hold back Saraleh from writing to him.

He had to go back to Alexandria and find out. Not another day could he endure it. He was needed there, he felt it, he must go. Araleh put in a request for compassionate leave. In a week he could be back. There was even good reason to send him, mule replacements were needed, supplies.

Trumpeldor himself recommended the leave, with urgency. A whole day, two days, no reply from the island. And still no letter from Saraleh. Then came the reply: refused. Request of Sgt. Aryah Tchenstokover not granted at present. Nothing else. A message from a typewriting machine on an island back there. With numbers and initials and not even a name to curse at, but he knew the name, it came back from that anti-Semite, Col. Whitbury, he was certain. And he spat at their "Not granted." He would show them, a Jew was not a wog to be kicked aside, to be squashed like a bug and flicked away. He would show them.

Gidon had never seen Araleh like this. A deep pitying misgiving came over him: see what happens if you are married and a soldier. He thought about those men whose lives were in soldiering, like the Irishman, like Josef too. Oh, there was much lively talk about the Irishman, a great one with the ladies; and Josef too, despite his arm or perhaps even because of it, women fell in love with him—Gidon had even wondered about Leah—and here on Gallipoli, Josef received packs of letters from women in love with him, especially two sisters in Alexandria. Yet both of these soldiering men, you could feel, lived their lives alone. It was true that many of the higher officers, Britishers of the upper class, even sons of the British nobility, usually had wives and families and homes back there in their England. But for those it was different. Such high and mighty persons, a man didn't even have to try to understand. Only through this suffering of Araleh's, Gidon understood some instinct in his own self that was holding him back from

womankind, as though all he saw before him in his life for
the present was war and soldiering, and therefore he must
not let himself fall into such a situation, such a torment as
Araleh's. Over and over Araleh searched every word of
that reply. "At present."—When else did he need to go to
Saraleh!

—But perhaps it did point to a reason, Gidon argued
with him. The Mule Corps was depleted at present, not a
man could be spared, the Irishman and Trumpeldor were
even going back to get more men and mules, and probably
that was why, just now—

So depressed was Araleh, he hadn't even known they
were going. Why, perhaps he could ask Josef to see Saraleh
for him—

At once, Trumpeldor promised, carefully writing down
Saraleh's address and telling Araleh he would send back a
message on the military wireless.

So they departed, the Irishman wearing his finest uniform, the one that had been especially tailored in London.
A few days passed. Araleh haunted the regimental message
center—nothing. Now he was certain of the worst, Trumpeldor had not wanted the terrible news to come to him in
a wireless. Guiltily, Gidon found himself staying away from
the bunker they shared, he could no longer bear to listen
over and over to Araleh's imaginings as he tried to read
what was meant by the void of silence. It was impossible
that Josef had failed to carry out his promise; he was a
man who never failed to do what he said he would do.
Only two things could have happened, either Josef sent the
message and it was held up, perhaps by that anti-Semitic
devil, Col. Whitbury or—

Gidon even began to fear that Araleh was going out of
his mind. Already Gidon had seen this happening in Dr.
Ashkenazi, who had volunteered in Alexandria. As it came
out that Gidon was half a veterinary, he had soon begun to
help patch up wounded animals, and then, in a flood of
casualties after a sudden Turkish attack, Dr. Ashkenazi had
seized on Gidon when he came for medical supplies. A
bombardment was under way; the doctor, as everyone
knew, had been unable to master his trembling during
shellfire—some people simply never got used to it. How
much he had aged in these few weeks! Suddenly Gidon
found the doctor begging him to help, the doctor couldn't

go on—the flies, they crawled in the wounds while he was operating—he had demanded sanitation supplies and they had not come—he was being undermined—and all at once he seized Gidon's arm and began sobbing. The next day when Gidon returned from his rounds, Herschel bore the news that the doctor had collapsed, sobbing and stabbing at flies; he was being sent home to Egypt.

It was this moment that Araleh seized upon. In a single instant, everything was thought of and worked out. Gidon alone need know. Gidon must somehow arrange to carry him on the sick roster. In the confusion of the present situation, with the two commanders away and the doctor leaving, it could be managed. In a week Araleh would be back. Only the time to reach Alexandria, to run home, and he'd return on the next ship. The hospital ship carrying Dr. Ashkenazi was sailing direct for Alexandria, and Araleh would put on a Red Cross armband and accompany the doctor. He had already mastered the company clerk's typewriter, he knew what forms to use, and during the mess hour, for a few cigarettes, the clerk's dugout was his.

How could Gidon prevent him? If Gidon refused to take even a small part in the scheme, Araleh would try anyway. To report his friend's intention, even if to save him, was a thing a man could not do. And what if Araleh should be proved right in his worries? Though Gidon realized this was a kind of infection of fears, by now he at moments caught himself seeing, not little Dudu's sick face but Saraleh's in the pallor of death, her eyes calling to him piteously.

Together he and Araleh helped Dr. Ashkenazi onto the hospital ship where the commanding doctor with professional cheerfulness took him in charge. Then, just at what moment Gidon hadn't even noticed, Araleh had slipped away, mingling somewhere with the masses of sick and wounded.

Indeed, as he told it later, he might well have carried off his entire scheme. He had managed the voyage, the debarkation, and had rushed home. Not Saraleh, not the child was there. An elderly couple from Petach Tikvah now was quartered in the room—but they knew where Saraleh was, she had gone to live with her father's friends, and hurrying in a carriage to the Musaras, Araleh found her. Oh, what a surprise from heaven! she cried. She was well. Tiny Dudu threw her arms around her abba's neck and wouldn't let go to give her mother a chance. Every day she had written him! Saraleh said. And Trumpeldor had been here only the day before yesterday to inquire after her! Yes! Josef had come himself!

As it turned out, the loyal Trumpeldor, having first failed to find her at the old address, had meanwhile been hurried to Cairo to recruit new volunteers for the depleted Mule Corps. But nevertheless on the way back he had fulfilled his promise to Araleh, and sent the wireless. The anti-Semitic Col. Whitbury, seeing the message, had in an impulse of human kindness gone in person to hand it to the anxious husband, and, unable to find Sgt. Aryah Tchenstokover, had thus tripped open poor Araleh's entire escapade. Here the colonel had come in person with the message in his hand, and all the while that bloody smart Jew had already carried out a scheme of desertion! Search orders were put on the wireless, and Araleh was picked up as he left the Musara house early in the morning. For one thing he thanked God, that Saraleh hadn't seen his arrest. Nor would anyone listen, much less believe, when he said he was on his way to a ship to return of his own accord. Put in irons on the vessel, he was led off, on landing, shackled hand and foot, to be court-martialed. By the time Trumpeldor and the Irishman returned with a hundred mules and word of a hundred and twenty-five new recruits to follow as soon as they were trained, Araleh's penalty had already been posted.

The deserter was to receive the lash, before the entire assembled Zion Mule Corps.

"You see, they consider us their equals," Herschel found it in himself to jest. "Just like a British soldier, a Jew may receive the lash."

Once before, the men had witnessed it, carried out before the entire regiment on a deserter, a Britisher, no less, found stowing away on a departing supply ship. All done in perfect parade order, the open square of men silent at attention, with only the cracking of the lash like an echo of shells from Achi Baba.

Already Trumpeldor had protested. He himself was at fault, he declared to the Irishman, for he had been slow in carrying out his promise to the man, and the added days without a message had aggravated Araleh's fears. Besides, as it was perfectly clear that Araleh had intended to return at once, this was not a desertion, but only absence without leave.

Doubtless that was Araleh's intention, the Irishman agreed, but unfortunately that bastard Whitbury had caught him out, the sentence was passed and could not be revoked. As Trumpeldor pleaded on, exasperation appeared in the Irishman. "Admit you're not the easiest race in the world to deal with! I took you on, and I don't regret it—your men have turned into good soldiers, I'll stand up for you on that score—I'll stake my whole bloody career. But goddammit, when you're caught out, you're caught out, and that's the game; fair or not, you take the punishment." No, the Irishman could not, would not go to Whitbury. If he were to make an issue of this incident, every damn previous nastiness would be thrown up again, from the Zion man who was caught profiteering on two bars of issue chocolate, to the blasted squad that had refused an order to lead their mules under fire. "I've taken care of these things in my own way, I know our boys and we all know there isn't a unit on the beach where such things and worse haven't happened, but damn it, Josef, we can't ignore the fact that there are plenty of staff officers who are Jew-haters, and never wanted this unit to exist in the first place."

That was precisely why, Josef insisted, Araleh's sentence must be fought—it must be shown as an exaggerated punishment resulting from prejudice. The man would clearly have returned of his own accord.

"How can we prove it except by his word?"

"His word should be enough."

"Forging orders. Deception and lying. The whole way. And you want me to insist on his word!"

"It's my word too."

The Irishman could no longer control himself. He too had been caught out, for his damned Jews. "It's your bloody unbearable stubbornness! The stiff-necked people! I don't wonder they would only give you a mule corps. That's what you are—a race of mules."

Their glares held like caught swords vibrating ungivingly. Then the Jew turned on his heel and marched out. From his tent Josef Trumpeldor sent his orderly with a letter resigning his commission and requesting to be severed from His Majesty's Service. He had been insulted as a man and as a Jew.

The shouted, heated words had been heard and carried through the camp. At first there was only a depressed sense of fatedness, that even with the best of the goyim the inevitable moment came. And if a man like Joself took it so deeply as to resign, the quarrel was beyond repair. Angriest was Tuvia the Cement-head. The entire corps should mutiny and demand to be sent back to Alexandria. "What are we proving here anyway, shoveling muleshit out of the trenches? Let them get gyppos! That's all they take us for!"

When the tale reached Araleh in the lockup, he sent word through the sentry: Tuvia and Gidon should come at once to the rear side where they could hear him.

They heard his voice through the wood. "Nothing must happen! You hear me?" Araleh's voice was calm, as if all personal anger had been strained out. "If we fail here, it will be worse than if the Jews had not come at all. Listen, Gidon. Go to Josef and tell him I refuse to have anything done because of me. They caught me and I will take my punishment. You hear me?" And he continued. "Everyone, every last man, must assemble and march to Josef and ask him not to resign. You hear me?"

Slowly a different mood grew. Herschel proclaimed in a mock Talmudic singsong, "After all, what did the Irishman call us but mules? Don't our own prophets call us mules in the scriptures? Are we not the stiff-necked people as he said? Is this an insult? The Irishman is already like one of ourselves, and if we can call ourselves mules, he also can call us mules—from him it is no insult."

The entire unit stood in ranks outside Trumpeldor's tent, while Tuvia, Gidon, and Nissim Abulafia from a leading Jewish family in Cairo went in to plead with him. As was his way in a discussion, the Captain listened without making any comment, only asking a few questions at the end. Turning to Gidon, he asked, "Gidon, did Araleh tell you from the first that he would come back?"

"With the first ship."

And to Tuvia, "He insists on accepting the punishment?"

"He insists."

Then came an interval of silence. Josef would probably send them away saying he would think it over, as was his habit. But when he spoke, he had already decided. "I will withdraw my resignation. I see that it was a personal reaction on my part and did not represent the will of the unit." Rising, he went out with them to the men. They were altogether less then four hundred now, but standing assembled at attention they looked like many, an army.

From where he stood, just behind the hero, Gidon heard Josef's caught breath as he saw his men, the full ranks, at attention. "You are right, chaverim, I'll stay," he said.

When the punishment took place, the men kept their eyes to the ground. It was all done to form. Col. Whitbury and his staff attended. The Irishman stood rigidly in his place, saluting their arrival. Even Josef. But the distance seemed further than usual between him and the other officers.

An English sergeant-major read off the charge and the verdict of the court-martial. Araleh was marched to the post, the blows were heard, but nothing from him.

With his eyes lowered, Gidon still saw it. As he saw the bared back of Araleh and the lash cutting the sunlight, he also felt some last thing being cut out of himself to make the Jew a soldier.

Araleh slumped over, but when the cords were undone, he did not fall. The regimental officers marched away. The Irishman gave his order. "Dismissed." Only Herscheleh spoke; between his teeth he muttered, "The gentlemen."

When he was returned, his back healed, Araleh was to the men the same Araleh who would always find a way to help a fellow get something he wanted, especially now if it needed a little cleverness against the British order of things. He liked, even, to tell of his adventure, of the part where he had outwitted them all, for in final account, had he not succeeded, had he not got home as he intended? The rest had been a stupid accident, and above all, he cautioned Gidon, Saraleh must never know of the punishment. There was an instant's calculation, now, in every little action Araleh considered, as though he first measured it by his own particular measure. It went with a new word that answered for everything—"Ourselves!" Nothing else in the world could be trusted. No stranger, no politics, no power. In the end, as indeed they had always known, it would be "ourselves."

17

OF THE Chaimovitch daughters it was Eliza, the well-favored one, for whom something special in life was expected, let it only be for the good, may no evil eye fall upon her because of her loveliness. From earliest childhood, Eliza was the one whose golden little head drew every hand to stroke it, she was the appealing little female child with the great velvet eyes and a heart brimming with love and helpful willingness. She was the one who without being asked took joy in running to fetch things for Feigel in the kitchen, she pumped water without objecting that this was Schmulik's task, and she took her greatest joy in carrying to the fields the basket that Feigel had filled with bread and tomatoes and cheese for the mid-morning meal.

In the winter months it melted your heart to catch sight of the girl's smoothly combed glowing head, beside the kerosene lamp, bent to her Hebrew grammar, while the soft light stroked her lustrous hair. It was a burnished gold, like a perfect Sabbath chaleh thickly braided.

Naturally Eliza was aware that she was the well-favored one among the sisters, and she had the grace to accept her fortune as though this were not entirely a personal gift, as though one well-favored daughter was the family's due, and since the luck and the role had happened to come to her, she must give it her best and fulfill it.

In every village there are a few girls like this.

"Show us your maidens" is the word of the visiting dignitary, prince, conqueror, and the judgment on a whole people, on an entire civilization, may well rest on these girls, the end product, proudly shown, most cherished and protected.

A man trudging home wearily from the fields, the strength burned out of his bones by the all-day broiling sun, beholds the young girl, his own daughter, moving about the yard, perhaps hanging out clothes to dry, with her bare arms aloft, with the softer light of the afternoon's end glowing on her skin, a ribbon in her braids, and his entire being wells over with joy. For this. For this young creature, calm, and still untroubled, innocent; let the world boil over with wars and cataclysms, only let her yet be protected from it and somehow indeed come to lead an untroubled life. For her it has all been done, she is the product. Her smiling face as she turns her eyes to him and says, "Nu, Abba"—this alone is enough, he is home from his day's labor—what is there to discuss? For this end a man long ago lifted himself up and journeyed here, and cleared rocks from the fields, and pounded the hide of a stubborn mule, and haggled with Syrian merchants from Damascus to receive another franc for his measure of wheat—see, behold the lovely daughter of our family, our people.

With her sisters Eliza was not overly vain. She carried her loveliness as though it were really some garment given for all of them together that it happened just now in her first bloom to be her turn to wear. True, this had always been the most troublesome aspect of her good fortune—to know that from her sisters all eyes would turn to her. There was Leah with her enormous thick-legged body—despite her great warm soul, she was no beauty. Perhaps, Eliza wondered lately, it was even because of her, Eliza, that Leah wandered away from home so much; sometimes when Leah was here of a Sabbath, and a chalutz working as a fieldhand for one of the Roumanians came over for a visit, Eliza had an impulse to disappear from the table and stay out of sight so that the man would learn to know her sister.

Another embarrassing and yet pleasing part of it was that if Leah herself, or Mameh, bought a new kerchief, or even if Malka Bronescu bought herself a bit of finery, all the girls wanted at once to see how it looked on Eliza, as though only then could its true attractiveness be assessed.

In the village, all the boys since childhood had been in love with her in their turns, though as it happened not one of them stirred her with the feelings she had read about and awaited. There had even been Gidon's Arab friend, Fawzi, whom she often caught looking at her with burning eyes, when he rode up to meet Gidon to go hunting. She had teased herself with dreams about what she would do if she happened to fall desperately in love with an Arab. But fortunately she had not been put to the test, it had not happened to her, and perhaps luckily, now Fawzi had been taken away to the war, for in this year of her flowering, who knew what could come over her?

To Dvora who was nearest to her and already twice a mother, Eliza sometimes confessed, on a Sabbath visit to Gilboa, about certain spells that came over her like . . . like intoxication from the scent of flowers, except it was as though the scent grew within herself. Dvoraleh sighed with her, and only said Eliza was coming into a time of her life when she must be careful, very careful.

Some of those who had been infatuated with her had given up and gone to other girls; one pair was already married. Also, some of the young men of the village, particularly the farm-helpers, had hurriedly slipped out of the country to avoid labor conscription. And strangely, where there had been so many young men in the land for every girl, now, in her bloom and beauty, Eliza found herself much alone and without a beau.

There was one whom she had not dismissed who had been in love with her now for two years and more, and she had often jested with Malka and the other girls, even jested with the boy himself, about his steadfast courtship, with a mock sigh declaring to him, "Don't give up! In the end you are the kind a girl marries, instead of all the handsome heroes."

His one fault was chubbiness. His face was pudgy like a kugel and his body was a pillow. Yet occasionally, in a strong shaft of sunlight, Nahum's face suddenly looked well-formed and handsome beneath that puffiness. And besides, he was highly intelligent. Even when he had come as hardly more than a boy, with his father, Reb Bagelmacher, to buy geese, Nahum had talked to her own father without timidity, giving sensible advice about the prices of crops, and entering at once into calculations over the citrus grove they were planning, advising lemons instead of oranges, since lemons could more easily be sold right here in Eretz so that the grower did not have to worry about export. How wise he had been, for now in the war the orange growers of Rehovot and Petach Tikvah were already in great difficultly, unable to ship out their crops.

Nahum was also very sentimental, and it was he who

persuaded her to call herself Shulamith. She had never liked the name Eliza, and since Shulamith was her second name, after an aunt on her mother's side, she had suddenly decided to adopt it. As an excuse and to win Leah's support, she declared it sounded more Hebrew. Malka Bronescu teased her: did she imagine herself the mysterious Shulamith of King Solomon's Song of Songs? But in the end all the young people began calling her Shulamith because it suited her. Only at home the family kept calling her Eliza, it simply didn't seem natural to change. Until she stopped answering to Eliza. Leah was the first to make the change, but she called her Shula instead of Shulamith, and then so did the boys; finally her mother also gave in, though Abba behaved as if he did not hear and simply kept on calling her Eliza. Only Yaffaleh, and the faithful Nahum, used the full name, Shulamith.

Naturally Yankel and Feigel, though they never said a word for fear of arousing the contrariness of the young, eagerly and anxiously watched, hoping that a match might develop. Not only was it that Reb Bagelmacher was well off with his hotel, but here at least was a good Jew, let the Above One grant that one of their daughters should marry into a respectable Jewish family instead of a communa. Or instead of becoming, the Above One forbid, like Leah, a who-even-knew-what in their modern world of free love!

Each time he appeared to buy geese, Reb Bagelmacher would ceaselessly beam on Shula-Eliza, and sometimes even go so far as a little cheek-pinch. A beautiful maiden gladdens the house, he would quote from some sage— everything he said sounded like a quotation.

—A long beard gladdens the mice, Nahum once mocked, but so that only she could hear it. Shula barely managed to stifle her laughter. This started a game between them; they would engage in conversations consisting totally of mock-wisdom, and in this mischief with its secretly amused whispers there began to grow in her a respect for Nahum's quickness and daring of mind, while in Nahum an already full-grown infatuation was deepened by the discovery that his Shulamith had wit as well as beauty.

It was a teasing kind of wit that in a girl less beautiful might have been a tongue with a cutting edge, but with each teasing remark—usually about his chubbiness—the look in her eyes assuaged him. "She has doe's eyes, and her tongue is an adder's," he mocked her.

"His mind is a sharp quill, and his flesh like a mattress of goose-feathers," and he had to laugh.

Yet when even teasingly Shulamith called him "my faithful," "my suitor," Nahum felt a balm under his smarting, and when she used him to fetch her little feminine things from the shops in Tiberias that he brought to her when he came for the geese, Nahum was happy.

Some kind of bond was growing between them, and Nahum had already determined in his soul that one way or another he would win her, while in Shula there was a certain calm because she knew without doubt that one boy was bound to her in his heart, that she could do whatever she wanted with him and not lose him; that unlike all the boys who were drawn to her by her beauty and who stared and tried to touch her here and there where she wanted and didn't want to be touched, Nahum was truly in love with her, the love one read about, like Levin's love for Natasha in *War and Peace*. So too in the end it was conceivable that she might be his, Shula joked to herself and even to him—if, for instance, everybody should starve in the war—and people were already beginning to speak of such horrors in Jerusalem and Tel Aviv—why then, a half-starved Nahum would become slender and handsome!

But though tales of want came from Judea, here in Galilee things were not yet difficult, and in Tiberias, though the season at the hot baths was poor, the Bagelmacher pension had taken on a sudden prosperity. Each week Nahum bought more and more geese.

The pension had been discovered by the German fliers, the same who had taken over half of Gilboa as their quarters. They could be seen in their automobiles rushing back and forth on the newly-built road along the lakeside, for which the Turks had made Abba cart stones on his wagon. In Tiberias, in their visored caps and their mirror-bright boots, the aviators strolled about, bored, along the one street, or ate fish at the Arab cafes by the shore. And this had given Nahum a thought.

One day he sought out Malach the carpenter to make him a signboard, bringing him words already drawn out in

German script. "Deutsche Speisen," it said, and Nahum had also traced the outline of a roast goose, legs in the air—this was to be painted above the German words.

"After all," Nahum explained to Shulamith, "Jewish cooking is German cooking, with maybe a little more schmaltz."

Reb Bagelmacher had at first hesitated. It was true that important goyish visitors had from time to time been brought to his dining room as guests by Jewish dignitaries, and they had always shown respectful interest when the kashruth laws were explained to them, and avowed the highest willingness to observe these laws at the meal; about religion, people of high importance were always respectful. The Belly, too, had appeared more than once to gorge himself on Mama Bagelmacher's roast goose. But to open the dining room to strangers, even though the German aviators were all officers, struck him as opening the door to trouble. From his own father he had heard of dreadful occasions in their inn—that had been in Russia before the family came here—when Cossacks had at knife-point forced him to serve them butter with their meat dishes, contaminating everything on the table.

"The Germans are not Cossacks," Nahum argued, "and those who can't do without butter will go elsewhere. Tateh, try it. You'll see, it will save us!"

One Friday, Reb Bagelmacher gazed over his near-empty dining room, and on Sunday Nahum hung up the sign. The first cutomers appeared almost at once, for the noon meal, peering into the pension with an air of well-intentioned curiosity. Pointing to the portrait of the brooding Herzl that hung in the entrance hall, one of them expertly informed his companions, "This is their Zionist Messias."

It was Nahum who explained to them that although the cooking was German, it was kosher. In good spirits they sat down, while the knowing one with an indulgent laugh explained to the others, "That means we can't have butter on our bread. But we can have goose-fat!"

The bird itself, from Yaffaleh's brood, well-fed on the Chaimovitch corn, seasoned with Mama Bagelmacher's spices and served with numerous side-dishes of pickles and cucumbers and sour tomatoes and even red cabbage, so

delighted the Germans that they called forth Frau Bagelmacher and laughingly declared that if this was Jewish
cooking, they would all become Jews!

On the very next day two huge motorcars filled with yel-
low-haired young officers roared into Tiberias, halting directly before the pension.

Their voices were loud, they raised their glasses and
toasted Kaiser Wilhelm, they toasted their high commander
Kress von Kressenstein, and the Roman Emperor Tiberius.
A pious Jerusalemite, who for many years had come regularly for the season at the hot baths, rose to leave the room
and would have departed forever, had not Nahum instantly
thought of arranging the glassed veranda as a special dining
room for the pension's regular guests. "How can we refuse
the military?" he begged, as one who would do nothing
that might hurt the Jewish community, and the Jerusalemite, who, like all steady customers, counted heads, to keep
track of how Reb Bagelmacher's affairs were going, sighed,
"Well, it's been a very bad season for you."

That very afternoon Nahum had to make a special trip
to the Chaimovitch farm for more geese. And presently it
proved Nahum's own doing that threatened to bring about
his undoing. For one day Yankel drove to Tiberias with a
load of potatoes for the pension, and Shula-Eliza rode
along to shop a bit in the souk and "breathe the air of the
city."

Nahum, such was his bad luck, was out when they arrived, and while Reb Chaimovitch and Reb Bagelmacher
made up their accounts, and decided between them which
side would win the war, agreeing that for the Jews what did
it matter, a Kaiser, a Czar, one devil was as bad as the
other, Mama Bagelmacher did her best to entertain the
beautiful Chaimovitch daughter and keep her there until
Nahum came back, surely at any moment. A bite, Shula
must take something in her mouth, a bite of something
tasty after the long ride, and not in the kitchen! Like for a
real guest, Mama Bagelmacher set out tea and cake in the
dining room, and in the moment when she left Shula alone
while she fetched some preserves to put in the tea—for
such moments are fated—the outer door was flung open,
and Shula looked up. A godlike young man stood there, his
shining head the sun itself, the blue Kinnereth behind him.

Now occurred that moment of astonished fatedness that

Shula had so often read about and had awaited in her soul.

It was for her he snatched off his officer's cap, and he now advanced in smiling politeness and made a request in German. More than once before in her life Shula had heard German spoken and found herself understanding most of it because the words were similar to Yiddish. Indeed, Reuven and Leah and the melamed and all the Hebraists were eternally disdainfully explaining that Yiddish was nothing but a jargon of German mixed with Russian. What the young god asked sounded to her like "Is there a goose here?"

And a laugh blurted from her. For as in a joke with Nahum she almost responded, "Yes, right here!" She already knew this would be true of herself, for the entire course of her foolishness, Shula told herself, was already clear as though written in a book. And doubtless he too at once sensed the fatedness, for while she was explaining that she was not of the house, in a Yiddish that she stumblingly tried to make sound dignified like German, the officer gazed at her with that growing glow of enchantment that any pretty girl knew she must beware of. "Excuse my German," she ended.

"Oh, but it is charming. But then what could not be charming, from such a source!" And before Mama Bagelmacher returned, he had learned her name; she repeated the full Shulamith and he exclaimed, "But naturally! I should have guessed! The Shulamite!" And even while Mama Bagelmacher stood there, he learned that Shulamith was from a farm, a place called Mishkan Yaacov—"Ah yes! The settlement by the riverbend." And after he had placed his order, for already tables had to be reserved, the young officer clicked his heels and made a half bow directed more to Shula than to Mama Bagelmacher, saying "Servus," while he withdrew with his eyes still on the girl. Boldly he added that he trusted they might meet again.

Shula knew she was flushing under Mama Bagelmacher's gaze. But nothing was said, Nahum's mother wisely did not even make her usual remarks about how for her part she could do without these German fliers altogether. Fortunately Nahum appeared just then so that his mother could suggest he accompany Shula to the souk as, with all the soldiers that were roving about in Tiberias, a decent girl could no longer go alone to the market.

The next day a plane thundered down low over the Mishkan Yaacov, sending the hens and geese into wild cackling circles in every farmyard. With one accord, all the boys rushed out of the schoolroom and Mati raced along the open street trying to keep directly under the airplane as it made loops and circles and even—he recognized—a figure eight. In front of the house he kept shouting to Shula, "Look! It's so low you can even see the aviator!"

She did not go out into the yard but remained in the doorway. He could not know which was her home, but she could see him; he had taken off his helmet and his shining head was now the sun in the sky. Yesterday, when he had clicked his heels in departing, he had spoken his name, Luft-Leutnant Gottfried and then something doubled, like the names of noblemen. Though to be so stupidly romantic as to be enchanted by a click of the heels and an aristocratic name, she certainly was not.

Mati was excitedly showing everyone, with complicated movements of his hands, the movements the plane had made. She withdrew into the house.

Hardly a week later, Bronescu was suggesting to one after another of the villagers when they came into his shop that it would be good policy to invite some of the German officers to a festive occasion when they could perhaps mingle and make friends. After all, the Germans, unlike the Turks, were a cultured and civilized nation, nor should people believe all the horror-tales about Belgium. It looked as though Germany would quickly win the war, and with the Germans in the land, something could be accomplished! The British, it was plain, despite all the might of their entire fleet had failed to break open the Dardanelles, and this was the turning point of the great conflict. The Germans and the Turks in their turn would clearly now prepare a truly massive assault on the Suez Canal; that was why the aviators were here, and this time the canal would be seized and the British lifeline would be cut. France would fall, Russia would be defeated. It was wise to be on good terms with the Germans.

Presently, the commanders in Nazareth and Tiberias and the fliers from the camp in Gilboa were invited to a Lag B'Omer festival to be held in the open center of the village. Not that Lag B'Omer had been such a festival in Roumania, but from the old-time Jews in Tiberias, the children

had picked up the custom of lighting bonfires on this holiday—what child will miss an excuse to light a bonfire?
And also since it was a custom to hold marriages on Lag
B'Omer, the festival would be a wedding celebration for two
couples who would be going under the canopy, one, a village romance on both sides, and the other, a son of a villager to a girl from a fine Sephardic family from Safed.
Quickly, let the boys be married. Each day the fear of the
Roumanians increased that their former homeland would
be dragged into the war; if on the side of the Triple Entente
then the boys might be deported or imprisoned, and if on
the side of the Germans and Turks, they could be conscripted for labor. A married man was still safer than a
single man.

Among the young people themselves, especially the girls,
it was said that the fever of war brought on the fever of
love. The bride from the village, Gerta Kolnodly, explained
to Shula that you suddenly saw with different eyes the boys
you had seen all your life. You saw them in danger of
death, and you suddenly became afraid that you would
miss everything that life was intended for. "Do you understand what I mean, Shula?"

Shula understood. Yes, she had felt something of that
herself.

The invitation to the Germans was made not without
opposition. Several of the mothers declared to each other,
why tempt fate? And in every kitchen they repeated to
each other the tales of Jewish girls led astray by Christians,
by Czarist officers and Polish noblemen. Sometimes the
wretched misled daughter returned unmarried with her
baby, or left the baby on the doorstep with a note, while
she herself was found days later floating in the river; here it
could be either the river or the Kinnereth. Sometimes the
nobleman even married the Jewish daughter, and many
years later a grown son, a Christian, wandered into the
town's synagogue, led by fate alone, as he did not know his
mother was a Jewess, and the wanderer would beg a sage
to teach him the Torah. And sometimes after many years
the daughter herself returned, usually to her father's death-
bed, to fall on her knees, her tears indistinguishable from
her neck-chain of glistening diamonds, as she begged his
forgiveness.

All these tales Shula heard with one ear, knowing they were intended for her, even though her own mama would only sigh and repeat to the neighbor-woman, "So is the way of life."

A few of the mothers even declared that if the Germans were invited to the festival, they would take their daughters off to Chedera, to Haifa, to Jerusalem, and some vowed they would keep them locked indoors at home. But as the festival neared, and the street was arched over with green branches, and the children dragged wood from rotted chicken coops for their bonfires, who could stay away?

The four musicians from Yavniel came on a flower-decked wagon, the open street was filled with townsmen and guests, and then a whole caravan of military automobiles arrived. Shula saw her Gottfried at once. He jumped out and came to her directly, bowing, whisking her around to the music, his hand pressing against the small of her back.

"I must be careful not to show I want to be only with you," he said after their second dance, and somehow Shula felt sure that Bronescu's suggestion of hospitality to the Germans had been connected with Gottfried's search for her. A little frightened by the young German's determination, she also felt both pleased and frightened by an oddly adventurous thought that came to her, that for this beauty that had been bestowed on her a special fate must be destined. Was she simply, like Dvoraleh, to marry a shomer, or a chalutz, and live in a communa or a village settlement? or even in Tiberias?

Luckily Nahum had not come; it was a busy night at the Bagelmacher hostelry, for many German officers, before going out to watch the picturesque Jewish festival, were gathering for festive dinners. Some planned to drive up as far as Meron, where the long-bearded long-coated Jews were said to dance all night in mad circles around the tomb of an ancient rabbi. Others had been invited to various villages.

All over the Yishuv it was being repeated now, that after all the Germans were a cultured people. Their young officers came from good families and could be trusted; naturally these young men had a longing for breathing the air of a civilized home where they might talk about literature and music and enjoy the presence of decent women. For other needs they could find their way; in Jaffa and other places there were houses of shame. "But let us not treat them as outcasts. It may well prove to our advantage to have friends among them."

In Mishkan Yaacov everyone agreed the festival was a great success. The Germans had behaved with the most perfect manners. Though the malamed let no one forget that anti-Semitism had even been made into a science by a German professor, these young men were of a new generation, and perhaps things would change.

In departing, Gottfried had kissed Shula's hand.

Then it was a cruise on the Kinnereth—the Sea of Galilee, as they called it. Organized by a whole group of aviators, it was to take place on a Sunday, and Malka Bronescu begged Shula to join the select number of girls who would enliven the excursion with their feminine company.

Cleverly, the officers had invited along the malamed himself, since he had discoursed so interestingly at the festival to their commander about the ancient synagogue ruins in the region. He would be their guide.

When one or two of the villagers objected that things were already going too far, since after all it was a Christian place they were going to, where That One was said to have preached, the malamed reminded them that it was nevertheless a synagogue, Kfar Nahum, which was now called Capernaum, indeed the most ancient synagogue in the land. Every Jew should visit it, only keeping in mind that it was ours, not theirs.

Though living so close by, Shula had never been there. It was said to be a most romantic place for picnics. Just then Leah was staying at home. "Ah, it's beautiful there," she said, in such a dreamy way as to make Shula wonder whether something had happened to Leah in that very place with her Handsome Moshe? And since Leah too had been invited, what was there to fear, what reason was there not to go?

They were restrained the whole way across the lake, the girls sitting in their little cluster around Leah, who kept them singing, sometimes getting the young officers to join in and learn the Hebrew words. But once among the ruins, Gottfried managed in a lane of fallen pillars to walk Shula aside, and then, lingering to examine closely a six-pointed star that the melamed had pointed out on a stone, he kept her separate from the others. Today he was no longer a cavalier pursuing a flirtation but a man making ready to show a woman his soul.

When they stood by a broken-off pillar, gazing out to the dream-blue sea, Gottfried suddenly remarked, very seriously, "You know, Shulamith, I am a believer."

He wore a hovering smile, as one who, had he approached too far, was ready to withdraw. Her heartbeat quickened as she kept on her face only the look of friendly interest and earnestness due to anyone who speaks of sincere belief. And Gottfried spoke to her of his beliefs the way a man tells innermost things, perhaps the story of his family, to the woman he hopes to draw to him.

She retained on her lips that earnest, interested smile which she had already long ago learned to use when a boy talked of things important to him, such as the speed of bullets or the number of horses in an engine; even if a girl did not understand, she could smile. But today Shula found herself straining to understand. Yet just when she felt she caught a glimmer of their strange Christian idea, the thought suddenly vanished among the glinting tips of the tiny golden hairs on Gottfried's arm when he moved it in the sun.

In all her young life this was really the first time she had spoken naturally to a Christian about their religion. In Russia, she had been only a little girl, and all she knew was to fear them. Their church in the center of the town was the place from which death issued for the Jews. The priests in their black robes and black cylinder hats were executioners. On Sundays, in times of quiet, she, together with her closest girl friends—with a pang Shula suddenly recalled them, were they still there in Cherezinka?—on Sundays they would peep from behind a standing wagon, waiting for the peasants to stream out, and if the band of goyish boys espied them, though these were the same boys they saw every day in the marketplace, the little group of Jewish girls would whirl around and run away in terror.

Of their Christian religion she knew almost nothing, Shula suddenly realized, except that far back there in Cherezinka the little Jewish girls had caught a story and puzzled over it amongst themselves, giggled over it, and solved it by laughing at the ignorant, gullible moujiks; it was true that you could get them to believe anything at all, even the greatest absurdity!

It was the story of the ikon they worshiped with candles before it, in alcoves in their houses, and everywhere, even in stone altars on the roads. Not the picture of the naked man on the cross with only a bit of cloth covering his secret part, but the picture of the mother and the baby. The moujiks all believed that the baby was conceived and born while their Matushka remained still an untouched maiden! How could any grown person believe such a thing? The stupid moujiks! And the little Jewish girls, whispering to each other the true secret about a man's seed, would burst out laughing. It was like grown people believing the story of the stork.

And yet even at that remote time something akin to a wish had whispered in her—if such a thing could be true? To have a sweet little baby of her own. Like the joy that swept up in her when she had helped to bathe Dvoraleh's newborn baby and felt the writhing naked little body in her hands. So, as a little girl, she had wondered about having a baby without the painful and ugly part of when a man tried to plant his seed in you, and it struck Shula now that this might be why all those millions and millions of Christians, the greatest part of the world she supposed, wanted to believe in such a story, especially the women.

So much was happening in Shulamith because of Gottfried's nearness that she felt confused and a little afraid. Always, because of her being the prettiest and because she knew she was intelligent too, Shula had felt a special protection in the world. For a moment now she lost this feeling.

"To stand here where the Christ himself stood and preached," Gottfried was saying with awe—but quickly, and managing to put a personal tenderness in it, he added, "— of course he was preaching as a rabbi to your own people—to stand here makes it all so real to me, more true than ever." And gazing into her face, he added, "Excuse me, Shulamith, perhaps I am offending you?"

"Oh, no." Her heartbeat was even more tumultuous, but Shula kept on her understanding womanly smile, and repeated what she had once heard Reuven say in a discussion with Leah, "Many things he preached are exactly in the words of other great rabbis of that time. And sayings of our prophets, too. My own generation is not very religious, I'm afraid—my oldest brother and Leah are freethinkers." Would he guess that what she had just said meant they believed in free love as well? She was flushing. Was Leah keeping her eye on them, she wondered.

"Naturally." Which part of what she said was he agreeing with? It was such a hot day, not a hamseen but a motionless heat; even by the waterside she felt uncomfortable, she was moist under her arms and below her breasts. He must feel so hot in his military jacket; should she ask him if he wanted to take it off?

"Naturally, the prophets," Gottfried repeated. "Since our Jesus came as your Messias, just as they had prophesied."

"Mashiach." She felt on safe ground again and smiled. "Our religious people are still waiting for Mashiach. Each day my father prays he should come already!"

"And you?"

"I? Do I pray for the Messiah?" She giggled now. "I am a bad Jew, I don't even pray." Then she added seriously, "Our religion is old-fashioned and prejudiced, a woman doesn't even count, if she prays or not. It is only for the men!" Leah should only hear, and be proud of her!

"Then you too are a freethinker?"

"Maybe worse. I don't think at all!"

"Oh, you have already shown me the contrary."

"Well, with our teacher in school we sometimes had discussions about such things."

"About freethinking? I thought the Jewish schools were religious?"

"Oh, he is religious, but he let us discuss, to convince us." She laughed.

"Do you believe in God?" he asked. How intimate and serious they were! She stopped laughing and giggling. "In God, yes." Suddenly she was sure. Their eyes met as though in beautiful agreement that this was the most profound, the one thing. "I don't even know exactly how I believe, but . . . My brother, the oldest one, Reuven, the one who is now in the Turkish army in Damascus—he is a true idealist, a vegetarian. He says that we ourselves, the Jewish people, we are the Mashiach. That we are the sign of God. That we ourselves must rebuild the Holy Land, because the Messiah is an idea and cannot be a person."

Gottfried pondered a moment. His smile became lighter, and, as if to get out of the deepest depths, he remarked, "I wonder, when Christ returns, will he again be a Jew?"

Then he hadn't really listened to her, he had disregarded what she said, as if this profound idea of Reuven's didn't matter. And instead the German began to explain to her the very first things about the Christians and their churches. To begin with there were the Catholics and Protestants—Oh yes, this she knew, she even knew that there was another big difference amongst the Catholics themselves, between the Russian priests and the Pope in Rome; the Russian pappas were allowed to marry, but the Pope's priests were not.

"Our Protestant preachers too are permitted to marry." Gottfried smiled, as though this somehow lessened the vast distance between them. He was a Protestant, a Lutheran, he called it, explaining that a Catholic priest named Martin Luther had been the first Protestant, for one reason because he protested against celibacy and wanted to marry.

She didn't know whether a laugh just now would be proper, yet something about the whole struggle in their religion being started by a priest who wanted to go with a woman was suddenly farcical to Shula. The Christians were really mad people, to make a thing of God over something so natural. It came to her to wonder, was their Yoshka ever married? Nu, but hadn't there been something about a beautiful woman who washed his feet and dried them with her hair? But wasn't she also a prostitute? This was not the time to ask. Perhaps she should really try to read something about their religion; after all, the Christians ruled the world, even though here it was the Moslems, and it was important to know about their religion.

"And there are other important differences," Gottfried was saying. "Our own Lutheran Christianity, we believe, Shulamith, is more like the way of Jesus Christ himself, without all the superstitions and primitive ceremonies that the Catholic church has added to it."

She made a schoolgirl nod. Their principal belief, he said, was that God sent to mankind his own son, the Messiah, but mankind was not then ready to give up sin, and this son, Jesus—"

"Yoshua," she said. "Yehoshua is a Hebrew name."

"Yoshua took into himself the sins of all mankind, and

suffered and died on the Roman cross to expiate those sins so that man could be cleansed and saved and again come into the realm of God—"

She concentrated, but could not quite understand this. He continued, "At the time of Judgment, Messiah will be sent down to us again—".

"Our religious people also believe Mashiach will still come," she said, to find another point of agreement. "In the pogroms all the religious Jews cry out to God, send us Mashiach already!"

He nodded, and became even more serious. "But you see, for you, Messias is only to help the Jews, and for us, he is for all mankind, the whole world."

This startled her; for an instant she was taken aback, for surely the Messiah should be for the whole world, for all mankind. "Isn't he only for the Christians?" she asked and saw in his face that now in his turn he was a bit taken aback. With this, her spirit returned to her, the little teasing touch was back in her voice, the secure knowledge of a woman that one could always bring boys—no, men—down from their lofty superiority.

Gottfried had responded with a soft appreciative laugh. "Touché!" he said. From reading somewhere, perhaps in a Russian novel, she recognized the French word, and joined his soft laugh, feeling victorious, and glad that they had somehow emerged from the most dangerous ground—religion.

Others from the excursion were coming toward them, led by a long-robed monk who must be the guide to the ruins; he was conversing with the melamed, who kept his head cocked in the pose of watchful but unprejudiced attention. Malka gave Shula a quick, gobbling smirk; Malka would be sure to ask if he had kissed her. At least Leah had no questions in her smile and only said they had missed a very interesting lecture.

Now Shula's nights were invaded by the sweet, insatiable longing. It had come. The girlish longings she had known before had been but a longing for this longing. Before, when she had touched her breast and her secret woman's chamber, it had always been with a defiant declaration to herself that this was only natural, but now she felt a tremble of shame, for now it was with the image of his face lying over her. And even worse, a certain curiosity grew, and though she could still manage to mock herself over it, the question would not depart from her mind. It was to know exactly what a man's thing looked like uncircumcised. —Oy, Shula, she would mock herself, this proves it isn't really love, only wantonness. But the curiosity would not go away.

She did not even know quite fully what a Jewish one looked like. Of course when Mati was a baby, and with Dvoraleh's babies—But after they grew? A few times she had inadvertently caught glimpses of Schmulik's, and of Gidon's before he had moved out of the boys' side of the room to his hut. Indeed, she had once even glimpsed it big, just as she awakened, and Gidon had rushed out and she believed that was why he had moved. Now even Schmulik was careful in dressing and undressing. On Dvoraleh's new baby, Giora, she had once, when the communa had agreed that Dvoraleh could bring the babies on a visit, seen his tiny penis standing upright, and Mama and Dvoraleh had given a special kind of laugh. But how was it on a grown man, when it became swollen and strong? This she never had seen. Even in the art book of famous sculptures that Leah had brought from Jerusalem, it wasn't shown this way but soft-looking and like asleep. In Reuven's kvutsa, boys and girls were being raised to be much more natural and unashamed before each other; perhaps when they grew up, it would be better, because hungers like this should not be allowed to influence a choice of love. Yet she wanted, she needed to know. It haunted her. In animals—the sight of it coming out of a horse put Shula in such confusion that she would hurry away. But after all in a man it did not come out of hiding like that, it was always there on his outside. But—she dared to think further—when in a man it suddenly swelled and lengthened—she even wanted to ask a man, was it painful?

—Poor dear Leah. Now Shula felt she understood the terrible longing that Leah must be suffering every night, all these years, for her man. Could the longing be even worse after you had once begun with the man?

An awful part of her curiosity and longing was a desire in her very fingers to touch that part of a man, to know just what that hardness was that came into it. Almost—so friendly was she with poor Nahum, that she even had a fantasy—almost she could ask him. As a true complete comrade. Simply to help her understand. He would sit quietly like an artist's model, and like an artist she would gaze calmly and study it, perhaps she would even touch it, just to know. This would be a protection for her, even against her own curiosity, so she would not do anything foolish as so many girls did merely because of curiosity and ignorance. But if she were to see Nahum's, it would still be only a Jewish one, a circumcised one. Shula dared not let herself try to imagine touching the other.

In the midst of the day, in the kitchen, in the yard, Shula would suddenly feel her dreamy spells coming over her and find herself seeing the sun-gilded tips of the little hairs on the back of her Gottfried's wrists.

Already Feigel had noticed, and worried, but she did not yet feel the time had come to speak.

In parting, the Jewish girls delivered safely home from the excursion, he had held her hand overlong. He must see her again, Gottfried had said, his eyes devouring her as though this need to see her was an actual hunger. And with an intimate pressure on her palm he had added, "Soon, my Shulamith." Then his head dipped in a knightly manner as he once again gave her hand a cavaliery kiss. For a fleeting instant she had been frightened because of that hungry gaze, even wary, but this must be a part of feminine nature before there came the fullness of love and trust. The fear vanished when he kissed her hand.

And now the flying officers in their turn invited the young ladies to a celebration at their quarters in Gilboa. Several notables too were invited, with their wives—not only Issachar Bronescu but Yonah Kolodnitzer, the mukhtar of Yavniel, as well. Since Mishkan Yaacov was the furthest away, it was suggested that their contingent remain overnight at the camp. As it was really in Dvora's communa, what harm could there be in this?

Yet one of the Roumanian mothers this time held back her daughter, and Feigel also mumbled. Yankel was away; again the Turks had commandeered him with his mules and wagon to haul things far down in Beersheba; perhaps if he were here, he would forbid his daughter to see so much of the Germans. Still, Leah would go as well, and it would be a visit to Dvoraleh and Menahem, who had been replaced here by another shomer. Since Nadina and Galil had been sent into exile, who knew where deep in Turkey, Menahem was needed in the leadership in Gilboa.

And Leah wanted to go there to hear—big problems were to be settled in Gilboa. The contract for guarding the fields of Chedera had been lost. The farmers could not pay; every week the Turks wrested new taxes out of them and also they had had to buy their sons out from labor conscription. Now those young men had revived their own secret society, the Sons of Nimrod, to rival the Shomer. They were not so much riding out on watch, but more like the old Bar Giora from the beginning, they were going to be like chieftains of Zion and who even knew what. The last time Leah had seen Menahem, he had laughed about them. The leader was a young poet, Avshalom Feinberg, son of that early settler from Rehovot who had first got the Baron to help the Yishuv. With the start of the war, this Avshalom had returned from Paris, and now he spent his days galloping around like an Arab sheikh. He was thick with the Aaronsons of Zichron—both daughters were said to be in love with him; their younger brother was one of the first in the Sons of Nimrod. Of course these fine guardsmen were hiring Arabs. The elders of the town had offered to keep a few of the Shomer's men to watch their orange groves, using the Arabs only to guard the eucalyptus forest. But in outrage the Shomer had withdrawn all ten of its men. Let the Turks cut down their groves for locomotive fuel! Let the Chedera farmers learn their lesson all over again!

In the south too, a few contracts had been lost; Zev the Hotblood had got together a band of watchmen in Ruhama and they worked for less than the Shomer. As always in troubled times, the organization itself was strained with inner disputes. Since Nadina and Galil were gone, the quiet Shimshoni had risen to leadership, alongside Shabbatai Zeira, and each had different principles. Zeira believed their task was guarding, and nothing else. For this his brother had died. Shimshoni, with his small, stony half-bald head and his narrowed skeptical eyes, was a close follower of Nadina and Galil, a social idealist still imbued with the mission to "conquer the soil," to bring ever new areas under cultivation, while also building up the ideal of the communa. The Shomer's men must be guardsmen but not guardsmen alone. Shimshoni was one of those who had pressed for the settlement at Gilboa, and now he pressed for newer settlements. For what was their aim, their higher purpose? Not merely to watch for thieves in the fields. It was twofold: to be prepared to protect the whole Yishuv, and always to pioneer new land. Shimshoni's plan just now was to take a group up north, to the high hills touching on Lebanon; there the Keren Kayemeth was buying a hilltop, and they would become the settlers. There, as Shimshoni pictured it, they would raise herds of sheep and cattle. This was the sort of man he was, something like Reuven, loving peace and solitude though he was one of the bravest of the guardsmen.

Menahem too was drawn to the idea of the new settlement, even in the midst of war—a deed of construction. Had it not been, long ago at Sejera, a dream of his closest comrade Yechezkiel, Dvora's Yechezkiel? From up there, near Mount Hermon, they could work as watchmen for the Baron's early settlements of Rosh Pina and Metulla; they could guard the whole north, and meanwhile build their own place. Yet could he take Dvoraleh and the babies up there, to live in tents again, and without a children's house? Nor did the members of Gilboa want to lose Dvoraleh, who was their expert on egg incubation. All this was what was to be decided, and Leah was eager to be there.

As the military motorcar arrived in Mishkan Yaacov for them, Gottfried himself was driving, and while the sisters got ready, he allowed Mati to sit with his hands on the steering wheel. Twice, Shula changed the headscarf she would wear for the ride, and in the last moment flew back to change it again.

First Gottfried complimented Leah on her flowing white gown, and then he made a sweeping, cavalier's bow before Shula, who wore a long velvet dress with lace ruffles at the wrists and throat that Feigel had brought out from among her rarely worn finery from Russia. Nu, even when a mother was dubious about what was happening to her daughter, she yet wanted to dress her in the most beautiful way. Admiring her, Gottfried remarked, "But won't you be very warm?" "What won't a girl suffer for her vanity!"

Shula sparked, and they were off. He sat her next to him; when the back of the motorcar became crowded with the whole Bronescu family, Leah also moved to the front seat, pressing them closer together.

It was Leah who did most of the talking, in a German even more Yiddish than Shula's. Gottfried expressed great curiosity about Gilboa itself; even though quartered there, he and his friends had learned little about the ways of a communa. He himself, he said, had socialist convictions, and presently Leah was explaining to him the looming question about a part of the group going to settle up north.

"I hope it is not because we are driving them out?"

"Not that at all!" she explained. "But among us it is a principle that as soon as one place is settled we should bring life to a new wilderness." And so at Gilboa there were those who had fallen in love with a far hilltop where the melted snows from Mount Hermon made a waterfall.

"Ah, yes, I have seen it! Beautiful!"—From his airplane. Nothing in the land was unknown to him. The Germans with their thoroughness!—Ah what an ideal pastoral life it would be, Gottfried said, in a place of such great natural beauty. He too was a romantic. He could even see himself remaining here after the war, to lead such an ideal life. And when he turned to smile intimately at Shula, Leah knew that this whole thing might become very difficult.

How quickly the motorcar had covered the distance that took more than half a day in the wagon! After the war, automobiles would come, the settlements would be joined by roads, and help could come from one place to another in no time at all!

As they arrived in the Gilboa yard, Leah experienced an odd sense of error, as when one knocks on a familiar door and a stranger appears. All was inordinately neat, as though the very ground had been brushed, and there was a gravel walk to the dining hall but—grotesquely—there was a flying squadron flag over the entrance, and a German flag flew from the roof.

"Perhaps the young ladies would care to freshen themselves?" Gottfried said, and led them again on a new gravel path to the dwelling cottages—past Dvora and Menahem's room, where an officer sat on the porch, reading. Of course she had known that the cottages were taken over, while the members of Gilboa lived in the barn and in various sheds. On the far side of the yard she could see a row of tents, the same tents that she had helped pitch on the day of the founding of Gilboa and that long before had been taken down. The chevreh were back in their tents, but at least, she knew, it helped their strained financial situation that the Germans were paying for their lodgings. Only the children's house had been left to the communa. Never mind. Let this but be the worst of the suffering brought by the war.

Leading them to what had been Nadina and Galili's chamber, Gottfried opened the door and stepped aside for Leah and Shula to enter. The furnishing was the same, even to the Arab water jugs and bits of ancient mosaics that Nadina and Galil had carried back from a walking trip to Caesarea. But yet the atmosphere of the room was entirely changed. Another officer, Gottfried's roommate, his arms filled with shirts and mannish belongings, formally inclined his head, acknowledging Gottfried's introductions.

"But we are driving you out of your room," Shula protested charmingly, and it seemed to Leah that her silly sister didn't even realize the irony of her remark.

"Please!" Gottfried had the grace to say. "It is we who have driven out your own people. I assure you we would have been quite satisfied in the tents, after all, we are soldiers, but this had already been arranged. At least for tonight you must take back your home. I assure you we shall make ourselves quite comfortable, don't fear." And with a gallant smile to Shula, "I will give you only a few minutes out of my sight." He looked at his watch, a fine instrument with additional small hands and complicated markings that Mati had marveled at. "A quarter of an hour?"

"Twenty minutes," Shula said.

"Not a moment more. Remember, we aviators are exact!" And he left them.

It was clear which was his bed, for beside it stood a photograph of his parents, the father resembling him. And even in middle age, how handsome a man!

Gottfried had, perhaps quite unthinkingly, set down Shula's little valise on his own bed.

Again, Leah glanced at her young sister.

Choking hot in that closed-up dress—perhaps in the evening it would at least become bearable—fatigued from the pounding ride and the tension of sitting so close to him, Shula wanted only to strip off the gown and lie down for a while. Leah had already taken off the blouse and was sponging herself at the basin. Latching the door, Shula started to undo the torturesome gown when there was a knock. "Please. I forgot something." It was he. Only putting a towel around her shoulders, Leah went to the door; her huge breasts against her camisole had left large damp circles. Before Shula could say anything, she had let him in. Gottfried went straight to his night table, slipped a little book into his pocket and was marching out. "Military secrets?" Shula had recovered her spirit.

"My diary," Gottfried blurted, surprisingly blushing.

"Love secrets, then!" she said.

He blushed even more strongly, with an effort at lightness blurted "Touché!" added confusedly, "Please forgive the intrusion," and rushed out.

Leah re-hooked the door. "How could you display yourself like that!" Shula snapped. Her big sister let out a roar of laughter. "It's not my bosom he's aching to behold!" But at last the tension between them was lifted. Shula pulled her gown over her head, letting out her breath with relief, and took the sponge. There was even cologne on the stand. Imagine, these German men! She used a bit, feeling naughtily intimate, and offered the bottle to Leah, who sniffed it and laughed. Luxuries.

In her petticoat, Shula stretched out on his bed. On the same little side-table lay a German Bible, and also, to her surprise, a Hebrew language book. Leah had already dressed and was going; she couldn't wait to see Dvora and also to run to the children's house to see Giora and Yechezkiel, and find out how Nadina's little Buba was faring. "Are you coming?"

"Go ahead, I'll come in a moment." An impulse had suddenly come over Shula; what would it feel like to be alone in his room as though waiting for him?

Opening his Hebrew exercise-book she saw his writing, filling in the lessons. It looked even and methodical. Handwriting was something a person couldn't disguise. Malka Bronescu pretended that she could read character from handwriting. Perhaps when Gottfried wrote her letters, she

would show Malka his writing—where the words were not
too private.

This time he did not let her leave his arms, laughingly
refusing her to his fellow officers except for his commander
and once for a dance with his roommate. Circling and circling in the waltz with Gottfried, she felt hypnotized. Sometimes she caught sight of Leah, who had made quite an
impression on the commander, and floated evenly by, like
a queenly ship at sea.

At one time, when the music halted, Gottfried led Shula
outdoors and upward on the slope of Gilboa, to where the
young pine forest began. A soft wind touched her cheeks
like the brushing of the tender feathery branches when she
looked up to the sky, that clear sky of Eretz over which all
the diamonds of creation had been flung. Just like the scattered diamonds on a blue velvet pad she had once seen in a
jeweler's shop—where could she have seen such luxury?
Not in Tiberias—there, you only saw at best bits of amber
and silver ornaments for Christian tourists. Then Shula remembered; far back when they had started on their journey
and come as far as Odessa to take ship, she had followed
her father and mother into a jeweler's shop where Tateh
intended to buy, for his wife's keeping, something they had
much spoken of, a "diamondl." In long discussions in
Cherezinka after Mameh had sewed the gold coins into Tateh's money-belt, the parents had decided on buying a "diamondl" as their last resource, a diamondl which Mameh
was to hold in case "anything should happen" on the peril-
ous journey, or in case starvation should beset them in Eretz, or again, in case a Jew had to flee with his family. On
a blue velvet pad the jeweler—a good Jew who, having
been recommended by their rich uncle, was sure not to
take advantage and sell them a piece of glass as he might to
a moujik—had then spread his diamonds. This, Shulamith
now saw in the sky. Tateh had only been able to buy a very
small stone, and it had been set in a brooch with tiny seed
pearls around it. How many times—such as the time when
all the cattle had been stolen from the village—had she
heard worried discussion between Tateh and Mameh, "Perhaps now we should sell the diamondl?" But it had always
seemed that there might yet come a greater disaster for a
Jew, though Shula also suspected, with a sudden perception

of Mamaleh's femininity, that her mother could not bear to part with her diamond brooch. That last time, Tateh had been loaned money by Reb Bagelmacher, who had even refused to take the diamondl as a pledge.

Why had all this memory come to her now, Shula wondered, and just then she felt again the feathery brushing upon her cheek, not the touch of the delicately wafted pine branches but of Gottfried's lips. And then on her mouth. It was a very tender kiss, and it gave her a great relief that it did not arouse her, not even the way the kisses of one or two of the boys in the village had done, boys she had quickly had to forbid. It was more like Nahum's at a kissing game that Malka had introduced when she gave a birthday party at her house.

And again Gottfried began to talk of religion! Yet it was true, the sky like this and the shadowy earth made you feel the mystery of God.

"Thus it must have looked to the Hebrews of old," he said, "to your Ur-father Abraham," he said, while she wondered what kind of an educated word that was, Ur-father? "In a place like this," Gottfried went on, "one can almost feel God speaking, as men in olden days felt or heard God's words. One believes."

His arm was around her. But as it was permitted in dancing with a man, why should this be different?

Beyond, across the flat Emek, the darkness of the earth swelled upward in the outline of a full breast perfectly rounded, and just then in the night sky a band of mist floated over it, like a thin batiste gown rising as a woman breathed; it made Shula think of Leah's breast when her big sister lay sleeping in their room at home.

"Tabor," Gottfried said quietly, in the voice of a lover careful not to disturb a beloved's mood. Then he said, as one quoting, "And the poor shall inherit the earth!" It must be from the words of their Yoshka, somewhere she had read it, and indeed Gottfried now added, "Tabor is believed to be the place of your Rabbi Yehoshua's Sermon on the Mount."

"I know," she replied. "You have a monastery on the top. For us it is the place of the song of Dvora the prophetess. My sister is named after her."

"A song of war," he said, but not ironically, and he began to speak of all the wars there had been on the plain before them, the Assyrians and the Crusaders and the Saracens and the ancient Philistines against King Saul; even Napoleon had marched here, "and you know it is prophesied that the fate of the world will be decided in a terrible battle that will take place here, the Armageddon."

Shula drew in her breath. Perhaps that final, enormous conflict was coming now, and she could see Gottfried in his airplane, no, not falling, not shot down wounded, she would not permit such false visions. "You remind me of my brother Reuven," she said to avoid those thoughts. "I remember when we first came on the way to the Galilee in a wagon, as we passed here, Reuven gave us the same lecture about all the wars. But you know, he hates wars, he is a pacifist," she added.

"You would not believe it, but I too hate war," Gottfried said, adding that he should like to meet her brother Reuven, he sounded remarkable.

"Oh, he is," and Shula wondered what attitude Reuven would take about what was perhaps happening to her? No, Reuven would be broad-minded and understanding.

Now Gottfried said, but not in a flirting way, that he was glad he had come to this land. When he had learned that a squadron was to be sent to Palestine, he had even prayed that it would be his own, for he had sensed that in the Holy Land was destiny. And he held her shoulders closely.

"Do you really believe your God answers your prayers?" she asked.

"Our God?"

"Jesus." Saying the name was a little strange.

Gottfried became reflective. "No, not exactly. You see, I don't believe a person or a spirit sits up there listening to every human request. That is one of our differences with Catholics, who believe in a more personal way, even in all sorts of saints as well as Jesus and Mary, and pray to them by name. But perhaps in a very great crisis something of our own spirit breaks through and in some way reaches a universal spirit—that is to me the Christ."

They were silent. Her heart was beating violently.

Shula made a slight move to go back, but as though desperate to hold her, to bridge the gap that his last words might have made between them, Gottfried said, "It was there on the Mount that Christ repeated the words Moses said on Mount Sinai, Love Thy Neighbor."

—He had really studied the Bible, she remarked.

—Did she know, he said, that it was Luther who translated the Bible into German so that all could read it for themselves? Because to the Catholics it was a forbidden book.

"No, I didn't know." Shula was really surprised. How ignorant she was of things after all important in a world ruled by the Christians. Perhaps then, their Protestants were coming closer to an understanding of the Jews, and one day there might even cease to be anti-Semites.

—Yes, he said. When you took away the superstitions, all the great religions had the same truth. They sought the goodness of man, in a union with God. And here in this land one really felt in some mystical way that it must happen, perhaps even now through the return of the Jews. He hoped after the war was won his country would administer this land, and help to bring this about; he would even like to remain here and take part, he could think of nothing more important in life, and he was entirely in favor of Zionism.

Shula gazed up into his face. Why had Gottfried declared this to her? Her limbs were trembling, but it was an inner trembling that a man perhaps would not detect even though he had his arm around her. She must go back now, she said, the girls would begin to talk about her. "You know how silly girls are," and before going they moved very closely together as one being, and the trembling rose all through her. "Dear one," he whispered. But then while clambering down, Gottfried had to take his arm from around her and she felt more calm; the danger that he had perhaps not even known about in her had passed for the time being.

When he opened the door to the room for them and bade them sleep well, Shula saw that the bedcovers were off and that the sheets had been turned back by his Arab, and for an instant she had a silly impulse to ask Leah to change beds. But when she was lying in his sheets (though it was certain that the servant had placed fresh ones) she would deny herself a daring, delicious moment of snuggling down, with her cheek on his pillow, as though turned to a husband for a good-night kiss. And the imagined kiss swept her blood, for in bed that was surely how things began.

Shula turned her face upward and lay rigid, forbidding herself. Excited, she could not hope to sleep. Then Shula was aware that her big sister too was wakeful in the dark. Shula wanted to speak. On her lips were the beginning words, Leah, are you awake? But a tumult was in her mind as to just what should follow.

Then she heard Leah's voice, "Shulaleh, you can't sleep?"

And the words that tumbled out in anguish, different from anything she had expected to say, were, "Oh, Leah, now I know how terrible it must be for you. And it doesn't go away, as people say, does it? Year after year I see that it remains in you."

After a long moment, Leah's voice came, not offended, not hurt, and even with a touch of humor within its warmth. "No, Shulaleh. At another sufferer I can't be offended. Only you don't know, may you never really know how terrible it is. And I only want to help you, so you should never know. So it won't be for you like for me. Or even worse."

At this, Shula's tears began, and even in the dark Leah knew it, though the sobs were stifled in the pretty one's throat.

"Has it really become serious, Shulaleh?" the big sister asked, and only then, to answer her, the sob broke out. "I know this sounds like old-fashioned advice," Leah said, "but perhaps the best thing is to stop it now, and not see him again."

"And you? Would you have taken such advice?"

"But he believed in everything I believe in," Leah said. "We might have had a life together here." And in her unended words it was as though she could not stop believing that that life might still come.

Shula said, "He thinks of remaining here."

"What!"

"He loves this land, Leah. This is sincere. And when the war is over, Germany would help the Jews to develop the land, and he wants to stay and be in the administration. He thinks there is nothing more important in life." She sucked in her breath, sharply, perhaps she had said too much even to Leah.

"All this he told you?" Leah did not even add, What if Germany should lose the war? Her mind was striving, searching—what did the man really mean? And if perhaps he was truly in love with Shulamith? That too had to be given consideration. Men, too, sometimes changed their lives for love.

A Christian. The cry from forever rose in her, "It will kill Tateh," but to this there was also a reply. It did not kill them. It deadened the hearts of such fathers toward their daughters, it was true, and could even deaden their hearts altogether, and yet in life, if a love of this kind happened to a girl, wasn't it more of a sin and even a greater imposition of suffering to destroy the daughter's love, to make her give it up for the sake of the father and mother, when it was she herself who would have so many more years to suffer? And even not counting the heartbreak of the man in the case!

And indeed on principle, Leah demanded of herself, since she was a freethinker and believed in all freedoms, could she rule out intermarriage? But if they were to intermarry with Christians, why had they come to Eretz? How devilish was the Master of Life, if indeed such there were. Against each thing you believed in was set another thing you also believed in. Almost at this moment she grasped what it was that her Moshe had tried to expound when he and Rahel argued over a rule called dialectics. A rule from Karl Marx. But a rule from philosophy—did it help you solve what was in a girl's heart, did it help you to help your young sister?

Leah tried to reach for wisdom, wisdom from somewhere, from her people, Jewish wisdom. Her father would remind her now, that there was the evil urge and the good urge, yatzer ha-rah, and yatzer ha-tov. Whatever had to do with sexual impulses was the evil urge to them, the pious. And love? Wasn't love on the side of goodness, of generosity, of giving oneself? Was the truth not rather that both were mingled, each always within the other, instead of at opposite poles so that you were drawn first by one, then by the other? Then where was wisdom? And was a woman's urge different from a man's? For all that Rahel insisted that men and women had the same needs, was the urge truly the same?

But she was racing far ahead. Perhaps, too, her worry would prove needless, perhaps this was only an infatuation of Shula's that would pass by itself. The real question was to know the man. And she must not be against him automatically, Leah told herself, merely because he brought with him such a disturbing problem.

Indeed, she asked herself, was she not already prejudiced against him because from the first some warning had arisen in her to be wary of the handsome German?

Yes, another Handsome One.

And then, into Leah's harried thoughts, came the voice of the pretty one. "Don't worry about me, Leah," Shula said from the other bed. "One thing you can be satisfied I learned, thanks to you—I won't do anything—with a man—unless I am married."

Leah could have leaped up and slapped her. Now it was to her own eyes that tears came. How could it be that no one, not even her own snit of a sister, understood? Almost, she could wish to let the girl get caught in the same torment, and suffer.

Meanwhile, Shula, to her own surprise, had slipped into a tender untroubled sleep.

Now came the phase of meetings in secret. Either it was only an infatuation or it was love, and until she was certain, she had to see him. And until she was certain, Shula told herself, there was no cause to bring torment to her mother and father. As yet, they need know nothing.

It was not easy for a girl in the house to absent herself, and particularly in these times when the roads were filled with soldiers, and mothers were more than ever watchful of their daughters. Leah wasn't at the house; again she had gone off to Tel Aviv to her friend Rahel to some mysterious work that fell on them now that Avner and Dovidl were away. No one was home to help Mameh in the house but herself. Then, as though heaven were conspiring, Yaffaleh just now came into her womanhood; her period was painful to her, and it was Shula who led the flock of geese down to the river. There Gottfried met her, and this time the kisses were passionate.

Under a certain stone, they arranged to leave messages, and again heaven conspired, bringing Gottfried nearer so they could have more opportunity to be together. For there was doubled and tripled military activity now at the Samekh station, and even while Abba had not yet returned with the wagon from serving them in the south, a Turkish officer came demanding the second pair of mules, to labor at Samekh. Unless Schmulik went with the animals, who knew if they would ever be returned, and in any case what work could he do at home without them? So he went, each dawn, and while he insisted he wanted nothing more than bread and cheese, Feigel each day prepared a whole cooked meal for him with a canister of tea, and Shula would take it, riding to the station on a donkey, insisting to her mother that in midmorning the road was so busy there was no danger for her.

There at the station, Gottfried managed to be, searching for crates of airplane parts, or loading munitions onto an Arab camel train, shouting and laughing at them, "Yallah! Imshi!" And when she was on her way back, he would already be waiting at their trysting place by the river.

They were seen—how could they not be seen?—by that same Bedouin boy with his goats; and at another time a shomer passed close by, but he could not have been certain the girl was Shula. Yet, a word here and a whisper there, until Malka Bronescu one day demanded, "Why do you keep secrets from me? Tell, or I will tell."

<hr />

Never before had Leah felt so close to Rahel, truly as though they were like their namesakes, the daughters of Laban. And if they did not have the same Jacob for a husband, Rahel ruefully jested, here they were, a Leah and Rahel with the same no-husband. Both their men were in exile, and who knew when and if they would return.

Only for those few harried months here, after their long separation while they studied in different countries, she in France and he in Turkey, had Rahel and Avner been reunited, and now Rahel turned more closely to Leah as if to know what happened in a woman, what would happen in herself, when every contact, even a letter, was cut off, and perhaps long years lay ahead, and a woman did not even know what might be happening to her man.

They did not speak so much of what was in their hearts, but it was simply this—this being with someone who was in the same situation so that one need not even explain

oneself, so that one always felt understood without words—
that helped.

For the moment, Rahel was living with her family in a
small house in Tel Aviv that belonged to friends who had
fled to Alexandria. Rahel's father had suddenly decided he
would at least try to grow their own food. In Jerusalem her
father had attempted to engage in his old business of paper
supply, but with the war this had failed and the man didn't
know what to do. Somewhat he reminded Leah of her own
tateh, except that he was not so strictly observant, and also
he was more of an educated man, a little higher in the scale
of worldly life. But one day he had bought a watering can
and a mattock, and marked off with a string a plot of land
in the sands behind the house. With her French diploma as
an agronome, Rahel decided she must test the soil for him
and spent an entire day going to Professor Volkansky's agricultural station in Ben Shemen to borrow a soil-bore; the
next day she carried back the samples and borrowed the
use of a laboratory to make her analysis. Meanwhile the
father lugged can after can of water out to his tract. At one
glance Leah saw the water was seeping away, but at least
let them try to grow what might grow here, and each
morning she labored planting cucumbers and carrots, and
pulling out the choking weed called yablit. Rahel helped.
The few early hours were most sisterly, but soon Rahel
would run off to her thousand projects and committees. She
was planning to bring out the journal again, underground,
and she was holding meetings with the Herzlia Gymnasia
group, those who had not joined the Turks to become officers; with them and some men from the Shomer, she
planned self-defense units.

For with each day there came more hallucinating tales of
the massacre of the Armenians in Anatolia, and each day
brought threats from Bahad-ad-Din to do with the Jews as
with the Armenians. Now he had begun to arrest the leaders of the Jewish community, even Dr. Lubin himself,
though Lubin was a German. It was said he would be sent
into exile in Turkey like Nadina and Galil. How would
Shimshoni's new settlement in the north be set up, without
Lubin's help? And in the midst of all there was growing
unemployment. In Jaffa there was starvation. Soup kitchens
had been opened, and Arab children appeared. No, you
could not send them away. And, as always, the worst was

the women's problem. Every day, more chaluzoth appeared
at the party's labor exchange, seeking work. Rahel was
having a special meeting on this problem with Mayor Dizingoff's emergency relief committee. But now there developed a new aspect of this problem. In Jerusalem, in Mea
Shearim, a Bokharian girl had been found chained in the
house because her father had seen her walking with a German officer. From the southern settlements, too, where soldiers were encamped for a new attack on the Suez, there
came awful tales, though about Arab girls. A girl of a good
Arab family had been killed with a knife by her brother for
consorting with the foreigners. And, Rahel told Leah, the
German officers kept seeking acquaintanceship in the Jewish settlements, because, they said, they were lonesome for
civilization. They heard the sound of a piano and knocked
on the door. They longed simply to engage in conversation,
to hear a woman's voice. With Jewish women, they said,
they could at least converse.

Leah sucked in her lip; of such things she already knew
too well. And that night after they had lain down, for Rahel had insisted Leah share her room, she talked and talked
with Rahel of her problem with Shulamith. Rahel pondered
the problem. "We cannot be like our older generation, opposed merely because of religion," Rahel said. Nor on principle could an enlightened person object on the ground of
race. The whole idea of their movement was positive rather
than negative, a creative building up of the Jewish self, so
that it would preserve itself without fear of the outside
world when a few dropped away, rather than have preservation maintained through fear and forbiddance. And over
and over came that phrase, "in principle"; in principle this,
and in principle that, until Leah began to imagine that Rahel would bring up the whole question of Shula at a committee meeting.

From the time of Solomon, Rahel pointed out, there had
been intermarriage, and even such a profound modern
scholar of Judaism as Martin Buber (Leah concealed the
fact that in her ignorance she did not know who he was)
was married to a Christian woman—though in this case his
wife had adopted the Jewish faith. "You know, that is a
point that would be interesting to study statistically," Rahel
digressed. "Whether when a Jew and Christian marry, the
woman is more likely to follow the man, or the man the

woman? I don't think the study has ever been done!" And
Leah had the impression her friend would leap from her
cot and hurry right off to try to find a book on the subject.

"You know," she said to Rahel, "he talks to Shula about
staying in Eretz and helping build the land. Perhaps, if he
is really sincere . . ." That was the first thing to be determined, if a man was really sincere.

The word jumped across the room, back and forth. Sincerity, yes, that was the question, the test. In everything.
They had arrived at the same point.

Leah fell silent and let Rahel sleep.

Then in the silence the ancient gnawing resumed in
Leah. Sincerity. And had not Moshe been sincere?

Once more Rahel said they must return to Gilboa. She
must consult with the Shomer about joining forces with the
self-defense committee of Tel Aviv. Some of the Tel Aviv
boys were excellent. On graduating from the Herzlia Gymnasia, two had even spent a season working in a kvutsa.
Though they were sons of businessmen and had only vague
ideas about creating "the just society," they could be won
over to the proletarian view. Meanwhile, she must make
contact with Nadina's printer in Safed for the journal, an
aged Reb who would never be suspected. Did Leah know
that the very first printing press in the Holy Land had been
brought to Safed in 1682? Perhaps this was even the same
one!

In all this, Leah felt, there was flight. Rahel seemed always to need to change her life, to hurry from one group to
another, to run away, to hide. Perhaps she even feared that
with Avner away, life might bring her too close to another
man if she remained in one circle, in one place? It was a
need Leah herself kept feeling, to run from one place to
another, only with herself it was perhaps the opposite, that
she had to move about because she was seeking for something to happen to her, rather than running away from it.

In Gilboa, Menahem too had brought home a tale. Did
Leah remember the Yemenite girl, Yael, the daughter of
Abadiya the shochet? —The girl who had shown her the
Yemenite dances? Leah asked. The same one. Exactly
how it took place and exactly what took place, no one
knew, but the girl, tempted to take a ride, had gotten into

one of the German automobiles. Yael swore by her life it was nothing more, but she had been seen, and when she came home, her father had whipped her across the face with leather thongs and all but blinded her. Yael had run away from home and was recognized in Tiberias working as a cleaning woman in the German hotel. Weeping, she vowed that she was innocent, untouched, but she would not return home lest her father kill her, he would slit her throat with his shochet's knife. And now she was to be seen in the cafes, defiantly and openly, sitting with officers and laughing.

—She wasn't the only one, Dvoraleh remarked.

—No, Menahem agreed, in Tiberias it was becoming a problem. The pious who lived on collection money from abroad were completely without means, starving, and their daughters had taken to loitering by the seashore restaurants.

Though it was not the same, in no way the same, from Yael it was not far to the problem of Shula.

Was the German sincere? Leah repeated to Menahem and Dvoraleh, that was the real question; perhaps here in Gilboa something more could be known of him.

"What can we know of them?" Dvoraleh said. "They stay in their world, we in ours." Then she added, "I believe he is meeting Shula in secret. He goes every day to Samekh." Perhaps from the word *secret* something came to Leah. That moment when the German had hurried back into his room to remove his diary. "Love secrets," had been said, in jest, and his face had reddened.

It was a shameful thing from which she shrank, and yet—if it were to save her sister? From the diary they might learn the truth of the man. Perhaps it would even point the other way, to sincerity and goodness and a true love. Or perhaps—and she already saw her vain little sister seduced, abandoned, sitting at a cafe in Tiberias.

"You know he told Shula he wants to remain here after the war. Suppose it's true. Suppose he is sincere and they should want to get married?" Leah found herself arguing.

Menahem stared at her, brooding. "True. It might possibly be love. But does a man himself know how much is true of what he says to influence a woman?" He was gazing at Leah so that she knew he was thinking about herself and Moshe; his eyes were full of compassion.

Hesitantly, so that she could draw back by treating it only as a joke, Leah said, "Perhaps he writes down the real truth in his diary." And she told in what embarrassment the aviator had snatched his "love secrets" out of the room.

So quickly did Menahem seize on her hesitant thought, that Leah herself was taken aback. Why not? he said. They ought to have a look into that diary. If Dvora and Leah felt that the fate of their sister was involved, why not have a look?

He became practical. The diary must not be taken out of the room but looked at on the spot. Gilboa's own women did the cleaning. Dvora might go in——But no, Dvora protested, she wouldn't be able to read a word of German.

—Rahel? Menahem asked Leah.

Instinctively Leah felt that Rahel would not do it. She would raise all kinds of principles about a person's private life, spying—

Menahem's dark look passed across his eyes. "Never mind, don't even trouble her." Perhaps, Leah said, she herself would be able to make something out. Their alphabet she could read. And German words she might make out from Yiddish.

With a kerchief over her head, and a pail and rags, Leah entered the room the next morning after the officers had gone off. The little book in its soft red-leather cover lay in its place. If he left it there so openly, surely it was not so secret, the other man must feel free to look into it. She could imagine the two of them sitting and talking about their conquests, their seductions. A touch of nausea came to her because of the way men are. Thoughts arose of the time she and Moshe had lain softly rocking in the bottom of the small boat on the Kinnereth, and again of that first time in the goren. Had those times not been sacred? And could it be——in some hut in Siberia, to a comrade in exile, or even to his woman there, that Moshe might be——She was trembling. Resolutely Leah opened the little book.

The handwriting was neat, like a good schoolboy's, and many of the words she could understand. She had opened it near the back, automatically, as one opened a Hebrew book, and almost at once she saw her sister's name. Her heart bounded in a leap of fear and shame, and yet she read on. By sheer force of her need, she managed to understand nearly all that was written.

"Is it really love this time?" he asked himself. Then came some words she did not know for certain, there was something long, poetic, the word kiss, Leah felt she mustn't read on— What was she seeking exactly? And then her eyes picked up a name—Genevieve. "Not really the same as with Genevieve—" It would be here.—Her sister's entire life. If she could only absorb the whole book in one glance, only know the meaning of certain words that were strange to her—leafing back hastily, she found the name again, Genevieve; he was in France now, he spoke of soon reaching Paris, there were other names on other pages, a Lisette for many pages, and here, a whole sentence she was sure of, "For me, the affair always has to appear serious." And then she came to an open page, like for a new chapter. He had just left France, he said, and there in the very first line, making her head pulse, were the words for which she had committed this shameful prying: "I leave France behind me with three maedchen the fewer."

Oh, why were men like that? Oh why? Leah could not stop the upsurge of tears. She didn't even know for whom, for what. Softly, as though it were some dead animal thing, she set down the diary in its place. The whole question and shame of having spied into it was gone, swept away in a sense of grief, of dismay. Oh, why wasn't she angry? "May his airplane crash into his grave!" Leah declared to herself, but even this did not help.

And how could she tell Shula? Hadn't she herself known of her Handsome Moshe that he was a seducer, hadn't Nahama even warned her "He's a heartbreaker," and had it stopped her from making a fool of herself and was she cured of him even today?

Also, she must be absolutely certain, she must ask Menahem the exact meaning of that word "Maedchen," or, perhaps better, Rahel.

The whispers about Shula Chaimovitch and the flier had come to the chubby Nahum as well by a hint from Malka Bronescu. And at once he knew which flier was meant. And it was here in his own place that Shula had first encountered the German.

Gay, excited over some aerial feat above the Sinai desert, the group of young officers appeared for the Sunday dinner that had become customary with them. Through the glassed porch, Nahum saw them approaching, that same golden-haired one in the middle of his comrades, talking animatedly, with the swooping hand-gestures of the aviators that Shulamith's little brother Mati had so quickly learned to imitate. Hurrying to the door, Nahum stopped them before they could enter. "I am sorry, there is no place for you," he said.

"But what is this! We always have our table on Sunday!" It was that same one, himself, Lieutenant Gottfried Schirmer-Hauptmann who cried out.

"We no longer can serve you here. I am sorry."

One of them laughed. Surely it was some kind of a joke. And Nahum could scarcely believe it of himself. Yet he stood erect in his doorway and barred it to them.

"Are you out of your senses? Who are you to refuse—" Another seemed about to push his way inside, and to Nahum it was as though in this instant his soul prepared itself to die. If only his mother would remain not near, and in the kitchen; at least the old man was at his shul.

Then it was the seducer himself who led his comrades away, saying, "With a Jew, one does not dispute."

When his mother remarked, how was it the German fliers had not come, Nahum only shrugged.

Early the next morning, two Turkish militiamen arrived and demanded Nahum for labor conscription. Old Bagelmacher was aghast. Had he not paid the price of a thousand francs for his son's release! But the military police stood with ears of stone for his words. Without further ado, they plunged into the pension, seized Nahum and marched him off, one on each side, his poor mother running after them into the street with a hastily snatched blanket and a feather pillow; young dolts on the street laughed, while elderly Jews stared in terror and Reb Bagelmacher ran to the Kaymakam. It was useless. He could not get to see anyone of importance. In the street, every Jew already knew all that had happened, the tales about Shula Chaimovitch, the German cry, "With a filthy Jew one does not dispute."

With his wagonload of potatoes topped by a rattan cage of poultry, Yankel drove into Bagelmacher's yard. But his old friend emerged with a countenance of thunder. "You can turn your wagon around and take it all back."

"What's happened? What is it?"

The wife came out behind the husband; glaring at Yankel, she snapped, over a sob, "He makes as if he knows nothing." And directly to Yankel, "Take your geese and your potatoes and don't come to us again."

Yankel stilled his rising anger. "What's come over you? Did I ever bring you a rotten potato?"

"Not your potatoes are rotted, but your daughter!" the woman screeched. "The harlot!"

Still something in Yankel told him not to release his anger. Binyamin Bagelmacher, his friend, was gazing at him with the deep eyes of a tzaddik who weighed every word before pronouncing judgment. "Be still," Reb Bagelmacher said to his wife. "Perhaps he really doesn't know. A father, like a husband, is the last to know." Already Yankel felt a tumult in his ears. He had had his misgivings, his fears, what with Bronescu's pandering to the Germans.

They told him. Even to the sneer uttered by the German anti-Semite, "With Jews one does not dispute."

And then they gave him the dreadful news of the conscription of Nahum. From such military labor as Nahum had been sent to by the Turks, Binyamin said in tragic sorrow beyond rancor, indeed in the torn voice of a man saying Kaddish, "From such labor, as we know, few will return alive."

Nor could Yankel at such a moment of bitterness, try to remind Binyamin Bagelmacher that his own son Reuven had nevertheless managed, even in their military labor, to be singled out for decent work in Damascus, and that surely Nahum with his cleverness—

As to Yankel's poultry and produce, there was no need for it, Bagelmacher was saying. The Germans would come here no more, nor would they be let in if they came. Yankel could take his produce and sell it in the market, even for higher prices.

The last words Yankel scarcely heard, for he had already turned the wagon and was flailing against the back of the mule the whip he should rather raise against the skin of the Germans or—as the enormity of it all came to him—on his own daughter, the one that had always so gladdened his heart, his favored one, his Eliza, no less a whore than the female offspring of that poor Yemenite, the shochet Abadiya.

The wagon swayed, crashed into potholes made by their motortrucks and their cannon, and with each lurch Yankel felt cries wrenched from him—angered and bitter reproaches against his Eliza, their Shula as he thought of her now, their Shulamith—it had all begun with that whorish name—and cries rose in his soul against his dear God, Gottenu! How could either of his loved beings fling him into such torments? With the Turks and the war, and the Turkish bandits dragging him away to break his back in the desert while the German pigs seduced his daughter, with his sons scattered in what ends of the earth who knew, and perhaps killing each other from both sides—why, why, with all his woes, did his comely one, his own favored one, have to heap these added burning coals on his head, coals of shame. "You—you—" the words burst from his mouth, he howled them out to the sky—"Harlot! With a German! An anti-Semite! A dog of a Christian!"

All the while Yankel was on his way home calling down his bitterness upon her, Shula, though she had no intuition of her father's anger, was pervaded by a guilty uneasiness. Half-hidden in Gidon's old hut of black stones, she was reading the forbidden book. It had been her own thought, with no suggestion whatever from Gottfried, that she must read the Christian Bible. Nor was she reading it with even a hind-thought, with even the remotest danger, of accepting their Christian belief. But again and again, after the intoxication of her trysts, she had asked herself, How can I fall in love with a man and yet remain ignorant of something so important in his life as religion is to Gottfried? On his side, Gottfried after all was not ignorant of the Jewish Bible. He knew each place that was written about, he had gone to visit places she had never seen, like the altar of Elijah near Haifa. In the same way he naturally also sought out places in the Christian Bible, as on their excusion to Kfar Nahum. (Why, it was Nahum's name! She never had thought of it. But what matter?) And once, when Gottfried strolled with her along the Kinnereth and they had passed a group of Arab fishermen whose nets hung drying from an ancient carob, he had remarked, "How true it seems when one walks along here, that Jesus said 'Follow me, and I will make you fishers of men.' They must have looked just like these fishermen we see here." Or again, when Gottfried told her another tale of the miracles of their prophet, Shula could understand, she could almost see for herself, how the Christians imagined their Mashiach walking on the waters of the Kinnereth; sometimes when the surface was so smooth and shining, with the sun's glow behind the figure of a man far off, perhaps standing in a low-laden bark, you could imagine he was walking on the water.

So it had come to her that to understand her Gottfried she must read the Christian Bible. But how and where would she secure it to read, without stories spreading that she was already about to become a convert? Of this in itself Shula had no fear; just as she was not a religious Jew, just so would it be impossible for her to become religious as a Christian. But her poor father was so pious that the mere whisper of his daughter's having accepted from their mission a copy of their Bible would be enough! The same way as only to be seen walking with one of them proved a girl was already seduced!

Nor could she ask Gottfried to bring her the book, for he too might give this a wrong interpretation. Even if she were to go in and buy the book in one of the shops in Tiberias that sold crosses and holy pictures—there too she might be seen.

Then suddenly it came to Shula that once, idling among Reuven's books in his room in the kvutsa, she had noticed it there in Russian. Of course this had not even surprised her. Their Christian Bible, Reuven told her, contained many interesting details about the way people lived in the Galilee in those days, and besides, he said, it was important for Jews to know about Christian beliefs. And Moslem as well, he had said, though he had not yet read the Koran. He meant to learn to read Arabic and study it in the original language. "If the Koran was about Eretz, you would already be studying it," she had joked, and he too had laughed. So her oldest brother, at least, would understand her.

A few days before, then, though there was now a new chaver in Reuven's place, Shula had gone to HaKeren, and finding the room empty, had taken the book, trusting that the new chaver would not notice before she put it back.

Often, lately, she had used Gidon's hut for moments of solitude. This much even her mother seemed to understand without questioning—a girl in her moods. "I'll be down there in the hut." Not yet had she permitted the hut to Gottfried as a trysting place, though sometimes she let herself daydream that he found her here and . . .

For more than an hour now she had been reading the book of their belief, with a doubled sense of uneasiness. First, that no one should chance on her reading it. Second, that her reading might not do something, as yet unclear, to her wondrous spell of being in love. At one passage and then another, it was as though she must ask Gottfried, "But this story—do you believe in it too?" And if he did, would it leave her still in love with him?

Much of the book, of course, was only grandmothers' tales. Tales of miracles, of wonders of healing, of making the blind see, and signs from heaven, such tales were in the Jewish Bible too. Like the parting of the waters, or the angels who told Samson's mother that she would give birth to a son, a Nazarite—was that the same as Jesus of Nazareth, she wondered? what did it mean? As with Samson, a holy man who should never cut off his hair? All the same kinds of stories, miracles like the walls of Jericho falling down—but hadn't Reuven once said, there in Jericho it had been proven that they did fall because of an earthquake? But then in their Christian Bible she came to the part that made her feel sick with disgust—the part where the Jews cried out that Jesus must be put to death, and they shouted, "We take his blood on ourselves and on our children forever."

But it was unimaginable! Suppose the Turks were hanging a Jew—no matter for what—could such an outcry ever be imagined?

Surely Gottfried did not agree to this!

Why was it in their book?

It was all like when there had been some puzzling subject in school, like when the melamed tried to explain the Bible story of creation, and also evolution, so they fitted together, but you really felt it was all imaginings from other days.

Surely these were imaginings of ancient anti-Semites. Even put there on purpose! Another strange thing about their book—after she read the story of their Yoshka once, she saw that it was told all over again, the same story. Four times. Why was this? Were they themselves in doubt? After the first time, Shula read more quickly, as it was all becoming familiar, only here and there some new miracles were added. But each time she came to the part about the Jews she felt nauseated, and yet read every word. In not all of them, she noticed, was there that awful part about taking his blood on our children forever. Perhaps the Christians had kept adding things. And they told the whole story four times so as to make it seem more true, and so as to make you remember and believe it, the way you repeated the same thing over and over to simple people, and the more they heard it, the more they believed.

And so Shula sat in the hut, on the stone bench along the wall. As by habit she had sat down on the same part of the bench she had slept on as a little girl, when the family first arrived.

Suddenly she heard a heavy tread, and—not Gottfried—her father was already inside! His face was in fury; with an involuntary movement, she tried to hide the book, but there was nowhere—and in the same flash it came to her that if she hadn't tried to hide it, he would never have noticed what it was. He carried the mule-whip, his arm was raised—this could not be happening! As Shula's eyes met her father's inflamed glare, her hands flew up to protect her face, the book fell, Shula let out a scream, "Tateh! No!" And as though the scream released his movement, Yankel's arm swung the whip.

He heard it strike her body, while some voice that had lain unknown in him shrieked out, "Daughter of whoredom!" Then Feigel, rushing after him as he howled out his rage, seized his arm with both her hands, hanging onto it with all her weight.

Even as the girl crumpled but also tried to seize the book, Yankel already knew what it was. The Above One, he was sure now, had sent him here with the whip. Yankel wrenched the book from Shula's hands, but his fingers shrank away from the hideous foul thing, and it dropped to the floor. Unclean! Tref! All the while his heart was weeping. Then it was true, all that everyone except himself must already have known was true, everything vile about her was true. The abomination was in his house. For this he had brought his children to Eretz. How long, how long had his house been impure, his daughter's body the vessel of foul seed? And Yankel's arm dropped, taken beyond anger to defeat; tears gushed from his eyes.

He hardly heard their womanish babble, their lies to confuse and soothe him, with Feigel swearing no, she is not—no—nothing has yet happened, Yankel—I believe her, Yankel, by the head of Mati, by the soul of Avramchick, I believe her—and then babbling some story that the girl was reading their accursed book only to see for herself what lies they told, how they taught hatred of the Jews. Yes, poor Shulamith had been attracted to the German flier, but from their own book she was better prepared to see them as they are, and not be blinded—

—Where had she got it?

It was Reuven's, Shula said, and Yankel's rage burst out anew —Reuven's! He might have known. All of them betraying him, deceiving him. And now in the middle of the girl's weeping and protesting and swearing her innocence to her mother, she even had the indecency to shout out against him; how primitive could her father be over the mere reading of a book, to come and spy on her!

Only then did Feigel seize her daughter, crying out, "Shula, he didn't come because of the book!" And Feigel told her what had been done to Nahum in Tiberias, because of that German officer of hers.

Staring at Feigel unbelievingly, Shula made her mother tell it again. And Nahum had closed the door in their faces? And they had cried "Filthy Jew" and sent the Turks to seize Nahum?

The girl sat, stunned, not even feeling the smarting from the blow of the whip. Her mother had at last drawn her father away, and they had left her sitting there.

In the following days her father did not look at her face, or speak to her. In the house the heaviness was unbearable. At least to Yaffaleh, Shula wanted to say something, to explain herself, but what could she explain? Schmulik in a boy's way tried to show sympathy, pumping water for her kitchen tasks, telling her news—yet how much of her story had come to him? That Tateh had beaten her for reading the Christian book?

And even poor little Mati kept looking at her, bewildered, as if he wanted to ask but dared not—should he cease admiring the flier in the air? Should he no longer want the German aviator to be victorious over every enemy in the sky?

A hamseen came, and in the oppressive atmosphere even

to breathe seemed not worth the effort. The image came to
Shula of Nahum, in this dread heat, made to lift iron
cannon-shells and carry them. This was what loving her
had done for poor Nahum.

She had to see Gottfried. Only once more. For one thing
alone—to have him do something about Nahum.

But to her note under their stone she found no answer. It
lay there. Had he been spoken to? Had he been driven
away?

Even Malka Bronescu was avoiding her. In the village
street, it was as though everyone were watching her the
way one watches a crazy person to see what insane thing
he will do next. The worst was that now her longing for
Gottfried was returning. Perhaps he had been hurt, even
shot down, killed. No, somehow she would have known; in
their vengefulness the Jews would have told her. Yes, that
was how she had just now thought of them, Tateh and all
the rest, "the Jews." And how could she be certain it was
Gottfried who had cried out insults against the Jews when
Nahum barred the door? She owed it to Gottfried to hear it
from himself. And how should poor Gottfried have known
that Nahum was in love with her? had always been in love
with her? All Gottfried knew was that the boy refused to
let him and his friends into the restaurant. So the angry
outburst from the Germans was natural. . . . But still, to
have gone and complained to the Turks? Could she be in
love with a man who could be so vindictive— It must have
been one of his comrades who had done it. But then Gottfried could have stopped it. What sort of man was this who
had taken her heart? How did a woman know what was
true in a man?

The sky and the sea and the yellow ripening fields, all
nature seemed so certain of itself, and would tell her nothing. Nor would God. For despite everything, Shula felt
there was God, yet neither God, nor nature—nature that
sometimes told you things through your own body—would
give her a single sign.

Was the longing a sign? At some moments Shula even
wished her father had continued with his whip until he had
whipped it all out of her, the way a dybbuk is driven out,
the way some of their nuns were said to whip themselves
when they had evil desires until they fell unconscious.

The silence, the silence around her. She was so used to

the village girls running in and out of the yard, to liveliness
and gossip, and at one moment it came to Shula with an
inner bitter laugh and then a gasp of pity, that now she
knew what it must be like to be an ugly girl, an ill-favored
one who was left out of everything. On impulse she went
down to the river to keep Yaffaleh company with the geese.

It was then that Leah came back from Gilboa, seething
with all she had found out there. Mama was alone in the
house kneading, her hands not as strong as they used to be;
Leah took over the task—where was Shula? And Feigel
told her the new woes that had befallen, the girl halfway to
seduction and conversion, the father raising a lash to his
daughter—could he even be blamed?—God alone knew
what was happening with the girl. Even though there was
something in herself, Leah thought, that had always been a
little envious of Shula's femininity and prettiness, even if,
for Shula's vanity, she had perhaps in some hidden part of
herself wanted the girl to suffer a little—it would have been
only a little, not deeply like this. How should she begin?
"Shula, let what happened to me at least serve some purpose, let it help you—"

Everyone was in the house, so the two of them couldn't
speak together during the meal, but Shula's eyes kept asking Leah something, and the moment they could go out to
sit under the grape arbor, she begged, "Is he there in Gilboa? What's happened to him? Leah, I haven't heard—"
Should she tell the girl at once what she had learned about
her fine Gottfried?

The fliers had been much away, staying in a new camp
near Beersheba, Leah told her, and Shula sighed in relief,
for his silence was explained. She pulled her dress from her
shoulder; in the waning light the reddish welt curved into
the cleft of her breasts. No, it didn't hurt any more, only an
itching. Did Leah think it would leave a mark?

Leah looked closer. No, she said, luckily the cloth had
protected the skin. They looked into each other's eyes, and
something like a foolish laugh and a pleading broke from
Shula. "I was only trying to find out, to know what they
believe, what they are really like. Doesn't a girl have a
right—she must try—or how can a girl really know the
truth about a man?"

Thus, Shula herself had given Leah the moment. "Shula,

believe me, there is something I did—it was from the same need—to find out—I wanted to help you to know everything about him. You remember when we slept in the room, and he came back to take away his diary? We joked it had secrets of love—"

Shula had sucked in her lower lip. Oddly, a glint of her natural liveliness, curiosity, even of girlish perversity had come into her eyes. "You looked into it!"

Leah nodded.

"He writes about me? Love?"

"About you, buba. And others."

"Oh."

"Your golden-haired angel from the sky, in his diary he counts them, two virgins in Belgium, three maidens in France. All he needs now is a Jewish virgin in Palestine! Then he could fly on to the next land of conquest."

At first shock, Shula only felt stone cold. Ashamed of herself.

Then she felt wary, yet self-possessed. She was her own self, her own self before she had let herself fall into that blind dizziness of love. Yes, she saw him running out with his little book of love secrets. No, Leah was simply not capable of making all this up. Yes, she now could see behind his pure blue eyes of love, it was as though Leah had torn open for her the pure blue skies that had hidden the truth—yes, you must tear open the very skies to find the truth you need. Shula saw herself like any stupid, silly, moonstruck girl. And there was even a lightness in her as she asked Leah for every detail of how she had got hold of his diary.

And then, while Leah told her, there came a thought that Shula did not really want, but it came. Suppose when Gottfried had hurried back for his diary, it had been because this time, with her, he felt different, because with her he felt truly in love? She mocked herself for this thought, and yet now that they were talking together so openly,—in so sisterly a way, she said, "But, Leah, you too, when it happened to you—you knew he had seduced one girl after another. And yet—"

Now the big girl drew in her lip. "Yes, my sister. I knew."

"And yet—even now you still long for him."

"Shula. It's like the kadahat. In some, the disease keeps

returning. You suffer the attack of fever again and again. But each time it passes."

Shula leaned close to her big sister. All at once she felt tears in her eyes, not for herself, but for Leah, and she hid her face in Leah's bosom.

When she found his note under the stone, Shula left word for Gottfried this time to meet her in the hut.

For the first moment she let him hold her and say how much he had hungered for her, and she gazed back into his adoring eyes, wondering if now she would see what lay beyond. How well-armed she felt! It was not only because of what Leah had found in his diary. Even more, it was because of what she herself had read in their book. Now she was no longer awed by them, the Christians with their high church spires and beautiful paintings and their mysterious cloisters with closed walls all around them, and their nuns all married to Jesus, and the knowledge that they ruled the greatest nations in the world. How could any truly intelligent people believe the grandmothers' tales they believed in? They must all of them in some strange way be self-deceivers or liars. No, she could not ever be taken in by one of them. And in giving him her lips she also felt reassured, she would be no more be overwhelmed.

It had been bad, bad, worse than over France—he poured out his sorrow to her—two of his closest comrades, she knew them, she had danced with each of them. Egon, the aerial photographer, and Kurt, the son of the Mayor of Cologne, Kurt, who had been in his squadron from the first day, who had gone through every campaign with him, Egon and Kurt, their plane had been hit and they had crashed in flames before his eyes, and burned to cinders in the desert near the damned canal. He had bombed the damned British ships in the canal until he had no more bombs, he had dived and strafed until he had no more bullets and no more benzine—

"But you too could have fallen!" Was there a real chill in her heart?

"At such times a man doesn't think of it."

They sat, holding hands, the dark fate of the war, of his comrades, pulsing from one to the other, and Shula could not yet bring herself to speak as she had meant to, of his incident in Tiberias with Nahum. Then as a soldier who turns from death to life, Gottfried took her face in his hands to kiss her gently on the lips, and after this it was he who asked, "Is something wrong?"

—A good friend of hers, Shula said, had been seized by the Turks for their labor battalions, from which few returned alive. When she told him the friend's name, it took Gottfried a moment to remember—Nahum?

"In Tiberias. In the restaurant."

He struck his forehead. Of course. "Where I first saw you. The fat boy."

"You didn't know they seized him the very next morning?"

Gottfried gave her an odd glance. No, no, he had not known. Not exactly. It came back to him now, there had been a misunderstanding, and it was indeed Kurt—poor Kurt—he choked, but mumbled, yes, Kurt had put in some sort of complaint. Since the young man was a friend of hers, Gottfried hated to say this, but it had been a question of insolence. Totally unprovoked. "He refused to let us into the place."

"You don't know why he did it?" Gottfried gazed at her, puzzled. She said, "Nahum is in love with me. And he heard stories about you and me."

"That boy?" She could see he held back a feeling that it was comical.

"Since we were little."

"Oh, I am sorry. I—I must do everything to get him released." He was gazing into her eyes with utmost candor. "My dear one, how could I possibly have imagined? Poor fellow. But how could a boy like that—" It was as though Gottfried now touched on something that all the world—that particularly persons like herself and himself—quite naturally understood, and indeed it was something Shula had felt since knowing herself even in childhood to be the loveliest girl in the village—it was like a natural law. The most handsome man and the most beautiful girl belonged together. Only here all at once she was ashamed of the assumption.

Now she added, "You let something out, about the Jews, Gottfried. Everyone heard it."

At this, though not about Nahum, he flushed. Then Gottfried gazed again into her eyes and said, "I am ashamed. It came out in anger. It was not myself speaking,

Shulamith, believe me. Unfortunately we have been brought up in this. I swear to you as a grown man it is not my way of thinking. Or how could I be here with you, my dearest?"

"I know what you are brought up in," she said. "I read your Bible."

"You read it."

"To try to understand you."

"You are wonderful!" His eyes, still resting upon her, now had that milky Christian look.

Then she spoke of the terrible lines in their book about the eternal curse on the Jews.

—But this was a working out of the divine will! Gottfried said passionately, still gazing at her. See, had not the Jews indeed been scattered all over the world? The prophecy was dreadful, he agreed. Only in divine things could there be such ultimate dread. And the Christians believed it because they had seen it coming true.

"And you believe this, too, that we are forever cursed?"

"My dear one, what was that curse? For refusing to accept the Messias. And what is the meaning of the Messias? Love. Christ is love, unbounded love. That is what we believe and what we teach, my Shulamith." His face had become exalted in that glowing way you sometimes saw on the faces of their nuns.

"And now that we are returning here," she said, "are we still cursed and doomed if we do not believe that he was the Messiah?"

It was in a different tone that Gottfried replied. Until now his words had come easily, like in school when you are ready with the answers. But now it was as though he were thinking, searching himself, from word to word. "To many of us Christians," he said, "the return of the Jews to the Holy Land can only be a part of the divine design, it is a sign that the return of Messias is near. Must we all believe that this return will again be an appearance in human form? Or will it not rather be in the spirit, the teaching of Christ? You yourself have spoken to me, Shulamith, of the interpretation of your brother—how I should like to meet him—that in his ideals and the ideals of his movement, the people itself is the Messias. Your brother speaks of the Jewish people. But when all the peoples of the world accept the ideal of love for one another, accept the ideals of Christ the Messias, and live by them—then Christ is returned within us, and the prophecy is fulfilled."

Was he saying this to please her?

All differences would be swept away, Gottfried declared in a kind of exaltation, or be swept upward into something higher, a beautiful civilization of justice, a culture that would be brought to the entire world, to all mankind.

"But how can you believe this when all over the world men are fighting and killing each other?"

He looked at her as though astounded and then with a tender patience, like a teacher who is surprised to realize that the brightest pupil has all along missed the main point, Gottfried explained: "But this is our mission in the war. It is we who must bring it to the world. This is how it will come in our victory."

The effect of his words on her was just like when she read in their book of their strange beliefs; what he said was so strange to her that Shula felt momentarily she did not know who he was. And yet she felt that perhaps something was missing in herself since—as in their book—all this was so clear and believable to millions and millions of people.

And then he said that even their love, love between a Jew and a Christian, was a symbol of the fulfillment.

And he embraced her. In his arms Shula was as two different persons, she was herself as she had been in previous times with him, an infatuated girl, and yet she was like a wise old Jew who has seen the ways of the world during thousands of years. And it was as though Gottfried, far back in these years, were some god-like Greek who had come to this very place by the Kinnereth and told a Hebrew maiden of their wonderous Greek deities, and she had looked on their beautiful, harmonious statuary as she had seen it in Leah's art book, while the conquering Greek had told how they were spreading their culture and civilization to all mankind, to the ends of the earth.

Quietly in his arms, Shula came to the second part of what she had prepared. "Gottfried, I must tell you something," she said, and though he pressed her ardently, she still felt in possession of herself. "You know my sister Leah had a terrible experience with a man she fell in love with, and I have seen her suffering. I would never be able to give myself to the man I love except in marriage."

His embrace did not relax. It even became more tenderly

possessive. "I know, my dear one. I would only want you like that." And he kissed her very tenderly, and she responded tenderly, not letting her mouth move on into the mad twisting and devouring of a few times before. This much she had attained on her way to womanhood, Shula told herself, and she had Leah to thank for it. She did not feel helplessly at the mercy of her desires as Leah must have been, or even of her curiosity.

As Gottfried did not go on to say any more about marriage, she did not speak of it either. As though understanding her and out of his higher love restraining himself, his kisses remained tender, slow, sweet clingings of the lips. Just as they were parting, Shula was almost tempted to remark, "Perhaps you'll write in your diary—one Jewish virgin in Palestine, still unconquered." Then she felt somewhat ashamed of her thought because of the way the knowledge had come to her. Let it all end quietly, without rancor. He would not come back.

Then a new thing happened. One day Malka told her that Nahum had come home to Tiberias.

Whether this was Gottfried's doing Shula did not know. And Nahum did not come to see her. She went to Tiberias.

When the dark young man came into the doorway of the parlor, there moved all through Shula something odd, questioning, as though she were a girl of the olden times, seeing a suitor brought by a matchmaker, and finding to her surprise that he was not as she had feared. She was a trifle ashamed, and afraid to feel happy. The sudden feeling confused Shula so that she let out a little giggle at herself.

Nahum had become slender. His mouth was no longer thick, but outlined as in miniature paintings from Persia, such as one saw in the souvenir shops, pictures of noble princes. His eyes appeared larger, and at the sight of her they glowed. Thus he stood before her.

18

THEN the locusts came. Mati was the first to remark on the low-hanging smudge in the sky, borne as though on the sluggish hamseen from the wilderness that lay across the Jordan to the south. It was too low for a cloud. "What is it?" he asked Schmulik—could it be billows of smoke from some distant fire, perhaps some enormous new thing of the war?

They were watering the young lemon grove, the saplings from Reuven's tree nursery at the kvutsa that Gidon had insisted on planting before he left for Jaffa. Now there were pale green leaves on the thin branches. They had to water the trees laboriously from barrels on a wagon, instead of from a motor pump. Even the kvutsa already had an engine for pumping water; it had been dragged by two teams of mules on a wagon all the way from Haifa. Just as Reuven had said, with the water-pumping there were now two crops a year instead of one, and perhaps there would even be three. Some day even here, they would have such an engine, a smaller one. Even without an engine, Mati pestered Schmulik to help him try to build a water wheel by the river. Already thousands of years ago, before the time of Moshe Rabenu, there were water wheels—the Assyrians and the Egyptians had them, you could see them in pictures in schoolbooks—all that was needed was an old mule or even a donkey to turn the wheel and fill buckets of water. Instead, he and Shmulik had to go down to the river with the wagon, and there Schmulik would hand up the full pails for Mati to dump into the barrels; then they would haul the water to the grove, and Schmulik would hand down the full pails for Mati to empty into the saucers around the lemon trees. The whole village said it was madness to water a grove in this way. Only Yankel Chaimovitch would be crazy enough to try to grow citrus here.

While Mati carefully emptied the water so as not to lose a drop, Schmulik stared at the approaching movement in the sky. He had never seen this. And yet, who knew from where, even from the Haggadah that he only half-listened to at the Seder on Pesach, there came to him a fearful answer: *like darkening clouds low over the land came the swarms of devouring locusts.*

Nearer now, Shcmulik could see how the cloud settled downward, like a vast blanket on the earth. Perhaps it would remain where it lay and not spread here to their own fields. But then from behind there moved another such cloud, and now the breadth of the horizon was becoming filled.

Even the mules had become nervous. Mati, the emptied bucket half lifted, stood transfixed, staring at the approaching darkness. Schmulik called to him, "Come!" and hurried the wagon homeward, as though racing against evil, the half-emptied barrels bouncing as the wheels leaped over the rocks.

Already the entire village was in the street, each asking the other what to do, what would happen, some merely staring at the sky and awaiting their fate: would the swarms pass over them, or settle on their fields and devour the half-grown grain?

Reb Meir Roitschuler, who since the death of Alter Pincus in the raid of the Zbeh had taken his place as the Torah sage, declared that this was in the days of the Pharaohs. The plague was not sent against the Jews but against the Turks. God was sending the plague on Djemal Pasha who wanted to seize all the grain for his armies.

Bitterly a chalutz who worked for the Zeidenschneurs remarked, "So should we smear our houses with blood, Reb Roitschuler, and will the locusts spare us enough grain for bread for our own needs?"

Reb Hirsch, the melamed, speculated that this was perhaps the rage of nature, upset in all its balance by the flying machines, the waves of the explosions and battles in the skies bringing the locusts in their wake.

A Yemenite known as Bronescu's Eliyahu, since he worked in Bronescu's fields, declared that he had seen this in his own land: the locusts would remain for three days on the fields, until all was devoured, and only then would they move onward.

Women gathered their small ones and ran inside and shuttered their houses, like ghetto Jews in the face of a pogrom. From the southward fields, the shomer galloped in. The locusts were already settling on the wheat, on young Mikosh Janovici's land, the very same fields that had been burned by the Arabs. "Every evil falls on me!" he cried.

"Every curse!" his wife raised up her arms to heaven. "Mikosh is a good man. What have we done to deserve it?"

"They move from one field to another," the Yemenite said, "until the whole land is bare."

From where, no one knew, perhaps from the memory of the great fire itself, the wall of flame with all the small beasts of the field fleeing before it, mice, lizards, centipedes, all crawling and flying things, there now came the cry, "Make smoke!" With smoke the pestilence would be driven away.

The whole village now, as in the days of the flames, streamed toward the fields. Wagons were brought out, madly snatched implements, flails, brooms, and tins of kerosene were loaded in. Even ahead of Janovici, the whole Chaimovitch family raced along, standing on their wagon.

At the approach to the fields, Abba halted the wagon and they stared in awe. Nothing green could be seen. What seemed earth was not earth, but a brownish skin woven of insects. A humming arose as though what lay before them was a process of life.

Children ran, dragging briars, dried thistles, clods of dung, whatever might burn. Smoke rose, people drew back with smarting eyes, but the plague lay shimmering, humming on the earth.

All at once, Bronescu's Eliyahu began to beat with a sickle on the end of an emptied kerosene can. Noise drove them off, the Yemenite said.

Everyone began to make noise, beating with stones, with sticks, on tins, on their wagons; children started shouting, women began a high-pitched kind of scream, "Away! Away!" and presently, indeed, a movement was seen, a corner of the earth-smothering blanket was lifting itself away, while an answering kind of noise, a weird high-pitched insect shrill somehow akin to that of the women, rose above the maddening, pulsating hum, and the mass of locusts hovered in the air, and then, to a great triumphant outcry from the people, the plague moved on. But in another moment the human exultation turned to a cry of rage

and dismay as the thick horde lowered itself, hovered, and
then settled on a field beyond. Rushing there, the entire
mass of villagers, as if possessed, resumed the din, shrieking, howling, beating on wagon-sides, on mattock-blades,
shouting. Then, like a swept-up tablecloth, a wider, larger
swarm of locuts suddenly left the ground; screaming savagely and beating louder, the humans advanced step by
step onto the field. The swarm continued to lift and they
ran under it, insensate, the children throwing stones upward. "Away!" they shrieked in a confused, laughing cry of
pursuit, and boys put fingers in their mouths and whistled;
someone fired a gun, and mounted men galloped under the
swarm, more of them now firing pistols and rifles, howling
imprecations upward, while those with empty cans ran
along, beating, beating, to keep the plague from realighting.

Even though each knew the beasts would only come
down again upon another field, there was a momentary end
to the sense of helplessness. They had found a way. Something could be done. Now each settler rushed to his own
land to see whether the plague was come upon him, cries
arose. "To us! Help! Come to us!" and some ran here and
some ran there, and the din and the shouting echoed from
all sides.

To help in the battle, the entire population from the cluster of Yemenite huts had been summoned, and they came,
beating on kettles, raising their voices in that raucous tone
of theirs, and from the center of their clamor rose up, most
piercing of all, the voice of Abadiya the shochet. Around
his cry, presently, the other voices died away, for Abadiya's
wordless howl had become a harsh incantation, and it was
no longer an outcry against the plague, but, with recogniz-
able sounds, with words now, it became an outcry against
man, against themselves, against iniquitous daughters who
had called down the wrath of The Name upon them all,
against the harlots who ran to the cities and fornicated with
the goyim in the land: "You shall take them to a place of
stoning and hurl stones upon them!" His body shook, his
raucous voice cracked, and he was taken by a paroxysm of
sobbing. The whole village stood as though transfixed in a
circle somewhat away from Abadiya, while the throbbing
rose from all around them on the fields, vengeful, grinding.
It was Leah who broke the spell, hurrying forward toward
the old man, but, as she would have touched him, he came

to himself, stiffened, and nearly hurled her off—the touch of a woman not his wife. Several of his own people led him away, elders from their little congregation with whom Yankel had a few times prayed before the synagogue in Mishkan Yaacov was opened.

Little was said of the outburst. Work began again to drive off the hordes. Now flails and rakes beat them from the earth. Shula worked with the others, telling herself her feeling of guilt was absurd; no one had even glanced in her direction. And in the end what had she done—nothing! nothing! And this insane Abadiya's poor little Yael—she too was probably just as innocent. Wasn't she scrubbing floors for a few groschen in Tiberias?

Hour upon hour the population stumbled after the swarms, beating, shouting. Already a large part of the furthest Chaimovitch field was covered; the family stood in a knot gazing at the hopeless task, not knowing even at what corner to begin. Suddenly, Mati had a thought and told it to Schmulik, and Schmulik, who would not leave off beating with his flail, sent Shula back on the wagon to the farmyard. "Bring a long rope, bring iron lids, empty pots, milk cans—put stones in them to rattle," he cried, and though she had never handled the mules, Shula lashed them homeward and gathered desperately whatever she could find.

The moment she returned, Schmulik, seizing the rope, began frantically tying together pots and pails, while Mati filled the pots with stones. Then Schmulik unhitched the animals and leaped on Chazak, kicking the sides of the mule while he dragged the rope with the whole chain of tins rattling on the ground behind him. The mule started to gallop. Mati climbed onto the second mule; this was his invention, even Schmulik proclaimed it—what a head on him, that little Mati! Wildly like cowboys they circled the horde of locusts, howling above the din of the dragging pails the cowboys cries that the American Joe Kleinman had once taught them. And there came a marvel: the horde rose up as though on command, and the Chaimovitch field, only half devoured, was clear.

In triumph the boys galloped on to help others, but presently the locusts were slower to rise, and then only patches lifted, and only when the hooves of the mules were almost upon them.

Some of the farmers were giving up. Janovici stood, exhausted, limp, by the edge of his field. He was mute. His wife, his two young boys, stood back a few steps from him. The woman looked at him. They did not get on well, it was known; often her shrill curses were heard halfway across the village. But now she said his name quietly, "Mikosh, come home, it is useless." He waved her away—with the children, too, go, go—and hesitantly they left. He stood there, his mouth a tight bitter scar, his face black with smudge, grimed with sweat. It was futile, each stroke was like striking the sea, but he could not halt, he could not give up, he trampled the locusts on the ground, he swung the back of his spade on them, all the while in a hysterical whine muttering curses.

Yankel to could not stop. A patch of locusts had returned on his ground and he flailed at them. Wiping away sweat that was running into his eyes, he raised his head for a moment and there came into view the shrunken figure of Sheikh Ibrim on the small gray horse he still kept for himself.

"Are they not on your fields?" Yankel wondered.

"If you drive the devil from your house, he will but enter the house of your neighbor," the Arab said, though with no reproach. And with a kind of wonder and pity, he continued, "Why do you labor, why do you exert yourself so? The end will be the same. They will devour all, and only then will they arise and go."

It was so. All was useless. Even as Yankel gazed around him, again a black cloud approached from behind, lowering itself upon the fields. His arms were heavy. Along the wagon path he saw the desolate settlers, hunched and exhausted, returning to the village. His own children still made an effort, the boys on their mules, the girls following in their wake; now and again the insects rose and moved a bit, only, insolently, to settle on the field farther on. Yet something in his blood would not rest.

"It will be as Allah wills," old Ibrim said.

It was useless to go against the will of God, and yet what was the will of God? Yankel groped in his heart for some cause for this punishment. Had he been unjust? And against some barrier in his mind there beat the vision of the moment of the raised arm that had struck down on his daughter. He denied. And even if there was a deserved punishment for him—then why the whole village, why the whole land? Why had God smitten the whole land of the Egyptians when it was their Pharaoh who was unjust? Or was it perhaps that each person in himself knows the injustice that is written against him, and that each must apply the curse to his own transgression?

Like his arm, his mind was heavy, he could not raise up his thoughts, yet just as the blood of his arm would not rest, so too his wearied mind throbbed on, to answer in some way, to do.

From the far end of his field, toward the village, a new outcry came. He saw Mati on the mule, riding toward him. "Abba! Abba! The grove!"

No, this he would not tolerate, not even from God. God or the evil one, wherever it came from. The good and the evil impulse—these were not only in man but in all creation. Why had he never understood this before? To the end of his strength he would storm against evil.

The lemon grove, with its tender leaves, the saplings they had planted here against all advice, he and his sons for once united, and with what labor they had nursed these saplings, each drop of water carried from the river. The grove from Reuven's nursery. Despite all their disputes, even at times his hatred of Reuven, it was though he were running now to protect the very life of his absent eldest son.

Among the small, tender trees, there was a turmoil as of Gehenna itself. Leah ran with a smoke torch, brandishing it wildly. An angry hum was over her head as the seething insects whirled. Mati and Schmulik had left the mules and were slapping with sacking against the locusts that covered the tree-trunks, trying even with their bare hands to sweep the devouring insects from the leaves. Yaffaleh too, and Eliza ran from tree to tree, striking noise from empty pails.

Schmulik had just managed to strip the beasts from one of the saplings, but like knowing evil beings now, they only hovered, to descend again on the small, half-chewed bud-leaves. Clawing at them, Schmulik let out a cry of despairing rage. Suddenly Feigel, to help him, undid her apron-strings and wrapped the cloth around the tree, tying it together firmly at the bottom of the trunk. "This one you won't get!" she shrieked at the buzzing locusts.

Within all his misery, a wave of gratification came up in Yankel, of affection, indeed of love, even of the rightness that still existed in the order of the universe, just as when they had first arrived here and had had to lie in the hovel by the river, and there Feigel had made a good Sabbath.— Woman of valor!—he could have cried,—*Eshet chayeel*— But he said, "That is the way! that is the way! We'll cover every tree! Run, bring clothes from the house!" Already he was stripping off his own shirt. "The pardess they won't get away from us!"

Again Shula took the wagon, her mother riding with her. In the stable, in the house, they first seized every old rag, an old blanket, a piece of canvas—but anything torn you could not use, even the smallest hole they would crawl through. With a great sigh Feigel opened the ancient trunk, drawing out her last tablecloth, the one she had saved for perhaps if Leah got married. Then even sheets from the beds—but still it was as nothing, two hundred trees had been planted, and now from the other room Shula came with her arms overflowing—petticoats. All of her own petticoats she had heaped up, and Leah's, and Yaffaleh's, and mother and daughter were seized with a kind of laughing frenzy—skirts too! every chemise! every nightgown! The entire Chaimovitch wardrobe! Let the whole village behold! Onto the wagon they heaped it all, and still it would hardly make a beginning. Then onto the field they came with their arms loaded, half-stumbling over the trailing ends of whatever they had seized, patched old sheets, petticoats, more aprons—would the voracious beasts even eat through the cloth? No, it was the green leaves they wanted, Schmulik said; from the covered trees they were easily driven away. —For once, Mameh declared cheerfully, it was useful to have so many daughters! But even Leah was somewhat taken aback as Shula wrapped around a tree her most feminine shift, the one with bowknots of blue silk tied all around the hem and neckline. "But, Shula!" she cried. "So then?" Shula responded. "And our washing we don't hang out?"

From neighboring fields there came over the last of the settlers who had not yet given up and gone home. They stared at the mad Chaimovitches, the boys sweeping the locusts from the saplings, the girls binding their petticoats around the little trees—could it really save them? But what had been fetched was soon finished; again Shula raced homeward. She ran to Malka Bronescu—from Malka, from her mother, from Shoshana Mozensohn, from half her schoolmates she borrowed petticoats, and as the craze spread, other girls came with filled arms, laughing. When Shula arrived again with the wagon, her father spoke his first word to her since their great trouble. This time she had even brought the velvet gown that her mother had given her, the one she had worn at the dance in Gilboa. Yankel saw her about to bind it around a tree. "It won't be needed," he said. "We'll find something else."

In the morning, from all the fields, the thrumming still arose. The locusts had not departed. Men hurried out to see the worst. And there, in the midst of the disaster, only the lanes of white garbed lemon trees, the Chaimovitch pardess, stood intact.

The pious prayed in the shul. Again and again during the day the settlers would go out to look at their fields, but the plague had not lifted. They would pass the Chaimovitch grove. They did not even laugh at the strange assortment of pillowcases, petticoats, sacking. A few scratched their heads, wondering whether the trees would not suffocate? Leaves breathe in air. Several times during the day, Yankel and the boys came and unwrapped a few trees, but all seemed in order. The crops were lost, all except the potatoes and turnips that grew under the earth. Though Leah had built a smudge fire all around her vegetable garden, it too was destroyed.

Later in the day Max Wilner came to see for himself the rescued grove, for the fame of it had already reached Ha-Keren. The kvutsa's own grove, the grove Reuven had planted, was totally devoured. Max gazed, nodding, with a wry smile, But even had someone thought of such a thing—"Our girls don't have so many petticoats," he said.

News came first from Yavniel, then from Gilboa, from Chedera, and from Petach Tikvah and the southern settlements. Everywhere, disaster. The curse was on the whole of the land.

Unceasing, the thrumming was in their ears. It had become maddening. And by now everyone knew what it promised; the locusts were mating, the females were burying eggs in the ground, and in twenty days, some said, in forty days, other said, the plague would be renewed, tenfold, a hundredfold worse.

What was to be done? How could they remain sitting day and night listening to the song of doom, helpless?

～～～

That he had best try to keep himself clear of the drunken rages of Djemal Pasha, Reuven quickly understood. A word from Aaron Aaronson was not lost on him. "As with all tyrants," Aaronson had remarked, when he saw Reuven installed in Damascus, "you do not approach unless you are summoned."

Installed on the grounds of Djemal's residence, in a stable-barracks of palace guards, he had almost at once been summoned by the Pasha for a tour of the grounds, an estate seized from a Syrian banker named Atassi who, Djemal shouted even now with wrath, had been plotting and conniving with the French consul to betray the regime. "We have the proof! We found the papers in the French consulate! Atassi escaped with the consul to Paris, but when Paris is taken, I will get him and hang him!" The graveled walk crunched under his boots. It was Djemal's way, Reuven soon learned, to shout to anyone, even to his house servants, about traitors and betrayers, as though he suspected them, too.

The walks were bordered by low clipped box-bushes enclosing formal flower beds—a classic French garden with pieces of statuary. "Where will you put your Garden of Eden?" The Pasha had not forgotten. "Here!" With his quirt he circled the area. "Bring trees of every kind! Pomegranates and oranges. Will Jaffa oranges grow here?"

"If the soil—" Reuven began.

"Make them grow!" And leading up to the residence there must be a lane of palms such as he had seen at Aaronson's agricultural station; let Reuven bring the finest palms from the Euphrates area, they must be transported full-grown. "Tomorrow you will take wagons, take a dozen men—"

Also in the city. At once the tour was made. There must be a new plan for the central square, more open space in the middle where there stood a giant oak.

"Ah, what a tree," cried Reuven. "Indeed it should have space to be admired."

—Twenty hangings at a time had been made from its branches, the Pasha cried. It was the governor's hanging tree. "But not for me!" How could one degrade such a tree by hanging traitors, criminals, vermin from its branches? "I put up a gallows."

Soon enough Reuven saw it. When he brought his laborers to the square, the gallows stood ready. Who was it for? No one answered. Only the elderly gardener, Musa, spoke to him with some freedom and self-respect; the laborers were not used to being talked to as equals, and feared to comment. Excited throngs were filling the square, jesting, shouting in a frenzy of eagerness. The culprits were traitors from high families, Musa said with equanimity, a doctor, the editor of a newspaper, they had been caught in their plottings, they had taken enemy gold to betray Turkey and rule themselves. All was politics, what could a poor man know?

Reuven did not want to see it; he took his laborers back to the Pasha's garden, but the next morning the figures were still hanging, their dried distorted faces above white shrouds on which had been pinned large signs announcing their treason.

All around him there was such lust in cruelty, Reuven wanted only to creep away, to be by himself. In a cafe he encountered a few officers from Eretz, most of them translators here; the cafes were filled with political whisperings, the Turks were threatened everywhere with conspiracies, independence movements—the Syrians had secret societies, the highest Arab commanders were said to be members; why had Enver and Djemal Pasha decided to stamp out the Armenians? As an example, to frighten the Kurds, the Maronites, the Druze. All were seething, plotting to strike for independence.

Deep in the garden of the estate, behind a brick shed, Reuven had started a tree nursery, and into the shed he now brought a cot, explaining that he must be constantly watchful of the tender shoots. Away from the barracks, he was at peace. What a paradise he had fallen into! How was he deserving of this?

Soon Reuven found that he could go off afield for days in search of rare plants to bring back for the garden, particularly when Djemal Pasha was away on army inspection. Vast movements were taking place, a score of divisions, virtually the entire Palestine army, was marching north to reinforce Gallipoli against the British.

In a deserted hollow amongst low arid hills, Reuven came upon a strange grove of trees. They were gnarled and bowed like ancient olives, but as he made his way closer, he saw a shimmering of rose-amber tints among the leaves. Instantly Reuven felt the throb of prescience, of ancient knowledge and foreknowledge, a current going back and forth in his very veins. The trees, he saw at once, bore a species of nut—pistachio, but longer and fatter than any he had ever examined, a variety all its own—and surely it stemmed from antiquity, this isolated grove that had somehow remained and perpetuated itself in this cupped enclosure. Through all time this grove had stood here waiting. This was his own. A discovery.

Standing beneath the branches now, Reuven held back his hand for a moment as though asking permission. His father, it crossed his mind, would have said a thanksgiving to the Lord for having permitted him this finding. Then he plucked a few of the delicately tinted shells, and opened one, examining the pale oval kernel, touching the seed to his tongue, gently biting, confirming the flavor, perfumed and sweet. It was a morsel that might have delighted a concubine of King Solomon; Reuven envisioned a slender, long-fingered hand with jeweled rings reaching into a silver bowl.

Taking soil samples, examining the topography, sensing the wind, Reuven made his notes. Then carefully he made cuttings. One day, returned to HaKeren, he would plant such trees; the kvutsa would export the nut fruit to France, to America—what a find, what a discovery! This was something to show Aaron Aaronson, but even to him Reuven would not reveal the location!

Hurrying back excited with his find, and seeing that Djemal Pasha's automobiles had arrived, Reuven could not put off showing his discovery, and sent in word by an adjutant.

In wrath, his eyes glazed, the Pasha fell on him: where had he been, on whose account was he wandering the land? where was he spying? twice he had been sent for—he should be summarily shot!

Foolishly, Reuven's hand was extended with a sample of his find. As he began to explain, the Pasha's quirt came down, slashing the open palm, the samples flying in all directions. Pistachis! Did he expect the army to be fed on pistachio nuts! Famine was falling over Palestine, a plague of locusts had descended. The crops were devoured.

—As for the Jews, Djemal cried, they could starve, whatever happened to them they deserved, and the Arabs too; they were traitors and plotting against Turkey. But his army! Where would bread come from for the army? An immediate survey was necessary to measure the extent of the disaster. As Reuven could not be found, he had set Dr. Aaron Aaronson to the task, and Reuven could consider himself fortunate that he was not sent to prison. Out! Out!

What would happen at the kvutsa? And to the family at home? Hastily, Reuven read what he could about the plague of locusts in the Bible; . . . *the Lord brought an east wind on the land all that day and all that night, and when it was morning, the east wind brought the locusts.* And then . . . *And the Lord turned an exceeding strong west wind, which took up the locusts, and drove them into the Red Sea; there remained not one locust in all the border of Egypt.* The swarms had appeared from the east on the prevailing winds. If only strong winds would carry them away! Even if he were there, what could he do?

He set to work planting his pistachios. What right had he, in the midst of disaster, to be gratified in his work? Toward dusk, as he planted the cuttings and the seeds in different samples of soil, Reuven heard the stomp of Djemal Pasha in the garden. At times at this hour the commander strolled. Now the tread came closer; the Pasha stood there, legs apart, with the defiant steadiness of the intoxicated.

Then carefully, like a colossus of Ashur, he lowered his bulk over the new plants and touched the tender leaves. — Was it true that the trees were thousands of years old? Where then was the grove? Malaala? He had passed in that region. In the direction of Mesopotamia.

And in a burst, seemingly without connection, the Pasha poured out angry words. Why was it he who was blamed for sending off the Armenians from their Anatolian villages into the wastes of Mesopotamia? Why did the whole world fall on him for atrocity? Not he but Enver Pasha was in authority over Anatolia! Only just now, supervising troop movements through the area, Djemal had personally issued orders for army bread to be distributed to the Armenian women and children on the roads. Bread which the troops would soon lack! But what else could have been done with the Armenians than to remove them? If they had not been cleared out entirely, they would have risen behind the army. At Erezum they would have let in the Russians! Year after year their fanatical leaders made risings! With their mothers' milk their children sucked in hatred of the Turks. And did Reuven imagine only the Armenians were plotting? The Maronites in Lebanon had fifty thousand rifles hidden away. He could have loosed the Lebanese Moslems on them and wiped them out, but he had refrained. Only their leaders were arrested. They would hang. As for the so-called cultural conference in Beirut, it was nothing but a mask for a secret nationalist organization; those plotters too would hang, every one of them! Even the Druze could not be trusted. And the Jews. Oh, he knew about the plans of the Jews. He knew about their secret army, the Shomer. Djemal's eyes impaled Reuven. He could have loosed the Bedouin on the Jews, but had he done so? He was not a man to massacre women and children. He was not a hater of the Jews. They were valuable people. The Moslems has always known them for a useful people. He would not destroy the Jews, but they must be careful. Just like others they had traitors amongst them. Where were there no traitors? Even among the highest Arab Moslems. Why had the Sherif of Mecca, the descendant of Mohammed, not yet confirmed the Sultan's proclamation that this was a holy war, a jihad? Could the Sherif of Mecca not realize that the Arabs together with the Ottoman Moslems could constitute the greatest power in the world? Yet in the attack on Suez the Bedouin horsemen promised by the Sherif had failed to appear. With them, it could have succeeded! Who could know but what that old dog Sherif Husein was playing a double game? It was said that one of his sons had been in contact with the English. Everywhere there was intrigue, deception, betrayal.

The eyes bulged at Reuven. Would the plague of locusts, Djemal suddenly demanded, spread over Syria? Would it destroy the wheat of Golan?

Reuven hardly dared speak. In some strange way, this tyrant, from the day of his rescue had made an omen of

him. The locust swarms were more likely to move westward out to sea, Reuven half whispered. All depended on
the winds.

On the fifth day of the plague, two horsemen galloped
into Mishkan Yaacov. One of the riders sat squat, riding
solid like a Napoleon; it was Aaron Aaronson, Leah saw,
and at once ran out to him, for this was her first sight of
the famous agronomist since Reuven had written how
Aaronson had rescued him from the hands of Bahad-ad-
Din. As would be his way, Reuven had not told the story in
all its brutality, but details had seeped through from Arabs
who had seen it—it was from death itself that Aaronson
had taken Reuven.

Alongside the scientist, on a more showy steed, boyish
and lithe, and as usual wearing a keffiyah, rode Avshalom
Feinberg. Politely acknowledging Leah's gratitude but almost brushing it aside, Aaronson came at once to his task:
the locusts. At a glance he had already measured the rav-
age. "You must call together the men. I will explain what
to do next."

Mati was already running to call Bronescu. Meanwhile
the riders must at least have a glass of cold buttermilk—
Feigel approached with the crock. Yes, he had seen Reuven in Damascus, Aaronson said, indeed only yesterday.
Reuven was well, she need not worry. "Your son is probably the happiest soldier in the war." Reuven had become
Djemal Pasha's own adviser. Oh, not for military matters,
but quite opposite—not to destroy but to plant. Not only
Djemal's palace garden, but the entire city of Damascus
was to be transformed so that the name of Djemal Pasha
would live forever as the creator of boulevards and parks,
and it was Reuven who was to devise and plan it all, sumptuous public gardens, fountains, and avenues of trees. "So
you see, what better task could have befallen a pacifist?"

Feigel glowed. And it was through him, this Aaronson
himself, she knew, that such good fortune had come to
Reuven; she knew also of the rescue from punishment,
though the full horror had not been told her. If Aaronson
had only let her, she would have kissed the man's hands.

He had not yet dismounted; from every yard the villagers were hurrying, their wives behind them, each calling

out to Aaron Aaronson the extent of his disaster—what fields, what plantings he had lost—how was he to live, where was he to get new seed, what was he to do?

Tersely, the agronomist gave orders. The mukhtar, Bronescu, must be the commander here, and they must act as an army, as one, to prevent the greater disaster that was soon to come. In three weeks the spawn would emerge. "The eggs are already planted in your soil in countless millions. The locusts may have seemed to you without number, but you must multiply them by the thousand thousands. Each pair of locusts has left thousands of eggs just beneath the surface of your soil. They will mature and emerge. The locusts ate what was green. The larvae will devour everything—you hear, everything."

Then what could they do? They must hurry and plow: plow day and night, not once but three times, five times, to bury the larvae so deep that they could not emerge. No, kerosene would not kill them unless the entire surface of the land could be flooded, and where would they get kerosene? Lye would be more destructive than helpful. Only plowing. "But if it is not deep enough, they can crawl out. If you see them crawling out, you must dig trenches, sweep them into the trenches and bury them. Understand?" He gazed around on their faces the way a general before battle anxiously, uncertainly, weighs the valor of his troops.

Their faces had fallen despondent. Instead of a remedy, what was before them was only more labor, more disaster. To plow five times, every inch of the soil, in the space of a few days—who had such strength? —The advice of a great expert, Mikosh Janovici remarked in Roumanian, but he himself probably had never put his hands to a plow even once. Catching the words, Aaronson replied in kind, in Roumanian, for were not the settlers of Zichron all from that land? The familiarity somehow dissipated part of the gloom. Dismounting, Aaronson cried, "Here, the expert who never put his own hands to a plow will show you something." Just inside the Chaimovitch yard, he squatted on the ground, peering close, then with the blade of his pocketknife, he made a little jab, and raised the knife to show them, on the tip, a tiny translucent bead, the insect's birth-sack. As everyone crowded near, Leah and Mati too knelt on the earth. The farmers, the children, the whole village pressed in, as Aaronson demonstrated how by a careful examination of the soil they could tell, as he had, where to find the eggs. "The female scoops a tiny hole with her tail, she deposits her eggsack, and scrapes earth over it with her hind legs," he explained. Absorbed as she was in his words, Leah could not help thinking about Aaronson himself. He was unmarried. It was said he had for years been hopelessly in love with the wife of his best friend, a doctor in Zichron. A strange man. How alone he must be.

Many now, with their faces close to the earth, were searching but could not find the tiny holes. The first to succeed was Mati. Yes, yes, that's it—they must dig them out, throw them in a pail and then bury them, deep.

"But there are millions! The earth is filled with them!" On her knees, Leah searched in a destroyed flower bed. The earth was liked a pocked skin. Something between revulsion and awe rose in her. Lifting out one of the tiny sacks she held it on her palm. A man's face bent close to hers, over the bead of life. It was Avshalom Feinberg, with that warm, excited intensity you always saw in his face. "Just think," he remarked, "if all the millions of human sperm were to germinate as well!"

He chuckled, and added, "Then we would *really* have wars, to get rid of all the grubs!"

"This war isn't enough for you?" she asked. He was another handsome one. It was said that first Sara Aaronson and then her younger sister had fallen in love with him, and for the sake of her stricken sister, Sara had accepted a match with a rich merchant from Constantinople and gone there to live. Avshalom and his Sons of Nimrod—enough trouble they had caused the Shomer in Chedera.

Aaron Aaronson was now starting out to inspect the fields, and as Leah followed, Avshalom walked beside her, leading his horse. His step was quick and light, like the animal's.

—Did she know that her young brother Gidon was fighting with the British? he asked. With a Jewish unit led by Josef Trumpeldor, in the terrible battle of Gallipoli?

No! Leah had not known. Of Trumpeldor's gathering a Jewish army in Alexandria, whispers had come. And that Gidon would join such an army was a foregone conclusion. But—in Gallipoli? One day, it was dreamed, they would appear victorious, here in Eretz driving out the Turks. But they were in Gallipoli? Was he certain? How did he know?

Ah, he had ways of knowing.

Then did he know more? How did he know of Gidon?

Gidon had been one of those mentioned, since everyone knew him to be a good fighter.

Mentioned? By whom?

Ah. Avshalom Feinberg assumed a mysterious air, but the air of a man who is drawing you on to ask more. The Jewish troops wore the Star of David on their caps, did she know that? he said. And their unit would be only the beginning. Perhaps after Gallipoli the British would even land them here in Eretz on the coast. The entire Yishuv should be ready to rise and join them, and free Eretz from the Turks! "Then the land will be ours. Only when we have fought for it and shed our blood can we claim the land as ours!"

But—to fight here openly against the Turks? It would be mad—Djemal Pasha would obliterate every Jew, as he had done with the Armenians. Already he kept threatening it, again and again he promised it!

Yet Avshalom's words raised an echo in her. Where had she heard them—almost these very same words about fighting for the land! From Dovidl, from Avner, before they were sent into exile. And from Galil too. "Only when we have fought and shed our blood for it can we claim this land as ours." And to secure arms. To be ready. But they had meant not to fight for the British. It was to be for the Yishuv itself. To save it, against no matter whom. When the test came, here in the land. And as for Josef Trumpeldor, everyone had understood he had left Eretz to join the Russian army. It was still the Russian patriot in him. The English were on the side of Russia, and therefore for him, the case was clear. And for Gidon and all those in Alexandria to join with him—they were young men, they must have been drawn into the war and they preferred to go together as Jews. Just as Dovidl and Avner had wanted the Jews to go together as Jews if they had to be in the Turkish army. In every country, Jews were fighting for *that* country. And it would be better if they could be together.

From the excited way Avshalom watched her, she knew he was following her every thought. No, Avshalom said, it was not the same for Jews to fight on one side or the other.

All Jewish strength must go to the side of the democracies, the French and the British. There it would count.

—Could Jews count at all, in this great world conflict? Leah wondered. "We are so small. We must only try to save ourselves, and continue our work. How can a few Jewish soldiers help decide the war, for one side or the other?"

Again Avshalom took on a mysterious air. "We can. There are ways where a few count as many." Then he stopped. —If she wanted, he added, he would try to find out something about her brother Gidon.

Vaguely, Avshalom let her understand that he had connections. After all, he had many friends in France. Perhaps in a roundabout way he could receive news. Through Aaron Aaronson, who still received letters that came on American ships, as his experimental farm was supported from America. And through American friends contact could also be made with the British.

Leah fell silent. Why she could not tell, but she felt wary, as one sometimes feels in an unfamiliar place. She felt as though she were being drawn the wrong way, perhaps. "Do you hear from Sara?" she asked.

"Aaron hears," he said. Then he added, "It's what she writes underneath the postage stamps, in tiny microscopic letters." He walked a bit in silence, then burst out, "If you want to know what Djemal Pasha and his partners are doing to the Armenians—before Sara left, it was agreed we must look under the stamps." It was an old Jewish device, even in Russia it had been used. "What you've heard is nothing, a few massacres. Like pogroms, you think. Let me tell you. A pogrom passes. This is something else. It is a complete plan. It is the annihilation of the whole people. To kill them all." It was done town by town, village by village, he said. First the men were taken away as though for the army, but they were murdered in a wood or a ravine. Then the whole village, children, old people, women, were rounded up and marched off, with horsemen with knouts to keep them moving on the road. "Wherever they pass, no one is allowed to come near them with food or water. They are driven eastward into the wilderness, and the dead and dying are left by the roadside." The two of them were standing stock-still now, and Avshalom, his face no longer boyish, cried out, "Not in one village, and not in ten, but already in half the Armenian towns this has happened, Sara writes. It is attested. Christian pastors have gone out and seen it. Only in the cities, the Armenians have not yet been molested. But the Turks will finish with those, as well. It is the greatest slaughter the world has ever known. And if the world knows, it does nothing to stop it. That's what I hear from Sara."

He flung the words at her as though to accuse her of having expected gossip of a lingering romance, a broken heart. "You're afraid they'll do to us as to the Armenians. The whole Yishuv sits trembling. And exactly because of our fear, Bahad-ad-Din will take whatever he wants from us, and when they have squeezed all they want out of us and are ready to repeat the Armenian slaughter on us, they'll do it. And no one will interfere, not even their cultured German allies."

She could not speak.

"Would the Armenians be any worse off if they fought back?" Avshalom demanded. It was said that in one city on the Russian border they had fought, and held off a whole Turkish army until the Russians came. "And that is what we Jews must prepare to do while there is still time."

—With his band of twenty Sons of Nimrod he would hold off the Turks?—

"Don't laugh." And by now Avshalom was altogether another man, flaming, fanatic. "Perhaps not twenty, but a few hundred could carry out a great deed. Seize a stronghold on the coast—the beach at Tantura, or better, the Crusader port at Athlit. The whole area there is virtually unguarded. In half a day the British fleet could reach us. With their landing secured by the Jews of Palestine, the British could cut straight across to Damascus—"

She could not help reminding him, had not he and his band even given up their guns when the Bahad-ad-Din demanded them? At least the men of the Shomer had managed to hang onto their weapons.

Avshalom glared at her. "You know well enough why we had to give up our guns. They had me and Alexander Aaronson, they had already beaten the soles off our feet. Then they gave us three hours before they would seize our sisters and turn them over to a barrackful of their officers."

In Gilboa the story had been told as a mere tale. But from Avshalom it had a different ring. And why else had

Alexander Aaronson at once taken his sister Rifka off to safety in America? "I saw my Smith and Wesson in the hands of an Arab in Nablus the day after I turned it in." Then with a fine Arab curse, Avshalom laughed. "Never mind, I bought it back, I have it."

Now he turned his face to her, serious, fiery. "Leah, this is no time for the Shomer to despise us, and we them. You are a woman of sense and everyone respects you. I plead with you, bring us together into one united organization to defend the Yishuv."

Perhaps indeed there was far more to him than she had known, perhaps because of old hatreds between the planters and the chalutzim, someone like Avshalom had been misunderstood. "Twice already the Turks have had me in their hands," Avshalom said, "and I vowed if I got away with my life, I would pledge that life to fight them."

Of one of his arrests she had heard only vaguely; it seemed to have been over a prank, for on an outing, a number of the sons and daughters of the orange growers had galloped down to the beach at Caesarea. Couples had wandered off, with only an occasional flicker of a lantern as they strolled. Near the ruins of Caesarea the Circassians had a village, and from there someone had spun a tale about Jews making lantern-signals to British boats. This tale had been embellished with further tales about camel caravans bringing stacks of Jewish wheat to the shore to be sold and taken off at night to enemy-vessels. As a result of the wild story, the Kaymakam of Nablus had raided Chedera, arresting a dozen young men, Avshalom among them, and it had needed the influence of Aaron Aaronson with Djemal Pasha himself to keep them from being hanged.

And now Avshalom declared, "Leah, when we lay in their dungeon waiting to be hanged, something came over me like a vision. After their lashing I had a malarial attack. I lay on a stone bench and I saw everything clearly as it could and must happen. The story about us that they invented—what is a story, Leah, but the inspiration for truth? The flickering lights on the beach, the signals to the ships—yes, that is exactly what we should do!" He would make contact with the British, with the French. Not at Caesarea, where too many Circassians wandered about, but at the ruins of Athlit. "Aaron's experimental farm covers the whole shore behind the ruins. Look, Leah, if the

Shomer works with us, we can prepare, and plan with the British, and on the appointed day, seize the ruins and raise our flag. It is an impregnable position—a hundred men could hold it against an army. And the Turks have no real army here—Djemal Pasha emptied Palestine for Gallipoli. While the main Turkish army is still held up in Gallipoli where your brother is fighting them, it needs only a small British force to land where we hold the shore. They could cut the Turks in two." Then he quoted Herzl, " 'If you will it, it need not remain but a dream.' "

Now she felt she understood Avshalom Feinberg. He was a poet aflame with a vision. "You have a great imagination, Avshalom," Leah said. "It would make a wonderful poem. Why don't you write it?"

He flung her an angry look. "In times like this one does not write poems," he said. "One lives them." And he walked ahead quickly, as though to rid himself, in disgust, of her lumpish lack of understanding. Then all at once he halted. Before them was the little lemon grove that her father had saved from the locusts. In their rows, the trees stood still attired in all their raiment, the patched sheets, the striped pillow cases, but more than anything, the white petticoats.

A gale of laughter burst from Avshalom. All his angry wild plans seemed forgotten. In delight he cried out something in English. "Petticoat Lane!"

When at last he stopped laughing, he explained to her; Petticoat Lane—it was a famous street in London. —And this that they had done, she and her father and the whole family, this was not a wild thing of the imagination? he demanded. This was not poetry? This was not impossible?

But it had saved the trees, she explained.

"Against a vast army of locusts that covered the earth, and against which nothing could stand. Except only a bit of human imagination, a bit of daring, Leah!" And he was changed again. Now his words poured forth not as a grandiose vision but in simplest reasonableness, as though there could be no other way of thinking. What future lay before the Yishuv with the Turks? Only famine, disaster, massacre. If the Turks won they would destroy every minority, impose Ottoman culture completely, as they had already shown was their intention. The beginning was already here, with Hebrew virtually outlawed, with even a Keren Kayemeth stamp a crime. But even aside from the Jewish fate, what kind of world could there be? All that was alive in the world, all that was new and fresh in the arts, the whole modern awakening as he had seen it in Europe—in painting, in literature and in freedom of thought—all was in the spirit of the French. It flowed out from Paris. To such a world their strength must go, win or lose, live or die.

She thought him a poet, he knew, an impractical man—but was such a man as Aaron Aaronson impractical? A scientist, a man of sober judgment. "He too has decided, Leah."

What was he leading to? What had they decided? What did he want of her?

"Our fate is with the Allies. In whatever way possible we must help the Allies." Perhaps it would not yet lead to a landing on the Palestine shore, but was not Palestine a battlefield nevertheless? Had not the Turks and the Germans already attempted to sweep down and capture the Suez Canal? "They will try again, you can be certain. The war is here, and we can be of great value, regardless of our numbers."

Had she not heard, in wars, of work carried out behind enemy lines?

The word for it came from within herself—spying. Leah did not repeat it to him; it was abhorrent. Even the clever look in his eyes now seemed to her to have become somehow besmirching, as Avshalom measured her response to his revelation. Oddly, he did not even seem to notice her immediate aversion.

—Why did she think they had come here, he and Aaronson? he asked her. True, to help the farmers against the plague—this, Aaron would have undertaken in any case. But it fell well for their greater purpose. From Djemal Pasha, Aaron Aaronson had received authority to go everywhere, he and his helpers, even to enter military areas. The disposition of the army, the fortifications, the condition of the food supply both for the soldiers and the civilian population, all this information must be gathered and sent to the other side. This was the great task—

Now Leah made herself say it. "You mean to spy?" She tried to keep out of her tone any shock, any revulsion over the word itself. When a human being opened his secret before you, when he was ready to put his whole life into the most terrible danger, because of his deepest beliefs, how could you shame him?

"In today's wars," Avshalom said, "it is called Intelligence. It is the way one person can serve with the weight of many. It is even a way to save the lives of many soldiers, when the battle comes."

She did not want to say it was wrong. But her head was shaking slowly from side to side. "It is something I could never know how to do."

Would she arrange, he suddenly asked, for him to speak with Menahem? "Don't fear—not about Intelligence, Leah." The sparkle had returned in his eyes. "Who knows, we and the Shomer might still lead a British invasion into the land, together."

Only Nadina and Galil could have decided whether even to bring such a question before the committee. And if it went before the committee, Menahem reflected, how long could the secret remain a secret? That was the great danger of the whole plan. It could not long remain unknown to the Turks. Such a one as Avshalom would himself give the secret away; he was impetuous.

Of the cause, Menahem did not need to be convinced; he had already calculated in his mind on which side lay the best hope for the Jews. Certain ideas had come to him, even of the sort Avshalom spoke about. At the Samekh station, how simple it would be for a wagon-driver to keep count of the war matériel coming into the land. Even at the Fuleh station, someone in a cigarette kiosk could see what army units, what officers, were arriving. Such information would be valuable to the Allies. And simply here at Gilboa, the number of German fliers.

Avshalom's wilder plans, such as raising the flag at Athlit—that was a poet playing at war. True, such landings had been made. Yet aside from all this, even at a minimum, the need for some kind of cooperation between the different Jewish defense groups for procuring arms, for readiness and a united resistance in case of another Armenia—surely for this purpose alone it was necessary to bring Avshalom's request before a meeting. The question was, how far should the shomer go?

He would have put it first before Shimshoni, who commanded in place of Galil, but Shimshoni's answer he knew

in advance. Straightforward, plain, Shimshoni detested the
sons of the planters and would never agree to work with
them. Perhaps better, if they went first to the Herzlia Gymnasia group in Tel Aviv with whom Rahel was in contact?

But meanwhile, as Avshalom had put it, suppose he
himself—suppose some knowledge came to him that would
be of importance to pass on? What should he do?

Troubled, Menahem came late to his cot. It was often so,
from late sittings, or from night duty, that even when he
was at home in Gilboa, he had hardly a word with Dvora.
Yet this night he sensed Dvora lay awake.

She too was troubled. Where was she to find feed for the
poultry flock? It might even come to the point where the
chickens would have to be slaughtered, and the communa
would have to feast on them.

Of the secret problem he did not tell her, but of the
problem of unity they talked a long while. It was a long
time since they had had such a good talk together, and
after a while Dvora came over to his cot and into his arms.

After the thrumming had ended, and the plague of locusts
had risen from the fields, hovered like a low cloud, and at
last floated away, all had lain barren and still. Not a shoot,
not a leaf on a vine, not a speck of green was to be seen
except for the patch where Yankel and the boys removed
the coverings that had saved the lemon trees. They returned home with the wagon heaped with petticoats, and
Feigel and Shula set themselves to washing and ironing,
first those that had been borrowed, tubful after tubful.

In the vegetable garden behind the house, a patch too
narrow for the plow, Yaffaleh worked, squatting low to the
ground as she dug out egg-pouches and dropped them into
a bucket. A few of her geese had discovered the delicacy
and their long necks bent into the pail as they gobbled the
eggs. In the larger garden, Leah plowed, burying the eggs
the way Aaronson had instructed. She must plant at once,
quick-growing beans, squash, carrots. Schmulik came, impatient for the mule and the plow. Abba with the good pair
of mules was already back in the fields. Into the dark they
labored and every day without halt, to leave no earth un-
turned, to bury the egg sacs.

Already the famine was acute in the cities. Wagons came
from Jaffa, from Jerusalem, merchants searching to buy the

few sacks of grain hoarded away from last year. Wheat was worth its weight in gold. Potatoes, turnips, anything, they begged.

To HaKeren came representatives from all the kvutsoth in the region, now numbering nearly a dozen, some dominated by the Poale Zion, some by the Poël Hatzaïr. No matter, in this they must act together. The real famine was yet to come, Max Wilner reminded the delegates, and in the wild speculation that had already started, who would suffer more than workers, the unemployed, the poor in the cities, and the low-salaried teachers? They must take certain things on themselves. All that they produced must be distributed under their own control. First they must supply those who were most needed in the Yishuv. Workers' kitchens, before any other consideration, must be assured of supplies. They themselves must ration their sale of milk, for children, for hospitals. He proposed a central cooperative to which they would all send their produce, eggs, milk, vegetables, grain when they had it, and from there the food would be sold according to their own priorities, without going through the hands of speculators.

For once, the two groups were in agreement. But what produce was there to distribute? The grubs were appearing, devouring all.

Mati saw them first, small white wormlike things dotting the compost heap. He called Schmulik. Under their very eyes the crawling dots were drawing together, forming a little mass, like ants forming an army. And the mass began to move.

This must be the danger Aaron Aaronson had spoken of. They had not thought of searching the dungheap for egg-sacs.

Hurriedly they began digging a trench. By full morning it was a frightening thing to behold—like a creeping white lava, the living, devouring, pulsing blanket smeared itself onward. Despite all that had been done to destroy the eggs, the grubs oozed upward out of the garden patches and began a creeping devastation of the new plantings. From yard to yard the outcry was heard. With brooms, the women tried to sweep the pestilence into hastily dug troughs, but even from those, unless they were full ditches, the white lava swelled outward.

On Leah's plowed field, they had not come up, but the neighboring vegetable garden, once the Kleinmans', was covered with the milky horror, and as Tsutsig Bronescu ran from one side to another with his mattock, his wife screamed that the flood was invading the kitchen, the house. And Leah saw one edge of that flow slowly extending, like spilled milk, in her own direction. With armfuls of straw, she hurriedly laid a barrier of fire, but unbelievably, as though commanded, the devouring wave divided itself as it neared the barrier into two prongs reaching out to encircle the line of flame. On one end, Leah ran, flinging down straw to extend the fire, on the other end Mati furiously chopped open a ditch, while Feigel came with a broom to sweep the worms into it.

In the field, Schmulik and Abba labored a second time to save the grove. From the hillside of Dja'adi, which had never been plowed after the locust plague, the white phlegm was rolling inexorably downward. No wrapping, no cloth could this time protect the young trees; at once they had understood this. The grubs devoured even the bark. Only a deep trench could stop the flow. Abba plowed as deeply as he could, while Schmulik labored with the mattock to dig the furrows deeper, pausing only to glance at the creeping whiteness—how long would it take? a day? Given a day they could dig their moat all around the grove.

19

AFTER the second wave of destruction there came pitiful, emaciated Jews on the road from Tiberias, Jews whose alms from abroad had long ceased, begging for something to eat, anything. In Mishkan Yaacov and in Yavniel they came to each door, begging for a crust to carry back, or their daughters would be lost, they said, and they told lurid tales of Jewish girls bringing home bars of Swiss chocolate, and crying out defiantly that they could not watch their little sisters and brothers go hungry. To the Chaimovitches

there even came Noach Abulafia the stonecutter who in the
first days had helped them to settle into their hovel. He
did not come to beg—he still had money—if they would
but sell him food. From their last stores, they helped him,
but he too told tales of Jewish girls . . . the shamefulness
was not to be believed. Something must be done, but what
could be done? He seemed to be speaking directly to Leah.
A plan was rising in her mind, but how to go about it was
still unclear to her. She must come to Tiberias and see for
herself, she told him. And later she was to blame herself for
not having gone at once. Perhaps in some way she might
have prevented what happened.

She blamed herself; the comrades in HaKeren blamed
themselves and held a long sitting with bitter self-
accusations. How could they not have seen, how could they
have shut their eyes to the misery only a stone's throw
away in the cluster of Yemenite huts?

The little employment the Yemenites had had to provide
their meager living had vanished; their own garden-patches
had been devastated, and now they sat with their families
and starved. Had they only come to the kvutsa and asked for
help—but it was not their way.

From Tiberias, Abadiya's Yael had come home bringing
lentils, flour, and for her little brothers and sisters, bars of
chocolate. It was all earned with floor-washing, she swore
by her eyes, by her soul. Only the chocolate came as gifts,
the German officers had so much of it; she had done nothing wrong—would she have dared to show herself if she
had done anything wrong?

Abadiya her father listened in silence to her words and
even allowed her mother to take the girl into the hut,
where her brothers and sisters happily devoured the chocolate. Yael slept that night on her mat.

In the dawn, the mother's screams rose over the tiny
settlement, and the young children ran from the hut, trembling and sobbing. What was seen was soon known in the
kvutsa, and in Mishkan Yaacov, and not long afterward in
Tiberias as well.

Leah was among the first to see the sight. Yael lay on
the mat, only a brown stain under her head, where the
blood had soaked through into the earth. The small pointed

head was askew like the head of a bird after the shochet's knife had cleanly slit the throat. Outside, Abadiya stood alone in a circle of men that kept a distance from him. His body was smaller than ever, shrunken on his bones, and his hollow face was upturned to the heavens, the earcurls dangling. His eyes wore the hard shine that you could not see into. Endless, his singsong continued in snatches of prayer, of psalms, ancient words in their Yemenite Hebrew. A few words she caught; sin-offering, and whoring of the daughters, and lift off Thy punishment from Thy people—

First Leah went to Nahama's Shimek at the kvutsa and saw to it that the new united cooperative, of which he was in charge, set aside each day a portion of milk for the children and the sick among the Yemenites. For once Shimek did not insist that he had to wait for a sitting over the matter, but on his own responsibility portioned out the first canister of milk. Then, bringing plants and seeds, she helped the Yemenites to start their gardens again. And only then did she go to Tiberias.

It was as everyone said—you had only to walk among the seashore cafes to see it. There were Jewish girls now, sitting not only with German officers, but with Turkish officers as well. They had given over completely, they were wanton and tref, the elderly Jews of Tiberias complained in rage; they pretended that it was for the sake of their parents, that the old ones were hungering, but it was told that one of them had even shamelessly brought home a portion of ham, and eaten it in the house of her parents! The entire house was tref! What should be done with them? Who could blame poor Abadiya the Yemenite?

Leah walked past the long row of cafes. Where had these girls come from? A few even had the look of chalutzoth! One or two she felt certain she had seen, perhaps at the Sejera training farm. Some turned away their faces, others looked at her with defiance in their eyes.

How could she begin? Two sat together, as yet without men—one was a slender dark girl who appeared Yemenite. Leah asked if she had known Yael. The girl gasped and half rose in her chair as if to run away. But from someone who had seen with her own eyes, the girl wanted to know what had happened, and Leah sat down with them.

On the further side of Tiberias, northward along the lake, was a cabin once used by a small kvutsa of plantation workers—Josef Trumpeldor had been among them, she recalled; they had set out a vast banana grove for wealthy Zionists who would come from abroad when the fruit was ready. But with the war, the work had been halted. In the open hut flies buzzed, and a stench arose from a few half-torn sacks of rotted straw. Was she not used to such beginnings? Only work was needed, yellow scrubbing soap, then mattocks, seed. Tomatoes, cabbages, lettuce, carrots, cucumbers—she could already see the girls hoeing along the rows. The girls would come. She would somehow bring those two frightened friends of Yael and others, one by one.

First there must be a few who knew how to work, and were leaders. Rahel might come. Perhaps Mama could spare Shula for a few weeks, and it would even be a good change for Shula. Nor did the thought fail to come to Leah that with Tiberias so close by, something more might easily grow between the pretty one and Nahum. The same thought undoubtedly come to Feigel as she urged Shula to go, go—the company of young girls would be livelier for her than sitting here in the house.

The Sephardi stonemason, Noach Abulafia himself brought Leah to the sage of their synagogue, who nodded and nodded as she argued how much better it would be for the daughters of the old Tiberias community to learn to grow their own food, rather than be tempted by the cafes. She would keep the strictest watch on the girls, Leah promised, indeed let them send to her only those who were already in difficulty at home.

—But would the kashruth laws be observed? the sage demanded. She was even ready to promise to keep kosher. —And the Sabbath? And all the other mitzvot? He eyed her ponderously. "Those who want to will observe all the mitzvot, naturally!" she said. "But I can't promise to force everyone."

The sage turned his heavy gaze onto Noach Abulafia, and sighed, as though to say, You see, I have uncovered their real intentions.

Nevertheless Noach sent her two girls, sisters, from the poorest part of the community; it was the same tale, they had brought home tref food and been driven from the house.

Within a week she had assembled ten girls for her kvutsa; they scrubbed and even whitewashed the cabin, and cleared the ground around it, and suddenly spirit was born and singing was heard.

To secure seed was not easy, aside from what she brought from home. Every grain was now as a drop of water in the desert. Leah appealed to Max Wilner; it was truly a matter of importance for the movement. These girls would not only be saved from a life of shame, shame for the whole Yishuv, but would be won over to their new way of life; they would become rooted in the soil, productive. The flow of pioneers from Europe was halted, how else could their movement grow?

Max smiled indulgently at Leah's familiar words. The record so far of transforming girls from the beggar halukah communities into productive workers was not such as to create optimism. And what did these girls know of planting? The seed would be wasted.

"And I? I don't know how to plant?"

—And who would guard their place? They were on the open highway. Things had become so bad that townspeople roamed the roads, pulling roots from the ground to appease their hunger.

"We will stand guard ourselves," Leah declared.

And stand guard they did, after HaKeren had allowed her corn to plant, after she had begged a loan from the Baron's agent, Jacques Samuelson, to tide the girls over until their first produce was grown.

In heavy shoes and men's jackets, her girls took their turns on guard duty at night, carrying their mattocks as weapons. Zipporah—the closest friend of the murdered-Yael—even showed Leah a dagger she carried, a decorated Arabian blade given her by a German officer.

It was Zipporah who proved to be Leah's first triumph. As though herself astonished, the girl confided one day as she worked alongside Leah that what she had most feared had not happened at all. She did not miss the company of men. "Not in that way." A girl could get along happily without their piggish doings. "Isn't it so, Leah?" she asked intimately.

"Yes," Leah said. "It's so."

In short order, Leah Chaimovitch's experiment gained fame. As the green shoots appeared, and the young women were to be seen in the rows, weeding, watering, even on their knees pulling out yablit, the weed that ran just beneath the surface of the ground, the whole of Tiberias sang with praise. Our daughters have shown us.

Why should Jews sit and hunger, while all around them there was earth? One after another, vegetable gardens were planted, while the bearded ones with their wives ran to Leah for seeds, for advice—ten generations in this land, and they had never so much as planted a carrot!

Over the entire yishuv the story spread of Big Leah and her meshek of girls, and how she had rescued several of the girls from a life of evil (though Zipporah went off after a time and was seen in the port of Haifa). Presently there were committee meetings in the Poale Zion cabin on the Tel Aviv shore; Leah was sent for, and she and Rahel organized a whole movement. A member was detached from Gilboa and sent to Jerusalem to supervise vegetable-growing on a plot of land opposite the Hungarian Orphans' Home—the land was owned by a good Jew in Hebron and freely loaned for the purpose. And thus in the very middle of Jerusalem, and also in vacant lots on Rothschild Boulevard in Tel Aviv, Jewish daughters were seen at their gardening.

With Shula too the hoped-for had happened. Not only did she recover her liveliness and good spirits, but where the girls had anticipated an atmosphere of drabness, expecting to go about dressed like Big Leah in lumpy workclothes and hobnailed shoes, here was Shula in a bright cotton duster, with a gay kerchief on her head, and every evening she would exchange bits of finery, or loan out her hand-lotion, or show them how to keep the luster in their hair, or suddenly, laughingly, she would be applying the Arab women's kohl to their eyelids.

On Friday evening there was always a gathering, and though it had seemed since the war that there were no young men to be seen anywhere, young men appeared. Someone was sure to bring a harmonica or an accordion, singing began—soon there was a hora.

Nahum came by on weekday evenings as well, and sometimes even in the day. Their very first produce he bought in advance, so that the kvutsa's debt was quickly and proudly paid off. Once more, the Bagelmacher pension was faring well—the Germans had returned, even some of Gottfried's band, though he himself was discreet enough to stay away.

Nahum would come by with a cart on Mondays to pick up his vegetables. One time, as he was about to leave with a load of large perfect cabbages—what a pity to feed them to those German fressers who lacked for nothing!—Nahum beckoned to Shula. Bending from the cart, he whispered that he had something that he particularly wanted to show her. Then he called to Leah that he would bring Shula back before dark. She sprang onto the cart and, amidst bantering cries from the girls, they made off.

Instead of driving toward the pension, Nahum turned upward on the hill that overlooked Tiberias. Near the top he swerved onto a set of wagon ruts that soon petered out. Still he maintained his mystery. Leaving the wagon, Nahum led her a short way down a goat-path, moving nimbly on his small feet, and presently Shula saw a black stone hut with a terraced courtyard covered by a grape arbor. Behind and above the house, where the hill rose sharply, was another terrace covered with vines, and further above that, a third terrace, and up there were some ancient olive trees.

An Arab who seemed as ancient as the trees came out to greet them, showing a few stubs of black teeth in his smile. He and Nahum talked for a few moments while Shula stood aside; this was a man's affair. How quiet, how heavenly was this place; perhaps the most beautiful view of the Kinnereth she had ever seen was from here, for the sea lay all whole before her, its surrounding hills like a glowing bronze frame holding an antique handmirror. Now Nahum drew out a money-pouch and counted large silver talers onto a stone table. There were Arabic phrases, touchings of breast and forehead, smiles and blessings, and then Nahum came back to her where she had seated herself under the arbor, petting a small nosy dog that had approached.

"I have it!" he said.

That he had been buying this place she had understood. But what for? What would anyone do with this mountaintop? Surely Nahum couldn't be imagining that it would one day be a home for them, even if he was now taking it for granted that he would win her. Oh, she did not quite like him to be so sure, but why else had he brought her here?

Nahum's face was beaming; rays seemed to emanate from the skin, as on pictures she had seen of the sun god of the Egyptians, Amon Ra. Nahum Ra, she would call him if things really went well between them; in all their years of knowing each other she had not until now felt an impulse to give him a nickname that would be private between them.

In a flood of words, as she stood now beside him, he was showing her his vision. Yes, he had brought this land; there were a hundred dunams here, and he had been buying it bit by bit with his own money that his father paid him as wages. When Salim died the land would be his. There was time. What would he do with it? One day he would build. An enormous hotel would rise on this site, like the luxury hotels of Europe, like the fashionable watering places such as Marienbad and Karlsbad where the crowned families and the famous and wealthy of all the world came for their cures.

"And what crowned families will come? The Yeshayahus of Jerusalem?" she teased him.

—Ah, but wait! Look at this view, was there any view in all the world that was more beautiful? Even the fabled Lake Como of Italy had nothing to compare with this!

"Nahum, you have been keeping secrets from me. I didn't know you had been to Italy."

Guests had told him—before the war there had been at the pension well-traveled Jews, even aristocrats from England, from Germany, and all had sworn there was no view in the world so beautiful as this. And did one need to be told? Didn't she know within herself—as he did—that nothing anywhere could be more beautiful?

"Yes," Shula said softly.

—And the hot springs, he continued. The hot springs were the equal of any in Europe, even better, even more curative. It needed only to be known. From the whole world people would come, for added to all this was the appeal of the Holy Land. See, Nahum said, after the war, whichever side won, this would be a changed land. The world of Europe and America would come here to Palestine. There would be automobiles everywhere. There would even be airplanes linking Palestine to Europe, and one day he was certain, to America! Airships would bring people from across the ocean! And a modern land would be built here, a modern land, not only a land of tillers of the soil. The dream of the chalutzim, with Jews becoming peasants again—that phase would soon be over. No, this would be a land of energy, of machinery, of electricity. See—see there—

And she saw, far down where the Jordan flowed out of the Kinnereth, where the river twisted like a hairpin, gleaming through the valley, down past Mishkan Yaacov, there where the Yarmuk joined the Jordan and the waters fell, tumbling in fall after fall. Down there a German engineer had studied it out and calculated it out, Nahum said, and not long ago, dining at the pension, he had told how a vast electrical station could be built, generating power from the falling waters, and from this the entire country could be electrified—everywhere there would be light, everywhere machines would turn!

At that moment, as though in response to Nahum's vision, they heard the roar of motors over the sea. An airplane came streaking the length of the Kinnereth, from the south northward until they could clearly see the black eagles painted under the wings—it was German. Then higher up came another—but that was a British one. No, there came two British airplanes.—Unfair! something cried in her. Nahum was carefully not looking at her, nor did he make the slightest movement, yet every question within him reached into her as though he had asked it.

Not now, not yet—she could not answer him yet. The battle was engaged. She could even see how the movements of the airplanes were as the fliers always described them after their return from battles. She could see Gottfried's hands making swooping gestures as he explained a fight to Mati, and Mati's hands as he in turn explained to the village boys, "You must get above and behind the enemy." Swerving, the German plane pointed itself upward. Good! Good! something cried in her. Good! They won't get you!

And then! Oh, look out! look out! For still another airplane now appeared, even higher in the air. Was it German? was it British? Three to one? No, no, unfair, unfair! It was so high up she couldn't see—

"It's German," Nahum said quietly.

As they plunged into their own trails of smoke, as matchlights of fire showed from their guns, as they swept past each other and doubled back, Shula could hardly keep track of which was which; at moments they seemed to hover shuddering in the air in a fearful almost-quiet; then the battle moved southward and the small distant sounds were like sounds from toys rather than great machines in a death-rage. The battle must be over Mishkan Yaacov, Mati must be watching—with those sharp eyes, Mati might even see if one of them was he.

Far up, one airplane hovered and then began to twirl, spiraling downward as they did sometimes in daring flying feats, as Gottfried had once done before her eyes, explaining afterward that it was not mere bravado but a way to shake off an enemy in battle. Only now the airplane did not straighten from its spiral but plunged with a trail of heavy smoke into the sea.

Shula had seized Nahum's arm, digging her fingers into it. He placed his hand over hers.

"German? British?"

"I couldn't see," Nahum said, still stroking her hand.

The remaining fighters were coming toward them—one, and two behind. The first rose, rose, and was opposite them—German.

Then it was the second German plane that had fallen.

Suddenly the two enemies half-circled and turned back, away, southward.

"They must be running out of gasoline," Nahum said. "The British are far from their base. They have never before come this far."

She still clutched his arm. Now she was able to turn her face to him. At once he said, "I'll take you down. Perhaps we'll be able to find out."

During the ride Nahum said nothing, concentrating on driving the cart quickly without overturning on the steep descent. The cabbages jumped on the bottom.

Where would they be able to find out? Whom could she ask?

"I'll pass their headquarters," Nahum said as though in answer. "Perhaps we'll see someone that one of us knows."

As they reached the edge of Tiberias, two German automobiles sped by. In the second one she saw Gottfried. He was leaning forward talking intently to the driver.

Nahum too had seen him. He turned the horse, at a walking pace, toward Leah's kvutsa. He still asked nothing.

The words gushed out of Shula of themselves, "Nahum, Nahum, marry me!"

She heard her own voice. It sounded shrill:

They were just past the Scottish hospital on the narrow lane alongside the lake. Nahum guided the horse into a copse, a place they had often strolled to from the girls' farm. The beast lowered his head to browse among the crevices in the rocky soil.

On Nahum's cheeks, tears were slowly brimming down. Shula too felt tears coming, and drew in a sniffle. After the kiss—not like anything before, not like with Gottfried, but a meeting of two beings, uncertain, certain, pledging their whole lives, questiong, unquestioning, a man pledging himself, not a man testing his masculine power—oh, now she knew—Shula said, "Dear one, I want to tell you—"

"No, no, you don't need to—"

"I want to."

It was all finished and it was all—all so small. "Nahum, believe me. Nothing really happened. I'm so glad at least of that."

"You don't have to tell me."

"I need to. It wasn't—just now when they fought—it wasn't as if it could come back, I knew it was really finished. But if it had been he who fell—"

"I still might have lost you."

A sharp breath overtook her. Could it be true? How much more of a person, a man, he was, than she had yet realized. It was good that your man should understand you better than you did yourself. "I might have lost you for a long time," Nahum amended. They drew back their heads and gazed at each other, not only loving, but measuring, probing, beginning to make their marriage. "Thou art not black, but golden, my Shulamith," Nahum quoted, returning to their old game of long ago.

"Thou hast hawk's eyes, my dove," Shula responded.

20

THE FIRST rains came, in Gallipoli as in Eretz, and they lay in mud. For weeks there were rumors that the whole bloody campaign was about to be abandoned, the troops withdrawn. Then, instead, a new regiment would be landed, a new assault attempted on Achi Baba.

The Mule Corps shrank to its hard bones. Even the Irishman was carried away to be hospitalized, seized by some mysterious disease that had come back upon him from his campaigns in Africa.

Josef commanded. Almost at once he assembled them and called for volunteers to become a fighting unit. The hard ones volunteered, enough for a full company. Soon the reply came down—they were more urgently needed as muleteers.

Josef would not remain sitting at headquarters but rode out with the forward supply missions—he would yet find a chance for them to fight, of that Araleh was certain.

In his head, Gidon wrote letters to those at home, sometimes at night, before sleep came, sometimes trudging alongside his mule. He found himself writing more to Mati than to Schmulik, especially if something happened that a boy would think of as real war.

—Tonight we really became soldiers, and Josef Trumpeldor was wounded, but that didn't stop him. We were taking ammunition to a company of Australians who were the farthest up, on the slope of Achi Baba, the mountain I already told you about. Suddenly on our right we heard shooting and shouting—

He broke off the imaginary letter. How could he explain the different ways a man felt? Just now he was lying in the dugout on straw-filled sacks over boards resting on large water-tins to keep them off the verminous ground; at least here, what with Araleh's using half the unit's supply of poison on their dugout alone, they had mostly got rid of the rats. Sometime perhaps he could tell all this—to Reuven? to Leah? Would he ever lie peacefully in bed with a wife, and let it all come out of himself? Sometimes in Gidon's longing different girls appeared, sometimes Eliza's friends—but she was much prettier than any of them, and with none of them had he felt at ease, with none of them had he felt "this could be she."

. . . So Josef, when they heard the shooting, had halted their squad, telling them to take up their rifles while he explored. They already knew. The Turks must be attempting one of their surprise sorties to overwhelm an outpost.

Dropping their mule-leads, the men lifted their rifles from the packs. The animals, long ago used to gunfire and shells, stood untethered, immobile hulks, spectators, with their bared teeth gleaming now and again in screaming laughter while the muleteers plunged on the flank of the Turks who were themselves plunging down on an Australian gun emplacement.

Cries, howling, only the language of curses in the dark helped to distinguish ally from enemy. Standing and shooting at blurs, Gidon heard Josef's enraged cry close to him, in Russian, *Pschakreff*! He was hit. But, pushing Gidon aside, he plunged on into the Australian trench; Tuvia and a few more men added themselves, shooting over the parapet at the blurs. Finally no more shooting came toward them, and in the trench too it stopped. Only then Gidon saw three Turks huddled on their haunches against the trench wall, two of them cramped over their wounds. They had reached their objective as attackers, and were prisoners, if not dead.

—Only then—he was writing it to Mati again—Josef examined his wound. He had a bullet in his left shoulder, you could see it, and he sat still without a cry while an Australian dug it out with a clean knife point. After that Josef ordered us to round up the mules and led us on to deliver the munitions. That is a hero.

Another tale he could tell Mati was how his own mule, Achi, also became a hero. —What! Mati would demand, pretending to be insulted that he had called a mule his brother, you called your mule Achi!—"Well, you can see I was thinking of you all the time." And he would rough Mati's hair. But perhaps it would be to his wife one night that he would relate how he had given Achi his name. They would be lying quietly side by side, and she would tenderly run her finger over the long scar high on his thigh, up there, where, as the fellows joked, it had "just missed." "Aren't you lucky?" she would say, and he would reply, "No, it's you who are lucky!" and they would laugh together and perhaps begin all over again to prove it.

It was a short time after Trumpeldor's wound, and hurrying across an open stretch of what had once been an isolated farmyard, they came under shellfire. A splinter from the very first explosion had hit Gidon's mule, and while the rest of the band dragged their animals to cover behind the ruins of the farmhouse, Gidon tried to undo the load of his beast, fallen thrashing to the ground. Suddenly the mule heaved around, biting at him savagely.

"Leave him! Come away!" Herscheleh shouted. "Who do you think you are—Josef?"

Nevertheless Gidon would not let go of the mule. Just as the strap came open the heavy pack fell away, he felt a slash across his own thigh, one with the thigh-wound of the animal, who, now freed, reared up. Gidon's thigh burned as though the searing iron still cut against it, but he pulled the mule across the splintered field to the shelter, and only then lay down to let Herscheleh tend his ragged cut.

"It's nothing, a deep scratch," Gidon insisted. He was blood brothers thus with the beast, and named him Achi. He would keep this mule for his own. "For a week" the letter to Mati would say, "we were limping on the same side. It was a joke to see us together. Araleh said he couldn't tell which was the mule."

Then he would tell Mati of Achi's celebrated deed. "Because of Achi we are famous for The Charge of the Zion Mule Corps!" Achi had become very clever, much like the cow they had at home, Klugeh. He kept to Gidon like a dog and was uncanny in scenting the presence of the enemy. On another delivery night, they plodded through a wady, climbed a ridge and began their unloading. It was a flank position, not active and the outpost of men, thankful for human contact, made the usual jokes about what exquisite delicacies the Zion boys had brought them, surely stuffed partridge with fresh-baked cream puffs for dessert. They gave a hand with the munition boxes. Suddenly Achi lifted up his head, screamed, and leaped across the trench and over the sandbagged embankment, plunging down on the other side.

—So you know what happened, Mati? From just where Achi ran into No Man's Land, we heard men yelling for their lives—Turks—they had been sneaking up and were right near the trench. Achi smelled them. Everybody started shooting, all the mules got excited and stampeded after Achi, some of them with boxes tumbling off their backs. The Turks thought it was a whole cavalry charge! Then the English jumped out and chased them and even captured the Turkish trench. So we became famous. It was the biggest joke of the war. The charge of the Zion Mule

Brigade. Only, we lost nine mules—they never came back. Except Achi. When I called him, he came, the only one. "Just like Klugeh," Mati would say.

But of what there was to see when the sun rose, he need not tell. Of the dead spattered on the slope, two mules among them. A Turkish soldier with his dagger still in his mouth between his teeth, the point sticking out beyond his widespread mustache. And the captured trench on the opposite slope, a crease in the stony earth, that four times had changed hands. As the men labored once more to reverse the embankment, they found it compounded not only of sandbags but of corpses, shredded uniforms and patches of flesh and decayed limbs all mashed together. Nor could it be seen which had been Turks or Australians or Scotsmen. Within the captured trench a haze of heavily gorged green flies lifted only slowly before them as they moved through, coming down again behind them like a sluggish fluid. Under their feet was a squash of maggots and mud and latrine filth; the mouth could not take in even a gasp of this atmosphere—it was like a partly dissolved compound of all this corruption. The men put cloths over their faces, and what entered their nostrils through the cloths was in a state barely gaseous; not an odor, but an encompassing, all-penetrating foul sweetness. It was, Gidon remembered, like the living putrescence released in the Huleh when Fawzi's hunting knife split open the belly of the slain swine.

How could you conquer an enemy who could subsist in this?

The English lieutenant decided not to hold the trench; it was exposed to fire from the Turkish position above. Twice it had been lost. Unless a major drive was intended here, it was not worth holding, and everyone knew the campaign was nearly over. Let this be left to Kemal.

They would be the last to be taken off, for their mules were needed to haul down cannon and to move what could be evacuated of supplies and stores.

All night long, groups of men moved soundlessly down onto the beach, then waited, squatting in their formations. Entirely different this was from the fiery disorder of their landing here. Now there was order, each man was in his place, though in some of the units—like their own—hardly a third remained of those who had come ashore.

A masterwork of evacuation, the generals said of it later, recounting the cleverness with which firing mechanisms had been widely deployed on the slope and actuated by water-drip devices the engineers had made so that all through the withdrawal guns went off, causing the Turks to believe that an attack was being prepared. In the end the English commanders talked themselves into believing that this last act of the terrible, protracted defeat had been a victory.

To the end Gidon labored. Cavalry mounts were embarked, and even the best of the mules. But over a hundred animals remained tethered to their stakes, among them many that he had patched up. His own Achi he managed despite the scar to push onto the barge under the eyes of Trumpeldor himself.

For the destruction of the imperfect animals, a squad of Gurkhas was borrowed; Gidon could not ask his men to do it. One by one the beasts fell. A few screamed and thrashed about, and to these Gidon himself, with his revolver, gave the *coup de grace*.

He had to run, plunging through the water as the mule barge was churning, pulling away from the Gallipoli shore, for the shadowy sea was already nearly empty of other transports.

Most were too weary to speculate what would be done with them now; Herscheleh argued that the Turks, freed from the battle for the Dardanelles, would certainly take their troops and send them sweeping down for a new attack on the Suez. And this move the British would be forced at once to forestall with their own attack on Palestine; thus at last the Zion men would be sent to fight in their own land. Not as mule-drivers this time. "No, as camel-drivers," Araleh sneered.

Josef sat pondering, breaking silence only to say that the unit must remain together. Whatever happened they must stay together. They had made a beginning, given a good account of themselves, and they must stay together.

On the faces of the few Nissims that remained you could see that they only wanted to get out, and stay home.

The answer as to their future was not slow in coming. Scarcely had they disembarked and reached camp when Josef received orders to disband the Zion Mule Corps. And now it even became clear that they had not fully been part of His Majesty's Armed Forces but only some sort of service unit attached to the military, a shade higher than gyppos. So this was why, Araleh raged, Saraleh and the other wives had not ever received the family allotment for soldiers. Nevertheless he had been subjected to military discipline and punished! Oh, the cunningness of them. Never again would they use him, Araleh swore. He would use them.

With the Nissims and the surviving boys of the mellah, it was well. They slipped off and went home. Some stopped to shake hands. Shaking hands with a man who had huddled against the side of a ravine with you waiting out a shelling—it was not unlike taking leave of the helpers from Yavneh and Tabor who had come when Mishkan Yaacov was under attack. But Gidon's real comrades were those from Eretz, and, the last, they remained tightly together.

"Don't accept discharge, wait!" Trumpeldor half-ordered, half-pleaded. He was going to see a still higher commander, and he would go on to appeal to the highest. Discharged from the hospital, the Irishman appeared, wan, but on his feet, to accompany Josef in his search for a reprieve. Let the Mule Corps be disbanded, yes, but let the Zion men be enlisted as a full fighting unit. They had earned it.

The Irishman assembled the remnants and made them a cheery speech. "Maybe some of them up there in the high command still don't know you are fighters. Well, I am the one that ought to know . . . never a finer or braver group of men—of course we had our little troubles, there would be something wrong with you and with me if we didn't, but the test is, would I take this command again? I'd jump at it! And not for the mules!"

They cheered, but they knew it was over. Araleh had already got himself discharged and gone home to Saraleh. For the rest of them, there remained the crowded little hotel rooms, the cots in the refugee barracks where the same faces were still to be seen. It had become a way of life; a cheder had even been established there for the children.

Only a handful still were kept in the army encampment, oddly enough because the mules had not been demobilized. The animals were needed for construction work. Staying on had become a mark of loyalty to Trumpeldor himself. Obsessed, he brought a new shred of hope every day. He had just received a letter, a telegram, a press cutting. Jabotinsky was making headway in London; even Chaim Weizmann, who could open the door and walk in on Lloyd George himself, was in favor of the plan for a Jewish fighting force. The bravery of the Zion Mule Corps men had been written about as far as Australia. And grim as it was to see the Allies now suffering setback after setback, Josef reminded his men that this heightened the need for every ounce of help, so that a Jewish unit must yet be accepted!

At last Gidon received word from home, indeed from someone who had been in the house, who had seen the family. One morning when he was on duty at the camp headquarters, a military car drew up and let off a civilian. Watching from the window, Gidon was certain he knew the man. The young man was well, even elegantly dressed, and he approached with an air of importance, of urgency. Yes, it was Avshalom Feinberg from Chedera. Gidon had always seen him before in a keffiyah, galloping around on an Arab steed. A Son of Nimrod! Had Feinberg too been deported? Was he perhaps coming here belatedly to join the Mule Corps?

The visitor had a pass to see Captain Trumpeldor. "But I know you," he cried to Gidon—"You're from Mishkan Yaacov—"

"Gidon Chaimovitch."

"You're related to a shomer—I saw you once with Menahem," he said with excitement, as though in his mind wheels were connecting and turning. "You're the fellow in the big fight there—the one who stayed behind."

Trumpeldor was out on one of his missions to headquarters, Gidon told him. Then he would wait, Avshalom said; for Josef Trumpeldor he would wait, and he looked at his watch as a man who had all sorts of things to do. Then at full speed he began talking, explaining, inquiring about the men, the fighting, which were the best men, all as though he had something important in back of his mind. How had things been with the higher command? Yes, he knew, high up there were those who had no use for Jews, a nuisance, not worth all the trouble they made, certain ones said. A whole circle of them. Old Egypt hands. Arab lovers. He chuckled. But certain others understood that the Jews could be of great use, some of the British had an excellent sense of history, and particularly in the intelligence service—

At last Gidon found a moment to interrupt; had Avshalom by chance heard anything of those at home?

Heard? He had even seen them, he had not long ago been in Gidon's own meshek, during the locust plague—

Of the plague Gidon knew, but nothing of how Mishkan Yaacov had fared.

"Pretty badly, terribly, like everywhere, but—Avshalom suddenly laughed. "Petticoat Lane!" he exclaimed. Gidon was puzzled. "Your father! Your sister, the big one, Leah! They saved the young lemon trees!"

"Yes?"

A sight! Avshalom related. Leah had got hold of every girl in the village, she had stripped the girls naked, and put their petticoats around the trees! Gidon too burst out laughing, his heart pounding with a strange joy, as if he were there at the triumphant feat.

Of Eliza's marriage, too, Avshalom told him. Not knowing of your own sister's marriage! And to Fat Nahum! And she called herself Shulamith now! And Nahum was getting rich feeding geese to German officers—

"Our geese!" Gidon cried, and he could have wept with homesickness, seeing Yaffaleh running away, out of sight, every time the Bagelmachers arrived to buy geese to be slaughtered for their pension.

Perhaps Gidon wanted to send a message home? He was going back soon, Avshalom said.

—Going back? How could that be?

Avshalom laughed his excited, knowing laugh. Not a letter, he couldn't take anything written, naturally, in case he were caught, but a message, even a few gifts. Though there would hardly be time for Gidon to buy anything—this was why he was waiting to see Josef Trumpeldor, it was urgent that he see him before he left. Already Gidon was pulling all his money from his pockets for gifts for the girls, Avshalom would know better than he what to buy—and for his mother and Schmulik—suddenly he began ripping off

his Shield of David insignia—the Mule Corps was finished,
anyway, this would be for his little brother, for Mati—

—What was to become of the Zion men? Avshalom
asked. This was exactly why he was here. And he plunged
into his own plans, talking rapidly, intimately, as to a
pledged comrade. Didn't they have the same ideas, the
same aim, to fight for Eretz? With the failure of the Gallipoli campaign there was not a day to lose, the British must
act more swiftly than the Turks, and the way was closer.
Ships they had. He had smuggled himself to Egypt for one
purpose, to urge them to organize an expedition. He and
his men would prepare a landing place. In Palestine he was
not alone. For months he and Aaron Aaronson had
planned this, they had organized a group of Jewish fighters—

—Their Sons of Nimrod, Gidon thought, but held back
from making a remark.

—What did Gidon think? Would the Zion men join?

—If there really was to be such an attack, if the British
would only take us—naturally . . . Gidon still did not
know quite how to respond.

And Trumpeldor? Would Trumpeldor send back word
with Avshalom to his friends in Eretz? "He has such influence. After all, Gidon, I'll be honest with you, I know you
people don't like us. The Shomer, the Poal Hatzaïr, the
Poale Zion—but all these things are in the past. They're
nothing. We all have the same aims. If Josef Trumpeldor
would send back word, if we could all join together and
seize the beach and the British would come, with your
fighters of Zion—can't you see it! We'll raise our flag at
Athlit!"

Gidon could see it as though it were happening. Hadn't
it been for a year his own vision, the vision of the whole
unit? Except they had not thought of the flag already there,
of fighters from inside the land already waiting for them.
But wasn't that too a clever idea? He knew the area—the
ruins of Athlit—deserted—why shouldn't it even be possible? Yet something within him held him back. It was too
clever, too daring a vision, the vision of a poet, and this
Avshalom was a poet, he had heard. Besides, it came to
Gidon, it was hardly for him to decide such things, it was
for the leaders, the Dovidls, the Galils. They had all been

sent into exile, he had heard. Who was left to decide? What would Josef say?

Yet the vision drew him. What was he doing here but rotting, no longer even needed for the mules—gyppos were being brought in to feed and clean them. And it was even said that the Russian consul had a list of all the men in the Jewish unit, and they might all be sent back to Russia, indeed Trumpeldor's Russian army pension had been restored. Instead of rotting here or being sent to Russia, imagine if he could smuggle his way back to Eretz itself, he and a whole band of the chevreh. And he could see them actually leading the capture of the ancient seashore fortress, climbing the jagged high wall to raise the flag atop the ruins . . .

"A whole shipload of you! You could be the vanguard!" Avshalom's eyes were drawing in his very thoughts. "A secret landing—I have good contacts with the British—an advance force—yes!" How many of them were left? A thousand? No? Even a few hundred could do it—And he had the right connections, here!

Perhaps he did have important connections. They had sent him in a military car. Besides, how had he got out of Eretz? And how was he going back?

New revelations poured from Avshalom. All year he had been planning how to contact the British. First he had hired two boatmen from Jaffa, but along the coast they had become frightened and had turned back. Then the American relief ship had appeared in Haifa, and he had smuggled himself aboard with false papers as a Spaniard, and when the ship stopped in Alexandria—here he was! At first the British command would not listen to him, but luckily he had run into a young Arab friend from Haifa who had taken him to the Intelligence Division, and there he had found an officer who understood. A Captain Walters. Walters desperately needed information from Palestine. He had seized on Avshalom and talked to him for a whole day. The disposition of the Turkish forces. Their armaments. Everything! The British had a few Bedouin bringing them information, a port-worker in Sidon, but what good were they? As Captain Walters had himself noticed, whatever an Arab believed you wanted to hear, he told you—while Aaron Aaronson, with his entry to Djemal Pasha himself, could secure for them every deployment, every plan, the

location of every military installation . . . With his bur-
bling laugh, Avshalom told of Aaronson's clever stroke: as
head of the war against the locusts, he had free entry everywhere. The poet dropped his voice. "Captain Walters understands the value of what we can do." The tone had become lower, conspiratorial, and yet with a strange candor.
The Captain was sending him back on a secret intelligence
vessel, disguised as a small freight ship. Every week this
ship would pass Athlit, and he had a code for making contact. A smoke signal. —In another moment, Gidon
thought, Avshalom would even reveal the code to him, but
Feinberg rushed on: thus, from both sides, from inside the
Yishuv and from here, the landing would be made ready,
and at the proper moment, a month at most—His eyes
were triumphant.

Gidon nodded. He still was not sure what to think; his
uneasiness had returned.

At last Josef appeared. Avshalom sat with him in his
office and it didn't take long. The military car had returned
and was waiting for the visitor. "I won't forget your gifts,
you can be sure," Avshalom called out to Gidon, as he
hurried off.

"Adventurism," Josef muttered. He had heard Feiberg
out and now he asked a few questions of Gidon. "You
know him? And the Aaronsons?"

"I went once with my brother Reuven to Aaronson's experimental farm. And he came to us to see Reuven's potatoes. He didn't go to Reuven's kvutsa because he was un-
welcome there."

Trumpeldor grunted. What the workers thought of those
Jewish effendi he knew. Yet if he could believe there was a
serious chance in Feinberg's plan he would work even with
them. Only what did it all amount to? Some captain in the
British Intelligence wanted to make use of Avshalom for
spying. Very well. Josef had nothing against such work behind the enemy lines. After all, was it different in moral
essence from sending out a scouting party? It was a tactic
of war. Let them gather intelligence. But anything of
greater scope—a landing, an uprising—would certainly not
be set in motion by a minor captain in the Intelligence Bureau. No. The English were simply leading this boy on.
Josef was convinced by now that from this band of British

high officers in Egypt nothing was to be obtained. They would use the Jews as mule-drivers, as spies, but not as fighting soldiers. His final discouragement had come this morning, and he was not in a good mood.

Even the last remnant here in this camp was to be discharged. The only promise he had been able to obtain was that if a nucleus of his men wished to enlist in a proper British regiment, they would be kept together. And if he eventually succeeded in the plan for a Jewish fighting force, these men would be transferred into it. This much he had obtained from General Butler himself, a friend of the Irishman's, but the promise had been given with the air of a man who humors you because he is certain there can be no such eventuality.

To obtain the right to such a fighting force, nothing more could be done here in Egypt; he must go to London. Meanwhile would the men stay together? The last of his men. What did Gidon think?

What else could they do? Should each man cast himself adrift in Alexandria? And yet to enroll in an army, to be subject to orders to go wherever he was sent, even if there was some general's promise of their being kept together, was a hard thing for each man to decide.

21

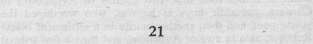

WHOSE story does not become entwined with history? With some, as with the Aaronsons and Avshalom Feinberg and all their tragic band, it becomes history itself. And then all who were at one time or another touched by the fated ones feel even more insistently the mystery of a chance connection, a decision made, that led to some seemingly fated end.

And so the Aaronson band entered history, and scarcely a family of the Yishuv but was to be touched, and some even destroyed, by the dilemma invoked by their choice. For who in the Yishuv, shrinking and becoming more interdependent each day, did not know someone who knew someone, who had not at some given moment had to decide whether to reveal or to be silent, whether to give shelter to the hunted and abhorred, or to keep the door closed? So ridden was the Yishuv to become, so profound was the moral shock of betrayals and counter-betrayals, that for half a century afterward these questions would be shrouded in avoidance.

To the Chaimovitches as well, virtually to each in a separate way, to Leah, to Reuven, to Gidon again, to Yankel, even to the boys, the question had to come.

As he had announced to Gidon, Avshalom Feinberg was brought back by Captain Walters' patrol boat, and in the moonless night rowed to the rocky cove of the Crusader ruins at Athlit; with all his baggage of gifts from men of the Mule Corps and from others in Alexandria, he clambered ashore, carrying also—in his head—a code of smoke signals that would be given by the vessel each time it passed, so that information that had meanwhile been gathered might be brought down and transmitted when the ship circled back at night.

All this in elation Avshalom Feinberg related to Aaron Aaronson, in the upstairs laboratory of the agricultural station. And then began their adventure, with its hiding places under the floor, its secret repositories in the walls, both here and in Aaronson's cottage in Zichron, across the courtyard from the family house. There came the growing chain of informants, first, two cousins of Avshalom's in Chedera, romantic boys as he was, who worshiped the young poet, and then another cousin in a settlement below Rehovot, also in awe of Avshalom, and then a few trusted Sons of Nimrod; and from Aaron Aaronson's side, a Jewish doctor in the Turkish army, and through this one, another, and so the chain grew. It was to have its name, later, at the height of its activities: the Nili, the group called themselves, putting together the first letters of each word of a Biblical line, *Netzach Yisroel Lo Yishakareh*, that is, literally, "The Lord of Israel Will Not Lie"; but "lie" is not the real sense of the phrase; perhaps it should be "misuse" or "betray" or "fail" us. And so they believed.

With the gifts and messages from Egypt, Avshalom was so reckless that he would seem to have been straining any promise of protection from the Lord of Israel. On the wrapping paper of the elegant box of loukhoums which he brought as a gift from Gidon to Shulamith, Nahum found printed the name of a noted Alexandria sweetshop, Groppi.

Yet who could find fault with such a messenger, one who had seen and spoken with Gidon and could describe to Mama how well and strong her son looked, and assure her that he had come out of the long battle unscathed and would now be safe! Feigel fingered and stroked the French-made crocheted shawl brought as his gift, and even longer she caressed the insignia with the Shield of David that Gidon had taken from his uniform and sent for Mati. From hand to hand this went, with Mati nearly bursting before it came at last to him, and only Menahem, in the family assembled to hear news of Gidon, was quick enough to stop the boy from rushing out to show the emblem to the whole village.

"Idiot!" Schmulik scolded him; Schmulik would have wanted the badge himself, though to him Gidon had sent an actual photograph of the whole group, his squad in the Zion muleteers, standing side by side with Josef Trumpeldor.

Only later was Avshalom able to manage a serious talk with Menahem. Now that he had made the contact in Alexandria, things would develop. What was needed first and urgently was information, to show the British Intelligence officer what Jews could accomplish. Most essential was information about troop movements, and Avshalom had already thought out a plan. Every rail movement into Palestine passed through Fuleh. Someone selling refreshments at the station could easily keep track. And Gilboa was close by. One of their women? Menahem was already shaking his head. The whole matter had been decided the first time Avshalom approached them, and the decision would not change; it was not even wise to bring up the question again, since secrecy was essential.

And what about Menahem himself? He agreed with that policy?

"Our task is to defend the Yishuv, as best we can. Not to place it in further danger. With that I agree, completely."

But Avshalom was not done. Something unsaid passed between the two men. Somewhere, at some point, Menahem must feel in agreement with the purpose and the plan. Menahem himself moved about a great deal, he might come upon useful information . . .

In the end there was this much: If ever there was something that, for the safety of the Yishuv, it was urgent for England to know, Menahem would make a personal decision. No, he wanted no codes, no encounters, no secret connections. "If anything of this sort should happen, I'll find a way to get it to you."

Already the information they had collected seemed urgent and vital. From one of the Herzlia Gymnasia graduates who had been made a Turkish lieutenant and was stationed as an interpreter in Damascus, Aaron Aaronson learned of a violent disagreement between Djemal Pasha and the German commander, Kress von Kressenstein. Fearing intrigues and revolt among Arab tribes, Djemal wanted to reinforce the outposts of the Ottoman Empire in Mecca. The German insisted on using all their forces in a massive second assault on the Suez Canal, with all possible speed. New squadrons of German fliers had appeared and were stationed in Dagania. Gaza was being fortified with heavier artillery—Avshalom had even obtained the details of the emplacements, the site of the guns. All this was coded and the papers wrapped in a package sealed in oilcloth, ready to hand over; day after day they watched the sea, but no smoke signal came. The time for two sailings went by. Surely something had gone wrong. The information would not keep. Suddenly Avshalom rode off and was gone.

On a smugglers' tracks south of Beersheba, the rider was stopped by a Turkish patrol. The local commander was unconvinced by the tale of a renewed locust invasion, and sent Avshalom under guard to Beersheba, presently to be turned over to the Germans; he might have been summarily hanged had not Zev the Hotblood, now a watchman in the area, heard of the arrest, galloped with the news to Aaron Aaronson in Athlit, and returned with gold, so that matters were at least delayed.

In this time, as long afterward became known, the contact ship's smoke signal had been changed. The British captain sent word of the change to his Arab agent in the port of Sidon who was to bring word of the change to the Jews in Athlit. But the message had not been delivered; perhaps the Arab had not wanted a rival among the Jews. In Alex-

andria, receiving no response from the eager Jewish lad
who had seemed so bright and promising and who had
even scorned the offer of money for his undertaking, Capt.
Walters decided to make one more attempt at the contact.
There was a growing urgency. It was becoming clear that a
campaign would have to be undertaken into the Sinai to
forestall further attacks on the canal. Specific intelligence
was needed.

Among the Palestine refugees in Alexandria, or perhaps
better, among the veterans of the Zion Mule Corps, someone must be found who was a good swimmer and who was
familiar with Athlit.

Soon the proposal came to Gidon. Josef was not against
it; it was Josef himself who had indicated Gidon, among a
few others, to the British captain.

The Zion men were now completely demobilized, most
of them housed again as refugees in the Mafrousi Barracks
where their stay had begun. Herscheleh had found a dwelling of sorts, a large room over a cafe owned by a Greek
Jew, and with Tuvia they all moved in, still using some of
their back pay; Josef did not want to leave for England
until his men were settled together in a British army unit,
but many were holding back. Discussions were endless. To
join up they had time. At least as long as the Russians let
them alone here. Who knew whether there would ever be a
Jewish unit?

"You join an army, it's like a marriage," Herscheleh
said. "Jacob was promised Rachel for his bride and he
woke up in the arms of Leah."

"Don't forget he got Rachel, too," said Tuvia.

The proposed mission was at least a chance to break
away from their endless, repetitive ruminations, from the
sense of uselessness. One thought troubled Gidon, however.
Once he touched the land, would he have the courage to
leave it and come back here? Or suppose he should make
his way inland across the Emek, home, to disappear, simply to stay there and go back to his work on the farm,
keeping out of sight of the Turks?

Like so many of the lieutenants and captains to whom
Gidon had carried supplies in Gallipoli, this Captain Walters seemed surprised that a man understood his instructions the first time; the captain repeated them with many

mind you's. At once Gidon saw there was no question of the dreamed-of landing of troops. It was information about the Turkish offensive with which the British were concerned. From Bedouin in the Negev had come tales of masses of Turks arriving, numerous as the sands in the desert. "Mind you, your Bedouin seemed to imagine the larger the number he tells us, the more gold he can demand for his information."

"We have a saying, he tells you what he thinks you want to hear."

"Right you are." But accurate and dependable information was urgently required. No point in keeping masses of troops sitting here waiting for a Turkish attack when they were needed right now on other fronts.

The captain had his nose in a dossier. A chap had appeared over a month ago, "One of yours"—meaning a Jew. They had arranged for him to go back to Palestine to send on information, but the signal had been altered, apparently he had not received the new code which was to have been brought to him by some bloody camel-driver. Gidon, then, was to deliver this new code to this Avshalom Feinberg, or Aaron Aaronson, whichever he could find, and bring back whatever information they had meanwhile collected. The new code was simple. A prolonged trail of smoke. That meant the boat would circle back and rendezvous the same night.

Though Gidon could not reveal to Araleh exactly what it was, Araleh advised him to take the mission. The pay was good, he needed the money, and the risk, from what Gidon said, was not great.

The vessel was battered-looking, a small freighter like the Greek tramp ships that carried lumber and iron and all manner of cargo around the Mediterranean. Only, its cargo space was half taken up by a large new engine; the vessel raced along the coast.

A young lieutenant gave him an oilcloth-covered bundle of clothing, a rubber-encased pistol, a knife. In a pocket of the trousers there were false papers; should he be picked up, he was an ordinary laborer. But in his few hours ashore, and at night, there would be little chance of his getting caught, so he was not likely to need the identity.

Every two weeks the Lieutenant made this coastal voyage; yes, he'd seen a good deal of rainfall this winter over Palestine. —Then the crops must be doing well, Gidon thought. If only the war would move quickly to an end, so that the Turks would not be there to seize the next harvest.

Enormous, solid clouds, like strangely shaped earths, rolled heavily in the night sky. The vessel was running in landward, and as in that distant night of long ago, Gidon could sense the density of the nearing land, the bulk of the Carmel, a great arm spread along the shore.

The engine only murmured now. The lieutenant stood by the rail and held out a whisky bottle. For politeness, Gidon took a swallow. Then he climbed down into the tender. They would row him as close as they could. He stripped off his clothes and tied the waterproof bundle on his head.

Now he saw the ruin emerging, blacker than the atmosphere. In those ancient times too the English had ventured here. It struck him all at once—what a strange thing for them to have done, those Crusaders. What had they needed to come here for? With Jews it was different.

There were rocks, half in, half out of the sea. The oarsmen were holding the bark steady for him to climb over. Gidon lowered himself; the water, though cold enough, gave him no shock. One hand still clung to the boat. To let go was to be alone. But swimming to Eretz—would they at home somehow feel he was near, that his foot had touched the land?

He swam easily, but the distance was greater than he had expected, and in the silence and aloneness, the black water and the black sky were one. He could not keep his head high enough to make out the bulk of ruined wall, and when a wave rolled over his head, Gidon even had to fight back a sense of panic, of being dragged back into the measureless void of tohu v'bohu. "No, I am not like that," he told himself. He did not have such imaginings, such fears. And thrusting about with his foot, he scratched it on a jagged rock and soon found bottom.

The rocks were slippery with moss; his hands gripped an edge of what must once have been a sea wall, and pulling himself out of the sea, Gidon, without resting, undid his pack and put on the shirt and trousers. Gazing back out to sea, below the clouds, he could discern a blot that moved—

the ship going away, to return at dawn. He stood up and turned to the dark land.

Below his feet was a tangle of thistles and broken stones; briars came waist high and scratched and clung. In Gallipoli, when at times he had gone on a lone mission with supplies, there had been at least his mule. And here in Eretz that time he had remained behind on watch over Mishkan Yaacov, there had been his horse with him. The howl of a jackal was welcome to him now.

Moving steadily, Gidon stood now against the single, jagged high wall that, as he recalled, was all that remained of the ruined fortress, though in the night the form of the wall was unfamiliar. Behind it would be a neck of land, to the left a shallow beach, on the other side the salt marshes. He must be careful there. Like that time with Fawzi in the Huleh marshes, a man could sink in. Behind the marshes, a few hundred feet of wasteland, and then there passed the main highway from Jaffa to Haifa, cutting across the fields of the agricultural station. On the other side of the highway, Aaron Aaronson's double lane of palm trees led to the station itself, where someone should be on watch in the laboratory on the second floor.

Not a lantern, not a sign of habitation.

Then, as he moved onto the fields, a sound came to Gidon. He stood entirely still, holding back an involuntary movement of his hand toward the pistol. A pistol against an army—what use! For what he had heard he identified now—it was the murmurous movement of troops, the long scuffling beat of an irregular march, marked with hoofbeats and wheels creaking, and as he came closer, the conglomeration of sounds was interwoven with scattered voices.

They were already here then, from Gallipoli. Almost, he could see that dead Turkish soldier with the bayonet between his teeth, risen and marching to get at his killers. The British had come away by sea, the enemy was moving down by land. Here they were.

Carefully, treading in a furrow of plowed earth, Gidon moved closer. A dog might discover him. Yet, compelled by the soldierly demand in him, Gidon could not but move forward until, even in the night, he might make something out.

Off the plowed field in an outcropping of rocks he found good cover. A stretch of the highway lay unobstruc-

tedly before him, and he made out the blur of a column.
How easily now, with a few machine guns here in ambush—had Avshalom's crazy landing been made—they
could have cut down hundreds!

But then? The numbers were unending. Sometimes when
Gidon thought the end had passed, and gathered himself
to dash across the road, a few horsemen would ride up, and
after them he would hear the tramping resumed from the
north. Again the forces would come, light artillery rolling,
and kitchens, and wagons of supplies, and after another gap,
files of men. At least a division he must have watched passing by. And in the night—for secrecy and also for haste.
And this was only one night and one route.

He moved laterally until he was opposite the palms. But
there was bad luck. A tent was set up beneath them, a
checkpoint. Gidon drew back into the field and considered.
To outwait them? To fail his rendezvous with the ship and
remain the two weeks until it would pass again, emitting its
signal? He could see himself in a day's walk crossing the
Emek; it would be better to go by day, a simple worker in
the land, and by nightfall reach Gilboa, Dvora, Menahem,
safe among his own, and the next day on a horse, home.

But if caught he would endanger them all.

It pulled, pulled on him. If he sat here until it was too
late for him to reach the vessel. He had only to sit, not to
move. At a certain moment it would be too late. Then the
choice would have passed by, it would be too late. He
could continue in his life only for himself.

But what he saw here was in itself important. He had
come upon information and must report it—that was urgent. It could not wait two weeks.

And his mission, the signal for Avshalom?

There on the field, close by where he sat, a plow had
been left. Someone would come to finish the field, one of
Aaronson's Arabs. If a message was left, tied to the handle
of the plow . . . The fellah, unable to read, would take it
to them in the station. It must be worded so that they
would understand, but no one else.

Over this, Gidon puzzled for some time. How could he
explain about the code?

In his pocket they had put a stub of pencil; everything
they had thought of—even a box of Jaffa cigarettes, taken
from a Turkish prisoner at the Suez. The British were

clever at this work. Tearing off the lid of the box, he wrote on it in Hebrew: "Avshalom! Passed by but missed you. I'll pass again in a few weeks, and we can sit down for a long smoke."

With his poet's imagination, Avshalom would certainly understand about the signal. Gidon signed, not his own name, but "Walter." He managed to fasten the bit of cardboard to the plowhandle. In the doing of all this, the pull of the land had somehow fallen away; he was engaged in a task. Yet as he made his way back to the ruins, there remained in Gidon a powerful wish to leave some kind of mark that he had been here; it was like the thought a man sometimes has: if he passes from the world, will there remain any sign that he once lived and was present in it?

Before the vessel appeared to pick him up, he had a bit of time, and he scratched with his knife the name Gidon on a stone of the ancient wall, among other names that had been scratched there over many years. One day perhaps he would show it to Mati.

22

IN THESE same days Sara Aaronson passed through Damascus, and there Reuven encountered her in the house of the Shalmonis in the Harat al Yahud. They were a wealthy family who traced their origins back to the time of the Dispersion, and their house was open, particularly on Sabbaths, to the scattering of Jewish officers who found themselves in Damascus. There was a daughter, whose fiancé, a captain, was posted far off in the forces in Yemen. An educated and refined girl, she was almost always seated at the piano—she had studied at the conservatory in Paris. Often some of her young women friends were there as well, but Reuven did not aspire to these daughters of wealthy families, and besides, they were always taken up by the clever and dashing types. Reuven came by of a Sabbath afternoon simply to be able to talk a while in Hebrew and to hear news from those who had lately been in Eretz.

This time, as it happened, there were only a few Sabbath

visitors—troops were on the move, everyone was busy. And Elisheva Shalmoni was seated not at the piano but in an alcove with another young woman, talking intently, while her mother served tea to the few other guests. Half-starting toward Elisheva and her friend, whom he seemed to recognize, Reuven halted in hesitation.

The visitor had raised her eyes. "Yes, we know each other," she said, just as he blurted—"Sara Aaronson." And, "Excuse me, I—your married name—"

With a fleeting, odd expression she said, "It doesn't matter, I'm Sara Aaronson."

Except for the burnished hair and the blue eyes, there was nothing of the plump, saucy girl who had brought him the botany book from her brother's library when he lay ill in their watchman's hut. The young woman's face was strained, pale, it soon came out that she had been an entire month on the way from Constantinople with endless breakdowns and requisitions of trains for the military so that long stretches of her journey had been made by carriage and even horse cart. But there are times when an explanation of physical strain does not erase an impression of suffering, of crisis, and so it was here. She must be pouring out her heart to her friend Elisheva; Reuven felt himself an intruder, and yet Sara Aaronson seemed eager for him to sit with them. She and Elisheva had known each other in Europe during their studies, she said. Had he lately seen her brother Aaron?

—Didn't Aaron know she was coming?

No, nor her family; it was a surprise or they would have stopped her.

Aaron was well, he was very active, he assured her.

Something seemed to be troubling Sara about her brother. "From his last letters" . . . she said, and broke off. When had Reuven last seen him?

It had indeed been nearly a month, and the incident was one Reuven did not feel he should relate to her. He had happened into Djemal's outer office just in time to hear the Pasha shouting as Aaronson emerged from his presence, "Don't come to me again! I have enough of your interference! Perhaps next time I'll hang you!"

Aaronson, as the one with the best access to Djemal, had come to plead for the return of the wheat that Bahad-ad-Din had seized in Jaffa from the relief ship sent by

American Jews to the Yishuv. In Jerusalem the highest
community leaders had pleaded with Bahad-ad-Din—to no
avail. They had turned to Aaronson, asking him to intervene with Djemal Pasha. Though Reuven later heard that
half the wheat had been returned, he had not seen Aaronson in Damscus since that day of Djemal Pasha's threats.

Ironically, he heard Elisheva just then telling Sara,
"Aaron has the greatest influence with Djemal Pasha."

"Oh, yes," Reuven said, "I even owe my being here to
him—he actually saved my life," and he began to tell of the
incident.

Sara Aaronson seemed to become more distraught,
though he tried to make light of it, but suddenly she broke
out, "Oh, they are so cruel! How can human beings be so
cruel?" and then there poured from her things she had seen
on her journey: the roadside littered with corpses still lying
unburied, dead children with their little legs like dried
sticks. She had seen entire Armenian villages burnt, empty.
In Constantinople they had known and not known. All
year she had been wracked by the tales. A whole million of
people, it was said, a whole people destroyed, could such
things be? And there she lived in luxury in the city and
heard these tales, and her husband became richer in his
war dealings and people said it was all exaggerated, war
horror stories. But why? why? her eyes were dilated; she
was talking to Elisheva, but her eyes spoke to Reuven, and
he began to feel shame that he was in Turkish uniform and
wanted to explain to her that he did nothing for their war,
that he was a gardener.—It was not only the usual hatred
of the Moslems for Christians; the Turks envied the Armenians. Sara was answering her own question: the Armenians were a thrifty people, their villages looked richer, so
now they were to be destroyed. Turkey was to be for the
Turks—one people, one religion, one land. And the Jews
would be next, everywhere it was said the Jews would be
next. That was why she was coming home. "It was as
though I were being called, I couldn't stay away—you understand me?" If anything should happen, she wanted to be
with her family.

Elisheva soothed her. It was dreadful, it was a cruelty
beyond belief, but between Turks and Armenians, it was an
old bitter hatred, and while there had always been anti-
Semitism here, she would not minimize it—how long was

it, only a generation or two since the terrible Damascus blood-libel in which one of her own family had been among the accused and had died in prison from their torture— still, today, even on the Turks there were restraining hands. Their own allies the Germans would never let such a massacre take place, and America too had a great influence, and besides, Elisheva was certain that the effect of the Armenian massacre throughout the civilized world was so ghastly that nothing of this kind could ever happen again.

For a moment Elisheva was drawn away to other guests, and Sara Aaronson, once more self-possessed, turned to Reuven. "And you, Reuven? It is a pity you have to waste yourself here. My brother had a high opinion of you as a horticulturist, I remember."

—Oh, he was fortunate, Reuven said, he did not have to take part in the war, and he was even carrying on his own work. Indeed, he had lately found something he wanted to show to her brother, perhaps she could take back a few samples? And he told of the pistachio grove he had discovered. The way she listened, a woman asking intelligent questions—after all, the sister of Aaron Aaronson—a balm, even a touch of Sabbath peace was returning around them.

"And you'll bring seeds back and plant them at home one day when this is all over," she said.

Something in this young woman drew him profoundly; whatever it was with her husband there in Constantinople, the husband of whose riches she had spoken so scathingly, she had had the courage to undertake this frightening journey by herself. She was running away, he now understood, to return to her people, and this moved him. A sense of love rose in Reuven—no, not in the man-and-woman way, but as sometimes for a chaver or chavera at home in the kvutsa who undertook some extra task not required of them.

Sara was worried about how to continue her journey, since all the trains were entirely taken over for troops. The next morning Reuven happened to encounter a pair of German officers who were going by special carriage as far as Jaffa and said they would be delighted to escort a Jewish lady. When he came to tell her of it, Reuven brought a twist of paper with some pistachio nuts for her to take to her brother, and in a lighter mood, Sara put one of the nutshells between her teeth and cracked it open.

"I may eat them all before I get home!" she said, almost gaily.

Only after her surprise arrival, in fashionable traveling costume in a carriage with two gallant German officers, and after the tumult of reunion and Sara's assurances that all was well in Constantinople—that the war was making her husband richer than ever, she had but to hint at a new luxury and he bought it for her—and only after the meal of good things that her mother spread out "in spite of everything," was Sara Aaronson able to mount a horse and gallop down to surprise Aaron at his agricultural station.

He was not there. His overseer, Salim, greeted her, seeming not even surprised at her coming. Her brother had gone on urgent business to Jerusalem. Salim seemed to be hesitating whether to tell her something more; then he brought out the note that had meanwhile been found on a plow in the field. Perhaps it was important?

—Walter? Who was Walter?

Salim knew of no such name. Sara thought it odd, a Jew named Walter—more likely a German. And why was it addressed to Avshalom? For a time she waited for Aaron; then she decided Aaron would now more likely return directly home to Zichron, and rode back.

He came toward evening and leaped from the carriage in surprise at seeing her, but through all the warmth of greetings, Sara felt her brother's tension. Perhaps it was because of her, perhaps he was not pleased that she had left her husband and come back to be one more problem for him? They crossed the courtyard to his own small house; she chattered a bit more about her journey, but still they were not completely united as in old times. Then she told him about Damascus, even brought out the little packet of pistachios from Reuven Chaimovitch.

Aaron was pleased. "He's right, it's a discovery! I've never seen such a tree in the whole region! What a fellow! Ten wars couldn't stop him."

But still Sara felt some barrier between them, and she suddenly slipped down with her head on his knees and let everything pour out. She would never go back to that stifling, meaningless life—she had debased herself, debased her body in marriage to a man who was nothing to her, whom she mostly despised—it was even unfair to him, to that spiritless well-meaning nothing; she could endure it no longer and had returned to live her life here. She wanted to be of use, she wanted to help Aaron; whatever he was doing, he was doing important things for the Yishuv. She had felt something in his letters—whatever it was, he must take her to help him.

Still he was silent.—Was he angry with her for coming? No, no, it would be good to have her near him, Aaron said. She was perhaps right in leaving her husband if all she said was true. But they must take time to think, and meanwhile he must go on urgent business to Damascus. When he returned—

With a puzzled instinct, Sara drew out the message that Salim had found in the field. Her brother studied it, and seemed to be drawing even further away from her.

—But who is Walter? And why to Avshalom? "Avshalom doesn't smoke a pipe," she laughed uneasily. And how was Avshalom? What was he doing? "You wrote he was helping you in your work?"

Just now Avshalom was in Beersheba, Aaron said.

Beersheba? What was he doing there? What was the mystery? And all at once Sara broke out; she was no longer a girl, she was a woman now, and she had taken her life in her own hands, and he need have no fear if it was about her and Avshalom—

Brushing his hand across his forehead, her brother said, No, it was nothing so romantic. Very well then, he would tell her. Avshalom was in prison in Beersheba. He had made a fool of himself in their work. The note from Walter was a note from the British—and the whole of it came out.

"Against the Turks? Good, good!" she cried. "Anything against the Turks, no matter how dangerous!" She had known it in her soul, this was surely why she had come!

But in Jerusalem today he had failed, Aaron said. Even the Jew with the highest connections there, old Ehud Yeshayahu, could do nothing to free Avshalom because the case had been turned over to the German military. The only chance was in Damascus.

She would go with him.

No. She must remain at the laboratory. In case there was an urgent message. Or if they came from Beersheba for more money. He needed someone trustworthy there, he did indeed need her help. Good she had come. From the family he had kept all knowledge of this work. In Damascus he would somehow find a way—her damned Avshalom was brilliant and courageous, but he was always getting himself arrested.

Reaching Damascus, Aaronson did not at once go to the palace; he was uncertain just how to proceed. To approach Djemal Pasha and plead directly for intervention for Avshalom was a great risk, it would be trusting Avshalom's life to the devil's capriciousness. Stopping at the Palace Hotel, he refreshed himself. A way must be found to minimize Avshalom's danger. The solution must exist, it was somewhere around him, he felt its presence as sometimes with a scientific problem when he stood in his library knowing the response was there—he had just to reach out his hand to the right book.

And coming from his room, he passed a small group speaking Hebrew. In his deep preoccupation, Aaron might have avoided them, but one caught his eye—it was Reuven Chaimovitch in his shabby uniform; and the scientist automatically turned back to greet him. The others were mostly from the labor settlements, but there was also the planter from Rehovot, Smilansky, who cried out, "You are just the man we need!"

They had been summoned by Djemal Pasha. He was demanding an impossible tonnage of fodder and grain crops for the coming summer, he even threatened to raze all the orange groves to make fields for growing animal fodder. Aaronson must speak for them!

Suddenly he saw his solution. He would be summoned. "If I appear before Djemal without being called, it will rub him the wrong way," he said. Reuven, however, might mention that luckily Aaronson was in Damascus and would surely be able to help about the fodder.

It did not take long. Reuven came running, and they hurried to the Residence.

"He was screaming at them," Reuven said. "He demanded a final figure on wheat, and they said they didn't know. He started screaming again, to bring someone who knew, and then I spoke of you. Djemal drove them all out and told me to bring you at once."

The first words the Pasha uttered were, "You're in Damascus and didn't let me know?"

"Last time you said you would hang me."

"Next time!" Djemal laughed, and demanded, "How much wheat and fodder can your damned Jews turn over to the army, if they don't hide it or smuggle it to the enemy?"

A huge new fodder crop, Aaronson suggested, could be raised in the orange groves themselves, between the rows of trees; this would not deplete the soil. Already Djemal's eyes were gleaming. "And this also," Aaronson said, "will release many fields now used for fodder to grow grain."

"How many tons of wheat? How many tons of barley?"

To compile such a report rapidly, Aaronson smoothly replied, he needed his chief assistant, who kept all his records. "Unfortunately, when I sent him south to survey the Negev for barley crops, your brilliant German friends arrested him as a spy. They are about to hang him, and so I fear I can bring you no report."

The Pasha bolted upright in his chair. One could virtually see the current of his fury diverting itself into this newly opened channel. The stupid, interfering Germans! The Ottoman army could starve, but the Germans had to discover spies in the desert! When the war was won with Turkish blood, it was the Germans who would try to take all the spoils. Djemal flung himself over his desk—already he was scribbling a telegram, his pencil nearly tearing through the paper. What was the name of this assistant?

"Avshalom Feinberg."

Reuven had remained standing near them, silent yet in some way included, hoping only that Djemal Pasha might not turn to him with questions, and that he might not unwittingly spoil Aaronson's purpose, whatever it might be. At first he thought the purpose was to gain time, but the mention of Avshalom Feinberg was like a shade raised, and Reuven inadvertently turned away his face so that Djemal might not see the emotion come over him. For Leah had managed, through a refugee family that had bought permission to stay in Damascus, to send him a note about Gidon. The Son of Nimrod, she said, had been in Joseph's land and had seen Gidon, and it was true that Gidon was with The Hero in the narrow place. The Son of Nimrod had even brought back gifts from Gidon for the family.

In terror that what he now knew could be read on his

face, Reuven only wanted to get out of that room, yet he stood, astonished at the dry way in which Aaron Aaronson went on to discuss agricultural matters with Djemal Pasha, who was now in an excellent mood.

Even when they were safely away from the palace, Reuven did not open the dangerous subject. Instinctively he felt it was well not to know more. Let Aaronson think that he, like the Pasha, had found believable the tale of Avshalom Feinberg's agricultural mission in the desert.

It was Aaronson who broke what was becoming an embarrassing silence. First, he complimented Reuven on his discovery; Sara had brought him the rare pistachio samples. Remarkable! Reuven said he was happy Sara had arrived safely. "I believe we have you to thank," her brother replied, "for finding her the transport and the gallant escorts."

It was only a piece of good fortune, Reuven said. As he had now been given an officer's rank, he sometimes found himself in their canteen.

Ah—it was good that he could move about among them, Aaronson remarked. The two had entered a public square that Reuven had laid out, and half deprecatingly, yet proud of the colorful effect, he showed Aaronson his floral design of the Turkish flag with its crescent and star in thick clusters of white carnations, and, surrounding the flag, a box-border cut in arabesques.

Abruptly, Aaronson sat down on a stone bench and motioned Reuven beside him. "You understood about Avshalom?"

"I have heard he was in Egypt. He even saw my brother."

"As for discretion, it is a quality lacking in him. He'll yet manage to get himself hanged. Except for your having me called in by Djemal, it would have happened this time." Then he discoursed, as when he discoursed about plants and soil, in the tone one takes with a colleague who has equal devotion, is equally absorbed in the same cause in life. Surely, like his brother Gidon, Reuven must understand in his heart that the only hope for the Yishuv lay in an Allied victory.

"I can only say this," Reuven replied, as one who owed a master full candor, "I am satisfied that what I have to do in my role in the war cannot in any way affect the military situation."

"Perhaps it could," Aaronson said. But to begin with, he wanted Reuven to understand that he was in no way under obligation to help. Indeed, Aaronson said, he had refrained until now from speaking to Reuven about this subject since he had not wanted to risk Reuven's feeling obligated because of the accidental service he had been able to do for him. Yet matters were now at so crucial a stage that they must overcome this scruple. As Reuven well knew, there were military tasks where the work of one man was worth that of hundreds, even thousands, in the field. Here in Damascus it was relatively easy for one who moved about freely in official circles to hear of strategic plans, of movements—

Already Reuven's whole being had tightened. "I cannot. I cannot. Don't ask it of me."

Aaronson halted.

"Don't think I suggest that what you may do could be wrong," Reuven blurted. "I—it's probably the highest bravery." Aaronson showed no reaction. "It is not that I would not want to help. Only there are some things a man knows he cannot do. Believe me, if it were that there was fighting in Eretz, that we had to protect our people, believe me, I would come, one way or another, and take up a gun." Sadly he added, "Though I am a pacifist."

Aaronson turned to him now with a curious smile compounded of understanding and respect, yet with something of pity too, as for an unfinished man.

"What little I did today, to help someone," Reuven stammered, "even had I already known the truth of the mission, I would still have done what I could."

"That will have to suffice for us then," said the scientist. "Perhaps such a situation will arise again where without actively joining us you can be of help." Aaronson stood up.

"I'll remain here a bit," Reuven said. "I want to do a little weeding."

"It is a superb formal garden, Reuven." Aaronson complimented him again, and with his brisk energetic stride, walked away.

"Good job!" their Captain Walters cried out gaily as Gidon ended his account of the troops marching southward. To these British, it really seemed a game. The captain jumped up with the notes he had made, so Gidon also arose. "Perhaps we'll call on you again."

Did he want to go again? For a week, two weeks, Gidon waited uncertainly, nervously, and then quite by chance in a cafe he saw the young Haifa Arab whom he had encountered in Captain Walter's office, before going on his "swim." Had the ship brought back any news from their friend Avshalom, Gidon asked.

Faud looked at him sadly. "Oh, bad luck." The little ship had been torpedoed on the very next run. Captain Walters himself had decided to make that run and had been on board. "We don't know whether he is alive or not. We just don't know." No, he did not think there would be another ship sent out.

Each day Sara sat for hours by the laboratory window, watching. The signal would appear, Aaron insisted. "They need us." Had not the British themselves sent a messenger who left that note on the plow to resume the contact?

Meanwhile the metal box hidden under the floor-tiles was filled with reports. Avshalom, freed, was ceaselessly on the road gathering material. Even in the prison in Beersheba he had learned things; Zev the Hotblood had smuggled reports to him, locations of encampments, and the numbers and units of the men, all of it in a Hebrew prayer-book. Now Avshalom and Zev were everywhere. With what spirit, with what joy, Avshalom recounted their escapades when he came to Athlit with his material. And Sara too must join in the adventures. He would take Sara to Jerusalem, to the Hotel Fast. She would flirt with a high officer, learn what was needed, and at the crucial moment—Avshalom initated some slavering colonel about to take her up to his room—he, her "husband," would appear and whisk her away.

Urgent material came into the hands of Aaron himself. Returning from a trip to Damascus, he declared he must quickly get word to Alexandria. German troops were being brought in for the Suez attack. It was planned for August.

And still the ship did not appear! Something surely had gone wrong again with the signal. There was only one solution, even if it seemed the long way around. Aaron himself must make contact with the British Intelligence. The contact must be established firmly, on the highest level. He must somehow reach England. From there, he would get himself stationed in Alexandria. Only then would the operation be certain. What they would send he would receive. Already he had worked out a code for Sara. She would use the watchman's hut on top of the hill in Zichron, in the vineyard. When there was material to be picked up she would hang a sheet to dry. It could easily be seen from a distance at sea.

Already Aaronson had planned how to reach Europe. Djemal Pasha was just now pleased with him, for hundreds of tons of fodder had resulted from his plan to plant between the trees in the citrus groves. He would ask Djemal Pasha for leave to go on a scientific mission to Berlin. It was even true that he needed to consult an expert there on the extraction of oil from the sesame plant. From Berlin he must reach a neutral country—a scientific conference perhaps—and from there he could escape to England. For the work at this end, Avshalom would be in charge.

In Berlin, Aaron Aaronson learned of the presence of an American rabbi on a relief mission to German Jews. By happy chance, Rabbi Judah Magnes was a member of the sponsoring committee for Aaronson's agricultural station. Perhaps the only one of the committee who would have done anything so decisive, Magnes arranged to spirit Aaronson into his own cabin aboard a ship returning to America.

The British, alerted, halted the ship in the Orkneys for a "routine inspection," and Aaronson was taken off under seeming protest, and delivered in London. There—a Jew from Palestine who offered an entire information network behind the Turkish lines—he was questioned and questioned.

Even from the deployment that he himself had seen on that single night ashore, it was clear to Gidon that British troops in Egypt must soon be needed to fight in Palestine, and so now he urged the Zion men to enroll at once in a British regiment. After lengthy meetings, they entered the Londoners in a body, nearly two hundred of them, the best that had been hardened in Gallipoli. But Captain Trumpeldor, with his one arm, was refused. Never mind. When the Jewish unit was finally created, he would surely be given special dispensation. He left for London, to join Jabotinsky in the campaign for the Jewish Brigade.

23

IT WAS the year of the golden harvest in Palestine. The grain was fat, the yield twofold, and this was the way of Allah, Sheikh Ibrim declared to Yankel Chaimovitch. Did Yankel not recall the flight of storks that had alighted after the plague of locusts was gone, covering the fields as with a white abaya? The fields were rich from the droppings of the storks that had feasted for days on the crawling larvae of the locusts; such was the way of Allah.

And even though the Turkish military police came onto the fields and counted the sheaves, and even though the tax-gatherers watched the filling of the sacks on the threshing floor, and even after half the sacks had been delivered to them, there still came the merchants from Beirut with their leather pouches filled with gold coins hanging from their girdles, and after they weighed the napoleons into the farmer's palm, and praised their Allah, even then a good farmer still could send a few wagonloads to Meir Dizingoff's committee for distribution to the needy, let the price not be thought of, and still put away stores in the ground, for who knew how long the war would continue and what would yet have to be endured. Far into each night Yankel and the boys labored at their digging and their carrying and their hiding away.

A second time they had attacked the Suez and been driven off; British warships standing in the canal itself had shelled and routed the Turks and Germans too, until they fled in disorder, staggering back over the wastes in the August heat, strewing their belongings all over the Sinai, casting away their rifles and their bandoliers of bullets, leaving broken wagons, dead mules and dead horses in their wake.

For the moment, as the summer ended and Rosh Hashanah approached, the war seemed to be in a pause, a moloch ruminating, digesting all it had engorged, gazing about for other chunks of mankind to swallow. There was even a

moment in the pause when the members of the Shomer
gathered in Gilboa, and despite all that had befallen and in
some ways because of it, young men flocked to be accepted. There was a new need everywhere for watchmen;
from the defeat in Sinai gaunt, wild-eyed deserters were
roaming about alone or in small groups. Every village
needed redoubled protection.

With the ranks replenished, Shimshoni at last succeeded
in his plan for the new settlement at the northern edge of
the land, at the foot of the Hermon. Though there were no
funds to buy his dreamed-of flocks of sheep, though the
Zionist office was closed and Dr. Lubin exiled to Constantinople, the members voted for his kvutsa to go up. In the
last moment Shimshoni appealed to the Baron's agent,
Samuelson, who had long lived in the northern district, in
Rosh Pina. The elderly manager took the task on himself,
and went to a neighboring sheikh with whom he had had
many dealings. The needed gold was dug out from its jar
beneath the courtyard. "Do not concern yourself, my old
friend. You will pay the gold back when you have it," and
on Succoth, Shimshoni's settlers went up with their tents
and their wagons and their newbought flock and their
friends to help in the Aliyah, Leah and Rahel among
them—how could they fail to take part in such an event?
Just as they had gone out years before, from HaKeren to
settle Gilboa, so they went now from Gilboa to settle Har
Tsafon.

It was as in the early days, cooking on stones, singing in
the sundown, tramping a wild hora far into the night: "If
not now, then when, then when!" and in the dawn opening
one's eyes to the breath-taking vista from the springs of
Dan down the wide flat vale of the upper Jordan, to the
hazy mirror of the Huleh swampland, and beyond to the
Kinnereth. Here all lay in peace.

From Dan to Beersheba now, the Shomer reached to
guard the land, as they constantly repeated to each other in
an elation of wonderment—they were actually making
these words come true. And it was toward Beersheba that
Leah now was called.

The moment had come when arms could be obtained in
considerable quantity.

From the further reaches of the Sinai, Bedouin were appearing with three, four rifles under their cloaks, picked up where deserters had flung them. In the Tel Aviv Gymnasia group with whom Rahel was in contact, Eli, the lad who had spent last summer working in Kvutsa HaKeren, put her in touch with a dashing young man named Dov who, as a paymaster for the Turks, moved freely in the southern region. Dov could act as their eyes in the field, he could deal with the Bedouin. What was needed was a safe place, as far south as possible, to which the weapons could be brought. A girls' farm in one of the southernmost villages, Gedera perhaps, would serve the purpose. And also serve to gether in the chalutzoth who were out of work in the area, and to grow produce for the Jews of Jaffa and Tel Aviv.

Though older, the village with its facing rows of settlers' dwellings reminded Leah of Mishkan Yaacov; she and her girls could occupy an abandoned house at the far end, and the house, too, with its pair of rooms, was of the same pattern as at home, and as in most of settlements. All but a few broken chairs the settler had carted away; behind the house stretched his modest grove, with last season's oranges still hanging shriveled on the trees.

Soon she had collected her girls, even a few who had stayed with her ever since Tiberias; Zipporah returned—how could Leah refuse to accept her? And presently the dwelling with its rows of cots along the walls and its window sills loaded with flowerpots looked like every one of Leah's habitations.

Menahem himself had come down to help deal with Dov's Bedouin, meeting them wherever indicated, driving a wagon filled with straw. At first the price was high—a camel for a rifle. Where could such sums be obtained? But Rahel hurried busily back and forth approaching notables in Tel Aviv, in Jerusalem, and Eli and his Herzlia Gymnasia group with their excellent family connections, set themselves to the task of gathering funds. Presently, as various Bedouin tribes began to compete with each other in offering arms, the prices went down, as low even as a few loaves of bread for a gun. Each week Motke the shomer from Petach Tikvah would come for the goods, driving off with a hidden wagon bottom stuffed with rifles, pistols, grenades, and munitions, to be stored in his attic. Sometimes Rahel, sometimes Leah, rode with him, sitting on the straw.

Once at Leah's kvutsa itself, there appeared a Bedouin who grinningly produced, from under his black abaya, two rifles of an unfamiliar sort. They were British. The Turks had withdrawn from the lower Sinai wastes, and the British had crossed the canal and were slowly extending their line toward El Arish.

Gidon's regiment, the London Fusiliers, was after all not among those who had crossed, for, with its small contingent of Zion volunteers, the regiment had been ordered home for refurbishment and redeployment.

Gidon Chaimovitch lay on his pallet among the rows of men breathing each other's breath in the iron hold of the troopship, wearing his lifesaver harness, and feeling a final loss of will; he was being carried, carried further and further from his place and purpose in life.

But Herscheleh still had breath to debate, and argued that this corridor to England might still be the best way to their purpose in Palestine, for, like the Jews who left Egypt with Moshe Rabenu, "we have only forty years of wandering before us."

Who could fathom the ways of history? A dozen years before, after the death of Theodor Herzl, a young Russian Zionist named Chaim Weizmann, a research chemist by profession, had as though by choice moved himself to Manchester, where chemical dyes, his specialty, were important in the weaving industry. Even in Manchester he had incessantly worked for his cause, explaining Zionism to prominent Englishmen, such as the editor of the newspaper, and among those who had listened, several were now in places of power.

In London now, strategists weighed and planned the fate of various lands, including Palestine, after the war. One member of the War Cabinet, indeed, had concluded with a sigh that the only way to protect the canal on the Palestine side was "to take Palestine ourselves." And then what should be done with it?

Annexation was too bald. And already secret schemes of partition of vast Middle East areas had been made with the French, with the Russians, agreements for areas of control, areas of influence, in the cutting up of the Ottoman Empire. Only the question of the Holy Land had not really yet been settled. Its allocation was vague. Now that the moment for its conquest was come, why not, after all, help the Jews to return to their ancient homeland, and through them, keep a hand on the area? The new Prime Minister, Lloyd George, was a lover of the Bible. Words of the ancient Hebrew prophets rolled from his tongue. The names of villages in Judea were as familiar to him as those of villages in Wales. And Lord Balfour, newly appointed Secretary of State, was one of the earliest to have been fascinated by the chemist Chaim Weizmann and his messianic dreams. And the adventurous Winston Churchill, too. All of them were taken with the sense of being as fingers on God's hand, in the final mystery of this Biblical cause. And it could be a highly useful maneuver, too. Why not set the Jews on the other side of Suez? What other people could be as energetic, resourceful, and loyal to the power that brought them back to their land?

There was also a Russian-Jewish firebrand, Vladimir Jabotinsky, come to London with his proposition for a Jewish fighting force; there was much to be said for that idea— Jews from all over the world would volunteer for it, thus binding themselves to the cause of England. And even Jews in enemy lands would be moved. Further, the millions of Jews of Russia and America would be so stirred, they would turn all their energy and influence to the cause, those in Russia to keep their country from falling out of the war, and those in America to bring their country into it. And just now, when the situation was strained and every ounce of help was needed!

Suddenly, in London, the campaign for a Jewish Palestine was making progress. An even greater vision appeared to the Middle East expert whose name was on the secret agreements with the French for dividing up the entire Levant. Sir Mark Sykes saw how not one but three submerged peoples could be awakened to help the Allies in a grand design of eventual self-rule: Judea for the Jews, Arabia for the Arabs, and Armenia for the Armenians—whatever remained of them after the massacres. Urging this inspiring plan, Mark Sykes was everywhere, bringing people together, tugging at the powerful.

When the torpedo struck their troopship, Gidon knew he would live because they were in sight of the shore of Crete and he could swim it. But Herscheleh had disappeared and, rushing down into the hold to look for him, Gidon found his chaver clutching his diary of Gallipoli, which he had gone back to rescue. But like that time under shellfire in Gallipoli, a paralyzing fear had overtaken Herscheleh. Dragging him up on deck, Gidon found the ship immersed in British calm. A troop of nurses, in perfect order, was entering the first lifeboat. Men were at their gun stations firing at the sea. Others were drawn up at their boats. Herscheleh recovered. Yet, entering their lifeboat, he again was seized by panic, and lost his balance, his diary jumping out of his hands into the water. With a wail, he would have leaped after it. "Let it be the diary instead of you!" Tuvia cried, and tumbled Herscheleh into their boat.

That was the one adventure of the voyage; the last troop of the Zion Mule Corps arrived intact, merged into the London Twentieth Fusiliers, in England.

Though hardly more than a company, they were at least together in their own barrack, and anyhow the long brick building was better than a row of tents, or stinking holes in Gallipoli. But to be far away now in England, under the name of a London they had not even seen, sometimes made Gidon feel as though his true being had sunk like Herscheleh's diary somewhere in the sea.

Not even Josef Trumpeldor had been there at the ship's arrival, and Tuvia and Herscheleh had resumed their predictions, begun in Alexandria when Trumpeldor had departed for England, that they would never find Josef again; they would melt into the vast substance of the British army and find themselves shipped off to France to be gassed or blown apart as numerals in a foreign regiment.

The inured shrugged: what did it matter? And Gidon too at times sank into this peculiar soldierly indifference, this sense that you withdrew to a degree from living, from the exercise of will, in order to preserve yourself for the time when you might yet live. Perhaps it was something like the enduring of a long prison sentence.

Then on only the second day Josef found them. On both sides there was hearty, bluff rejoicing. So they'd had a spill in the water! Oh, yes, he had known, even though the movement of their troopship was of course a military secret and he was still outside the military—never mind—the efforts to establish the Jewish unit were progressing, and he would soon be with them again. He and Jabotinsky had

secured an absolute promise from certain very high persons
in the government that if they could present a list of a
thousand Jews ready to volunteer for the Jewish regiment,
the unit would be officially established. The campaign for
volunteers had begun. So far, however, only a few hundred
signatures had been obtained. Things were complicated. Interference and opposition came from strange, unexpected
sources. From Jews themselves! Never mind. Jabotinsky
had high connections and Chaim Weizmann was helping
him with even higher connections. Now that the Zion men
were here, as a nucleus, the campaign would really get under way.

At times, the peacefulness of the English countryside,
even now, when Britain was deep in the war, aroused in
Gidon a great swollen-hearted longing. When would his
real life ever begin? This longing that came over him could
even feel physically painful, as during moments when he
might be walking with Herscheleh down one of the country
lanes, between autumnal fields on which sheep were grazing, and not far off a farmer plowed behind a thick-necked
Belgian percheron with heavy hocks—ah, what an animal,
benign and powerful, a solid part of their clean British
world with its compact moist soil. So painful was his longing then that Gidon would grow glum and cross at anything Herscheleh said, until they went less and less together
on their walks.

Nor did they go often to the pubs. Gidon somehow
could not find a link to the British in their pubs, and would
mostly remain sitting in a corner with Herscheleh, Tuvia
pulling hairs from his nose. Drinkers they had never become. Even in Gallipoli the Zion men's alcohol had been
traded off by Araleh for good things to eat.

The English villagers were friendly, as by some rule they
had made for themselves to be friendly to foreign soldiers,
but they were so careful not to intrude on you with personal questions that all human contact died out in games of
darts or observations on the weather; "a bit of bad luck,"
they would say if the war news was disastrous, or "jolly
good" for a victory.

Here in England as in Egypt, Jewish families, learning of
the presence of a group from Palestine, issued invitations
for Sabbath Eve. But the feeling was not like in Alexandria.

There, the Jews after all were not Egyptians but Jews. A wealthy Sephardi with his silent-footed black servitors was, in his home, still like a sojourner in Egypt. Here the British Jews were British; Gidon hardly felt a Jewishness among them. They had sons in the service, and intelligent well-educated daughters; those who invited the Zion boys were British Zionists, it was true, and they all devotedly read their weekly *Jewish Chronicle,* and they never failed to remind you that Theodor Herzl had received his very first public support from British Jewry when he arrived from Paris to lecture about his plan for a Jewish state. Yet Gidon somehow could not imagine these people or their children living in Eretz.

They were good Jews and most of them were observant, though still one did not feel it was the real thing like in Mea Shearim. They began their Sabbath Eve properly with Kiddush and the blessing over the chaleh, and managed with their war rations to provide a Sabbath-like meal, mostly fish and boiled potatoes, yet a British Jew's Friday evening display of Jewishness almost made Gidon feel a little surprised.

As Tuvia was a belligerent unbeliever, Gidon and Herscheleh usually went together, and they would dutifully recount their stories of Gallipoli; the Charge of the Zion Mule Brigade that stopped a Turkish surprise attack was their best. There was also the pathetic tale of the frightened Yitzik who in the end was posthumously awarded the D.S.O. for hanging onto the leadrope even after two bullets had gone through his arm. (He had died of dysentery.)

Yet it was always still fairly early when they departed with a "Good Sabbath to you." Sometimes they walked from the West End to Whitechapel, to the hangabouts of the other Jews, the ones the British Hebrews called "those fellows." Thousands of young Russian Jews had got to England to escape the Czar's armies.

Usually their British hosts would refer to "those fellows" in crisp but self-mastered disapproval, "They are beginning to present quite a problem to us." But on one particular night their host had broken out in cold anger, for these "Russian draft-dodgers" (they were not referred to as Jews) had had the audacity to organize themselves into a society and had issued a broadside openly opposing induction into His Majesty's armed forces! Inevitably, the public had reacted against all Jews, despite the above-average presence of British Jewish sons in the various services. In Leeds, the window of a kosher butcher shop had been smashed. "Really now, I believe we should confront these Russian immigrants with a plain choice: Join up or go back where you came from! The Czar would have them in uniform one, two, three—you can count on that."

"What I don't understand," said the wife, "is how they can brazen it out in public. How can any man with an ounce of self-respect walk about in mufti while the sons of this land are fighting for him—that I can't understand! And mind you, perhaps they have reasons to have no love of country where they came from—after all, they fled the land of pogroms, and I can understand that they might not want to fight for the Czar even though he happens to be our ally. But England has given them refuge, and for them to refuse to join up is disgraceful."

"The worst of it is that most of them look like the common idea of the Jews, the unfortunate ghetto type, and that makes the problem all the more conspicuous."

"I don't blame those that hate them," said the daughter. "I find it difficult to keep from hating them myself." Her husband was at the front in France. Two sons of the family were also in the service; one of them had been gassed and was in hospital. "It's a pity we Jews are judged by the example of such as them, and not by such as you," the daughter said to Gidon and Herscheleh.

Yet, perversely enough, it was when he found himself among "them" that Gidon felt more at ease, more with his own kind. Not his own kind as he was today—these men were familiar to him from long ago, from before, from when he was a boy; they were still arguing in the same hotheaded way in Yiddish as when he had listened in Cherezinka, to Reuven and his friends in their endless dispute about the revolutzia. Whitechapel was filled with them, the street was in a constant turmoil of movement, of clusters forming and dissolving; the tea shops were packed with them, and everywhere you heard Yiddish and saw Yiddish papers.

When his own family had gone to Eretz, and other Jews had gone to America, large numbers had come here too. They were the schneiders, tailors working in clothing manufacture, and it was from among these immigrants that

Trumpeldor and Jabotinsky expected to recruit their Jewish army. Only, as Herscheleh the Newspaper had at once sniffed out, everything in this respect was topsy-turvy—as could always be expected where Jews were involved. It was, Herscheleh said, like when they themselves had come to labor in Eretz only to find that the Jewish planters refused to use Jewish workers. The schneiders among whom recruits were being sought were exactly the ones who refused to fight.

To begin with, the schneiders of London answered you, had they wanted to fight for Zionism they would originally have gone to Palestine and not come here. "Why should we kill ourselves to make a Jewish nation if we are going to be like all other nations, with an army and capitalism and downtrodden workers?" If you answered that what the Jewish nation was going to be like was up to those who came there, and that your own brother and sister were part of a communa, they sneered at "Fourieristic idealism and romanticism that led nowhere." Others, a bit less hostile to Zionism, declared themselves to be followers of Ahad Ha'am, who had come from Odessa and was right here in London preaching against nationhood.

First, the philosopher declared, came the creation of a center for Jewish life, of Jewish culture, of Jewish ideas. But the revolutionary schneiders went further. Nationhood was already a thing of the past. The triumph of the world proletariat would do away with nationalism, so there was no need for Jews belatedly to embrace it! But all these arguments were as nothing when you came to the anarchists, the pacifists, the Mensheviki and the Bolsheviki. They could talk even Herscheleh under the table. Many of them were followers of the firebrand of the great revolt in St. Petersburg in 1905, a Jew named Trotsky. Even Gidon remembered about him—how, after the uprising was crushed, Trotsky was put on trial by the Czar's police, and the whole of Cherezinka had worried for this Jewish revolutionist—even the older, pious Jews who cursed him for an apicoiras, a godless renegade, had worried for him. Gidon remembered how all the boys in his Talmud Torah had cheered and rushed out into the street in their excitement when word came that Trotsky had escaped from Siberia. This same Trotsky was here in London, or he had just been here, who the devil knew, but he had many passionate followers among the schneiders, only waiting for him to give the signal for the international workers' revolution. According to them, on one great day all soldiers everywhere on both sides of the war would drop their arms, refuse to kill their fellow-toilers, and that would be the end of it! So why, of all things, start a Jewish army?

The revolutionists had their gangs, too. Only a few weeks before the Zion company had arrived, indeed perhaps at the very time when Herscheleh and Gidon and the rest of the boys were struggling in the waters before Crete, a gang had appeared at a recruitment meeting called by Trumpeldor and Jabotinsky. Tomatoes and rotten eggs had flown, and rocks too, and the editor of Jabotinsky's paper, a small, near-sighted Zionist, had had his glasses broken.

This at least, Tuvia declared, was something for the Zion boys to take care of. The toughies were known as Chicherin's Boys, after a Russian revolutionist—not even a Jew—in exile here. Chicherin's Boys came to Zionist meetings, thirty or forty in a gang, hooted, howled, started fights, and prevented speakers from being heard.

Yet despite their anger at these hooligans, Gidon and Herscheleh were drawn to Whitechapel, to the cafes where you got tea in a glass instead of in a mug with milk, and where you could even get a piece of golden lokshen kugel, or a knish. Just the odor alone of these tea shops evoked a far earlier state of being, a homeyness that reached back to before their life in Eretz, that was in a childhood time of a bobeh, a zaydeh, in Cherezinka.

Soon enough they got into violent arguments. The schneiders were not too eager to pick up acquaintance with men in uniform, and at first Gidon and Herscheleh felt a ring of avoidance around them. Their Shield of David insignia had been replaced with the patch of the Twentieth London Fusiliers, but once, a tall, red-pocked fellow with glittering, knowing eyes, and a little sneer behind them, remarked, "You're speaking Hebrew?"

And so it began. Not that the fellow could speak Hebrew—only, he said, a vestige from cheder, for luckily he had fled from there in time! But half in English, with Yiddish words—complete Yiddish phrases thrown in when the talk became heated—all the usual arguments came pouring upon them. No, chum, he wasn't wearing any uniform, no, thank you. He was making them, and at good wages, too,

but when it came to fighting, he was waiting for the capitalist powers to kill each other off, and preserving his
strength for the great day. "On the barricades, I'll fight!
For the people, I'll fight!" And there were twenty thousand
like him here. Not only did they escape conscription, as
foreign subjects, but certain taxes they escaped as well, and
where, he wanted to know, where did they and the Zion
army people get their nerve, coming here and upsetting the
applecart?

At first Gidon heard the words without anger, the way
he might have listened to a singsong recitation in cheder—
this revolutionist was even swaying back and forth like a
yeshiva bocher. All this talk was the same as in Cherezinka, the Bundists with their world revolution against the
Poale Zionists.

All the boys and even the girls had been in one youth
movement or the other. And it was the old slogans of the
Bundists that now came sputtering forth between forkfuls
of kugel; in the years in Eretz, Gidon had forgotten them,
so now the slogans had the ring of snatches of song from
childhood: imperialism, world struggle, downtrodden masses, chauvinism, militarism, bourgeois bloodsuckers. "At
home"—the fellow meant in Russia—"would you fight for
the Czar? And here in England is it different? Czar, King,
Kaiser, they're all the same, even if they make war on each
other, they're allies against the common people, and anyway they're all cousins, the lot of them. The English have
to uphold Czar Nicholas and his whole band of parasites,
his Rasputin, his Okhrana, his pogromists. You Zionists
are a bunch of dupes. Allegiance to His Majesty's Government! Tfoo! It's against your royal highnesses, not for
them, that we'll offer our lives—may all of them choke on
their own blood!"

And then the schneider began to fling questions, chal-
lenges at them, flinging out the answers as well before they
could open their mouths. Who was Herzl? A lackey of the
capitalist press, an assimilated bourgeois Jew who had himself escaped his people's tribulations and who saw the Jews
only as miserable scum, as a relief problem. "And even
worse are your false socialists, your so-called Labor Zionists, your Borochovs with their mixed-up Marxism . . ."

Gidon was no great reader or theorist, but under the
incessant outpouring he was becoming red-faced. Let Her-

scheleh answer, let them throw names of writers and books
at each other, Kropotkin, Bucharin, Plekhanov, *Das Kapi-
tal, Rome and Jerusalem.* A circle of hangers-on kept
growing behind the Bundist, grinning as he waved his long
arms to emphasize each point he scored. "Lackeys, that's
what you are! Fighting the capitalist war against your own
brothers in the international working class, bribed and
bought because those clever ruling bastards allow a mere
Jew to put on a uniform and get himself shot up for them.
Jewish fighters! Actually you're traitors to your class, a
bloody bunch of moral cowards!"

At this, Gidon leaped up. "Shut your bloody trap!" he
shouted, and got off one hard slap at the fellow's mouth.
For a second the fellow teetered in his chair, his arms flailing for balance. Herscheleh too had leaped up. It was no
band of revolutionary toughs such as Chicherin's Boys that
they faced, but a circle of startled Jews, many with eyeglasses, a few fat-faced, but most with the thin-lipped look
of the half-tubercular shop worker, the skeptic, the self-
educated reader of books, the listener to discussions.

"Stop! Boys, please! Not by me! Not in my place!" the
proprietress was begging, in Yiddish. To the Bundists she
cried, "I begged you a thousand times, don't quarrel with
soldiers!" And to the muleteers, "I beg you, leave."

Gidon and Herschel shouldered their way out, while imprecations rose behind them, "Catspaws! Traitors to the
working class!" And then a surmounting shriek in Yiddish,
"Shlemiels!"

From somewhere within himself a long unused reply
spat out of Gidon. "Vantzen!"

Once outdoors, he agreed with Herscheleh, those vermin
weren't worth a bruised knuckle.—It was a long, long time,
Gidon reflected, since he had been completely disgusted
with Jews.

When they reached the barracks, a peculiar feeling came
over him of returning to his own world, with the foul civilian world shut out. The smell of metal, oil, men, weapons
and gear. The solid clean foulness of the soldiers' own language, the familiar eternal cardplayers, and even the narrow cot. You knew where you were.

Tonight there was to be a big meeting in the hall above
Goldwasser's restaurant in the heart of Whitechapel, and,

with a few dozen other muleteers, Gidon would attend in mufti.

Over the stairway entrance was a huge banner in English and Yiddish, with the name of Jabotinsky in high flame-tailed letters. The sidewalk was crowded; Jews were arriving, most of them on the elderly side, accompanied by their corpulent, corseted wives, hurrying eagerly as to a free show. "You've never heard Jabotinsky speak?" Gidon caught a lip-smacking voice. "Oho! A tongue of gold! If he wanted to sing in the opera he would become another Caruso!"

But already at the entrance disputes seethed. The stairs were half-blocked. Young men from the revolutionists' table at Goldwasser's, and a number of their girls—who, with their eyeglasses, all seemed to resemble Nadina of Gilboa—were pushing leaflets into everybody's hand. "Militarists! Murderers!" he read. An arm yanked at him. "What do you want to go in there for, comrade?" Behind, a squat, middle-aged Yidl with a pointed beard cried in Yiddish, "Let me through! Hooligans!" "You can go, who stops you!" they laughed at him. "Such as you can join Trumpeldor's army."

All those pushing their way inside seemed to be above military age, good-hearted little shopkeepers, loyal Zionists, each of whom doubtless had the Keren Kayemeth's blue collection box in his kitchen. But once in the hall, Gidon saw a scattering of younger faces, some looking serious. Perhaps there would be a number of undecided and from them perhaps a few would come forward to enlist. But there were other young men, with their smirk of impatient belligerence, sitting in twos and threes. Wherever these were clustered, Gidon and Tuvia placed a few of their own boys on the aisle. A reserve they kept in the rear.

Josef Trumpeldor spoke first, after an introduction by an important British Jew, a member of Parliament, who called him "The Modern Maccabee." In his military jacket, with an odd assortment of Russian and British insignia and decorations on his chest, and the Shield of David of the Zion Mule Corps on his cap, his artificial arm straight at his side and the other arm held just as stiffly, Josef was like a statue of himself. And just as nobly statuesque were the things he said, in English phrases he had memorized, delivered with a heavy Russian accent that brought sympathetic chuckles

from the middle-aged. The good Jews gazed at him
proudly, and here and there Gidon saw a girl with that
moist, rapt look that Josef evoked in young women. Even
the revolutionists sat quietly, as though their strategy was
to let this one pass. Among them, Gidon's eye caught sight
of the tall talker of a few Fridays ago, the one he had given
a good smack in the mouth. The glitter of recognition was
returned to him, not marked with any promise of vengeance but with a pitying scorn.

A notion passed through Gidon's mind. What if Josef,
the real Josef, suddenly let go at them, the Josef of shellfire
and the trenches, roaring a foul *pschakreff* and flinging a
cannonade of soldiers' curses at the fearful and cowardly,
blasting them out, the way he had landed a good kick on
Herscheleh the day he was frozen in fright? The thought
made Gidon grin, and Herscheleh, beside him, demanded
what was the joke.

Josef soon concluded, calling every man to arms,
straight, soldierly, direct. "Jews, we have fought for every
cause but our own! Numbers of our best men have died
and are dying every day in every army in the world. At this
moment they fire at each other from French and German
trenches. But at last we can fight as Jews, for our own
cause, for our own land! Can any man find anything wor-
thier in life on this earth?"

There was applause, many of the older Jews gazing
around with indignation at the young radicals who sat un-
responding. Then a single, jeering voice rose up, "Go give
them your other arm, chum!"

A shocked hall-wide gasp, a young woman's voice crying
"For shame!" a rumbling, and trouble might have broken
out. Trumpeldor remained standing, rigid, livid, but Jabotinsky had leaped forward, his words chopping down in
scathing strokes on such contemptible, worm-soft coward-
ice, like the flying strokes of a chopping knife on a noodle
board, ripping the dough into slivers, and plop goes the lot
into boiling water.

From all around the hall came sighs of pleasure as he
gave it to them, the hooligans, the troublemakers, a disgrace to their people. Suddenly the orator pulled from his
pocket a crumpled leaflet—theirs. Loudly, he read
out their own slogan and argument, " 'Jews! Why Fight to Create a New Ghetto? At last, we Jews in democratic lands

have attained equality, justice, an equal vote, an equal place in the schools. Why again separate ourselves as Jews? If fight we must, let us fight in the English Army as Englishmen, in the French Army as Frenchmen, yes, even in the German Army as loyal Germans.' " And then, without a shred of emphasis, the orator read out the signature, " 'The Society of Jewish Trade Unionists.' " As though startled, he read it again, " 'Jewish Trade Unionists.' " And in mock puzzlement, Jabotinsky reread a previous line, " 'Why again separate ourselves as Jews?' "

Oh, he had caught them! The hall rocked with glee over the master stroke.

"Perhaps," the orator remarked when the laughter had at last gone down to a bubble, "perhaps this splendidly logical leaflet was written while standing on his head by that renowned upside-down philosopher, Moishe Kapayer!"

This set them off again.

And now in all solemnity Jabotinsky repeated, "Why separate ourselves as Jews?" and began to give the answer.

In Egypt a year ago when Gidon had crowded with the rest of the fellows from the deportation ship into an unused stable in the refugee compound to hear the famous journalist, he had listened to much of this same oration, but it was like music to hear it again. It swelled, it vibrated, it pierced. The devoted elderly Jews who had come to hear the great orator wept tears as he described Kishinev with the slaughtered laid out in rows in their shrouds, and they sighed with pride as he told how Jewish boys had revolted against the supine ways of the older generations, and secured weapons, and mounted guard in Homel, in Odessa, even in Kishinev itself. The listeners breathed deeply with naches as he told how Jewish members of the Shomer rode on their steeds, guarding the settlements in Palestine, and they sat erect with wonder and admiration as he declared how he himself had made a wrong judgment, how, in Egypt last year, he had refused to join Josef Trumpeldor when Jews were offered acceptance into the British army only as muleteers. But those very muleteers of Zion had become a symbol of valor in Gallipoli! Among your famous Scottish regiments and your famous Australians, and your famous Gurkhas—none of whom feared to ghettoize themselves in their national pride—there had arisen the name of the sons of Zion. The Shield of David on their caps had become among the most respected of emblems amongst the toughest of fighting men in the hardest of campaigns. And many were the men of Zion who had given more than their arm, their two arms—they had given their lives. And because of this, Jews were now to become a fighting brigade. Only by fighting and winning back their own land from the Turks would they overcome the age-old stigma of the ghetto. For what was a ghetto? A tolerated corner in a city that belonged to another people, in a foreign land. A land of your own, a city of your own, was no ghetto. Was London a ghetto to the Englishman? Simply this, then, was the object of Zionism, of the Jewish Brigade. Already the Jews were building their own city—Tel Aviv— in what would one day, by the grace of the remaining, mighty right arm of Josef Trumpeldor and of the men who joined with him in the coming battle—be their own land. By such courage would their own city one day stand in their own land.

The orator paused to allow the wild, joyous response free rein. Then he resumed: And who were these very British patriots who disdained to fight as Jews? There were two kinds: the social revolutionists, and the sons of the big capitalists. Strange bedfellows. What did they have in common?

First, let it not be imagined that all social revolutionaries were against the idea of a Jewish fighting force. On the contrary—the very originator of the fighting force was a social revolutionist, and he was present here on the platform—Josef Trumpeldor, Zionist *and* Communist, for such was his declared philosophy. The nucleus of the Jewish fighters in the Zion Corps were stalwart settlers from the kvutsoth and the cooperatives of Palestine, the only place in the world where true communism was being lived and practiced.

What then was the difference between pro-Zionist social revolutionaries, and anti-Zionist social revolutionaries? He didn't have to tell them. Both kinds were here in the hall. One kind wanted to remain Jewish, right through and on after the world revolution, just as French revolutionaries wanted to remain French, Germans, German, and British, British. But the Jews, and perhaps only the Jews, had another type amongst them—those who wanted to disappear as what they were. They wanted to disappear as Jews. Internationalism for the sake of the world revolution was their excuse. All other nationals of course understood that internationalism was a union of nationalisms. What else? Only the Jews who hated being Jews wanted to disappear into the international revolution. They were, quite simply, ultra-assimilationists. Their argument really had nothing to do with the social revolution. This was simply an excuse. To their twisted souls, the cry that there would be a ghetto in Zion was, under the guise of idealism, a way out of being a Jew.

Oh, it was nothing new, even in social revolutionary circles this argument had been put forward at the very beginning, seventy-odd years ago. Karl Marx was a Jew who didn't want to be a Jew, who hated it. He had been born into a converted family, yet found himself known as a Jew. And so, as a substitute for the Jewish Messiah, he invented the internationalist utopia. Virtually a cofounder with Marx and Engels of the whole Communist theory and theology was another Jew, Moses Hess. But in the midst of it all, this one had discovered for himself that he remained deeply a Jew, and had turned to the idea of the return of the Jews to Jerusalem—without ceasing to believe in socialism. Socialism was in no way contrary to national peoplehood. So much for the first group, the revolutionists.

And what of the second, the sons of high capitalism, likewise opposed to Zionism and the Jewish army? As with the socialists, so with the capitalists; this opposition hardly embraced all of them and it had nothing to do with their economic status or philosophy. Here in London you had one Rothschild who was a supporter of the Jewish army, and another Rothschild who put in its way every obstacle he could muster. It was not their capitalism that made such men anti-Zionist. It was, exactly as in their socialist enemies, the craving to disappear as Jews, to assimilate. The same hatred of their origin—an old, old phenomenon among us—Jewish anti-Semitism.

Let them assimilate, let them disappear. It could be done. Even with comparative ease. Human beings were amazingly adaptable. They could live without a sense of smell, they could lose their eyesight and live, they could live after half their internal organs were removed, and they could live without their souls. But as for him—he respected a thousand times more a man who honestly lost his limbs in battle than a poor wretch who wanted to cut out his own soul because in this brutal world he encountered imbeciles and wretched bullies who spat on Jews.

Oh, those sick souls! There was Lionel Rothschild using all his wealth and high connections to block the cause of the Jewish army. There was Sir Edwin Montagu screaming with rage against Zionism! Why, such goyim as Lloyd George and Winston Churchill, Lord Balfour and General Smuts were better Zionists than these soul-sick Jews, nor did they need to have the reason for the creation of a Jewish army explained to them. "Our worst enemies come from amongst ourselves, those who are *unknowingly* victims of anti-Semitism, those Jews who want to cease to be Jews, who are fearful of being what they were created to be. They are so sick that like miauling infants they thrust away, they go into a fit of rage at the cure that is brought to them."

His tone changed.

So much for the assimilationists. But there were others who held back from enlistment in the Jewish unit, and for a very comprehensible motive. They didn't want to get killed. And even better, they didn't want to kill.

With them he could reason, even materialistically. True, they had found themselves a haven here in London and been able to stay out of the war thus far. Perhaps they did not realize that British young men as well didn't want to kill and didn't want to be killed. But there were times when one's choice was not entirely free. And their own choice too, he now had to inform them, would soon cease to be so free. For the Russian Ambassador to England, Count Nabokov, was being pressed from both the Russian and the British sides as to their status. The Czar was demanding that they be sent home as deserters. And the British were embarrassed to have their hospitable land used as an escape-ground by tens of thousands of men of fighting age who were the subjects of their Russian allies. As they all well knew, diplomatic talks on this unpleasant subject had been going on for some time. "But I myself have very recently spoken with Ambassador Nabokov and can report to you the unpleasant news that any day now you may be seized and shipped back to Russia."

There arose a bitter murmur of anger, hostility, wariness, as though he were playing some kind of trick on them.

Waiting until it had subsided, the speaker demanded now in the voice of a hard and practical bargainer, devoid of idealism: Was it better to be thrown into the half-starved, ill-equipped armies of the Czar, where men were cheaper than bullets, the cheapest of cannon fodder, and where in addition to everything else they would find themselves among their ancient, unchanged comrades, the illiterate anti-Semitic moujiks and Cossacks—was it better to be spat on and beaten up there, as Zhids, or was it better to volunteer here to fight together with fellow Jews, the men of Zion, for one's own people, one's own land?

Something flew through the air and spattered against the table. Amidst outcries, catcalls and screams, rotten vegetables pelted the platform. The speaker brushed muck off his shoulder. Trumpeldor had leaped up to protect him, but Jabotinsky did not budge. Gidon and Herschel plunged into their row and collared a pair of Chicherin's Boys. The Zion squad from the rear of the hall had already pushed down the aisle.

No fight was offered. A dozen of the troublemakers were speedily ejected. People settled back in their seats; Jabotinsky resumed: "I appreciate the eloquent attempt at a counterargument . . ."

But the mood had been broken. When he ended and called for volunteers for the Jewish Brigade, scarcely twenty men, at least half of whom had been primed before the meeting, came forward toward the platform.

It was a dreary English winter. In the day, Gidon's platoon were drilled as though they had never seen battle. Everything from the beginning, left turns and present arms and the strictest saluting. Leaping over barricades and climbing walls, marching with full pack, all with a double relentlessness.

After the wearying days, a few times they went to London to police the recruiting meetings. But it even seemed as though their numbers instead of growing were becoming smaller; one after another of the volunteers from the mellah, who had never really seemed part of their group but had perhaps joined as a way to get out of Egypt, now managed to have themselves transferred here and there where things appeared safe and easy. A few habitual complainers got themselves shifted, and so did a few good men who had become embittered over the lack of response of the Jews in England and now declared they were sick and tired of the whole idea of the unit—the Jews of the Diaspora weren't worth it. Until only the hard core remained, scarcely more than eighty.

"It doesn't matter," Josef would repeat his famous phrase at every defection. It was even better, he said.

He had still not managed to get himself inducted. But he would come out every few days to tell of the progress being made. A full plan for the Jewish regiment had been submitted in writing to the War Ministry with the signed support of two cabinet members.

It was the worst time for Gidon. Even Herscheleh had deserted him, having at last picked up with some girl who worked in a nearby munitions factory. Herscheleh was always sneaking out on borrowed passes; the shikseh was married, her husband at the front, she didn't dare be seen with a man—a foreigner was safer for her—and each time Herscheleh came back from her and described the shameless things this proper English girl had done, Gidon was plagued with images. A few times he went whoring, only to pick up a dose, as they said: cursing the world and the vileness of creation, cursing himself, he got caught in short-arm inspection and confined to barracks, and took out his bile on a squad of schneiders. For now he had been given a squad to train.

Despite everything, recruits had dribbled in, a number out of genuine conviction, "real English" Jewish lads who were about to be called up and decided they might as well volunteer for the Jewish unit. But most of his squad fitted the typical picture of the sallow, thin-lipped, hollow-chested schneider. The Russian Embassy had indeed sent out registry forms to all the immigrants, and while their Chicherin instructed them to ignore this and sit it out, a certain few were coming to volunteer. Having come, they retained their own attitude. They were argumentative over every stupid regulation, and too often right. And though they had made up their minds to do a good job of soldiering once they were in, the schneiders were not militarily endowed. They tripped over their feet, while their fingers, so nimble on a sewing machine, became thick on a Lewis gun.

Or else they were overeager to obey precisely. In his own squad one day there arose what came to be renowned as the response of a true Jewish soldier. As Gidon marched his greenies, calling left, left, left, he noticed one of them half-hopping, half-stumbling. Halting the squad, he growled, "Don't you know your right foot from your left?" To which the willing schneider replied, "You keep saying left, left, left—on my left foot alone, I'm trying, but I can't march."

Though he himself hated drill and saw no more use to it than they did, Gidon drilled them until their knees buckled. Indeed, he became the proverbial tough drill sergeant. One day when he heard a schneider call him anti-Semite under his breath, a little glow lighted in his heart. He had them! The were becoming soldiers. Their compressed, bitter little smile of Jewish resignation was turning into the soldier's sneer of inurement. One night, when he saw a few of them meticulously cleaning their rifles on their own impulse, and exchanging advice about different oils, Gidon suddenly believed again that the whole plan would succeed.

On a cold sleety morning just after he had started training a new squad, an additional recruit arrived from London and was sent out to join them. The movement of the approaching soldier reminded Gidon of someone—head stuck forward, and a hasty step. It was the journalist himself! Jabotinsky had enlisted!

Before Gidon could even have a thought about it, the recruit halted before him and saluted, declaring, "Private Vladimir Jabotinsky reporting for duty, sir," and the entire squad was agape. Already they were arguing over the event—Jabotinsky was doing it so as to give an example before the world. No, he himself was escaping deportation to Russia. No, they couldn't deport him, he was a journalist. Then why join, when for the Jewish army he was more useful outside than as a simple soldier?

"You don't salute a corporal," was the first remark that broke out of Gidon. Then he barked the squad to attention. He sent the new man into the line. From Jabotinsky's expressionless glance, Gidon knew he had handled it right.

Many times they had exchanged a few words. Once, as far back as the Alexandria days when the journalist had moved into the Mafrousi Barracks and was sitting around with some of the chevreh drinking tea, he had even asked Gidon a few questions about his family.

The drill continued. In no time it became clear that the new recruit was a case of bad coordination. Compared to the orator even the schneiders were born soldiers. He couldn't adjust his stride, and he was so intent on catching orders that half the time he was ahead of the line in executing them. Finally, Gidon hit on the idea of sending him aside and assigning Herscheleh to get Jabotinsky started. But this too had a flaw. Herscheleh naturally tried to seize upon this opportunity to hold discussions, while Jabotinsky kept constantly calling his instructor back to instruction duty.—He certainly wasn't going to be used as a common soldier in the war, Herscheleh would tell him, so there was no point in troubling themselves over punctilio. —No, Jabotinsky would insist, he wanted to be a correct soldier.

In the barracks a worshipful young Zionist who had a cot in the corner offered to give it over to the orator so that he would have a bit of privacy, but the famous one refused.

There were soon many jests. A special detail would have to be sent to fetch his mountains of mail. In the middle of drill a runner would appear with a message for Private Jabotinsky to call the Lord of the Admiralty, Winston Churchill. Or perhaps Chaim Weizmann. In the end Gidon solved all the problems together by assigning the famous man to barracks duty. After sweeping out, he could sit and read, and write all his memoranda to the government.

Yet the presence of the orator made a change in Gidon. It was not, despite all the jokes on the subject, that he felt any self-importance in being the one who gave orders to Vladimir Jabotinsky. And it was only partly because a new feeling of interest had come into the barracks, with the bits of half-secret news that the leader let out after his visits to high offices in London, and with his caustic descriptions of the fantastic lengths to which certain highly placed "frightened Jews" would go to place obstacles in the way of the official creation of the Jewish Brigade. Nor did Gidon feel any particular quickening when Jabotinsky let it be known that this one or that one of great power had been won over to their cause. Gidon did not even share in the gloating when one morning Herscheleh came running with the London *Times*, reading out a leader in favor of the creation of a Jewish fighting unit. Fine and good; Gidon did not need the London *Times* to convince him.

What was it then, that was breaking through the apathy

that had begun to engulf him? Gidon found himself really trying to unravel this. Was it because the enlistment of the orator somehow demonstrated, as some insisted, the "worthiness of the plain soldier?"—Like that old man Gordon in the kvutsa who made a whole philosophy about laboring with his hands on the soil? That wasn't it, either.

He wasn't a hero worshiper; it made Gidon feel uncomfortable when, after an impassioned speech in the city, Jews crowded around the orator and wanted to kiss his hands. Especially as he felt the orator rather liked it. There were even certain ideas that the leader didn't often talk about to the crowds but that Gidon heard voiced in private now and again that vaguely troubled him. It was not only a Jewish army to fight for the Jewish land that was being raised, but see—in the entire Levant, what was to be found? Backward and primitive Arab tribes, scattered over vast areas as large as the whole of Europe. A Jewish nation would bring the Middle East into the modern world, it would reach out as in the days of Solomon, it could reach from the Euphrates to the Nile; Jewish brains and energy would draw upon the untouched resources of Mesopotamia, of Arabia—the vision was broad, ambitious—and what was wrong with having vision? Yet something in it rubbed Gidon the wrong way.

Then despite all this, just what had been brought alive in him by the leader's presence as a soldier?

Perhaps it was the nearness, the spectable of a man pressing on with ideas, projects that had simply risen up from within himself. Gidon could not quite think it out, but this was his feeling. That he had begun to go down under the sense that man was too small in himself, that a man ended pushed into this line or that by the enormous powers that ruled the world. But now the other feeling had come back, the feeling of personal worth. What was Vladimir Jabotinsky but a journalist who had come to the refugee barracks in Alexandria and been seized with an idea for a Jewish army? Even here he was still nothing but a soldier in a foreign army. Yet only because he had the will and was sure of his ideas, he was able to make the high ones listen, able to press forward even to the highest. Though Gidon never felt that within himself there was any great force of this kind, the nearness of it lifted him from apathy.

Presently a whole new fever arose. All at once the newspapers were filled with dispatches about upheavals in St. Petersburg. The newest recruits coming from London brought in Russian and Yiddish papers, and the schneiders snatched them from each other's hands; they became like excited monkeys in a cage, chattering without stop, hopping from one cot to another, starting arguments in the middle of the night, in the midst of drill, speculating, what was happening there in St. Petersburg? Was it the revolution at last?

Jabotinsky would be called away for days at a time; was he not after all a Russian journalist, an expert? It seemed his knowledge was needed in high places.

There were strikes in Russian arms factories, soldiers were said to be in mutiny, it was said the Duma had been dissolved, no, the Czar's ministers were dismissed, the Czar had abdicated, no, he had withdrawn his abdication, the Czarevitch had been crowned, no, there was no Czar at all! And suddenly it was official, it was true; the Russian Czar had abdicated, there was a democratic government, and among the very first laws was one providing complete equality for Jews!

The schneiders paced the barracks, trapped here, cursing themselves for having only a few weeks ago bound themselves to this army—you could see that everything drew them to Russia, to the great events. But some of them already argued that the revolution was no revolution, it was only a movement of liberals and the bourgeoisie; everything would remain in the same hands, the hands of the aristocracy and the capitalists. And for proof—here was their new "revolutionary" government declaring that Russia would continue to fight the war alongside her allies, and with renewed vigor.

Jabotinsky came back from the city bringing Trumpeldor. First they tried to answer everybody's questions, but then they sat in a corner with their heads together for hours. It was no secret that Josef had a new plan altogether. Why wait eternally for the mighty British to decide to permit the Jews to have an army? Instead, he would now go and raise a Jewish army in Russia! He must go to St. Petersburg. In the new government, he knew this one and that one. In the Duma and even in the Central Council, here was a Jew and there was a Jew, in the highest offices. If Josef did not know them, then Jabotinsky knew them.

Everyone was flocking back to Russia from exile, from Switzerland, from here in England, even from America. Just now, Josef pointed out, another of the exiled leaders of the 1905 revolution, Pincus Rutenberg, had passed through London on the way back from America. From the very start, this Rutenberg had been with Jabotinsky in the idea of creating a Jewish army; he had even gone to America to spread the idea. In the new Russia he would have great influence. He was after all a veteran social fighter! With Rutenberg's connections, Josef Trumpeldor was certain that he could quickly receive authorization from the new government. A hundred thousand Jews would answer the call overnight! For in Russia was the very heart of Zionism.

—Had he forgotten, Jabotinsky argued with Josef, while half the company hovered around them, had he forgotten that the Russian Zionist Congress itself only last year had passed a strong resolution against the formation of a Jewish army? And the journalist burst into a tirade, describing how his oldest, closest friends and supporters in the Russian Zionist movement had turned against him and shunned him. Precisely because of this he had then come back to England—

"But now it is all different! A year ago they were afraid. Now everything is changed!" The new Social Democratic government was sure to welcome Josef's plan, for the Jews would bring new spirit into the war. He would lead ten divisions through the Caucasus and capture Constantinople for Russia! And then the Jewish army would sweep down through Syria into Palestine, while the British army came up from Egypt, and they would smash the remains of the Turko-German forces between them, a hammer and anvil. A hundred thousand Jewish soldiers would remain to become chalutzim, settle in the land and rebuild Palestine!

—A fine vision, but unfortunately Josef was being unrealistic, the journalist retorted. With a burst of quotations from Russian newspapers, from experts in London, from Bolsheviki and Mensheviki, he showed that the very cause of the Russian revolution was war-weariness. Entire army units were simply turning around and leaving the front. The Russian people were sick of the war, and if the Jews even attempted to revive a fighting spirit, they would be answered with pogroms such as had never been seen in the worst Czarist days. If the Kerensky government persisted in continuing the war, it was certain to fall.

Besides, where would Josef get his hundred thousand volunteers? Those Jews who were already in the Russian army would still be with their units as long as the army held together. And those who were already out of the army were certainly not going to go back in.

"They will! They will!" Josef cried. "For their own cause, they will fight!" At least in Russia there was a chance, a good chance, while here every obstruction had been placed in the way and the whole plan looked hopeless.

"No! We are on the verge of success!" Their plan was now already on the desk of the war minister himself, recommended for approval. The Irishman had already been alerted to command the first Jewish regiment. He would certainly commission Josef as second in command. While if Josef, instead, started off to Russia, even before he got to St. Petersburg the provisional government could fall apart. Kerensky had only the shakiest coalition behind him. And it was the Bolsheviki with their anti-war slogans who would topple him. And then Trumpeldor, arriving to call for a new war campaign, might find himself in a cell in the Peter and Paul Fortress, rather than in an army headquarters. Finally, did Josef really believe the British would make it possible for him to go to Russia at this juncture?

And there it was the soldier who came forward with a political answer. Why shouldn't they? he demanded. On the contrary! If the British were worried that Russia might fall out of the war, they would welcome his proposal to awaken the millions of Russian Jews, inspiring them to win their own land. They would help keep Russia fighting.

"Ach, you are only hungry to go back to Russia and see the revolution. You're still a Communist!" Jabotinsky cried, half exasperated, half in sympathy.

Long after their chief had again left for London, the men were still at it: What the Russian Social Democrats would do, what the Cadet party would do, what the Bolsheviki would do, if this, if that, what the English would do if this, if that. The devil take them all, Gidon thought. Why couldn't Jews do what Jews had to do, and an end!

Then—hardly a week had passed—another great new thing. America! If Russia was falling out of the war, Amer-

ica was coming in! The sky had opened. With every
Tommy in the camp you had to drink to the Yanks. The
Hun was finished now for sure. Once the great giant from
across the seas planted his feet in Flanders, it was all over
for Fritz. It might still take a bit of a while for the Yanks
to get over here, granted, but all that was needed now was
to hang on, and it would be the Kaiser they'd be hanging,
in Berlin!

In the new, excited discussions, the schneiders had already added an American Jewish army to their ranks. In
their enthusiasm they saw enormous troopships filled with
Jews already on the way across the Atlantic. Trumpeldor's
Russian Jewish army too was embarked, crossing the Black
Sea, sailing through the Dardanelles, never mind about
Gallipoli, the straits would be conquered as he sailed to-
ward Eretz Yisroel! And they themselves were afloat,
crossing the Mediterranean on British war vessels. Con-
verging, these invincible Jewish armies would march up to
Jerusalem, and plant the flag of Zion atop the Wailing
Wall.

24

EVEN a glass of tea had become a rare luxury. The familiar Wissotsky packets had disappeared from the shops, as
had all else except for scant supplies of chick peas rationed
by the committee of notables. Even olives were kept in the
rear.

With her girls, Leah raised mint for tea. First they supplied the weak and the sickly. Everyone was gaunt; Leah
herself had grown thin, and on her last visit home Shula
had joked that, as with her own Nahum, it had taken a war
to make Leah beautiful.

And Leah added to the jest, "Yes, and just when there
are no men."

Who could be concerned in these days over romance,
over personal matters? The entire Yishuv was shriveling,
dying. In the cities only half were left. Some had escaped to

Egypt, some even to Damascus, but the rest had died, who knew from what, from disease, from starvation.

Among the Arab villages it was not as bad, but bad. The fellah who had a bit of earth to till still managed to hide away enough grain for his pittah, but the wage-workers now wandered about with hard, sometimes frightening, looks in their eyes. More and more of the orange growers had abandoned their groves; they had no benzine for their irrigation pumps, and where, to whom, would they sell their oranges?

Even here with their vegetable farm inside the village a night watch had to be kept over the growing cabbages, and each night the girls went out two by two. One night, dashing Dov the paymaster made a hurried stop, awakening Leah to leave not only two more British rifles that Bedouin had sold him, but a wondrous gift, a package of English tea that had been bartered along with the guns. When Dov left, Leah took it into her head to bring out a jug of real tea to the girls on watch—tonight it was Rahel who watched with Zipporah. So as not to come on them suddenly and give them a fright, she marched boldly on the gravelly path just inside the lane of cypress. Suddenly she heard a shriek such as she herself had let out on a famous night on watch long ago in the Aaronson vineyard in Zichron, when she had heard scraping sounds, and caught a pair of Arabs loading clusters onto their donkeys. Running forward now, the tea half spilling from the spout, Leah was brought up short by Rahel, holding the famous little pistol that Avner had left with her, with Zipporah behind her with a rake.

"Oh—it's only you!" Zipporah cried.

"I almost shot," said Rahel. And then, in relieved anger, "Leah! I've begged you a thousand times! Why must you wear those men's shoes!"

It was the sound of the hobnailed boots that had frightened them.

"And I spilled half the tea. Real tea."

The incident became a watchword with the girls whenever anything frightened them. "Don't worry. It must be Leah in her hobnails, bringing tea."

For Chanukah Leah decided to have a party. "Why should life be so grim?" Zipporah kept insisting. Hunger, war, fear, loneliness—enough! There were several young men in the village, after all, a few farmers' sons with exemption papers, and even a few chalutzim who had good hiding places. Two of the girls had their sweethearts among them and saved food for the boys, who slipped over to stand with them in their turns on guard. A system had even been established—one couple on watch, the other "resting." That still made two on guard, didn't it?"

But most of the girls were lonesome, and if word of Leah's Chanukah party were spread to Rehovot and Beer Tuvia, surely more young men would appear.

Though there were no potatoes for Leah's celebrated latkes, she had saved a little oil and promised to make eggplant pancakes that could not be told from the real thing. There was no sugar—who had seen sugar in a year? But they held back from the marketing cooperative a portion of honey from their hives. And on the morning of the party a farmer's wife, Rifka Belman, astonished the girls by bringing a full crock of milk. It tasted of oranges, for her husband was one of those who at least made use of part of his wasting crop by feeding oranges to the remaining cows. Rahel brought a few bottles of wine from Rishon, and they had dates and figs, enough to make a show on the plates, and really heaps of almonds from the grove.

When the time came to dress, Rahel, who from nowhere had produced a gown with Yemenite embroidery, plagued Leah—for once!—and sat her down and arranged her hair in an upward billow such as she had seen in Paris just before the war. Then, for what to wear, Rahel pulled out the old suitcase from under Leah's cot, and, underneath a torn sweater that even Leah could no longer put on, she found the long, loose white-wool abaya made years ago for Leah's swan dance.

"But what's this!"

"It was for the visit of Chaim Nachman Bialik," Leah blushed.

They made her try it on. Studying the effect, Rahel pulled off her own embroidered belt and tied it around Leah's waist, high under her breasts. All the girls gasped. Suddenly it was a fashionable gown. "C'est la mode Empire!" Rahel pronounced, and Zipporah fetched a glittering Spanish comb to put in Leah's hair.

Now the whole little kvutsa began adding ornaments and rings and bracelets to beautify their Leah. "Oh, she's a queen!" a tiny one, Pnina, cried out. "Oh, I'm going to sew myself a gown just like hers!" Leah kept protesting, laughing, but they held up a hand mirror for her to look into, and Zipporah insisted on putting kohl around her eyes: "Sit still!" The girls were having such a happy time, she submitted to everything.

Finally, perfection achieved, the girls commanded her to parade up and down for their approbation. Already hoof-beats were heard—men were coming!

Before they could even see who had alighted there burst in Zev the Hotblood, crying "What! A party, and you didn't even invite me!" He had come along with a boy from the next village, the round-faced, red-cheeked Naaman Belkind, son of one of the early Bilu families. "And I brought my cousin too," Naaman said, with a mixture of shyness and pride, as his cousin was Avshalom Feinberg. And with Avshalom there had to be the Hothead, for since Zev had saved him in Beersheba from being hanged as a spy, they were seen everywhere together.

Before Leah, Zev halted agape. "By my life!" He made a sweeping bow of homage to beauty. "Avshalom, speak! Even in Paris has anyone seen such as this?"

"Why Paris? Not even in Jerusalem in King Solomon's day!" responded Avshalom.

All the girls were gawking at him, and the first remark from his lips did not disappoint them. This night would be bright. There would be glowing words, and feelings would rise and flash between men and women, and at least for tonight they would not be only girls making their shrill liveliness amongst themselves; already there was heard that lower womanish laughter that holds promise.

More young men appeared, a harmonica and an accordion played, several couples were in the yard and a few were wandering down the cypress lane, where Avshalom, with Naaman clinging to him, was the center of a small group around a stone bench. Avshalom was singing a song in French, and Rahel was joining in: "Sur le pont d'Avignon, l'on y dan-se, l'on y dan-se—" Inside the house, another group had somehow got to singing Yiddish songs—"Oif'n pripitchik" they were singing, and passing on to Hebrew songs of the chalutzioth. Soon the hora would begin out there in the yard; Zev the Hotblood had already received a few slaps on his roving hands, and at one point

Leah even asked Avshalom to take away from Zev the bottle of arak he had brought, from which he kept taking swallows.

Avshalom poured some of the liquor into a tumbler and, mixing it with water, watched it grow cloudy. Did she know this was also a favorite drink in the cafes of Paris, he said, particularly with artists and poets, though there it was made with absinthe and was even stronger than here? And he recited the praise of absinthe by a French poet, Baudelaire.

Now they were sitting together talking. Leah knew very well that nothing was likely to happen between them, for many reasons, not really his lack of height, but rather, that Avshalom was betrothed to the youngest Aaronson girl, the one who had been sent to America for safety. And also he was said to be in a deep entanglement with Sara. Everyone knew there had been something between him and Sara even before he fell in love with little Rifka; it was even said Sara had married and gone to Damascus so as to free him for her sister. But now it was said Sara had come home not merely on a visit, but had really left her husband. Not only Rifka was gone from Zichron; Aaron Aaronson was mysteriously no longer to be seen—he had gone to Berlin, it was said. Thus Sara and Avshalom were much alone together at the agricultural station. Everyone talked of them. Sara was no girl now but a mature woman. Even Rahel didn't keep back from this bit of gossip. In the course of her flitting from place to place, she had not long ago gone to work with her agronomy diploma in Aaronson's laboratory in Athlit on the classification of plants; but no sooner had Aaron gone off on his voyage than Avshalom had dismissed her from the station, as though he wanted no strangers there.

Slightly as she knew Sara, Leah could not imagine her as a woman who took love lightly. Sara was of a strong and serious nature and Avshalom too, despite his flamboyance, was of a serious nature. Though he liked to pose as a man of extravagant experiences, and would often remark enigmatically that he had enjoyed *everything* that was to be found in Paris, such things were only what was expected of a handsome and dashing poet. His true self, she felt certain, was profound, and passionate. It could not be said of him, as of her own Handsome Moshe, that he lightly set out to break women's hearts, that he misled young girls. Here in this room every girl would tell you, yes, she could fall in love with Avshalom Feinberg! But it would only be like innocent, excitable girls chattering to each other over the picture of a famous actor. And that was all that Avshalom would reveal of himself—an image.

This was also why Leah felt that nothing could happen between Avshalom and herself; his soul was hidden, it was pledged, whether to Rifka or Sara or both. Alongside him she felt a joyous excitement, not particularly sexual, but a great stimulation, a meeting with a person who raised her out of her day-to-day life—a poet, an artist. Others too had been to Paris, even to America. Rahel could speak of Paris, the museums, the theaters, but Avshalom really belonged inside that world of culture, of art, of a living civilization. Sometimes Leah's heart longed for it, with a longing almost as strong as her longing for a man.

"You knew her!" she cried out as Avshalom happened to speak of the famous dancer, Isadora Duncan, of her sitting near him amongst a circle of young artists and poets at a cafe. "Oh, what is she really like?"

"Why," he gave her a measuring look, the way Yosi the sculptor had once done at the Bezalel school, "Why, she is just like you!" he laughed. "When I came in and saw you in that dress, I felt something like a recognition, and that's it! Yes, Leah! She even wears a gown like this, she had it made in Greece!" He chuckled with pleasure. Leah ran and brought him the book Rahel had given her with drawings and photographs of the dancer, and Avshalom quoted lines that a French poet had written about Isadora, and translated them for her into Hebrew, and gazed again on Leah, crying out how much alike they were, and this seemed to carry her a little distance into that other world.

"You long for it, don't you?" he perceived. "You hunger for that world of art and civilization."

"Ah," she confessed, "and then I put on my heavy shoes and go out to work in our fields. To our generation it fell to begin from the beginning and remake ourselves. Later perhaps we can come to such things."

"You still go on repeating all this!" he cried. "And I—I am not of the same generation? My father was a Bilu. Thirty years ago he spoke the way you do. I know, I know that our families are already supposed to be the bourgeoisie in Eretz. Ach, Leah! Sacrifice is wrong! Everyone should live out to the last urge what is in them! Leah, after the war everything will be possible here, even civilization. The Turks will be gone, the country will open up, what a land we will build! Not only another Jerusalem, but another Athens, another Paris, another London, another New York! That is what we must make here, and not a land of peasants. Why don't we all work together, Leah, your people and ours?"

He was agleam with excitement, his entire being glowed, his fire was leaping across to her, yet it was not the flame of a man-and-woman union. She knew—who did not know, how long could it be before the Turks would know?—the dangerous way that he and the Aaronsons had taken. About the details she had not wanted to know. Now out of a sudden fear for him and out of love, too, Leah asked, "What brings you here, Avshalom?"

"—And a caravan of Ishmaelites took Joseph on the way to Egypt," he quoted, his mouth remaining partly open, his eyes dancing like those of a child bubbling to cry out his secret.

Her heart fell. Of his mysterious trip of nearly a year ago to Egypt, everyone pretended to accept the tale that it had been a love tryst, that Avshalom had managed to reach Alexandria to see Rifka before she sailed to America, and that he had made his way back on a fishing vessel. That was when he had brought so many gifts and greetings. But then why, only a few weeks ago, had he been caught in the desert in what must have been an attempt to cross the lines and reach Egypt again? Only Aaron Aaronson had been able to save him from being shot as a spy. And now? Was he mad enough to try it once more?

Leah had put her hand to the scarab Avshalom had brought her from Gidon in Alexandria. "But for you we wouldn't know what had become of my brother," she remarked.

"Soon I'll be able to tell you more."

"Avshalom. Why, why? This time if you're caught, they'll hang you." Aaron Aaronson wasn't even in the land to help him if indeed any help would then be at all possible.

No, he would not be caught. This time it was not so far to go. The British were already partway up the coast, near

Raffa. He had to reach them. He had secured the entire plan for the defense of Gaza. There were heavy German guns. He must warn the British—their attack should be by way of Beersheba, not Gaza. Around Beersheba the defense was light. Besides, he had to establish regular contact with them. The contact had been broken off. A signal had been arranged for a ship to stop at night at Athlit.

No, no, why need he tell her of this? But he tumbled on. The British had left a note on a plow, about a new signal, but it was already a long time and no ship had come. Therefore he must go to them, he must reach them, he must show them that the Jews had not failed them.

She felt terrified for him.

Did Sara know he was going?

"She's worried to death over Aaron. We haven't heard a word since he left. Perhaps I can find out something there."

"There? From the English?" Leah was puzzled.

"Where do you think he went?" His gaze was triumphant.

She couldn't speak. It was all somehow wrong, wrong. He tumbled on. His old plan—a British landing, an uprising. Her group must join. He knew they were gathering arms—

—No, no, he didn't understand. How many times had it been decided, the arms were to defend the Yishuv, it was not for the Yishuv to enter the war. Suddenly she seized his hand—why must it be he, Avshalom, who should take this deadly risk? Just now he had spoken to her of the mistake people could make with their lives, of the wrongness of turning everyone into a chalutz—let the peasants be peasants, let the soldiers be soldiers, let the poets live as poets—then he too! let him live his own role in life!

"But it is, it is my role!" Avshalom cried, so vehemently that a few heads turned to look at them in their hushed discussion. "It is exactly for me, Leah. Action is the poetry of life. The most concentrated, the most daring action becomes poetry." He spoke of Byron, a British poet who had fought for the liberty of the Greeks, and did she know the great French poet Rimbaud? "Rimbaud flung himself into the world, he vanished into Africa, among smugglers, among brigands—he was living his poetry."

"Sara doesn't know you are going," she said.

Avshalom's face became quiet. He shook his head; his

eyes grew pained. All was without pretense now before her.
And a dark intuition came to Leah; this was perhaps the
very cause of Avshalom's flinging himself into such danger.
Both Sara and Avshalom were driven souls, and if doom
did not come to them, they would pursue it.

He was pressing her hand, almost as though clinging to
it. As though from within her own thoughts, Avshalom
said, "I'm such a one. And so is she. And you—no, not
you. You are of the earth, Leah." It was not to make her
less; it was even in envy.

He was perhaps about to add something, a message for
Sara, but Zev had found them. As the Hothead approached, Leah had a misgiving; Zev would say something
gross and loud, he was drunk, he would destroy all the
feeling that had come to them here. But instead Zev spoke
with gravity, each word like the careful step of a man who
realizes he is tipsy. "Don't worry about Avshalom, Leahleh, he is going with me. And as everyone knows, nothing
in all hell ever happens to Zev, the foulest of men."

The fire had died down, the young men of the village
had gone home or to their hiding places; Avshalom's pink-
cheeked young cousin Naaman, who had hardly spoken to
a girl all through the party, but had taken refuge in singing
around the fire, again dogged his steps, reminding him that
he must get some rest. Then Naaman too must know of the
journey.

They were mounting; Leah had an impulse—she must
give him something, and she looked around the room. Every scrap of food had been consumed, but in their kitchen,
she remembered, she had put away a few provisions for the
girls for tomorrow. She hurried, and took from a jar a
handful of dates, always good on a journey. Beside his
horse she reached up her hand in farewell and left the dates
in his palm. "The woman of the earth!" Avshalom chuckled, and with a sudden movement bent over and kissed
the top of her head. Leah's heart quivered, and she felt a
dread rush of sorrow. "Ride in peace, Avshalom!" she
cried as he moved off, the last to leave.

Then nothing was heard, neither of Zev nor of Avshalom. During several weeks the thought of Avshalom
rarely came to Leah's mind, though twice his young cousin

Naaman passed to ask if they had perhaps heard mention of him from the Bedouin with whom they had contact.

It was a bitter season; the planters dismissed the remaining watchmen from their groves—what was there to watch? They allowed Bedouin to come in freely and take fruit from the trees, full camel loads that were carried down to be sold, it was said, already to British soldiers.

Everyone was short-tempered. Even in the shul in Ness Ziona, it was told, a fight had broken out between a dismissed watchman and a planter just after the singing of "Come, O Sabbath Bride." Everyone knew the watchman, Pinya Bosnowitz, a steady man, with four young children, long established in the village.

Suddenly seizing hold of the planter's sleeve, he begged, "Take me into your yard in place of the Arab family. I will take care of your stable, my wife will work in your house, my children will work for you, we have nothing at home to eat, I can't go home and look in their faces." The planter tried to pull his arm free, and they fell to screaming at each other. "No, no, I won't let you go—"

"What do you want of me! Go to the committee!"

"You let a Jew go hungry and the Arab you feed!"

"God in heaven, what has one to do with the other! He has been with me since I came to Eretz!"

"Take me too! I won't let go of you!"

Pinya grappled with the burly, gray-headed planter. The worshipers pulled on one, on the other, crying, "A shame! Not in shul! Quiet!" and suddenly Pinya burst into tears, then Gruzman as well. Pinya left off and went home; later Gruzman sent his boy with a Sabbath chaleh. Such things were happening.

The Turks too were becoming nervous and more strict. Yet rifles were accumulating in the deserted old cabin in the grove, though Dov twice came into danger while bringing more. He had secured leave for a few weeks, using the time for arms-gathering, but once as he drove his cart overloaded with heavy gunnysacks a wheel snapped in a mudhole in the midst of an Arab village. When he went into a cafe for help, a military policeman was there and came out to look, asking what was in the sacks. Only Dov's nerve saved him, as he told the girls when he arrived. "Military supplies, what else!" he had roared, and sent the gendarme to fetch him two Arabs with donkeys so that he might get on with his supplies, while leaving the wagon behind to be repaired. That same week, coming from a second trip, Dov related to Leah how he had suddenly seen before him a checkpoint at a neglected crossroads. Fortunately a military convoy appeared behind him and he managed to smuggle himself into the midst of it, passing unnoticed. So urgent was the work that he overstayed his leave, and only a warning from a Jewish clerk in the Jaffa headquarters that his absence had been noticed saved him. With an elaborate tale of a malarial attack, Dov went back unpunished.

To get the arms onward to Petach Tikvah, Rahel resorted to the old ruse, stuffing a pillow over her stomach and stretching out on a bed of straw that covered the rifles. If they were stopped at a road-post, she groaned as a woman in labor being carried to the hospital in Petach Tikvah.

The war was steadily coming nearer. The British were building a whole railway line up the coast to carry their cannon, and also laying a pipe to bring water all the way from the Nile for their troops.

One day Leah and Rahel came to an urgent meeting in the party's cabin on the shore between Jaffa and Tel Aviv; Eli, from the Herzlia Gymnasia group, proposed that they organize "Standfast" units in case of evacuation. Suddenly cannon bursts were heard. Rushing out, they saw a British warship facing Jaffa. Could it be the invasion? Had Avshalom really succeeded in persuading the British to his plan?

But the British warship turned and departed.

In a few moments a chaver came running from Jaffa. The large military ironworks had been hit directly by the shells, and nothing else. "They knew exactly where to shoot. They must have spies."

Like Leah, Rahel too had at once thought of Avshalom. Suddenly now she understood why he had sent her away from Athlit, she said. The laboratory was surely their secret spying headquarters. "Can you imagine, Leah, three months I worked there every day with Aaron Aaronson, and nothing entered my head! How they must have laughed at me!"

Then Avshalom must have reached the British safely, Leah concluded.

Two more weeks went by, and one day as she was bent,

carefully pulling out an endless, stubborn length of yablit, Leah raised her head and saw Sara Aaronson coming toward her between the rows. Straightening up, Leah went to meet her. Sara was well dressed, in a gray riding skirt and smart boots, and her face was composed, though as she neared Leah saw a slight quiver pass over her lips. At once it was covered by a firm smile.

At least let her not be uncertain of friendliness here, Leah thought, and so she hurried to Sara, beaming, crying "Shalom!" and taking hold of both her hands. How cold they were. "What brings you to us?"

"I came to see you, Leah."

"Come inside! I'll make tea."

"You have tea?"

Alas, the real English tea was long finished. "From herbs. It's good. I'll give you seeds, you can grow them at your agricultural station."

"Oh, you'll have to show me how to plant it. I'm all alone there now."

"Why, I just poke it in the ground with my finger. It comes up quickly but needs weeding."

Fortunately all the girls were out working, so they could have a quiet hour. When she had settled Sara and put the kettle on, Leah said, "You've heard nothing from Avshalom—don't worry. It's a good sign. If they had been caught, we'd have heard. And nothing ever happens to Zev, the mamser."

Sara gazed on her, her eyes never leaving Leah's form while she distractedly unbuttoned her short jacket; then she began talking in a different voice, not that of a visitor nor that of a daughter of the Aaronson house, the sister of the world-famous Aaron Aaronson, but instead the voice of a chaverteh. "I don't know why I came to see you, Leah— Yes, I know. It is not only that he was here on the last night before he left, that you were the last one he talked to—yes, his little cousin Naaman told me. You know, Naaman idolizes Avshalom. He noticed that he sat talking with you for a long time." Only a few days ago the boy had come all the way to Athlit to know if there was news of Avshalom. "He's more worried than I am. But they should have been back weeks ago."

—And the shelling of the ironworks in Jaffa, had not

that been a sign that Avshalom had reached the British?
Leah hesitated to ask.

"Naaman wants to go among the Bedouin to find out if
they were seen, I had to command him not to go. I left him
at our station on watch so that I could come here—I
wanted to talk to you."

How alone she was. Sitting there day after day on watch
for a signal. Her brothers were gone, her sister was gone,
and now Avshalom too.

And yet, now that she was here, Sara didn't seem to
know how to speak, how to confide what she wanted to
confide in another woman, a friend. Suddenly she was
speaking of Reuven, of having seen him in Damascus, as
though she had simply come to convey his greetings and
bring news of him.

"You know your brother made another discovery, an ancient grove of pistachio trees. He gave me samples to take
back to Aaron and Aaron was greatly impressed. He is
such a gentle person, such an idealist, your brother!"

Then perhaps it was this, Leah thought, between Sara
and herself—the bond of love for their brothers. For all at
once the barrier was gone, and Sara was talking, talking
and easing her heart.

"Leah—even though when I was still a young girl and
imagined I was in love with Avshalom— But you know
now when I think of it, the happiest times of my life were
when my brother Aaron took me along with him and we
searched in the mountains and in the desert for different
plants, and at those moments when we found something—
You know the feeling too? Sometimes I brought Aaron a
wildflower—once we even found together the black orchid
he had been searching for, we saw it at the same moment
among the stones of an abandoned well—at such a moments I was happy. Really happy. You too—you came
with your brother to Eretz and you worked together in the
fields, even in our own vineyard—I remember that was
when you and I first met, when Reuven was recovering
from a kadahat attack. And still, wasn't that the happiest
time of your life, no matter how hard it was?"

"It was good," Leah said. "But then—when with my
chaver—when I went out and worked together with him,
when we made the first harvest in the kvutsa all of us together, and he and I worked side by side—"

"I know, I know!" Sara cried with a thankfulness in her voice. "Then on such a night it was love."

So it must have been with her and Avshalom in their secret work, since her return from Constantinople, and it was this she had come to share, to feel again, to confirm, through another woman who had felt things she had felt. And she had come, to be in the place where Avshalom last had been. An impulse came over Leah to cradle her, to weep for her.

Sara was telling her now, "Before, when we were so young, Avshalom was always trying to say clever things, to show off his riding—I thought he was superficial, and when he began to impress Rifka, and how could he not be drawn to her, she was so lovable, a kitten—I suppose I was offended, I let him go, yes, I let him go to her. But I wasn't even a woman yet." The tremor flew over her lips.

Sara plunged into the story of her marriage. The empty, monotonous round of teas and dinners . . . and then tales of the massacre of the Armenians began to be heard. "What was maddening was the Germans. My husband did business with them and high officers came to the house, diplomats. For them it was not even hatred, it was not even religion. It was a principle of racial purity! The Turkomans had a right to purify their land, to make it one, there should be no other blood but their own—can you believe it!" And her husband would listen calmly and even seem to agree with them, until she could no longer endure it.

Then she was speaking of love. Even our body which we trusted to tell us could deceive us. Even with her husband her body had sometimes carried her away. Yet now Sara felt she knew. It was as Leah had just said, it was when everything joined together, not only the body, but what you believed in life and what you did in your life. "Now since I came back, when we go out on a task together and Avshalom will not stop—he will risk everything to find out what we need to know—then when I see him returning to the hotel, and from the light in his eye, I know he has succeeded, and meanwhile I too have learned something we need from one of their bragging officers, oh, then we have such a joy together!"

Sara had fallen silent. A melancholy came over her face. "Perhaps we had no right—Leah—do you believe in punishment for sin?"

But not for love! Not for her honesty! Could such a terror still have hold of poor Sara? "But with Avshalom—" Leah began. Then she smiled broadly to Sara. "Perhaps God isn't too religious, either, about such sins," she said. "When they struck the ironworks in Jaffa, wasn't that a sign that Avshalom had arrived there to them safely?"

Again the trembling came over Sara's lips, and her voice was small. "It was my brother Aaron who carried the information of the ironworks."

When Sara started homeward, they embraced like sisters. Sara's hair was just below Leah's lips and Leah restored there the kiss that Avshalom had bestowed.

It had been his last, for Avshalom Feinberg's body lay somewhere under the sand, beyond Raffa, in a hole not too deep, only as deep as might be scooped for the planting of a tree. The Bedouin did not care for the labor of digging. And already the place could not be found. From Alexandria, Aaron Aaronson had sent search parties to the area. He had learned of the death from Zev.

At long last cleared and enrolled in the British Military Intelligence, Aaron Aaronson had been sent out to Alexandria—only to find suspicion, and chill, and even a belittlement which he could hardly endure. Accustomed at least to being received everywhere as a man of stature, a world-renowned scientist, he found himself left to wait hours on end in one anteroom after another, only to be interviewed finally by some subaltern who had received no instructions and could give him no answer.

Once he had been questioned about his geographical knowledge of the Sinai. They were, he knew, laboriously laying a pipeline from the Nile in preparation for their attack on Gaza; eagerly he pointed out on the topographical maps sources of underground water, if they would but dig. Called back to the same office, he was introduced to a long-faced young Englishman parading himself in an abaya, a Captain Lawrence who had, just before the war, made a survey of the Sinai area under some pretext of mapping for a geographical society; Aaronson took an instant dislike to him. Indifferently the young surveyor remarked that he did not care to gainsay him, but still rather preferred to take heed of Bedouin tradition as to water sources in the Sinai.

It was a brief and hideous meeting; later Aaronson learned that the abaya-wearer was involved in some far-reaching intrigues with the ruling Moslem of Mecca, the Sherif Husein, and that camel-loads of gold were being dispatched to stir up an Arab rising there in the Hedjaz so as to occupy the Turks during the British advance into Palestine. If so, Aaronson proposed, what about fostering a Jewish activity behind the Turkish lines? Wasn't it high time to contact his group?

Jews? They only smiled.

Then suddenly one day Aaron Aaronson was sent for, and brought to a military hospital in Port Said where a wounded Jew from Palestine had spoken his name. There lay Zev. He told of Avshalom's death, a stupid death, maddening in its needlessness. A death so mean and paltry, against their high purpose.

More than a month before, eaten out with waiting for the British signal, Avshalom had set forth with Zev to reach the British lines. Deep in the first night they had passed with their Bedouin guide beyond Raffa into the wastes between the Turkish and British outposts that were penetrated only occasionally by patrols. A night mist had come down on them; their guide, becoming uncertain of the sand drifts, had advised bedding down until daylight. At dawn a whole troop of Bedouin appeared and began a violent dispute with the guide. Avshalom tried to intervene. It concerned a blood feud, Zev had made out, between the guide's tribe and these others. The guide had entered their area and they meant to take him. The terrified man started to run. Shooting broke out. Fearful of being seized and betrayed to the Turks, Zev and Avshalom had tried to hold off the entire band, but once the firing started, they knew they were lost. Himself twice hit, Zev heard Avshalom gasp that his bullets were spent and he too was finished. Crawling to him, Zev said, he found the poet dying, and then he himself lost consciousness. Under the burning sun, he had awakened only to find everything vanished with the mist, the Bedouin, the camels, even the body of Avshalom. In the end, as he crawled on, a British patrol had found him.

Only then, in the hospital, had Aaronson broken out in rage at their months of delay, shouting at the Intelligence officer, "But for all of you, he would be alive! I was already in Alexandria weeks before he left Palestine! If you had let me send a signal, he would never have started on this insane journey!"

From that day forward the operation was under way.

Aaronson himself could not reappear in Palestine. Zev, recovered, would be sent back on the contact ship. He and Sara must take command of the gathering of information. Every two weeks the ship would return to pick up their material. Aaronson would remain at Intelligence headquarters to interpret it, and to transmit particular tasks to them. As for Zev's absence of a few months, who would have noticed, since he was always moving about? To those few who secretly knew he had gone off with Avshalom, he would explain that Avshalom had made his way to the other side and was training to become a flier in a French aerial squadron. This everyone would readily believe.

And what should be told to Sara?

"The truth," Aaron said. "To Sara alone."

Then began the effective work of the Nili. Sara Aaronson and Zev circled the land, gathering up from their ring of helpers the required information. Daringly, as though to carry on Avshalom's ways, she returned to the hotels frequented by high officers. Now it was Zev, resplendent in fine new clothing, as the husband, a wealthy merchant, who appeared to carry her off at the crucial moment. Their packets of information were prepared and were picked up by a swimmer from the contact ship, one of the Zion men who had remained in Alexandria. Presently he too began bringing greetings and family messages and then gold napoleons from those in Alexandria, until it seemed that the entire Yishuv must be aware of the contact, and the secret could not but come to the Turks. Among the community leaders, whispered discussions were held, some insisting that a stop must be put to the whole Aaronson affair. And then, instead, there arose a desperate need for it.

Just before Passover came what had long been dreaded, an order of banishment. All Jews must at once depart from Jaffa and Tel Aviv.

No, no, it was no Armenian slaughter, there must be no panic, the Emergency Committee pleaded. This was clearly a military measure. A British attack on Gaza was now expected and the Turks did not want Jews in the area. As well, perhaps, for the Jews.

Only a few caretakers were to be permitted to remain, for the whole town of Tel Aviv. Hastily, Eli and Motke of Petach Tikvah assigned Standfast units to hidden posts in locked-up homes and shops, as additional guards.

Already every road and lane northward was packed with carts, with pathetic lines of trudging exiles, with overladen mules, donkeys and the last horse-carriages. In orange groves beyond Petach Tikvah, as far as Kfar Saba, tents were springing up, huts made of mats such as the Bedouin used in the Huleh, booths of straw, none failed to observe, such as were dwelt in by the Israelites of old, the tribes that followed Moshe Rabenu into the Sinai wilderness. Attempting lightheartedness, some declared, "So, we will have Succoth all year around."

But more numerous were the prophets of doom. They awaited the massacre. "No! With us it shall not be!" the resistants proclaimed, and Menahem and Motke secretly distributed the accumulated pistols, rifles, grenades, to picked men in each encampment.

Committees held incessant sittings, and somehow by Seder night a spirit of survival was developing. No massacre had yet taken place. There was even a distribution of matzoth. "I feel like in a prison of the doomed," a wit declared, "after the hangman has passed on to another cell."

Then began a new phase for the Nili. From America, from England, Jews sought for a way to send relief to the thousands driven from their homes. But America had just entered the war; her ships could no longer approach, nor was there even an open way to send money. Gold would have to be smuggled in, and only through the fortnightly trips of the contact ship, the *Monegam,* could this be done. Through Aaron Aaronson in Alexandria, on each voyage of the *Monegam,* now, there came several herring-kegs filled with gold napoleons. The coins had to be carefully selected from prewar mintings; the kegs were dragged ashore in the night to be buried by Sara and Zev in the Crusader ruins until the gold could be transmitted to the Emergency Committee. Well into the summer this work went on.

25

HALF-RUNNING despite the noon heat, there fell in upon Leah and the girls, in the new place close to Rehovot to which they had had to move, the dark-skinned Chemda from Gilboa, daughter of the younger Zeira, who had been slain in the earlier days of the Shomer. The girl was near collapse, her delicate features drawn tight with desperation and exhaustion combined. Refreshing herself only with a few gulps from a water-jar, she hurriedly told Leah her mission—a message must reach Jerusalem at once. The Nili were caught. The last shipment of gold coins, turned over by them to the Emergency Committee, must not be found in official hands in Jerusalem, or the whole committee, the entire Yishuv would be implicated.

Troubled by rumors that had risen over the disappearance of Avshalom, his young cousin Naaman had gone into the desert to search for word of him among the Bedouin. Naaman had been arrested; he had collapsed in the hands of the Turks and named the whole Nili band. Sara Aaronson was being tortured in Zichron. Arrests were under way everywhere. If the Turks found the Nili's gold in the hands of the Emergency Committee, the Yishuv would be annihilated. And the coins could be recognized.

There had been an act of carelessness: in the gold sent up to the Jerusalem committee there were coins minted only last year. This warning had come from Zev who had managed to elude the Turkish searches in Zichron, and then had disappeared. The gold napoleons must be removed from the committee's office in Jerusalem. "Leah, Leah help me. I tried to get to Jerusalem. I tried for hours at the station, on the road. I can't find a way."

When Zev's warning had come to Gilboa, they could not decide whom to send. An older person would be more likely to be stopped. A man least of all could be risked. Chemda had volunteered, and now, she cried in agony, she was failing. As far as Ramleh she had come by wagon. In Ramleh she had even managed to get onto the Jerusalem

train, but before it left the station the military police had
gone through the carriages and taken off every Jew. She
had been locked in the women's part of the station where
an Arabess had begun to search her. "I gave her money
and she let me out through her own little corner, in back. I
was afraid to try the train again. There were some military
trucks, and a driver was going to take me—I was even
going to risk it, but an officer came up and they began to
discuss something. They kept looking at me." She had
jumped off. In the streets Chemda had tried to hire a horse,
even a donkey, running from side to side of the square,
until she noticed that a Turkish policeman had his eye on
her. "When I left Gilboa, Rahel told me that if I couldn't
manage, I should come here to you," the girl said to Leah.
"Rahel herself wanted to go, but they wouldn't let her."
From Ramleh the child had half-run all the way here.
"Leah, what should I do?" she begged.

"Never mind. It's not a task for you," Leah quieted her.
"I'll go."

You lived your own life, and if you made a mistake, you
alone might suffer. But from time to time something came
and locked itself upon you, a burden and a trust where you
dared not make an error. The chaverim would appear with
a sack of rifles and put it in your keep; until they took it
away, you did not belong to yourself. Things that for yourself you could never have managed to do, you found ways to
do.

Leah set out at once. Her first thought was of Pessha
Mendelowitch who kept a stand at the Hulda station, and
for whom she saved out tomatoes when she could. By short
cut the station was an hour's walk away. Leah had not for
a long time gone in this direction—it bordered on army
encampments.

Already the land seemed to be disintegrating before her.
Here was the very grove where she had first gone to work
in Eretz, these were the very trees she and Reuven had
planted when Moshe had got the contract for their little
kvutsa. Abandoned. The leaves were curled on themselves,
shriveled. Then came fields of brambles, riven with open
crevices as though even the earth itself had been ripped
under some giant lash. Then there were not even brambles;

the earth lay desiccated, broken. The world was dying away here, edging away into something else, into some cruder, earlier order of existence.

This gave way to the landscape of war. She was in the midst of an endless disordered encampment, of wagons tipped over because of a missing wheel, of scattered heaps of ammunition boxes, of stray mules snuffling the barren earth, of piles of refuse, clusters of tents, scattered men turning to stare at her, their eyes redrimmed, their cheeks black with stubble and grime, their gaunt bodies half-bare in the heat. To avoid them, she veered, only to find herself in the stench of latrine trenches; raucous calls came from squatting soldiers, their laughter filthy as the smell. She veered again, toward a clean patch of earth that even looked as though it were freshly raked, and pulled back, nearly losing her balance as her feet trod onto softer earth, for these were graves. So shallow were they that the mound of each body could be made out as under a thin blanket.

Though Leah knew herself to be deemed strong and self-reliant, it was a feminine terror that invaded her legs, the terror of a woman finding herself alone in an existence made totally of men, where the slightest pretense of a world composed of men and women, of families, was absent. The terror was cutting off her breath. To work among men, even to do man's work, to hammer, plow, tread the soil in man's shoes, all this she had done as a woman. Her strength had been but a pretense. That she did man's labor did not help her here. Here she was plunged into their true world where men totally removed themselves from their bond with womankind, where all energy was turned into one substance, the substance of destruction and death. No one could enter it and live.

Then this hysteria had passed, and Leah saw with clarity. She was emerging into a different area of the encampment; there were larger tents, in straight rows, and passing among them she saw a figure in a white dress, a nurse. This was the hospital section, then. There were signposts in German.

Her legs still felt somewhat strange, empty, almost as after love. But now she was taking longer, firmer strides, and her fright was sealed away. There, directly before her, was the railway siding, and, as a sign of good chance, she saw that Pessha's kiosk was open. Soldiers of all grades, officers too—German, Turkish—hundreds of men were milling around, and along the tracks stood a train with flatcars carrying cannon. Wagons and trucks were everywhere, loading and unloading.

Pessha stood in her kiosk, a bundle of a woman of no age, the kind men no longer saw as a woman, her skin cracked and lifeless, and her eyes alert only with suspicion over the confusion of coins offered to her. On her stand was a large jar from which she sold glasses of sweetened water, and behind her on barren shelves were a few boxes of cigarettes. From under the counter, only to certain ones, Pessha sold bread and cheese.

"To Jerusalem?" She gave Leah the short nod of those who understand an urgency. With her head, Pessha motioned toward a stout Arab wearing broad Turkish mustaches. "I'll speak to him. Don't give him more than three francs. At the last moment he'll put you on somehow." Pessha thought there would be one more train before nightfall.

But before Pessha could find a moment to slip out and speak to the trainman, the entire area burst into tumult. A whistle shrieked—not from the train—and men raced in every direction. Leah remained standing confused, as she saw men hurling themselves beneath the halted train; Pessha was pulling her by the hand, and as they reached a shelter trench, an airplane sound overwhelmed all the others; the sound hammered down on them and the airplanes swooped down—five, more—over the railway tracks. Dustmounds were flying upward, bombs must have exploded; Leah had half-jumped, half-tumbled into a trench so filled with men that there was no room to fall, and Pessha was still pulling her somehow, among the massed bodies, into a side-pocket, a covered-over place, dark, but alive with men's cursing. Out of the corner of her eyes as she was pulled from the open part of the trench, Leah saw, on the earth above, a horse and the boots of a rider; the horse reared, then tumbled, and through all the exploding noises of the war, she seemed to keep on hearing the cracking of the man's bones.

As her eyes grew accustomed to the shelter's gloom, she saw faces that, a moment ago, around Pessha's stand, had looked idle, or weary, or some even cheerful, or comradely to each other; they were now one distorted face of fear and rage. How had she lived so close to man's war these months and years and not known, not seen its face? The raid went on. In an endless unbroken curse a German officer befouled the British aviators. "Where are ours?" Where was Shula's Gottfried, to sweep the English from the sky? Leah hardly knew which side she wished, here at this moment, to be the vanquisher. Perhaps it was true that the Turks and Germans were nearly finished. If what was left of the Yishuv could endure only a little bit longer it would be saved.

One officer lit a match and stared at her. "What are you doing here?" he demanded. "Who are you?"

"She came to help me," Pessha said quickly, and at last the match burned down.

The shooting petered out like a dying argument, and the men began to clamber from the trench. Men's hands were on all parts of her to help her; it didn't matter, except that she noticed how quickly the sense of this had returned. She was above—the horse and rider lay before her in a mud of blood. Two of the flatcars were overturned with their cannon cargo spilled, and men were pulling out mutilated bodies from underneath.

She had lost Pessha. The urgency of her task was upon Leah again; would a train still go to Jerusalem? Pessha was once more with her, seizing her hand from behind. "Come." Leah could remain for the night in her house, the English had crushed the tracks, there would be no train.

But Leah could not go backward. She would stay till the track was repaired. With a glare Pessha marched away. "Don't give him money until he puts you on a train."

The sun was down to its last hour. Along the rails, an officer was shouting to a few labor conscripts who had appeared. Leah walked forward; perhaps she could learn how long it might take. No one answered her or even raised his head; the laborers were like dead beings making movements, but without life.

Not far beyond, Leah saw the red-tiled roof of a two-story house. But this would be on the site of Hulda, where, that first year, they had planted the Herl forest, after Reuven had torn the Arab-planted saplings from the ground. A kvutsa had settled there. Without any plan Leah walked onward alongside the tracks. It was at least in the direction of Jerusalem. But even if she walked all night she would not arrive there in time.

Just before her, on one knee, was a tiny old Jew with his trouser-leg rolled up. Blood showed. A Yemenite, with ear-curls and the spare straggly beard they had, he was moaning in his throat. She bent to the wound. His flesh was so stringy and spare, you wondered how it could bleed; a shred of bomb had cut him. "Come with me, at the kvutsa they'll clean it and bind it up."

Leaning on her arm, he could manage to limp along. "A thousand blessings on you, daughter of Israel." Might her womb bear fruit. Might she live to see her children's children's children, down to the last of whom, and into eternity, he lavished his blessings. Though surely still in pain, he moaned no more but only blessed her. Who knew, perhaps he was Elijah the Prophet.

All the trees, she noticed, now were but stumps; the Herzl forest had been cut down for train fuel.

They had reached the gate. Just inside it, piles of iron rail and portions of machinery covered the yard. There were army tents; soldiers, laborers stirred around. Then, further, Leah noticed several battered motorcars and even an enormous lorry. Who knew? Perhaps Elijah's blessing was indeed at work.

From the doorway of the kvutsa's building, someone cried out "Leah!" A girl held up a lantern; the girl was one of her own, from the first gardening farm in Tiberias! Chava— Yes, Chava-Hates-Eggplant they had called her. As Leah sang out the nickname, they laughed, hugging. Before anything else, Elijah's wound must be tended, and again things fell out well, for Chava herself was the kvutsa's first-aid girl, and as they washed the Yemenite's leg, counting each droplet of water, several of the chevreh clustered around and all was related. The army had quartered a repair station on them; the army mules drank all their water while their own few remaining cattle were howling with thirst. They had no well of their own so water had to be fetched in barrels from the well of an Arab grove owner who raised his rate every day. Meanwhile Chava's chaver, a capable looking lad with reddish freckles, naturally called Gingi, begged Leah to convince Chava and the rest of the girls that they must evacuate. The British would surely bomb this place because of the repair station.

All through the meal of soup and chick-peas, with a tea made from some sort of wild grass, the arguments were passionately repeated: the girls would not leave without the men, the men would not leave and abandon the farm. The girls argued, "There's nothing left but a few cattle, and we can take them along," but also it was known that if the men so much as stepped beyond the gate, the Turks were likely to seize them for labor service. Within their grounds they somehow had protection through the German motor-vehicle repair chief, whom they helped.

On this Leah seized. Might any motor vehicle be going to Jerusalem? She must reach Jerusalem, it was urgent.

Gingi understood. He went off, quickly returned. It was well. And this very night!

Leah must get a few hours of rest, they insisted; she could use the cot of their watchman. In the still-dark they woke her, pressing bread on her for the journey, and led her to the enormous lorry. Stacked on its body, now, looming above the tents, were upended airplane wings that had been repaired here. A middle-aged German was the driver; without questions he accepted Leah, only warning her that she must get off before the checkpoint at the main highway; she would find him waiting for her a distance ahead.

The German handed her some kind of army jacket; in this, should a sentry hold up a lantern, she could pass. He was about to boost her up the high step, but Leah swung aloft like a man, and heard an admiring grunt.

Yet when he stopped for her to drop off, and she circled through a field alone in this nowhere, a dark speck of humanity moving in this dark night, known only to one being, this laconic German driver who might not even wait for her, Leah found herself whispering, "God help me." Could there be a God? In all this absurdity, could there really be a God to devise fates that hung by such slender chances? And overhead the sky, the wondrous sky of Eretz with its boundless quiet, with its clarity and beauty that in times of agony spread healing over your heart . . .

The truck was there waiting. At long intervals the German made remarks. He had a daughter her age. "Huebsches Maedchen." Large like her. How he loved his machine. The Jews made good mechanics. Arabs were good too; if they wanted, they could be clever with machinery. But—and he imitated their indifference—"In'sh Al-lah."

As the mammoth vehicle slowly ground its way up the tortuous road on the climb to Jerusalem, her whole body was bending forward as though to help it. Before seven probably no one would be at the Emergency Committee's office. Still, suppose the police came early and broke in? Now the lorry was impeded by a tangle of donkeys and army wagons. Now by another huge vehicle, even slower than theirs. At last they were passing the brickworks at Motza, to climb the final height. At the edge of the city, the German halted; here she must get down. As Leah thanked him he said, "Your people is the people of God. May your people be saved."

His truck was about to enter a military compound. As the gates were opened, there swarmed from the street, from all along the compound fence, wraiths of religious Jews in their black capotes, haggard, clamorous, trying to squeeze alongside, into the area, begging bread, bread, each of them desperately holding forth some last possession, a silver spice-box, a ring, and one snowbearded Hasid even snatched off his gilt-rimmed eyeglasses to thrust them at a passing soldier. The guards, using the sides of their rifles, swept them back like rubbish, the wretched Jews stumbling over each other, gaunt, ravenous, and beyond insult. Again they darted close, to each soldier who came out or approached they fastened themselves, pleading, begging. Along the barbed-wire fence Arab children, all but naked, pressed themselves, calling inward, their small hands thrust through between the barbs, even little girls carrying emaciated babies on their backs were begging, baksheesh, baksheesh, lechem, bread, bread. A wave of children rushed toward Leah, clutching, pleading. In her kerchief was the chunk of bread Chava had given her. Leah halted, thinking to divide it, to give half to one of the famished Hasidim. But as she began to unknot the scarf, the wretched children grasped at her hands, tore at her fingers with their talons; they tore at each other to get nearer, and suddenly the tallest of them clawed the bread out of her hands and fled, the howling pack behind him.

So it was in Jerusalem.

Among the names of advocates and importers on the doors along the second-floor corridor of a long, important looking edifice on Jaffa Road, she found that of the Yeshayahu Brothers, who were part of one of the fine Jerusalem families of "before," before even the first Aliyah, a family listed at the head of every charity, of every school and hospital committee, a family respected both by the religious community and the Zionists. It was the elder brother, Ehud Yeshayahu, who now headed the administration of relief.

Behind the railed entry was a desk with nobody yet there, but at a high bookkeeper's stand Leah saw an elderly Jew who must have just opened the office, for he was pulling on his black half-sleeves. He looked calm, so nothing could yet have happened, she had arrived in time.

With a broad well-tended beard and a silken skullcap, he was a specimen of the fine-looking old-style Jew, the scheiner Yid, and he leaned over his ledger like an eager scholar over his Talmud. "Is Mr. Yeshayahu here yet?" Leah asked.

The bookkeeper glanced at her with the reproach of a worshiper at an interruption—and from a woman! "And who asks?"

"I'm sent with an urgent message. From the committee in Gilboa."

He turned now and faced her. His eyes had the sad yet steady gaze of those who see beyond you to the ways of the Eternal, that are beyond questioning. Leah's heart sank.

"He is arrested," the bookkeeper confirmed. "They already came yesterday."

Even her father would not accept God's will with such calm but would cry out!

Leah's eye fell on a large iron safe that stood in a corner. "They took the gold?"

The man too turned and gazed at the safe; she began to feel angry at this fine calm Jew. Then Leah noticed something about the safe itself. Over the edge where the door closed into the frame was a blot, a large wax seal.

"Dr. Yeshayahu raised the legal question," the Jew explained with a tone of delicate appreciation. "Since he is holding the funds in trust for the community, how could he surrender the keys to the safe until the police brought a

proper order? Therefore they sealed the safe until they secure the document. But him they took away."

Then everything was meanwhile in this one's care? "We
must remove the gold coins!" Leah cried, explaining why.
When would the Turks come back? Today? At any moment?

The bookkeeper was still gazing at the iron box as
though God's law lay encased there. "It is true that the
Jews of Jerusalem are perishing of starvation," he repeated,
as in a Talmudic argument with himself. "And this gold
was sent by our brothers in America to buy food and save
them."

Now he turned his gaze on her, and his eyes were filled
with pain. "What I have seen in the Holy City!" he said.
"In the Arab shops there have appeared Jews with Scrolls
of the Torah in their arms, to be sold for a measure of
lentils. And the Scrolls the Moslem shopkeepers have torn
into scraps to be used instead of old newspapers for wrapping vegetables. Perhaps because we have profaned the Torah, God has sealed off the money sent to save us."

"Reb Yid!" Leah cried. She didn't know where it came
from—perhaps from Tateh. "Doesn't God command us
above all to save life?" And suddenly she saw that the seal
was stamped with the Moslem crescent. "Is this the seal of
our God? Shall we wait with folded hands for the will of
Allah? Doesn't God demand of us that we put our hands to
the task and help!" At this, behind his startled gaze, she
saw an uncertainty. "Who has the key to the safe?" Leah
demanded. "You?"

"No, no," he cried. But she saw that he knew who had
it. Softly the good Jew said, "It was I who was made responsible for the seal."

So it was fear. Of God or the Turks, what did it matter!

"Listen," Leah said, "it is not only by hunger that
Bahad-ad-Din can kill our people. Do you know why the
Turks came here for this money? Do you know how this
money got here?" What Jew did not already know the secret of the Nili and the gold?

"The Yeshayahu brothers had nothing to do with your
spies!" he cried. "Even Djemal Pasha has respect for the
Yeshayahu family."

"God in heaven!" Leah burst out. "Aaron Aaronson too
Djemal Pasha respected. And the Turks are at this moment

torturing Sara Aaronson to death. And if this money is found here it will give them an excuse to accuse the entire Yishuv, the Emergency Committee, everyone, of being part of the spy ring. They'll hang even your Yeshayahus. Massacres will begin. We must break through the seal at once. Tell me where to get the key. The money must disappear. Don't worry about your safety—I'll take you away, we'll hide you."

He made no move. But then Leah saw something else coming into his eyes, a certain little gleam. She recognized it from far back, from some sagacious Talmud-wizard in the old country, the gleam that came when a Talmudist found an interpretation, a way around something that seemed forbidden. "Perhaps God has put another way into your mind?" Leah asked.

"After all, the authorities don't yet know what is or is not in the safe," he said. "If the brother of Ehud Yeshayahu should give you the key, then perhaps there is a way to deal with the seal."

"What way?" Leah stared at the wax imprint. Could they perhaps cut through it with a thin blade and then, heating the tip of the blade, try to melt back the wax when they closed the safe again? No, they could never hope that the seam would not show. "But what are you thinking of?" she asked.

Now that his scruple was gone, or that he saw a way to get out of things safely, her Reb Yid was altogether changed, quick, clever, decisive. Oh, these pious Jews! You could always find a way to work with them!

"The problem is," he said concisely, "to know how to seal it up again with the same seal."

She did not quite follow. Could he obtain the official seal? Bribe someone and borrow it?

"An artisan," the bookkeeper revealed his thought. "With wax. The way a silversmith makes an imprint and then a copy of a medallion."

And he even knew a silversmith nearby who could make such an imprint. Only, he himself must not leave this office.

Leah ran, but found the metal shutters of the shop shut down. In a doorway sat a pallid boy with long earcurls. Where did the silversmith live? The boy shrugged. Gone, gone away.

Where, who else? And just there, in this very street, Leah saw, as she gazed around in desperation, was the courtyard where she had once stayed with Rahel, among the Bezalel students, among the stonecutters. In a corner of the yard Yosi the sculptor had made souvenirs for Jerusalem visitors, little plaques from molds of plaster. Elijah's blessing was still with her! For there he was, the same Yosi, the baldness higher on his forehead, there he stood, whistling and grumbling, hacking away at a block of stone. Behind him in his narrow cave of a room, even as she approached, Leah saw, as always in Yosi's room, some lazy-looking girl on the cot. As though not a day had passed. And before she could tell him what she so urgently needed, Yosi demanded, What did she think of his stone? An abstraction, he proclaimed it. The newest movement from Paris. And the abstract movement would be perfect for monuments in Eretz! Since images were forbidden by the everlastingly interfering rabbis, here finally was the answer! "Yosi," she broke in, "you are needed." And quickly she explained.

"Why not?" Yosi said. She had come to just the right person. And from a table cluttered with tools, sketches, bits of food, he collected his materials, explaining all the while that he had managed very well through the war—the damned Germans, bless their stupidity, were addicted to antiquities, and he made for them the most authentic antiquities, and if the English should come, never mind, they too had a passion for antiquities. Before Leah could drag Yosi off to his task, she had to admire several clay figurines, women with snakes between their breasts. "Terafim! Leah, you don't even recognize them? You don't remember? The little household gods stolen from Laban by whom? By Leah and Rahel!" He laughed at his jest. Now as a test she must point out to him which of the lot was a real, which a new antiquity? "Later, later." "Only one second. Which is the old one?"

"This! Come already!" she pointed at random.

"You see! That one is my own! A perfect re-creation!" And he followed her at last.

Kneeling before the safe, mixing plaster in a saucer, grumbling and whistling, Yosi did his work while the bookkeeper hovered over him, frightened, yet pleased that his plan was practical. Meanwhile the good Jew told Leah where she must go for the key—to the other Yeshayahu brother in their bank.

It was a small distinguished place, not the sort of bank ordinary people might go to, but with a hushed atmosphere as if the important financial affairs that made the world turn were conducted here. Through the arabesques of a wrought-iron grille, a clerk at last took her message, and departed to the rear. A few more clerks sat rigidly at their desks, their eyes following her as though she brought nearer the terror they were expecting. Now the first one returned, opened a gate, and led her to the rear chamber, where sat the other Yeshayahu brother, Raphael. A soft-cheeked man with a short, silver beard, and wearing a velvet kippa, he spoke to her in a solemn Biblical Hebrew. There had been many arrests in the night, his own turn might come momentarily. He must already have had some message from the bookkeeper, for the banker knew her mission. Yes, on his desk—Leah had heard there were a few in Jerusalem—was a telephone. The banker now took a small key from a desk-drawer and handed it to her.

"One more problem you may not have considered," he said. "When the safe is opened by the authorities, they must find some sort of funds inside." He was, he said, assembling the largest possible amount on such short notice, in Turkish pounds. Part of this he could already entrust to her.

In a moment, while the banker spoke to Leah of the darkness of the situation, of the recklessness and irresponsibility of the spies, of their unforgivable crime in involving the innocent leaders of the community with their gold from abroad, the first clerk entered carrying packets of currency. Leah tied them in her scarf. The banker did not forget to have her sign a receipt.

Yosi had already taken the impression in fine plaster. Now he cut away the wax seal. He must hurry to his workshop to pour lead and make the duplicate stamp, but he lingered while they opened the safe. He just wanted to see all those golden napoleons, Yosi said.

There were several small leather pouches. Still, Yosi had to open one and pour out the gold so as to feel it on his palm. "Go, go!" Leah screamed at him, but he examined a coin. It was indeed stamped 1915. No artist would have been so careless, he laughed. Tossing the coin onto the bookkeeper's stand, he was finally on his way. They locked the door behind him.

What if the police should come right now? It had been foolish to open the safe until all was ready, the substitute money, the new seal, so that only a moment would have passed before the safe was in order again. "At least," Leah said, unbinding the kerchief, "put in these packets." How long did it take to melt lead? Should she perhaps rush to Yosi's, to hurry him?

A knock came. But it proved only the bank clerk with more packets of money.

Then she heard Yosi's whistle. He had indeed worked quickly, the devil. As he melted a stick of wax and pressed in the new seal, they hung over him. Perfection! Yosi leaped up, so pleased with himself that he seized Leah in a bear hug, the pious bookkeeper even looking on with tolerance.

"What'll you do now with all this dangerous gold?" Yosi laughed.

"Take it away, take it away!" the bookkeeper begged.

"Maybe I'll melt if for you into antiquities!"

If only she could agree! But her task was not ended. The money was to be brought back to Petach Tikvah for hiding. Again Leah signed a receipt, which the bookkeeper secreted away as he bade her farewell. In Yosi's toolbox the little sacks were carried to his workshop. How easy it would be to leave it all there amidst the litter of stones. Instead of feeling elated over her deed, Leah felt a dreadful weariness now, and the burden was still clamped on her. Such complicated actions as this were not in her nature. And how was she to get back? She was not clever, she would yet stumble.

Yosi made tea, real tea he had gotten from the Germans. He bore up her spirits, he thought of a thousand comical plans for transporting the gold, while that girl of his still lay curled there on the sofa as if it was all of no interest. Then, like a teacher who has decided the children's play hour is over, the girl remarked to Leah, "There should be an ambulance going down to Ramleh. If you want, I'll try to arrange it for you."

She was a nurse at the Hatikvah Hospital. "Don't you

remember I always prefer nurses?" the sculptor jested. "Our Jewish nurses are easy game, they like to pretend they're cultured."

Still with her lazy air, the girl went off and brought back a nurse's uniform that Leah could get into. And for the bags of gold Tanya produced a medical supply satchel with Red Cross markings all over it, borrowed, she explained from a Christian mission nearby. They covered over the leather pouches with bandage rolls, and carried the satchel to the rear of the hospital where an ambulance stood waiting. Soon came the stretcher with the patient, an elderly notable from Ramleh. Leah took her place as his nurse, and thus began the return journey.

After depositing the patient in Ramleh, the driver, a Polish Jew who sensibly asked no questions, delivered Leah and her baggage to Petach Tikvah, leaving her, as she asked, in the outskirts, for there was no need for him to be troubled with her exact destination. Shouldering the medical case, she plodded through the groves to the house of Motke the shomer, where the secret store of rifles was kept.

With relief and joy they fell on her. Trust Leah! "I told you she would do it!" Motke cried to his wife, Bluma, who had been certain that Leah was arrested. Poor young Chemda, returned from Leah's kvutsa, had been accusing herself incessantly for letting Leah take over her mission; red-eyed, she fell on Leah's breast. The Turks were all over Rishon; they were arresting everyone even remotely connected with young Naaman's family.

Lifting the satchel to carry it to the attic, Motke nearly slipped on the ladder under its weight. "Never would I have dreamed I would be so glad to get rid of so much money," Leah laughed as she steadied him. But Bluma, already ladling out kasha for her, had dreadful things to relate. A wagon had appeared with news of Zichron.

In the choking hot attic, Bluma's voice reached up, shrill, disembodied, a keening of timeless horrors. Leah saw, as Bluma cried it all upward, Sara Aaronson lashed to the gatepost of their yard, and, astride his horse, the Kaymakam of Haifa, Hassan Bey, not the Turkish Hassan Bek, but another butcher just as evil, coldly watching as the lashes struck the girl across her breast. As though Bluma saw it, her voice told of Sara's bodice red from blood soaking through, soft-fleshed Sara Aaronson, round and milky, and as Bluma's words still rose to her, Leah saw the father, old Ephraim Aaronson, flung on the ground in the dust of his gateway. Like her own father bearded and gnarled, the settler lay there; a decent man he was acknowledged by all, despite his following the ways of the Baron's settlers when it came to Jewish labor, for nevertheless Ephraim Aaronson was a man who went out with every dawn and worked with his own hands among his vines. Old Aaronson lay in his gateway before his bound daughter, and when the tormentors paused in the lashing of Sara, they continued on him with the long whip used on bullocks, and she called out to him, "Be strong, hold strong against them!"

Then Sara's father shouted out to her, "Is there need for you to teach me, my daughter? Have no fear."

Through the entire first day not a scream, not a whimper came from the father or the daughter, it was said, but on the second day, yesterday, Sara's screaming began, and rent all Zichron, and the Zichronites closed and shuttered their windows so as not to hear, so as not to see. But Sara's screams pierced the walls of stone, as she cursed and reviled her tormentors, crying out to them that the British would soon destroy them, and that Hassan Bey and his overlord Bahad-ad-Din, and each of their executioners would be remembered and would receive his due when the British victors arrived. The entire civilized world, she cried out, already knew of their barbaric massacres, and everywhere the Turks were loathed.

In the police house and in the synagogue the elders of Zichron had been locked up as hostages. Arab servants, venturing through the deserted lanes, brought back word of the tormented men flung one after another across the table in the police house, the soles of their feet bared for the bastinado. To their pleading, to their protestation that they had known nothing of the Nili, that they themselves were totally opposed to the spying, Hassan Bey cried out, How? They had known nothing of the spying? and yet they had been opposed to it?

All, all were responsible. And until the master spy Zev was found and surrendered, all of them would be held. And if Zev, the paramour of Sara Aaronson, was not found and surrendered, then there was no telling how far Djemal Pasha would go. Let it be remembered that the Armenians had done nothing even half so treacherous, and let the Jews think deeply of the fate of the Armenians.

—The Armenian fate could begin there in Zichron, Bluma's keening voice reached up to Leah, and Motke, bent double under the eaves, his face livid as he labored to push the troublesome box deep into the hiding area, uttered a growl of confirmation at each dire prediction his wife called upward. The entire population of Zichron would be driven onto the roads, across the Jordan, across the Hauran, into the wastes of the desert to perish.

Nothing would help unless Zev was found.

Zev had escaped, it was said, from the cellar of the Aaronson house. A servant told it. As soon as Hassan Bey appeared, Sara had commanded Zev to flee, she had even managed to send down a loaf of bread to him, wrapped in her head scarf.

"I have no pity for her! She had no shame!" cried Bluma. "As for him, Zev always brought trouble everywhere. And now disaster! If he entered this moment, I would give him over to the Turks."

"Better dead," Motke muttered, and straightened to climb down. In the kitchen Bluma stood, her face drawn in bitterness. "Who gave them the right? How could they take on themselves to do this to the entire Yishuv! And the way they flaunted themselves, it was certain they would be caught, driving shamelessly everywhere together in her carriage, staying together in the best hotel in Jerusalem, spending gold napoleons like coppers! Who gave them the right to have all Jews branded now as traitors and spies? Where one morality falls, all morality falls," she declaimed righteously. "Adultery and spying, it all goes together!"

"Bluma!" Leah cried. "You yourself have told what Sara is suffering. What she did, she did not for herself but for the Yishuv, for the Jews. Is this a time to besmirch her? And as to the gold, how many Jews would have starved but for this gold? Haven't we ourselves received a share of it and used it to buy arms? Oh, poor Sara." Leah could not touch the food before her—she found herself leaning on her hands in sudden convulsive tears, in an anguish of desire that all this, all these years of war, and dread decisions, and smuggling of weapons, and constant fear, all should be wiped away and only the early days of heroic struggle and labor and even malaria and exhaustion should return, that she might be nursing her brother in the hut in the Aaron-son grove and sensing his young man's yearning, as the young daughter with a face of clear butter came to lend him one of her brother's precious books.

Suddenly the need came over Leah to be gone from here. She must go home to Mishkan Yaacov. The searches, the horror, would reach there too. Whatever happened to the family, she must be at home with them when it came.

Only, her task was not finished. At once when she arrived, the eldest boy of Motke and Bluma had been sent off to tell Eli, who now came hurrying. The Tel Aviver praised her, listened to tales of the wax seal, laughed delightedly, his clever eyes showing he was filing away the scheme for future need. But as for now, the napoleons must at once be sorted out, the telltale ones hidden away until the Turks were gone—

"We can buy arms with them right now, the Bedouin only bury the gold, anyway," Motke intervened.

Eli shook his head. Just now not the slightest risk could be taken. But the coins of pre-war vintage, the safe ones, must go at once to the Emergency Committee here in Petach Tikvah.

"What for?" Motke roared. "Those frightened Jews in Jerusalem turned the whole lot over to us, good and bad. Leah risked her life to bring it. The Shomer can make good use of it all."

The funds had been allocated for relief, Eli insisted. "It's up to the Emergency Committee to decide where this money goes."

"No, it's up to us!" Motke insisted. "I tell you we stand at the brink!"

"And you think I don't know it?" said Eli. "Motke, this is no time for quarreling with the community notables."

"I piss on your notables! They have money of their own hidden away. When those fine notables in Jerusalem had to put some money in the safe, they found it quickly enough."

"Paper. You know you can't buy food with paper."

"When Bahad-ad-Din comes after us, we need guns more than food."

"Motke, you complain that the Nili should not have made decisions on their own. Nor can we. You can come and talk to the committee yourself. Only don't piss on them, Motke. It won't help."

It was young Chemda then who had a suggestion. "Why shouldn't we give the coins that are safe to the committee, and the rest we can keep for arms?"

Leah kissed the girl's clear little forehead. Again they clambered to the attic, Motke holding a lantern while his boy snaked into the narrow hiding area and pushed out the coffer. Then, sitting on the floor in a circle around the lamp, with Eli and Bluma on watch below, they opened the leather pouches and made two heaps of golden coins, Chemda and the boy vying with each other to read out the year marks. Despite all that threatened, a calm came over Leah, almost as though they were a circle of comrades in a kitchen shelling peas. And this was a thing to remember, she told herself, that amidst the worst agitation such peace could come in sitting together at a simple task.

At last Motke and Eli went off to the committee with the pouches of prewar coins. In no time they were back, Motke in a rare mood of hilarity. "Out! Out!" he mimicked the shrill Yiddish of a city father of Tel Aviv. "Take it away or I'll throw it all into the Yarkon!" Not even these "safe" coins would they touch. Even the astute Dizingoff had wanted none of it. Nor should the gold remain anywhere in Petach Tikvah. Searches were expected momentarily. "If they find your guns, it's already bad enough."

"For the guns," Motke remarked, "our brave notables know that only we would be arrested. But for the gold, they too."

Anything that could be connected with the Nili must vanish. "Take it away, take it away!" the notables had screeched.

The leather pouches again lay on the table. Quickly Leah packed them back into the medical case. But now what to do with it all?

As if in answer there came a double-gallop and a wheel-whir known to all of them. "Dov!"

The paymaster's carriage snapped into the small yard; Dov sprang down from one side and from the other, Menahem. And what goods they brought! Even Menahem was sparkling as he quickly took down a sack which he would not even entrust to Motke, carrying it into the house by himself and lovingly laying it on the table. Folding down the neck as gently as a man undressing a bride, he let them stare. A machine gun.

Their first. Speckless and bright.

Studying the weapon with his sharp, matter-of-fact gaze, Motke's boy Eytan said, "British."

Dov gaily knuckled the boy's head. From the disastrous British attack on Gaza. Right now everything could be bought. They had ten good rifles, too, with plenty of ammunition.

"You see!" Motke shouted. What could be done with this gold!

—But the British had failed, then? Leah asked.

—Thousands killed, Dov said, a stupid general. He could have pushed in, but at the crucial moment he had lost his nerve and withdrawn. "But they will come back, the English will come back." He must at once report to his headquarters. On one foot, he listened to the story of the gold. No question, Eli was right, it must be taken to Gilboa. Menahem agreed. And giving Leah a pat on the shoulder as he would a man, Dov cried, "Good work," made a smart Turkish salute, and was gone.

Better chance the ride at night than in daytime, Menahem decided. From the Emergency Committee itself he managed to borrow a carriage. Motke would come with him. "Take me too!" Leah cried; she had to get home, home, an end to all these adventures. Menahem glanced at her, still in her nurse's dress. Good, all the better. Into the carriage. The Red Cross case she placed under her feet. Rifles were stored beneath the driver's seat, and topped by a layer of feed.

The whole way to Chedera they were not stopped even once. Perhaps it was the fine looking brougham, like a doctor's, and the nurse in white.

There was no wind. The air lay close, signaling a hamseen for tomorrow. Menahem had boldly taken the top down and Leah's uniform gleamed. Now and again they passed an encampment, a control-post, a dozing sentinel. "Night is best," Menachem congratulated himself.

Before Chedera, Menahem pulled up, resting the horses, and debated with Motke. Half awake, Leah heard. They could take a bypath avoiding the town, but if they were challenged, how to explain it? Besides, Menahem argued, Chedera had already undergone the spy search, half its men were arrested. Again he decided on boldness, and trotted the horses forward.

Alert now, Leah recognized many houses in their stillness. Down this lane the Schneirsons lived, cousins of Avshalom Feinberg; both of the sons and the father had been seized by Hassan Bey. What grief must lie on the mother—surely she sat there in her darkness, awake within her silent walls. If one could but stop and speak a word of comfort. And then the Feinberg house itself, a tomb. She saw Avshalom on that Chanukah night, in her girls' kvutsa, his keffiyah flying as he galloped away, so filled with life that his little cousin Naaman could not believe his death and had gone into the desert to find him. And this had brought all the disaster. Leah couldn't breathe. Each silent house as they passed seemed now to be shrunken in a waiting terror, for half the Nili had been from here.

Menahem was rigid, clinging, she knew, to his fury at the bungling lot of them so as not to feel pity for them. The silence tightened in the carriage.

And then they were on the road, going past the collectiva at Karkur. Leah felt her breath returned. The worst was over.

From the roadside a figure sprang, directly before the horses. The animals shied, half-rearing, the carriage rocked. Menahem managed to control the startled animals, but the attacker seized their bridles, crying hoarsely, "Menahem, don't shoot!"

It was Zev.

Menahem pushed down Motke's gun. Zev's voice, in a croak of desperation, still carried an echo of his old, boasting tone. "I knew the gait of your horses!" Now beside the carriage, he recognized Leah. Whatever it was, she tried to fling it off, but Zev's whole being had already made a claim on her. He raised his leg to mount. "Keep off!" Motke leveled his pistol.

"Take me with you, hide me!" The desperation was addressed to Leah, while his words were to the men. Despite the revolver, Zev sprang onto the mount-step, clinging to the carriage. Motke's pistol butt came down on his forearm, Leah heard the thud, but Zev clung. "Ride, ride," he gasped to Menahem. "You can't leave me!" His eyes still hung with terror and pleading on Leah, pleading out of a puffed, ravaged face, but to the men he managed even a threat in his tone, "You know it's too dangerous for everyone, for you to leave me here."

"With a bullet through your head we can leave you," Motke said.

Zev's eyes left Leah and he faced the two of them. This now was the other man in the wretch. He held his head erect. "I'm unarmed, Motke." And then the boaster rose up in him, his words poured from Zev in a feverish jumble of arrogance, even of madness, yet with the glitterings of nobility that made little stabs at your heart nevertheless. "What have I done that is so evil except risked myself day and night for two years for the cause of the Yishuv? What have I done but fight for us in the way most dangerous to myself? All, all of you now, you only want to live through the next few weeks until the English save you. And I? When every last one of you finally realized that our fate was with the English, you only went and hid, you stuck your heads in the ground, you didn't even move a finger but only waited. You, chaver Menahem—you admitted a year ago when we asked your whole Shomer to work with us—you yourself agreed that reason was on our side. And in your heart too you yourself would have become one of us, deny it! I know you too well. How many nights did we do the rounds together! But you were loyal to the decision of the Shomer. Good. Fine. Noble. On us, everyone spits— spies, vermin. But the gold we bring, oh, that's kosher enough even for the exalted Dizingoffs and our Turkish-ass-lickers in Jerusalem—" But how could he know? How could he possibly know it was here in the wagon? Could they still have spies that had known her every movement today? Impossible. And yet something uncanny enwrapped them all, as though the carriage, the horses, they themselves, were become a substance of the night, a black haze mingling the real and the unreal, in which even your past actions, even your thoughts, were in some way mingled with what was visible and clear. Just as some strange force had caused Zev to spring at the carriage, had made him believe he recognized the hooves of Motke and Menahem's horses from afar. A hundred coincidences, a handful of pebbles flung into the sky, had formed themselves into a chain, and drawn all of them together here in the middle of the night on this road through the silent wady.

"To deserve our land we must fight for it!" Zev mocked.

"And who has carried on this fight? Who but we? Yes, spies. In a war, one spy is the worth of a thousand, ten thousand men. Who told the English ships where to strike in Jaffa, at the armament yard? Who gave the British aviators the locations of encampments for their bombing? And I—what evil have I done? Did I betray anyone? Was it I who babbled and brought down Von Kressenstein and Bahad-ad-Din and all their spy-hunters on us? When I was ambushed in the desert with Avshalom and we shot out our last bullets, so we could get to our allies with the plans for the defense of Gaza, when I got two bullets in me, and was also left for dead, was that evil? Believe me, I would prefer to have died in place of Avshalom. But I lived and I accomplished our work." He half turned to Leah. "If it had been Avshalom who lived, is Avshalom a man you would have despised? No! a hero. But Zev is a lout, a braggart, a traitor, a spy, shoot him down like a hyena."

"Enough, enough!" Leah couldn't endure it. "Take him! It's not for us alone to decide."

"It's not for us to decide?" Motke whirled around with fury—as though he could execute her right along with Zev. "But *you* can decide! You can decide for everyone to risk their hides if we're caught with this slime in the carriage, or even worse if we get to the kvutsa and the Turks are sitting there. Then every last chaver will hang. That you can decide for us! With his women this schvants could always save himself!"

Tears of rage, denial, bitterness over gossip—and why shame?—all of this together choked her. It was all so unworthy at this terrible moment. Leah felt paralyzed, but Menahem had turned on Motke. "Enough!"

"I swear to you if we're stopped, I'll say you captured me." Zev had caught the moment; it was his begging voice now.

They were still over three hours from Gilboa. Even without the hunted man, if they were stopped and the guns were found, and the gold, they were destroyed. Perhaps with the spy bound as though captured—

"We can't remain standing here!" Menahem cried. "All right, tie him. Get in!"

Zev had already leaped in beside Leah. Her heart contracted a notch tighter. The foulness of him, to have run away leaving Sara—Even this thought he caught in her. "I

swear to you I refused to leave Sara, she commanded me to
reach the English. I swear to you I am not that much of a
swine. She commanded me."

Motke had flung her a rope, and it was she who had to
tie the wrists that Zev extended with a movement suddenly
arrogant. Avoiding even touching his skin, Leah bound
him.

"The feet too," Motke angrily instructed, and Zev with a
snort stuck out his feet for her. His boot struck the medicine chest. Uncannily, the same way he had divined that
the oncoming carriage was theirs, he now divined their errand. He took in her nurse's uniform. He pushed the chest
with his foot and sensed its heaviness. "Our gold!" he cried.

His eyes had come alive. "Our gold you'd save, but not
me." No one answered. Motke sat clenched, clearly with
all his strength holding back his urge to put a shot into the
jackal and make an end.

Menahem lashed the horses. Zev squirmed this way and
that, his shoulders and legs pushing at her while he kept up
a wild incoherent incessant monologue, his voice sometimes dropping so it was only for her, sometimes rising for
the men, too. "Leah, believe me. Between you and me
there was always something, we understand each other—"
Even in this extreme moment, a low note of suggestion
crawled into his voice—the wretch, the vermin, how could
she still pity him?—"Leah, you are a real woman and I
respect you. I swear to you I would give my soul to exchange places with Sara at this moment. But they had already seized her and she sent down the servant, she commanded me to flee and the truth is, it's the only chance for
her too—as long as they don't catch me, they will keep her
alive. If I can only get word to the English, believe me
they'd come, they'll send a warship straight to Athlit,
they'll land a rescue party! Leah, everything they say about
Sara and me is filth, lies. I worship her, I respect her. I
worshiped Avshalom—when he lay dying in the sand, I
wept over him, I wept like a baby, the only time in my life
I wept and wept. I lay over him to protect him and shot at
them until I was hit twice and I believed I was dead. You
know what that is? To believe you have died? And then I
was gone, nothing. Leah, you at least believe me. Sara and
I went everywhere together to carry on the work. How else

could we do it? Would the German officers in the Hotel Fast babble their secrets to me? But in the end she wouldn't have to go with them because she would pretend she was with me. That's why I had to buy good clothes and even wear rings, to show I was rich, an important man. I swear to you, just as it was with yourself, nothing happened with Sara. I love women, I have made some women suffer, I have given some women joy, but I am not such a coward as to leave a woman to save myself—" and on and on, in a tormented kind of truth, in self-pity, in arrogance.

"What chance did I ever have to learn anything? I have a good head, Sara herself said I could have studied and become somebody—" It could yet be. Appallingly, Zev believed everything could yet be; he would change, he declared, he would become a decent man. In a week, in two weeks, the British would launch their great attack, they would finish with the Turks, his information was absolutely certain.

She did not even tell him of the defeat at Gaza. What use would it be?

"Hide me, Leah, get them to hide me. I tell you I know, I've seen the plans of battle, I know when they will strike. Sara must hold out. She is strong. Hide me. The British have surely already understood what happened here. Aaron Aaronson is in their headquarters in Alexandria, did you know that? A rescue ship is already on the way. I will lead them to her, I will free her." His voice pitched higher. "Only I can save Sara!" He harangued the men. "You want gold to buy arms? I'll bring you a barrel of gold. Two barrels. I've got it all safely hidden, don't worry. Work with me, and I'll buy not only rifles but cannon—"

Suddenly Motke whirled on him with the foulest of Bedouin curses. "Shut up! Shut up or I'll finish you off!"

For a moment Zev remained silent, though eying the back of Motke's head in the way of a man who notes down in himself how he will one day even the score. Then he began a half-whispered pleading to Leah, a new plan, she must persuade Menahem to help him to get to the north. To the Druze on the Hermon, above Metulla. "With the Druze I'm like a brother, they'll hide me in the hills—" Her flesh began to quiver from the night chill that had come, or was it from contact with Zev?

At the gate the watchman was alert, he had heard them nearing. It was Young Avram on duty, a lad from Kovno who had been sent to Siberia while only in the Poale Zion youth movement; after two years, he had become the expert in making false papers for escapees. Finally he had made a set for himself and managed to reach Eretz on the very eve of the war. "Leah, Good! Chemda found you?"

"That's all taken care of," she began, but he was already staring at Zev.

"Yes, it's him," Menahem said, "the jewel himself. Take him up the hill and stay with him. Guard him well."

"Who's in command here?" Zev demanded. "Shimshoni?"

"Get out of sight!" Motke snapped.

Young Avram had already grasped everything. "Quick. Hassan Bey will be coming today. Yesterday he cleaned out Merhavia. They took away seven."

"Who?" Menahem gasped.

Young Avram began naming them. The settlement was stirring. Across the yard a few chaverim came hurrying toward them, their tea mugs in their hands; there came Chemda's mother, whom Leah quickly reassured that the girl was safe.

Avraham Halperin, the secretary since Shimshoni had gone north, had reached them and was staring at Zev. "What's he doing here?"

"Thank Menahem!" Motke blurted.

"He jumped on the carriage. We have to decide what to do with him."

A few men had gathered, but they kept a distance from the pariah. Zev's face quivered in an attempted bravado, even a kind of greeting to those who had once been his comrades.

"Only for a week, hide me—" he began.

"Avramaleh," Avraham said to young Avram in his urgent half-whisper, "at least change his clothes. With his fancy clothes he can be recognized a mile away." The secretary then motioned them toward the hill. Hurry. Then he waved everyone close. "Chevreh, I beg you." Absolute silence. Those who had seen Zev were already too many. There would be an immediate sitting of the central committee.

Dvora had come running to Menahem. "Leah!" she was surprised.

"And at home?" Leah demanded.

"It's still all right." Late yesterday, a Yavniel man had passed by and given news of Mishkan Yaacov.

The medical case, the weapons, were already being carried off to be hidden. From every side Leah heard stories of the havoc in Merhavia, beatings, pillage. Each chaver seemed to be inwardly girding himself for their turn here, and every chavera somehow kept trying to hold her man in sight wherever he was at work.

Leah hurried up to the committee room, above the cheder ochel; it was used also as the room of Rahel and her sister Shoshana, the nurse. Rahel, wakened by some sense of emergency, was just getting out of her cot; Shoshana was up and dressed. "What, you're joining me?" she laughed at the sight of Leah's uniform. The story tumbled out.

Calling, "Girls, all right?" Avraham the Secretary came up with Menahem. Motke followed, insisting this was not an affair of Kvutsa Gilboa alone, but of the whole Shomer. Shoshana quickly excused herself and left. Leah too wanted to leave, but Avraham insisted she must remain to help establish exactly what had happened.

—If it was an affair of the Shomer, Rahel said, then Shabbatai Zeira, the field commander, must be summoned from his farm in Sejera.

"It would take hours!" Menahem pointed out.

And what of Shimshoni, up north? Shimshoni was the deputy for Nadina and Galil in exile, Avraham Halperin reminded them. Clearly Avraham did not want to be burdened with this decision. It concerned not only the Shomer, but the whole Poale Zion. He looked to Rahel: after all she was the deputy for Avner.

—And did the party, Rahel asked, have the right to decide for the whole Yishuv?

"God in heaven, do you want to refer it to the next Zionist Congress!" Motke shouted. Here and now they must decide what to do with the bastard, and quickly.

All the same arguments poured forth anew. This time Motke tried to speak more calmly. "It's only blind chance that threw him into our hands."

Menahem's eyes were remote as though searching behind the darkness of chance. Was there perhaps some intention? Perhaps some use could be drawn out of what had been put into their hands?

"Yes," Motke cried. "Deliver him to Nazareth and all the searches will stop."

"In his hatred, if we turn him in, there's no telling whom he will implicate," Avraham said. "All of us, and even Dizingoff's whole Emergency Committee, to get his revenge."

"If he had any decency, he'd kill himself," Motke half-shouted. Then, lower, "Yes. We have to show him that that is the only solution. And if he doesn't see it, we have to help him to do the job."

Rahel had buried her head in her hands.

"We haven't any cause to decide such a thing," Menahem said. "Unless in the face of his capture."

"Then what do you suggest, chaver?" Motke demanded belligerently.

"Perhaps something Zev himself begged for. If we take him north, take him under guard, then if he can get to the Druze, he's off our hands."

Avraham the Secretary raised his head, as did Rahel.

Motke cried, "Are you crazy? A thousand to one we'd get caught on the way."

A commotion arose from the yard, feet pounded on the stairs. The Turks already? It was again Zev, who burst in with Young Avram behind him, hanging onto him by the half-ripped sleeve of his shirt. Glaring from one to another as though he could read each one's decision, Zev shouted, "Who made you my judges? You threw me out of the Shomer—today you have no right over me! Let me go! I'll get away! I got away from them every time before!" Wilder than in the carriage, in a state of frenzy now, he tumbled out tales of escapes, from a German colonel in Jerusalem, from the Bedouin in the Sinai Desert when he played dead. In Egypt he had been received by the commander-in-chief! If the Shomer had but listened to him and Avshalom, and risen against the Turks, the English would already have freed the land! The Yishuv spat on him, but the British would award him their highest medals!

From boasting, he suddenly took the tone of a bargainer. "You want gold and guns? Hear me. Two barrels full of napoleons. Safely hidden, I'll lead you there. Full to the top, the way they sent them to us."

Rahel was glaring at him, and now Leah saw him as though through Rahel's despising eyes. Though Young Avram had removed Zev's fine boots, and given him old work clothes to replace his expensive riding costume, thick gold rings were still imbedded in Zev's fleshy fingers, and despite his last days of terror and hunger, there remained an oiliness about his face, a desperate guile. In Rahel, Leah saw a tightening toward judgement, decision, something that she herself, Leah knew, could never muster.

Zev had caught what was happening in Rahel. "Despise me!" he flung at her. "I'm too much of a man for you. Does that give you the right to kill me?"

"To some men," Rahel said, pallid, "it would be better to be remembered for having the courage even to destroy themselves rather than to have their entire people destroyed."

Zev wet his lips. "No!" he roared. "You dry bitch! No! I won't kill myself to solve your problems. Before that, I'll take a chance on hanging—and the lot of you with me!"

"Be quiet or I'll end the problem right now." Again Motke had drawn his revolver.

"Better take him out," Avraham Halperin said to Young Avram. "Take Gershon with you and keep him in the cave until we decide."

Zev obeyed, only casting back a last glance, murderous, lost.

They had to decide. If only Galil were here with his quick clear mind. "There are three alternatives, it seems to me," Avraham the Secretary began ponderously.

Leah could not bear it; she went to the door. Suddenly Rahel jumped up and joined her, clutching her arm. "Decide without me," Rahel mumbled to the men, almost sobbing. "I—I can't be fair to him."

Quiet lay over Gilboa; each man had gone to his labor, following the example of Avraham Halperin who continued with the task he had begun a few days before of manuring a harvested field. On the threshing floor, an old mule continued its endless circling with the grinding board, while Rahel, a keffiyah binding up her hair, joined Avraham's wife, Guta, in winnowing the chaff. There was barely a breeze, the straw drifted down lazily and dust hovered in their eyes.

Leah worked with Dvora, carefully filling the water-troughs in the chicken-run. It was long since they had felt so sisterly. Dvora was pregnant again—just the start. Despite the difficult times, so were several more of the girls, Dvora said. For one thing, the kvutsa believed that with the population of the Yishuv shrinking, it was needed. And for herself, she always felt better when carrying. Yes, in regard to the children, she bore the arrangment better now, Dvoraleh said, the present metapelet was understanding of mothers and really tried hard not to have the children attach themselves to her. And after all, working here in the poultry run, she was quite close to the children's house. And it was not as in their first infancy when, wherever she happened to be working, it was as though a magnet in her breast was drawing her back to her baby. Only—

—Only what? Leah wondered. How could she give Dvora an older sister's advice when she sometimes sensed herself far from being a whole woman?

"Only, Leah, there's something missing. It's not like at home in a family when a child half the time is under your feet and you even want to give him a slap, and then he is so good you could eat him up, and it's all one thing together. Yes, that's it. Here, the children have their life and we have ours. You know, the children, the monkeys, the older group has even started a kvutsa to imitate us. Nadina and Galil's Buba started it—they hold sittings and send us resolutions and demands." She laughed. "Their deepest life is together, with each other, their chevreh, and when they come to the parents in our hour for them, it's almost like playacting. That's what I sometimes feel."

"Then could it be not the right way after all?" Leah asked of this way of life.

"Who knows?" Something of Dvoraleh's girlish simplicity and wistfulness had returned, softening that tightening line of her mouth with its worry creases at the corners that had come from her constantly peering at her chicks for signs of the dread fowl diseases that periodically swept the flock. "You know, Leah, I'm all the time with my poultry," her half-laugh rang out, "and sometimes I feel like I've become one of them, instead of a member in the kvutsa. I know which one pecks which one, better even than I know about my comrades."

"Like I am with my flock of girls," Leah said, at once feeling a need to get back to them.

"At least you are all day with your girls, they are human beings! Better than a flock of chickens! I pass my days here hardly saying a word to anyone, and I'm sure I'll soon begin to cackle!"

"But after work, when you have the children—and Menahem—"

"Menahem is away so much. And even when he's here, he's always at a sitting, and you know I am really not one to take so much interest in discussions." Dvora was confessing a kind of loneliness, Leah realized, that she herself sometimes also felt, even amongst her girls. It was the last thing you would have expected of life in a collectiva. Both sighed.

"Dvoraleh, it's all right between you and Menahem?"

Only an instant the smile hovered uncertainly before widening. Yes, it was well. As though she had just measured and decided. Though Menahem was a strange man, with his silences. And indeed, intimately, woman to woman, Dvoraleh asked, just as if Leah, being older, indeed knew more of life, did any woman ever truly understand what was going on in a man?

So they worked on, and talked, as though to attest that all would continue, all their little problems would continue, this life would continue, as though thereby to exorcise the impending doom.

Yet at last night's lengthy sitting the operating committee had spelled out the order of continuation: if Avraham Halperin were arrested, and if his replacement were arrested, and the third, down to the fifth . . . Several of the younger men had been sent into hiding, so that the farm was nearly denuded of males.

Still the Turk did not appear. The whole morning, not a rider on the road, not a wagon passed by with news. But by the back pathway from Merhavia came Nathan Ben Schmuel, son of their arrested mukhtar; the boy was hardly older than Dvoraleh's Yechezkiel, and to Avraham Halperin he handed over a note. "Burn everything," it said. And the boy added, "The Turks even seized our school-books."

As everyone came in for the noon meal, they gathered around a notice that Avraham had put up by the door. All Zionist documents, all letters, all membership cards and papers must be destroyed. Throughout the meal people kept running to Avraham with questions. Diaries? Diaries too. A precious complete file of Brenner's *Awakener?* Yes, yes, everything. Because of the finding of such material, several of the men in Merhavia had been arrested. One of the girls asked, "Even love letters?" Avraham Halperin considered, then ruled solemnly, "As long as the Poale Zion, the Poël Hatzaïr, or anything Zionist, isn't mentioned—"

Rahel was in a bewilderment of sorting. A whole satchel of Avner's papers was open on her cot, notes he had made on trips through the Galilee in the old days when he could find time for such excursions and they had wandered on foot together to Arab villages, tracing Arab names to ancient Hebrew sources and wondering whether these were not families that, in the seventh century perhaps, had accepted the Moslem religion in order to survive, and, unlike the Marranos later in Spain, had lost all trace of their Jewish origin.

How could she burn Avner's notes? "Let me take them, I'll hide them at home," Leah said.

Then there were old letters he had sent Rahel when she was still in Russia, about the movement, the problems, the party—there was no time to read them over to see which were dangerous, yet as something caught her eye, Rahel would stand there reading.

Dvora was more practical, piling together booklets, Menahem's copies of brochures by Borochov, even Herzl's portrait, even the poems of Bialik, a whole basket for the flames, keeping aside only her pamphlets about poultry, in the English that she had learned to read, though Leah pointed out that anything in English might be dangerous. And also, a pitifully thin packet of love letters, remnants of Yechezkiel . . .

Already the children were leaping about the fire. How can you keep a boy from enjoying a bonfire, Rahel remarked, even if it is consuming your own youthtime? Chaverim kept running up to Avraham with letters, books: "Must I burn this too?" And then the four-year-olds, given things to fling into the flames, began dancing in a ring around the fire, and a crazed spirit of perversity, defiance, took hold of them all. Rahel joined hands with the tots, Leah joined hands with them, Dvoraleh with her little Yechezkiel and Giora. For the children, the chevreh made a game of it; let the fire burn. Better paper than the whole meshek! Let it burn, and Bahad-ad-Din and Hassan Bek and Djemal Pasha should burn in a fire too!

As night fell, three good horses were saddled; Menahem and Yaacov the Kurdi, a nephew of Shabbatai Zeira, a real bandit of a rider who knew from childhood every goatpath in the Galilee, took Zev between them, and all three with their faces half-covered by their keffiyahs rode northward by obscure pasture trails, avoiding the Nazareth region, passing through venerable olive groves, mounting onto the wilder rocky areas of upper Galilee, headed toward Har Tsafon. There let Shimshoni take him in charge and decide whether he might escape to the Druze on Mount Hermon.

And as the three men rode, the peaceful night-spell of the groves, the scent of the spent heat like dissipated anger, the presence of eternity in the stars, the breathing of their mounts, and the quiet exchange of knowing words about horses erased the pressing consciousness of their errand, until they were as a trio of the Shomer in the old days picking their path, perhaps discussing the ways of the Zubeida tribe whose sheep grazed these hills. It was from them Shimshoni had bought his first flock, but it was a mistake in Menahem's opinion; these fat-tailed sheep were a poor profitless strain, and instead Australian sheep should be imported. Australian sheep were for the plains, Zev argued, but the Druze had an excellent mountain strain that might be blended with Zubeidas. Yaacov the Kurdi told of an old Zubeida sheikh, said to be a hundred and ten, who had purchased a bride of ten, not yet quite ready for use. "Never mind," said the sheikh, "I am providing for my old age."

This led to other tales, and so they rode, Zev recalling with Menahem the time they had ridden the rounds together at Mishkan Yaacov, and then telling a few tales of his famous nighttime "tea parties." Ah, Roumanian women! And then it was Bedouin women, and Christian women who were crazy for Jewish men, and a certain nun in Nazareth who had opened a rear garden gate to him.

"Ah, grandmothers' tales!" Menahem said.

"Indeed, indeed," replied the incorrigible Zev, telling a tale of a grandmother and her daughter and the thirteen-year-old granddaughter, all to be enjoyed together in a certain house in Beirut. "By my life!" he swore, he had done it. So in amity the men rode between Meron and Safed, gazing down on the distant black-mirror surface of the Kinnereth, and up ahead to the pallor of the snow-topped Hermon.

Later, on a nearing height, Yaacov perceived the glimmer of the night lantern of Shimshoni's settlement.

26

PASSING the gate to Gilboa, there rattled a wagon with a whole family from Zichron, a townsman fleeing to a cousin in Yavniel, halting only to cry out, "Sara Aaronson shot herself."

In the fourth day of her torment. Live coals in her armpits. Her fingernails wrenched out. The skin beaten from her soles, her feet like butcher's meat. Then Hassan Bey allowed her to go to the bathroom, in her brother's house, and there a small pistol had been hidden, and Sara Aaronson shot herself in the mouth.

Now that no more could be learned from her, the fury would fall on every Jew.

An oppressive lethargy covered the kvutsa. As with the doomed who await the executioner, every movement felt futile. Though Avraham the Secretary stubbornly continued with his manuring, the work otherwise fell off. The women gravitated to the children's house, and even when two small girls became hysterical, the metapelet did not drive out the mothers.

Why didn't Hassan Bey appear here already, and an end!

Leah sat with Rahel, with Dvora, talking of poor Sara Aaronson. To them she revealed much about that last time

Sara had come to her in the south, in deep hunger for a woman's friendship. How alone, how alone Sara must have been in her marriage in Constantinople, and then in her frantic secret labor of the last year, and now in her dying!

And still the search did not come, but word did come of a train of prisoners. Young Avram, driving the water-barrel wagon filled up at the springs of Ain Harod, plunged into the yard with the barrels jumping on the floorboards. The horror he had seen! A train halted on the tracks while the trainman foraged for firewood for the engine, and young Avram, hearing unearthly howling, had driven nearer. Four closed animal cars, with human hands reaching out from the airhole high in each car. Voices calling out in despair, and when he answered, one face appeared, hoisted up to the hole. It was an aged notable from Jerusalem, a Sephardi.

"Yeshayahu?" Leah cried.

"I think so. They called out so many names I can't be sure."

"Our own members?" Rahel demanded. "What of Misha, the party secretary in Jerusalem?" Avram didn't know.

"They are packed eighty in a wagon, no room even to sit. They said their feet are chained. They are dying of thirst—I gave them water. They've had nothing to eat since the day before yesterday. As far as Jeneen they were forced to walk, in the hamseen, roped together, with the irons on their feet. Chevreh, through the boards I heard men sobbing. I promised on my life I would come to Damascus to help them. Even on the way to Siberia, I didn't see suffering like this." Young Avram's voice was choked. "The train is still standing there."

All the bread they had they threw into a wagon, and cheese, cucumbers and tomatoes, and half the kvutsa ran behind the wagon along the tracks. There was the train. Through the boards, voices called. Coins were passed to the guards, the people of Gilboa pressed themselves against the train, climbed on each other's shoulders to reach the apertures, from which bits of paper, messages, were being dropped down. Misha, the Jerusalem secretary, was indeed inside; he managed to get his face into an opening. "Chevreh, you are our only hope." The train began to move.

Running alongside, Young Avram kept shouting, "I'll come to Damascus! I vow it!"

In the last moment Avraham Halperin galloped up. He had brought a few packets of the gold coins and managed to pass them through an opening.

Cries came back to them, a tumult of last messages, pleadings, a maddened shriek joined with the whistle of the engine, and after it, a prolonged Job-like wail.

What could be done? Any instant their own doom might arrive. Men and women found themselves standing dazedly in the yard or continuing absurd, meaningless tasks, like Guta ironing the Sabbath cloths.

Mounting to return to Petach Tikvah, Motke had a last bitter word for Avraham the Secretary. "I want nothing more to do with it. We should have turned him in. We still should turn him in. But one thing for certain. Every chaver who laid eyes on him had better be got out of here before Hassan Bey arrives." He rode away.

In this last, all agreed Motke was right. Upstairs in Rahel's room they hurriedly planned. Rahel must leave. Leah must leave. She could run with Rahel across the back fields to Merhavia, it had already been searched and was comparatively safe. From there she could get back to her girls. But what of the family at home? She was being pulled in two different directions.

And Avraham Halperin himself? He was the mukhtar. If the mukhtar was missing, the Turks would be enraged. He would remain at hand—up in the cave on the hillside, Avraham declared. Young Avram could hide there as well.

Motke, instead of heading homeward, had circled back around Mount Tabor to ride to Sejera where Shabbatai Zeira lived with his mother on their farm. The Kurd came only rarely now to the sittings—he was not one for discussions—yet after Shimshoni wasn't he still commander?

Shabbatai listened to Motke's whole account and swiftly agreed. That the Nili had spied against the Turks did not trouble him; there were various tasks in war. That Zev was a man once cast out of the Shomer did not weigh strongly with him. For himself, the Kurd had always believed in the Hotblood, a good rider, a good rifleman, his one fault women. But all this was of no account in making the decision before them. The fate of one was outweighed by the fate of all.

Together he and Motke rode to Nazareth. With the Bimbashi, Achmed Bey, the Kurd had had many dealings. Even the finely inlaid Damascus coffee table in Achmed's office was but a small gift that attested to their long friendship. But just now Achmed was not occupying his imposing headquarters. He had generously insisted that Hassan Bek take over his office. Achmed's aged coffee-bearer led them to the Bimbashi's refuge at the end of the corridor, a dank hole without even a rug.

The Nazareth chief's eyes were red; he was shrunken and in bad temper, but some instinct turned away his abuse from the two Jews. Instead, muttering what might be taken as an apology for receiving them in this barren closet, he burst out over the pandemonium in the courtyard with Hassan Bek's riders coming and going with their shoutings, curses, and whip-cracks. What blind geese, what rabbit-spawn were the whole lot of Hassan's men, when one wolf of a Jew could bite their behinds and run free!

Agreeing, Zeira deposited his coffee cup on the tray and moved his stool somewhat closer to Achmed Bey. "Difficult times, Achmed Bey, difficult for you and not easy for any of us."

Ah, everything was in the order of a man's work. Difficult, easy, a man's work must be done.

"We have always wanted to be helpful. For after all are we not in the same work? Are not our interests the same? Lawfulness, order, and peace."

A measuring showed in Achmed's eyes, as though to say, he appreciated Zeira's people. Let Hassan Bek tear apart every Jew in the land, they were a clever, hard lot and would yield up nothing until they were ready. There was Hassan Bek's five-hundred-pound reward for the capture of Zev the Hotblood, now doubled to a thousand. But it was not for this the Jews might want to arrange something, he was certain. And he was just as certain that Zeira's Shomer would know where Zev was to be found.

Soon the Bimbashi at Nazareth understood the bargain that was being suggested. It was best that the hunted Jew should not be found by a Jew. The reward could naturally go to those of Achmed's own men who brought in the spy. Or his body.

So it was agreed. And why need Hassan Bey know any-thing of this helpful effort? If it succeeded, let the glory come to Achmed Bey, as was only just. Nor, of course, did his vistiors really know of the whereabouts of the spy. "If we knew, would we protect him? Didn't we ourselves throw him out of our ranks for the troubles he caused in Mishkan Yaacov?" Well did Achmed Bey remember. "We are fighters, not spies. Hear me, old friend," said Zeira the Kurd, "what does a hunted animal do? He creeps home-ward to his lair."

"Beersheba?" Achmed's eyes measured Zeira—was this but a hoax?

Motke glanced over to Shabbatai. The thick-headed goyim! Achmed didn't even know that Zev came from Me-tulla.

"I'll send up a whole troop," the Bimbashi cried, "and tear the place apart from wall to wall."

Shabbatai smiled as at a figure of speech. With the ap-proach of a whole troop of hunters, the wolf might be alerted and run off. But suppose one officer went up, and brought back the wolf or his body?

Then, with the hunt ended, Motke put in, surely the vi-cious Hassan Bek would depart from here, his searches would be halted and all the hostages returned to their homes!

Achmed leaned forward, and touched Motke's knee. "He who makes a promise for another binds neither himself nor the other," he quoted. "But if a highwayman is caught and the robberies cease, there is no need to continue to search for him."

It was Achmed Bey's youngish brother-in-law who rode off with Motke in a carriage large enough to bring back a man's body.

Serene as a white-haired god the Hermon sat, and in the lap of the god were sacred wonders, groves and caves, sanctuaries where men might breathe the stillness of peace and feel in their breathing how good this earth could be.

From an opening in the mountain rock, a stream issued and became a pool, and from this again issued a stream, bordered by grassy banks where a man could lie still and hear only the music of the water. A grove of ancient trees stood eternally waiting for the rites of worship to begin again, and nearby, in the face of the stone from whose mouth water rushed out, just there where it came from the mountain form, men long ago, not knowing how else to show the awe and wonder they felt in this place, had cut an alcove as deep as a human body, and here in the ancient days, it was said, even before Abraham passed this way from Hauran, the pagans in their elation offered life-blood so as to be at one with their god.

Not too far away was another such place of awesome beauty. The Chimney it was called, perhaps also a place of worship and sacrifice even more overwhelming than the tender grove. Here the torrents of melted snow had first, atop the height, cut a wide smooth stone basin, and then over one edge spilled downward, through centuries cutting a chimney-like chasm, the water plunging the depth of a mountainside and flowing away at the bottom in a narrow stream. Deeper and deeper the chimney was cut until the water fell fifty times the height of a man and then flowed away between bushes and wild vegetation to join the other streams that form the Jordan River.

In spring the abundant waters from the upper basin did not seem to fall but rather to leap outward in a great shimmering wall of water, vitality itself, and no one who lived here, no one who came here, ever outgrew the spell of this sight. But in the heat of high summer the water only brimmed over the lip of the upper basin enough to keep the wetted inside of the stone chimney darkly glistening.

Down along the valley near the converging headwaters of the Jordan lay an Arab village called Halsah, a small place with only a few footpaths between the earthen dwellings. An outer lane led to the sheikh's house, made of stone and standing higher than the huts.

His courtyard was open, and here they left the carriage until it should be needed. On the rug of the guest chamber, Motke and his companion were welcomed by the sheikh and his three sons—the sheikh himself, a broad-girdled man with the look of a confident bargainer, the sons all three with the heavy-lidded eyes of the kif-smoker. Through Halsah passed hasheesh traffic from the Syrian fields.

After the formalities, and over the second cup of coffee, Motke's companion Sayed, the fierce-looking young brother-in-law of Achmed Bey, Bimbashi of the Nazareth District, honorably known to all of them here, explained that they sought a traitor, a spy and bandit, believed to be hiding in this area. Instantly all three sons as one leaped up, ready to mount for the hunt; with Allah's help, this bandit would not escape them, for, in this region there was not a mole but they knew its hole. Motke could already envisage them clattering into Metulla, storming each farmyard—and with the sanction of the police! Praising and thanking them, he explained that it was a matter of law for the officer himself, the excellent Sayed here, to capture the spy. All that was asked was the sheikh's hospitality, as Sayed would wait here with the carriage, so as not to draw too much attention, while Motke himself went forward to make some inquiries.

There were glances all around. Much was understood. There was an inner affair here among the Jews. And Motke went on foot up the grassy slope above Halsah.

Climbing toward Shimshoni's kvutsa, he already saw their broad flocks; the dream was well on the way to reality. Perhaps he too would have been wiser to have taken his wife and children and withdrawn with this group to this farthest corner of the land. Already on the lower of their two hills they were constructing a second meshek; wood was still plentiful hereabouts, and a pair of chaverim were constructing a stockade fence around a half-finished stone house with a large yard. What did it remind him of? Pictures he had seen in his children's schoolbooks of the stockades of American cowboys.

Motke approached the two lads—he did not know either one. Uncertain whether everyone in Shimshoni's kvutsa would be aware that the Jewel was hidden among them, Motke started on something else. "It looks like a fort you're building."

"All the better. They'll respect us."

"Are they giving you trouble?" His head motioned to the village below.

The first lad shrugged. "No. In the main our relations are good. The sheikh has a passion for Maria Theresa thalers and keeps begging us to buy more land."

"But the sons are annoying," the other one said. "They're always coming around, give us this, give us that— whatever they lay their eyes on, a teakettle, an iron rake."

"As for your Jewel," the first chaver said dryly, "he's

right in there!" The lad pointed to the half-finished dwelling within the stockade.

Had they lost their wits, here? Didn't they understand what was going on over the entire Yishub?

"Don't fear." The second one had read his thoughts. "From up here we can see anyone coming from any direction, a long way off. . . . Do you want to pay him a visit? On top of everything, he can't bear being alone."

"No." It was enough having to carry out his task; he needed no discussions with Zev. "Where's Shimshoni?"

Above at the upper farm, where else?

What could Motke have explained to Shimshoni? That an arrangement had been made to deliver Zev, for the safety of the Shomer and the whole Yishuv? Or perhaps only that Zev's being here was known, that an Arab had seen three riders arrive, and only two going away, and that it was impossible to hide the Jewel any longer? Let him go. Perhaps he could even save himself and reach the Druze.

With his unwavering small eyes in his round, compact head. Shimshoni listened to what Motke told him and said, "Then do you want to tell Zev yourself what has been decided?"

Motke would not flinch from the task as he would not blink under Shimshoni's gaze. Together they went back down the path to the lower hill, where these idealists were continuing to build while the whole Yishuv was on the brink of destruction.

In a wall-hollow between the kitchen and stable, a secret place for storing arms, Zev stood. At the mere sight of Motke, he comprehended. Instead of breaking into rage, he turned to Shimshoni the face of a man who sees his death. "I won't, I won't—" he began.

"Achmed Bey from Nazareth has sent a man to Halsah," Motke said matter-of-factly.

"You brought him."

"Then why would I not simply have turned you over?"

"You're afraid of what I'd say if taken alive."

Then Motke said, "Sara's dead. She shot herself."

Zev's eyes went from one to the other, from one to the other. "You're lying, to get me to do the same."

Shimshoni said, "Zev, you understand what it would

mean if you are found among us. Besides, your only chance is to leave here."

Still his head turned from one to the other. Then Zev's eyes became dull and his head dropped. "Where did they bury her?"

"Her father buried her in the vineyard," Motke said. "Old Aaronson by himself."

Zev drew in his breath. "I'll get out after dark."

Below in Halsah the gendarme, Sayed, and Sheikh Jibran with his eldest son Ismael had enjoyed several more coffees and sweets while the meal was being prepared. There was nothing that Sayed knew of his mission that remained unknown to his hosts. The hunted one had received much gold from the British; as was well known among the Bedouin in the Hauran, the British were lavish with their gold. For a pair of Turkish ears a man could dip his fist into a sack of napoleons and keep all he could draw out.

The Yahud hidden here must still have gold on him. Far more than the thousand paper pounds that was to be paid for his body.

Sons-in-law of the sheikh also came now to sit with the guest, and Sayed repeated his tale. The eldest son, Ismael, rose and went off. He was an impatient man who roamed much. Three riders had passed on the heights the night before last, a shepherd had seen them. Only two had gone back, in the day. Now he understood.

Ismael roamed the few miles between the hill settlement of the Jews and their older village of Metulla. The way curved above the gorge to the top of the Chimney; behind the saucer-like top of the waterfall lay Metulla, and behind Metulla rose the slopes that led to the Druze. A fugitive attempting to escape to the Druze would have to pass this way. Ismael stationed himself and waited.

Motke meanwhile had returned to the Arab village to fetch Sayed and the carriage. In this way, in this space of time, he might be giving Zev his chance to escape to the Druze. So he would believe.

After dark, Zev had told them, but when the hammering stopped, he stepped halfway out and saw the two chalutzim climbing to the upper farm. Now he was before the open space of the partly stockaded compound. That foul Motke could be as cunning as himself, and guess that he would be starting earlier to elude their trap. But no shot struck him as he moved beyond the grounds. In dartings, he made his way around the slope of the kvutsa's hill to the Metulla side. But there the hill was barren rock, a kind of marble that, in his boyhood, some of the Metulla men had spoken of one day quarrying. No shrubs to give cover. He must move swiftly down from this. Quickly, for he heard a carriage from below.

As Zev scuttled across the Metulla road to reach the growth above the gorge, his form was for one instant visible.

Motke was driving with his rifle at hand beside him. Sayed had his rifle at ready and raised it and fired. In the same moment came a reverberation from above, another gun. Ismael, both understood.

The figure had vanished. Zev must have fallen, struck, and tumbled into the ravine. Ismael came galloping from the top of the Chimney, waving his rifle in the excitement of the kill.

Clutching at roots and stones, Zev tumbled downward until he lay at the bottom. Not yet killed. Instead of terror or even an engulfing pain, an exhilaration shot up in him. As that time with Avshalom in the desert, here too he had not been destroyed. No! He was not to be destroyed. The sounds came back to him—two, three guns? or an echo? In his boyhood, when he first was brought here, the settlers had made much of the pogrom-orphan from Kishinev. The mukhtar of Metulla's own boy, Yechiel, had taken him down here to show him the echo in the Chimney. They had stood down here shouting and shouting; Yechiel had even taught him some Arab curse words, and they had listened with joy as the words, together with their own laughter, came back to them. But later he had hated Yechiel, a "good boy." Yechiel was still in Metulla. Could he risk showing himself to him?

They'd be coming down for their kill. His body. Motke and Shimshoni too, he didn't doubt, and maybe a third to make sure. Why wouldn't he have thought it of Shimshoni? All of them, the lot of them, he would gladly sign their execution. Afraid to execute him to his face, they had made him run like a hunted rabbit.

Zev's fingers felt for the wound; where neck and shoulders joined blood was spreading; the bullet had passed through the flesh. From the stream, he splashed on water. He still had Sara's kerchief, a last talisman from her hand; escape, live! He tied it around his neck, making a knot in the armpit. He was able to stand. Carefully, Zev trod in the stream, the other way, downward. Where the bank was thick with high reeds he hid, to regain strength.

Soon he heard them up there crashing into the ravine, might they break both legs and their heads. It was good and dark now. He heard their cursing and their calls to each other and the high far echoes. One was Motke. Two others, Arabs. So he was sold! The three hunters had clambered down to the bottom, but as he had reasoned, the idiots were going the other way into the narrowing crevice of the Chimney. They thought they would find him there, cornered.

Now was his time. The slope was not difficult here. Scrambling up on the further side, Zev circled far around behind Metulla to one of his old boyhood hiding places among the rocks. From there he could see the outlines of his uncle's house.

With his hands Motke felt along the foliage perhaps for some pressed down place where the body had fallen. The sheikh's son would not leave them to go searching downstream. Afraid he would miss the gold. And Sayed kept muttering they had hit not a man but the devil, a shaitan.

When a gallows broke, wasn't the doomed man left to live, Motke asked himself. The underflow of disgust he had felt all along was now bile in his mouth. Why had he done it, why had he felt so impelled to ride to Shabbatai Zeira? No, but Shabbatai had agreed it was necessary, imperative to save the Shomer, the Yishuv, to save even Zev himself from prolonged torture, as he would surely be caught in any case.

They had wound their way to the Chimney now, the narrow high hollow, rising until its black glistening wall was lost in the dark, but you saw far above the softer darkness of the sky, and even stars. Tomorrow there would be no hamseen. The aroma of pines and fresh water filled the hollow, constantly refreshed by the trickle sliding down the walls of the Chimney. How could mankind incessantly find ways to disturb this serenity? Motke felt as though he were Cain with the finger of God stretching downward to point him out at the bottom of this black hole.

"We'll wait in the carriage for the morning light," he said. "It is useless to search for him now."

From across the yard Yaffaleh rushed to welcome Leah, rolling her large head against Leah's bosom so as to press first one cheek and then the other to her sister, until Leah laughingly pulled back her youngest sister's head to look into her face. In joy at Leah's coming, the face was radiant. "Leah, you'll stay here? Oh, we were so afraid for you in all the searches. If they come here, we can hide you." Laughing, Leah kissed her. —And Menahem and the young Zeira from Gilboa, she asked, had they passed? Perhaps yesterday or early today? —No, they had not been seen.

In Yaffaleh's eyes Leah saw another plea. "Be with me, stay with me, I am stifling," and in that moment, Leah thought, "I'll take her back with me to be with the girls for a time, it will be good for her."

Mameh had emerged, beaming with relief. "Leah, you are not mixed up in all this trouble with the Aaronsons?"

"Na, Mameleh." Leah smiled broadly in denial, in reassurance. "You know our kind of work is different."

But Feigel was worried that some of those who were caught might reveal how there had once been gifts from Gidon.

"Before they could beat one word out of me," Yaffaleh cried, "I would die like Sara Aaronson."

Leah stroked her. "Poor Sara."

"What they brought down on the whole Yishuv!" her mother said.

"Mameh, they were trying to help. They kept the whole of Mea Shearim from starvation."

"The Above One will judge them, not I," Feigel said, and then added, "Leah, don't defend them before him"— Tateh—"his eyes see only the evil they have done."

He and the boys were still cutting in the field, for without help they were late in the harvest. Giving Mameh quick news of Dvoraleh, of the grandchildren, Leah found herself a scythe and marched out. She could see them, Schmulik and Tateh advancing evenly step by step, and

Mati behind them with a pitchfork. As she gave Mati a hug, and began to swing her scythe, Leah nevertheless saw her father smile deep in his beard, content that she was home. He would ask her little, only, "Nu, Leah, how are things in the south?" And she saw that he was already calculating; he would have to send back a wagonload with her, wheat for the refugees banished from Tel Aviv, and Tateh was already struggling with himself as to how many sacks he would load on.

But presently Yankel spoke what was on his mind. Had she heard no news on the way, of the hunted one, might his name be erased from Eternity? And with each stroke of his scythe her father's strong old arms seemed to be cutting down the maker of disaster. "Already when he was the shomer here, he all but destroyed us, and now the entire Yishuv will have to pay for his evil. Why didn't we let the Arabs make an end of him! To meddle in the wars of the goyim, that has always been our undoing—didn't Jeremiah cry out against it? And because the king did not pay heed, Babylon came upon us . . ."

He had gone back to Yiddish, and his querulous sing-song seemed to reach her from the huddled lanes of Cherezinka. With all her love, with all her admiration for the labor he had brought out of himself in this place, Leah could not remain in the field and listen to his bitterness, though Schmulik worked on as though he did not hear, Schmulik the young ox. Besides, Leah had to hurry over to HaKeren, she had messages, instructions, and two heavy baskets of "eggs" to deliver; she would take Yaffaleh along for the walk.

"Leah, good you came." Max Wilner greeted her in the whispery voice he used when things were grave. Word had already arrived about Gilboa. The searches had taken place. Three arrested. Avraham Halperin among them; he had come down from his hiding place. But worst—the old woman, Rahel's mother. Not finding Rahel, whose name was on his list, Hassan Bey had become enraged and seized the old woman. His men flung her to the ground; defiantly she had at once taken off her shoes, presenting her bare soles to the Turk. "I know nothing. But proceed in your own savage way."

They had pulled her up and hauled her away with the others.

There was more. One of the captured Nili from Chedera was dead in the Nazareth prison. The Bek had hung the body from the cell bars, so as later to declare he had killed himself. He had been beaten to death, everyone knew.

In the first daylight Ismael quickly found the traces of the fall, and the spot where the body had turned on the foliage. There were bloodstains, he cried out joyously, he had not missed! But then the trail vanished as though the shaitan had been lifted from the earth.

The Nazareth gendarme, Sayed, turned his eyes on Motke with that particular look of suspicion that was kept for Jews. Had there been a trick in all this?

—They must search in Metulla, Motke said, where Zev had relatives, "Let me go in alone," he managed to persuade them. "From me, they won't hide anything."

The woman didn't wait; she came running toward Motke from the farmyard, gathering together her wrapper, her hair uncombed, her face in stupefaction. "He was here, he was here in the night. I beseeched him, Zev, go, I always knew he would bring agony in the world. I begged him for the sake of my children, Zev, go—" and then, as though she still could not fully believe it—"He went."

It was his aunt who had raised him here, a poorish, neglected place with half-broken implements lying about the yard, a wagon with a missing wheel. Two girls still in their nightgowns appeared in the doorway, and their mother screamed at them, "Stay inside! . . . He's gone, he went, I swear by the heads of my daughters, I don't know where, to the Druze perhaps. I only bandaged his wound, it was bleeding." She showed him where, on the shoulder by the neck. "The width of a finger more, and it would have been all over for him," she said with a sorrowful puzzlement, meeting something in Motke's own eyes—wouldn't it have been better? Was it God's intention that had been spoiled by some error? "From when he first came to us, I tried my best with him, I swear to you—an orphan from Kishinev!" As if everyone else, too, hadn't made allowances all his life for this. "But Zev was never anything but trouble."

Deep in the night she had opened her eyes, and there he was, the Jewel, standing over the bed where she lay with one daughter on each side of her, the way she slept every night since the Turks had dragged off her man with the only good wagon and the mules. That this moment would come, she had known as soon as Zev's name spread over the land and news reached even to Metulla that Zev was the chief spy, the hunted one. She had known he would come here, if only to show himself in the height of his doing, evil or good, the way he would always show himself after his childhood misdeeds. The chief spy, the hunted one! And there had arisen in her the anger, the exasperation, yet also the bitter tinge of admiration that he evoked even as a boy. She was not his aunt in truth, but his older cousin, and when he had arrived among the group of orphans, it was to her the Jewel had fallen. And her husband, more of a decent Jew then, for it was before he had gone bitter, had accepted.

Now in this deep night, Zev stood in her room like a nightmare. Everyone, the Turks, the Shomer, the whole land—who would not at once think that he would try to come here? And to defy them all the Jewel had done it.

As he stood there, Malka put her fist in her mouth. In the kitchen, sleeping on the floor, lay two watchmen posted in Metulla by the Shomer to strengthen the guard against Turkish army deserters and marauders. How had he not awakened them? And her daughters would awake. "Zev, they'll scream. Hide in the outhouse. I'll come to you."

A long moment Zev hung over the bed. Why was it required of him again to set himself in motion? He had reached home. Between the two watchmen on a straw mattress on the kitchen tiles he had safely passed, knowing nothing would interfere with this destiny, knowing he would enter Malka's room. Something in him had even known that his cursed uncle would not be there. But the two girls in the bed he had not expected. Perhaps because of them he at last now turned and made his way back soundlessly again between the two sleepers and then across the yard; the outhouse door still hung on one hinge; Zev sat. His arm heavily rose and brushed the flies from his wound.

Tumultuously it was as though he were arranging all that had happened to him so he could tell it all to a woman. Her form hovered toward him, the kindly goyish neighbor woman in the blacksmith's yard in Kishinev who thrust him into the shed among the sacks of coke, to hide until the pogrom died down. Saraleh, when she thrust him down the ladder to the cellar in Aaron Aaronson's cottage, and then sent down a loaf of bread wrapped in her kerchief. He would unburden himself of all that had happened to him; she would hold his head and the throbbing tumult would be soothed away. There was no Sara any more, but the mother in Mishkan Yaacov had thrust him into the great dark oven. When all was safe, Big Leah had come, and again in the carriage Leah had saved him. To Big Leah he was relating it all, not his wife, long ago she had gone back to Janovici, her whining he did not need. The woman would come, who was she?

It was Malka who came to him; she held a basin of water, and after the laving, she spread balm on his burning wound, the same balm he recalled from years ago after the thrashings. Malka kept telling him he must go, this was the first place they would search, he must go, why had he come here, it was foolish; and in the same voice Malka kept repeating with her eternal stupidity, "Where will you go?" This same stupid flat voice—how it had always enraged him—and again it was to Zev as though he were relating all this to the real woman, saying, "Even when I was a boy, I would become so angry, I'd spit on her and run away."

Suddenly he cried out to Malka, "Listen, the British are sending a ship for me. I have two barrels of gold hidden in Athlit. Malka, hide me, I'll buy you a hundred cows from Denmark, I'll build you a big new house, hide me, bring me food, keep me hidden only for a week—"

She was staring as when the troublesome boy had told her his wild tales. "Wait one moment, Zev," she whispered and hurried back to the house.

Now a profound knowledge of his whole life swept over Zev, and he saw it clearly and knew how he would explain it to the real woman. That which had impelled him to come creeping back to this house was a mistake, an error of the kind that life thrusts on you, and he was now finished with this mistake and could go. But in the same clarity Zev knew that he had not the strength to climb to the Druze, and also that the welcome of the Druze was an illusion. Would he not be hunted there at once? He must go the other way, southward, he must reach the British.

She was returning; she carried something.

A loaf of bread.

"Quick, go now. Oh, where will you go?"

A tale, something from cheder, came to him. From the days of Abraham. Bread. They brought you bread. As a welcome, for the welcome guest. In his life everything had always been turned around. Zev took the bread from her hands and without a word slipped into the darkness.

"Don't tell them he was here, no one saw him!" Malka begged, and for Motke as well it was best to deny.

"He has not been here, she swears it by her daughters," Motke declared as Ismael and Sayed swarmed in. "Besides, how could it be? Two men slept on the floor, her daughters slept in the bed with her."

They burst through the house, angry. The thousand pound reward. And the gold on the body. From Halsah came horsemen, the sheikh himself and his other sons and his sons-in-law. Through all Metulla they galloped, in every house they searched and pillaged, while Sayed with two of them, surrounding Motke, climbed on their steeds up the mountainside to the Druze. The mukhtar declared the Jew had not been seen.

In rage Sayed bethought himself of the kvutsa. It was there the trick on him had been planned. Now Har Tsafon was invaded. The sons of Sheikh Jibran had become Sayed's deputies, the kvutsa was ransacked, Shimshoni was seized and put into the carriage—at least some Jew; Sayed would take back with him.

"He could not have escaped, he was wounded, we will find his body," Motke kept protesting. One more chance Sayed gave him. Again they searched every hole in the rocks, the tunnel that led to the Chimney, the caves. At the end, Sayed turned wrathfully on Motke and had him bound and flung into the carriage with Shimshoni. Ismael and his brothers rode behind. The return to Nazareth began.

27

BEFORE the disaster deepened, there was just time for a rider from Har Tsafon to reach Shabbatai Zeira. The Kurd took the failure on himself. He would not hide or flee. It was he who had made the decision to go to Achmed Bey in Nazareth, and he would go again. The story must remain exactly as he had given the Bimbashi to understand. Men of the Shomer had captured Zev and held him in Har Tsafon, while he, their chief, had come to Achmed Bey. The earlier complications at Gilboa need not be known. Motke could be counted on not to reveal it and endanger the rest of the Shomer. Therefore Menahem and Zeira's own nephew who had escorted Zev to Har Tsafon must at once be securely hidden. The error was that too many had been too tender-hearted; they should have finished Zev off on the spot.

In Nazareth, Shabbatai Zeira was arrested. The Bimbashi Achmed Bey, and his blundering nephew Sayed had been swept aside as Hassan Bek took all in his charge. Whoever had not been arrested of the Jewish leaders must be seized. Every shomer must be seized. And from Nazareth to Gilboa came the most gruesome tales. The "specialist from Beirut" was in attendance, a doctor who watched as men were brought to the verge of death and then gave them respite, so that the torture could begin all over again. If any emerged, it would be as broken men.

Only if Zev were found might it all come to an end; if he was not dead and devoured by hyenas, he must be found; the entire Yishuv was now desperately searching for him.

When Leah brought Menahem's food to him that night in Gidon's cave, she saw at once in her brother-in-law's eyes that peculiar glowing melancholy that came upon him where hatred and bitterness came to others. The look was not of despair but of the sick-heartedness one sometimes feels in the face of insensate suffering, as at the side of a doomed, fevered child. Nor could one have the solace of accusing God, of questioning God, since God was no longer believed in.

As was his way, Menahem spoke only of what moves should still be made, in a dark voice but with his thin bitter smile. From his yeshiva days he had retained at least one rule against sin: despair was forbidden. First, Leah herself must not remain here in Mishkan Yaacov but had best at once leave the Galilee. If, because of the new tumult about Zev's escape at Metulla, the searches had not yet reached Mishkan Yaacov, they were still certain to come. And though neither Motke nor Avraham Halpering would reveal anything of her presence that night in the carriage, what might happen if she were apprehended here, arrested, and beaten? No, another Sara Aaronson was not wanted. He had thought everything out. She had best return to her girls and remain as though she had been there all the while. She could return there on a wagon with sacks of grain from her father, and if stopped on the way, she was bringing wheat for the refugees. Schmulik must ride with a rifle to protect the grain, and then he could bring back the mules and the wagon.

Climbing down, Leah's limbs were heavy. Below spread the village, and the kvutsa, and beyond were the fields of two more kvutsoth that had grown in these years, and also of the village of Kinnereth, there lay all the golden clean oblongs of harvested fields, the green squares in fodder, and the winding pale green lanes of eucalyptus that she and Reuven and the chevreh had planted knee-deep in mud; all lay so peaceful.

What wrong, what evil had they done in all this? Were they still to be driven out to the Armenian fate whose threat had never been lifted from them? How could—not God—but mankind, the world itself, permit all this endless cruelty?

And what had been done about the Armenian fate? Two years had passed, and who spoke of it, except those who feared it for themselves?

Then Leah drove all this from her mind. No, she was giving way to panic, she was lacking in courage.

All day Zev had lain hidden high in the Lebanon hills, in

a cradle of stones heaped around him. At night he had moved westward, to reach the sea.

The sun reached the stones and when it rose high, reached into his wound. He felt the flesh healing. Malka's bread was half finished.

His thirst grew. He scarcely knew the region except that far down there must be the Litani. Could he show himself, even to a stray shepherd? All would be hunting him now, the Jews themselves, the Shomer added to the Turks, and for the gold on his head, the Arabs. The mark of Cain— he could have laughed at such children's tales, but still, Cain wasn't hanged—God only sent him into exile. What did even the Bible know of what could be done to a man, by men? Then Zev cried at himself, "Idiot." In their good days when he and Sara had frequented the hotels in Jerusalem, she had taught him one thing, "Don't imagine everyone knows about you all that you know about yourself." Oh, she had such intelligence.

And only now the grief for her broke through in his heart. A long time, he lay still. She seemed to come and say to him, "Foolish one, do the fellaheen hereabouts even know that in the world a vast war is taking place?"

If he found a cluster of houses around a stone well, could he not appear by the well, saying he had lost his way seeking a short cut to Zidon? Water, then olives, goat's cheese, pittah, even dates—he had coins on him still.

Thus, walking in the nights, Zev on the fourth day came in sight of the sea, and through two more nights, following the shore, came below Haifa. It was as though a charge of strength flowed up into him from the familiar earth. The night no longer was night to him; just so it must be to a blind man when he is in his familiar room. There he moves freely.

How many nights had they lain together waiting among these rocks of Athlit, for the blink of a ship's light? Zev hastened into a half-run, as though the outline of the British vessel must surely be out there, discernible beyond the high jagged outline of the ruined walls. He could almost hear Sara, as always running with him, falling behind out of breath, calling, "Wait for me."

For a moment he stood still from the blow of her absence, just as he used to stand waiting for her to catch up. And then he moved on. She herself had sent him bread. "Live!"

Each thing that had happened since contained a sign. Alone he had escaped them all, once again, and here he stood unhindered in the very place where they should have been waiting to trap him. Saraleh, here I am! The sign of fate was absolute. To have reached this far meant he would succeed to the end.

With the British he would return, a commander of advance troops. The first he would search out would be Motke, and—a blaze of fire. Even before the Turks, before Hassan Bey and Hassan Bek, he would cut down the whole pack of his own, Shimshoni too, the "Idealist," and all the "fair" ones. Only Menahem had been half decent, perhaps because of Leah's influnce there in the carriage. Menahem he might spare.

At a half-run, Zev came to the ruined wall. Close to the base, the fourth large stone—he clawed at it, heaved it over. Here, he and Sara had dug.

Nothing. Only Sara had known this place. In the last, might she have sent their trusted abu, hoping still to buy off Hassan Bek with a barrel of gold? His wound throbbed. His strength flowed out like tidewater. Zev let himself drop, mindless of the sharp stones. Let the waters come in and sweep him out, this was the bleak jest he had known awaited him, all his life.

There was one other place, but what use to look? Then something returned to him: A time Malka had caught him stealing a few bishliks from her jar of house money, and the uncle had beaten him until the rod broke. As soon as his wounds half-healed he had taken every coin in the crock and fled Metulla forever. Zev pulled himself up and made for the second hiding place. His fingers tore through the layer of earth and almost at once felt the wooden cover of the keg. Yes! the top was still nailed down. With stones, with torn fingers, he pried it open. Even in the night the luster appeared. One keg for him. The half of what they had put away. Sara had thought of him even in the end, she had left this untouched for him.

And this time there came a flow of tears.

Filling his pockets, Zev covered the rest, for this too was an assurance to himself that he would vanquish, he would return and yet be rich. With a heady recklessness he even made his way toward the agricultural station. Who knew? Once before the English had manged to leave a message.

The highway was empty as he had known it must be, for him. There in their lanes stood Aaron's palm trees, their distance perfectly measured by Aaron Aaronson himself in the planting. The whole area lay still; the fellaheen had surely quit this place as accursed. And here he, the hunted one, walked freely.

The door was open, its lock smashed. Papers, books, broken jars, specimens, dried excrement, a smell of spilled chemicals and urine.

Upstairs, the same. The bookcases where they had kept tea and biscuits for their long vigils, all broken glass.

Behind the agricultural station rose the Carmel; at the top was a village of the Druze. Zev climbed the slope. On the outskirts of the town a rider was just emerging from his yard. With words in their own tongue, Zev stopped him; the Turks had just seized his mount, Zev said, and he had far to travel. He had gold, he would pay a good price for the horse.

In the face of the young Druze, Zev saw that his luck still held. The Druze asked no questions. Though he would not sell his own mount, he brought out an excellent mare from his stable; Zev even bargained a bit to make everything seem normal. And a large, warm pittah was fetched, together with several balls of sheep-cheese such as they made.

At last he was mounted again!

As though an insect were crawling on her skin, the sense of a prowling presence came to Leah in her sleep. Wakening, she listened, hearing nothing but the breathing of her girls. Yet she sensed the presence.

Not far off, perhaps in the lane on the other side of the dense acacia bushes, she heard a horse neighing. Then she heard a tiny scratching, a fingernail it could be, on the pane behind her cot. As though someone knew where she lay.

And still her girls slept in their weariness.

Leah put her face against the window. Above her pots of

geraniums, in the dark glass, she could make out indistinctly the form of a head. She knew. It was he. Even through the black pane the huntedness came to her.

Taking her hobnailed shoes in her hand, she moved barefoot between the two rows of girls. Their breathing made the air of the room heavy but not unpleasant. Like the summer night air at home when she had slept in one room with all her brothers and sisters.

Outside the door she still moved barefoot, keeping to the cabin wall, but she did not find him. Then he moved out from behind a cypress, and caught her hand. His skin was like burning iron.

Her first hushed outcry was, "You're feverish." Then, "Are you mad, twenty girls are in there, it only needs one to wake and scream."

"Water," Zev murmured.

"Wait behind the acacias. I'll bring it."

Slowly his fingers unlocked from her arm. His eyes hovered over her face. Leah moved with him, half-supporting him, as far as the break in the acacia wall. "For the horse too," he gasped.

Just inside the cabin entrance they kept a tall jar of water; Leah gathered a tin cup, a pail. She found him by his horse. Her eyes had adjusted to the dark, and she saw now that his face was hollow, stubbled, he was half starved and in a malarial attack. A dirty scarf was around his neck, with dark patches, dried blood. "They shot at me. My old comrades. Motke tried to assassinate me." He gulped more water. "Nothing can kill Zev!" he half-cackled. "I got away. All the way from Metulla, I got here."

From the other end of the land, wounded, hunted by everyone. For an instant there coursed through Leah, unwanted and denied, that peculiar unquenchable self-pride of a woman to whom a man has made his way despite every peril. And she wanted to cry back, "No, no, Zev, not me! You are mistaken." It was not through feelings of that kind that she had made the men take him into the carriage. Even now, he must not imagine it.

They could not remain in the open lane. If caught here, he endangered even the girls. "Come. Hurry." But the horse? A horse's neighing might attract a dog. Tomorrow Leah could say she had bought the animal from some Bedouin, to haul their produce. "Wait." She would tie it up in their lean-to. But in the morning—what to tell the girls? Last night there had been no animal. How? From whom? She would make a mystery of it as though it had to do with the transfer of arms. Ask no questions.

In dazed weakness Zev followed her into the grove. Luckily the old watchman's hut was no longer used for arms. Ah, if the Turks were to comb all the abandoned huts in all the groves, whom would they not find!

A half-rusted padlock hung on the door; Leah had the key.

Inside they felt their way to a small pile of empty sacks. Zev could hardly stand long enough for her to spread the burlap on the earth. He slid down then, and at once the shivering overtook his body; his knees pulled up; doubled, he huddled into a ball.

Then the tale poured from him. Again and again Leah attempted to hush him, attempted to leave, promising to return with food, with quinine, but each time she tried to rise up, the fingers clawed at her skirt, her arm, with the fierce strength of the fevered.

All, all, the betrayal at Shimshoni's Har Tsafon, the two watchmen on the floor at Metulla. Bitterly he told of his homecoming. "Malka—a mother to me, she drove me out." The mountain nights alone, hunted, and at last the ruins of Athlit, and of the empty hole where the gold had been, under the rock, and casting himself down in despair to be carried away by the tide. And then the second hiding place. "It was there! It was a sign!" As though fed on each escape, his pitch rose, from the bitterest hatred to his old unconquerable boasting. Nothing could kill him! Alone against all the hunters! On these last days and nights, passing through the thick of them! Only the fields for shelter. Not a drink of water. But he would live and revenge himself on his enemies.

Then, as if all was proven, all was concluded and certain, "Leah, I have gone through the flames, and believe me, all the rot of me has burned away. Leahleh, only one week, two weeks, keep me here until the English come. You—for me you were always the real woman. Leah, I have gold. I will buy a pardess of a thousand dunans. You will be a queen. All the others, what are they, nothing, a man's passing need. Only Sara I revered, and she, she was far above me, she was not like us of the ordinary earth. All the others—nothings. They would let a man die. But a woman, a real woman—" and amazingly his tongue fell into the chant of the Sabbath blessing, Eshet chayeel, a woman of valor, what is she—and Leah found herself choked, even weeping, not for him, but with tears slowly coursing down her cheeks, tears for she did not know who, for Sara, for the train of prisoners, for the miserable starved Turkish deserters who came begging for bread, for Avshalom who had ridden away from here to his death.

Zev's head was in her lap; a new, violent trembling had come over his body, his words had fallen away, she heard his teeth striking against each other and she held his head, but his body thrashed as though the limbs would break. Then she slid down on the earth and held him against her until at last the thrashing subsided and he slept, the poor, fevered, hunted one, the hated one, the mistaken one, the braggart and the weakest of men.

When word came to Hassan Bek in Nazareth that the hunted one had again escaped, his hurling fury was such as one read about in despots of ancient times. It was such that among his blasphemies his commands could not be heard, his servants and subalterns fled his riding whip, he raged through the corridors, the stables; unable to remain in one place, he mounted and clattered off with a troop to make arrests in person—every one of the Jews was a traitor, a spy, he would tear their secrets out of their flesh. That treacherous Jew, that shomer that had been brought back from the north, let him hang by his feet until the truth tumbled out of his mouth—a shomer, they were all in it, he would castrate the lot of them! Let every house in every settlement be searched, let that lying conniving Kurdish Jew from Sejera be sent to Damascus, there Djemal Pasha would know how to burn the truth out of him, and that fat fool of a Kaymakam in Tiberias, that Jew lover, Azmani Bey, who had not made a single arrest, let him move his fat carcass, what was he waiting for, Hassan Bek could not be everywhere at once—out! out! send the fat-belly out to scour the settlements.

Mati would be the least likely to be noticed, a boy carrying bread and cheese and a jar of water as though for himself in the fields, and he was still small enough so that his head could scarcely be seen above the high brambles when he climbed.

His uncle Menahem the shomer had moved from Gidon's cave, for sometimes sheep and goats grazed nearby. It was now Reuven's cave that he was hiding in, the one Reuven had explored long ago, letting himself down with a rope tied around a big rock above. The cave had only a small mouth in the face of the height, and Reuven had said that in the times of the Romans, Jewish fighters had hidden inside there.

Menahem had already caught sight of Mati approaching, and now gave a bird whistle.

Making sure there was not a goat or a sheep on the hillside, Mati moved closer along the cliff wall, so even a watcher could not see; he was careful not to leave a trodden path in the brush. Directly below the cave he looked upward. In the half-light his uncle's face appeared, the height of three men above him, and then Menahem let down the rope for the provisions. But what Mati had been puzzling over was how Menahem got into the cave the first time, after he had seen a shepherd too close to his other hiding place. Menahem hadn't even had a rope; it was Schmulik who brought it to him after he heard the bird-whistle signal from the new place.

"How did you get in?" Mati asked.

"What do you think, Mati?" his uncle answered, as a test.

"Did you climb down, or up?"

"Find out." Slowly, Menahem pulled up the food.

The boy stood, carefully examining each crevice in the rock. His uncle was not like a teacher who, if you don't give the answer right away, makes you feel you're a stupid.

"I am a human fly," Menahem whispered down. Only with children did he sometimes show such playfulness.

It was true, Mati considered, that flies oozed out a stickiness so that they could walk on walls, and upside down. Perhaps the men of the Shomer had discovered how to make such a substance and stick it on their hands and feet—no, that was foolishness.

Something in Menahem's look made him study the rock sidewise. There Mati saw a faint ridge. It would be very hard, but a man could creep along there. And also Mati saw crevices where a man might work downward from the top, clinging with toes and fingers. Then he could inch sidewise, and thus the cave could be reached. Why had he not seen this until now? "Sidewise," he gave the answer.

He even made a plan. One day he would come still earlier and surprise Menahem with a visit inside. But his uncle saw his thought. After the troubles were over, Menahem said, Mati could come here one day and try it.

Mati knew it was because of the spies that Menahem had to be hidden, and that Leah had had to leave quickly, though they did not belong to the spies. The secret name was the Nili. The chief was Zev the Hotblood. With Schmulik, Mati discussed it—if Zev should come here, would they hide him?

"Don't talk stupidities," Schmulik replied.

"We hid him in the stove, the other time."

"He wasn't a spy then. He was a shomer."

"Maybe he will come here to hide. What would we do?"

"He won't come here."

If Zev was hiding up in a cave, would they bring him food and water?

"If the Turks caught you, they'd hang you."

"Even the Turks don't hang children."

Schmulik snorted and muttered a dirty curse, the way he did when he couldn't find an answer.

"Who are we for, the Turks or the English?" Mati demanded at last.

"We're for ourselves."

"If you knew where Zev was, would you tell?"

"Idiot!" his brother growled.

When Azmani Bey came, it was first to the kvutsa, and Yaffaleh happened to be there; she had come to borrow a salve for mule-sores. The Turks came clattering into the yard; before the Kaymakam's carriage rode Hassan Bek himself on a black horse—she knew him from what everyone said. With his glittering uniform, his sneering face, this could be no one else than the terrifying Bek who tortured prisoners until they killed themselves, as Sara Aaronson had done. And after the Kaymakam's carriage rode eight gendarmes. Like the time they came for the conscription. But this time was surely worse.

Instantly, HaKeren was in turmoil. The eight soldiers

seemed a whole army, they stomped into every dwelling, into the barn, drove their swords into the hay, shouted, reviled. Rushing past Nahama into the children's house, they brandished their pistols even at the infants.

Every male had to come and stand in the yard. Watching from the kitchen, Yaffaleh saw the prophet-like Old Gordon—She had read his writings in the *Poël Hatzaïr*; Gordon was against all wars, and a vegetarian like Reuven. He had a thick, tangled grayish beard like Tateh's, and as the Old One walked calmly across the yard, Yaffaleh herself saw how a soldier planted a kick to send him stumbling, then laughed. Gordon picked himself up without looking at the soldier and went to stand with the others.

The Bek was cursing them all, spies, traitors, every last one of them would hang in Damascus unless they produced the escaped Zev and every last Nili spy. Hoisted out of his carriage, the Belly too stood in front of the chaverim; from Max Wilner he demanded where was this one, that one— he knew them all by name.

"Conscripted for labor duty, you took them yourself," Max Wilner replied, again and again. Even Reuven, she heard the Kaymakam ask for.

"But he volunteered—he is working directly under Djemal Pasha's orders, in Damascus."

"You have arms. Where are they hidden?"

"Only the two rifles permitted for our watchmen."

"And twenty more, not permitted. You received them from the Shomer. They were bought with gold from the Nili."

"If we had arms you would have found them."

Behind the kitchen, Max Wilner's chavera, Hemda, pushed a large bowl of potato peelings into Yaffaleh's hands. "Here, quick, take this slop and feed the chickens." As Yaffaleh took hold of it, the bowl by its weight nearly fell through her grasp, and at once she understood. Walking to the chicken run, she scattered a few peelings, while careful not to uncover the grenades. No one had followed her. Yaffaleh hid the grenades under straw, let the hens hatch them. Now she must run to Mishkan Yaacov to give warning.

"What's befallen?" Feigel cried, though she knew. Feigel always knew beforehand, and taking the jar of salve that Yaffaleh still carried, she set it aside and began to prepare for their coming—honey-cake, and the few eggs she had saved, allowing herself only the solace of curses: may they swallow their own teeth and may their teeth devour their stomachs, she cursed; while she furiously ladled out honey: may a swarm of live bees inhabit their throats; and as she uncovered real butter: let her last morsel be sacrificed to the Belly and perhaps he would not take Tateh away.

Already the news flew and the anxious villagers rushed into their yards and out of their yards, the terrified wives called and sent children with messages. Bronescu came out into the street wearing his tarboosh and begged for calm. Since Roumania had finally entered the war on the side of the Allies, he and all the others had become Ottomanized.

Feigel kept Yaffaleh in the kitchen with her, and from the window Yaffaleh saw them coming just as she had seen them entering HaKeren, the Bek on his black steed, the Kaymakam's carriage behind him, and the rows of mounted gendarmes.

Bronescu welcomed them to the feast already spread. The table was waiting, he said with a flourish, good news of such guests travels on the wind beforehand.—We are old friends, loyal subjects, he called the fat Kaymakam to witness; whatever must be done we shall accept and remain loyal. If there are traitors in the land we will be the first to help hunt them out!

The Bek dismounted, glancing at Bronescu and the villagers with suspicion but as yet without rage, showing that a civilized man does not respond with barbarity to a hospitable greeting, but that a proud Ottoman is not to be deceived with servile flattery, either. Let every man be brought before him, he commanded.

"Some are in your service with their wagons at the station, and the rest are in the fields harvesting grain for your army."

"Grain to hide from us! No Jewish tricks! Bring them here!" He motioned toward the Kaymakam, who had a ledger on his knees. "Every last one is written down in his book."

A chortle came from the Belly. Already, Azmani Bey was lifting to his mouth a slice of Feigel's white bread thickly laden with chopped eggs and onions. "Oh, I know this village well," he said. "The fat of the land is here, milk and honey!" And turning to Bronescu, "Your Jewel, as you call him, he was shomer in this village. Your women used to hide him from their husbands, eh——! But you won't be able to hide him from us!"

"We drove him out, Azmani Bey, you know it—he was nearly the end of us—this is the last place he would come to, God forbid it!"

"Tea in the middle of the night," the Kaymakam's voice rose to a sly, obscene giggle as he said to the Bek, "Better take the women for questioning too! And what about his wife's family? He was married here!"

"His wife has long ago left here, as you know, your honor," Bronescu smiled.

Just then, Feigel brought another pitcher of cool buttermilk for the soldiers, and the Belly called out to her, "What of your daughter, the big one? Where is she?"

"In the south where she lives," Feigel said firmly.

"And your son-in-law, Menahem the shomer? Where is that one? He was not found in Gilboa. Where the devil is that devil hiding, eh?"

Hassan Bek himself was now glaring at Feigel. "I know nothing of Menahem's whereabouts," she replied calmly. "But I can tell you where is my oldest son Reuven. He is in Damascus in the service of Djemal Pasha."

Yankel was brought in just then, two soldiers with the noses of their rifles prodding him from the field; he carried his scythe over his shoulder. Behind the soldiers came the two boys, Schmulik too with his scythe; all the way from the field he had kept muttering to Mati, with one stroke he could slice the legs off them!

A dozen men of the village were taken away, Yankel among them, and even the melamed. Beseeching and wailing, their women ran to Bronescu, to the Kaymakam; they kept calling, each to her man, in Roumanian, in Yiddish. Who knew if they would ever see each other again, each called, and each begged her man not to make a hero of himself, not to do anything foolish, and the men kept calling back instructions for the livestock, and to whom to go for help in worst need. And so the little band was marched away. Who knew why this one had been seized and not that one? a golden napoleon squeezed into a fat palm, a jar of goose-fat from Golde Roitschuler as the Belly was hoisted back into his carriage.

The Bek sprang onto his horse.

The women clustered around Bronescu. No, no, it would not be like in Zichron, he reassured them, gold had passed, perhaps the men might have to remain a few nights in Tiberias, but surely they would not be dragged to Damascus. He himself would go to Tiberias tomorrow, he would speak to his friend Azmani Bey, once the Bek had departed; the Belly was not so evil, it was only a show he had had to make for the Bek.

Still they besieged him. The melamed's wife worried, her husband needed certain pills—yes, Bronescu would take them to Tiberias himself. They followed him into his house, and to each Bronescu promised all would be well. He promised.

Feigel sat in her corner. The children had never seen her exactly this way; Mameh was sobbing. When Yankel had been sent off with his wagon as far as Beersheba to serve the Turks, she had only cursed them with a wife's curse, and packed hard-boiled eggs for him, and even cursed the fate that had turned her eyes to Zion when her sister begged her to come to America. What devil had entered into her? It was she more than Yankel—in her longing for Reuven and Leah, she had dragged the family to the bottom of the world, here. But now Feigel sat bereft of her last strength, she sat and let sobs come.—A stubborn man he has been to me, she was keening, as though certain she would see him no more.—And to our children he has been hard. But though his sons are good boys and good workers, what joy have they given him? "If he never comes back to us," Feigel suddenly admonished Schmulik with a trembling voice, "you will remember that each of you left his ways, you did not follow the ways of your father, that you betrayed his beliefs, and what good is it to a father to have sons who do not follow him, and daughters who do not listen to him? He is a pious man, and even I did not help him to bring his children to follow him—"

Then, all at once, with a little gasp, Feigel leaped up from her chair, her energy returned in one burst. "His tfillim! They took him away without his tfillim and his tallis!" Darting to the shelf, she seized the embroidered bag.

Feigel scanned her remaining children. Something told her not to send a boy. Yaffaleh would have to go. "Yaffaleh, Tateh won't rest without them." This could not wait for Bronescu's journey tomorrow. Surely a few other women would be setting out, and Yaffaleh must go with them. She must also go to her sister, to Shula in Tiberias—the Bagelmachers had influence with the Kaymakam. "You'll go, Yaffaleh. Be careful."

28

AFTER the iron-barred door closed upon them, the conjectures and disputes ended. Be still, shah, one had to listen to the stones, to listen, yet without wanting to hear how bad would be the shrieking. But not a sound came through the black stones. The curses on Zev, on the Nili, started up again. Where had they taken Tibor, the first to be questioned? What would they do to a man? How long—

Until Tibor was flung stumbling back against their bodies into the crowded cell. His mouth was bloodied, but still Tibor wore a twist of his habitual ironic grin—he had endured. Those same two butchers did it, Tibor said, the two who dragged you out from here. It was before the Belly himself. Azmani Bey sat and questioned as though not seeing what they were inflicting on you. First, kicking, cuffings, a fist on the mouth. Also the whip, a rider's whip. No, not to him on the feet. On the back. On a bench the Belly had there. Seven, he had received. About the railway station in Samekh, the Belly demanded. When you worked there with mules, to whom did you tell how many trains and what was in the trains? Such things. Then about Zev.

Others took longer to return. Some were thrown back into the dungeon, their feet bloodied. Some were sobbing. On the wallbench, the men laid out the worst beaten. Old Gordon hurried to each one, "It will pass, it will pass, you

see for you it is already over and done with, and the pain
will pass."

There came a long interval. Would no more be called
out? Was it finished?

The Kaymakam had gone to his meal. Let the Belly feed
all night long. Perhaps they would be left in peace until
morning. Perhaps Zev would be captured somewhere and
the tortures would be over.

Already a yellow-eyed jailer had "received," and small
bundles, packets of food, candles, messages, even Yankel's
tfillim bag had been thrust into the stone chambers.

Yankel sought a corner and recited the benedictions. Behind him he heard them starting their chalutz songs. They
were gathered around Gordon, and it was their Hagalili
they were singing, the way Leah sometimes sang it on the
stoop of a Sabbath, when first the girls, then Gidon used to
join, in the days when the children had all still been at
home. Sometimes, just like the men here now in the cell,
they would go over to Hillel's song, "Im ain ani li, mi li"—
"If I'm not for myself, who will be for me?" It had been a
joy to his soul to lie quietly after the Sabbath meal and
hear them on the stoop, knowing Feigel had admonished
the children to sing low so as not to disturb Tateh in his
nap.

The chalutzim were gathered around their philosopher,
Gordon; at first Yankel resented the man, their Tolstoy,
their sage, also a vegetarian, from whose writings Leah was
always reading out loud with sighs of enjoyment and
smackings of her lips, and Reuven too was one of those
who sat at his feet in their collectiva. A man whose fame
was that in his elder years he had come to Eretz to labor
with his hands. Then what was the great wonder of it? Had
not he, Yankel, done the same? —An aristocrat, a learned
man, a relative of Baron Ginsberg, no less, the richest Jew
in Russia. And behold Gordon leaves his entire family
there, and comes to Eretz to be a simple laborer on the
soil. —And is there more virtue in leaving your family behind than in bringing them with you to Eretz? But he must
not be unjust, Yankel told himself, for later, he had heard,
Gordon had brought over his wife and children, and there
had been tragedy, sickness, the wife had died.

From song to song the chalutzim continued, and now,
even as sometimes with the children at home, Yankel heard

the low, plaintive, familiar melody, "Eliyahu Ha-Navi," the Sabbath song of longing for the Mashiach. Even with their atheism, they had turned it into a song for themselves. Oh, let Elijah come already, bring Mashiach, it was time. They were strange, these godless children; in the midst of their godlessness, they were Jews.

In the candle-flicker, Yankel saw Old Gordon standing before him with half-opened lips and a half-smile on his face, the simple curiosity and friendliness of Jew to Jew, as though to say, "Well, and how goes it with a fellow Yid?"

"I know your sons, I know your daughters, Reb Chaimovitch, I've heard you have a fine meshek. Nu, it's good for us to meet at last, though not in the best of places!"

To Yankel's own surprise, a lively response rose to his lips. "Why not? If Jews no longer come together in the synagogue, even a prison is good if it brings them together."

A prolonged shivering moan arose from a body stretched on the bench, and Gordon quietly remarked, "If God hears prayers, they will reach his ears from here as well as from the house of prayer."

"He hears, he hears," Yankel said. "Only we, we don't hear, and heed."

The other man's eyes met his with a kind of warmth and patience that made Yankel reflect, if this Gordon were not so mixed up with the unbelievers, you could take him for a tzaddik. "No, we don't always heed," Gordon agreed. And just then the Belly's two tormenters plunged in amongst them anew, and glared from the one graybeard to the other. "The old one!" they commanded.

"It must be for me," Gordon said; before Yankel could move, he stepped out.

Now complete silence fell.

When the door again opened, he was being dragged by the two guards; they cast him in, and the men caught him in their arms. His sandals were thrown in, and the bolt was heard across the door.

Gordon's beard was matted with spittle and blood; his bare feet flamed from the bastinado. But as the chaverim carefully placed him on a pallet of sacking, he gasped, "You see it's not so dreadful. A few blows and it's over. A Jew can endure."

—And if they demanded of Yankel where was his son-in-law Menahem the shomer? —God seal my tongue, Yankel prayed; his turn had come.

～～～～

Distantly, from his cave, Menahem had seen the movements from HaKeren, from Kinnereth, and then in Mishkan Yaacov. He had seen that there were arrested ones led away. None at the kvutsoth were burdened with knowledge of his hiding place. Leah knew, but only about the first cave, and she was far off. Also the boys knew. Yankel was not to have known, but perhaps, in his way, Yankel knew. Let it be. But who, who had now been taken? In his mind Menahem went over each chaver in each kvutsa. It was useless to speculate nor could he go down even in the night to find out. The Belly was sly and might have left a gendarme behind for just such an occasion. He must still wait.

Waiting and solitude were part of his life, but never yet had he passed so long a time unbroken, except for the moments with young Mati. And perhaps tonight because of the turmoil even the boy would not come. No. Mati was already a chevrehman; no matter what, he would come.

At the rear of the cave was a ledge cut in the stone, in what remote century, who could tell? Menahem lay there in a kind of half-trance he had taught himself long ago when passing the nights on watch. His mind roved, making distant plans. Clearly now all was broken—the Shomer, the Yishuv. But one must think beyond. In a month, in a year, the Turks would be defeated and the English would rule here. From the vast outer silences of the world, one nevertheless caught echoes of the great waves of events. The great thrusting wave first generated by the Germans against Paris had fallen short. Then the great wave generated by the British against Constantinople had fallen short. Twice the Turks along with the Germans had stormed against the canal, and fallen short; twice the British had stormed against Gaza and fallen short. Last, in Europe, the Germans had mustered their fullest strength and stormed again against Paris, but left the goal unreached. And from where would they renew their strength? From the Russian front? There, it was said, they had plunged far, and every barrier was gone, and yet this had not availed. Through the whole length of Jewish habitation, as it happened, from Danzig to Odessa, they had swept. But could they regather this spread-out energy? Meanwhile on the other side there was an inexhaustible new ocean of strength, for the Americans were coming. Thus the final, conquering wave would have to be that of the Allies; no matter how long it took, no matter what back-and-forth movements still took place, this last added strength would conquer. On this he must calculate. The Allies would rule here. And then what was left of the Yishuv must gather itself together and rebuild itself. Waves of new energy must come, and this time fully build the land. There would be no more restrictions, no more barriers, no more need for coming into the land by stealth; the great dream would at last be realized.

But from where would this new energy come? Without a vast new wave of young chalutzim, how could the land be rebuilt? Would the builders come from the lands of the victors? English Jews were hardly Jews, French Jews would not come, American Jews would send money, but few would come, for most of them were the same Jews from Russia who had in the first instance decided to go to America and not to Eretz. Where could the masses of new chalutzim come from except Poland and Russia?

And here was the impenetrable, the tohu v'bohu, the tumultous void, the darkness as dark as this cave. What was happening, what was happening there with their revolution? Would it prove good or bad for the movement? Would the young Jews all flock to the banner of the Bund, lose themselves in the Russian revolution, and scorn Zion?

Menahem thought back to his own time, to the endless arguments and even the bodily assaults, in his own circle— what was more important, the revolutzia, or Zionism? And now that they had had their revolutzia, though only bits of rumors seeped through—Jews had already been given full equal rights it was said—would this draw them away from Zion? Would it be enough for their dream, merely to have more civil rights in Russia?

Though no one had letters, no one had newspapers, tales had come through Constantinople, from the Zionist bureau there, filtering down to the Jews in Damascus. Many Jews were prominent in the new government in St. Petersburg, it was said. The social revolutionist Pincus Rutenberg, a good Zionist as well, was rumored to have returned from exile and to be high in the Kerensky government. Also, it was rumored, Trumpeldor had found his way back to Russia, and surely Trumpeldor would not forsake the movement. Yet how could one know what was happening there? One had to go there. Could someone, in some way, perhaps get to Russia? And on this, his mind could spin, on strange schemes to penetrate the impenetrable.

Deeper in the night, Menahem fell into a different contemplation; fragments of thought, like ends of threads long broken off, seemed to cling there in his mind.

Why was darkness created, and night? It came back to him that from the black and nether side of life must be drawn the very substance of light and life. So the Cabbalists had comprehended the secret; the roots of life fed in darkness. It was needed that he should lie here in a black cave so that illumination would rise within him. Thus the darkness would shine for him, his solitude be lifted, and he knew that he was one of those to whom a spark of destiny might be shown. It was then that Elijah came.

Elijah who had dwelt in a cave on the Carmel—Elijah entered Menahem's cave and approached him on the stone ledge. He was as Menahem had always imagined him, though long ago renouncing such imaginings, counting himself a rational man. Nevertheless even a rational man could conjecture on the visions that had come to Jews in the past, to Moshe Rabenu, to Saul, to David, to Samuel, and to Elijah. As always, Menahem saw, Elijah wore his garment of skins, girdled with a thong, and his staff was from an ancient olive. His lips were wide and red, and he moved quite close into the alcove, as a man who has intimate, secret matters to impart.

"He cannot yet come down," Elijah said of the Messiah, "because the Unnameable has not yet given him a body. But as you know," Elijah confided to one who had been a yeshiva bocher, "there is a way to bring down Mashiach even before his time."

So powerful was the yearning of Messiah to come down, as he witnessed this time of terror and knew the full need for his coming, as the outcries and the pleading and the prayers of the tormented and hunted came to him, so deeply did he suffer even for those who like Menahem were becoming disillusioned through witnessing the agony that God permitted to be inflicted on His own children, to the very point where they had to cease to believe in God, where they had even to deny God—so eager was the Messiah to come down, that a spark from the flame of his soul had escaped, and this spark Elijah carried.

"It is here within my breast," Elijah said, and in sublime awe Menahem perceived the spark. Even while his rational mind protested—what grandmother's tales, what childhood bobeh-meises had come back upon him—tonight, in this vision, the Messianic spark glowed and burned within Elijah's flesh, and illuminated the ages, into the time to come.

So it must have been across the generations at all times when the Messiah could not endure the waiting, at all times of deepest torment in the world. A spark of Messiah it must have been that moved Shabbatai Zvi along his Messianic path, until the spark dimmed, and he erred and knew fear and bowed to the will of a Sultan and became a Moslem. And had it not also been a spark carried down by Elijah that entered the body of that well-bred Jew of Vienna, Theodor Herzl, and through him brought the mission of Messiah almost to completion, until Herzl too flawed and was ready to gather Jews into another land than Israel? Just so, Menahem knew, Elijah's spark was now reflected into himself, and he would go forth and lead Jews to Eretz. He would go forth, Menahem knew it, from this cave where Elijah sat with him, and he would bring Jews from other lands, by the impulse from Messiah, into the homeland.

When daylight came, Menahem noticed that he had lain on a scorpion. It had not touched him. Had he been superstitious, he would have taken this as a sign.

After Yaffaleh came with the evil news, Nahum had not wasted a moment. In a way he had long prepared himself for troubles of this kind. Though not a great reader, Nahum was a fairly constant reader of biographies of the great. This was a good way to learn about useful qualities in life, and Nahum had already begun to put into practice some of the points he had picked up from such books. In a biography of the powerful Rothschild family, which one of the German officers had left with him, Nahum had been struck by the way the Rothschild fortune had begun. The founder had been an ordinary moneylender in the ghetto of Frankfurt-am-Main, but he had developed a hobby of coin collecting. When he met the Duke of Baden on a small business affair, this old Rothschild had learned that the Duke was also a coin collector, and thus there had developed an important connection that began with a simple mutual interest. Now in this, Nahum explained to Shula, there were several lessons. Could she perceive them? "To develop mutual interests with important people?" she said.

That was one principle. Good. But what was an even deeper principle?

Shula liked to make occasions for Nahum to display his clever thinking to her—he enjoyed it so. Especially when she honestly couldn't see as far as he saw, he was delighted, and then she could ask of him anything she wanted.

"Look," her husband explained, his eyes glowing, "it shows that a man will do a big thing for a small thing, if the small thing really pleases him."

How had he jumped to that? His conclusion truly interested her.

"Why, the Duke's coin collection was a hobby, no? A small thing."

"Perhaps it was a big collection?"

He laughed and patted her. Touché. But Nahum explained nevertheless: "Even a big collection would be a small thing compared to the Duke's vast business interests. Yet he turned his whole fortune over to Mayer Anschel Rothschild for management because they were both coin collectors. Thus a small thing brings a big one."

Her husband's cleverness never ceased to surprise her. But Nahum wasn't finished with what he had learned from the Rothschilds. "The important thing is to know what people really care about. A hobby is something like being in love. You can touch a man deeply through his hobby."

"So how can you ever have all the same hobbies as every one you want to do business with? You won't have time for the business!"

"You don't have to have all the hobbies, Ketzeleh." Even without being himself a coin collector, if Rothschild had simply learned that the Duke loved old coins, he could have found some for him, and this also would have worked.

—But didn't everyone know this rule? Shula asked. To get on the good side of people? Sometimes Nahum was funny—he made himself a whole system out of what every-body naturally knew.

Still, perhaps the way her Nahum did things was a little different. She saw how it had begun with the fat Kay-makam. Once when Azmani Bey had been invited for a holiday dinner, the Turk was still stuffing himself when everyone had finished. Papa Bagelmacher drew out his gold watch to look at the time. It was a beautiful watch he had inherited from his own great-grandfather who had been a watchmaker in Lublin, and the Kaymakam's eyes swam over it as though it were another of Mama Bagelmacher's apricot dumplings. Might he look at it? Papa took off the watch and chain. All at once the fat one's sausage fingers became delicate as the feelers of an ant; he opened the back cover, the inside lid, and his mouth worked as though to lick up all he saw. Then he drew out his own watch and showed it also was unusual, it had moons and suns on the face. Everyone admired the timepiece, but Nahum had really become interested and had asked questions. There-upon the fat one drew out a second timepiece; this one was amazingly flat, and thin as a Maria Theresa thaler. Azmani Bey sat there for another hour discoursing about famous watches, and when he left at last, the Kaymakam invited Nahum to come and see his collection.

Nahum went the next day, and on his return told Shula all sorts of things, really intriguing. Could she imagine, the Belly had an entire special room filled with a collection of watches and clocks. He had a long shelf of books from France, Germany and Switzerland, about clocks alone!

Then what? Must Nahum become a collector of old watches and thus a Kaymakam?

Nahum patted her. Ay, Ketzeleh, didn't she see? The next time they needed something important from Azmani Bey—

"You'll give him your father's old watch?"

—No, but at least, she wasn't entirely stupid, he said.

Just so, Nahum began keeping an eye out for old watches. To linger in little jewelry shops, to look at beauti-ful stones, moonstones, rubies, gave him pleasure; here in Tiberias there were only a few poor stalls with heavy silver-work, but in Nazareth where Christian tourists stayed, there were shops, and already long ago Nahum had be-

come a good friend of the son of a shopkeeper, a Nasha-
shibi who kept a clutter of things in his trays. Yassir, like
himself, took pleasure in fine stones. And as two young
married men, they had knowing jests for each other.

Once Nahum brought Yassir a remarkable set of French
postcards that a German flier had traded him for three bottles of the best Rishon brandy. The photographs were
hand-tinted. In return, Yassir, another time, drew Nahum
into a back room and there showed him two bronze figurines that could be coupled and uncoupled. They laughed
and laughed, handling the pair in turn, making many positions.

Since then, Nahum had developed the habit of picking
up from the counter trays curious timepieces that villagers
occasionally brought in, and only a few days ago Yassir
had pounced on him as he entered, "Nahum, I have something especially for you!" With joyous anticipation in his
eyes, he drew Nahum to the rear, and even before the boy
brought coffee, took out from a velvet pouch a thick gold
watch—but wait! Yassir opened the back, and with his giggle, offered the watch to Nahum's gaze. There, in the silvery steel movement, a busy little manikin with each stroke
drove his member between the legs of a silvery minikin,
and in the next stroke withdrew. With moist lips, the two
young husbands kept gazing at this wonder.

And so when Yaffaleh told of the arrests, Nahum was
prepared. Yet the matter must not appear as a simple
bribe; for Nahum to rush to the Kaymakam would not be
the right way.

But how could they wait? Tateh might at this very moment be under the lash, and who knew what he could endure?

"Besides the gifts that Avshalom Feinberg brought that
time, from Gidon in Alexandrea," Nahum asked, "what
more could he reveal to them?"

Yaffaleh was silent.

"And Leah?" Shula said. "How much did Tateh know?
Of her doings? Of arms? He isn't supposed to know anything."

Then Yaffaleh said, "It's about Menahem."

"You are hiding Menahem?"

Nahum's father put his hands over his ears and ran from

the room. The mother kept half sobbing, "We can't leave him there! The fat one is a monster. He will beat everything out of him!"

"Tateh won't speak," Yaffaleh said. "He will be like old Aaronson."

Like the old Aaronson. But the Aaronsons had done what they had done, while Tateh had raged against even the first whisper of doing such things.

"I'll find a way. I'll find a way," Nahum promised.

As with old Aaronson, it was happening to Yankel. By their two devils he had been summoned, and he also like Old Gordon had walked a pace ahead of them so as not to be prodded. He found himself standing there before the Belly, who even greeted him with a "Shalom, Reb Chaimovitch" followed by a weary sigh. "That you would not be foolish enough to hide the Jewel in your oven once again, I know, Reb Chaimovitch."

The pig. Even the tale of the oven had reached his pig's ears, but it was already long enough ago to be a tale that everyone repeated. Yankel too sighed, a sigh far more profound. It did not rise, like the Kaymakam's, from an afternoon's weariness at being obliged to listen to the futile shriekings of grown men, but from centuries of standing thus, before the Inquisitor, the Cossacks' hetman, the Graf, the Baron. "Not in the oven or even in the outhouse, as your excellency knows. Nothing but disaster has ever come to us from that one; we drove him from the village, and ours is the last place he would come to, to hide."

"He was a shomer. And every member of your Shomer," the Kaymakam giggled, to show how easily the secrets fell, "each one took a blood-oath to protect his brothers to the death. Your son-in-law Menahem is one of them."

Already Menahem. "But the Shomer also threw Zev out, and Menahem was the first to vote against him."

"Then why did your chief shomer let Zev the Hotblood escape, in Har Tsfon?"

What did he, Yankel, know of such things? Was this even true? That the Jewel had escaped, this was the cause of all the misfortune—but—allowed to escape? Yankel felt whirled around as by a sudden wind. Could Menahem have anything to do with such a thing?

Of Menahem's being hidden now in the cave he was

aware, though even this had not been spoken of to him. Nothing was spoken of to him. But did they think that he had no eyes in his head, when Mati slipped out over the fields before dawn?

The fat mamser had already smelled the wind of doubt and fear that assailed him. Now the questions came as from a dozen adders' tongues, as though from a host of inquisitioners. His daughter—the big one—had she not been home last week? Why had she suddenly departed? Where was she now?

Of her he could easily tell, that he sent her with food for the families driven out from Jaffa and Tel Aviv. And there she would remain, to help.

And where was his younger son—the sharpshooter?

"Gidon? Long ago Bahad-ad-Din seized him with the shipful of Jews in Jaffa, and sent him away, and it is as though he had vanished from the face of the earth."

"Indeed, Reb Chaimovitch? And you haven't heard from him since?"

What could this Pharaoh know? Of the gifts brought by that reckless, insane one, that Avshalom Feinberg, whose babbling mouth was now finally stopped in death? In sudden anger Yankel wanted to shout curses over all those meddling idiots whose intrigues and spying and self-importance, together with all their heroism, had now enmeshed and entrapped him. How could he safely answer? He would be caught by a yes or a no. Not a word! He would stand as Akiba before the Romans, let them flay the flesh from his body!

—And the Aaronsons? Had he not known them?

"He came in the time of the locusts. He came to everyone, to tell how to overcome the plague of locusts. Djemal Pasha himself sent him!"

"And your eldest son—what is his name?"

"Reuven. But he is in your own service, in Damascus." And what does he tell you from Damascus?"

"We have hardly heard from him in the whole war."

"Reb Chaimovitch, Damascus is not Alexandria in Egypt."

"Only now and again, a word that he is well."

—Perhaps Yankel was tired, standing? There was the bench, to lie down. Sometimes one remembered better, lying down.

Let it come. Why should he escape what God had ordained for Jews to suffer? For the first stroke, for the fire that arose in its wake across the soles of both feet, he was well prepared.

Azmani Bey had fallen silent as though to let Yankel hear the descending rod. Each slash became a streak of fire, and then his feet were entirely bathed in flame. The words of prayer did not come to Yankel, only a groaning, with an inner, rumbling, drawnout *Gottenu*.

There were not even questions between, to give him respite. If he had been asked again, Menahem? Would there come out of him, at some time, the word—cave? The word was *pasul*, forbidden, it was outside of the whole range of things that existed in the universe.

A high-pitched shrilling from the fat one reached him. "You still have nothing to tell me?"

"Gottenu, ratteveh mir!" came from the Jew.

Yankel did not know it when the guards dragged him back to the dungeon, to haul out some other Jew.

When his soul returned to him, Yankel heard the talking around him. Some said it would be done every day until the Jewel was found. Others said they would all be sent to rot in Damascus.

Then they were singing again. Deep in the night a madness seized them. Their torn feet tramped on the stones. In a candleflicker Yankel saw the old one, Gordon, his beard tilted to the Above One, leaping in their hora. "Chai! Chai!" they chanted. "Am Yisroel Chai b'li dai" Alive! Alive! The people Israel lives without end!

Nahum had decided on the best way. Placed in a velvet-lined jewel box of Shula's, the gift was dispatched that same evening by an Arab servant to the Kaymakam residence, high up on the ridge overlooking the sea, not far from the site Nahum himself had purchased for the future. Around the timepiece was a note from Nahum saying he had only now returned from Nazareth where he had seen this in a shop, and he was hastening to send it on for Azmani Bey's collection, so that not a moment of enjoyment might be lost.

The next morning Yankel was called—the first. He had just completed his prayers; to his surprise a minyan had

formed, Gordon among them. Thus, Tibor, the bitter hu-
morist, declared should any of them die, he could even expect a fine Kaddish.

Somehow, Yankel managed to walk on his feet before
the two tormentors. The other prisoners watched him with
apprehension, and Gordon even touched his sleeve and
said, "With God's help."

But Yankel Chaimovitch was not brought back to them
in the crowded stone-walled room. Already another had
been called out, and the men feared for Yankel. Then, from
outside, through a grating, they heard his voice, "Jews! Be
of good heart!"

—A favorable sign for all of them, Gordon declared.
And he took Yankel's tallis and tfillim in his care, to bring
back to him as soon as they were all free.

⁓

For three nights Leah had taken the night watch on herself; this much was not unusual. But how long could he be
protected? He had emerged from his fever and lay drained
and limp. Yet, Zev talked. His words began before she had
even fixed the door back into place, and between swallows
of water he talked, and as he chewed his food, Zev poured
out his life, his triumphs, his wrath, returning to go over
each detail if he had omitted the smallest item; he poured
his life out to her at though he were leaving it in her keeping.

His shame at certain things he had done, women he had
misled. Even the disease of shame he told of, though while
it was on him, he swore he had abstained from Jewish girls.
And his boasting. In Alexandria he had sat with the highest, the strategists of the war. On their secret ship he had
been carried from Athlit to Alexandria, they had sent for
him, and there among the highest in the Intelligence, with
Aaron Aaronson himself, he had given advice to their generals. Thus he could tell her each step the British would
soon take. With Aaron he himself had planned the attack,
marking for the British on their map the site of each Turkish encampment. An odd Britisher was there, a pipsqueak
who wore Arab clothes, and came and went with camel
saddles filled with gold for the Arabs of the desert. It was
said that he had led some Bedouin tribesmen in blowing up

a few Turkish trains that had high officers riding in them.
Ah, Zev had told them, he could send them word when
there would be a train with Djemal Pasha himself riding on
it! And so he had done. The train was exploded, and but
for a stroke of luck Djemal would have been killed. How
did the British know that Djemal was on the train? Ah, a
pigeon flew!

What to believe, what to half-believe, what not to believe, it did not matter to Leah; there had indeed been rumors that poor Sara Aaronson had been caught because of
a pigeon she had sent off with a message, a pigeon that had
come down in the wrong place, in a police officer's dove-
cote in Caesarea. And thus she had been caught. Though
others said it was because of poor Naaman, caught searching for Avshalom. To all these tales Leah gave only half an
ear; what did they matter against Sara's death itself?

Or, it would be of his childhood Zev would speak, how,
already a boy with urges of manhood, he had spied on his
aunt and uncle. . . .

And so she let him pour out his fevers.

But soon among her girls whispers and giggles spread;
when she went out on watch, an impudent one whispered,
so Leah could hear it, "Why does our Leah keep taking the
night watch? Do you think she could be meeting someone?"

It would not be many nights before one of them would
slip out after her.

When she warned him that it could not endure much
longer, Zev himself declared he had already thought of this.
And his plan was ready. He was well. He had but to make
the last stage of his journey, and just as he had passed
worse dangers, so he would pass this one; she need not fear
for him. "Leah, you must bring me a keffiyah and an
abaya."

A keffiyah she had. But an abaya? If she were to start
asking for an abaya among the Arabs who worked in the
village, suspicion might be aroused. Then Leah had a
thought: there was her white gown, flowing like an abaya.

The next day a newly disturbing thing happened—the
horse disappeared. Doubtless it had been stolen by a deserter.

At night when she fetched Zev the keffiyah and the
abaya, and told him of the theft, he became highly upset. It

was bad luck. He would go at once, he would go on foot as far as Nebi Rubin in the sand dunes. There, with Sheikh Abu She'ira, he would be safe until the English came. Many arms he had bought from the sheikh. And that clever Arab would understand it would be well for him, when the English arrived, to have harbored such a friend.

In the garments, he looked a true Arab. At the door, Zev's face suddenly became grave. "All I said to you, of us, Leah, I said knowingly. The fever only helped me to say it."

"I understood, Zev," she said and made him a smile, but without assent.

He would return to her, Zev insisted.—What need at a moment such as this to deny him, to gainsay him? She kept her face quiet. She must not fear for him, he insisted again; two bullets had not killed him when Avshalom fell. And in the north the executioner's bullet had not killed him either.

Yet Leah saw death in him. She saw it with heartbreaking certainty. And she let him speak, and let him strengthen himself against his fear, while she held back tears, and trembled with the same tender dreadful pity as on the night of his arrival here when the man's fevered body lay against hers.

Carefully, Zev replaced the lock on the closed door behind them. Then he stood erect, still not quite able to move off into the night, and in the terrible pity she hid in herself, Leah saw that the white abaya was also like a shroud.

Zev mistook her trembling because she smiled to him. With the wide sleeves of the abaya engulfing her, he cupped her head in his hands and kissed her on the mouth. It was a tender kiss, a kiss of love, and from her despairing heart Leah returned the tenderness.

She too had brought him a loaf of bread.

When Zev's form was swallowed in the grove, Leah's old dread superstition returned over her, that like one who unknowingly carries the germ of a disease, she carried death.

By evening it was known. The entire village was in the street as though released from quarantine. Everywhere Leah heard them making gallows-jokes. The fugitive had been seized as he came in sight of the tents at Nebi Rubin. Before he could even call out for Abu She'ira, two young tribesmen recognized him, rushed upon him, felled him, took his gold, stripped him naked, tied him, and carried him triumphantly to their sheikh, crying out, "The reward on his head is ours!"

Bound and trussed, wrapped in sacking, the Bedouin delivered Zev the Hotblood to the Turks in Ramleh and received their ransom; in chains he was taken to Jerusalem where Bahad-ad-Din himself awaited.

The hunt seemed ended, true; in Zichron the elders who had been locked in the synagogue as hostages were released and allowed to go home; in Tiberias the dungeon was opened and Old Gordon led out the prisoners, singing. But Max Wilner and Tibor were not among them; they had been taken to Damascus, and of the hundreds more imprisoned in Damascus there was not a word. Not one shomer had been released, not Shabbatai Zeira in Nazareth, not Motke, not Shimshoni. Every shomer in hiding must remain in hiding.

Rumors came that Zev, revenging himself, had named the entire Shomer to Bahad-ad-Din as accomplices of the Nili, gathering arms to open the land to the British. Other tales from Jerusalem had it that, on the contrary, Zev had named no one. Who had harbored him in his flight through the entire length of the land? No one. He had hidden himself in the fields. He had bought food from Arabs. Beaten to tatters, some said, Zev had spat out his teeth in blood at Bahad-ad-Din and defiantly cried that the whole Yishuv awaited the coming of the British like a bride awaiting her bridegroom! And the Turk had shrieked, "Let the groom come! He'll find no bride for the wedding!"

A great battle was coming, everyone was certain. An oppressive fear spread. Even deserters were hardly to be seen—many had been shot on the byroads, even in the fields. Dov in his paymaster's wagon did not appear. Leah could no longer endure it; she must unburden herself, she must find Rahel. One morning she set out and walked the whole way to Petach Tikvah.

Motke's Bluma opened the door, with only a sour, mumbled Shalom. Of Motke there was no word, nothing. This was the doing of Zev, that beast should never have been left to be taken alive. Finally Bluma sent her little girl to show Leah the hiding place of Rahel.

Again, a hut in an abandoned grove, the ground overgrown with weeds. And what would you expect, finding Rahel? There at an upended crate she sat over an open English dictionary, copying out words for when the British would arrive! "To learn English is now of the first importance!" she burst out, even before all the heavy problems flooded out between them.

"No, no, don't blame yourself," Rahel declared after Leah's unburdening. "Leah, I too was unable to judge him." Suddenly Leah began to weep, in great, uncontrollable shudders, her shoulders, her breast heaving, her large face twisting, while she tried to stifle the sounds. How could she have come here to add on her foolish sorrows to Rahel's when Rahel's own mother was among those taken off to Damascus? Her friend was holding her, Rahel's small hands and arms around Leah's big hulk, and Leah felt more foolish still, but it was just everything, everything, no longer even knowing what love was, and perhaps total destruction coming, and Rahel kept soothing her, "Na, na, Leatchka, it will soon be over—"

"So—alone—" broke from Leah's throat.

All at once Rahel too had given way and was weeping. For a long, long moment, without any effort to control themselves, the two of them let the tears flow, and it was such a good cry, such an easing, until they were able to look at each other, still sniffling, and then like silly schoolgirls half-laugh at each other's red face. Jumping up, Rahel cried, "Listen! I found wonderful news! Avner and Dovidl are coming!" Running to her cot, she seized a magazine, thrusting it open, before Leah; there, underlined, Leah saw the names of Dovidl and Avner. In German. The Zionist magazine was still appearing in Berlin, and this issue had arrived half a year ago to a subscriber here in Petach Tikvah! And Rahel had come upon this item: the Poale Zion leaders, it said, naming Dovidl and Avner, were busily organizing a chalutz labor brigade in America.

—Didn't she see what it meant? Rahel glowed. A brigade. It meant they were organizing fighters! America was now in the war, on the side of the British. They would organize fighters, exactly as had been agreed upon, the night that Dovidl and Avner were expelled from the land. The two-point program. To organize pioneers, and fighters. This was a clear message for those who knew of the plan. A message from Avner and Dovidl! Who knew but that Jewish fighters were already in the south with the British, already coming near, already before Gaza!

—Then Gidon, too, would be coming! Yet under Leah's excitement there stirred again that sense of something deeply, profoundly wrong. "Then, Rahel," she said, troubled, "then it was they who were in the right—Avshalom, Sara—the Nili—and Zev? And we who made the wrong decision?"

Momentarily Rahel was taken aback. "Ours was the right decision at the time. For here, for the Yishuv," she said slowly. "Yes." Her other voice, the sharp, confident voice of a well-prepared student reciting, repeated it. "In every decision, time is a decisive factor." And Leah felt her throat again choking up with that awful feeling of helplessness, of the cruelty and stupidity of events, and of human sacrifice.

29

—IN LIVERPOOL, Herschel read from the English newspaper, angry Tommies had beat up a number of Russian Jews.

Gidon was sick of the whole thing. He would as soon go out and beat them up himself. The schneiders were not joining.

Then one fine day the Irishman appeared in the barracks, in blooming health, slapping the backs of his veterans, damn right he remembered each one! Herschel, the old rumormonger! Gidon, the old reliable! Yes, here he was, to take command of their Jewish regiment! definitely on the way! No mules this time—real soldiers! "You lads are mules enough in yourselves!"

In rapid-fire order now came official decrees. Conscription of aliens was at last a law. Either or. The schneiders would have to enroll for service with the British or the

Russians. A few days later came the military decree forming a Jewish regiment.

Hinting about even greater pronouncements to come, Jabotinsky rushed to London. Instead came a new hullabaloo. A delegation of highborn British Jews, headed by Lionel de Rothschild, had called upon the Minister of War himself. How, they asked, could the fighting reputation of forty thousand true British Jews, present in all the British forces, be allowed to depend on the dubious quality of the reluctant Russian-Jewish tailors now being pressed into the so-called Jewish regiment? Nor, they objected, should there be any special Star of David insignia! British Jews were British, they wanted no religious or racial designation! It would be like wearing the yellow badge!

Finally, they objected, why should such a unit, if created at all, necessarily be sent to Palestine, instead of being available like any other fighting force for any front on which the High Command saw fit to use them?

Jabotinsky returned dejected. These British Jewish Lordships had had their way. No, the Jewish force was not totally erased. But the word "Jewish" was to be erased. Nor would there be any Star of David insignia. At least not for the present. One day, if they distinguished themselves in the field, it would be forthcoming.

Then what was left? What were they?

Herscheleh saw the notification in the message center. "You know what we are?" he brought the news, announcing it with an exaggerated British intonation, "we're the Thutty-Eyeth Lohndun Fuzzileahs."

And he saluted smartly.

Yet the schneiders were arriving now. An official recruitment office had been opened. The great Yiddish playwright, David Pinsky, had composed a fiery pamphlet, which was sent out by Jabotinsky to the War Office's list of 35,000 Russian Jews. Some came, preferring to be with Jews rather than to be conscripted. Some came, admitting they were tired of the cold British stares in the streets. A number had received white feathers in plain envelopes in the mail. One recruit cried, "What could I do? My own mother chased me out of the house!"

No one had yet been deported to Russia. Nor, despite the overthrow of the Czar, were the schneiders eager to go back. After one of the recruitment meetings, Gidon came again upon his long-nosed friend Pekovsky, who laughed, "We're not in a rush to go back to be popped into the army there, either. The true revolution is against the war, comrade. So far what they have there is a fake revolution. We just intend to sit it out. Nobody will force us, you'll see. The Russian commanders don't really want a shipment of Jews—real anti-war revolutionists, at that."

And yet, in spite of the erasure of "Jewish" from its name, the news of a Jewish army being formed had spread to the ends of the earth, and volunteers began to appear from all corners of the Empire, even from as far away as Singapore. The newspapers reported that American Jews, too, were forming their own regiment, and were already training in Canada. Then one day Jabotinsky brought word from Trumpeldor in Petrograd. He had won the approval of Kerensky's war minister, and was raising a Jewish army of a hundred thousand!

In the midst of all this came reports of a big new campaign in Palestine. A new commander had been sent out, and this time Gaza would be taken.

A fresh panic seized the veterans from Eretz. They would arrive too late!

Sometimes, as he trained his sewing machine operators, Gidon thought that might be just as well. Perhaps those British Jewish lords had been justified in their fears about the fighting quality of the schneiders. When it came to bayonet drill, his recruits turned green. In Yiddish, in Russian, Gidon howled at them, "The Turks would rather drive in a bayonet than a bullet. You'd better get your own in first!" Mercilessly he made them lunge into the dummy and twist the blade. "All right, you can look at me as if you want to do it to me, I don't care. But learn!" Herscheleh, now also an instructor, had his own system. "What's a bayonet? Only a big needle. Push." It didn't work, either.

Even on the rifle range they had scruples. The Irishman had a special target made with a red tarboosh that moved up slowly into sight. "Look," Gidon explained, "when it comes up, like from a trench, you take aim at the lower rim of the tarboosh and hit him in the head. Understood?"

"Understood."

"So repeat what I said."

"When it comes up, I take aim at the bottom of the tarboosh, and I hit him in the head—God forbid!"

Jews!

Then, at the low point of discouragement, came the Declaration. From the Orderly Room, a schneider came running out to the rifle range, waving the *Jewish Chronicle*. Palestine for the Jews! A Jewish National Home was backed by the British governemnt!

So this was the big, startling event that Jabotinsky had been hinting about. The squads fell into disarray. Everyone who got hold of the paper read the announcement out loud. An official declaration from Lord Balfour to Lord Rothschild. The good Rothschild, Edmond.

Dancing over the field, the men were slapping each other on the back like Englishmen, shooting their rifles into the air like Arabs, yelling and even weeping. At last Gidon knew that everything he had done in coming here was right. Oh, these British! In spite of everything, how decent they were, how good they were! They understood the Jews!

Already the men were discussing: Wait, wait don't get too excited. Clearly it is good politics for them. Maybe it is all a political trick? Here, see what it says exactly. A Jewish homeland. Does that mean a nation? It can mean anything. Yet questions were raining on everyone from Eretz, on Gidon, on Herscheleh, on Tuvia—could a man really make a decent living there, in Palestine? And how bad was the heat, was it bearable? And what about the Arabs, could one live with them?

In the excitement, Gidon would have dismissed his men from drill, but all at once his schneiders leaped back into their ranks, "Come on! Don't waste time!" Never had he seen such a transformation. They couldn't wait for their turns on the shooting range.

In the following days the recruiting too was transformed. Jabotinsky's meetings were packed, crowds sang Hatikvah and God Save The King, the blue and white flag appeared in every shopwindow in Whitechapel, and even in shops in Piccadilly.

One day, receiving a new batch for training, Gidon was astonished to recognize among them his bony-nosed revolutionist. As he read out his name, Nathan Pekovsky, Gidon couldn't resist asking, "What brings you here?"

Pekovsky looked him directly in the eye. "Well, comrade, now that we Jews are going to have a nation, I bloody well want to make sure it's international."

On the barracks wall, a detail map of Palestine was pinned up. Herschel, now posted to headquarters, came running a dozen times a day to move the pins. Gedera was captured! None of their original Zion group was from Gedera, but they had a pardessan's son, Zussman, from Rehovot, and he took to dogging Herscheleh's footsteps. The day Herscheleh called out "Rehovot!" it was Berl Zussman personally who ran to the barracks and moved the pin; you would have thought he had captured the town himself.

To the south the whole night was filled with wagons, carts, cannon, horsemen, Turkish forces hurrying to reinforce Gaza, and in the midst, coming the other way, there was a tangle of wagons piled high with bedding, chicken coops, children, Jews from Ruhama, from Gedera, in flight before the battles. Now was the dangerous hour for which Eli and Rahel, Dov and Menahem had prepared the hidden weapons. In each village, chalutzim and sons of grove owners together took their posts each night to prevent pillage and murder and rape. From Eli's Gymnasia group, three young men arrived to protect Leah's kvutsa of girls. Everyone was in a fever; there was even some merriment.

Heavy early rains fell, all was mud and bog, and into this like a flashflood into a wady there suddenly came a flood of defeated Turks, stumbling and lashing and staggering past the village, leaving only a debris of wounded, of broken men and broken carts, of mud-covered crawling wraiths begging for bread.

Gaza, that had twice thrown off the English, this time was taken. As Zev had said it would be. Such force, the fleeing Turks related, had never been seen. From the enormous cannon of their warships, there at sea, from swarms of airplanes, from crushing masses of artillery brought on the railway they had built, the British had buried the Turks in fire.

And more. Dov, in the midst of the Turkish retreat, two wounded Turkish officers flung across his cart, halted for an exultant whispering. Beersheba too! British cavalry, uncountable in number, had swept around Beersheba to reach for Jerusalem. With the butt end of his officer's quirt, Dov drew it all for Leah in the mud before the cabin door, reminding her that such also had been the path of the scouts sent by Moses into Canaan: In an arc from Beersheba, up through the Hebron hills, where even today you found the same large wonderful grapes of Hebron that the Biblical scouts had carried back to Moshe Rabenu!

And Leah could almost hear poor miserable Zev exulting: Through Beersheba! Just as we told them!

Was he yet alive? Would he know, before they hanged him?

Then a whole day of emptiness passed, hushed, still as Yom Kippur.

The night too was without movement.

Then, in the early daylight, from the hill at the furthest edge of his orange grove, Smilansky came running. He had gone out to his grove. Only Smilansky would be stirring at such a time. And there, at the gates of his pardess, he had found Arabs from Nukeiba, waiting with large baskets strapped onto their donkeys—to buy oranges!

Oranges?

"They've come!" Didn't anyone understand! British soldiers were already buying oranges from the Arabs of nearby Nukeiba!

Still the British did not appear, but instead, at midday, from the north there came back a line of Turkish cannon. Children were pushed indoors. Shutters were hurriedly closed. The girls sat together in a circle on their cots and Leah tried to start them singing. The cannon were ranged on the hillock at the edge of Smilansky's grove, and now the firing began. The British were sure to return the cannonade, and the town would become a battlefield. A shellburst was heard toward the Yemenite quarter. Then, just as strangely, the firing ended. Mules were dragging the Turkish cannon back through the mud, in the ruts they had made when they came. Shutters opened again, then doors. Children ran after the Turks, jeering and laughing, some, from a safe distance, even daring to fling gobs of mud. The whole village was laughing. And the next day before the sun was high on the very hill where yesterday the Turkish cannon had given their last bark, there appeared three horsemen from the south. Soon it was a wild holiday, a Purim feast! The first three rode down into the town—

giants! they rode on high steeds, and wore broad-brimmed hats like pictures of American cowboys, and when the entire population of the village engulfed them, they alighted and stood taller than the high heads of their horses. Australians! Australians, the cry spread. The word evoked gales of laughter. WHo would have thought of this? Australians! The soldiers themselves laughed. From "down under" they proclaimed, drawing circles in the air to represent the globe, and thrusting their hands underneath. From the bottom side of the earth!

Gottenu! It was a jest! God in heaven was a jester! Australians he had sent, instead of the Messiah! Who had even known of them! Were there Jews in their land—down under! —But why show such ignorance? Right here in Rehovot there had been a planter who had moved to Australia and settled there to grow sheep; had everyone already forgotten him? Laemel Weiskopf. An uncle even remained here, old Sholem Weiskopf.

By now, more of the giant cavalrymen had arrived, and in the hubbub there came a great cry—"He knows Weiskopf." A soldier had recognized the name. "Owns a boot shop in Melbourne," he said

The town dignitaries in a body were advancing toward the liberators, led by the rabbi bearing bread and salt on a silver salver.

A young officer appeared and graciously accepted the welcome offering, making a little speech in English. Masha Weiskopf, who had been studying English (as everyone knew, the rest of the family had quietly been planning to leave Eretz to join the brother in Australia) now translated the officer's words into Hebrew. "We Australians, the youngest people on earth, are proud and happy to greet you Hebrews, the oldest people on earth!"

Applause burst out. What a beautiful speech! Several of the enormous Australian horsemen surrounded Masha to speak English with her; bottles of wine were being handed to the men, "From our own grapes! Yes! Our own vineyards, our own winery!" And all the while, a complete army was entering. A row of gray mud-spattered automobiles appeared, stretching back out of sight. Young boys were already racing down the road to count them. There were huge motor lorries, pulling enormous cannon, bigger than even the biggest German artillery. What army in the world could stand before such machines!

In the outbreak of joy, of pure happiness, all problems vanished. By evening the Australians were encamped in tents among the heavy-scented orange trees. In the town hotel, officers and councilmen feasted at a long banquet table, and in every house soldiers sighed blissfully, some with tears in their eyes, "White tablecloths! Real crockery! Home-cooked food!" Most of it, they themselves had contributed from army stores. And their eyes never left the movements of the women, the mothers, the daughters, but no one need fear. They gazed in a kind of awe, almost in disbelief.

In Leah's kvutsa, four men to each girl had collected, and because of the size of the troopers the cabin seemed about to burst its walls. From somewhere a music box with a horn had appeared, a Victrola—a scratchy thin voice sang English songs. The machine was not unknown, even in Rehovot several of the orange-growers possessed Victrolas, but to have one right here in the kvutsa—! Already great wonders were arriving.

Soon the men's voices drowned out the machine, "Ta-ra-ra-boomdeay!" they sang; was that English? Great laughter exploded at the question. Now they sang "It's a long long way to Tipperary" and several of the girls solemnly tried to learn the words. At their mistakes, there was even greater laughter. Then the girls were teaching songs to the men— "Hava Nagila"—Masha Weiskopf was trying to translate the meaning. Soon cots were piled one on the other, couples were dancing, and an Australian with a farmer's large hairy-knuckled hands stood before Leah, indeed above her, so huge a man that she had to turn her face upward to his! What a curious joy coursed through her. So this was how feminine little girls felt, always turning up their faces. How sweet it was! And the Australian roared something to his comrades that brought gales of friendly laughter, while the fellow put his arm around her waist.

"What? What did he say?" she called to Masha.

Her cavalier repeated his cry. "A real woman! A man-size woman at last!"

But what was happening, could the soldiers at last tell them what was happening in the outside world? Leah led her cavalier to a corner where Masha and another trooper sat down with them. "Jerusalem by Christmas!" Leah's giant cried, continuing to beam his broad, good-natured smile on her. "That's the order, my girl!"

Their Christmas—it came soon after Chanukah. And Chanukah was barely a month away!

"And the Jewish army?" Leah asked. Did he know? Had he heard of a Jewish army coming from England, from America? She could already see Dovidl and Avner, marching with Trumpeldor and Gidon at the head of vast Jewish hosts, carrying the blue and white flag of Zion. As they arrived, the men of each settlement flocked in behind them, swelling their ranks, marching on to Rishon, to Ness Tsiona. They freed Tel Aviv, they marched on Petach Tikvah—quickly they must come, surely the British would let them go forward first, in the forefront, to free Jerusalem.

The Australian's eyes had become dense, like some schoolboy's when he tries hard to understand a subject he has not been told to study. "Why, no, ma'am." —Why, no, he hadn't heard of any such unit. They had an Indian unit just behind them, Gurkhas, no, not Indians from America! They were Indians from India. And with this, he guffawed happily, draining his wineglass.

But there had been fighters from Zion with the British in the great battle for Constantinople, Leah said. Still the Australian was puzzled.

"Gallipoli," she said.

"Ah, yes." His face lighted, then darkened. "Gallipoli," he repeated. "That was a bad one." His own company had not been there at Gallipoli, but many an Australian had fallen.

"My brother was there," Leah told him. "My younger brother escaped from here to Alexandria, and the British made our boys into a Jewish unit, the men of Zion."

"Right you are, my girl," but he was still foggy.

"His name is Gidon," she said, and suddenly a glimmer came into his face.

"Gidon. Gideon, that's how we pronounce it. Gideon! That was a great Jewish fighter in the Bible!" He became solemn, gazing at her with a new admiration. Jewish fighters. Hebrews. The Hebrews. Gideon! Joshua! King David! Raised on the Bible, he was. Say! It was here! Right here! "David—and Bathsheba!" he cried happily. Now he had his bearings. Now he was back with this great fine girl.

With moonish radiance, he burst out into a declaration, pointing to Leah, pointing to himself.

"What does he want?"

"He says he wants to take you back to Australia," Masha translated.

Laughingly, Leah thanked him. No, no, no, he was in earnest, her suitor declared. His name was Arthur. And for some reason he brought out his soldier's paybook. Arthur Selwyn. He began to describe his sheep ranch. The man's eyes were so earnest, his face was so decent, so good—oh, if one could only embrace a life so simple, so clean, so free of the Jewish struggle.

One more desperate question, Leah tried. "And Russia? The revolution in Russia?" Had these soldiers heard any news?

The baffled look returned to Arthur Selwyn's face, only this time with a touch of suspicion—was she perhaps making a joke of him? Shaking it all off, he sprang up, he wanted to dance. "Come on, my girl, what do you say!"

Though Leah's face still held a smile, the man caught the momentary dark in her eyes. "What's wrong, Leah girl? Aren't you happy? We've got the old Turk on the run for you!"

Happy? Yes, yes, she was joyous. How could she be so ungrateful! Yet it was like being told a dear one was saved, would live, and yet knowing the fever still remained there in the body, and who knew when it might rise anew?

"Muchrachim l'hiyot sa-mey-ach!" the girls were singing, and Masha was translating, "Sa-mey-ach—it means happy. Happy, happy we must be!" Army boots stamped, the walls shook, heavy feet learned the hora, the circle swelled, bulged out through the open cabin door, "Sa-may-ach" the shout rose high with heavy men's voices roaring and the girls' voices shrilling above them, "We must be," "Muchrachim! Muchrachim! Muchrachim!"

30

ALL morning Reuven worked by himself with his mattock around his pistachio transplants, sending his helpers to other tasks as though this were something that required his hands alone. The feel of the mattock, the steady stroke of his labor, somewhat helped him, keeping down the tumult. What was done in the square he did not want to see.

But late in the morning he was called to accompany a group of high officers from Constantinople for a tour of the Pasha's gardens, to show them his rarities. And then they must tour the avenues and be shown the flowered embankments, the fountains and the long park, the great pride of Djemal Pasha. There was no way to avoid the central square.

As the motorcar approached, the sounds from the crowd rolled toward them in waves like from cannon bursts. "Yahud, Yahud," and as they came closer, "Traitors, death, death to all Jews!" Reuven sat rigid, silent. Did these officers know he was a Jew? They made a few remarks amongst themselves; he tried not to hear but heard—was he craven? should he announce, Sirs, I am a Jew? The car plowed steadily into the multitude. Gesticulating, shouting with sudden spurts of laughter and outthrust arms, people half-clambered over the vehicle, pointing with enjoyment, triumph and anger to the gibbet as though these high officers would answer their cries and at once issue the command, Hang them all! Hang every Jew!

Quite close now, the car brought them amidst the inner circle of spectators who stood transfixed, gaping as though they expected something more to happen, some added gratification.

Not high above their up-angled heads hung the two figures in long white gowns like shrouds, their heads askew as in some inquiry, but in a different way—wrenched. On the death-garments large placards were affixed proclaiming their crimes. Traitors. Enemy spies. Jews.

The boy Naaman, Reuven had not known; his round young face had a look of protesting surprise. But Zev was himself, his face excited, his parted lips about to break out with some astonishing proposal that would save him.

One of the visiting officers carried field glasses and offered them now to Reuven. Was it brutal irony? Almost absently Reuven raised the glasses toward Zev. There were flies over the dead man's mouth, in his nostrils, and crawling over his open eyes.

That night a great need came to Reuven to be among Jews. Not merely to seek out a few of those from Eretz who were, like himself, in the Turkish army; this was rather a feeling as though to stand in a crowd around the door of a shul, to immerse himself amongst Jewish folk, and it led him to the Harat al Yahud.

The street was barred—at least Djemal Pasha did not want a pogrom. Reuven's officer's uniform was enough, though he thought he heard one of the guards mutter something to his companion after letting him through.

Hardly a sliver of light could be seen from the heavily shuttered windows high in the walls. His own steps in the ancient deserted lane almost unnerved him.

At the Shalmonis' it was the voice of the master of the house himself that came from behind the thick carved door in a hesitant whisper, "Who?" In their salon Reuven saw a few like himself in Turkish officer's uniform, men he half-casually knew, one or two stationed in Damascus as translators, interpreters. Also there were a few well-connected community leaders from the Yishuv who had, instead of being sent to prison, been ordered confined to the city. And there was the brother of the exiled Nadina, the tall engineer from Haifa, Lev Bushinsky, indispensable to the Pasha. For the rest, it was the Shalmoni family, in an atmosphere of dignified calm. The daughter, Elisheva, was at her piano turning over music, though she did not play. It was in this room, with Elisheva, that he had sat with Sara Aaronson.

"Has the city quieted?" Shalmoni asked, and Reuven said, "The streets are quieter. The cafes are full."

"Here it has been quiet," the mother said.

"We are protected," the daughter remarked dryly.

"It's just as well," the father said. "Anything could have

happened. Today convinced me nothing has changed in our compatriots."

Never before in this house had Reuven heard the father even indirectly refer to the Damascus blood libel of eighty years before. Though everyone who came here was aware that a Shalmoni had been among the community leaders accused, the family did not speak of the ghastly case. The avoidance of the subject, Reuven had always comprehended, was in no way out of shame, but was rather an aristocratic silence, in the way that high-standing families did not call your attention to their wealth and honors, either.

"We have not seen you for a long time," the mother said. "I hope it must not always take an evil event to bring you to our house."

He made the excuse that he had been away on an expedition, and on their questioning told how this time he had brought back cedars of Lebanon; the daughter took a lively interest and made him tell more. Elisheva even remembered the pistachio grove he had discovered and that he had given samples to Sara. When she spoke Sara's name her voice was unflinching.

It was indeed many months since he had come to their house. Reuven had told himself he did not really feel at home in this atmosphere of an ancient, important Sephardic family; and also that this house was perhaps somewhat dismal because of the blind uncle who sat at the Sabbath table with his fixed smile of the sightless. But more truly, Reuven admitted to himself, it was because he had begun to be drawn to the daughter. It would only have brought pain.

There were far more suitable men than himself among the Jewish officers, better educated, more polished, and indeed handsome. He had seen this one and that one begin a campaign for Elisheva; a captain had even performed piano duets with her. But nothing had happened. It was declared she was engaged and that her fiancé was at a distant front in southern Arabia. This could explain her cool self-possession.

She was not aloof. In the way of finely bred people, as he had noticed, she spoke to everyone with a show of real interest in their lives—just as now she asked every detail about his trees. Elisheva Shalmoni had been educated in

France and liked to discuss French literature and music. Reuven knew little of either, and in the general conversations on Friday evenings he would often fall back on: "I must read that . . No, I never have heard Debussy."

But increasingly his eyes had been drawn to her. Today, perhaps even because of the tragic atmosphere, he let his gaze rest on her. Elisheva was indeed like a bird, delicately boned, and with a hovering air as though she might at any instant fly off. Her face was formed in the long oval of the Sephardim, with a narrow long nose that at first had seemed a flaw to him, and she had tawny hair with a touch of reddishness not unlike Sara Aaronson's. Others were always remarking on her color, seeming to find it surprising in an ancient Sephardic family, but after all in the Yishuv, Reuven remarked, many children whose parents were black-haired were being born even totally blond and with blue eyes. "My own nephew is blond, like a Scandinavian," he said, and it was his first personal reference.

Like a returning ghost, the subject of the Nili had again arisen: had they done right or wrong? Little was said of Zev; the taint was on him even now of having tried to escape while leaving Sara to the torturers.

"Sara acted like a heroine," Lev Bushinsky remarked. "She will live forever like a heroine of the Bible."

"Perhaps it would have been as well to live out her own life," Madame Shalmoni said quietly. "I do not mean to detract from her heroism."

Elisheva turned away her head.

—and even Zev had in the end conducted himself with dignity, the engineer said. He had watched it all. Zev had thrown off the guards to mount the scaffold himself, and he had shouted out his wrath, shouted that the British would hang his enemies, every one of them, shouted until the words were strangled in his mouth.

Some of the tension seemed to pass from among them, as though at last now the description that they needed to hear had been heard, the worst had passed. "See what their heroism has led to," the mother sighed. "They meant well, undoubtedly, people like the Aaronsons, but it is a danger for all Jews."

"You had only to hear the shrieks of the bloodthirsty mob," a young officer began.

"I heard them," Elisheva said. She was looking at Reuven; her face was white and he felt a tremor from her as though a bird shuddered in his hands. So that only he might hear, she whispered, "Oh, poor Sara."

"You heard them? You went out?" her father asked, alarmed.

"I couldn't keep her," the mother said.

"Spying is a part of war," Lev Bushinsky resumed, "and a spy knows the risks he takes." Arabs too had been hanged by the Turks, in Jerusalem itself, he reminded them, for spying.

"Yes, but this doesn't put all the Arabs in danger. The Arab spies simply did it for money, for themselves."

The Turkish command was particularly on edge right now, Bushinsky reminded them, because at any moment Jerusalem—

All around there was a sharp intaking of breath like a backdrawn cry of joy. "You've heard something?" Shalmoni asked, but in a neutral voice.

"I believe the British have had heavy losses, but the attack continues."

Their eyes shone, but no one asked more.

Reuven hadn't noticed her movement, but, indeed like a bird, Elisheva had lighted closer to him. They could talk between themselves. "If only Sara could have lived to know this," she said.

"Yes."

"I must be romantic—I even imagined, at the time she was here, that you were perhaps infatuated with her when she was quite young."

He was startled that she had sensed something so hidden in him, and that she had actually remembered it. Her eyebrows were a straight line, making her gaze even more direct. "Forgive me if I intrude."

"Perhaps I was, in a way. When she was just a girl. I didn't know it could be so noticeable."

"Oh, I notice things about people. I remember I noticed when you used to come here Erev Shabbat, you didn't eat meat—you're a vegetarian, an idealist." She wasn't mocking.

"Oh," he deprecated, "some ideals are not so difficult to live up to."

"You live in a commune. That's an ideal. Only—" she paused, half-puzzled, half-troubled. "It's like what they were saying of Sara. She was an idealist, but did that idealism make everything right?"

He couldn't answer.

"In a commune you share everything in common," she said, as though not quite certain what it meant, and added in an effort at lightness, "Even wives, people say!"

Reuven was a little disappointed that she should repeat such foolishness.

"Have I said something foolish?"

"You said others said it." He tried to pass it off. But now she earnestly kept asking more and more about the life they led, and her eyes became fixed on him with a kind of growing question. "But, Reuven, if, as you say, there are so many more men than women—more chaverim than chaveroth—and if all that we imagined was so foolish—then—then what do the other men do? Those that have no chavera?"

Something within him was in flight now. "Well, we are vegetarians." He flushed.

The subject had awakened such self-consciousness in both of them that for an instant she seemed to take his words literally. "Oh. You mean—" She was on the point of asking, he saw, whether being a vegetarian really diminished carnal desire! As her eyes looked into his, she grew quite red, and laughed at herself.

It was as though he caught himself up, in flight from her inquiries, for a wonderful thing in his life might be happening here, and he must not run away, he must face down his shyness. If only Elisheva would not ask things directly about himself! And that she sensed this too and now put her questions less directly was a second step in this wonderful happening. The more delicate exploration of each other had begun under the pretense of generalization.

"We women are always led to believe that for men it is much more difficult, even unhealthy to abstain. Though of course modern women see this only as a masculine ruse so that men can claim the biological need for a double standard. That's why today women are demanding more liberties. Still, though I do believe in equal rights for the sexes—"

"Yes, our women demand the right to do the same work, even to plow," Reuven said. "My sister was the first!"

"Oh, no, thank you!" Elisheva's laugh was musical, unaffected, a trill.

He was suddenly overwhelmed with longing for Leah. "Of course she happens to be large and strong, she's taller than I—" But why should this girl be interested in his sister? Reuven returned to the general subject. "I too—the idea that a woman should make free with herself like so many men—I know I could not love such a woman. But I do believe in equality, then if a man expects purity in a woman, he must bring her purity too."

He had said it, he had virtually revealed himself, and he did not turn away from her gaze. A welling up of wonderment, not yet allowed to break through for fear she might be mistaken, remained for a long moment in her eyes. But she did not pry further, she did not ask the definitive question of him. How good of her to know that it was not yet time. With a sociable smile, Elisheva turned to pick up the conversation with the other guests, as though apologizing for this tête-a-tête.

But when Reuven was taking his leave, Elisheva remarked that he must not again stay away so long, and then added that she would indeed like to see the rare trees he had planted in the Pasha's garden.

"Whenever you want to," Reuven said.

And so out of the human destruction of this war he was perhaps yet to be blessed with love. All the tormented nights throughout his younger years, all those frustrated years through which he had held himself continent so as to come unsullied to his bride, all would prove to have been the true way for a union without flaw between them. But what dreams was he permitting himself! He was already envisioning her returning with him to the kvutsa, but how could Elisheva live such a life—she was delicate, fastidious, a girl who had studied in the conservatory in Paris. Other chalutzoth, it was true, had come from homes of luxury and fine families, women like Nadina, yet when he thought of the Shalmoni house, of the richly laid table, the dishes served so smoothly you scarcely realized how they came to be there before you, and set against this the clamor of the cheder ochel, the jostling and clambering over unsteady benches to find yourself a place, the flies, the slop-pan on the torn oilcloth, and worse, the common toilet, and everyone noticing you coming out, and Elisheva was a girl so reserved, so private—

Reuven sensed all this as though the crisis had already come. He imagined her bravely trying to accept all the hard and ugly things of their life, as though he heard her final desperate cry, "But, Reuven—to have the chevreh know even when we—even every intimate thing we do in our room together—I can't—I can't!"

But somehow he would help her, and Dvoraleh and Leah would help her, and perhaps—

How foolish it was to dream so far. Yet really foolish? He knew; this time he felt sure.

Scarcely a week had gone by when Elisheva came in her carriage and found him in the garden. Reuven had not dreamed it would be so soon. He had been wondering how soon he could go again to their house.

She had indeed come to see his plants, she said, but first also—this a little breathily—she had a message for him. A man had come to the house who wanted to see Reuven. His name was Menahem. He was to be found in the Harat al Yahud in the Gelman house.

The Gelman house Reuven knew, for it was from there, from time to time, that he had been able to send word home to the kvutsa and to the family. Far less imposing than the Shalmoni house, the lower part of it was occupied by the widow Hadassah Gelman whose husband had been among the first members of the Shomer to fall. Upstairs were several rooms rented out to refugees and emissaries from Eretz.

On the second door, as the widow had instructed, Reuven knocked, and for an instant failed to recognize the gentleman who opened the door—a well-dressed gentleman, with a Van Dyke and a pince-nez. Menahem chuckled briefly. First, without explaining his presence, he gave the family news. But why had Menahem come here?

"The eye of the storm is sometimes the safest place." Despite the end of the Nili, men of the Shomer were still being hunted. But it was not to hide that he had come here. "I spent a month hiding in your cave. Now I have to work." It was his way not to say more of that month of hiding. Well, his eyes were somewhat affected, these glasses he wore were really necessary; still, they made a serious impression, eh? Good. He was here as a wealthy Jew from Constantinople, head of the Committee to Aid Jewish Prisoners.

Reuven remained puzzled.

Menahem asked, "You know Young Avram from Gilboa?"

"I heard he was here," Reuven said. He didn't personally know him.

"Avram has already made some contacts. We need a little help."

So that was it. But what help could he possibly be? With Djemal Pasha others—for example, the engineer Bushinsky—had far more influence. Within himself Reuven begged that Menahem would not ask him to do something he would feel obliged to refuse.

"Don't worry." Menahem knew Reuven's scruples. "I'm not going to ask you to eat meat." What he wanted was simple. Reuven had only to request the authorities to allocate to him a number of prisoners as day-laborers in the city's gardens. As many as he could possibly justify and even a few more. Ay, what a fellow was Menahem! "How many do you think you can ask for? A few dozen?"

Rapidly Reuven reviewed every project he had under way. Yes, he could justify as many as twenty-four men.

Menahem had already noted down a list of those who most urgently needed to be brought out into the open air. Somehow, with gold, Young Avram from Gilboa had found his way to the keepers of different prisons. He had even secured lists. The Palestinian Jews were mostly in the Chan Pasha and the Kishleh. Each name on the list was a pang. Shimshoni. Tibor. Many had yet to be traced. "Max Wilner?" Reuven asked. Menahem shook his head. As yet untraced.

Forty had already died from typhus, from beatings; some were suicides. Out of the Kishleh, nearly two hundred had been deported to Central Turkey, it was said, God only knew where. Among them were twenty-nine from the Shomer, nearly half the organization. It was rumored, Menahem said in his monotone, that they had been sent as labor conscripts to the front in Erzerum, near the Russian border. Motke from Petach Tikvah was among them—if indeed he was still alive. If there could be some way to find out . . .

His eyes were fixed questioningly on Reuven. "No, such things I have no way to find out," Reuven said. This mad brother-in-law of his could take it on himself to go all the way to Turkestan to search for them. "Max too may have been sent there," Menahem said.

"Max," Reuven repeated. All their contentions, the deep plowing, the shallow plowing, the bitterness over his long futile experiments with the potatoes—all this seemed so trivial now. What right did he have not to risk himself? "If I went myself and asked Djemal Pasha—"

Now it was Menahem who shook his head. "Reuven, you're not to risk your position. We need you where you are."

The very next morning, with a legitimate order for thirty laborers, he presented himself at the Kishleh. There, making no sign of recognition, Reuven saw two well-dressed men, Menaham and Young Avram, being escorted obsequiously from the Commandant's office, where doubtless another gold-filled cigarette pack had been left to be pocketed.

In the mass cell he now entered, with the list Menahem had given him, there rose voices of broken men, pleading in hoarse whispers. The list had even the name of Professor Shatz, the museum builder, and only by his eyes did Reuven recognize the wraith that responded. Men lying on the floor clutched at his feet. "I'll come back for you, I'll find a way," he half-sobbed.

At last Reuven led out the selected ones—a strange selection for laborers, feeble, tottering, feverish. He would have them sit far back in the garden, in the sun, with pruning-shears in their hands.

The troops moved on, others came, cannon rolled through, planes streaked overhead; it was said the English had reached Jaffa, reached Petach Tikvah, that Jews were already returning to Tel Aviv, under British rule!

The mayor of Rehovot came to Leah; a cultural pageant was being prepared, would she and her girls take part? In the British cavalry was a Rothschild, a high officer, and the town was inviting him to a feast of honor; he would visit the colony founded by his father, the Great Donor, Ha-Nadiv.

"No, not his father, his great-uncle," Masha Weiskopf corrected; she had become the liaison on all things to do with the British. "This one is an English Rothschild, the Nadiv was the French Rothschild."

"Nu, does it matter? A Rothschild is a Rothschild."

Yes, yes, gladly Leah would do it, and perhaps it should be for Chanukah, a festival for Chanukah? Indeed! the mayor agreed, and Leah began to think of it—it must be something surpassing, something wonderful. But each day she could only think—how far were they already? Almost to Kfar Saba, some said. And when would the troops of Zion come at last! A Rothschild, and other Jews, it was true, were among the British, but where were the troops of Zion? Would Trumpeldor come, she wondered. One day a caravan appeared from the south, a camel caravan without end, seeming to stretch back as far as Egypt, the animals in their unperturbed plodding appearing to have continued since the days of Joseph and the Ishmaelites. Only, instead of burdens of spices and silks, there shone from the side of each beast the reflections of petrol tins.

In the field opposite Leah's kvutsa, the caravan halted. Swarms of Arabs—no, these were Egyptians, even blacks from the Sudan—began to unload and pile up a mountain of tins, with shoutings, thunderous collapsings of giant pyramids, imprecations, laughter. And riding up, a neat, smallish Britisher in a sun helmet, carrying a swagger stick, quickly restored order. Suddenly the young Britisher shouted, "Leah! Shalom, Leah!"

Araleh!

What didn't Araleh have to relate to her! The veils of destiny were drawn aside at last! Instantly, the news of Saraleh and the baby—two now. Well and safe in Alexandria. See, he had photographs. And Gidon? Through the whole of Gallipoli, like brothers! Safe, whole—yes, thank God this much she had known, Gidon had sent a message with Avahalom, poor Avshalom Feinberg. The Nili had been caught, she related; Sara was dead, Zev was captured, hundreds were in prison. Yes, Araleh knew, he had heard in Alexandria. —But Gidon? In England. England! Yes,

for nearly a year. And had Araleh heard from him? Now
and again a letter. Gidon was well, she had nothing to fear,
he might even soon be in Eretz, he was in the new Jewish
regiment—

Then it was true! A Jewish army!

—Wait, wait! With a quieting up and down movement
of his hand, Araleh motioned her to be calm. His lips in a
twist of skepticism, he related how it was with the British.
Trumpeldor's men of Zion had been wanted and not
wanted, they had been soldiers and not soldiers; under fire
they had proven themselves, only to find that they were
auxiliaries, porters—their wives not even entitled to aid if
they were killed. But never mind. Perhaps in England it
would be different than in Egypt. Two years it had taken to
win the right to have a Jewish force. Trumpeldor had wearied and gone back to Russia to raise a Jewish army
there—

"Is he coming?"

Who knew? But from England it was at last said the men
were coming. The same commander, the Irishman of the
Zion Mule Corps, would be leading them.

Then Gidon would be coming! It was as though at any
moment her young brother would be standing before her.

"Ah, not so fast," said Araleh. They would have to come
through Egypt. That the commanders in Egypt would send
the Jews to capture Jerusalem—of this he had his doubts.
With the British—though it was promised the unit was for
Palestine, the Jewish soldiers would still be lucky if they
did not find themselves fighting in the trenches in France.
"The first time, too, we thought we were sailing for Palestine, and found ourselves in Gallipoli."

Still her spirits were so joyous, Leah could only laugh at
his doubts.—And he himself? After all, here he was!

Ah, said Araleh, he had learned his lesson, written in
stripes across his back.

—No!

Yes, to her he could reveal it, though Saraleh still did
not know and must not know. Then Araleh told her his
tale. He had learned; and henceforth to no power would he
swear allegiance, "only ourselves." Now, he was a contrac-
tor. They needed him, his Arabic was good, they paid him
well, but no one could lay a rod on him. He was his own
man and could leave.

Still, nothing Araleh said could dampen her joy. He had always been a difficult one, even in the early days of the kvutsa. And Jewish fighters were coming, it was true!

—And his in-laws? Araleh asked. The Zuckermans, she was certain, had been in Petach Tikvah among the refugees. Araleh rode off to look for them.

Where, how, could they join the Jewish army? In each village young men hurried after every British officer who rode through the street. They gathered and discussed marching in a body to the British commander. No need to wait for Jewish troops from America and England—here they were, on the spot! In Rehovot they flocked to the house of Smilansky the writer; despite his age he would be the first to join, he declared, and names were taken down. All of Leah's girls demanded to be put on the list to be nurses, even to be fighters!

A sitting was being held to determine how to proceed, and Leah hurried to the workers' house on the Tel Aviv shore. "My mother is free!" Rahel greeted her. Just before the flight of the Turks, a message had come from Young Avram, who was in Damascus trying to help the prisoners. It was because of Zev, Rahel related, that her mother had been freed—at least one decent thing he had done. "They brought her before him to be identified. 'What do you want of this old woman!' he cried out. 'This is not Rahel, it's her mother. She had nothing to do with anything. She knows nothing. Let her go!' And they let her go, she is free in Damascus!"

Then Zev was still alive. They hadn't hanged him?

"They hanged him a few days ago. With Naaman," Eli said.

Leah turned her head away.

Then, just outside, she saw a British officer, hesitating in the doorway, an immaculate, refined-looking man, wearing glasses. "Sholem Aleichem," he said, and stepped in, introduced himself: "Captain Ned—well, Nathan Hardin." He apologized if he was interrupting.

In a formal, Biblical Hebrew, such as had been used here years ago, at the beginning, the Captain explained that he was a barrister from London, and that his task in the military service was civil administration; though he realized he was somewhat beforehand, as few Jews had as yet returned, he had not wished to delay his first sight of Tel Aviv.

Soon they became at ease with him, and more flowed from this refined British Jew. A good Zionist, he knew everyone—Weizmann, Sokoloff, Zangwill, Jabotinsky—the whole struggle for the Jewish army he related to them, and with him Leah even felt free to ask about the hints Araleh had given that in the high command there was no liking for Jews. Smiling with a tinge of regretful but civilized tolerance, the Captain assured them—not really at the very top. Of course, everywhere there were bound to be some who didn't like Jews—yet after the Declaration, how could the British be doubted!

The Declaration?

The Declaration of the Jewish National Home! Palestine! At their dazed faces, the Captain caught himself up. But of course it was quite natural that in the midst of the fighting it hadn't yet been made public here. Very well, perhaps he was indiscreet, but he couldn't keep from sharing it with them. And the Captain quoted, having apparently memorized every word. " 'His Majesty's Government view with favour the establishment in Palestine of a national home for the Jewish people . . .' "

Messiah! In their own days! They were living to see it! Rahel too, Leah saw, was weeping. If Avner were only here! And Dovidl. But surely they knew. Surely in America they knew.

"The whole world knows!" the Captain assured them, beaming.

If Sara Aaronson could have known, Leah thought. And Zev, before they hanged him.

"A Jewish nation could protect this side of the Suez Canal," Eli observed. "'A great political stroke, too, for the Allies. To win the help of every Jew in the world."

—Exactly, and the point had not been overlooked, Captain Hardin agreed. And just as Jewish wealth and influence all over the world could help, so the Arabs too were being drawn into the British orbit with pledges of a vast kingdom. Just as the Jews looked to Jerusalem, the Arabs looked to Mecca, and the direct descendants of Mohammed, in Mecca, led by British officers, were already raiding the Turks, across the Jordan. Oh, he smiled in pride, the British were clever statesmen. And a certain amount of idealism must be counted into it, as well.

Why not? Could there not be good, as well as evil, in politics? Why was it more realistic to doubt than to believe? Leah asked herself. Why shouldn't she believe, and be happy?

Perhaps it would be best for the moment, Captain Hardin added, not to talk of the Declaration, not to raise excitement, until it was officially announced. Doubtless the General was holding the news back for a great occasion, such as the capture of Jerusalem.

On that very same day, when Leah returned home to her girls in Rehovot, glowing and bursting with the great news but managing to keep it within her, there was Araleh just returned from taking petrol supplies to the commander's headquarters. And there he too had heard a momentous piece of news. In St. Petersburg a second revolution had taken place, the real one. Armed workers, commanded by the Bolsheviki, had seized power!

Instantly Leah saw her Handsome Moshe among them. Free!

Oh, these were truly Messianic days!

Every few days, some of Reuven's men were changed for others, to breathe a bit in the open. Each evening in Menahem's room lists and plans were made. Young Avram and Menahem managed to be received by a certain Kadi, a whole box of chocolate-covered gold pieces was presented, a plea was made on religious grounds, and lo! they had permission to send in kosher food to the Jewish prisoners. In a warehouse belonging to the Shalmoni brothers, a kitchen was opened. Elisheva came to help, and there Reuven saw her, a kerchief around her head, stirring huge tubs of soup. "You look like a real chalutza!" he said.

Tables with benches were set out in the warehouse, and each day now, when Reuven led his men there for a full noon meal and even an hour of rest, he lingered in the kitchen and spoke with her. How good it was, he told her, to see even the most emaciated of the men in the prisons coming back to life, as decent food was brought to them.

Then, more even than the food, it was a piece of news that imbued everyone with new force. Young Avram came upon it in a German newspaper only a few weeks old that he bought at the stand in the Ottoman Palace Hotel. Great Britain, it said, had made a desperate political gesture, in the form of a proclamation in favor of Zionism. A so-called Jewish National Home was to be fostered by the British in Palestine!

Oh, if they could shout aloud, dance in the streets! Mama Gelman, working in the kitchen, flung her arms around Young Avram, and then Elisheva flung hers around Reuven. It was their first embrace.

No matter that the article went on to sneer at the crude British effort to secure the help of world Jewry by promising them Palestine while they did not yet possess it and were being thrown back with great losses. Here was Herzl's dream, a great power supporting Zionism. And not a word of this Declaration had the Turks allowed to come out! Clearly they were afraid of its effect. The Homeland would come to be!

Each day, while the men rested, Reuven and Elisheva sat together in a quiet corner they had found behind sacks of supplies. Reuven felt in a state of repose with her now, as when a delicate plant could be seen to have taken hold, and to be growing. The story that she was engaged was not true, Elisheva revealed to him; she had let it spread, she admitted with a mischievous sparkle, because it made a protection around her. A protection from whom? Oh, men and their devices.

Another day she said quite seriously, with a real effort as though she had made up her mind to overcome something in herself that was a barrier between them—that engagement tale—in a way it was not entirely untrue. No, she was not betrothed. But some other thing had happened with a man, and because of it, she had wanted to protect herself from men. Then, as one half-scornful of her naïve self, she told of how she had once fallen in love in Paris—of course in Paris a girl had to fall in love—

For a moment Reuven feared it would be the common tale, the Paris seduction, and he even began in his heart to be ready to love her nevertheless. If she had once given herself out of love to a man, it was as his own sister Leah had done.

But it was something else she wanted to tell him. "It seemed that all the while he was courting me and telling me his love, he would go home to sleep with his mistress." Elisheva uttered a rueful laugh over her own foolishness, and yet her eyes questioned him with uncertainty about all men, even himself. "You see, I knew the ways of Paris, but it seemed to me that a—he was from our own, from a fine Jewish family—it seemed to me that Jews didn't behave that way . . ." Her self-conscious laugh, begging him. What was she really trying to explain to him? "Of course I know they do. Here, my own brothers. I was silly to be so upset. Oh, perhaps nothing would have developed, and I would not have married him in any case as, aside from a girl's infatuation in Paris, there really wasn't anything to hold us together, he wasn't even musical . . ."

Momentarily Reuven's heart fell, what did he himself know of music? But she caught it up—"I don't mean educated in music, that's not important, but responsive—" This he was. And she returned to her story: "The idea that this way of behavior was so natural for a man, that he wasn't even ashamed of it—it made me ashamed. I—I'm not one to have many confidantes. But you remember poor Sara. She was in Europe then, and we were friends, and she laughed at me and said the man didn't exist who was like what I wanted. Pure. So—" Elisheva stopped, and then as one who decides to complete a confession, no matter what the embarrassment, she said, "I told Sara I would wait until I found such a man." In that moment, Reuven almost shouted out to her, "Yes! Yes!"

Elisheva had mustered the strength to look into his eyes. "If this was my condition, Sara told me, I would be an old maid. And that's what my mother thinks is happening to me. She keeps inviting all these handsome young men to the house. I know what they are like, what they all do about women. So I let them believe I am engaged."

Still Reuven sensed there was more. He must wait for her to reveal herself, before he too should reveal. It was not that she was so strictly moral, she said. Nor was it that she disdained the physical act, but—on the contrary—and it came in a half-whispered outburst—it was because such men had made something dirty and diseased of it.

Was it only this? Was her search for a pure man nothing more than a fear of disease?

"Oh no, no, Reuven, you must believe me, if I loved a leper, I would go to him without thinking of contagion. But when—when a disease comes from a degraded act of love, then it is really unpardonable, loathsome. And so, when you said—what you once said, when we discussed equality of women, about respecting your future mate—" There were tears in her eyes. They could do no more in this corner than reach their hands to each other and they let them remain clasped. In a moment Elisheva lifted her head resolutely and said, "Reuven, you know, my own uncle, Leon, the one who was born blind? Only after I was away in school, in a class in physiology, did I realize it was syphilitic."

Now a tenderness rose in him, a reverent sense of something growing between them that was altogether personal, that had no relationship to the war or their stations in life or even to Eretz. Still, her troubled sense of purity too was somehow linked to all the other plagues that were nourished by man's good impulses turned evil, to all that he himself wanted to heal in the world. Just so her greatgrandfather in the Damascus blood libel had been a victim of another human pestilence, born of the perversion of religion. Reuven felt that his entire being was growing, that with Elisheva he would enter into complexities he had never admitted into his life as a chalutz, and that this was part of the wonder of love that was at long last opening to him.

Her hand was moist in his. Was it possible for two people together to refuse the self-degradation and pestilence of the world of man? "People laugh at idealists," Elisheva said, "but why shouldn't idealists too have a right to live in their own way in this world? Even in the midst of war, Reuven—you grew gardens."

His very soul was touched and rejoiced. "You don't believe that I have been a coward?"

"A coward! You, Reuven!"

He shivered at how close he had come to never finding her, how he had failed several times to recognize his bride who sat there by her piano waiting for him. A Hasidic tale came to Reuven's mind, the tale of the Jew who for year after year sat before the gateway to the palace of the King, waiting to be admitted for an audience. At last, grown white with age, the Jew asked the guard, "When may I go in?" And the guard replied, "But I am guarding the gate from others. For you, this gate has always been open. This gate was made for you alone to enter."

Now the image came to Leah, for the festival. Eight girls in white, she would have, for the candles, and the ninth, the torch-lighter, would be weaving in and out in a pattern of flame. Oh, she would make something beautiful.

But on the days before the event, news was bad. The Turks had ceased their flight and established a strong line; the Yishuv was cut in two; none could pass to the Emek, to the Galilee—every contact was severed. Heavy rains fell, and Araleh appeared again, unshaven, exhausted. The battle was desperate in the hills. His camels were useless, slipping and breaking their legs on the wet rocks. The British cavalry was halted, he could not bring up enough water to them for their horses; the Turks had cannon high on the ridge at Ramellah and were slaughtering the attackers. A Rothschild had fallen, Major James, the one for whom the mayor had planned the feast.

Then, on the very eve of Chanukah, an awesome thing happened. Late in the afternoon, a motorcar appeared, filled with British Jewish officers, Captain Nathan Hardin among them. They came from the commander's headquarters, and they brought news of the capture that very day of Jerusalem.

Jerusalem, on Chanukah!

Who could cope with such a strange event?

The heart nearly burst with the wonder of it.

Streaming to the synagogue, the pious and even half-pious cast glances of triumphant scorn and pity, too, on the doubters and godless ones, the apicoiresim encountered on the way. So great was the joy that numbers of these atheists even came to the shul, standing at the edge of the crowd of worshipers.

—Did Abba know, Leah wondered. Surely such news must be carried on God's wind to the pious. Jerusalem, on Chanukah!

Yet it was as though God had allowed an imperfection to remain. Had Jerusalem been freed by Jewish arms on this day, could even the worst atheist retain a single doubt?

Still in a kind of puzzled, muted awe, Leah clothed her girls in the candle-sheaths. The entire population now, in Sabbath clothes, was gathered outside the shul. Long and eloquent were the discourses over the miracle. None failed to describe the symbolic sacrifice of the fallen Rothschild, surely the Yehuda Maccabee of our own time. And though willingly Jewish blood would have been given in place of each British hero who had fallen, surely by the design of the Unnameable there had been blood from men of far-off lands, of races from all the world, from India, from Australia, from Scotland: was this not a sign? Since the nations of the world had again and again destroyed the Holy City, as they had again and again carried off the people of God to slavery and exile, was it not a symbol of the coming of Redemption that soldiers from many far nations of the world had been brought here to open the way for the restoration of Jerusalem?

Such a fervor of wonder had seized them all, Leah felt some token must burst out from her, to mark the event, and suddenly she knew. Pulling aside the quickest of her girls, Shoshana, Leah instructed her to hurry as far back as the crossroad to Jerusalem, and from there the girl would come running with her lighted torch!

The eight girls in their white sheaths Leah had arranged on the steps of the synagogue. And now Shoshana could be seen from far, torch aflame. The multitude divided for her. Up the broad steps the girl ran, to where the mayor stood amongst the group of notables and British officers. Into the hands of the startled mayor Shoshana thrust the torch, crying "Yerushalayim!"

"Jerusalem is free!"

What sobbing, what exultation broke out! As though they had truly only this instant heard the news. At a whisper from Leah, the mayor knew what to do. He stepped before the row of girls, and lighted each candle, torch to torch.

Then in chorus her girls sang out the psalm of jubilation:

Were our hearts filled with song as the sea is with water,
Were our tongues loud with exaltation as the roaring billows
    of the sea—

Yet we would be incapable of rendering sufficient thanks to
   Thee,
O Eternal, our God and God of our fathers—

They were living again in the days of Yerushalayim.
Nothing had happened in all the centuries between.

Now the Yemenites began to chant and clap hands, their
women began to ululate, and the whole population jubi-
lated.

The congregation's leader, Reb Gedalia Feitelbaum, began to chant the Kaddish for the fallen. "Yisgadal," and the
voices fell in with him, a sea of solemn voices. Captain
Hardin too knew the Kaddish in Hebrew, and the unbelievers half-remembered, many women knew the words and
even children from religious homes solemnly moved their
lips.

With each word, Leah repeated in her mind a name:
first, this Major James Rothschild who had fallen; then
Sara Aaronson's name rose in her mind, *praised and exalted;* and her own baby brother Avramchick who had died
of malaria, *extolled and revered;* and Dvora's fallen beloved Yechezkiel, and Zev's name hovered there, and Avshalom Feinberg too, and the murdered American settler of
Mishkan Yaacov, Joe Kleinman, then all, all, each huge
Australian who had fallen, and the English soldiers, and
the passive, dark little souls from India, and even the
wretched, famished Turks.

～～～

All the churchbells in England, in France, in Rome rang
out the victory, *Jerusalem, Jerusalem.* In Notre Dame special services were held: it was as though the Crusades had
triumphed again, the Holy City was restored to Christen-
dom, and in the most perfect, the most meaningful time, as
a divine gift, for Christmas.

31

ONE could not yet go up to Jerusalem. The British were even stricter than the Turks. It was Yosi the sculptor who could tell of the capture of the city; coming down with Araleh's supply train "for a breath of the sea," Yosi regaled the girls with his irreverent account.

Though he did not pretend to be a military authority, Yosi said, he knew every stone in the ancient walls and fortifications. As the British fought their way up the wady, the Turks mounted the thick walls rebuilt four hundred years ago when they themselves had conquered the city. At this, wailing and woe broke out in Mea Shearim, the bearded ones calling to mind the days of the ancient Roman siege, when for three years Jerusalem starved, and, as related in Josephus, a demented mother devoured her own child.

And what Jew did not know the brutal words uttered in the face of the British advance by Bahad-ad-Din—"Let the bridegroom come, he'll find no bride."

And so Yosi had prepared himself a hiding place in a cellar beneath a cellar, had brought water there, and all the food he could lay his hands on, though more than three months of siege he could not have managed.

Then came the weeks of intensive battle for the approaches to Jerusalem. Why was it, Yosi mused in an aside, that the world's cleverest generals always selected the worst weather for their greatest battles? Napoleon had defied the Russian winter. And here the British high strategist was assaulting Jerusalem in the season of torrential rains.

Nevertheless it was related in the city that the assaulting soldiers clung to the rocks, lay uncovered in the mud, but did not fall back. And then the German commander, Von Falkenhayn himself, took over the defense of Jerusalem. A change of commanders in the midst of battle was, as even a peaceful artist knew, a bad military sign. Or should he say, for the Jews it was a sign of hope? The outcome of the looming battle Yosi knew for certain when a certain German officer, a client of his named Von Papen, came and roused him from his cellar. A fight had been raging back and forth for days on the heights of Nebi Samwil. Now this Von Papen had no time for bargaining and hastily paid, and in gold too, for one last ancient statuette, a genuine one, whose price he had for months been trying to bring down. Thus Yosi knew the siege was all but over.

Next came the day of the high-piled motorcars, carts, even overloaded camels and donkeys. Last sweeps of pillaging. And after that the day of strange quiet. Would there indeed be no crushing bombardment, no hunger? From a military point of view, after all, what was Jerusalem? The German strategist, Von Falkenhayn, had decided to withdraw and rebuild his tattered forces on a more suitable line.

And so, Yosi related, the mayor of Jerusalem, removing his Turkish tarbush, went out with a white flag along Jaffa road, seeking to surrender the city, but found no one very near. At last, in the defile, the mayor espied a British soldier darting from rock to rock. But the modest sergeant declared it was not for him to accept so historic a surrender, and sent the mayor further down the vale. After several such encounters, the wandering mayor reached a colonel who bade him wait while an inquiry was sent back to General Allenby's headquarters. At last came permission for the colonel to receive the historic surrender. Jerusalem was free.

The official entry did not yet take place, but by late afternoon shop-shutters in the souk rattled upward; in Mea Shearim, Jews were venturing out of their cellars, boys with flying ear-curls darted through the lanes, a few stalls opened—it was the eve of the first night of Chanukah. And that night, Yosi said, was more beautiful even than—than what? all he could think of was a fantastic opera-ballet with candle-tips dancing in the dark, that he had seen in Vienna before coming to Eretz. Where the Hasidim had all managed to get candles, after these years of darkness, who knew? But you walked through the lanes of Mea Shearim and from behind each half-open shutter you saw the first Chanukah candle burning. Even he, atheist that he was, was led to believe that in each house there took place a miracle like the cruse of oil in the Temple. All those tiny points of light, many of them from half-cellars and dun-

geons where the poorest lived, were, as a Hungarian Hasid
had once explained to him, like sparks of the universal soul
of God. In some of the half-cellars were the shtiblach, the
homey prayer-houses, of the small congregations; they were
packed full on this Chanukah night, and as though from
within the ground, singing arose. Courtyard gates stood
ajar, all around the yards on every floor, candle-lights
shone. Yosi had then made his way into the Old City and
followed a pair of Jews in their fur hats and long capotes
down to the Wailing Wall. Two and three deep along the
narrow stone corridor before the Wall, Jews stood, each
wrapped in his tallis, swaying; the Wall rose high into darkness, and along its base, little Chanukah lamps had been
placed, and the tips of light caught the hollow cheeks of the
praying Jews, their ear-curls, their eyes. "Ah," Yosi said,
enjoying the girlish faces with their parted lips, "on such a
night I have the soul of a Hasid!"

And two days later, Yosi had witnessed the official ceremony for the liberation of Jerusalem. It was not as though
the bridegroom had arrived to find the bride missing, he
declared wryly—it was simply as though the Jews were at
the wrong wedding.

True, a full-bearded rabbi in a fur-rimmed hat had been
procured from the Jewish quarter within the Old City
walls, and the rabbi was flanked by long-beards in their
gabardines. But what were they, as against the phalanx of
white-robed priests, and black-robed priests, and the troops
of kadis in white abayas, each with the ribbon-wound tur-
ban of a haj, and the bishops, and the Greek and Armenian
and Russian popes with broad sashes and bejeweled crosses
and silver and gold embroidery, all assembled in the square
by the Tower of David—which, he reminded them, was
after all a Moslem minaret.

And the Arab notables in western suits, and the English
bishop, and the Roman Catholics, and more friars in white
cowled gowns, and even a few Jewish notables who had
escaped arrest by Bahad-ad-Din, wearing high silk hats.

Then up Jaffa Road came the parade of conquerors, liberators of the Holy City, the generals on their steeds, dismounting before the gate. True, they might have ridden
through it, using the gash once opened in the wall for Kaiser Wilhelm on his visit, the time when Theodor Herzl had
hurried to Jerusalem for a sign that Wilhelm the Messiah

would persuade the Turkish Sultan to open Palestine to the Jews. But no Britisher would be so crass as to enter the holy area astride a horse. Dismounting before the gate, the new proconsuls entered respectfully, on foot.

And there before the Tower of David, as orations were made and tokens of honor exchanged and blessings offered and bells tolled, with a rabbi also reciting a blessing, there Yosi said, he could see a strange comprehension dawning on the faces of the Jewish notables. Why, this was a great Christian event. The Christians had returned as in the days of the Crusades, and driven out the Moslem rulers from the City of David.

—Cynic! Idiot! The girls fell on him angrily.—And the Declaration? And the Jewish army that was on the way from England? And the volunteers here in Eretz who were being officially enregistered now, to clear the divided land of the Turk? How could he be so cynical at a time like this!

"Chaveroth! Chaveroth!" Leah cried out, laughing. "Don't tear him to pieces! I happen to know that Yosi himself has volunteered!"

All the church bells in England had rung out the victory, *Jerusalem! Jerusalem!* On the barracks map, the pins had been moved from the Yarkon river-mouth outside Tel Aviv, up beyond Petach Tikvah, then back to Ramleh as the Turks seized it again, then forward again, and up to Jerusalem and down to the Jordan at Jericho.

Along the coastal plain the line bulged forward as far as Kfar Saba, and there it angled across the hills of Samaria, and reached as far as the Jordan, and stopped. So it was not all ended. There was still time. Gidon's own part of the land was still to be freed, and he could still envision himself, at the head of his London tailors, bursting into Mishkan Yaacov!

His schneiders were not so bad now. Even among them, many kept avowing, "At least they left us half of the job!" In training, the same thing had happened to the conscripts as to the volunteers before them. After a few weeks, their bodies were different; one day the feel of a rifle got into their hands.

Through the worst of the winter the front would not move, Gidon felt sure. General Allenby had learned his lesson in the December rains, crawling his way up to Jerusalem; now he would wait. And before Palestine's rainy season was over, the 38th Fusiliers might at last be on the move.

So it was. One day the Irishman assembled the entire battalion. From Herscheleh they already knew, but for the good Irishman they shouted their joy as if he brought the news fresh to them, announcing that their movement orders had arrived.

A fever of packing began, while Nathan Pekovsky snorted, "Congratulations! We can still have the privilege of dying in the Holy Land!"

Yet when they entrained to London for the send-off parade, there was Private Nathan Pekovsky polishing his buttons. "I wouldn't do this for Lenin himself," he groaned. "Next thing you'll even have me putting on tfillim."

With bayonets shining, as Pekovsky said, "like a flock of outsize needles to advertise the trade," they formed up, the mounted Irishman at their head, his medals covering his entire chest. Jabotinsky, a lieutenant now, led off Gidon's platoon, tossing back proud little ironic remarks when he could.

Ah, the Irishman cried down to him, "Josef Trumpeldor should be with us!"

"Don't worry, he's right now parading his Jewish army through St. Petersburg. He'll meet us in Tiberias!"

There in the reviewing stand was the Mayor of London himself, for were they not a battalion of the Londoners, and beside him stood a bald beanpole in striped trousers—that was Lord Balfour of the Balfour Declaration—and the most British-looking nabob was Sir Herbert Samuel, and there was the ruddy Lionel Rothschild, the same frightened Jew who had kept them from getting their Star of David insignia, cheering now as though the whole Jewish fighting force was his own idea.

And all along Whitechapel, in the windows, on the roofs, Jewish girls throwing kisses, Jewish wives weeping, children waving blue and white flags, Jewish mothers dashing into the ranks with packets of cookies. Across an entire house-front was a banner of the Jewish Trade Unions, the same fellows that had passed a resolution against the forming of a Jewish unit—"Hail to our Jewish Fighters!"

"Your old comrades must think we're off to defend St. Petersburg!" Herscheleh remarked to Pekovsky.

The surprise came in their passage across France to the Mediterranean. Wherever the train halted, morning or night, Jews appeared, girls with flowers and cigarettes and coffee. Groups of middle-aged French Jews alongside the tracks sang "Hatikvah," uncertain of the Hebrew words. At each stop the Irishman would make his speech about his pride in leading the first Jewish army since Bar Kochba!

In one city—Nancy—some Jews even called out the name of Jabotinsky, and he too made a speech—in French. And what now came over Jabotinsky! In the Italian port where they waited to take ship, Taranto, he went off with the English rabbi, their chaplain, and sought out the town synagogue, and there they unearthed an ancient Torah, to carry along, Jabotinsky declared, to protect them from U-boats!

Thus they arrived safely in Alexandria, still in time to rush to the front and free Mishkan Yaacov.

Instead they entrained for Cairo, and again the parade to the Great Synagogue, and the parade before the British High Commissioner, a General Wingate, and again the Jewish community's hullabaloo, and one-two-three they were in a tent camp outside the city. What for? For training.

How long?

"How long were the Jews slaves in Egypt?" Herscheleh retorted. If Herscheleh had no news, he had jokes.

There had not even been time for Gidon to seek out Araleh and Saraleh in Alexandria. Perhaps they had already gone home to Jaffa? But almost at once, Araleh appeared in the encampment, grinning, filled with news for Gidon, for all the old Zion men from Eretz. Only a week ago Araleh had seen Leah! In Rehovot, in her kvutsa where she trained girls in agriculture, "She's training up a wife for you," he laughed to Gidon. "She's got one all picked out." No, to Leah herself nothing had happened, though a big Australian wanted to marry her. About the rest of the family he couldn't say. "The land is sliced down the middle like with a knife." But probably on the farm things weren't so bad; throughout the whole war the Galilee had not fared too badly. No, no one could get through to them, the Tusks were solidly entrenched on their line. But things could soon be moving; he was here to buy more camels. Oh, Araleh had learned his way around with the British, he was well paid. Saraleh was fine, the children were blooming. Did Gidon and the men know—in Eretz too a battalion was forming, everybody was trying to volunteer, thousands. And what madness, what disputes! Some argued that with half the Yishuv still in the hands of the Turks, then if Jews in the British half joined their army, Djemal Pasha would kill every Jew in Galilee. And there were still hundreds of prisoners in Damascus over the Nili affair. The entire Shomer was destroyed—

Menahem—?

Araleh hadn't heard. But a few had escaped capture. Everything had to be started again from the beginning.

They remained in Egypt, training. In the damp, debilitating heat of the season in Egypt, a disintegrating spirit set in among the men. With half of Palestine already freed, why at least couldn't they be sent to train there, in Eretz?

From day to day, incidents ate into them. Each occurrence could be explained as a mistake, an oversight, an army entanglement—like the lack even of sufficient rifles. And why could they not be supplied with a Victrola for their recreation tent when the Gurkha battalion alongside had two? For the Jews, even chessboards were unobtainable! Restiveness and resentment grew, each incident became proof of anti-Semitism. It wasn't General Allenby himself, went the rumors, but his adjutant, and a whole inner circle among the officers.

From the Irishman's headquarters, Simon Levitas, the typist-clerk, a "real English" volunteer, brought a report. "Our Moses has asked to see Pharaoh." The Irishman, Simon could tell them, was an old chum of Allenby's, from service in India.

"And what was Pharaoh's answer?"

"Not Pharaoh answered. His servant, the Keeper of the Door, answered that the answer would come, as soon as Pharaoh had time to deal with the Jews."

As for Gidon, he fell back into the inured emptiness he had learned in these years of soldiering. "War is waiting," he would repeat. Oddly, here in Egypt he had been seized with an eagerness to read. It had come on him after a number of taunts from Nathan Pekovsky, who one evening flung a book at his head, "Here! Maybe something will penetrate." It was in Russian, by Maxim Gorky, about his own childhood, and to Gidon's surprise he couldn't stop reading.

The men had pooled their books, making a tent into a library, and there he sought for things he liked. Political books, theories, were not for him, and Dostoyevsky, that everyone said he should read, he didn't like—there was too much talk, talk, talk, with philosophic discussions that were meaningless to him. Pushkin—even Tolstoy—these were schoolbooks from other days. But real books about real people's lives, of these Gidon couldn't find enough. Pekovsky brought him the memoirs of Kropotkin. And the books of the American, Jack London. And also he liked books about traveling, about different places in the world, America, Africa. And a book about Palestine, too, he devoured; it had been written by an Englishman who had lived among the Druze in a house in Dahliat el Carmel near Haifa, and had wandered everywhere.

Once a week Gidon went with Herschel to a brothel, again a superior one which Herscheleh had discovered. It was French style, with a large open salon where girls of all colors, from Europe, India, Africa, hovered about in their French underwear, and you could look them over and choose. Some even sat quietly on a bench waiting without pestering you.

Gidon never felt at ease, examining girls like that, like in a slave market. Pekovsky said, and the second time, as Gidon glanced over the row, a little black girl put her hand to her breast as if to ask "Me?" so he nodded and she came to him. It went well enough; when he tried a few words in Arabic, she babbled happily. She was Sudanese, she had been here only five weeks, she was fifteen, her father had sold her in marriage to an old, old husband—with her hand she made the sign of a beard down to the floor—so she had run away— But Sudanese did not have long beards, Gidon said, and she laughed and tweaked his nose. The following week, no sooner had he and Herschel entered the place than the same girl ran to Gidon, seizing him by the hand—he was hers! This time when the servant knocked for time's up, she called a curse through the door, and even at the second knock, she sent the servant away, getting up only at the third, when the madam herself complained through the door. And the girl didn't even wheedle

for extra money. Was it really that she enjoyed it so much
with him? Oh, his Halina laughed, she could zigzig with
him all the time! And she instructed him to come on Mondays, because then business was slow and he could stay
longer.

Gidon would have liked to try some of the other girls,
but then Halina would feel offended. Only once he managed, as she was occupied when he arrived, but the next
time she pouted and scolded him, he should have waited
for her!

Still, even if this might be the way she behaved with all
her steady customers, the weekly zigzig made him feel
cheerful. Presently she instructed him that he should come
late, so as to be the last, and he would then not have to get
up out of bed but could stay with her the whole night.

Something in this made Gidon uneasy. Never yet had he
fallen asleep with a woman in his arms, and while each
time it was an effort to get up and dress and leave, it was
as though if he stayed all night he would be endangering,
perhaps spoiling, something that he should not risk, as
though he would be betraying the as yet unknown girl who
might one day be his true wife. Yet he could not stop imagining it, how it would be to fall asleep, and half-wake and
feel Halina there, and do it again and fall asleep again. At
last he gave in and arrived on a Monday at midnight.

He was spared the betrayal of his future wife. There was
a new crop of girls, and Halina was among those who had
vanished.

But even though they were enjoying the fleshpots of
Egypt, the Jewish soldiers were not content to tarry. With
Passover came still another incident. Not many of them
were observant, but Passover was a different matter, and
Passover in Egypt, while they waited to march into the
promised land—their British-promised never-never land, as
Herscheleh dubbed it—was an anticipation over which
even Nathan Pekovsky could not sneer. Yet, despite increasingly frantic applications from their rabbi, the requisition for matzoth remained unfilled. At the last moment, on
the morning of the seder itself, the Irishman with the rabbi
roared into Cairo to the Jewish quarter to buy matzoth.

Most impressively, the seder was held, with the entire
battalion at the long board tables rising with military preci-
sion to their feet to recite, "In each generation each man

must look upon himself as though he, in his own person, went out from bondage in Egypt."

Never before had Gidon understood it.

When the mess sergeant put in the bill for the matzoth, it was returned with a note that these were special rations which the men must pay for themselves. It was the last straw. Small groups of grumblers were to be seen, putting their heads together in secretive discussions. Among the schneiders there was an added bitterness, for now that the Bolsheviki had made peace with the Germans, the revolutionaries in the unit were constantly being twitted—had they chosen to go back to join the Russian army instead of joining the Fusiliers, they would now be clear of the war, instead of having perhaps still to go into battle and get themselves shot to pieces.

One morning the Irishman came bursting out of his headquarters with a face of rage, shouting orders for an immediate full assembly on the parade ground. In tones of brass he read them an order from the High Command. Since several requests for transfer to labor units had been received from his men, the Jewish battalions were to be broken up; the troops would be assigned to various labor auxiliaries.

"So you want to be slaves!" he shouted into the silent, dumbfounded ranks. "You want to remain slaves in Egypt!"

Oh, he knew the source of this order. It came from themselves! From a crew of cringing cowards among them! He did not blame the High Command, where certain officers had all along predicted that Jews would not fight. He was simply ashamed. Ashamed.

His voice had all but broken. "No, I am no Moses. Moses was one of yourselves and a Prince in Egypt. But as I stand here, so Moses stood before your ancestors. Moses knew there were renegades and cowards among them, worshipers of the golden calf, the fleshpots of Egypt, but he knew also that the greatest part of the Hebrews were good men, ready to undergo every hardship and every risk, so as to deserve their freedom in the land God had promised to their forefathers.

"I have commanded Jews. In the Zion Mule Brigade we also had the normal amount of bad stuff that you will find in any army, among any people. The snivelers and the gold-brickers. But what finally came out of that Zion Brigade was a band of men to make an officer proud. Therefore I was proud to come back to lead a Jewish fighting unit. I know that there is none, not one, among my own Zion men, who asked for this transfer. And I know that among the rest of you the far greatest majority will prove equal to the Zion men, and that, if we are given the opportunity in combat, we will earn the insignia of David that has been promised us. And that is the way it should be. We should earn it in battle. And no small group of renegades, connivers, and grumblers should be allowed to take away from you the opportunity for which so many have petitioned and waited, and which has been hailed by your people all over the world and by the whole world as a great step of justice for your oppressed people. No! no clique of communists, cowards, and anti-Semites, even if they are Jews, will succeed in destroying this unit."

Therefore he commanded all those who had signed petitions for transfer to labor units to step forward from the ranks.

Ten men stepped out, Nathan Pekovsky among them.

"Are you just plain cowards or do you have any kind of reason or semblance of an excuse? Go ahead and speak freely. I authorize you."

Pekovsky was the spokesman. "Sir," he said, "we do not consider ourselves cowards. But to get maimed or killed is just as distasteful to us as to anyone else. And to get killed or maimed while fighting for an army that does not want us in its ranks, under a High Command that uses every opportunity to humiliate us and discriminate against us, a command to which you yourself, sir, have protested as to anti-Semitic actions, that is plain stupidity."

The Irishman answered without rage, gravely. "I admit there is a degree of discrimination and anti-Semitism in the army just as there is in civilian life. And that is why we are here. To fight it. You are mistaken when you say that the army does not want you in its ranks. We are here because His Majesty's Government wants and has decided to have a Jewish force to participate in freeing Palestine. It is the Government's declared policy to foster a Jewish National Home in Palestine. The whole world is aroused and inspired by the fulfillment of God's promise, in this plan. And you men are in the forefront of it all."

"The whole world may be aroused and inspired by it, but the commanders in this area seem never to have heard of it, or they don't want to hear of it, or they want to kill that plan!" Pekovsky replied, and this time Gidon felt the entire ranks stirring. Wasn't it true? "All the way up to the top! They are all anti-Semitic!" Pekovsky challenged.

"Not at the top. You are wrong, and I will stake my army career on it!" the Irishman shouted. "I give you my word as a British officer, the Commander has not got a breath of anti-Semitism in his soul. There may be some dirty conniving in the echelons—all sorts of conniving goes on in every army—and we have got to be men enough to stick it out and root it out! Instead, what do you want to do? You want to confirm their anti-Semitic views. You want to prove for them that Jews are cowardly and shrink from battle. You should not have needed me to remind you that Moses himself had the likes of you to contend with! Now I want every man-Jew of you to withdraw his request, and I will personally go to the C-in-C himself and get this order canceled!

"Let me tell you now, you will have anti-Semitism at every step. Of course there is Jew hatred, here, there, everywhere! Isn't it to fight this that you joined the Jewish battalions? Will you turn tail at the first whiff? Let me tell you, you will be fighting the Turks in front while the anti-Semites knife you behind. You still want to quit?"

He strode closer, marched along the line, pausing before one and another of the rebels, face to face. Never had Gidon heard the Irishman so passionate, so open with his men. Let him believe himself Moses, let him enjoy the adoration of highborn Jewish ladies of Cairo, let him spend his free hours drinking whiskey with his fellow goyish officers—never mind, he was a man who had got to know the inside of the Jew.

"Who is it exactly that doesn't want you in the army? If you are not wanted, why has the High Command detailed your own leader, Lieutenant Jabotinsky—thank God he is not here to witness this heartbreaking disgrace—to go ahead to Jerusalem and recruit Jews from Palestine itself for our battalions? Why has Colonel Rothschild"—another one of the "good" Rothschilds—"been detailed as a recruiting officer for this outfit in Palestine? Why is a second battalion, the 40th London Fusiliers, on its way right now to join us?

"Do you think that I myself haven't been advised by some of my so-called friends in the service to quit the Jews if I don't want to ruin my career in the army? Do you think we didn't have to contend with the same rotten undermining sabotage from this same army clique when it at last condescended to enroll Jews even to be mule-drivers? We came out of Gallipoli with colors flying; why, the name of the Zion Mule Corps was uttered with the same respect a man gave to the King's Mounted. And I promise you when we come out of this campaign, they won't sneer about my Jewish Tailors—they'll say Tailors the way they say Anzacs!

"Now I don't know where anti-Semitism comes from. I can say this to you, I've known the C-in-C for years, I've campaigned with him, I've messed with him, I know him not only as an officer but as a man, and I can swear to you he is a man who deeply loves his Bible and has the greatest respect and admiration for the Hebrews. He has commanded men of all creeds and colors. He has no prejudice. Whatever nastiness we run into because of prejudices, if it reaches his ears, he will straighten it out at once. Oh, we'll have nastiness. An army has its nasty side. There are a million ways to undermine you. Orders and papers go through dozens of hands. A subaltern, a clerk, can turn the C-in-C's own intentions upside down. Much of the time, I know and you know, it cannot be traced. Pigeonhole this, misdirect that. You men have got to have the patience of your race.

"Now you can march out of here one day soon as free men fighting for your historic homeland, or you can go back to carry stones for the pyramids.

"What do you say?"

He halted before one of the rebels, a real beak-nosed Jew with a squint, Bobkeh he was called, a no-account, one of those who had joined out of fear of being sent back to Russia. Bobkeh's eyes darted to Pekovsky, but Pekovsky stood rigid as though to declare the proof would be in an honest choice.

"Look me in the eye!" the Irishman commanded.

It seemed incredible, indecent, that in this single moment the fate of the entire enterprise might depend on a Bobkeh.

Then, his head lowered, the same Bobkeh took a step backward as though not even to decide but to disappear into the ranks. The commander strode to the next man. One after another the rebels stepped back. A few even before he reached them. Pekovsky too in his turn. Only the seventh man, eyes averted, and the eighth with some defiance, declared they still wanted to transfer.

When the ranks were dismissed, those two hurried to make their packs. The camp atmosphere had changed; even the other eight rebels stayed aloof from the "traitors"; without a goodbye they disappeared.

Morale became better. Chaim Weizmann himself appeared on a visit; Herscheleh reported that he was on a journey to Arabia, to meet with the Emir Feisal who had risen with the British against the Turks, and to make a treaty over Palestine. With Weizmann came Aaron Aaronson from the Intelligence Section.

In level tones, Aaronson related to the assembled men how the Turks had tortured his sister, and his father in her sight, until Sara destroyed herself.

Gidon believed he had seen her once. When he had gone with Reuven to Aaron Aaronson's experimental station in Athlit, had she not been there? And on that night when he had swum to the ruins and left a message on the plow handle—perhaps that same bit of paper had come into her hand. For an instant there came over Gidon a shock of long-delayed fright. How lucky it was that he had not included, as he had wanted to do, some word, some sign, for the family at home. They too might have been drawn into it all, his own sister Leah like that poor Sara Aaronson.

And the other one, who had come, here in Egypt, to see Josef Trumpeldor—Avshalom Feinberg the poet, all excited and sure of himself, with his great plans for a landing! He had even taken back gifts for the family.

When Aaron Aaronson finished telling his story, Gidon had an impulse to go up to him and say who he was, and that it was he who had left the message at Athlit. Yet he held back. Something about the famous scientist, something in the way Aaronson spoke, made him hold back. Though Aaronson had spoken before everyone of the whole tragedy, it still seemed to Gidon that if he came up to the man, he would be intruding on a private sorrow. When the scientist spoke it was like a report, almost as though it had not happened to him, and yet if you went up and talked to him it would be different.

The Irishman was speaking now. "These were your forward scouts, behind the enemy lines. It was their mission to face the enemy before you, and how nobly they fulfilled their task! They were Jewish soldiers, men! They were the first of you!"

After being dismissed, the men spoke little of the Aaronsons. Why was it? As though some curse would be awakened by speaking of their fate.

32

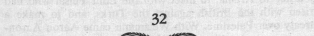

CEASELESSLY Menahem brooded. He must get the prisoners out, he must bring them back to Eretz, why else was he here in Damascus? And in the end, with Young Avram, he devised a plan. There was a railway hospital car that brought wounded and sick soldiers from Samekh to Damascus and carried them back when they were well. Into that car, disguised as recuperated soldiers, prisoners must be smuggled.

On the hospital car rode a German doctor whom some believed to be a Jew, though he never spoke of it. Menahem had made his acquaintance when the German fliers were stationed in Gilboa.

Young Avram was now on such good terms with the prison commander who consumed cigarette-packs of gold, that the Prisoners' Relief Committee was given approval to send in its own physician. This was a well-connected Jewish doctor of Damascus who even secured permission to send sick prisoners to the military hospital. From there, when cured, they were expected to report back to the prison. It would be a simple matter for an officer in uniform, such as Reuven, to take the discharged patient and escort him, instead, to Mama Gelman's. And at Mama Gelman's he could change from his prison clothes into an army uniform, ready for repatriation to Palestine in the German doctor's hospital car.

Records were scant, confusion was great. Still, Reuven reflected, it was technically a betrayal. But it was not, Elisheva argued, any sort of military betrayal, it was merely the saving of life. True, if there should be an inquiry, Reuven's head would fall. It was this risk that made him feel worthy of the joy that had come into his own life.

At Mama Gelman's, German uniforms were made ready, as well as identity papers prepared by Young Avram's expert hand. Once Reuven brought the prisoner from the hospital, he was turned into a soldier, then Elisheva would go for a stroll with him, a loving couple parting tenderly at the railway station, where the German army doctor would slip the lucky man into the hospital car. At Samekh the soldier would descend, walk to Dagania, and remove his uniform. Thus several surviving members of the Shomer were returned to the Yishuv.

Passing one day through the corridor of the military hospital, Reuven stood aside for the cart bearing the night's cadavers. Something caught him back. Not so much a sound, it seemed to him later, and not a movement—he could only describe it, when he spoke of it to Elisheva, as a sign of life. Hurrying after the cart, to where it had been left standing by the rear door, he leaned over and saw three cadavers, tangled heaps of rags with tangled clumps of hair and beards, through which one could make out a patch of emaciated cheek, a desiccated pair of lips. There he recognized the remnant of Max Wilner.

The body was but part of the cart-heap of wasted bones, but the forehead gleamed, even larger than before under the taut skin, the hair having far receded. As Reuven leaned over the cadaver the tongue seemed to touch between the dried lips, and Reuven whispered, "Max? You live?" In a whirled ferment of anguish and memory and grief, their animosity and strife and all they had nevertheless done together, all merged now in Reuven into a surge of will that this comrade-antagonist must live, must survive. The intelligence packed there behind the high forehead, how could it cease to work? Then under his hand, on Max's brow, Reuven felt the warmth of that determined brain still functioning.

The eyes slowly opened, and recognized him.

All that had ever stood between them was dissolved.

Fearful to leave Max even while fetching a doctor, as

though the current of tenacity to life depended on his remaining close, Reuven at last managed to catch the attention of an orderly down the hall. Eventually a weary doctor appeared. This afterbreath of life happened sometimes in typhus cases, but the man would die anyway, he said. Yet, insistently, Reuven got Max removed from the death cart, returned to a bed, tended.

—What had they fought over? The depth of a furrow. The buying of a water pump. How small this seemed, Reuven told Elisheva, beside the new sense, the exquisite sense, of brotherhood that had engulfed him in Max Wilner's miraculous return to life. All these divisions in life, arguments, splitting into factions—"When we get home, if we can only remember, and stay together . . ."

"Yes," she said, never moving her eyes from his face. "Reuven, it's certain? When you go back, you'll take me?"

From the happier air of her daughter, Mme. Shalmoni had already understood, and though not overjoyed, she was not hostile. Every effort had been made to put a suitable match in Elisheva's way, the years ran swiftly, and in the Sephardi community Elisheva was already viewed, though with puzzlement, as an old maid. Well born, attractive, with Parisian chic, an accomplished pianist—what was wrong? "Modern girls are choosy." Her mother resorted to that common excuse. "On a modern girl a match cannot be forced." But still . . .

And so Mme. Shalmoni did not discourage what she saw happening. Though Reuven was an Ashkenazi and from a small settler's family, it still could be pointed out—as she managed to pick up from among the Palestine refugees—that an uncle in Russia was a man of importance, the owner of a sugar mill. Even if, with the revolution in Russia, the uncle probably was rich no longer, still . . . And Reuven himself was a very serious young man, an officer and a favorite with Djemal Pasha himself. The Shalmonis had never been followers of Herzl, yet Eretz Yisroel was in their hearts. Moise Shalmoni had believed rather in the method of Baron Rothschild, in the gradual establishment of settlements without upsetting anyone. But see, the Zionists had actually succeeded in securing a Declaration from the British. And though Moise Shalmoni was in no way disloyal to his country, still, if the British should, after all, with the American colossus at their side, complete the victory in Palestine, it would be useful to have family connections on that side too. In the future it would perhaps even be men like Reuven Chaimovitch the idealist who would be influential, just as in Russia it was now the revolutionists, the laborers and peasants who ruled. It wouldn't hurt, Moise agreed with his wife, to have a link amidst the socialists.

Sara Shalmoni led her daughter Elisheva into discussions. Yes, she was deeply interested in Rueven, the girl said, in that modern way that answered but didn't answer you. In his kvutsa in Palestine, Elisheva said, Reuven was conducting agricultural experiments. Though he had never had the education of an Aaron Aaronson, he had great gifts as an agronomist. He had discovered ancient pistachio trees in the forsaken wilderness and transplanted them, and "Do you know, Reuven was the first to raise potatoes in Palestine when all the other agronomists, even Aaronson, had failed!"

"Since when are you interested in growing potatoes?"

If it had not been for the potato crop, half of the Yishuv would have starved to death in the plague of locusts, Elisheva informed her.

The mother was not really a creature of prejudice. After all, was raising potatoes so very different from dealing in dried figs? And this Chaimovitch had created a garden of wonders for Djemal Pasha. With the help of the Shalmoni family, he could perhaps be sent to France after the war to study agronomy, and become as famous as Aaron Aaronson.

"Oh, Reuven wouldn't go away to study unless his kvutsa sent him," Elisheva said, and tried to explain to her mother how life was lived in a kvutsa.

Sara Shalmoni was troubled. "But are you marrying him or his kvutsa?"

Indeed Elisheva was still a little frightened about her ability to live such a life. About joining her life to Reuven's she had no question, yet it would also mean joining her life to that of his entire group of chaverim. Logically, Elisheva asked herself, was that so different from the usual form of marriage in society, where you accepted your husband's family and the society he moved in? As Reuven explained, a kvutsa was like a family, only somewhat larger . . .

The most difficult part for the women, he said, was in regard to the children, for in the kvutsa, though of course the parents were the closest to their own children, still the children belonged to the whole kvutsa. The kvutsa even decided when and who should have children.

Yes! she agreed. Yes. To change the whole structure of society! The family was a tyranny too. Look at her own family. Her eldest brother had accepted an arranged marriage and compensated himself by keeping a mistress. Her second brother was miserable in the family business.

But another thing made Reuven worry about her. "So much of your life is music. We don't even have a piano in the kvutsa."

"Why, I'll bring mine!" Elisheva said. The Bechstein was her very own, a homecoming gift when she had returned from Paris.

"But, you see, in the kvutsa it won't be your own. It will belong to everyone."

"Of course! Why not!"

And if someone else wanted to use it just when she wanted to play on it! "Reuven, my dear one, I'm not a baby. Only one thing I must tell you—"

"What?" He was a little worried.

"I refuse to become a vegetarian!" And her laughter sang out.

But one thing she did ask of him, with a certain shyness, and only for the sake of her family. Could they have a conventional wedding here, with a rabbi and all?

When Elisheva made known to her mother that a wedding was in order, Sara Shalmoni began again with her optimistic plans of what could be made of a man like Reuven. As soon as the war ended, Elisheva could go with him to France for his studies. "But, Mama, we will live in his kvutsa." Now it was Mme. Shalmoni's turn to protest. A commune! Did Elisheva with all her clever learning know what sort of a life that meant? Like the Bolsheviki in Russia! The women were common property. Men and women bathed together naked in the communes in Eretz Yisroel, she had heard it from the banker Raphael Yeshayahu himself, in exile here. And as in a kvutsa they never knew who was the father of a child, the children were raised in a separate house, like orphans.

It didn't help to laugh. "Mama, does Reuven seem like a man who has led such a life? His own sister is married and lives in a kvutsa—you have met her husband, Menahem, and they have two children—" Her mother was not convinced. In the commune, as there were not enough women, a chavera was expected to belong to several men—

"Mama!" She could hardly talk for laughing, and then her mother was hurt, and so to assuage her, Elisheva told her something she at once felt she should not have offered even to her mother, but it was done. "Do you want to know the truth about Reuven? He is almost thirty years old and he has kept himself—as a woman tries to keep herself. He has waited to find the woman he loves." Angry at herself for having revealed Reuven's most intimate privacy, she broke into a sob.

An astonished softness came over her mother's face; the face became younger, and some deep longing, rising up from her girlhood, came into it. "In the old days," Sara Shalmoni said, "you know boys and girls were betrothed early, and they were married very young, so that for the boy too—his betrothed was the first. And among our pious men—you see, that is why it is a sin for a man even to look at another woman than his own wife. That is why they turn their heads away, so as not to be tempted." She sighed. "The truly pious ones, they lived their whole lives together, one man, one woman."

As it was in time of war, it was quite understandable that the Shalmonis should hold the wedding festivities on a modest scale, even as Elisheva insisted. But yet it must not seem they were in any way disappointed in the groom, and therefore Sara Shalmoni decided exclusivity would be invoked; only the oldest and most distinguished families would be invited, and word would be discreetly spread that Djemal Pasha himself would attend. On the first hint, "Surely your Reuven could ask him," Elisheva fell into a silent anger and would not speak to her mother for two whole days. Then she declared there would be no wedding at all, she would go off and live with Reuven in his kvutsa as many other couples did, unmarried. But when Reuven got out of her what was troubling her, Elisheva was astonished to find him unperturbed. "After all, if we are going to do it for your parents, why not do it as they wish?"

One day the Pasha came to the garden in a good mood. The Bolsheviki had taken Russia out of the war! Now all the forces could be turned against England! Presently Reuven remarked that he was about to be married and would be most honored if his commander would look in on the festivities.

The Turk gazed on him with a growing leer, as though for the first time he accepted Reuven as a complete male. "You are the only Jew who has never asked me for anything!" he declared.—And whom was Reuven marrying? Into the Shalmoni family! Djemal Pasha whistled, and stared again at Reuven, as though searching for some mark of concealed but amazing prowess. Who could comprehend the Jews? A nobody from Palestine—and the Shalmonis.

Now, Reuven said, he would even ask for something more. Could his family in Palestine receive travel permits to come to the wedding?

All went well. In Gilboa there was not an opposing voice to Dvora's being given leave for the wedding of her brother Reuven, particularly as this would be an opportunity to send with her the last of the hidden napoleons, desperately needed by Young Avram and Menahem in their rescue work. As to the children there was considerable discussion, for though a reunion with their father was of importance, the metapelet felt that such a drastic change of environment, with the introduction to a wealthy bourgeois manner of life, would be altogether upsetting to them, especially at their impressionable age.

Even leaving the children behind, Dvoraleh later thought, was to the good, for after the self-consciousness of the first hours, the meeting with Menahem was like a renewal. Never had they really been together like this, almost secretly, in the privacy of the room from which Young Avram had departed, and in a large city, with its wondrous gardens, and elegant shops and the lively cafes to which Menahem took her. Here for a time you could almost forget the war. And the sumptuous home of the Shalmonis. It was even richer than the great house of her uncle in Cherezinka.

Though all longed for Leah—oh, how she would have enlivened things—with the land divided in two, it was sadly doubtful if she even knew of the marriage. And Yaffelah too, who had gone with Leah to her kvutsa before the arrival of the British and had of course been unable to return home, oh, how she would have loved to see Reuven married. It fell to Dvoraleh then to be closest to Elisheva, and tell her from a woman's side about life in the kvutsa, and this too was good, for they took easily to each other and would sit for hours while Elisheva asked endless questions and Dvora replied with the simplest frankness. Only to Menahem Dvorah revealed some doubts. "Elisheva wants to, she has the greatest good will. But I don't know. It will be hard, hard for her."

As for the mothers, though Sara Shalmoni was not really taken in by the bits of information Feigel at once began to let drop about the importance and wealth of her side of the family in Russia, she soon perceived what this woman's life had been like in coming to Palestine with a large brood of children and little more than the clothes on their backs. She decided that Reuven's mother was a real heroine. Yes, a real person. Yet Mme. Shalmoni determined that she must in some way protect her own daughter from such hardships. Perhaps, she suggested to Feigel, Reuven would agree, for the sake of the good it would do to Eretz Yisroel, to go to Europe and study agronomy? Perhaps his mother knew a bit how to manage him? "Oh, he's stubborn," Feigel sighed. "Gentle, but more stubborn than a mule."

"Exactly like Elisheva."

"Indeed a pair."

Both sighed. Though Sara Shalmoni's was not a sigh of resignation.

As for Yankel, just as he had known for twenty years in Cherezinka how somehow to retain his dignity in the rich house of his brother-in-law, so here. He spoke little, but not deferentially. These Sephardim did not intimidate him. Perhaps they smiled behind his back at the Russian Jew who had become a peasant; at one meal, the talk turned to the plague of locusts and he let himself be led on and told the whole story of the battle to save his pardess. Now the trees were bearing fruit. After that, it was all easier.

The smoothest of the new family relationships turned out to be that between Elisheva's brothers and Reuven's brother-in-law Nahum. This young man could move to Damascus tomorrow and go into business with them, one of the brothers chortled. "And how long," Elisheva whispered wickedly to Reuven, "would it be before Nahum took over the business?"

Though it was "for the families" that they had brushed aside their resistance to a ceremonial wedding, when it took place they admitted to each other they were not sorry. The entire Jewish community of Damascus crowded into the great synagogue. This wedding had become an expression of a whispered hope, for here a member of one of the oldest families was being married to one of the new Jews of Eretz—and wasn't this a sign?

When Reuven was led up to the chupah between her father and his father, and while Elisheva, a white dove, was led around him by the mothers as though winding and binding them together, he experienced an elated sense of annealment to eternal ways. He did not stamp on the wineglass, but simply pressed it down; he saw her eyes through the veil and knew she understood the more intimate meaning of the breaking of the goblet and why he had done it gently.

The festivities had not tired them. They mounted to what had been her own chamber, facing the inner courtyard with its fountain. In each was a kind of vow, a prayer that nothing should mar the culmination.

From the barracks talk of men, bragging or filthy or even longingly sentimental, from solemn male arguments about just how to bring a woman to the point of ecstasy, Reuven knew that the principal thing was not to be hasty; he had heard so many jokes about the quick ejaculation, and about the woman left lying unsatisfed. But he was certain he could control himself, in all these years had he not held back, held back, and almost always conquered his urges?

How thoughtful of his dear one—she had changed her room for him! The feminine things were gone, the frills and the delicate colors, the curtains were different and—as he noted it, Elisheva buried herself against him—a large bed replaced her maiden's bed. During the long kiss his fingers sought to undress her. "It's too complicated," Elisheva whispered and slid away to her bathroom. It was for him now to undress and Reuven did so in haste so as to avoid any awkward moment, then lay down on the bed; she did not make him wait but flew out to him; in the lamplight he only glimpsed her nudity and she was quickly against his body.

Without the foam of her clothing, her form was so slight, the small breasts, the little naked feet, the smooth fragile limbs like a gazelle's, his palms ached with tenderness. Then Reuven felt through the length of her small body a slight involuntary shudder. As though to apologize for it, she clasped herself closer to him. It must have been when she first felt his member against her. Her mouth clung to his in ardor, in desperation, and she drew him over upon her. But he could not enter. They murmured endearments, "I know," "I'll try not to hurt," "Don't worry about me, my darling," even with a touch of sophisticated laughter, "I must have waited too long." He must not press, he must only let her feel the touch of it, and the tenseness there would relax, and just as a flower does, her petals would slowly fold back and open to him. As Reuven imagined this, an uncontrollable throbbing came, and the sperm. In the same movement, her body shuddered, but her arms tightened around him while she half-moaned, "No, no, don't be sorry, it's my fault." And it was she who recovered first, was able to make light of the accident. They really were both such innocents. Yet Elisheva was conquering a repulsion, he sensed. She lay quite still, the spent fluid on her thigh; awkwardly he hurried to bring a towel. Then they lay side by side and tried to make light of it. Her hand lay over her sex as in famous paintings of nudes. A thought of how stupid he was came to Reuven—surely he had known he must first arouse her. But she had been so ardent. Softly, Elisheva began to laugh. She was watching his member as it slowly of itself rose. Reuven too began to laugh. Still the consummation did not easily take place; she whispered "I'm trying," and he entered with the greatest caution, waiting after the slightest penetration for her muscles to become accustomed and to relax. It took a long while, but a great sigh of relief, of accomplishment, arose from both, and within the wondrous pleasure an enormous relief that though each had waited so many years, everything was well. They lay still, hands clasped. After a moment, Elisheva raised herself and said, "See, there's even a little blood. No, no, darling, it didn't really hurt. In the old days, a servant would hurry out with the sheet and show it to all our relatives!"

But then, despite her bravado, a dreadful thing happened. A whiteness came over Elisheva. She tried to hold back, she sat, rigid. "What is it, dear one?" he cried tenderly, alarmed, but she had slipped out of bed to her bathroom. Reuven too rose from the bed and half-crossed the room, hovered, asked if she was well, and felt an anger at the course of civilization in man that could even mar the beauty of so wondrous and long-withheld a natural experience. He heard the tap-water. At least she had not fainted. He must be watchful, Elisheva was so delicate. In a few moments she came out, reaching for his hand, her body still seized at moments by small shudders. "Forgive me. I'm so ashamed. It must have been the champagne." They were both able to laugh a bit. Then they lay tenderly with their arms around each other and knew that they really were married, that they could love each other, even in touches of ugliness and inadequacies of the flesh. Slowly Reuven began to feel eased. It was like this really to be loved, to be wed. They slept peacefully together.

Their lovemaking became better, even bounded into playful lust, to little perversities that they explored still with a bit of shame, though sophisticated enough to know that such delights were common.

Those months, into the summer, Djemal Pasha permitted Reuven to live at home, and the months passed as though some divine dispensation had been made for the married couple to be absent from the world of horror. Even the war in Palestine seemed to drowse.

33

THE NIGHT long, in open flatcars, passing through the Sinai, who could sleep? All was eerie emptiness, the sands as though made of mist, and at intervals from near or from far-off, who knew, a camel-bell, or a chanting. And at one time, on the ridge of a dune not far from the rail line, a long caravan in silhouette, returning the other way, to

Egypt. "They always go at night so as to avoid the heat," Gidon explained to a cluster of Whitechapel Jews.

Inevitably the Bible experts had to remark this must be in reverse the path of the Ishmaelites carrying Joseph into bondage, and Nathan Pekovsky's sarcasm had to emerge, from the heap of men huddled together against the night cold, "Nothing has changed, brothers—bondage it is, whichever way they carry you."

But few were in this mood, perhaps not even he. "It took Moses forty years, and we pass in a single night," a schneider singsonged in wonder. Another, half-religious, said in considerable awe, "Look. From the engine, a pillar of fire." And when daylight came, he pointed to the puffing smoke. "A cloud by day."

Tensely Gidon with Herschel and Tuvia watched for the first sign of the settlements. The schneiders too were now infected with this eagerness. As strips of green appeared beyond Raffa, they asked, "Jewish?" No, these were Arab groves. Then, after the next patch of emptiness, "Jewish?" Approaching Gedera, Gidon pointed. "Jewish, Jewish, ours," and they gazed.

Some men began to sing to the tune of "Tipperary," "It's a long, long way to Yerushalayim." Then you saw more and more red-tiled roofs, real houses, they were approaching Rehovot, and suddenly a pair of small boys came running alongside the train yelling in Hebrew, "The brigada? The Jewish Brigada?" From fields near the tracks, men and women came running, others on mules, riding alongside as long as they could, calling out questions, names. At any moment Leah might appear—hadn't Araleh said she was now near Rehovot with her girls' kvutsa?

Then Gidon saw a girl, a girl with bare feet, her braids flying, riding a good horse. She wasn't one of the daughters of grove owners, that couldn't be. How she rode! Gaining on the train! All the men calling to her! Close enough now so you could see how her cheeks were flushed. Her eyes so clear! And she sang out a great Shalom to them, calling over and over the old familiar phrase, "all honor to you"— "Kol hakavod! Kol hakavod!"

Her voice had the freshness of her face, her bare arms; the one glimpse of such a girl made his whole heart glad. Gidon even recalled Araleh's half-jest, "Leah has a girl picked out for you!" And why not, why shouldn't this be one of Leah's girls! Gidon tried shouting to her, "Listen! Do you know Leah? Big Leah? The one who runs the girls' kvutsa?"

For an instant he was sure the girl was trying to race closer to him to hear what he was asking, but all the men were calling out, gesticulating, laughing, throwing kisses to the girl; the train swerved where she couldn't follow, and she turned to gallop back with her news to Rehovot.

Leah, and with her Yaffaleh, and all the girls, half the village carrying wine, cakes, fruit, with children running ahead waving little blue and white flags, were already crossing the fields to where it was rumored the men would be encamping. "I think I saw your brother!" the mounted girl cried out. "I think I heard someone ask for Leah." And in the same breath she answered questions from all sides. "Oh, all fine-looking! All handsome!"

Aviva was indeed the one Leah had hopefully picked out for her returning brother Gidon, and so constantly had Leah and Yaffaleh spun the girl tales of the heroic Gidon, of the time he had remained alone on the hill to guard their entire village, of his magic way with sick animals, that Aviva as she galloped alongside of the train might even have had a romantic notion of catching a first glimpse of her destined one. Daughter of one of the early "fighters for the Hebrew language," a Jerusalem schoolteacher named Rabinowitz, who had changed his name to Yerushalmi, Aviva had been sent down to Leah quite definitely so she might prepare herself one day to become a settler's wife. A girl of such openness, such immediate warmth, she at once took everyone's heart.

On this day all the girls were brimming with the wildest anticipation. For several months they had flirted and danced and been pleasant with the British and Australians—and been tempted as well—for the men came so achingly hungry for a scent of decent girlhood they were ready to fall in love and even to vow to become Jews and remain in the land. Endlessly the girls had whispered and confided amongst themselves and restrained each other's impulses, while Leah exhorted, "Wait till our own boys arrive." She herself had had difficulties with another great lump of an Australian who came and sat and stared at her and sighed. Even Yaffaleh, always the last to be asked to dance by the foreign soldiers, let herself dream of the time when the Jewish army would arrive; she always pictured them as marching into Rehovot with Josef Trumpeldor at the head, riding on his horse. More she did not dare.

Detrained in the dusty Arab town of Lud, the men were marching under full pack, but briskly, on homeland soil at last. It was a lengthy march, but as they approached a large army camp across the Jerusalem highway the wave of welcomers surged toward them.

Nearly four years Gidon had not seen his sisters. With the huggings and blurtings of news and outbreaks of laughter, there was already a sense of resumed connection with Leah, as though never broken, and the sense of some tender, puzzled response to Yaffaleh, now become a stubby, thick-legged girl with heavy, enormous breasts, who could find little to say but kept very close to him. In the midst of recognitions on all sides, Gidon's eyes kept wandering to catch sight of the girl he had seen on the horse; that Aviva was her name he already knew from Leah, for—as though fatedness had laid a second finger on him—she was indeed one of Leah's girls.

"On the horse, yes! She told me she recognized you! I said look for the most handsome . . ." Leah called out, "Aviva!" and there was the girl in a circle of men, but her eyes at once spoke to Gidon, Wait, wait one moment, it's you I'm coming to!

"Leah has all her girls ready to fall in love with you, but I know which one it will be," said Yaffaleh.

He gave her another hug. Gidon wished he could say something easy to Yaffaleh, about all the boys falling in love with her, but already there had come a heaviness he remembered from when she was a child. "Isn't Trumpeldor leading you?" had been Yaffaleh's first cry just now; it was as though a promise had been broken.

Again Gidon asked about Mameh, Abba, about Eliza's baby, he still could not imagine beautiful Eliza married to Nahum the butterball. And Dvora's little ones? And Menahem? And all at once Yaffaleh's eyes met his in such a way that an enormous protective pity welled up in Gidon, and he felt it was for her he had come home. Beyond all the patriotism and Zionism, this sister somehow desperately needed him; though he didn't understand what it was that was lacking, he must try to help her, if a brother could.

In this camp, word spread, they would remain only a few days before leaving for the front lines. For months in Egypt they had pressed for it, even the reluctant Bolsheviks had caught the impatience, as though to confront the worst and have it over with. But now Gidon wished there were more time.

Though dead tired, that same night several of the boys walked with him to Rehovot. Leah's cabin was a bower of climbing, flowering vines. The girls had put on freshly ironed dresses, and done up their hair. A Victrola played, not the eternal "Tipperary," but music.

Aviva sat down with him and his sisters, and soon they had Gidon relating his experiences. At the other end of the room a hora began, and Leah took Yaffaleh to join. Then Aviva unfolded a sheet of paper. "Yaffaleh wrote a poem for your homecoming," she said.

"But why didn't she give it to me herself?"

Aviva smiled and began reading the poem. It was about the tiniest things of nature that you never noticed, a tiny snail, a pebble pearly with dew, and today each tiny thing glowed to her "for my brother is coming home."

On the last words, Aviva lifted her eyes to his, and he knew she was already one of the family, she understood all his tenderness and apprehension for Yaffaleh. The poem brought back a moment long ago when he was sitting by the Kinnereth fishing, and Yaffaleh, a child, plump, her skin always a bit sweaty, suddenly dumped herself into his lap and whispered, "I love you."

—Poor Yaffaleh Aviva was saying, things would be difficult for her, not really because she wasn't the most beautiful of girls—other girls no better-looking were sought after by men—but because Yaffaleh was over-sensitive. "She doesn't know how to take things in an ordinary way, everything has more meaning for her. Even if she were a beauty, she would suffer. Perhaps even more." Aviva had put into words what he felt. They glanced at Yaffaleh dancing in the hora, but the moment the circle broke up, she would be by herself. Again Gidon felt the aching need to help Yaffaleh, but now there was a stronger ache in him, to draw close to this girl beside him and hold her. He wanted to say how from the moment he saw her racing alongside the train on the horse . . . But Aviva herself started it, laughing—Had he noticed her on the horse?

And then it was easy, he even said it to her—about his feeling from that first moment, that she was racing right to him! And Aviva only flushed slightly and chattered on, telling the story of their horse.

It was the same horse that Zev, the Nili, had used before he was captured. The night before Zev was caught the horse had dissappeared, and the next day, strangely, it had come back to them. And then they were talking familiarly of all sorts of questions—the English, did they really mean to give the Jews a state?—"No one will give it, we must make it," Gidon repeated, and she felt exactly the same. Oh, unquestionably at last she was the one! If only he had a few more days to be near her.

First they were posted in a shell-pocked khan on a hill-top not far from Nablus, across a valley from the Turks. They extended their barbed wire down the hill, they made night patrols. At eight o'clock each morning a bombardment was received from across the valley; Herschel declared this made him homesick for Achi Baba. Even the schneiders in a few days became so acclimated that they refused to stop their pinochle games in the courtyard to take shelter during the cannonade.

Sitting on watch, Gidon wrote Aviva letters about the kind of life he wanted one day to live, and here at each mail call it was he who received more letters than anyone! Aviva too wrote about the kind of life she wanted when the war was finished, and she too preferred a farm village, a moshav, to a kvutsa.

Then they were on the march to new positions. Perhaps something would be starting soon. It was over half a year since the capture of Jerusalem, and there had been no effort to drive the Turks from the rest of the land.

From Jerusalem they started downward to the Dead Sea. In the pulsing heat of early August, with full packs, they marched on the highway of crumbling earth, keeping their lines widely spaced so that each would not swallow the dust of those ahead. But the dust from their own feet filled their mouths, and blinded them as well. Now and again in the heat haze as you tramped past, a figure was seen fallen to the ground. You passed on, clinging to your own endurance. Your knees must hold and keep you from toppling at least until the descent was finished, at least until the flatland before Jericho.

—So the Jews wanted to show their mettle? Very well, someone in the command headquarters must have declared with a diabolical delight, he had just the place for the Jews.

One advantage Gidon knew he had over his comrades: he came from the Jordan valley, he had lived his youth at the other end of this earthen gash that stretched from the Kinnereth to the Dead Sea, his body had been tempered in this furnace. But for four years he had lived in other climates, and his body had changed. And at this end the Jordan valley was far deeper below sea level than at home; the air here was more oppressive, each breath had to be brought in at the command of his will. He could even follow the course of the dry burning air drawn down into his body the way one follows the level of very hot water when dipping gradually into a steaming bath.

Sweat blinded him, and he was uncertain whether his vision wavered, or whether Herschel on his left was wavering on his feet. Now his companion was missing. Herschel was stretched on the ground. Gidon managed to put a water-bottle to his lips, and though Herschel knew to be careful, he could not stop gulping and Gidon had to pull the canteen away.

Through the haze the Irishman's voice came from above where he sat his horse. Gidon had nothing against the Irishman, yet there are times when to a foot soldier the sight of a man on a horse, no matter who he is, brings an automatic revulsion.

From long before Gidon's ears were well accustomed to the Irishman's code regarding his men. "When it comes to my men's legitimate rights, I'll fight the whole bloody King's Army for them, but no soldier in my command can expect to be coddled." With one glance the mounted commander had satisfied himself that there was nothing serious here. "All right! On your feet! Let's get on with it!"

The chaplain too had reined up, and while Herschel's eyes were still glazed, and Gidon was helping him to rise, the Irishman engaged the rabbi with a display of Biblical erudition. "They say, now, this is the place where Elijah was fed by the ravens, the *orbim*. That's Hebrew for ravens, isn't it? But elsewhere in the Bible, the Rock of Oreb is described as being not here but in Gilead. Now, Gilead was where Elijah was raised, and where he would naturally flee to when he had to hide."

The rabbi agreed there might be a contradiction as to the location.

"Gidon," the Irishman asked, "as I remember, don't you come from Gilead? Do you know the whereabouts of the Rock of Oreb?"

A thousand ravens should eat him, the Biblical scholar! Gidon was loosening Herscheleh's packstrap, maybe he could managed both packs for a bit. Through the heat-shimmering air more words filtered down. "Now didn't the old Hebrew tribes name themselves after certain places? Couldn't there be a tribe named after the Rock of Oreb, where they lived? Wouldn't that name be Orbim?"

"Yes, indeed," said the chaplain. "I see what you are getting at."

"Exactly," said the Irishman. "The ravens—the orbim who fed Elijah with meat and bread, couldn't they have been Hebrew tribesmen called Orbim? Instead of ravens?"

"Quite a thought, " said the chaplain. And Gidon could have shot the two of them. He had got the pack off Herschel but Herschel, wobbly and dazed, was trying to pull it back.

Just then the chaplain reached down and lifted the pack, placing it across his saddle. "All right," Gidon thought. "You're reprieved."

In his mind Gidon found himself already writing about the incident in a letter to Aviva. All the time now he was saving up incidents to tell her, like when a man comes home from labor in the fields, full of things to tell his wife.

And then he saw himself at home, in the meshek. Only it wouldn't be as a son on his father's farm. At long last he must start his own life. Could he get land and begin a meshek of his own? Because of the Balfour Declaration, Jews would be helped to settle more land, and surely the soldiers would come first. Or should he go back and finish learning to be a veterinary? Could he now take the time? A sense of years wasted like this bleak wasteland around him came over Gidon.

They reached the banana groves of the Jericho oasis, a green island in the engulfing desolation; they drank from the fresh water springs, and moved onward. A new energy came to Gidon. He was now marching homeward! Only a day's ride up the Jordan valley, if they once broke through, was the meshek and the family.

Still another day, and they had come as far as the Auja, a stream with live sweet water flowing into the Jordan. Here Australians were encamped, cavalry. Doubtless soon there would be the big attack. Perhaps it was for this the 38th was being brought here. And then it would be over.

—Not at all! predicted Nathan the Red. They would be sent to Europe, to another front.

"Impossible!" Tuvia argued. They had enlisted to fight here and here alone.

"There's only one way to be sure of that," Pekovsky said, "and that's to get yourself killed here. You won't have to try."

Beyond the Auja, they had moved into the desolation of desolation.

What could nations find to fight over here? Nothingness, emptiness. And were there really men with rifles hidden beyond the yellow ridges, and were there really cannon imbedded behind the emptiness? Even on Achi Baba there had been signs of habitation, ruined houses, stone castles built by men.

The column turned onto the bed of a dry wady, trudging, automatized; only red-rimmed eyes could be seen in these walking slabs of dust. Further up, a trickle of fluid appeared among the stones of the wady. Despite forbidding commands, men knelt and took the bitter water on their palms, touching it to their thickened parched lips, if only at once to spit out the stinking sulphurous muck. Between high barren chalky walls, they struggled, further into the ravine, careful now to stay close under the cliffs, so as not to be seen by the Turks who were said to be entrenched on the opposite heights.

Further, still further, into the barren narrowing chasm, as though they were filing into a deep open grave.

A single stunted tree stood out bleakly, mockingly, from the bed of the wady, and there, amazingly, a figure emerged, an English officer. In shelter against the chasm wall, his file of men waited to be relieved of the position.

Between those arriving and those leaving there passed

hardly a word. Only, "How long?" a London Fusilier asked in his Russian-Jewish accent.

"Seven years," a Scottish voice croaked.

That was for seven days, the longest that any man could endure in midsummer in this gehenna.

"Any action?"

"They let you die on your own, mahn."

The ghouls filed away, some with bitter smiles, not even of pity.

There were trenches of sorts, stone troughs, holes, Lewis gun replacements. And still further up the wady the position petered away in last stretches of barbed wire, and then into a sulphurous marshland where the dregs from some upper watershed must have sunk festering under the dead mineral-sour earth, to bubble up in nauseous springs.

The ravine was called the Mellallah. It was an airtrap; the pulsing, oven-baked atmosphere they had breathed along the Jordan valley lay stuffed in this gorge like a stifling blanket around your head. Each movement of a man's limbs seemed an effort against shackles. Each uttered word was against a weight of stone.

Slowly unpacking supplies from a donkey, Nathan Pekovsky stared before him. From nowhere a few flies had appeared, circling laboriously. Like some tired fairground ride grinding to a stop, the movement of the flies diminished, and then, from midair, the insects fell dead.

"Where men die like flies," Pekovsky remarked.

But if flies could not live in the wady, mosquitoes managed. Soon slapping was heard. Now Gidon recalled, in the line of Scotsmen they had replaced, the glittering unfocused eyes. Kadahat was here.

Other men had lived through it. For a week, for seven days like seven years, they would endure.

But at the end of the second week, no relief column had appeared. Already they had stayed in the Mellallah longer than any other troops during the heat.

A stray Bedouin appeared, as they had a way of doing, from nowhere—who knew, perhaps he was paid by the Turks to count the number of troops here. A cigarette? he asked, and then Gidon talked a bit with the passerby. No, he was not from here, but from up there—his head gestured, vaguely. In the months of heat, he said, no Bedu ever made camp in the Mellallah. No sheep, no dog, could live in this wady.

They had been dumped here and forgotten. They were the tail end of the army, holding a meaningless position.

Not so, the Irishman told them, they were the extended finger. Like every military man, he had to prove that his was the most strategic, the pivotal point, and he drew them patterns in the dust. From its juncture with the Jordan, where they had entered, the Mellallah forked at a forward angle several miles inward to the salty marshland. On the enemy side the ridge overlooked the Jordan, and directly across the Jordan was the high plateau of Rabat Ammon— need he remind them that Rabat Ammon was the ancient Biblical stronghold of the Ammonites? Today it was held by large Turkish forces. And they, the Jewish troops here, were like the advance guard of King David.

Even Nathan Pekovsky remembered his Bible well enough to recall the tale of Rabat Ammon and of the hapless cuckolded warrior sent to fight there. "Put him in the forefront of the battle that he may be cut down." Whoever it was at headquarters among those British Bible-quoters, the anti-Semite had found just the spot for the Jewish battalion! On the opposite ridge above them were several thousand of the enemy, enough easily to annihilate the thinly strung-out men. The Turks had only to pour down between the widely-spaced emplacements of the London Fusiliers, and finish them off.

Against this possibility a constant watch must be kept. At one spot the wady-bed was wide, and in the middle a strange pillarlike formation rose to a height level with the top of the enemy side of the gorge. From this point the Turks could be well observed. Here Gidon one night took his turn on watch with Nathan Pekovsky.

During these weeks in the cursed Mellallah they had changed toward each other. In this barren chasm each man felt his flesh, his very self, akin to the elemental rock from which the winter torrents had ripped away any last leaf of a living organism. Here, on the days when no mail arrived, even Aviva receded from Gidon's reality. And the family and the farm that lay so short a distance ahead were as absent to him as though they were in Iceland.

Bluish moonlight lay over the bottom of the wady; no

Turk would move down on such a night to attack. But aware that men were sitting on this isolated salt pillar in ceaseless watch, the Turks might expend a few artillery shells, and like a chance meteor one might fall upon them. Or would it be chance? Was even a meteor chance?

So speculated Nathan The Red. Gidon only half listened. Some men had a constant need for profound and philosophical explanations, as though this would silence the unanswerable absurdity of men's doings in the world. When other men kept pondering, why should they be fighting here over these barren rocks, Gidon answered himself, Why not? A terrain of battle might as well be barren stone. All the better. Less was destroyed.

Still, Nathan philosophized, "Who are the Ottomans? Who are the British? Why do they drag themselves here with so much suffering? What am I doing here?"

To which Gidon had to answer, "You are a Jew." —For us alone, he said to himself, this struggle has a direct meaning here.

"You believe in God? You believe the God of Abraham particularly wants us here?"

"I don't know what God wants. But I want," Gidon said. "And if some way there is a God, and he put this in me to want—it is the same."

"If it were only that simple for me," Nathan said.

"All right, I am a simpleton. Even those books you gave me to read haven't made me wiser."

Nathan's face, in the cold light that made everything look like stone, was graven into a tight-lipped ironic grin, the look that some men have when trying to hold in the pain of a wound. "You know, Gidon, it is somewhat because of you that I am here."

He entered into a long recitation, partly the tale of his life, partly an argument with himself and over himself. Back and forth, a Jew, a worker, Karl Marx, exploitation, nationalism, internationalism and a word that Gidon had now and again heard, but never understood—dialectic. This time it meant for Nathan Pekovsky, he now saw, the war within himself as his desire swayed from one extreme to the other: to be a whole Jew or to be rid altogether of being a Jew.

What was a Jew but a relic of the distant past, an anachronism, an atavism, a victim of a primitive tribal religion that had taken such a grip on a certain Semitic clan that it held its group together right on into the modern enlightened world?

But there was also another term; Gidon had sometimes heard it, with half an ear, in discussions as far back as Reuven's kvutsa, and again in that restaurant in Whitechapel: "historical imperative." If you peered deeply enough into the machinery of history you could come to understand exactly how the wheels interlocked, and even how the machine, if correctly manipulated, would in the end bring mankind to the realization and control of justice on earth.

For Reuven's friends, the idealists in the Poël Hatzaïr, this meant, first of all, that the Jews had to be brought back to Eretz, and there through a life of socialism and justice they would show the whole world how to live. The way it was written in the Prophets. And for Nathan's Bolsheviks, it meant the same thing, except that only the workers and farmers of the whole world could bring it about.

The Zionists in Eretz and the Bolsheviki in Russia really only wanted the same thing, a world of social justice where ordinary people could no longer be hoodwinked into making war on each other. "And why am I fighting here, instead of fighting for the revolution in Russia?" Nathan demanded.

"You came here to make sure that the Jewish land would also be part of the workers' revolution," Gidon reminded him. "That's what you yourself told me when you joined us."

Nathan laughed at the recollection.

"I remember even the first time we met, and I gave you a good smack in the teeth," Gidon said.

And Nathan rejoined, "When a man argues most fiercely, you can know it is because the other side's ideas also exist in him and he is shouting them down in himself. I will be honest, chaver Gidon. In London my crowd thought we really might be pushed into the Russian army. So I thought, in the British army I wouldn't starve and freeze so much. You see I was too smart for my own good—that I would be burning here in this gehenna I was too stupid to foresee. I even thought, why fight in the Russian army where I would be despised by the moujiks as a

Jew? and I didn't realize that we would be despised by our British commanders just as brutally. That is why when the Russian army quit the war, and I saw what a fool I had been, I tried to get myself transferred to a labor battalion. Eh! I miscalculated the historical imperative, my friend. . . . And at heart I am really a pacifist. Like all Jews."

The thought came to Gidon that it was true of Reuven, but was it true of himself? He saw again the Zbeh crossing the river, riding toward him, and in his trigger finger he again felt the tension. What could a man answer? There were those who said Jews were not so much pacifists as cowards. For hundreds of years in Europe they had bowed their heads and hidden themselves from pogroms rather than fight.

"When we have to fight, we fight," Gidon said. "But there are also peoples who simply like to fight. To the Bedouin, war is their soul. They attack you for nothing—because they like to fight."

"But the Arabs who attacked your village that time— you say to steal and kill—didn't they themselves believe they were fighting for their land?"

"The Zbeh? They came from over there—" he waved to across the Jordan. "This side was never their land. They attack the fellaheen the same way, for their cows and their horses."

"And the fellaheen here? Hasn't there been trouble since the beginning?"

—Small troubles. "A fight now and then—it's not the same."

"And you don't think they care if this land becomes a Jewish nation?"

"Why? They'll be better off with us than with the Turks."

"Suppose they get the idea that Palestine should become an Arab nation?"

The words came as a half-surprise. Was Nathan taunting him? Or was Nathan Pekovsky after all a kind of a traitor to the Jews? "But why on earth?" Gidon replied. "Arabia is over there—" in those vast stretches on the other side of Jordon, where the Arabs had always been, from the time of Ishmael. There they had their Mecca. There Arab tribes were raiding the Turks. The British were arranging it all—

the Arab chiefs would become kings over Arabia, and the Jews would have their nation in Palestine. All this seemed natural enough. And hadn't the whole world approved the Balfour Declaration?

Nathan was silent. It came to Gidon, how much more difficult it was for Nathan with all his complicated ideas and doubts to be fighting here. Nathan's mind sometimes went one way and his heart the other. The Jew in him had won out, but his mind wasn't satisfied.

And it was just this that Nathan presently began to talk about, in the mood that was upon them. "You know, Gidon, I was married in England."

"I didn't know. You're still married?"

"No. It lasted a year. With an English girl I met working in our shop. A shikseh." His wry smile came as though to anticipate, "Now you will say of course." And he added, with a half-laugh, "She wasn't even a socialist." And, as though Gidon had asked for more, "I said to myself, the hell with it all. The British are a good decent people—you know I admire them. The revolution seemed far away. All a man could do in this world was have his little family—as Voltaire wrote, cultivate his garden. Stay out of their imperialist war. A little garden in England." He chortled. "Gidon, when she put up the Christmas tree, I felt ashamed of myself."

"So you should have married an atheist."

At this Nathan roared with laughter. "She was! An atheist like me! And she had put up the bloody Christmas tree! So here I am."

He laughed so loud he would surely bring a Turkish cannonade onto their pillar.

With brooding eyes, eyes even of envy, the men watched the first malarials being moved out on camel slings. That same night, Gidon took a work party forward into the swamp, slipping beyond the last edge of barbed wire into no man's land to dig a drainage ditch to help against the mosquitoes. And the following night, they dug on even further, until all at once Gidon glimpsed the form of a sentry. The man was leaning against the gully wall on the opposite side of the swamp. Gidon motioned his men to freeze. The sentry too was motionless—and staring at the form, Gidon realized the Turk was asleep, standing up. No wonder;

nothing ever happened there. Tuvia was in the squad, and now he slowly crept over, sprang and seized the Turk, dragging him back a prisoner. The man's outcry brought rifle-bursts, and a schneider fell in the mud. Tuvia, remorseful now over his heroism, managed to carry out the casualty. The schneider was wounded in the chest, who knew if he would live.

For a few days Gidon remained depressed. He had lost a man. It was their fourth week here, and the sense of suffocation was immeasurable. Another afternoon a schneider went mad. Leaping out of his hole, he tried wildly to clamber up the opposite wall of the ravine, uttering animal screams.

Six more malarials were evacuated.

No other troops had been kept in the Mellallah even half as long. The Irishman rode back to the headquarters on the Auja to protest. "At least, for him—he can ride out of here," the men grumbled. At the Auja the water was fresh and cool from the spring.

Who could say their long, unrelieved watch here was not spite?

The Irishman came back, called together his officers, and explained something. He had noticed troops thinned down all along the line, so perhaps indeed no replacements were available, as the commanders had said. Besides, there were careful, secret movements going on. He smelled a coming action. A master plan was being put into effect. He had noticed several signs of his old friend Allenby's favorite strategy, the same tricks Allenby had used before the big attack on Jerusalem. The Irishman had seen a large camp of empty tents and learned that campfires were lighted there at night. There were even dummy supply dumps and false cavalry corrals with dummy horses to deceive aerial reconnaissance. Friends at headquarters had told him of troops making false marches and countermarches to stir up clouds of dust, more tricks for the enemy observation. At least the Fusiliers were lucky to escape the dust-making marches.

What could it all mean? Bluffing, to prevent an enemy attack on their thinned-out lines?

At least the deadly apathy was now broken. Heavy shells rode overhead toward the Turkish positions. The barrage even brought down deserters, exhausted, embittered men, who crept into the gully and surrendered.

Now, daring sallies were ordered, half a squad at a time, as far as the enemy outposts. In one of these a man fell, shot through the head, and trying to recover the body, another man was wounded. Both were London conscripts.

—He had known these fellows would prove themselves! the Irishman cried out, and sent back to headquarters a recommendation for decorations. The dead man was Yitzhak Zimmerman, a friend of Nathan's, and one of the ten who had in Egypt tried to transfer to a labor battalion.

Heartening news came. The second battalion of Jews had arrived and was stationed behind them, on the Auja. The lucky ones. But merely to have them near canceled out the envy. And, besides, this surely meant real action after all this waiting. The 40th London Fusiliers were even commanded by a Jew—Colonel Margolies, born in Rehovot! His family had moved to Australia; there he had entered His Majesty's forces, fought in France, become an officer, risen to colonel. A real one.

The day came when the Irishman galloped back from headquarters in tremendous excitement and assembled his officers beneath the lone tree in the wady. He had been handed their objective! They were to capture a ford across the Jordan, several miles up from the mouth of the Mellallah. Who knew but what it was the same ford where Joshua and his men had made their crossing, to circle behind Jericho! But now the Hebrews would cross in the reverse direction and circle behind the Turkish army in Rabat Ammon!

Then it had come. The final battle to clear all Eretz of the Turk was here. They were in time to take part. Suddenly Vladimir Jabotinsky, who had been sent to deliver orations at recruitment meetings in the British half of the Yishuv, returned to his platoon. A final sign. Action.

The next morning a sudden troop of mounted officers appeared, and the astonishing word passed among the Jews that General Allenby himself had come to their Mellallah. Captains and lieutenants, buttoning their tunics, were hurrying to the Irishman's tent. Even the most demoralized of the men began frantically to prepare for inspection. But just as suddenly the commanding general's party rode back. What had happened in the tent? Word filtered down. Jab-

otinsky himself confirmed it. —Can we trust the Jews to
fight? the General had asked the Irishman.

The bastard anti-Semites!

"What did he answer?"

The Irishman had said he was now losing two hundred
men a week from malaria, but if the battle took place while
there was still a Jew left on his feet, that Jew would fight.

There were even a few who argued—after all, if the C-
in-C himself on his busiest day, the eve of the attack, had
come in person to make sure of them, they must be of
some importance!

In the dusk they moved in file to the dry mouth of the
Mellallah, and then along a ledge, parallel to the Jordan
banks, northward. Behind them only the thinnest holding
line had been left.

The attackers squatted in clusters and waited. Gidon,
Herschel, Tuvia, Nathan, hardly said a word to each other.
Gidon wished Herschel or Nathan would at least make
some of their bitter jokes. So far this was no harder than a
patrol, he told himself, no worse than the quick stabs they
had made in the last week. He was an old veteran of war.
He would not fail.

Gidon had thought of writing but had not written the
letter to be sent to Aviva should he fail to come back.
Never before had he wanted to do such a thing; in the end,
even now he had not done it, because if anything should
happen, perhaps such a memento of him would make it
harder rather than easier for her to turn to a new life.

From close behind them their mortars rose up. It was a
good job, a full-scale inundation to clean any entrenchment
on the banks near the ford.

How many were they here? Two companies. A solid barrage of shells sent in reply to their mortars could spatter
the lot of them here. Still, to secure the Jordan crossing—it
was a task of which Jews would forever be able to say, "It
was our men who did it."

With daylight they moved carefully, watching the riverbank. Still they had attracted no fire. It was not entirely a
good feeling. Gidon kept imagining some clever-eyed
Turkish captain with his glasses on them waiting devilishly
until from specks they grew larger, came closer, closer,

waiting for the instant when they could be mowed down.

At last they were ordered to stop moving. They lay down now, each with the nesting movement of squirming his body into the earth, and then settling his elbow for his rifle.

To their volley of fire, directed into the ragged clumps of reeds on the other side of the river, there came only a few scattered shots, followed by a burst from a single machine gun. Nothing reached them. The Irishman rode up to their front line the way Trumpeldor would have done. Ah, what Josef would have given to be here!

To Gidon's squad the honor—"Scout ahead." He heard Nathan mutter in Yiddish, "A shainem dank." Thank you handsomely.

An enemy trench, almost stumbled upon, was empty. It had the stench of abandonment. Climbing out, they got their breath. Gidon glanced around to make sure of Nathan, Herschel, Tuvia. He had always looked first for Herschel, but today it was Nathan. Herschel could take care of himself, from Gallipoli.

A knot of men were around a Turk, on his belly in the brush. His mustache quivering like that of a terrified mouse, the wretch had been huddled in a shallow hole waiting to surrender; his skin was covered with sores, he stank. With abject imploring motions, the starved relic of a man tried to seize Gidon's hand and kiss it.

Gidon gestured across the river. Many?

No no, not many. The prisoner made a gesture—departed.

Sending Herschel back with the prisoner, Gidon scouted along further, almost to the designated crossing point. All at once a volley came from the other bank. Perhaps twenty rifles. He lay with his men behind one of the flat-topped cones of salt-rock that rose in this landscape, resembling pictures of the strangeness of the moon. But the mounds gave good cover. All his men were intact. They drew back a way to the shelflike outcropping. Presently the whole company moved in with them. A few Lewis guns were emplaced, raking the opposite bank. No return fire came. Looking down into the glistening swift water, you could see the stones of the ford; it was even shallower than the ford at home—a wagon could cross. On the Turkish side, the bank was broader, leaving no cover as far as the base of the heights. Strangely, no shelling came from up there.

The Irishman motioned. To Jabotinsky the honor. Weighed down with a Lewis gun, but appearing in this moment of attack determinedly calm, the orator took Tuvia and a few other men. No need to feel slighted—Gidon watched the group carefully working down to the riverside. From across the ford, a heavy machine gun opened fire, but again the mounds gave the squad good cover, and from along the ledge the entire company blazed at the enemy position. The gun was silenced.

Not long after, you could see the forward men emerging from their cover and making their dashes across the open space as far as the water, waiting there behind a clump of rushes.

Good. The rest of the company in small clusters moved down, and darted across the open area, from mound to mound, like children playing a game of follow-my-footsteps, reaching the river edge, flopping to the ground, surprised, each in nervous exhaustion at finding himself whole.

Still on his mount, the Irishman picked his way to them. Hastily they set up strongpoints. Like Moses signaling to Joshua, the Irishman raised his arm as a signal for Jabotinsky. Jabotinsky set his foot into the water. His gun almost unbalanced him, but he moved from stone to stone. He was across. Quickly the men followed, knee-deep in the rushing stream. Gidon passed over.

Now they held both banks. Men laughed, clustered together, made remarks, had to be dispersed to set up positions. And still no counterattack.

It began to feel eerie, alone here.

They explained to each other. Surely the Turk had been lightly strung out and taken by complete surprise. The Turk was assembled far below opposite Jericho. He had not imagined a crossing so far up to the north. Some strategists said he had not imagined a crossing at all to the other side of the Jordon. The Turk and his German generals believed the attack would be directly forward into the Emek, into the Galilee. Still, they were so few to have crossed, the enemy could react and wipe them out like a bunch of fleas.

At last a movement from their own side. Thunder on the earth—cavalry! Chator's Mounted!

Unceasingly the New Zealand troopers clattered across the ford, their commander waiting on the far side with the Irishman, watching the avalanche, shouting jokes at each other, "The London Tailors' Bridge!" while the mounted men swept on, zigzagging up the cliffs of Ammon onto the plain, circling on the top, howling and waving aloft their weapons, their broad cowboy hats, rearing their steeds, and charging onward.

Tales of enemy havoc came tumbling back. Materializing behind the main enemy position, Chator's Mounted had surprised the Turks into a wild rout; they were surrendering by the thousands, their officers among them, Germans too.

The crossroad town of Salt was taken. The way was open to Damascus.

And from the Palestine side of the Jordon came snatches of news of equal triumphs. The 38th's own rearguard, catching up with them now as the second Jewish battalion took over their old positions, told how Allenby's broad stratagem had succeeded. Von Kressenstein had been completely fooled. All those campfires and dust clouds had led him to believe the main British drive would be forward to the Galilee, and for this he had kept his reserves there. Meanwhile with muffled hooves, at night without dust or the spark of a fire, the British had stealthily moved masses of cavalry toward the coast, and in a sudden wave swept down to the sea, overwhelming the Turks, ten horsemen to one. Never in history had there been such a clean quick defeat! There on the Sharon plain and in the Emek, as here on the Moab plain, entire enemy regiments were surrendering. The British were advancing as fast as they could travel, with no resistance before them. All Eretz was again united.

Home, home, the way must now be clear, and the urge tugged at Gidon; it was like some halter-rope pulling him the opposite way while he stumbled forward with the battalion in the wake of Chator's cavalry. Blackened flesh of dead mules, dead soldiers, the litter of spilled ammunition boxes, ration-tins, soldiers' packs with their innards strewn about, and bands of Bedouin scavenging, children, women, older men, tearing off clothing from the dead. Now and again a famished half-alive Turk came crawling like some half-smashed fly, crawling toward them, making enfeebled motions with his hand to his mouth for water.

They must march and secure the town of Salt. Their own sick must stumble on with them, for a man dropped behind could not last long among the excited scavenging Bedouin.

Some of the men began throwing off souvenirs they had just picked up. Soon they were throwing away their emptied canteens. Their mess gear. Their hard rations. The pace slowed. This was worse than the march down to Jericho; this was uphill. A crushing, full-pack, endless climb. Some victory! There had to be rest halt. Without an order, the entire column fell prone, directly on the path.

Something approached. A motorcycle. A messenger. Dazedly they heard a command passed along. Countermarch. Change of order. It was not the town of Salt but a place called Zumerin they had to guard. A prisoners' camp. Up on your feet, turn about, and march. This was triumphal victory. With his palms, Herschel pounded the ground in exhausted bitterness. Tears were halfway down the crust of his cheeks. Most of the men lay as though never to rise. A sobbing rage was in Gidon's throat—all this burdened way for nothing, he could have been half the distance home. Not even in the blundering night marches with his mules in Gallipoli, when some idiot had packed the wrong loads and he had to return, had he felt such bottom bitterness. But he must rise to his feet and urge on his squad. He must pull one man after another to his feet. Even Herscheleh.

Only one thing was certain, one thing upheld him. This time he was pointed in the right direction, and somehow he would continue and go home. Let them shoot him for it. And even as they moved on, it seemed in a dazed way that Aviva would also be there in Mishkan Yaacov, awaiting him.

How it was accomplished no one could explain. If it were a march to a rescue, if a battle hung in balance—but only a blunder, a countermarch! In the numbness of exhaustion, with failed wobbling knees, in tremor, they reached the mud-hut village.

The Irishman's adjutant actually complimented them. A military feat. In twelve years of service he had not witnessed such a lengthy march and countermarch, and under highly adverse conditions! They were real soldiers and he was proud to be their officer.

In the night, fever outbreaks began. Two of Gidon's men were delirious, and in the morning a third lay retching out the victory.

A few huts were cleared for the sick. The doctor, himself packed full of quinine, his pupils dilated, appeared and tottered among the stricken. Meanwhile an endless, uncountable line of prisoners stumbled into the compound, herded by mounted Australians brutally healthy, waving their wide-brimmed hats with cowboy whoops.

The Irishman had galloped back to staff headquarters, and now he brought them word, they were being given a new name. Not yet the Jewish Brigade, no, not quite. But they were no longer the London Fusiliers. They were now named Patterson's Force. His! They and their sister battalion, the 40th, and when the third battalion, the volunteers from Palestine who had been sent to Egypt for training, became ready, they would all at last become a full brigade. And then, the Irishman trusted, his Jewish fighters would finally receive their promised special insignia, the Star of David.

The crowning victory of these days, he said, was according to Biblical prophecy. "Ha-ah-tereth!" he pronounced the Hebrew word for "the crown." Surely they all knew that these Hebrew letters stood for the numerals five, six, seven, and nine. And in the Hebrew calendar this was the year 5697! The Crown of Victory! Ha-ah-tereth!

"He too is being given a new name." Herscheleh was still able to jest in his fever. "He is now Chief Cabbalist of His Majesty's Forces."

Now it was guard duty over the prisoners; Gidon walked behind a detail of the stronger ones as they carried out those who lay dead on the ground of their compound to a burial trench.

Not yet could he make off from this pestilential hole, not while Herscheleh was down. No way to help except to sit by him and talk of home. Only a bit more to endure, and then home; the great new days of the Yishuv would begin.

Late in the afternoon, as he sat there, Gidon felt his arm gripped in the iron fingers of the enfevered. "Let us go,"

Herscheleh whispered hoarsely. He too had been planning it: they would take horses and make off!

"Not yet, Herschel." Gidon had to hold back his friend from what he himself so wanted to do. "When your fever is gone, we'll do it."

"I can do it now. I can make it, I know. Going home I can make it." With one of those excesses of wild energy, he even wobbled upward onto his feet; Gidon caught him in time to break his fall.

The droves of prisoners kept coming; even with the masses of dead carried out each morning, there was not enough room in the compound for the surrendering horde.

Herscheleh was able to get up now and nagged Gidon each hour—they must at least put in a request for leave. Had Gidon forgotten their plan?

Jabotinsky had vanished again on official tasks in Jerusalem. Gidon approached the adjutant.

"Chaimofsky"—this one had never got his name right—"don't think I fail to understand your feelings, but how can I give anyone leave at this juncture? Twenty men are down—I haven't got a single officer left on his feet." Wearily he motioned to an order on his table. "On top if it all, I'm to send a detachment back with prisoners, so as to make room in the compound. I haven't got an officer to send."

As the major lifted his head, their eyes met and it was done. "All right, Chaimofsky, take half your squad and escort them." The eyes remained impenetrable. This major, Gidon had never been able to measure. He was correct. He seemed to regard the whole business with the Jews as an odd bit of experience, one of those curious things that happen to a man in a war that he would no doubt afterward tell about amusingly. Was he for or against? Gidon never knew. But a disciplinarian he was. Break a regulation and there was no pity. It was he who had come on a little Tunisian, Gedalia Mograbi, fallen asleep on guard duty one night, and reported him without mercy, though they had been on a forced march all that day. And when a court-martial at regimental level automatically sentenced Gedalia to be shot, the major had not even put in a clemency request. It had taken the Irishman himself, at the last moment, sending a motorcycle rider with a personal plea to his old friend Allenby, to save Gedalia's life. Strangely, when Gedalia had returned to the ranks, the major had called him in to tell him he was glad he had been saved. "He really seemed glad over it," Gedalia repeated, puzzled.

So now, Gidon hardly knew what to make of the opportunity the major had given him. Surely the Englishman guessed what he intended to do.

"You're to deliver the damned wretches to the Jerusalem compound," the major instructed. "I'll prepare your orders. It should take you three days to get them up there and two days back. No monkeyshines," he added cheerfully. Again the impenetrable glance. "Well, the state they're in, make it five days to get there. Dismissed." Gidon saluted. Perhaps the bastard had a heart after all.

He would be mounted; at the King's Highway he would turn off, leaving Herscheleh in charge. Herscheleh was well enough now; he could ride in the supply wagon. In Jerusalem wait for Gidon to get back from Mishkan Yaacov, and then take his own turn for a quick visit home. To reach Chedera he had in any case to pass through Jerusalem.

"If there are any questions while I'm gone," Gidon said, "just tell them some prisoners escaped and I went after them."

Their line of prisoners could hardly move even at a crawl. These ragged remnants of men, who could have the heart to urge them on? And what difference did it make? Let their slow steps drag to a halt every half hour, let them take a whole week, a month to climb up to Jerusalem. As the column reached the old Roman highway, Gidon made off.

34

IN THE feverish evacuation Reuven had his own task. With the first news of the complete rout in Palestine, Menahem and Young Avram had begun their preparations. It could only be a matter of days until Damascus fell. The Widow Gelman's house was to be the assembly point. One of the Tel Aviv Gymnasia group, who had been stationed

with the German staff officers as interpreter, brought word
that the Germans had already commandeered a hotel in
Aleppo and would be evacuating before the end of the
week. Damascus would not be defended. This would be the
moment for Jews in the Turkish army to remain behind.
Civilian clothing must be prepared. As for the prisoners—
here was a dangerous situation. It could even be that in a
last moment of madness the Turks would take them along,
drag them out on the roads. At least the work-parties must
escape. On the eve of the capture of Damascus they must
not be returned to the prison. Reuven would bring his gardeners to the warehouse and they would have to be hidden
in various homes in the Harat al Yahud. The same with
Bushinsky's "engineers." Indeed, both Reuven and Bushinsky should ask for double the quota on the pretext of needing men to build fortifications. Even with small sums of
gold in these frantic days you could ransom out half a
prison. Young Avram had found a kadi who was already
preparing for good connections with the coming regime,
and understood it would be well to be able to show that he
had saved hundreds of prisoners who had been victims of
the Ottoman rulers. At the proper moment he might persuade the departing prison commander to leave the gates
unlocked.

Despite orders for gathering them at the edge of the city,
ragged, bloodied soldiers were drifting in and wandering
dazedly through the streets. Military vehicles crammed
with personal belongings were departing northward; inlaid
Damascus coffee tables, French chandeliers, were seen balanced atop suitcases and huge wickers of food. A convoy
was lining up at Djemal Pasha's palace. Reuven fled out of
sight deep into the garden. Behind a toolshed he had prepared his own cart for evacuation, and now he began to dig
out certain saplings from his nursery, date-palms of the
most valuable strain that he had brought from along the
Euphrates, cedars of Lebanon that he had kept in special
soil. His pistachios. Each plant carefully wrapped now in
damp burlap.

Djemal's convoy was gone. Before dusk, Reuven assembled his band of gardeners and marched them to the warehouse. In pairs, in threes, they were quickly spirited down
the lanes of the Jewish quarter. To Elisheva, that night,
after she had guided her last group of prisoners to a lodg-

ing, Reuven mused, "I am not certain Djemal forgot to
have me called for the evacuation. He never forgets the
slightest detail. Perhaps it was intentional."

"Reuven, I love you for it, but we mustn't always believe
in the good of people. It can be dangerous." She kissed him
softly. Who knew but what this might yet be the last night
for all of them in Harat al Yahud?

- Before dawn scattered firing could be heard. Suddenly
the city was in jubilation. Arabs ran through the streets
firing off rifles as in a fantasia. Riders galloped through,
keffiyahs flying, shooting into the air and occasionally at
some poor left-over Turk in a tarboosh as he darted into an
alley. From a high small window, the Shalmoni family
peeped out and saw a belated Turkish officer dragged from
his horse and quartered.

Then came a clatter of cavalry. A roar arose, "Feisal!
King!" "Feisal! King!" It became a chant that pervaded the
city. The Bedouin chieftains with their wildly joyous followers were spreading through the avenues, riding horses
into the shops.

Menahem stood behind the heavy street door to the
courtyard. Singly, in pairs, the former Turkish officers,
wearing civilian clothes, slipped up and gave the agreed-
upon knock.

It passed well enough. Among the Jewish notables from
Jerusalem who had been confined to the hotel was one who
had long been acquainted with the Hashemites of Arabia,
and who managed to greet Feisal even as he paraded into
the main square at the head of his warriors. Thus, in the
general looting, Harat al Yahud was relatively unmolested.
As prisons were burst open, Jews of Palestine along with
Arabs were free to go.

Several hundred men had already been assembled at the
warehouse. Only one subject was discussed—transport.
Trains there were none. Every last donkey, every cart, had
been commandeered by the evacuating Turks. Anything on
four legs that had been hidden away was to be bought only
with gold. All at once, impatient ones were declaring they
would start off and walk!

The countryside was in wildest disorder; to be murdered
on the road for a bundle of belongings, after all they had

endured—no, it was not to be thought of, not to be allowed.

But if they all marched together? All at once, Young Avram was turning it into a plan, an exodus.

From the wealthiest families a few hidden vehicles were borrowed for the weakest, for the sick. With the conquering tribesmen, Menahem managed a triumphant trade of several ornate clocks for a dozen donkeys. Smashed carts were dragged from the streets into the courtyard, the wheels remaining on one transferred to another.

Who ever beheld such a convoy! All were delirious with the end of captivity, with the news of the whole Yishuv again united, with reports that a Jewish Commission headed by Chaim Weizmann was already on the way to found the Jewish homeland! Flags of Zion were prepared, and Shabbatai Zeira even painted himself a banner carrying the ancient Hebrew words that had been the secret oath of the first defenders of the Yishuv:

> In blood and fire Judea fell,
> In blood and fire Judea will arise.

Reuven was somewhat uneasy over this, but Menahem shrugged, "After all that he has been through, what can it hurt?"

Young Avram, a veritable commander, formed them up along the narrow lane of the Harat al Yahud. Many were missing. Avraham Halperin of Gilboa, known to have died, Tibor the Comical also, and Motke from Petach Tikvah, sent off to labor, who knew where, but see how many were here! Reuven had pulled his two-wheeled cart with the seedlings all the way from the palace garden. He was prepared to pull it by himself, marching between the shafts, the whole distance to Eretz, but at the Shalmoni house there came a godsend.

When Elisheva laid a lingering hand on her piano to take leave of it, her father could not bear her look of sorrow. "No! Take it with you!" he cried. "Take my carriage-horse—later on, Reuven can send it back."

And so the carriage-horse, carefully locked away in the rear of the stable, was brought out and placed between the shafts of the cart. Menahem and Reuven and a whole crew of volunteers raised up the Bechstein and carried it from

the house. The seedlings were momentarily set down from
the cart, and now the men hoisted up the piano. Jehovah
was still with the Jews, and the vehicle only shuddered, but
stood whole. Between the massive piano legs and all
around and atop the instrument, Reuven placed his burlap-
wrapped seedlings, and Elisheva's baggage. Then, in a last
inspiration, Young Avram even made room for the piano
stool, and with Elisheva seated at the keys, a Hatikvah
such as had never before been heard burst forth from the
throng on Harat al Yahud, starting their march to the
homeland.

In jubilation, three days later, they marched over the
bridge at Bnot Yaacov. From Rosh Pina the old settlers
and their sons and daughters came riding, greeting them as
heroes. From there onward the march was a festival: more
and more riders appeared; carts, wagons, donkeys were
fetched for the weary; garlanded children with flags of Zion
led them into Tiberias, and only as they approached Kinnereth, was there one small untoward incident.

The entire kvutsa had come out on the highway before
the gate; even the infants carried banners welcoming the
homecomers. There, totally bald now, thin, but recovered,
upright and beaming, stood Max Wilner, who had been
smuggled home on the hospital train. And there was Old
Gordon, striding at the head of the welcome party, his
beard flowing. Suddenly he halted. He had seen the banner
held aloft by Shabbatai Zeira.

"No! No!" the prophet shouted. "Not blood! Put it
down!"

After all, it was but the Biblical slogan of the first defenders of the Yishuv. How many had spilled their blood!
Shabbatai's own young brother killed. And wasn't it true
that from blood and fire Judea was now arising?

"Not with blood!" Gordon shouted. "Not here in the
kvutsa!" Planting himself before the gate, the old Tolstoyan
declared, "Unless it is thrown away, I won't let you in!"

Zeira at first only laughed. But he too was stubborn. The
crazy old pacifist! Angered, the banner aloft, Shabbatai
strode past the gate and continued on his way on the road.

Let him go. Almost all of the others turned in at the
gate, at least for a respite, a refreshing meal. Already the
chevreh had engulfed their own members returning. Reu-

ven! Imagine, Reuven Chaimovitch at last with a chavera!
Truly the days of wonder and joy had arrived!

Pausing only to rest his mount, Gidon continued through
the night. How he loved this horse! What a good-hearted
animal, responding as though he understood why his rider
hurried.

And in the morning, here, from the opposite height, this
was how the Zbeh must have gazed on them, the gleaming
tempting oblongs of cultivated fields on the other shore of
the river, the two rows of houses and barns. How the trees
had grown! So high were the cypresses, the eucalyptus
rows, that he couldn't even see the house itself. But he
could make out a dark green rectangle among the field—
the pardess!

And further up the river, the fields of Reuven's kvutsa,
and behind HaKeren a whole new cluster of buildings, a
new commune, even two of them, and also Dagania—fields
on fields!

Gidon drew a full breath, almost in apprehension of the
longed-for moment that was upon him.

Riding down the escarpment, and across the ford, Gidon
felt his heart bubbling.

It was just the time for the morning pause when the men
came in for the full breakfast. Schmulik and Abba might be
coming in from the field—but it was a neighboring Roumanian woman who first caught sight of the rider, gave a
second glance, and cried out, "Isn't it Gidon?"

The surprise was nearly spoiled, but only the excited
tone of her cry, and not his name, had been heard in the
yard. Mameh came to the door for a look. Then the whole
household was upon him.

But they were all here as though awaiting him! The
whole family! Sisters, brothers, wives and husbands, they
kept tumbling upon him as though the surprise had been
prepared from their side, not his! Leah was here—how
could Leah have known he was coming? And Reuven came
hurrying from the house, home from Damascus already,
and not at the kvutsa, but here! Such a tumult, and so
many arms clutching at him, while the girls let Mameh in
closest—her whole face was trembling, the cheeks trem-

bled, how she had aged! And oddly what she first said after clutching to make sure all his limbs were really there on him, both his arms, his shoulders, his chest, his neck and cheeks—and after pulling herself back to study his eyes, as he smiled into hers—Mameh blurted out, "Ach, Gidon , all my teeth are gone." As he hugged her, it came to Gidon that in all his grown life he had not hugged his mother.

The girls in turn seized him, kissed him on his mouth "for once!" It was true, he had not ever kissed his sisters either. Dvora was here from Gilboa, with her little children, and Menahem was here—it was like a great birthday party. Once he had been to such a surprise party in England where everyone had assembled in secret and then rushed out at the feted one when he arrived, shouting "Surprise! Surprise!"

The most diffident was Schmulik—a man! he hung back grinning and at once began taking care of the horse. And about Mati there was a joke—he had shot up so, that Leah had to cry out to Gidon, "You don't recognize Mati!" And Eliza—no, Shula—she had changed her name just before he left but he hadn't got used to it—here she was, a plump young mother, though the same beauty was there on her face, only rounder. "Now I know who Yoram looks like, he's the exact image of Gidon," she cried to Nahum, her husband! Already bewildered, trying to absorb in one gulp the changes in the family, Gidon saw a stranger come out of the house, a delicate-looking young woman who at once went over to Reuven, and Reuven introduced her as Elisheva, his wife. Reuven had a wife!

All soon became clear. They had really not all been gathered here waiting for him, though Leah declared she knew in her bones he would be coming today. "Didn't I say to you—" she took Yaffaleh to witness—"I have a feeling Gidon will come today?" It was for Reuven and his bride they had all gathered; only yesterday Reuven had arrived with her at the kvutsa, from Damascus; a whole exodus had arrived of the prisoners at last freed from Damascus. Menahem and another chaver, Young Avram of Gilboa, had arranged the whole thing. In the tumult Mati began to tell Gidon a complicated story of how Menahem had hidden in the cave, and Gidon only then noticed his father standing in the doorway, with a true patriarchal smile behind his beard,

standing there with a "Baruch haba," and they went toward
each other and embraced.

Who could help feeling then that they were all placed
here to repeat what had been, long ago? The strength that
went into his own hugging, the strength that came from his
father's arms, was like some utterance, breaking out from
the deepest reaches, some enactment that spoke words they
didn't know how to say: son, father. Perhaps that was why
words and prayers were from some ancient time written and
made ready for you, the words to utter for each occasion.
Gidon heard something smothered in the beard—it was
surely Abba's favorite Shehechiyanu prayer, thanks that
they had reached and seen this day—and then he heard, "My
son, my son," and a shimmer of happiness rested like the
Shechina, the religious would say, over the Chaimovitch
yard. In spite of all, here they were. They had succeeded in
staying alive, in remaining a family.

Gidon followed his father into the house; the old man
picked up the cut-glass Sabbath decanter which had somehow lasted all the way from Cherezinka without breaking,
and set out the tiny brandy glasses, saying "Nu, son, a
schnapps." It was the first time in his life that his father
had offered him a drink, pouring a tiny brandy-glassful for
himself also, and for Reuven, Menahem, and Nahum, and
then for Schmulik and even Mati. "L'chayim!"

The family had been in the midst of the meal. "Fortunately there's something on the table!" Feigel cried out, and
what wasn't there on the table, prepared for the eldest son
and his bride, and now the second son had come home! All
the delicacies Mameh kept sliding onto Gidon's plate, while
Yaffaleh brought him eggs scrambled with onions, and cucumbers in cream sprinkled with little green bits of parsley,
and Mameh's own warm bread—she must have been baking all night—and herring with boiled potatoes and butter—famished indeed he was, from the long ride and from
the weeks of dry rations in the Mellallah. And where in all
these years had he tasted such dishes? And in sputters Gidon told them of the Mellallah, the battle for the river
crossing, all. Mati had run and fetched the Star of David
from the Zion Mule Corps to show him—No, the battalion
didn't yet have a Jewish insignia, though it had been promised. A whole side-explanation to Menahem and Reuven

about this, while he folded a potato latke with cream in the
fold and stuffed the whole into his mouth—an old trick of
his, that made Mameh swell with happiness just to see it
again. Then Gidon demanded news of the cattle, the crops
. . . "What have we to complain of, we lived through it!"

And as he ate on, he heard how it had ended here, the
same story as everywhere, the wretched famished Turks
suddenly running, and Mati told of a stray figure, a German officer begging for civilian clothes, he didn't want to
be taken prisoner, and they had given him some of Schmulik's old torn clothes—then all at once one day, silence,
stillness, not a soul in sight—and then a strange horseman
on the ridge, joined by another, a whole troop riding down,
giants with broad hats—the Australians had arrived. Only
just a week ago it was, but already life had changed, a new
world!

At once Gidon had to go out to see the barns, the fields!
the whole Chaimovitch family trekked over their land.
Here was the lemon grove that Abba had saved from the
locusts, covering them with petticoats—the story was famous all over the Yishuv. This year the trees would bear
fruit, the green nubs already could be seen forming on the
branches. And wait! He must see what Reuven had
brought back from Syria on his wagon—a date palm! Now
at once, this was the moment to plant it, and the entire
family turned back to the yard for the ceremony. Schmuel
and Mati dug the hole, Leah pumped buckets of water,
while Reuven carefully unwound the burlap from the roots,
explaining it was the best species, from where the two great
rivers, the Euphrates and the Tigris, had their confluence,
and where the legendary Garden of Eden really might have
been. In ancient times this species of date palm had flourished all down the Jordan valley, and if this tree took hold,
then as soon as there was peace in the whole of the Levant,
they must go back, beyond Damascus, and bring wagonloads of such date palms and plant them, for this was the
veritable tree of life.

Now Reuven and his wife Elisheva put the tree in the
ground, and at this moment Leah remembered with a
broad smile to tell Gidon, "Aviva sent a big shalom if I
should happen to see you. She's gone back to Jerusalem,
you'll find her there." Gidon flushed. He felt his mother's

eyes on him, and Yaffaleh's, and Shula's, then Dvoraleh's too.

Reuven and his bride straightened up; Mati tramped down the earth, Dvora's little Yechezkiel and Giora also jumped up and down on it, and Nahum even asked the old man to say a brocha. Everyone was glad Nahum had thought of it. How old was Abba now? Gidon studied his father, the beard was only streaked with gray. The shoulders were stooped, not in weakness but from labor. A real peasant, he looked. When they had first come to Eretz, Gidon remembered, he had already then thought of his father as an old man. Abba must be—what? fifty-five?

The entire population of Mishkan Yaacov kept circling through the yard—Reuven married, and into a fine wealthy Damascus family! And Gidon home, a fighter in the Jewish army!

In the afternoon, the young men went out to the furthest fields, Reuven, Gidon, Nahum, Schmulik, Menahem, and they let Mati come, as well. At one moment his brother-in-law Nahum led Gidon up the old rocks, he wanted to show him something. Mati did not stay behind—the whole day he clung to Gidon's side.

Climbing quite nimbly, Nahum reached a viewpoint. Look! It was the view toward where the Yarmuk joined the Jordon, and there, just before the juncture, Nahum pointed out a small island, as though Gidon had never seen it. It was there he had cut timber for the lean-to for their first mules. "That's my island!" he laughed to Nahum.

"Why not?" Nahum said. "Now it could be." Ths island and the long stretch of wasteland beyond—they were jiftlik, Nahum said, Turkish crown property; doubtless all this would be taken over by the new British government. And the entire bend beyond, where the Jordan valley was joined by the great Valley of Jezreel, the wide area all the way to the ancient Beit She'an—imagine the whole of it cultivated with lemon and orange groves, and groves of Reuven's date palms—all this! The British would surely take over all this crown land, and, according to their Balfour Declaration, they were bound to encourage land settlement by Jews. And about all this, Nahum had something in mind. What were Gidon's plans after the war?

He had thought a little, naturally, Gidon said, but as yet—

"You'll soon have to decide."

"Who knows?" Many of the men, and it was Jabotinsky's idea too, thought that the Jewish Brigade should be kept together, that the men should remain in the service so that it would be they who would be assigned by the British to establish order in the land.

"You want to remain in the army forever? Let others go in now, all the boys are volunteering. You, you've done your share, more than anyone. You have earned the right to start your own life."

Nahum had pierced to exactly what Gidon had been thinking, even in the same words that were in his own mind. He had earned the right to start his own life. Well, still, first he supposed he would come home and help Abba and Schmulik with the meshek. How many years could Abba have left for such heavy work?

"Believe me, Gidon, it never is good when you are fully grown—and you may want to get married—to share with your father. I'm in my father's business, and though we get along well, I know a grown man needs his own life. You want to be on your own. And you won't be satisfied like Reuven to be part of a kvutsa."

How could Nahum know his nature so well? "I thought first," Gidon said, "of perhaps finishing my veterinary studies."

"Perhaps. It is a good profession and will be much needed. But listen to me, Gidon, it's limited. You can earn a decent living but—it doesn't grow. And besides, big things will be happening here."

Nahum had talked with German engineers who come often to the Bagelmacher hotel. All the inventions, all the great strides, that had been made in the rapid production of war machinery, airplanes, motorcars, even the newest things, the tanks, all these would be turned to new uses in peacetime. The tanks would become tractors to pull farm implements, in the place of mules and horses. It would be a world of machines, even in farming. 'Of course," Nahum said, so as not to seem to be exaggerating, "a good veterinary will always be needed, for cattle and for poultry too—" Dvoraleh could tell of the wonders that were happening with poultry raising, especially in America where the incubators were turning into vast chicken factories.

But the best plan, in Nahum's view, was not to shut oneself into a small farm or into a profession that wouldn't grow. Now with the British, great things were going to happen here in this land, and here they were at the very beginning, and the best would be to be among those who made the great things happen. To seize hold from the very start.

Gidon didn't quite understand what Nahum was getting at, though he knew of course Nahum had always been clever. Now his brother-in-law explained his plan. Suppose they were to acquire large tracts of land, not only the government lands, the jiftlik, but lands that could be bought. And over all this area they would develop vast banana groves and citrus groves and date-palm plantations!

"But it takes years for trees to yield fruit. Who has so much money, to wait?"

"American Jews."

Nahum had worked out a complete plan. He would sell the plantations by sections, to American Jews and to English Jews; they would send money for the development, and when the trees bore fruit, everyone would profit. "Every Jew outside of Eretz should want his little piece of the Jewish homeland. Why should schnorrers collect pennies in little tin boxes for the Keren Kayemeth? Instead of coming to American Jews as beggars, we'll come with a business proposition. That's the way to do it!"

Glowingly Nahum explained each detail—he had it worked out with land costs and labor costs and the price of fruit and the profit to the Americans as well as to the company. "But suppose the British don't let us have the jiftlik lands?" Gidon asked.

"All this part you can leave to me," Nahum said, smiling confidently. What he wanted of Gidon was that he should undertake to manage the plantation. They would be partners.

It seemed far too large a thing to think about as yet. But Nahum went on, disclosing even greater visions. Did Gidon know how great a drop there was in the Jordon waters, just below them?

"A hundred and forty-six meters," Mati interposed.

—This little sprout was clever, he carried everything you wanted in his head! Nahum exclaimed. The German engi-

neers had studied the entire question of building a hydroelectric station there, and generating power. Of course it was
not the first time it had been thought of. But now all these
things would be possible. From that one hydroelectric station here you could light up the whole of Palestine. The
entire country could be modernized and industrialized—a
Switzerland! This was, Nahum reluctantly said, a plan beyond his own scope, it would have to be carried out by a
government or by great capitalists, but, even so, it would
open wonderful possibilites. The irrigation ideas that Reuven had had for intensive cultivation of the area could easily be carried out with electric power for the pumping of
water. Men and machines would pour into this valley for
such a giant construction scheme as a hydroelectric station. Tiberias would be the nearest city, and Tiberias would
grow. Huge modern hotels would be needed—nothing like
the little Bagelmacher pension. He himself in his own right
already owned a wonderful hotel site, near what had been
the Kaymakam's residence. He had a headful of plans. The
Tiberias hot springs themselves could be developed into a
world-famous health resort, a fashionable watering place
like Baden-Baden or Karlsbad. Indeed it was because of
these hot springs that the Roman Emperor Tiberius had
first built a palace here, and given the name of Tiberias to
Lake Kinnereth.

When Nahum went abroad to sell sections of their plantations he would also raise capital to build a new palatial
bathing establishment over the hot springs. Just as soon as
the war was finished, he would travel to London, to New
York; he would make a study of the fine luxury hotels of
Europe and America—

Under Nahum's spell, Gidon began to see the entire
Jordan valley studded with giant factories like in England;
below them would flow lighted roads, motorcars, tram-
ways. Why not? Hadn't Reuven too always pictured the
valley as densely populated, a vast, scientific Garden of
Eden?

From the hydroelectric plant, Nahum said, the Kinnereth's fresh water would be pumped into irrigation channels
as far as Jericho. Even the hellish wastes of the Mellallah,
as Gidon had described the place, could be made to bloom.
"Think about it. Get out of the army as quick as you can.
We'll go to work!

35

BEHIND the Jerusalem railway station Gidon found the compound to which Herscheleh was to have led their convoy of prisoners, a flat stretch of open ground already muddy from early rains, like some immense garbage dump on which clumps of human refuse had been left, with hardly a wire around the area to mark it off. At the gate there was no record of the convoy. As well—they had not yet arrived. So as to avoid complications over the convoy, he had remained at home only a single day, even though Herscheleh would have known how to handle things.

A half-hour's ride down the Jericho road, he encountered the column, with Tuvia in charge. "Good you came." This morning Herscheleh had been unable to get to his feet—dysentery combined with another malarial attack. "I took him in the wagon to the field hospital."

The hospital itself had proved hard to find, but at last Tuvia had discovered some Red Cross tents near Rachel's Tomb. Tuvia's eyes told enough—with Herscheleh, it was bad. He had not been able to stay with Herscheleh until a doctor came, because here he had left their two thousand prisoners resting by the roadside with no one in charge; should an officer have passed by and asked questions, they would all have been in the soup. He had only just now come back.

The whole way had been bad, Tuvia said. A sudden freak shower had come, just when they began moving up from Jericho. Chilling nights. On the climb, prisoners had given out and been left behind. Others had fallen dead, a few dozen. Herscheleh's fever had returned.

Tuvia's dry dull tone made Gidon feel frightened over Herscheleh, and guilty. If anything happened to Herscheleh, it was his fault. But what could he have done more than Tuvia? Still, if he had not left . . .

Wheeling back up the steep ascent he had to lash his tired horse. Once they reached the vast stretch of hospital tents, it took some time to find Herscheleh. There was no field hospital facility, the clerk insisted, for Patterson's Force, whatever that was. The Londoners didn't belong here, either. "We are attached to Chator. Oh, damn it, go look around for yourself if you want."

Toward the far end of the camp, in a long, gloomy tent where sick men lay in their blankets on the rain-damp ground, he found men from the 38th. Didn't they even have cots? Had anyone seen Herscheleh? "For cots you have to go back to Egypt," a voice croaked, "that's where they sent our cots. To our Palestine volunteers." It was Herscheleh. At least, if he could still joke, he wasn't dying.

But as Gidon knelt by his friend, his dread returned. Herschel's face was bloodless. The forehead glistened, but the eyes, after that first gleam, were lusterless. A stale odor enwrapped him.

There was no doctor for this section. Their own doctor was back at camp. There was not even a nurse. A few of the men who could move about brought water, rations. Alongside many of the sick, their rations lay uneaten on the tin plates on the ground. Herscheleh's, too.

Gidon hurried back to the administration hut. A doctor? "My dear fellow, we're helpless," a subaltern told him in an Oxford accent. "We're overrun. If you can find a doctor anywhere, do let me know."

Where could he turn? He must do something, do something. Never had Gidon felt such an anguish of helplessness. Find a doctor in some other detachment and bring him here at gunpoint? Hurry to Jerusalem and seek among the streets, among Jews—where is there a doctor for a Jewish soldier? Meanwhile Herscheleh might die here, untended, on the wet ground.

Gidon hurried back to the tent. "Listen to me, Herscheleh, I'm going out to bring a doctor." His friend's hand fastened onto his as though clingling to life; Gidon feared to take his own hand away. There was no strength in the handclasp and the skin was astonishingly hot.

Then Herscheleh began to talk, clearly, calmly, as though he had no trace of fever. He asked all about Gidon's visit home, asked about each sister and brother, about the farm, and said, "I can imagine what a feed your mother made for you!" He was interested in the tale of Reuven's marriage and of the piano brought the whole way from Damascus. And then, when he heard of Nahum Bagelmacher's ambitious plans, "It's an idea," Herscheleh said, even with a trace of his old irony. "Why not? Every American Jew should have his orange tree in Eretz. A very good idea. What do we need socialism for? Why didn't Ber Borochov think of something so simple and practical? So you had a good visit home."

—He'd better hurry up and get on his feet, Gidon admonished, so as to take his own turn to go home.

"No," Herschel said calmly. "Anyway, it's not so important." All Gidon's fright returned.

For all they had gone through together, Gidon knew little of Herscheleh's family execpt that he had relatives in Chedera.—Next to nobody, he had there in Chedera, Herscheleh now said—a farmer he had worked for had been decent to him, and who was from the same shtetl in Russia, maybe even a remote cousin.

Then, without a change of tone, Herscheleh was saying things Gidon could not quite follow. "If you believe in the theory of a fixed amount of energy in the universe, never destroyed but only changing in form, then it must also be from the inanimate to the animate—the inanimate is also a repository, a source of life energy . . ."

As he rambled, Herscheleh's voice became urgent, delirious. Now he was saying his father had been an anti-Zionist, and a landlord, a moneylender, so he had run away from home. His words merged back into Yiddish. "Tsion," he said, "you know what it means?" And he repeated with a feverish cackle, "Tsi—ohn" as one said in Yiddish, for trying on a garment, pull it on. And at his own jest, he remained silent for a moment, as though indeed trying on the meaning. Then he quoted, in mock-Oxford English, "How odd/Of God/To choose/The Jews," and began a rambling discussion in bits of English, then Hebrew, then Yiddish, then a phrase in Russian: how could anyone pretend to be an atheist, or even an agnostic, and yet be a Zionist? "Everyone of us here has the soul of a yeshiva bocher. We only substituted the concept of history for the concept of God. What are we doing here otherwise?"

Herscheleh's hand seemed to be slipping away. Gidon began to talk urgently of the ideas that had come up among the men for a settlement of veterans, not necessarily a kvutsa, but not a simple smallholder's village, a moshav, either. "Your idea, Herschel, a cooperative, half like a kvutsa, but where families would live each in their own house with their own children . . . Have you written out the plan yet? We must present it as soon as possible. Listen, we can ask the government for land, for jiftlik. Three-fourths of the whole country is jiftlik, did you know? I never thought it was that much. My little brother knows the figures exactly, he knows everything, that one—Mati. Listen—" Gidon couldn't tell if Herschel was hearing him, but he went on. For such a plan, they'd have to find girls, get married . . . Remotely Herschel's voice came, "I never found anyone. You found someone at last."

"You had that girl in England," Gidon said, to say something more, anything, anything.

"Gidon, Gidon—remember that time, the schneider on the rifle range that said, 'And then you shoot him in the tarboosh, God forbid!' Oh, our Yidlach. Oh, I love the Jews." Then, intimately, in his old knowing way, he whispered, "I know the best places . . ." Then after a long exhausted pause, "So much to be done . . ." he lapsed into silence.

His eyes closed. But there was a thread of pulse. He lived. Was it a coma? Sleep?

Could he leave Herschel even now and go search for a doctor, or should he give up and only sit here waiting for the death! Gidon squatted there on the ground, fearful that if Herschel awoke and found he was gone, it might make the final difference. And where would a doctor be found? In the depths of the hospital tent, Gidon caught sight of Simon the typist, still on his feet. "Watch over him. If he wakes and asks for me, say I'll be right back. I've gone to find a doctor." Simon nodded, and added with a weary shadow of a grin, "Ever see so many Jews and not a doctor in the lot?"

Whatever it was, Simon's feeble quip, or even some despairing need in himself to get out of the dreadful tent, Gidon hurried away, riding toward the Old City's Jewish quarter. It was closest. And there he had Aviva's address—who else did he know in Jerusalem? Her people would help him find a doctor. With the army it was impossible; he'd have to force his way up to headquarters itself, the devil knew where.

The lane lay close against the Old City wall, and there

when he asked the name, "Yerushalmi?" a boy with ear-
locks pointed to a wooden door to a walled courtyard. It
was locked, but Gidon found a cord to a bell that tinkled
within; at once he heard quick steps coming across the
stones. Aviva's, he was certain, and she opened the door
and pulled him in with a swift delighted kiss on his cheek,
then fleetingly across his lips—the first time. At this moment he could not feel the joy of it without guilt over Herscheleh, though he kept his arm around her. "Aviva, I have
to find a doctor at once," and he explained.

The courtyard was crowded with flowers around tiny
vegetable beds; Aviva had learned well from Leah, he
could not help noticing. At the rear was a narrow house
with an outer stair of worn stones; at the landing, a toddler
was already trying to come down to them, eying Aviva
with a half-frightened, daring grin as he wobbled down the
step. She rushed up and caught him, "Amnon! No!" with a
hug; the mamser couldn't be left alone for an instant—she
was tending him, their mother had gone back to teaching.
The doctor—it would be difficult, he was overwhelmed, the
only one left in the Old City, but he was a good friend of
her father's—"I'd better go with you." Amnon couldn't be
left, she'd have to take him. And she had to write a note
for her little sister who'd be coming home from school. The
room was walled with books, and on the floor stood several
large glued-together jars, finds from her father's searchings.

He'd better tether the horse in the yard. The child trotted between them holding a hand of each; as they turned
into a more crowded lane, Gidon hoisted Amnon up on his
shoulders. The doctor's flat was just inside the Jaffa gate
and at least he was there. The waiting room was filled,
Jews, Arabs, some squatting on the floor. But they let the
soldier through; Aviva knocked on the inner door and
called, "Dr. Plotzker, it's Aviva Yerushalmi. Excuse me—
an emergency." In a moment the door opened; a stout Jew
with a skullcap on his bald head peered at Gidon.

Aviva explained. "It's his chaver, he's dying."

"They won't let me into the camp without a pass," the
doctor said. "I've already been turned away by your British
lords. Get me a pass, I'll come."

"But with me, I'll get you in—"

"They're strict. It's no use wasting my time. Get me a

pass." To Aviva he added, "Regards home," and closed his door.

Then came another tormented half hour, trying to find the right place to secure a pass. Aviva with little Amnon he sent back. At the military civilian administration, crowds, queues, and then in sheer luck, from behind the barrier, Gidon heard his name called, and it was Fawzi, from home, from Dja'adi, laughing at the encounter. "Gidon! By my life!" Pulled behind the rail, he was pummeled, embraced.

Through hardly in the mood, he had to exchange complete news of home. "Your sister Leah, the big one—" A few years ago, Fawzi laughed, he had encountered her here in this very office when he worked for the Turks. Oh, yes, because of his reading and writing they had given him a good job, and besides his cousin from Jerusalem was high in this office. Also now with the British. Fawzi was learning to read and write English, he was to be an interpreter. Maybe his grandfather would again reward him with a fine horse!

At last Gidon was able to mention the pass. At once! Fawzi would get his cousin Haj Amin to sign it. "I'll say it's for an uncle of yours." Good luck for Gidon's friend. They must meet again, and go hunting in the Huleh like in the old days. Soon he was going to take a party of English officers there—they loved to hunt wild pigs. They did it in India, they said; only, could Gidon imagine, the mad Englishmen, they would not hunt the boar with guns, only with spears!

Pushing his way through the thronged lanes, half-running, he at last got the doctor. On the way to the camp the doctor told him, with interposed strings of Yiddish invective, how efforts had been made at least to send volunteer nurses into the field hospital to care for the Jewish soldiers. Refused. Incredible. A scandal. He could not fathom the military mind. Naturally one had to be grateful to the British for deliverance, and perhaps in time when the military administration was gone . . . But Weizmann himself after only a few months had given up and left; with the military in charge, there was nothing he could do. No use. Then suddenly the doctor emitted a heavy sigh and echoed his own last words, as a summation of philosophy.

"Against certain forces in human society, as in nature itself, it's no use."

And when they arrived in the long tent, so it proved. Herschel had not awakened, Simon told them. Shaking his head, the doctor stooped, opened Herscheleh's eye, closed it, shook his head again, glanced at Gidon. "Don't blame yourself. You did all you could. It would have been the same in any case." From all sides there were calls to him. "I'm really not allowed—" but he hurried from one man to another. A few he gave pills from his bag, muttering the whole time, a shame, a scandal.

Gidon made his way back to the convoy to tell Tuvia. They led their stumbling mass of prisoners to the compound.

Later, Aviva's whole family was at home: a brother of fourteen in the youth movement who eyed Gidon with respect and was shy about asking questions; a little sister who tried not to stare at him; the father with gold-rimmed glasses and a thick gray-speckled mustache, who said Gidon must come on Shabbat for a walk and, just outside the Old City wall, he would show him what he believed to be the real site of David's citadel; and the mother, compact, energetic, not old-fashioned like his own Mameh, and yet a balabusta, he could see, and making him feel already as one of the family. To the father he spoke of the ruins that Reuven had found above the Kinnereth, and the teacher became excited—now it would be possible to go to the Kinnereth again! He wanted to meet Reuven.

"He's only done his searches by himself," Gidon said. "He always calls himself an amateur."

"But I too am only self-taught," Aviva's father said, with his resigned sigh.

"Peretz, you know more than all their professors," his wife declared.

Peretz Yerushalmi shrugged. "The books anyone can read, and the material is all around us."

Suddenly Gidon was thinking of Herscheleh, the reader. A bitterness came over him, and in spite of the nearness of Aviva, he wanted to leave, to rush out anywhere. They were trying to ease him, to talk—the mother talked of why they lived here in the Old City; as they were not religious, they had at first been a great shock to their neighbors; she even told a few half-humorous incidents of Hasidim spitting at them. But to her husband, only the Old City was Jerusalem. Peretz would not think of living outside the walls, and she too had come to feel that way; it was not really unpleasant once you got within your own courtyard, though the smells—

Aviva suggested a walk. Taking his hand as they went out into the lane, she kept silently along with him. A weeping was welling up from within, but Gidon held it back.

"Do you know what," he heard her say, "have you ever been up on the walls?" Still holding his hand, she led him alongside the wall and there they came to stairs rising up to the very top. "Look," she said—on each stone step the moonlight lay. Aviva went up first. "We played here when I was a little girl," she said, her hand still reaching back in his.

Above, the top of the wall was wide enough sometimes for both, sometimes for one. The parapet, with archer's slits, was low enough so that they could see over it, everywhere around. In the village of Sylwan a few lamps showed, and above it, the regularly spaced lanterns of an encampment; looking downward, they saw a steep rocky ravine, the bluish light veiling the bottom as though it were not the solid earth down there, but an opening into unknown depths.

"The vale of Hinom?" he asked, though he knew—the valley into the nether world. Across, on the opposite slope, were the tombstones of the Mount of Olives, the low, irregular markers like an ordinary field of rocks. Would Herschel have wanted to lie there, even if he was supposedly godless, rather than one day be reburied, as they had promised at the field hospital, in some military cemetery?

"You're thinking of your chaver," she said softly.

Gidon turned slowly with his back to Hinom and the mount of graves. They had still not let go of each other's hands. For a time they looked into each other's faces. The cast of the moonlight on her cheeks, over her mouth, made her seem part of the eternal stone, and the unfathomable words from Herschel's delirium echoed to him. For a moment he seemed to grasp it all, to understand, from her hand still in his, from her eyes seeing within him. This time Gidon let the tears brim over.

She moved and was close against his side.

Then Gidon told her he was unclean. He told her how, long ago, even before the war, he had lain watching the Zbeh come closer and had slain two of them. Aviva seized his head between her hands, "Gidon! It is not a retribution! You hear me! You must never imagine it is a retribution! That is forbidden." Her voice was no longer a girl's, but like the voice of someone—a teacher, a mother, a woman—who has a right to tell you such things. "Gidon, it is forbidden!"

He looked downward on the inner side of the wall, and, partly because of his remaining teariness, the inner city that lay there was diffused, softened, so that it was like the surface of her cheeks, her face, glowing with life within. At the wonder and beauty of it, Gidon drew in a breath of awe, and a soft pressure from her fingers told him that she too felt this eternity.

Nearest them lay the small domed stone roofs of the houses of the Jewish quarter, the domes rolling from each other like a rippled sea, and beyond rose the larger domes of the mosques that stood over the Temple site, both the gold and the silver ones indistinguishable in color, luminous in the cast of the moon, and beyond and inward within the continuous encircling wall the entire Old City was a unity of low, small repeating roof domes, and rising from amidst them, so many spires and minarets, while between in the creases of the lanes a few lantern lights glimmered.

Gidon wondered again, had Herschel ever, perhaps before the war, seen it from here—this beautiful sight, of a forever that had been made by man? But now, when he thought of Herschel, it was without such bitter grief, now it was a calmed sorrow.

It seemed to Gidon that he for the first time understood them all, the chaluka Jews, living on alms, then the early Zionists, Aviva's father with his battle for Hebrew and his love for this place, his own father, and he understood why he himself was here. And not only their own generations, but long before. These were Turkish-built walls; David's walls had been perhaps not exactly here beneath them where they stood, but, as Aviva's father said, on the hill just behind, the hill of Zion—yet Gidon knew they stood on David's walls, and the enclosed city that lay below them in a magic silence was David's city; the remnant called

David's tower, though a mosque, was a tower of David's citadel; the vast luminous Moslem dome was a dome of the Temple, and the spires and minarets that arose so thickly from the Christian and Moslem quarters were no intrusions—they were included in the Jewish eternity of this place, as was the death of all the defenders who had fallen here under the Roman onslaught, and before, under Nebuchadnezzar's onslaught, as was the death only today of his chaver Herscheleh. Therefore he felt a more peaceful sorrow in this moment.

While he stood there with Aviva, another couple passed, their arms around each other's waist as they kept close together on the ledge. As the pair walked slowly, half-entranced, beyond them, there was a fleeting expression on Aviva's face, not a smile but an acquiescence, even touched with a kind of "forgive me" because of Herschel. This then was a place where lovers came. And Gidon let his eyes acknowledge it all to her; surely Herschel would have been glad of it so. Suddenly their lips came together in love, in sorrow and tenderness, in apology and yet in an outcry; Oh, God, what can you want of us, what can you expect of us when such utter beauty lies upon the earth, when such craving grows in our hearts, frightened of our own calling to each other?

Then they walked on along the top of the wall, sometimes passing motionless couples embraced in the casements, their own hands still sealed together, for it was not yet the night to put their arms tightly around each other. But all along their sides their limbs brushed and sometimes clung.

Where the life in the barracks, before, among the little nucleus of old comrades who had been together since Gallipoli had been a refuge to him, in Alexandria, in England, even in the Mellallah, it had now suddenly become unendurable. Perhaps it had been Herscheleh who had held that life together. But now every coarse jest grated on him; an entire seraglio left behind by the Turks had been discovered in Salt, but the tales of it only disgusted him. In another week, the war with the Turks all at once ended. Now the urge to get out, to go home, to start his life with Aviva, was a continuous torture. But even the speculations, rumors, discussions of demobilization were a torment, for no one really knew the slightest thing for certain.

They were comfortable in abandoned houses, the food was better, things were far better now for the sick—their own medic had gone to Jerusalem, made a great row at headquarters, and the sick were now in hospital. Much good it did the dead.

Gidon's head was crowded with images of how the real part would begin with Aviva. Their first time he must make beautiful. She was ready to come to him, and perhaps they should even simply get married at once and not wait until he was out of the service.

The battalion was moved back to Sarafend. Who knew but what they might still be shipped off to fight in Europe?

She was going down to help Leah, Aviva wrote; the owner of Leah's last farming place had returned, and Leah was starting a new girls' farm on the other side of Tel Aviv, on the sands toward the Yarkon River.

In the midst of it all, the whole war ended. In Europe, everywhere. There was peace in the world.

For Sabbath Gidon got a pass and found Leah's new meshek, a half hour's walk across the sands; what a place for a group of girls! He was suddenly almost angry at his sister, but Leah laughed—he needn't fear, they were infested with "protectors." If he delayed, one of them would steal Aviva away.

Aviva laughed softly.

Gidon had a new plan to talk to her about, a plan that appealed to him more than Nahum's grandiose ideas. Araleh and Saraleh were back, taking care of the Zuckerman hotel in Tel Aviv. Tonight there was a meeting with Araleh about a settlement for veterans. He had made a complete plan for a cooperative such as Herscheleh had used to talk about. Araleh himself wanted to go back to the soil, he said; he was not made to be a hotelkeeper—besides, as a construction expert he would be useful in building the settlement. Saraleh too was eager. Tuvia had put down his name, and even Red Nathan, and a dozen more of the best.

First, Saraleh had Gidon and Aviva eat, not in the hotel's dining room, but with her and Araleh and the children; she had insisted on having her own quarters behind the hotel, a real home. And from the first moment, as Gidon came in with Aviva, she beamed her approval. Now

Gidon knew he had of course never been in love with Saraleh the way he had thought in Alexandria. A poor lonely lout's hunger. How lucky it was he had never said anything, always restrained himself because of his friendship for Araleh, though women know these things. At least now he had no need to feel ashamed. They drank toasts, a l'chayim to peace, a l'chayim to Gidon and Aviva, another to Araleh and Saraleh, to the new cooperative, to the homeland!

Later others came and the whole meeting went off like a dream of amity: a few good arguments, but not a single quarrel, everyone intent on showing how well they would be able to get along together. All would be modern, with the latest agricultural machinery from America, to be used by each member in rotation. They would have big fields in common, but vegetable gardens and poultry for each family individually. They would buy seed and materials together and sell produce together. All was so peaceful that Araleh even remarked, "Chevreh, it is all too good—next meeting, let's have some bitter disputes!"

But one problem did arise. Wives.

For practical reasons, it was suggested only married couples—"or even not so married," someone jested—could become part of the group.

"What is this, the old Baron's kind of settlement?" Tuvia growled.

But how would a man manage his share without a wife?

—With someone else's wife!

—No, chevreh, seriously—

And, seriously, even Tuvia agreed it would be a need. "A need in more ways than one. Seriously."

—Well, then—

"Don't worry, the way it's going with the British, before we can get out of the army to start the settlement, we'll all have wives, even grandchildren."

After the meeting had broken up, and one after another had said his Shalom and gone off—Tuvia the last, lingering as though he expected Gidon to come along with him—Gidon remarked, "I'm staying over. I'm sleeping here in the hotel."

Aviva had sat with him through the meeting, and then gone off a bit with Saraleh; now she returned and took

Gidon's hand, and they went up to their room. Already in the afternoon he had passed by and arranged it all with Araleh, and taken the key.

As in all the rooms, there were six cots.

"Never mind!" he said. "It's for us alone."

"You paid for them all?"

"It's a wedding present from Saraleh and Araleh." They fell upon each other.

Only a few weeks later they arranged an actual wedding, with the canopy and all. Word had spread that married men would be the first to be demobilized, and besides, why wait? The wedding was to be in the open, in the Yerushalmi courtyard, with the rabbi of the Jewish battalions performing the ceremony, so that even the pious neighbors could scarcely find fault.

The day before the event, already on leave in Jerusalm, Gidon encountered Fawzi and told him the news and invited him—how could he not have thought of it before!

—A toast! Fawzi cried, and they sat down at the Alhambra. Fawzi ordered whiskies, he had learned from the English what to drink. Sparkling with joy as though it were for his own self, he told tales of marital prowess, told the joke about the village simpleton who found himself unable to perform with his bride and exclaimed in puzzlement, "But just a moment ago I wanted to make sure, so I went with a sheep, five times!"

Jestingly, Fawzi offered to take Gidon to a very good place where he could learn a few tricks for the wedding night—was he sure he knew what to do? A wonderful place, only English officers went there. French girls, the best. And Jewish girls were very good! His eyes sparkled as those of a man knows whereof he speaks.

—Arab girls too, Gidon said, and they jabbed each other laughing, while for an instant the memory came to Gidon of the little Sudanese prostitute in Cairo.

—And in England, Fawzi demanded, English girls?

—In England—Gidon didn't know why he was about to say it, but it was as though it brought Herscheleh here with them—in England, the little factory girls who had husbands away at the front, oh, they were wonderful.

Fawzi licked his lips. All their camaraderie had returned. Soon they would go pig-sticking in the Huleh with his British colonel, Fawzi cried, making the gesture of sticking the pig, and laughing intimately, between themselves, as he repeated the gesture in obscenity. Oh, the English! The colonel was even going to take him to England to become very well educated, and when he returned here, he would be an important man. Oh, the English, they were great friends for the Arabs!

—For the Jews, he wasn't so sure, Gidon said.

"Oh, the Jews don't need so much help! You are clever! You are all rich!" Fawzi said. And with a sly grin, he drew from his pocket a sheaf of typed pages, bluish hectographed copies, like a pamphlet of some sort, and handed it to Gidon, watching as Gidon read.

It was in English, but with some odd words even in the title, so that at first Gidon could hardly understand. "Protocols." What were "protocols"? He glanced further. The secret meeting of the Elders of Zion. What did that mean—Elders of Zion? Zionists or what? A whole list of names followed, the Chief Rabbi, Rothschilds, Herzl—and the meeting took place in the cemetery in Prague—what was this?

Gidon looked up at Fawzi, who had a delighted expression, as when someone catches you out. "But what is this, where did you get it?"

"How you are going to rule the world! The Jews!" Fawzi slapped him on the knee. Hesitatingly, Gidon joined in his laughter.

The colonel had given these papers to Fawzi. The colonel had brought the booklet from Russia where the English had sent him with arms to help the Russians that were fighting the Bolsheviki. These papers were translated from a secret Russian book.

In each country we shall have all the gold. With the gold in our hands, the rulers will have to do as we say—
We shall take all the women as we choose—

"But it's crazy," Gidon said.

Fawzi chuckled. "That's what I say to them. Some Jews work hard, they are poor like us." He leaned in, as when sharing talk about women. "My cousin Haj Amin says it is all true. He is highly educated, in Cairo, in the University, in the Al Haram. He is a Huseini from Jerusalem. Oh, very rich. Already he has made the pilgrimage to Mecca, he is already a Haj." Then Fawzi leaned forward as though to share the best part. "He says the Jews want to drive us out from the land!"

But why should such a thing be said? Where was there any sign of it? Were they not living peacefully side by side in Dja'adi amd Mishkan Yaacov? had anyone been driven from his land?

Then, as though here too a secret plan had been caught out, like the secret plan of certain Jews—not Gidon's kind!—to rule the world, Fawzi spoke of the Declaration. Did it not say Jews should have this land?

Gidon felt safer. "But the Declaration is for Arabs too. It says we should have a homeland, yes, but nothing should be taken from anybody's rights, that lives here."

Ah?

And Fawzi shrugged. It was all politics, he laughed, and talked of women. Did Gidon want to know a way to make certain whether a bride was a virgin? Gidon flushed. In such matters, Fawzi said, he himself would be old-fashioned. When he married, if the girl was not a virgin, he would send her back at once to her father and demand back the bride-money. Then perhaps her brothers would kill her.

They laughed together and drank up.

Fawzi came to the wedding and was not the only Arab. Peretz Yerushalmi too had invited Arab friends, several antiquarians of the Old City, and a teacher of Arabic from his school, and everyone kept seeing to it that they were not left standing to a side. When the festivities were at their height, Fawzi and Gidon and Schmulik and other lads formed a line and, as in the old days, Fawzi led them out in a debka.

Never had Gidon thought of himself as popular. The Irishman had come, and half the battalion it seemed, filling the courtyard and the little street; the entire family had come from Mishkan Yaacov, Mameh overburdened with packages and pots filled with good things to eat, and Leah had brought her whole kvutsa of girls up from Tel Aviv, Aviva's chaveroth. Of all the weddings, Shula declared, this was the most joyous.

It was a season of marriages. Even Rahel's! For at last, from their long waiting in Egypt, there arrived the third battalion of the Brigade, with Dovidl, and Avner. At once the two of them summoned a sitting in the party's cabin by the sea, arriving late, as they had received no pass and had had to sneak out. So many problems were on the agenda there was hardly time for a proper greeting.

Dovidl was married! He had married a girl in New York, a nurse, and already a baby had been born, a girl he had not yet seen.

Here Dovidl stood before Leah at last, and the same old impulse returned between them: they both burst out laughing. "Nu?" Dovidl said. "And you, Leah?"

And she? What could she say to him? That she was still a big fool, secretly dreaming of the day her Handsome Moshe might appear, as a few Russian Jews had begun to appear, after walking the whole way from the Caucasus?

—What a sight he was in uniform, she laughed, and Avner even worse, his leggings loose, his belt awry. Dovidl gave his comical shrug, and the sitting began—so many problems—who knew where to start? Avner had come with an agenda and a whole prepared plan. Unity must be achieved first of all, a single workers' party; an assembly of workers must be prepared, for they, and not the merchants and notables of Tel Aviv, must become the leading force in the National Home. Behind them they would have the whole force of the Poale Zion in America, and they must send a powerful delegation to the next Zionist Congress and be sure to capture places on the crucial committees. They must also send delegates to the World Socialist Congress and not become isolated; they must be a part of the world movement and have the movement behind them. Here at home there was the whole question of security. The Shomer was broken, half the men had returned with their health forever impaired. Besides, a new, broader organization was needed, one that would include the Herzlia Gymnasia group of Dov and Eli. And also the men of the Brigade—

A whole side-discussion began. The Jewish battalions must not disband! There was Jabotinsky's plan for them to be turned into a militia—

—But at least, leaders like Avner and Dovidl must be

got out of the service! It was absurd that they hadn't even
been able to obtain a pass to come here!

—Yes, and if the meeting didn't soon end, they wouldn't
be able to get back to Sarafend tonight and would be
thrown into the brig in the morning.

"Wait!" Leah interposed. There was perhaps a way. Her
brother Gidon had got married and it was true this had
helped, as Gidon was about to be given his discharge!

Misha, the secretary, who had lost his voice in the Damascus imprisonment, called out in his hoarse whisper, "Chavera
Leah, is this a proposal that Avner should get married?"

To everyone's astonishment, Avner, in the midst of the
laughter, announced from the chair, "If it helps, I am ready
here and now."

What was happening here! Suddenly the sitting had become a wedding! Young Avram from Gilboa arose to suggest they be married under the Jewish law of two witnesses.
It turned out that Avner even carried with him a wedding
ring bought in America and inscribed with Rahel's name
and his own. Standing with Rahel before Dovidl and Shimshoni, Avner declared he took Rahel unto him for his wife.
In recognition of equality of the sexes, Rahel in her turn
declared that she took Avner to her for her husband. Leah
was the first to embrace Rahel, engulfing her. Rahel clung
to her and sniffled.

And Leah herself? She was truly now the last.

It was Menahem who, at the next sitting, proposed the
mission to Russia. From those who had managed to come
through, one or two at a time, little could be learned. They
told of small groups of chalutzim meeting here and there.
One of them had heard of a conference that had been organized, was it in Kovno? by Josef Trumpeldor. But where
Trumpeldor was now, he had no idea. All Russia was tohu
v'bohu.

There was no doubt someone had to go there to make
contact, and to start a new stream of chalutzim flowing.

Then Leah rose. —What about chalutzoth? Women were
desperately needed. The experience of their own generation
had shown that with such a shortage of women, many of
the men did not stay. A woman should be sent there, too.

Both she and Menahem were selected. But how should

they go? With what papers? Russian ports were blockaded by the capitalist powers.

In Constantinople, Menahem was confident, he could find a way. Constantinople was occupied by the French, and just now they also held Odessa. Perhaps by that route? But how should Meneham and Leah even get to Constantinople? "Combinations" must be found.

Several kinds of identity papers were prepared by Young Avram. Leah even found her old Russian documents; she would be returning to seek her faimily. No, better—to take part in the revolution.

Finally, through Avner's political maneuvering in the Zionist Commission, urgent requests were made by the Commission to the military government for a safe-conduct for a pair of delegates to a labor conference in Constantinople.

36

IN CONSTANTINOPLE, Menahem soon managed. A busy black-market traffic to Odessa was being carried on by small vessels, and in one of these charterd by a Jewish lawyer from Moscow, who had escaped to Odessa and was trafficking in dried figs, bolts of cloth, olives, whatever he could find, they sailed. Menahem passed from the ship as a sailor. A woman—who noticed a woman, even such a large one? Leah walked ashore in the company of the Moscow lawyer who had just completed his arrangements with the customs inspector. What did it matter how much you paid, he laughed—in Odessa there were no price limits. Anything you could bring in you could sell for any price you named. Indeed he had noticed that Menahem was a clever man, and if perchance he wanted to go into business— fortunes could be made on a single trip. Fortunes.

There they were, before the great broad stairs that led from the harbor up to the city. Down these stairs, fourteen years ago, she had hurried with Reuven, in their departure for Eretz! Menahem too was filled with memories of the harbor, from his sailor days.

He walked swiftly, he knew just where he was going. Before the courtyard entrance of a large gray building, neither impoverished nor affluent looking, a pair of young men lounged, distinctly chevreh, on watch! It couldn't be—but it was true. In the old headquarters of the Jewish Self-Defense League—they were still here in the same backrooms! Young Jews. Defenders. Zionists.

The emissaries from Eretz were surrounded, hugged, deluged with talk, questions, inquiries, names. Was it true—a Jewish nation? And could they really get in? How could they go? What were the conditions in the land?

Here, things were in a turmoil. The French had come a few months before, but it was believed they would leave. Perhaps soon. No, they interfered little, and at least they kept off the roving bands of murderous Ukrainians. The Ukrainian nationalists were everywhere, killing Jews, seizing entire areas from the Bolsheviki, from each other. The Whites too were said to be on the march from their stronghold in the Caucasus. But here in Odessa, the Jewish Defense was holding fast. In this place, they had a garrison, a kitchen; many slept here. In the city, turmoil. Jews had fled here from Moscow, from Petrograd—starvation in the cities. Money had no value. Speculation, madness. Some lived like kings. The old Zionist leaders were still here, they would meet them. Trumpeldor? Not here in Odessa. It was rumored that he had come with a kvutsa as far as the Crimea and was on the way to Eretz.

Even before they had half-adjusted themselves and begun to make lists of contacts in various towns, the event came—overnight the French evacuated. Boarded their ships and sailed away. The next day the Red Army was in the city. It was better, it was worse. The Jewish camp remained unmolested. A red flag went up. Black marketeers were being arrested, shot. Many of the speculators were Jews, but who could defend them? The best was to sit quietly until there was a semblance of order.

Leah could not sit quietly, now that the way was open. What of their mission? They must go to the centers of Jewish life, they must find what remained of the movement.

Menahem could not leave; he was already involved in complex, secret negotiations to charter a ship. In the end he agreed that Leah should go. A lad named Meier, who knew his way about, was going to Kiev, just now freed from the Ukrainian separatists.

To wait in the station for a train was hopeless, Meier said. Among the thousands besieging the station, it would take a week to pass through. However, he knew the place where the engine stopped for water.

Even there, the ground was covered with those who waited. Peasants with bundles and wicker crates, townsfolk with suitcases. Why did people move about, where were they going, did they all have a purpose as she had? A day and a night on the ground, but at last they were successful. As the train approached, they pushed themselves so close to the tracks that they might well have been pushed under the wheels. Meier would wiggle his way between elbows and legs, and into the crack he made, Leah would press with all her bulk. Now the lad scrambled to the roof of a boxcar and she climbed up on his heels. To make room, Leah took a peasant woman's huge basket into her lap.

Before Kiev was Cherezinka.

And yet, in the early morning, as the train bumped on uneven rails through the region of her childhood and from the cartop she saw the endless vista of the fields of wheat swaying in a broad slow movement as though the great skirt of heaven had brushed over the land, it was hard to keep thinking of all the dreadful things that had happened and were still happening here in the Ukraine, and instead Leah's heart rose in anticipation of her childhood home.

On the roads she could see the peasants driving their long dray-wagons, the same sort as were used in Eretz after all, and in the fields she could see the squat women in their many broad skirts and cover-aprons, with their kerchiefs on their heads, bent over as before, as always, and the squat moujiks trudging in their boots. Then how could it really all be changed?

At last the train made the halt at Cherezinka, and the station hut looked the same, unpainted, mean and small, but even more dilapidated, the windows half-boarded up or stuffed with rags where panes were missing. But once she had scrambled down to the earth and turned her head to look this way and that, Leah saw that war had passed through—many times, as she had already heard. Petlura and his pogromists, and the Reds, and again Ukrainian bands, and now it was once more the Reds; they had seized everything, they arrested, they shot, but at least they put an end to pogroms.

A militiaman examined the travel pass that the lads in Odessa had arranged for her. He screwed up his eyes for a moment, then shrugged and waved her by. On her first steps along the familiar central street, Leah half-expected at once to recognize people she had known, but not a face seemed familiar. Red flags hung from various buildings; she recognized the apothecary's shop, but the Jewish name on the sign was gone. Here and there lines of women stood, with market bags, and that air of long patience—they didn't even seem to be gossiping. A few faces she almost knew—but she wasn't sure. Now she turned into a Jewish lane, her heartbeat quickening. Surely here she would see old school friends, neighbors—and she'd hurry to the big house of her uncle, where she would find everyone.

First, here was the courtyard where she and the family had lived. This house too had been owned by Uncle Kalman the Rich; considered an excellent building, it had four stairways spaced around the courtyard, and dwellings for some thirty families, all told. As Leah passed through the wagon gate, she felt relieved—the yard was the same. There in the center stood the low-branched apple tree over whose fruits everyone used to quarrel, and two small boys sat on a branch swinging their heels over the heads of four little girls who were playing, just below. Such pretty children! Leah could have swept them up in her arms to carry them straight back to Eretz!

"Who are you!" one boy called out in Russian, not Yiddish, and already a young woman was running from a washtub—still in the same place by the pump—calling incredulously, "Leah!"

It was Marusha, the daughter of a neighbor from her own stairway. Two of the little girls were hers, and a life-story tumbled forth, even as Marusha spirited Leah into her flat "before everyone seized her." She lived with her mother and father, the glazier—no, he no longer had the shop opening into the yard, but at least he had been accepted into the glaziers' artel; Marusha's husband had been killed in the war fighting for the Czar, she said with a bitterness that seemed to embrace both the Czar and her dead spouse.

"You remember Pinya the Philosopher, as everyone

called him—he was always with your brother Reuven, he too was a young Zionist—if he had only gone with Reuven he would be alive today—I married Pinya. How is Reuven—is he married, and you, Leah?"

But swiftly engulfing Leah's answer, Marusha's words tumbled on, not even giving Leah a chance to ask about her own cousins, her Uncle Kalman; the Germans had been here, yet somehow everyone here in the house had got through the time of the Germans; then the revolution—but then came Petlura, savages, the foulest of scum—the whole yard was a gehenna, blood, dead Jews.

"They raped me, too, they found me and dragged me out and raped me here on the stairs—" Marusha sucked in her lip just like when they were little girls and did something naughty. "I was lucky, only one of them, and then he took me for his—I begged him, if it must happen, then not on the stairs. But we never speak of those things and now things are better."

Yes, she now had a good friend, a comrade, a Red Army man, and he was very fond of her children, and they were very fond of him, though—and this time with an intimate whisper, a secret between them as in the old days, her mother must not know, "Leah, he's a goy!"

They had reached Marusha's door. From her mother, in a long singsong interspersed with sighs, Leah heard that very few Jews were left in the building, the Russians had sent them all away during the war and few had managed to come back; as to Leah's uncle, he was no longer the landlord, the building was appropriated, and she didn't know what had become of him—though she said it with an intake of breath that left Leah uncertain what she meant. This was no longer a Jewish courtyard. "Others" had taken over the flats.

Then the mother gazed on Leah with watery, compassionate eyes and whispered, "They killed him."

Her huge powerful uncle, the house-owner, the mill-owner, the loud Kalman before whom the entire family trembled? Who had killed him? the Germans? the Petlurists? No, no, even with those bandits he had managed, he contributed gold. "But when the Red Army men came, they shot him." The woman said it without comment in her voice; so it was, and Marusha again uttered her little giggle.

After a moment Leah asked—her cousins?

Oh no, not them. Nor her aunt.

—Where were they, then? Again, Marusha's mother sucked in her breath.

—And her school-day friends? Leah recalled several names from their youth group, the Tzirai Zion Club, had Marusha heard from any of them? In those days Marusha had come now and again to the meetings, it was there that girls met boys.

Oh, she had long ago forgotten those things, Marusha said. Now there was the revolution!

But perhaps some of their old friends were to be found? Perhaps some of them still dreamed of coming to Eretz Yisroel? "Now all can come! The doors are open! We have a Declaration—it will be a Jewish land!"

The mother seized Leah's arm. "Truly? Is it all true?" It had been whispered, but no one believed it. And now she wanted Leah to tell her how it was with them there, and at each detail, of the farm, of their cattle, of the cooperativa and Reuven's Garden of Eden, she clucked her tongue and sighed, "And Eretz Yisroel will really become a Jewish land?"

Suddenly Marusha rattled out, "The British imperialists have seized Palestine, and Jews are helping them to protect their Suez Canal and their colonial empire!" Then again she giggled.

It was necessary at once to register her presence in Cherezinka, and as Leah inquired for the commandatura, she was given a familiar address. But—it was her uncle's mansion!

Naturally enough, since they had liquidated the capitalist counterrevolutionary, they had taken over his big house. And there in the grand entrance hall Leah found, sitting behind the broad mahogany table with carved legs that she remembered from her uncle's library, a comrade secretary to whom she addressed herself. On the walls there still hung several huge gilt-framed paintings of which her uncle had been proud, a portrait of himself in a frock coat, and opposite it a painting of the prophet Elijah with a tangled gray beard, wearing an animal skin. There was also a vast painting of Moses on a thunderous mountaintop, with a streak of lightning illuminating the stone tablets of the

Ten Commandments that he held aloft over his head. Strange that they hadn't taken down these pictures. Indeed the house looked undisturbed, even cared for with respect, yes, a possession now of the people. And this gave her a feeling of approval, even of kinship to the revolutionists, though surely it might not have been really necessary to shoot her big, loud uncle. It was Kalman Koslóvsky, people said, her mother's brother, that she resembled in her great size. But perhaps Uncle Kalman had done something foolish. A provocation.

The comrade secretary, studing her ancient Russian document, suddenly arose and disappeared down the broad dim hall. Would there be difficulties now? Leah scarcely had time to speculate before she saw the comrade returning, followed by an officer who stepped quickly around the table and came to her. But it was her cousin Tolya! Fine-looking, erect, with steady half-narrowed eyes as analytical as ever, and on his face, even while he was smiling there remained his characteristic look betokening the seriousness of life.

"Leah! What brings you here!"

He took her at once into the library, which was his office. The hebrew volumes had disappeared from the glass-doored cases, which now held official-looking publications and dossiers. Extending his pack of cigarettes, then lighting one for himself, Tolya settled back and gazed at her, his examination speedily measuring many things—his eyes showed an objective approval of a strong-looking female, then they were the eyes of a thinker cataloging the forces of history, and then, as if the analytical part was concluded, they were even the remembering eyes of a cousin with whom she had grown up.

"First," Tolya declared, "since you undoubtedly will hear of it if you have not already heard, I must tell you that my father was liquidated as a class enemy."

"I've already heard."

"At the time, I was not here. I was fighting on the northern front against Kolchak. However," he added, as a man who makes no exceptions in the face of truth, "my poor father unfortunately remained to the end a slave of the belief among his type of Jew that you could buy your way out even of historical necessity."

She didn't reply, and as this disposed of the question,

Tolya now gave Leah news of the rest of the family: his mother was well and was living in this house as always— Leah would see her presently; a few rooms had been reserved for their use, for he and his wife and children also were housed here. Yes, he had two boys!

Though curious, Leah did not feel she should ask if his wife was Jewish; however, Tolya let this fact drop out at once, with an ironically understanding smile, as though to say it was merely a happenstance, but that he was in any case quite tolerant of such sentimental remnants of long inculcated but fortunately disappearing tribal atavisms.

"Well, Leah, you didn't really make your way back to us on such a difficult journey only to find out what has happened to the family and to your old school friends," Tolya said with his smile.

No, naturally, she said, she also hoped to find out what had happened to her friends in the movement. That was to say, her movement.

Oh, not much was heard of it nowadays, young people were so busy with other things, there was so much that was urgent to do, the revolution had so many enemies. But Zionism was by no means illegal, he said reassuringly; indeed, he had heard that in the Vilna region there was a certain amount of activity.

—Had he by any chance heard of the whereabouts of Josef Trumpeldor? Some said he had been arrested.

Tolya laughed his tolerant laugh. Oh, their hero was free, he could assure her. "But what do you want, Leah? He arrives here in the midst of the first phase of the revolution, when we were pressed on every side, when our first need was to get out of the capitalist war, and he talks of raising an army of half a million Jews to march through Turkey and conquer Palestine! After the October revolution I seem to remember some Bundists had him arrested at one moment, but never mind, he was let out almost immediately; he organized the Jewish Self-Defense in Volozhin and I'll say this for him, they did excellent work against the Whites."

Where was he now? Did Tolya know?

Of this he had no idea.

As for himself, Tolya had served his exile in Siberia—oh, come to think of it, even there in Irkutsk he had encoun-

tered one of her chalutzim, a fellow who had had enough
of it and returned to the revolutionary movement—

Instantly all that Leah had been pretending to ignore in
herself was a-clamor, shouting Moshe's name within her.
She even felt she was blushing. Yet she held it all back until
after she had asked Tolya about his own years in Siberia,
and until she on her side had related, without opening the
way to ideological discussions, the story of each of the family in Eretz. And then she even exchanged with him the
meager bits of information that each had received through
these years about those of the family that had migrated to
America. Since the end of the war, Tolya's mother had received one letter from her sister-in-law in America, carried
here by a townsman who had hurried back from the capitalist paradise to become part of the revolution. Aunt
Hannah wrote that they owned their own automobile, Tolya snorted. Now Leah asked again about his Siberian days,
and about that fellow from Eretz he had encountered, had
he perchance been a tall one called Moshe? She was flushing.

The measuring and recording look had returned to his
eyes. "A tall one, yes! The Handsome Moshe they called
him!" Her cousin waited an instant for the effect on her,
smiling, then added that by another coincidence he had
even known this Moshe afterward, in the October days.
"He did excellent work." And it even happened that Comrade Moshe had been sent to this very same region, in the
campaign to clean out the Petlura gangs, and if Tolya was
not wrong, this Moshe of hers was just now stationed in the
town of Pogorna. "You're not going to try to convert him
back to Zionism!" he said with an indulgent chuckle.

Tolya took her upstairs; her aunt lived in the former
bedroom, turned into something of a bed-sitting room, and
there she had placed the great samovar. Aunt Minna sat
straight as ever; it was from her that Tolya had his eyes of
cool judgment, but her cheeks were of a remarkable softness that carried Leah at once homeward to her own
mother. It was the look of Jewish women who tenderly
hold to their own woman's wisdom, while they endure un-
complainingly the stupidities and brutalities of a world carried on by men. Now she brought out the letter from
America that told of children who were first in their class,
and of a growing manufacturing business, and, thank God,

a good living and asked about the dreadful happenings they had heard were falling upon the Jews in the old country, and declared since at last now the Czar was fallen, might his name be blotted from eternity, they all hoped the family had not suffered and hoped for good news, and that one day the whole family might be able to meet again.

Without Jewish sighs or groans, her Aunt Minna now told of all that had happened to their relatives near and far; once even nodding and declaring that Leah's mother had after all been the wise one, in taking her children to Eretz Yisroel. This she repeated with a cool side-look at her Tolya; then she added with an air of one acknowledging what was just, that things were better now, for it had to be said for the Bolsheviki that they had made anti-Semitism a crime, and indeed many Jews were high up—on the highest rung Trotsky himself, and Kamenev, and Zinoviev, and this one and that one, and the wife of this one and that one, so Jews no longer had anything to fear from the government. If only her poor husband had listened to their son . . . And she straightened her back and pressed her lips together and was calm.

For four days Leah stayed with them, for she could not allow herself to run off to satisfy her foolish longing without first working here on her mission. From one courtyard to another in Cherezinka she managed to thread her way to members of her old-time youth group. So much had happened to each one, how could they have held together? In one or two she encountered a wistful reawakening. But this one could not convince her husband, and that one had aging parents to care for . . .

She must look to the younger generation. Only when Leah had managed to gather nearly a dozen lads and girls who listened with wonder to all she told of the communes, and agreed to meet together and study Hebrew with a veteran of the Poale Zion she had unearthed, and to perhaps form their own little kolhoz and practice growing vegetables, did she decide she had good reason to go on to Pogorna, as there had been a lively Young Zionist movement there even in the time of the Czar.

And to get him off her mind so that she could work wholly on her mission, in Pogorna Leah went directly to find Moshe. He was, her cousin had told her, a commissar of agriculture, organizing collective farms, and the central administration building was readily pointed out.

At first, Leah decided, she would only get a look at him, just to find out her own reaction. She even had the door to his section pointed out. Then, scolding herself for such juvenility, she decided she would walk directly into that office.

Just then the door happened to open; Leah heard his voice calling out cheerfully after a pair of young kolhoznicks who emerged laughing. She walked into the room.

There he sat, the same Handsome Moshe, his black curly hair perhaps slightly receded, his form exuding energy as ever—no sign of Siberian suffering, she saw with relief, or of war injuries—and before she could form more of an impression, he had leaped up, cried out her name, and was embracing her with a full kiss on the mouth, and another, while bursting out to his comrades with a great joyous laugh—she had scarcely noticed there were several more tables in the room—two men and a woman— "Excuse me, comrades! My greatest love has just walked in, returned to me out of the past!"

The two men chortled broadly; the woman, who was middle-aged, made a pulled-down mouth over the incorrigible Moshe and his many loves, and the Handsome One cried, "No! This is not for the office!" and bundled Leah out of the room, calling back, "I'm going on an inspection!" The men laughed, while the woman comrade groaned as though to say: What can you do with a rascal like that?

Keeping stride with him down the corridor, Leah already felt a liberation all down the length of her limbs. For always, walking with men of average stature, there was a restraint even on the size of her steps. Beaming sidewise at each other, they still didn't speak; all there was to say and ask was in such a tumult, the many subjects were like a crowd at a door blocking each other, each trying to get out first, and meanwhile the sheer tumultuous sense of their physical closeness seemed to overwhelm everything.

"Siberia agreed with you," she declared.

"Oh, Siberia, that was a long way back. Before the revolution!" he laughed. She had spoken in Hebrew, he answered in Russian. Doubtless his Hebrew was rusty—how many years had passed?—As though she wasn't aware!—it was almost as long as the number of years Jacob served Laban—No! what a muddle was in her head—yes, that had been fourteen, and besides the comparison didn't really fit, no, not at all.

"We could go to the canteen—" he hesitated. "No, the devil, a restaurant is no place for us to talk." They were outside the building. He gazed on her afresh, grinning appreciatively. "Leachka! How did you manage to get here!"

"I came for our women's movement," she declared, her beaming face belying her, virtually admitting she had come to find him. "But I couldn't resist going to Cherezinka to look for my family," and she told how her cousin had known of him and had got travel documents for her.

"Oh, Comrade Tolya, oho! With papers from Tolya, you can travel on the Moscow Express!"

But they still hadn't really spoken to each other. A dozen times Moshe had been stopped by comrades with problems to straighten out, but now that they were in the open air, he drew her aside, and, as they gazed at each other, she could hardly longer beat back the real question: Was he still with the one from Siberia, was he really married? And whatever the answer to that question, she had also to know from within herself now that she was near him again—was she forever fated, or not?

"I know!" Moshe cried. "I know where we will go!"

He called to a guard near the entrance. In the sentry-box, the soldier picked up a telephone, giving the crank a few turns, and she heard him tell a Comrade Anatol to bring the machine for Comrade Mitya. Naturally Moshe would have taken a party name.

"You are high up!" she laughed. "An automobile!"

"I have to do field work," he chortled, the old Moshe who always managed to arrange things.

"And all this time you couldn't send me a letter?" She couldn't stop beaming, and it was not really a reproach.

"The Czar allowed me one letter a month, so I wrote home."

The recollection of the first touching letter from his mother swept upon her. "Only from your mother we knew you were arrested. Moshe, she wrote to me so tenderly. Your parents are all right?"

"All right," he replied matter-of-factly. "Luckily Father

didn't do anything foolish and I was able to get him legitimized as an expert in hides."

The automobile, a battered but meticulously polished vehicle with a patched top, halted before them, and they squeezed into the back. Moshe gave instructions.

"Where are you taking me?" she laughed.

"On your mission!" he laughed back, but would tell her no more, and as he settled into the seat, their thighs molded as one, and she felt Moshe's arm pressed by their closeness against the side of her breast.

They turned their faces to talk to each other; instead their mouths met, and in the sensation it was as though layer after layer of longing dissolved away within her, as though the prolongation of the contact of their lips was in itself a necessity, a part of the intervening years of separation dissolving away, like a lump of sugar held in your mouth the old Russian way while the tea seeps through and dissolves it, and this must be given a certain length of time.

The vehicle had already passed through the town into the open flat countryside where stacks of reaped grain stood at intervals. A quaint notion came to Leah—in the land of the proletarian revolution, she and her lover had met to kiss in a motorcar driven by a chauffeur!

How long was it since she had thought of anything so lightheartedly!

Simultaneously they broke off the kiss. Now they could delay questions no longer. —And the revolution? she asked. —And the chevreh in Eretz? Moshe asked.

And when Moshe started describing the revolution, how even with Kerensky the prisoners had at once flocked back from Siberia, she had to keep interrupting, "But *you*. You got to St. Petersburg and then? Where did you live?" She still could not make herself say "with whom?" And why didn't he himself speak of that part of it? Perhaps after all that part with his Kati had ended? Perhaps after all it was unimportant?

On her side, Leah told of how it had been for the chaverim, Dovidl and Avner deported, Galil and Nadina sent off into exile in Turkey's own Siberia, leaving their child in the collectiva—

"They have a child?"

"And you?" It had come out of her.

Yes. He had a little boy— And they gazed at each other

with faces that said, we are mature. We must be honest
with each other.

"I will admit to you when I first found out you were in
Siberia, I was about to leave Eretz and go there to join
you, Moshe. And then I heard you had a chavera there
already."

His hand covered hers with an honest, friendly grasp.
"Leah, I would a thousand times have preferred if it was
you that came to me there." And, "But you know I am not
the kind of man who can remain long without a woman."
She did not draw away her hand. Then he inquired, "And
you?"

Instead of replying, Leah asked, "And she?" Coyness
was not in her, but she could not leave herself altogether
helpless by at once telling him the truth about herself. And
it would be as though she were making a claim on him by
revealing her long chastity.

"She?" Moshe repeated.

"The one who came to you in Siberia, isn't she the one
you knew even long before in Odessa? And she is now the
mother of your son."

"Yes," he said, still holding her hand and gazing frankly
at her, "Kati. She and the boy are in Kiev. Kati is in the
housing administration."

"And so you are married."

Still keeping his eyes on her, Moshe nodded. "We registered our union."

"And you still have to do with other women, the Handsome Moshe," she remarked, as over an old friend's inevitable foibles. But even while she concluded it was finally
broken between them, an image came to Leah of a broken
candle still held together by its wick, and who knew, if
lighted it might even be melted whole again. Moshe had
nodded to her last question as well, a helpless wicked boy;
it was as though to her alone, not even to his wife, could he
show himself, as though they two had a truly profound understanding that engulfed more than a past sexual expisode.

His marriage seemed somehow to recede into another
such sexual matter, not much deeper than the rest, and
perhaps leaving open for them the profound relationship
that went beyond.

To Leah it was as though her soul were passing through
a swift series of adjustments, of comprehensions, beginning

with the simple self-accusation, "But, foolish one, you knew perfectly well that Moshe couldn't have remained alone and unattached. And even before you started on this journey you knew that you had to meet him, not so much to find out his own condition, whatever that might be, but to find out in what way and how deeply you were still bound to him. In coming this far, you already admitted that even his being married might not release you. So now you have arrived at this point and you must find out what remains."

"And you?" Moshe repeated. "I thought of you often and much in these years, Leah, and I am not saying this only to please and to appease you. Nor will I pretend that I never also remember other girls, from before. There are some that I remember with great fondness and joy, as I hope they remember me, even if they are married and faithful to their husbands. But when I thought of you, it wasn't always so much of our love-making, though, truthfully, Leah, and I don't ask what other experiences you had, but what happened between us was as good as ever happens between a man and a woman. At least my philandering serves for me to tell you this. But with you it wasn't only sexual memories, it was all sorts of things. In the kvutsa once, the time your face was covered with smoke and smudges from cooking over the stones, and you screamed at us in a real fury, a real Chaimovitch rage, that the kvutsa once and for all had to buy a stove! And the boys were so terrified, they agreed so quickly that you burst out laughing, and said it didn't matter, you didn't want it!"

He chuckled softly, as though all that in Eretz had been his true life, and she had been the center of it.

"So you don't really intend to come back?" she said.

The same honest gaze as before met her eyes. "I can't say, Leah. Something within me keeps believing that one day I will go. Sometimes it is as though I am hearing someone relate the story of my life, and I hear them say, 'And then Moshe suddenly gave up all he was doing and went back to look for his chavera, Leah—'"

She laughed at his playacting. "You see, instead it was Leah who came to look for you."

"No, truly it might have been the other way—" Was he again only the charmer, Handsome Moshe who said to each girl what she wanted him to say to her? He went on, "Leah, as for my life with Kati and Volya, I can tell you it is not fundamentally this that holds me here. Well—perhaps Volya—"

"She wouldn't come with you? Kati?" It had been hard to speak the name.

Moshe considered, but briefly, as one who has already considered and only re-examines. "No. If it came to such a decision. She is so deeply Russian—and even when the revolution is secure, there is still the whole new society to build. You understand."

"Who understands better then we in Eretz?"

"And I—" Moshe blurted with the touch of helpless admission that—oh, curse the ways of nature—was a lovable trait in him—"I want to do both." Just as he wanted every woman that attracted him.

All along the road were marks of war. Red Army units were moving, with long plodding lines of horses pulling supply wagons, each with a cannon attached behind. Or else there would be an encampment in a field. Petlura had been driven all the way out into Polish territory, Moshe said, resuming his other voice, the voice of a commissar, confident, contemptuous of the enemy. There were other nationalist bands not twenty versts away, but they and remnants of the Petlurists were just now busy fighting each other. All the better. Let the hyenas and wolves kill each other off.

The automobile turned into a by-road, and not far before them Leah could see, reaching above the poplars, the pointed roofpeaks of a baronial estate house.

"I'll tell you where I am taking you," Moshe now said with a kind of teasing satisfaction that she still had no idea, and as though this were the real answer to her last question. "I was able to requisition this estate as a training farm."

Startled, her heart suddenly became flooded with love, love after all; Leah gazed into his face for confirmation. "For our chalutzim?"

He nodded. "You already have nearly fifty youngsters here, for your labor battalions."

What a conniver! The old Moshe! She glowed at him. He had really brought her on her mission! "Girls, too?" Leah asked.

"Boys and girls."

"Oh, Moshe, Moshe, I see you haven't lost your gifts!"

He looked so pleased, and there was such an attraction in his pleasure, that Leah, startled by something happening in her body, blushed violently. It was as though the devilish Moshe could be aware of a throb that had come within her sex.

From every direction they came hurrying—how eager, how young, with such good faces—see, despite all that had happened, there were real Jews here still! The girls were in blouses, peasant skirts and work boots—how on earth had they learned this was the way girls now dressed in the kvutsoth! And the boys—several of them had in their eyes that untainted idealistic look that Reuven had had, while a few others had around their mouths that bitter thin line of disappointed idealists who nevertheless saw no other way in the world; still others kept their heads cocked a little sidewise, like Dovidl judging you and planning.

Without a moment to think out what to say first, Leah found herself in the salon of the estate-house, a large parlor with a huge glass chandelier and an ornate ceiling painted with naked cherubs flying about; there were red velvet-covered sofas, and in the corner stood a grand piano. And—startlingly—on the walls were banners inscribed in Hebrew with quotations from A.D. Gordon, from Borochov; and on a flag with the hammer and sickle embroidered inside a Star of David were the words *Zionism and Socialism*.

Before replying to the storm of questions, some in hesitant Hebrew, most in Russian, she was trying first to find out a bit about the leader, whom Moshe had brought to her, a long-headed fellow somewhat older than the others, old enough to have been a soldier in the war. From Kiev, he was, as were perhaps half of the chalutzim; the rest were from Kamenetz, from Ooman, from shtetlach in the area. Yes, their leader said, he was in contact with a few other chalutz centers. What was needed was a united program, he himself had attended a meeting where Josef Trumpeldor had spoken of this—No, that had been six months ago, but recently he had heard that Trumpeldor had left for Eretz to find out about the possibilities for immigration. The difficulty in this area was that not everywhere was the training of chalutzim permitted—

"It's an agricultural school here," Moshe interrupted, "to bring back Jews to productive labor on the soil."

"Right here you see we are lucky." The leader, whose name was Koba, grinned appreciatively at Moshe. "But if we had happened to get an old Bundist in the commissariat—Oho!"

Then all at once she was standing behind a table to lecture to them, to answer their questions. Some were seated on tapestried chairs, which they handled most carefully; several girls sat on the floor at her feet, and in addition a few plain chairs and a roughly made bench had been carried in. Questions flew at Leah, and while Koba tried to control the meeting, sometimes, if it was an ideological question, a comrade would start answering for her, and cross-arguments would develop, and Leah had to cry out laughingly, "Nu, chevreh, it's just like a meeting in a kvutsa at home—everyone talks at once. So now you know what life is like in Eretz!"

—Was it really to be a Jewish state? Was there a democratic Jewish governing body as yet? Could the workers gain control of the future Jewish state—would this be possible under the British imperialists? Was it true that smoking was everywhere forbidden on the Shabbat? Were the women fully equal in their rights? What was the agreement between the Arab leaders and Chaim Weizmann? Would the Arabs really allow Jews to become a majority in Palestine? Could the British be trusted? What were the best crops to cultivate?

Leah was talking in something of a jumble, she realized; if only someone like Dovidl were here to explain it all in orderly fashion. She had started by telling of when she had first arrived in Eretz, of the first kvutsa, of the family's own meshek, of her sister married to a shomer and living in a collectiva, and the children, and also of another of her sisters married to a hotel owner's son in Tiberias. To the upturned faces of the girls, she talked of her own training farm for chalutzoth.

Was a kvutsa the same as a kolhoz? someone interrupted, and someone else answered, "You fool, in a kolhoz the members receive wages and live separately. We here are more like a kvutsa. You can see the difference—the moujiks of the village here are forming a kolhoz."

"No, I want to hear from the chavera herself—!"

All Leah's blood was warm, her energies streamed out of her, called forth by their eagerness. Just when she had left Eretz on this voyage, she told them, one of her brothers— the one who had fought in the Jewish battalions—yes, there had been Jewish battalions in the British army in Eretz— this brother and his friends were starting a new kind of settlement altogether, something between a kvutsa and a kolhoz. "We are experimenting with many ways, we are trying to find the right way for each person."

Were there Arabs in the kvutsa?

No, she said, but they must not misunderstand. "We would not refuse Arabs, surely not on principle, but it is not their way. They have their own way of village life, but perhaps some of their young people will want to change." Her broad smile came back. "We have so many problems—this is all still to be. You too will help to work things out, when you come!"

As in every group there would be one to whom you found yourself talking, one whose face seemed to drink in every word, and here it was a girl with a sprite-like face framed in short cropped hair; a girl who kept nodding at everything she said.

—The kvutsoth were spreading, Leah kept explaining, but also capitalists and merchants were arriving in the cities, there was even land speculation in Tel Aviv, and there were the old schnorrers in Jerusalem—

"But I don't understand," a young man interposed. He had a dense, troubled face. "What kind of country will it be? Socialist or capitalist? Religious or what?"

"We don't know yet how it will come out, because we are only beginning to make it. So when you come, you will take part in making it the way we want it, too." That was why they were needed right away, to make it their kind of country, and not a land for speculators and exploiters, and that was why she had come to them . . .

Until the meal and through the meal and after the meal, the cluster with its excitement and warmth was around her. The borscht was good—"What do you eat in Palestine?"

Not borscht, she laughed.

"Why not?" She hadn't thought about this. "Yes, we grow beets. But we eat more—some of the crops of the land, lighter things for the hot climate, some things we learned from the Arabs.

—Did it ever happen, a girl asked shyly, that a Jewish girl married an Arab? There was a bit of laughter. Had she nothing else to think about? "But why not!" the girl persisted, flushing.

"Then why not an Arab girl and a Jewish boy?" one of the boys demanded, half-teasingly.

"But seriously," the chavera persisted, "I only asked on principle."

Well, Leah explained as best she could, naturally there were cases, more in the older cities perhaps, you heard of it now and again.

"Just like intermarriage anywhere," one of the boys answered for her.

"But you see—" Leah tried again, "they have deep family customs, their matches are arranged between families—"

"Like ours in the old days—"

"We would like to bring them into the more modern way of life, but it will take time and it is not for us to push them. We have so much to do among ourselves—"

By now the cycle of questions was being repeated over and over, and long after the meal they clung around her. Her presence, Leah saw, was at last proof to them that all they were preparing for really existed. That was the main thing. She was "from there."

Finally the group thinned, the youngsters going off to bed, and only the leader, Koba Lederman, sat with Moshe and Leah over a last glass of tea, discussing his problems with Moshe, chiefly problems with the moujiks who kept making claims on their fields. These were the fields that had once been reserved for the estate itself, and were now given over to the training farm.

—Never mind, he'd settle it, Moshe assured Lederman. Those cunning Ukrainian peasants wouldn't get anywhere with him. And Moshe rose.

The sprite with the cropped hair had still been hovering about, bringing them tea—Manya she was called, and clearly she was Lederman's chavera. Now she and Koba led them up the curving stairway and opened a door on a palatial bedroom, preserved untouched. This was for the guest from Eretz.

No, no, Leah laughed, she would feel utterly out of place!

But they insisted. She was putting no one out, they all had
good beds, she needn't fear—and she must not deny them
the opportunity to honor a chavera from Eretz with the
baronial bedroom!

The enormous bed, piled high with a feather quilt, was
covered with a crocheted spread, and above all was a regal
canopy. Lederman and Manya were backing out of the
room. Of Moshe nothing had been said. True, there was a
wide sofa by the window, also prepared with a pillow and a
feather quilt.

Leah went to the bed, tested it with her hand, and
laughed, to cover her whirling uncertainties. In a way the
regal bed was like an approval even from on high. And it
would be hypocritical to pretend that this day could end in
any other way. As soon as she had come into his presence,
even before the explanation, in the automobile, she had
known that no matter what she learned of his present life,
she would have to extend herself into this experience, this
final test, this release, whatever it would be. Perhaps simply a sexual luxury. This one night at least she would put
out of her soul all the troublesome questions, and simply
gratify her body. After so many years.

And so Leah turned into his arms and filled her mouth
with his. Let there be no talking while their hands began
undressing each other. Then it needed a moment of separation to finish the clothing, still in silence. She was
naked first. Folding back the crocheted spread and the
sheets, she lay, her body full and glowing in the lamplight,
and silently watched Moshe's last movements, half turned
from her. As his buttocks became bare, her womb contracted within her, and as he quietly mounted and his face
was over hers, and she felt Moshe entering her, the contracted womb relaxed, and the sigh of eleven years of absti-
nence was released like the first breath of a body coming
into life, and at the same time as a heavenly surcease and a
surmounting of all the lesserness of what a person did with
his life. Even a light lewd thought, from a Yiddish word,
came to her—all this long way she had been carrying her
frauenzimmer to him, like a small sealed jewel box, and for
Moshe alone it was opened.

Even during the first interval they hardly spoke, except
for a "Nu, Leah?" and a "Nu, Moshe?" their eyes gravely
questioning how deep it might be with them, while their

hands again slowly and luxuriously stroked in long smooth movements. Then the lamp guttered, and this made them laugh, and he entered again.

In their repletion, in the darkness, it was Moshe who finally felt compelled to speak. "Don't misunderstand me, and don't be offended, Leahleh—but with you I feel even more as with a wife than with my own wife."

Her heart caught in a beat of ecstasy that momentarily erased all the errors of eternity. Yes, Moshe had felt the need to say this, to say something so good to her that it would seal the night of their reunion. And even so she must not allow it to have a meaning in regard to the rest of their lives. Not yet.

Then perhaps in the same need to give assurance, the same desire to seal away forever this achieved and beautiful time, she responded, "Moshe, you asked me something before, and I didn't answer. Moshe, I don't want you to feel that I imagine what I say gives me some right to you. But the truth is, in these years—I never had another man."

He was quiet, and his hand sought hers and grasped it. "But you are a passionate woman, Leah. I—I simply feel— I feel honored by this, Leah. Yet surely you understood I wouldn't have asked such a thing of you."

"It wasn't for you. I suppose I have a high idea of myself. Or I was afraid that this—in the body—would cease to have a meaning. If I gave in simply to desire. I never in my thoughts imposed the same on you. I suppose it really is not the same with a man as with a woman, because with men—it doesn't happen to you inside of you. It is something you release from yourself."

"Perhaps," Moshe said. "As you say, in a man the desire for release drives him, sometimes it doesn't matter where. And yet I believe such times haven't destroyed in me— when I am in love, it is simply not the same as when I am only driven by the need of a woman."

"And how many times have you been in love?"

"With you. With Kati." Her heart stopped. "And I don't pretend to you that Kati and I no longer love each other. It is not the same as in the beginning. But it is love."

"And no others?" She forced herself to keep on, though everything had been answered.

"Well, there was one other," Moshe said quietly. "The very first one."

"And what happened? It stopped?" Perhaps something from him would yet help her.

"A person should always keep something for his own self alone." Moshe's voice was so removed, she didn't know whether this admission had brought him closer to her, or made everything false. Was this why something within her had always felt that in the end he was unreachable?

He resumed talking. "Leah, we are trying to make a revolution in man himself. A political revolution, to achieve freedom, yes, to free our whole selves. Here and in Eretz, it is really the same, it is the same universal revolution, isn't it? To tear away all pretense and dishonesty, between men and women as well, so that people will be able to be what they truly are, and to be completely honest with each other." Was he really being true now? or were these only words that he liked to hear himself say, to have a feeling of profundity? "So I can tell you, as a man, as a male, I don't want to be a slave to a Czar, or to a capitalist, and I don't want to be a slave to my own schmekel either. I don't want to have to make pretenses or tell lies to some vain and stupid female just because my schmekel is dragging me on—but that is how it often is with a man. Maybe women aren't dragged so much by their sexual demand. Right now because women have equality, we say that they are the same as men and have the same force of desire as men, but really it doesn't seem so to me." What was he trying to tell her? Their moment of intense understanding seemed to be dissolving away into some kind of discussion . . . yet even this was not without comfort. It was the sort of talk that sometimes came in the kvutsa when you felt utterly comradely and honest, it was perhaps the sort of talk that happened between a man and wife, accepting each other as by nature different beings who cannot ever entirely be fused yet who entirely respect and love one another, and with this they drift off to sleep. She would let the problems go for the time.

He was away early, gone back to his post, and all day Leah worked in the fields with the young chalutzim, mostly the girls, little crop-headed Manya never leaving her. All day Leah heard their life stories, Manya telling how her mother had cut her hair and dressed her as a young Hasid, her breasts tied flat—good they were small—and two curls left for payes, see, the ringlets were still there, though brushed back into her locks. And thus as a Hasidl she had escaped violation when Ataman Grigoriev's brutes stormed into their town. Oh, he was the worst, worse than Petlura. Their house had been burned down, yet the whole family, hiding with a peasant, had survived, and then when Makho had driven out Grigoriev, they had emerged and gone to Lvov, but Petlura had come and seized Lvov. Again she had dressed as a young Hasid. Petlura's men were drunk, wild. On horses they burst into every yard, but if you managed to hide, in a few days it was over and not so dangerous.

"Like a pogrom under the Czar," Leah understood.

But fleeing again, they had fallen among the Whites. It was an army. You heard them marching into your street. Then they closed off the whole block. Then they marched to the first house and closed off the courtyard, and then mounted up each stairway to each door, soldiers with bayonets—and into each flat, into each room—they took everything, the bedding, the cooking pots—what they didn't want, they smashed, the pictures, the glassware—if they felt like killing, they killed—they seized hold of a woman and three or four soldiers would hold her arms, her head, and then one after another, they changed places—

"Don't speak of it any more."

"I saw it. I saw it."

"I know, I know." And Leah taught her how to move along the ground with least effort in a squatting position so as not to be bent over all day while weeding.

Moshe returned at dusk.

Presently she went with him to a meeting he had arranged with the peasants of the village, and Leah listened with admiration as Moshe explained and cajoled, reaching behind the suspicious eyes of the older ones, even salting or sweetening his words with Ukrainian proverbs, as needed. The situation was far from easy: their grain had been requisitioned; though they had been paid, the price had been set by the Soviets and they were discontent. Yet somehow Moshe turned them to discussion of a school; of course the teaching would be in Ukrainian.

"What of the manor? Put our school in there!" a stolid young man demanded. "It was promised to us."

"You'll have it. The Jews won't be there forever!" He said it with such good humor, as one who understood them, indeed as one of them, that she did not resent it, especially as he added, "The Jews want to go, perhaps even more than you want them to leave!"

It was all a kind of playacting, she could see it was nec-essary, and when the meeting ended and they came away, Moshe explained that the situation here was still very deli-cate, a few—like that young man—were good communists and therefore had to be taken seriously, as the rest of the village was still honeycombed with Petlurists and every other brand of Ukrainian nationalist. Therefore he had had to emphasize Ukrainian culture. He was deep in the prob-lem, and Leah told herself that of course Moshe had to speak of the young Jews as "they" and not as "we." In the situation anything else would be absurd.

Moshe must have known how the moment troubled her, for now he said "we." "Leah, do you realize how we need you here?" In this single day she had restored the morale of the entire training farm, which had been slackening—indeed a number of chalutzim had left. The old, Bundist arguments were making headway again. Jews would sim-ply be a cutural unity within the revolution. But not sepa-ratist nationalists. Now, for these youngsters, she was the answer. She must be the one to clarify things. She must go through the entire district—he would arrange a mission for himself so that he could open the way for her. They would go to Zhitomir, even up to Minsk. Yes, at this junction in history it was here in Russia that she could be most useful.

And as they walked, Moshe expanded his thoughts with-out any allusion to their personal relationship, but only in the excitement of the cause they shared. For they must look at it in the largest perspective, not only from the Pal-estine scene but from the situation of the whole Jewish peo-ple.

"How many are we, Leah? Despite all that were starved and slaughtered, and our young men killed in the war, we are nearly five million here in the old Jewish Pale. And in the entire world we Jews are perhaps fifteen million. In our greatest dream, even with the most intense development of the land, four, at most five, million can be supported in Eretz. Then what happens to the remainder of the Jews?

Will they be lost to us? Will they all assimilate in different lands in a generation or two?"

But this was an old question; from the earliest discourses of Ahad Ha'am it had been debated. The answer was that the Jews of the Yishuv, of the Jewish state that would now soon arise under the British—they would be the core of Jewish life. Not the old Russian Pale of Settlement but Palestine would be the heartland of Jewry, and from there the new kind of Jew would go out to the Diaspora, to teach, to fortify—

"Exactly. And you are the first emissary—you are already here! You saw the effect that you have on the youngsters?"

It was not yet a dismay that was creeping up in her, but a curious uncentered doubt. This was a discussion in which they both seemed to have the same honest passion—the very purpose of their lives. And what Moshe said was true. She would dispatch kvutsa after kvutsa from here to Eretz. She would win their tongues back from Russian and Yiddish to Hebrew. And even if there was a touch of cunning, even if there was a breath of opportunism, in this for Moshe, even if it enabled him not yet to have to make a decision about his own life, indeed even if it made it possible for him for a time to have two lives, two wives, one in Kiev and one to travel about with, why should she not, in the very nature of a woman, seize every circumstance to win her man—yes, win him from the other woman, from the other, the non-Jewish life? If such was the condition into which events—or history, as they called it—had put her?

This was not like herself, not like the self Leah had always seen as herself. But perhaps she had been wrong, naïve, unfinished, still a romantic idealistic girl despite her brief early experience with Moshe. Now, the reunion had proven that the bond—some sort of powerful inexplicable bond—still held, with him as with her. His plan she could understand—Moshe always found a way! His plan was to give himself time to search out, to test, his full relationship with her, for Moshe's case was more difficult than her own; Moshe had a child now that he would have to leave. Yet Leah felt that his union with her and with Eretz would prove to be the true one, it would grow stronger; like every plant, it had a full right to be nourished and given its natural growth, and one day it would bear its fruit.

Down the lane of trees as they walked back, lights awaited them—how like it was to approaching the kvutsa late at night long ago, in those weeks when they would go out into the field to lie together, and return for supper, famished. Moshe had the same recollection, for he took her hand and said in Hebrew, "Remember the time Araleh was the night watchman and nearly shot us?"

Tonight too they were challenged by a guard; one of the young chalutzim started up at their approach and called out in Russian, "Who is it?" Then the boy quickly murmured, "Oh, excuse me, comrade" to Moshe, and, with a winsome knowingness said goodnight in Hebrew to Leah, "Layla tov, chavera."

All Moshe had suggested continued to ferment in her over the next few days. It was true she must go on to all the other training farms, perhaps even prolong her mission. Here, the youngsters were already excited about starting on the way to Eretz, and long sittings were held every night. Should the entire group leave in a body? No, the farm must not be given up, but kept as a training center, constantly replenished. Then came arguments as to who should go in the first group? Lederman and his Manya wanted to go, but wasn't he indispensable here, to train the next kvutsa? Manya had already changed her name—Leah helped her to find just the right Hebrew word—Mayana it would be, springing from "water"—a water sprite!

And as for herself, before going north, Leah worried— shouldn't she first report back to Menahem?—Why consume time traveling back and forth, Moshe argued; she could send her report to Menahem with the first group, and meanwhile, he and she could go on to some of the other centers. That was what was most necessary. "Besides, running back and forth from here to Odessa is dangerous. Who knows where the Whites will be tomorrow?"

They were upstairs in their vast bed, but they had been conducting the discussion as though it were impersonal. Only at the last, about her staying on, his voice changed with a tinge of selfishness, and a little wave of gratification went through her.

"No, I really ought to go with them," she repeated, and

her body turned to his as though already to store up love
against their temporary separation.

Moshe covered her; then, just as he began to enter her,
he said playfully, yet masterfully, "You'll see, good old
schmekel will convince you to stay!"

And in that instant everything broke.

Her body reacted involuntarily and thrust him out. His
own word, the coarse word that in the playful reaches of
love was only a further intimacy, a laughing mark of joy
and freedom, this word had now thrust itself into her as her
enslavement. Not by the schmekel would her life be decided. Not by the demand of her sex.

"But, Leachka, what is it?" Moshe said, as though he
didn't know. He was still lying over her, she could feel his
thigh muscles taut, and his member almost touching her
sex lips; she could even feel its throb, and in astonishment,
even grief, as over some tragic revelation, Leah knew she
must not allow her lips to draw it back in. Instead, by an
act of will, she made her hips pull away from him. No,
Moshe was not an honest man within himself, he was a
conniver, a twister, she had always known this, but now
she must pay attention—he was a man who deceived even
himself about his final beliefs.

At her pulling away he reacted with masculinity. "Don't
be foolish!" and thrust himself in, his force pounding insistently within her to master her. Instead an agony augmented in her, a cry in her soul, "It's not *him*, it's not
him—after all, he is not really the one."

Her body rolled from side to side, as much through agony at her discovery as to avoid him; her shoulders rolled
as in the keening of sorrow, and her head rolled away from
the driving pressure of his mouth. The words repeated
themselves within her and in the sway of her mourning,
they emerged half-muffled, as from a delirium, moaning to
the man, "It's not you. After all, Moshe, it's not you." This
was the true answer to what she had come here to find; the
first answer had been one of a seven-year hunger.

Now he altered his movement so that uncertainty came
creeping back in her. Moshe lifted his weight from her,
slowly withdrawing, not in the way he had used to do so as
to give her the greatest, the most unbearable pleasure, the
slow withdrawal almost to the very end while her inner
lips throbbed and waited in exquisite suspense for the in-

stant of reprieve, when instead of going completely out, the withdrawal would at the very last tip of contact turn into a wild thrust reaching through her to her very heart. No, Moshe withdrew carefully as though he were respecting whatever strange notion had come over her, and did not want her to feel his movement, did not want to take this sexual advantage to influence her decision.

And at the very tip of contact he was gone; his might did not come down on her again, nor his sex thrust back into her; this was perhaps the dissolution forever, it was perhaps the immeasurable emptiness that a chavera had described to her after an operation in which the womb had had to be removed. And now he was lying, off of her, in careful separation so that no part of his skin touched hers.

What had altered? Perhaps she was entirely mistaken about him; but all at once Moshe had appeared to her as a person somehow sinister. That he was clever and adaptable and able always to find a way to arrange matters, she had always known, and it had seemed a resourcefulness, even a good quality in him. But now it suddenly appeared as of a low order in human morality, close to hypocritical, akin to his readiness to flatter and even deceive a girl, some orange-grower's daughter, or any creature with breasts and a vagina, that he momentarily craved, in order to get inside her. All at once Moshe no longer seemed a strong personality, but appeared to her as a man of weak character, puzzled that his "final argument" had this time failed.

Yet another, womanly part of her argued back that she herself was at fault, that in full womanhood this itself—the discovery of a loved one's shortcomings and even weakness of character—was part of what made him endearing. Did her mother not love her father despite all the absence of joy that was between them? Never in Leah's whole life had she thought there was an absence of love; her mother knew his irascibility, his narrowness—and look at this clumsy body and the potato-face behind the untrimmed beard; yet her mother, Leah was certain, felt a full tenderness and respect for her man.

And so perhaps she herself was at fault that a great wave of compassion did not rise in her to engulf the very weakness that she had suddenly felt in Moshe, a compassion to carry her beyond what had been a blind girlish attachment, and a lust, and even something of hero-worship, to a profound and all-embracing womanly understanding.

But a new thought came and caused her to recoil from herself in shame. Was not this the deep understanding that his wife Kati felt for him?

Moshe had remained silent; all that was unsaid throbbed between them. Yet when he spoke it was not on a wave of these thoughts, and did not help her. For he carried on from the moment before all this had happened in her and had caused a watershed in her life. "After all," Moshe said, "I myself was sent here on such a mission as yours, even before the war, and I suffered for it in Siberia, but I am continuing this mission now in whatever way I can manage. Then what is wrong with your remaining here, to join in it? That is all I suggested, and if you think it was only out of selfishness, so that I can live two lives, believe me, Leah, you can remain and carry on your work without seeing me and I will still help you all I can. What is between us as man and woman is another question."

Even this, which should have touched her, now left her with suspicion. Could Moshe truly mean it, or was he deceived by his own ruse? Poor Moshe, he wanted it both ways. And the only true test would be if she went back home, and then, should he come to recognize it was the Zionist way he wanted and that she was his woman, then he would come.

This thought too instantly tormented her as being perhaps a woman's wile: to go away to make herself more desired. Perhaps the more honest way would indeed be to give themselves more time here to be together, until he could decide which was his true wife. And why was it necessary that the true wife should turn out to be the one who was bound to the way of life he most desired, whether in this land or Eretz? Perhaps there too was a profound tragedy between men and women: that a person's life partner, and a person's life did not always go together.

She was already losing that clear vision of Moshe that had come to her, and slipping back into the illusion, seeing him as a man tragically torn between ideals. Leah arose from the bed. She stood undecided, there in the large luxurious room, and slowly her eyes became accustomed to the dark, as must his; he must be looking at her naked body standing there. So she reached and drew on a petticoat, feeling his puzzled gaze on her all the while. Then she went and lay down on the couch-bed by the window.

It was strange, but she dozed off and didn't know how much time had passed; in her troubled consciousness, she lay in something like the nighthaze that you felt when you had to get up for the milking, but still half slept; the pre-dawn light would then come brushing like a veil of dew over your body, and she felt it now, the tenderest caressing on her skin along her thigh.

His lips moved there; Moshe was kneeling alongside the couch, and his head moved along her bared thigh, and gen-tly his hand raised her slip. Languorously Leah felt his lips brushing over her belly and beneath the curve of her breast. Her entire body burned and trembled while she yet pretended to herself to sleep, until his mouth touched her nipple, and she gasped.

"No, no it's not right, it's not fair to do this to me! No!" Leah moaned, while the hollows of her hands ached to stroke the black curly hair on his head, and in anguish she seized his hair and put his head away from her, his mouth away from her breast.

Then Moshe went over and sat on the edge of the large bed. She arose and dressed, and Moshe dressed too.

37

FOR SUNDAYS, Moshe went home to his wife and son in Kiev—by Friday this week he had left, and for a few days Leah knew she would not confront him and could in some measure of calm examine her feelings.

But in happy excitement the chalutzim were trying to organize their own trip to Kiev for a remarkable cultural event. It swept up Leah as well. The dancer from America, the same Isadora Duncan, the one in the book Rähel had brought her from Paris—this dancer had come to Russia to offer her art for the revolution, and on Saturday night she would dance at the great opera house, now the Palace of Culture, in Kiev.

The head of the training center's culture committee, Siomka, had gone to the city, and had managed, by sleeping all night in front of the ticket bureau, and by every manner of connivance, to secure twenty places, actual seats, and seven more standing places, which some wild street child had somehow got hold of and had sold to him at double price, snatching his last rouble and running away, even before Siomka was sure the tickets were valid. He only prayed they weren't counterfeit.

It would take four hours each way by wagon; two full wagons were going. Wild arguments broke out over the allotment of tickets. Some had been bought with private money. The chaverim even took to hurling insults at each other, "son of a bloodsucking landlord!" "work-shirker!" "pampered bourgeois!" At first Leah kept from intervening so as to see how they would manage with such a problem, but now Lederman turned to her. How were such things decided in a kvutsa in Eretz? In a real kvutsa, she told them, even if a chaver received mony from home as a gift, or even if he worked outside for wages, as did the members of the Shomér, it was all given into the common fund and used according to what was decided by all. In a situation like this, there would be a lottery for the tickets.

Mayana and Koba Lederman were already writing names on slips of paper, and Leah was asked to draw out the lucky ones—twenty-six names.

—Hadn't they made a mistake? There were twenty-seven places in all.

"A guest is not subject to lottery!" Lederman decreed. And Siomka added, "And don't tell us that is how you treat your guests in Eretz, or we'll remain here!"

Leah had already her name on a slip, but Mayana pulled it from her fingers and tore it to bits. Tears of love came to Leah's eyes, and giving in, she reached down into the bowl for the first name.

Little Mayana was one of those who had given her private ticket into the pot, and at the end, when her name hadn't been drawn, she could barely hide her anguish. Trying to make light of it, she put her hand in the bowl to see what might have come out next, and read out "Mayana!" But somehow the sheer bad luck of it made her feel better instead of worse—now she could really blame a malevolent fate! "Leah, you have to dance every dance for us when you come back!" she demanded, remembering Leah's account of Bialik's visit.

Singing the whole way, shouting greetings to all they passed on the road, peasants and Red Army men alike, they reached the city and crowded into the opera house. So exhilarating was the atmosphere of the surging, excited mass that, even with the tumult of the ticketless outside, still trying to find a way to get in, even with the pushing and pressing together, it was good. Instead of showing irritation, the crowd raised still higher their wild feeling of a shared fantastic event, an achievement—they were here! The mixture in the crowd of strong-faced workers in their white Sunday blouses, of high ranking officers and plain soldiers hardly distinguishable from each other, of eager, bright-faced girls with hair freshly washed and braided—with all this there gushed up in Leah a love for Russia, even a momentary nostalgia, an inner cry of joy at the success of the revolution, that only slowly resolved itself back into her own particular world—We too will achieve!

And as to the program, never had her soul been so entirely drawn out of herself, and yet never had Leah felt her soul so entirely fulfilled, so replete. From the first measured strides of the flame-flowing figure moving toward her, toward each, toward all, toward her alone, Leah was transformed as though she had passed through some instantaneous reincarnation and was a greater being, and that being was moving toward herself, as herself, and yet as the universal soul in triumphant movement toward a victorious humanity.

She was in a daze. How was it done! It was only a woman walking! How could she ever show it, how could her spirit carry it back to the young people who had not seen this tonight?

In the moments between the dancer's different creations, Leah sat in an elated trance. The hall was a-roar with cheering; she too was cheering, shouting *bravos*—she even joined in excited comments with her young chaverim; such purity, such simplicity, such elemental strength! and how strange it was that this woman, this spirit from America, should be the one to come here to give the perfect expression to the revolution itself. And it was true as to this ample woman, this flowing form, this Isadora Duncan—that

in some essence she, Leah, resembled the wondrous dancer, was formed in the same way, of the same creative
urge—only how much more harmonious and powerful was
the urge of the woman on the stage!

Through this thought something else was stirring to clarity in her—why people danced before altars, danced before
gods, why Miriam, the sister of Moses, danced, why David
danced before the Ark; how it was that man, a creature
with four limbs that were made as in so many other creatures for useful movements, beautiful and pure as they were
in a deer, a horse, how this human creature could take
these movements of the same four limbs and body, and
seem to free them from the limits of the flesh, to declare
the poem of the entire universe through bounds and turns
and unlimited combinations, seeming freed even from the
fatedness of gravity! And through this woman, Leah knew
why she herself in the movements she had found instinctively for her simple festivals had never felt weariness,
never felt effort, or heaviness of body, but only experienced
a sacred sense of purity when she danced.

So she was carried, still in this excited mood, into the
intermission, when she surged again within the exhilarated
mass, and there she encountered Moshe and his wife. She
had surely known within herself that he would come here,
and with his Kati. In its compressing movement the crowd
brought and held them all three together, churning them
slowly in the multitude, unable to separate from each other
until, in the same churning of the mass, other bodies would
momentarily intervene, and the crowd-movement would
carry one or the other of them apart . . . all this, in itself,
with the inner rhythm of a dance.

Their faces, Moshe's and Leah's, were directly toward
each other as when heads are held gripped by a photographer's clamp, immovable, and so she exclaimed "Shalom,
Moshe!" And against him, a head reaching hardly to his
shoulders tilted upward; Moshe introduced his life comrade, Kati, and to Kati he said, "This is Leah, the one I
told you about, the emissary who has just come from Palestine."

As though in concert with their encounter, a tight inner
swirl of the crowd now turned Leah so that she faced toward the young woman. Moshe's wife's face was framed in
glossy black hair, with a straight part in the center. The

eyes were a cool gray, and large, intelligent. Set in a delicate face with very white skin, there was a small, precisely
shaped mouth, the lips a trifle thin, but of a surprisingly
lively red that gave the whole face, in spite of its intellec-
tual look, a burning sensuality.

Kati looked indeed the typical woman of the revolution,
even a good deal like Nadina at home without her glasses.
And Leah was relieved to find in herself no feeling of hostility, or envy, or jealousy toward this woman—only a curiosity. Perhaps it was good that their encounter had come in
this way, when she was so filled with the exaltation of the
dance, when her spirit was lifted so high that a human entanglement was only of another, a lesser order of life. In
this one look at Kati's face, while the crowd held them
inflexibly toward each other, the whole of Moshe's life was
clear to Leah; all that she had only vaguely sensed before
had nevertheless been true; he was bound in his union with
Kati, he was the weaker, she was the strong one, and so it
would remain. It even became clear to Leah that in some
way long ago when Moshe had undertaken the mission to
return to Russia it must have been in the way she too had
brought on for herself such a mission now; he had felt compelled to search out and test a former entanglement, to discover if he could be free of Kati, just as she had needed to
search out whether she could be free of Moshe. But all
lives are not the same. He had not been free, and she
would be free.

She was not even troubled as to how much about herself,
and what, he had told his wife, his life comrade. That was
already their affair in their life together. For it was surely
clear that Moshe would never "finish his work here" and
come back to Eretz.

The young woman, with her head uptilted, was talking
to her of the performance: did Isadora Duncan fulfill all
her expectations?

"Oh, more! It's immeasurable!" Leah said, and Kati
agreed it was an extraordinary experience, a cultural
triumph.

"The most remarkable aspect, as you must have noticed,
is the transcendence, the freedom from technique. Moshe
tells me you yourself have a talent for the dance, and have
even revived a whole Hebrew form of agricultural folk
dancing from Biblical times—"

"Oh, no," Leah laughed. "I only made up a few little celebrations for our holidays."

The head, even in the tightly-packed multitude, bending and tilting upward again, examined, measured Leah's entire form. Then Moshe had most likely told her everything. "You know, there is something about you like her," Kati went on, and tilted her head toward Moshe, as though to confirm a description he had given her. Moshe smiled broadly, letting the women talk, and Leah momentarily wondered how it was for a man standing close thus to two women each of whom he had entered. Her thoughts wandered on: it was after all not uncommon, not even unnatural—two wives had lived with Jacob, Rachel and her own namesake, Leah, and even today in Dja'adi among the Arabs—she had once asked this question of the two wives of a villager. The women had come down together to Mishkan Yaacov to work in the potato harvest. It did not trouble them; they had readily explained to her the place of the first wife and the second, and of the children of each. But then what of Kati's way? When Moshe had arrived there in Irkutsk, hadn't the story come back that Kati had been the companion of another comrade, and had lived with him, and then decided on Moshe? Could a woman do this, go from the bed of one man to another, and remain whole in her self? But everywhere such changes were made, Leah reminded herself, even in the kvutsoth; she was romantic, naïve. And yet she could not accept it for herself.

The multitude all at once pressed the three of them against each other and Leah felt a shock of abhorrence. No, she wanted none of such complexities, she yearned for a simple, total union without torment, for a life on the earth, a cleanliness.

". . . But what is most remarkable is the way she moves so easily from the classical ballet to movements that come directly from ancient Grecian urn-painting, and then to our own Russian folk-dances! And then to what is modern and entirely her own! She is the incarnation of the universal, the international, and even shows us the unity of the human masses throughout all history!" Kati declared, her tilted head turning from one to the other, and even including people close by who were catching her words.

"It was a miracle that I had the luck to see her before I go back," Leah said. Let Kati know.

Now Kati burst out with great sincerity and warmth, on the establishment of a country for the Jews. It was of the utmost importance for the world movement itself, what Leah was engaged in doing—to bring to Palestine young people who would carry forward the world revolutionary movement there, and help make sure that Palestine would not hopelessly fall under the sway of capitalism and imperialism, enemies of the revolution. Also, the real question of the Jewish masses and the liquidation of the age-old pestilence of anti-Semitism, implanted by the reactionary church and the Czars, remained a great task here in Soviet Russia. And Kati tilted her head to Moshe.

The crowd was now pressing them inward toward the hall, and at one point the mass separated into two streams. Leah was divided from Moshe and his Kati. Her side was slower, and at one moment she glimpsed them again, in the far aisle. The crowd had thinned there, and she caught sight of Kati, a diminutive figure in advance of Moshe, her hand reaching back to him, while his head stretched above the line, turning this way and that. Just for an instant there flashed before Leah an image of a tall-necked camel being led by its driver; then she was ashamed of making fun of Moshe. He meant much to her, after all, and this was like belittling her own self.

When the concert was over, when she had stood to the very last, applauding and crying "Bis!" calling out for one more, one more encore, she finally let herself be carried along by the crowd to the outside. With the roars of human joy and acclaim and gratitude for the release of their souls still holding her in her trance, Leah found herself with the mass that lingered before the theater as though to cling to their experience, and then she was with the chevreh in the wagon, everyone still talking of what they all had felt. The two wagons were already moving through the streets, the singing had begun; they sang a Red Army song and the Marseillaise and the Internationale, and the clopping of the hooves was a drumbeat to their singing; then, almost as though dutifully, someone started "Hatikvah," and at the end a girl's voice said somewhat wistfully, "Who knows when we'll see such a thing again, as tonight. In Palestine we'll be far from such experiences."

"We'll build our own opera houses!" one of the boys stoutly declared.

"Before opera houses we have a whole country to build up," another proclaimed, like a real chalutz. Then they were singing "Anu Banu Artzah," and "Yahalili" and homey Yiddish songs and the "Volga Boatman's Song." Half-stretched out on the bottom of the wagon among them, legs all tangled together, and as one breathing body with them in the dark, Leah felt at peace. She opened her eyes to the stars. Truly in Eretz the sky was different. Truly it was deeper, more mysterious, more filled with stars. But just the same she might be riding like this in a wagon across the Emek, in a wagon filled with her girls chanting these same songs that had now turned from horas to a more dreamy, wistful tone, "Eliyahu Ha-Navi, Eliyahu Ha-tishbi—"

And so through the long hours of the night, feeling a peaceful exhaustion, a great cleansing, and a sweetness perhaps like a woman after childbirth, Leah sensed herself being carried homeward, and she drowsed.

The sky had already emerged into a gray dawn when the wagons turned into the lane toward the manor house, and at once Leah sat erect with a start, and the chalutzim too; one by one, their puzzled questioning faces turned to each other, to her. Had something happened? Was it a smell of ashes, of death that hung over the lane?

A few snapped branches dangled like broken limbs from the trees. The dirt road was scuffed as by many hooves. Their own horses seemed to balk, and then they were whipped into a run. Several of the boys leaped from the wagons and rushed forward.

They burst into the silent house, and the others, from the arriving wagons, were already crowding behind them as they stood gaping in the archway of the large salon. A sound, unformed, compounded of sobbing, rage, groans, and something like a deathrattle, choked in their throats. The slaughtered bodies had not even been covered. Four lay there, hacked with swords, Lederman decapitated, and two boys with huge crosses cut in open flesh, and what had been a girl, disemboweled, her head a blood-clotted mass of hair so that at first glance no one was sure, then her sister shrieked "Essie!"

All the girls were pulled away quickly, outside. In the stench of the befouled room the carcass of a shot horse sprawled halftangled in the collapsed ruins of the grand piano. A dragpath of blood went through the double doorway and the hall, where the attackers must have taken away some wounded of their own.

Other chalutzim were found—two on the stairs, Yankel Kollowitz and Stashu Gebinder—they had been on guard, armed with pistols, they must have fought. Leah mounted past them through a debris of smashed mirrors, ripped paintings, broken furniture; in the first sleeping room the dead lay in a cluster as though herded together and chopped down. The door of the baronial bedroom was open; there on the canopied bed was a small form, bloodied strips of ripped clothing streaming away from the flesh. On the naked thighs of poor little Mayana were dried blotches of blood. The small breasts, sliced away, hung by a last shred of skin. Over the face was a large embroidered feather-pillow.

The clear-eyed young Commissar from the village had already arrived. Seven survivors were in his own house, he said. He had heard shooting soon after midnight, but had arrived too late, and had only been able to take away the survivors, two with saber wounds. One couple luckily had been out in the fields. Petlurists had attacked the house, coming he didn't know from where—small bands were still active in the area, made up of peasants who then disappeared into their villages. Certainly none were from here.

The wounded could not tell much more. Suddenly the troop of horsemen was upon them. The outside watchman had been cut down with a saber. Yankel and Stashu had fired from the stairs and hit one or two; the leader on the horse had been killed, they believed. Two girls who slept in the attic had escaped by hiding on the roof.

The bodies, seventeen in all, were ranged and covered by their comrades. Two members went to Kiev to notify the families of those who were from there.

At noon came a detachment of Red cavalry. Depositions were taken. Moshe arrived the next morning; he had only learned late at night in Kiev of the massacre. Kati came with him. Several of the parents from Kiev arrived, and from the nearest town with a Jewish cemetery came an elder of the chevrah kadushah, the sanctified burial society. There were hysterical discussions over the burial, but at last it was agreed to bury all the victims together in the town.

Solemnly and in sorrow, Kati declared to Leah that the Red Army would hunt down the nests of the remaining Petlurists, and that the revolution would root out anti-Semitism even from the Ukraine. Four Red cavalrymen were posted in the manor.

Leah remained only a few days more with the remainder of the chalutzim until she felt steadied enough to go on with her journey. The sense of mission gave her no rest; she had now to erase the knowledge in herself that the mission had partly been an excuse to find her former lover, and that she had dallied because of her personal problem. Day and night she held sittings with the chalutzim, planning which should start on the way to Odessa, and how they would manage the journey, selecting a responsible one for each group of four, instructing them where to find Menahem. Then she set out on her further journey, saying only a friendly goodbye to Moshe in his office.

Without rest Leah traveled, wherever she could squeeze her way onto a train, or clamber onto a roof, waiting half the night in one station or another; she found her way even as far as Vilna, found a dozen little groups of one sort or another in various towns, here and there a training farm that Trumpeldor had started several months before, and from each place she was on to the next. Through her the scattered groups were beginning to link themselves more firmly together. Were they really wanted in Eretz? Could they really enter Palestine now? Would there be work for them?—Yes, yes, come, come, and especially girls, young women, come! She would welcome them onto her own training farm, the movement must grow, they must build a Jewish workers' land.

In some areas the young Zionists were already in grave doubt as to how their movement here would fare under the Bolsheviki; in some towns where the hostility of the Bund-ists was unabated, the chalutzim met her in secret, for who could tell when their movement would be declared illegal?

At the end of two months Leah started back to Odessa, with six young chalutzoth clustered around her all the way from Minsk, with enough adventures and difficulties and even comedies, with false papers here and flirtations there, with crossings through forests from Red zones to White zones and back again to Red zones; and in the meantime Odessa had been seized by the Whites, and for the last crossing a peasant smuggler took them in his wagon as though they were a bridal party, all dressed up and singing. At last, one fine morning, she marched her girls into the Jewish Defense House where a cry went up, "Leah!" and from every corner young pioneers she had sent on the way flocked to her, relating all their adventures.

The whole band from the manor rushed to her, theirs was the first claim, she was theirs! At the training farm, they told her, a Red Army commissar had after all discovered that one of the older peasants had called in the Petlurists; they had intended, after killing all the Jews, to seize the manor house and its lands. But recently a large new group of chalutzim had arrived there from Kiev for training. Moshe had sent them. He had been transferred to Kiev itself, to a higher post.

Here everything was ready for going up to the land! Aliyah! Didn't she know? Within the week! She had arrived just in time! A whole ship had been procured by chaver Menahem. Three hundred chalutzim and chalutzoth would be carried direct to Eretz!

When Menahem appeared, he greeted her with that dark smile of his eyes that was for things well done in spite of all difficulty. He knew already all she had been through. And only little by little, mostly from others, Leah put together the story of his own journeys in these months, even the story of how he had been arrested in Red territory and sentenced to be shot, and how he had been rescued by a squad of young Zionists dressed in Red Army uniforms, arriving with false papers for his transfer to another jail. All this Menahem shrugged off as adventurism. But all the way as far as Rostov he had revived the movement and gathered chalutzim, and in the Crimea he had picked up news of Josef Trumpeldor. "He went across to Constantinople, with his own kvutsa, about a dozen, on a small Greek cargo boat, not long ago."

And still there fluttered through her foolish heart—as

she well knew it to be—that old, never entirely dismissed possibility that one day, with Trumpeldor . . .

"You saw your Moshe," Menahem remarked. And it was enough, nothing more had to be said, her brother-in-law's glance was a complete understanding, as though he had squeezed her hand in sympathy. Nu! There was much to be done. He was over his head with the problems of chartering a ship—the whole affair was one of Menahem's complicated accidents. He had espied the vessel lying in the harbor, a derelict of war, the ownership hard to trace, but, by a chance meeting with an acquaintance from his old days as a seaman, Menahem had made a connection—and the end of it was that he had raised money amongst some of the staunch old Odessa Zionists—Odessa, after all, was the heart of the prewar activist faction—and so the vessel was leased, and repaired and painted, and would be carrying Jews to Eretz! Even more, in London there had been pressure put by Chaim Weizmann through high members of the British government on their military government in Palestine, and official permission was as a result actually in hand for the immigration to begin! The chalutzim would arrive in this new era with valid entry papers in their hands!

And so they boarded the ship, with flags and amidst orations, sent off by Bialik himself, who vowed he would soon come, and with the giant activist Ushishkin and all the staunch Odessa leaders sending them on their way, and promising that a great wave of immigration would follow for the building of the homeland.

Not only their own youthful labor brigade was on the ship; there were also entire families, like her own family on their Aliyah, and there were several Jews from Eretz who had been back in Russia and been caught by the war. They were now returning home, and, arriving at the last moment from the Caucasus, there was even Motke the shomer from Petach Tikvah! The Turks had sent him to the far Russian front in the region of Ararat, and Motke had escaped to the Russians by crossing the mountains in the snow; he had reached them half frozen, and his right leg had had to be amputated, but here he was, alive! Going home!

The voyage was one continuous song of joy. But impa-

tiently Leah longed for her girls, for Mati, for the whole
family, and she worried about how things were with Yaffaleh. How different this voyage was after all from that first
time, with Reuven, the two of them virtually alone among
strange people in a fetid Turkish vessel, uncertain even if
they would succeed in entering the land. Fourteen years of
her life had gone by and only now, perhaps, was she grown
to womanhood, coming home to the land that was freed,
and she too had been freed within herself.

This time her real life would begin.

38

—THERE! There, already!—Leah pointed out, her young
immigrants crowding around her, thronging the rail—
there it was already, the large building looming into view
like a castle on the sands, that was already the Herzlia
Gymnasia of Tel Aviv! And as the ship moved closer, they
could even see, there, along the beach, there, the hut with
the red flag flying—that was the workers' place, the center
of their own Poale Zion!

Several young chalutzim even cried out they would leap
over the rail and swim ashore to be a moment sooner in
the land. All along the sand children ran, accompanying
the ship, dancing, waving little stick-flags of Zion.

From Jaffa harbor the Arab boatmen came as always,
plunging outward in their barks; instead of the ancient terror, what a homecoming joy to see them! Speeding in advance came a motor boat flying a British flag; on the dock,
amidst more flags of Zion, a delegation stood—Leah could
already make out the lanky form of Avner, and Rahel was
beside him.

But even across the remaining stretch of water there
came to Leah something disquieting from Rahel—from the
way she stood, and, in the growing nearness, from her face
itself, though she smiled.

With the second breath of their embrace, Rahel spoke.
Only five days ago, at Har Tsafon in the north, an attack.

Josef Trumpeldor was dead, and among the five others—
—Not Gidon!
—Yaffaleh.

And so with the tumult of welcomings and orations around them, Leah and Menahem listened to the explanations of how the defenders had fallen, while in Leah's mind a whole other sequence of events had to be pressed back, the dark sequence of deaths that seemed to pursue those she touched, those she loved. No, no, she must not succumb, she must fight off such a fantasy, there was so much of death in man's world, it came everywhere, it touched everyone, no one brought it on.

But the accusation kept returning. In some way it had been Yaffaleh instead of herself who fell with Trumpeldor. "She loved him," her words broke out to Rahel. Why she was telling this, out of all her grief, she couldn't think, but she told of that moment long ago in Mishkan Yaacov when Josef had come by, and Yaffaleh, then only a child, had served him at the table, "and I saw it happening in her, oh, Rahel, as sometimes you see it happening in a little girl, she fell in love."

And so it must have remained all secretly within herself, and so it must have been that Yaffaleh had gone up with a group of young people answering the call sent out by Trumpeldor for reenforcements when the disorders grew acute up there at Shimshoni's settlement in the north.

The whole of the tragedy Leah heard, sitting in a corner of the Poale Zion hut, from Gidon's friend, Nathan and the Red, who had fought in the battle and made his way back. A month before, Nathan had received his discharge from the British, though Gidon still waited. With a few others of the newly discharged men, Nathan, too, uncertain what he was going to do with himself, uncertain whether to go back to England, had gone up in answer to Trumpeldor's call, printed in the workers' journal. Even, Nathan shrugged, with the thought of trying life and perhaps remaining there in the kibbutz.

Quietly, no longer with the biting anger she remembered in him, Nathan related the events—not as one resigned or removed, but as one who has at last met the full depth of his people's circumstance, and accepted the challenge to share it. Only two months ago, Nathan said, Trumpeldor had managed to reach the Yishuv from Turkey, coming alone while his kvutsa waited in Constantinople.

Already the trouble had started up north, and there was much discussion among the different parties and the Yishuv leaders as to whether shimshoni should not evacuate. The troubles had started not distinctly between Arabs and Jews, but between the British and the French. The former allies were already at loggerheads over this area, and their strife had fallen on the Jews. It was now known that from early in the war there had been secret treaties between the British and the French to divide the entire Levant when Turkey was defeated. Each was to have political and commercial control of a certain area. The borders in Palestine had not been too clear, and now the French were pressing their claim to the whole of upper Galilee, to be ruled from Beirut. They had occupied Metulla and planted guns on the hills.

The British had not entered the area, but certain sheikhs who had been in their pay during the taking of Damascus had begun to raid the French outposts. When the French retaliated by shelling a few Arab villages, a rumor spread that their observers were stationed in the Jewish settlements. The Arabs became threatening.

Since Shimshoni's two settlements were isolated, they could not be defended except by considerable reenforcement, and where was the strength to come from? The Shomer was broken. The best young men of the Yishuv had volunteered for the Jewish Brigade and had not yet been released. Just as the Yishuv was trying to organize itself, with the old dispute raging anew between the two labor parties, the Marxists and the non-Marxists, there had come the question of the evacuation. Arriving in the land, Josef Trumpeldor had issued a passionate appeal for unity among the workers, and then gone up to take command of the defense of Har Tsafon.

Again and again the Arab chieftain, Khamil Effendi from Halsah had appeared at the lower farm, claiming that French officers were hiding there. He had been allowed inside the compound and had found no one. Yet tension grew. Twice, men of the settlement were fired on as they plowed. Arabs in the area had been heard angrily declaring they would destroy the settlements. They had been excited and restless ever since last year's capture and plundering in Damascus.

Josef had sent out his appeal for reenforcements, but even Jabotinsky had argued that the outposts had to be abandoned. With a few other veterans, Nathan had decided to go up. They had found the spirit strong, but supplies dangerously low. For a few weeks things were quiet. From the kibbutz of Ayeleth HaShachar, a day's journey below in the valley, food and some ammunition arrived. The old colony of Metulla had suddenly been evacuated by the French, and Josef had moved in a small detachment to protect the settlers there. A messenger had got down to Ayeleth HaShachar with a new appeal for reenforcements and this time a youth group had come, marching in singing, Yaffaleh among them.

Yes, Nathan said, she had been in good spirits, happy. He had often been on guard duty at the lower farm, at Tel Chai, where she had worked in the fields and in the kitchen.

Then, anew, a plowman had been shot at in the fields and wounded. One of the chevreh, running to his help, had been killed. The flocks were brought into the compound; every defense post was manned.

The next morning Khamil Effendi had ridden up to the gates of Tel Chai together with several of his sons and nephews, all in full fighting regalia, with rifles, bandoliers and Damascus daggers, once more demanding entry to search for French officers. Lower on the slope, ominously, clusters of villagers could be seen. When the guard refused to open the gate, calling back for instructions, Khamil had drawn his dagger. One of the defenders had fired a signal shot, and from the upper farm, Josef, at breakfast, had rushed down with a few men, Nathan among them.

"Khamil was still shouting at the gate. Another Arab kept cursing, yelling, that the Jews had hidden a spy there once before, he himself knew it, and we were surely hiding enemies again."

—That had been for Zev, then. Leah did not bring it up.

"Trumpeldor talked to Khamil and agreed to let him inside alone. I myself was posted behind the house, in the barn." Altogether there had been hardly a score of defenders.

The sheikh had mounted the outer stairway to the small

chamber on the roof; three men and two girls, among them
Yaffaleh, were there in the room, sorting ammunition.

Trumpeldor waited at the foot of the stairs; suddenly
from the upper room came a cry from one of the girls,
"Josef! He's taking my revolver!"

"Fire!" Trumpeldor shouted. A moment later, Khamil
had thrown a grenade and fired his pistol into the room.
The five were killed.

Of Josef Trumpeldor's death, too, Nathan told. Struck in
the abdomen as he ran to close the gate, he had been hit
twice again before he could be pulled into the dwelling. "I
saw him hit, Leah, it was as though he shrank together."

From his first wound, his intestines pushed out; Josef
himself had pressed them back in and supervised the ban-
daging. "These are my last hours," he had said, appointing
another commander. All day while the battle continued,
Josef had remained conscious and given advice.

From the upper farm, a last handful of men came running, managing to disperse the crowd of villagers who had
surrounded Tel Chai. Under a white flag the Arabs had
been allowed to remove their dead from the field, but the
truce was broken when one of them picked up a rifle and
firing began anew. An attacker hurled a flaming bundle of
straw onto the roof, but Nathan and a comrade managed to
crawl up and fling it off, throwing several grenades after it
into the crowd of attackers. With this, the attack was broken. Silence came.

"Only then we went into the upstairs room and found
the dead. She died from pistol wounds—it must have been
quick, Leah, she couldn't have suffered long."

So it had been. With his old bitter irony, Nathan added,
"It was my first real day of battle. What was in the Brigade
was different."

At the upper farm there was a doctor, and he had come
at nightfall. Trumpeldor still lived; they had put him on a
cot and started toward Metulla in hope that the doctor
could operate there, but on the hill halfway between the
two farms, Josef began to gasp, they had to halt.

A convulsion went through him; he gasped a Russian
oath, and his favorite phrase, "It doesn't matter." There on

the hill the dead had been buried, the men in one grave, the two girls in another, alongside.

Nathan had finished. Leah was thankful he didn't attempt to console her. After a time, she told him about Russia.

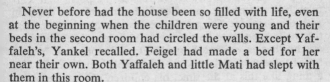

Never before had the house been so filled with life, even at the beginning when the children were young and their beds in the second room had circled the walls. Except Yaffaleh's, Yankel recalled. Feigel had made a bed for her near their own. Both Yaffaleh and little Mati had slept with them in this room.

Once more today bedding circled the walls, and little ones bounded underfoot, though trying to keep a quiet and solemn air because they knew there was a death. The soul of Yaffaleh, as Feigel said, had called together the whole family again.

There were the three children of Menahem and Dvorah, Menahem at last returned, together with Leah from Russia, and Shula's little one was walking and climbing everywhere while she carried her new baby in her arms. Reuven and his Elisheva would return to the kvutsa to sleep, and Gidon would stay with his Aviva in the old hut by the river; for a death in the family, the British had given him leave.

Yet though the house was filled, Yankel felt their departure already; after the Sabbath they would all leave, dispersing over the land; and another thing he knew, a thing they had been discussing amongst themselves: when they left this time, they meant to take his youngest with them. His yingel, Mati. He and Feigel would be left virtually alone with only Schmulik the ox. And wasn't Schmulik too only waiting to get married, to become the master and take over the farm, and be the one to make decisions while his father stood to the side?

So it would be, so Yankel felt it coming, and was no longer stirred up by the thought to struggle against it, for the last blow had taken his strength. Of Yaffaleh he was the one who spoke least, though what did any of them know of a father's thoughts and feelings? Of all the girls, she was the

one who as a little child would put her hand in his without
wanting anything of him.

When all were gathered after the meal, Reuven brought
out and placed on the table the little notebook of her intimate thoughts and her little writings that Gidon's army
comrade Nathan had found there in the house of the battle
and brought home to the family. They talked about Yaffaleh: how sensitive, even how gifted she had been, and when
all were hushed, Gidon's Aviva recited the poem that Yaffaleh had written the day when Gidon returned in the train
with the Brigade: The whole world, even the insects, even
the snails, seemed to be singing to Yaffaleh, "because today
my brother is coming home." Never before had Yankel
heard these words of hers; they had not thought to tell him
a thing like this at the time, his children did not know his
heart.

The lines were true poetry, Reuven's Elisheva said in her
clearly studied Hebrew, and, leaning across to the notebook in Reuven's hand, she read out another poem Yaffaleh had written:

> When dark falls, there the hut sits
> squat and heavy, a lump on the earth.
> It seems ugly and repels me.
> Then a lamp is lighted within,
> And all is changed . . .

Elisheva's voice caught in her throat, and across the table
Yankel saw Leah's large cheeks beginning to break into
twisting movements, the way even as a little girl her grief
would first show, before the tears came.

"It is she, it is Yaffaleh herself." Shula's Nahum was the
one to say what had come to all of them about the poem.

Heavy, a lump on the earth. Yankel knew the child had
thought of herself in that way, and time and time again at
night before sleep came, he and Feigel had talked worriedly together of their unfavored youngest daughter, and
what could they do? A father perhaps does not show much
of his thoughts to his daughters; perhaps they imagine he
does not know of their inmost feelings and worry about
them; but from their mother he knows all that is happening
in each one, and all this weighs on his heart. In Russia a
Jew had often to go on his voyages, a merchant, to bargain
for timber or for horses, and on his return he brought a

little fur muff for this one, a headscarf, a ribbon, for that
one, and with the gift and a kiss on the head, Tateh was
home again. But how had he and Feigel not worried about
their large-grown Leah, and how had they not discussed
and weighed and feared before they let her go off with Reuven to Eretz? Perhaps she had thought it was of no concern
to her Tateh? And here in the years when Feigel and Leah
had discussed what should be done for Yaffaleh, had he not
known from Feigel every word, every fear, about Yaffaleh's
dark moods and her friendlessness? All at once, the image
returned to Yankel of Yaffaleh standing before the great
poet Chaim Nachman Bialik, with the bouquet of flowers,
and, just as she had written in her own last little poem,
Yankel again saw the illumination that had been in her
then, a lamp lighted in the squat little house of her being.

And who of all his children had been the one to come all
the way to Tiberias with his tfillim for him in the prison?

And only three weeks ago, when she had marched off
with the Herzlia Gymnasia youngsters from Tel Aviv who
were going to join Trumpeldor—then she had looked to be
a happy young girl. Though all through the night before he
had spoken his misgivings to Feigel, when Yaffaleh alev
hashalom had marched off happily, Yankel had felt it was
for the best.

And who could tell, when a soul has such times of darkness, whether a death at a happy time is not for the best?
The death itself is God's to decide; man cannot dispute.
Yet sometimes a man must choose his course, and so must
a woman, and Yaffaleh, knowing her danger, had chosen to
go, and who could tell what was best?

Yankel at times took a pinch of snuff, and now was such
a moment, not to disguise his tears, but simply that the
momentary convulsion in his chest and lungs brought him
a kind of new breath, a clarity.

In this new breath, his thoughts moved out to the fates of
those who had remained in Russia, as Leah had told of
them. Feigel's brother, the rich Kalman Koslovsky, stood
against the wall of his sugar mill and shot, and his son
cold-bloodedly remaining there in the house, an officer in
their service, with the mother a prisoner upstairs—no, he
did not feel his revenge on Kalman, yet he had his
thoughts. His own sons, Reuven, Gidon, no matter how
distant they were from him in his beliefs—no, they would

not have served him with such a treachery after his death, no, they were still Jews.

And at least one thing in their Bolshevik land had happened for his daughter Leah: she was finished with "that one." So the word had come to Yankel from Feigel, "It is finished."

He peered now at Leah.

In olden times, Jacob, standing amongst his stalwart, tallgrown sons as Yankel imagined them—did Jacob the Patriarch feel himself augmented, more powerful in the surrounding strength of his sons, or as he grew older, did he fell shrunken before them?

Reuven had never stood taller than Yankel, yet now Yankel felt bowed and cramped under the hardships and blows that had befallen him; Gidon was a bit taller and he had such a clear strength over his whole being that Yankel felt diminished; Schmulik was broader of shoulder and as tall as Gidon—yet, however it had been with Jacob of old, Yankel did not feel his own strength expanded through his sons. And with daughters it was even more strange until their children grew about you. When Leah had been young, a girl, her largeness had seemed even pitiful to him, for to his mind there had always come the image of a man leading away a large acquiescent cow. But now here she sat, a huge, powerful woman, and even before her Yankel felt diminished.

What would become of Leah? Their eldest girl, unwed. True, among the chalutzim and in their kibbutzim an old maid was not so ended a matter; yet sometimes, talking with Feigel, a great pity came over him that for their daughter the new ways had had to happen, and that matters could not have been arranged, a passable marriage perhaps in the simpler ways at home.

Leah's eyes had the pained darkness in them, perhaps not only about Yaffaleh, to whom she had been the closest, but surely also because of Trumpeldor. Yankel had not needed Feigel's few remarks, that time years ago when the hero had visited the house, nor had he needed the mention of Trumpeldor's name now and again in the war years when Leah had stopped in at home, to know that within the big girl the hope had remained of a possibility. Perhaps indeed she had even been secretly in love with him. And as Feigel had said of poor Leah's fate, no sooner had she freed herself of "that one" and come home with the possibility alive, than she had found Josef dead.

His daughter's eyes had met his, and Leah let him gaze into hers until a profound undertanding passed between them, as though all his thoughts were acknowledged, the heartaches interchanged from one to the other, as though she even felt for his sense of waning power amongst his offspring. And yet it was Leah who led in the plan to take away the young one, his yingel, Mati; it was she whose ears had been filled with the pressing arguments of the melamed that the boy must be taken to the gymnasia in Tel Aviv to study and "become someone."

In Yankel this had awakened the whole war of his life. A father's pride he had, pride that the boy was bright, even gifted in learning; what Jewish father would not be proud, even though it was worldly learning rather than Torah?

In the old days it would have been simple; he himself had been judged gifted and sent to a good yeshiva. From the yeshiva a gifted young man made a good match and then engaged in years of study, or became a rabbi in a town better than his own. Except that he himself had been drawn into commerce, and so had wasted much of his life.

But what did it mean today to go away and study and "become somebody?" What "somebodies" were needed here, except good men of the soil to build up the Yishuv? An agronome, then? The yingel was not inclined that way, so much. His gift was in mathematics, they said. A professor somewhere? Was it for this they had returned to the land? In his bones Yankel felt that the boy's going away would turn out wrong; and yet he had to ask himself, wasn't it also because he was loath to let the young one go? The one born here. His last. A willing and good-tempered lad. None of them could know what gladness it brought to a father's heart simply to have the boy walk beside him in the field.

And there was the fierceness with which Mati had defended the field of grain, that time the Arabs had left the mark of the dirk in his back. It was here, here on the land that the son born here belonged.

Before the argument could begin, Yankel betook himself to the shul. While he was away, they all would be feverishly debating their plans and deciding who should approach him. And he—with whom could he talk of his problem? Even were he to go to Tiberias for a talk with his friend and marriage-relative, would he be understood? Binyamin Bagelmacher was after all still a merchant; their family had returned to Eretz, but not to the soil.

In the shul Yankel found Reb Roitschuler with whom, in the last years, he had become friendly. While the rest of their Roumanians had never made him feel he was more than a tenth man for the prayers, Roitschuler often asked news of his sons, his daughters, indeed of late there had been dropped words regarding Schmulik and Reb Roitschuler's granddaughter Nuta, now seventeen. The girl was, it suddenly struck Yankel, in appearance not unlike poor Yaffaleh, a short girl with a round face and heavy round legs and large breasts. Her beauty was in her long nut-colored braids; as Feigel and the village wives kept saying, Nuta's hair was so long she could sit on it. The possible match seemed suitable, though of course it would have to seem to happen of itself. Schmulik was known as the best farm worker in the village; Nuta, Feigel noted, had more than once on a Sabbath stroll made some excuse to enter the yard to marvel at Yaffaleh's flowerbeds, or to ask for a recipe; she had surely cast her eyes on Schmulik, and from his side too—he clearly did not look away from her.

During the prayer Yankel stood aside with Reb Roitschuler, and after his townsman again with heavy sighs had commiserated with him on the tragedy, and spoke of the ways of the Above One, Yankel let out what was troubling him about the plans for his youngest boy.

Reb Meir Roitschuler was nearly ten years older than Yankel; the hair of his beard was wiry, and he held himself erect so that, while of the same height as Yankel, he looked taller. He spoke with a deep slow voice, with the weightiness of a sage, though Yankel in his heart had never felt certain that the Roumanian was a true man of wisdom. Only now, in the tumult, grief, and doubt that engulfed him, the older man's words carried the solace of practical matters, of thoughts much like his own.

"Wherefore the great haste?" Reb Meir began. "If your boy is to enter the gymnasia, it will not yet be until the holidays in fall."

"True," Yankel said, "but they argue that the examinations come soon, and he would have to prepare at once. Our melamed does not even have the books for him."

"The books can easily be obtained, and the boy could prepare here, and still be of some help to you. You have now lost your daughter, and but for Schmulik will have to do everything alone. How will you manage? Your fine flock of geese—" Roitschuler spoke almost as one of the family—"isn't it now Mati who takes care of them?"

Yankel only nodded; of Yaffaleh's flock of geese he could not bear to calculate.

But Reb Roitschuler continued: Mati was not as yet Bar Mitzvah, he remarked, "and even though we know that in the end he will turn away like his brothers, at least let him learn Torah until his Bar Mitzvah. He can go a year later to the gymnasia."

True. And yet from the other side it had to be admitted that the Bible in its entirety, his children knew; they might not know the prayerbook, but it was a strange thing how well the unbelievers knew every footprint written of in the Bible.

Reb Roitschuler nodded in agreement at the puzzle, and then gazed a moment into Yankel's eyes. "I do not decry worldly learning," he said. "When has a Jew decried honest learning? But to go away there is time. There is always time. It is almost," Reb Roitschuler mused, smiling faintly into his beard with a different kind of commiseration, "as though his brothers and sisters . . ." he left the thought hanging. But he picked up the thread further on, repeating ponderously, "And Joseph became a great man, in a foreign land."

With the allusion there came to Yankel a shock of recognition. Was not this his own premonition, his own fear?

The boy was so eager, so avid for knowledge, once he started on the way, would he not go further and further?

What would there be for him to return to here?

As he walked ponderously homeward, Yankel knew they would already have settled it amongst themselves while he was away in shul. And soon, with the Sabbath over, they would all begin going away, dispersing, Reuven and his wife to their kibbutz, and Shula with Nahum and their little ones in their carriage to Tiberias; now with the British at least it could be said the road was safe even at night. To-

morrow morning it would be Dvora and Menahem and
their children going off to Gilboa; they had arrived on a
wagon of their chaverim on the way to a political meeting
in Kinnereth, and to return home they would borrow the
farm wagon, all of them together, Gidon and Aviva taking
Leah onward to Tel Aviv. And the certainty came to Yankel that Mati too, they must already have decided, would
be carried off with them in the wagon.

Dark had come, but at least in some things they still
respected him, they would not light the lamp on the Sabbath until the proper moment. The children were in the
yard making a contest of it, Dvoraleh's little Yechezkiel
cried out the first star in the same breath as Mati, and Mati
even let him cry out the second, but when it came to the
third, the one that counted, Yankel knew Mati would not
be so generous. Intently, everyone scanned the skies; Yechezkiel's little brother Giora at one moment cried, "Look,
look!" but it was the same pale second star that had already been counted, and in that very instant Mati cried
out, "There!" pointing, and his eyes, so sharp, like a Bedouin's, had perceived what it took everyone else a full moment to make out, a remote twinkle, a third star almost
directly overhead.

Giora for consolation was allowed to strike the match,
and then Yechezkiel applied it to the new pressure lamp,
which sizzled alight.

Finally the discussion must come. Turned away, Feigel
was preparing a hot cup of tea for him, and when she set it
down Yankel saw that her hand was not steady. Scanning
their faces, he knew it was Nahum that had been selected
to make the argument. This already was irksome. They
must have decided it should not be Reuven because with
Reuven he always quarreled. And why not Menahem? No,
already Nahum had begun with his smooth smile, the husband of his favorite daughter, the son of a pious household
still himself pretending to a bit of piety—oh, Yankel knew
him. At least his own unbelievers made no pretense, but
Nahum still wore his yarmulkeh in the house, though Yankel had caught sight of him more than once smoking his
cigarette on a Sabbath with the rest of them behind the
barn.

Smilingly, Nahum put forward all the arguments, Mati

meanwhile keeping his eyes away from his father. As Yankel knew, the boy was so gifted for learning, the melamed himself admitted he had no more to teach him; with his mathematical gift, who could even try to play chess with him any more?

Therefore they had de—Nahum nearly said *decided*, but changed in mid-word—they had *discussed* a plan. The cost would be as nothing, since Mati could stay with Leah at her girls' school at the edge of Tel Aviv; it would not be too far for him to walk to the gymnasia. As to the fees, Nahum himself was ready to advance the cost. For it would amount to a wrongdoing to fail to provide opportunity for a child who had such capacities . . .

Already Yankel inwardly flamed. Was this an allusion to Reuven? If Reuven had been able to study at a university, he might even have become another Aaronson, everyone was always saying. And what had become of Aaronson with all his learning and achievement? He had sunk half the Yishuv into torture through his brilliant ideas! Suddenly a storm of words broke out of Yankel—words that he would not have intended. "Mathematica! Calculations!" he cried. "All that is for commerce! For schemes and combinations! For merchants!" He flung out the words recklessly, at Nahum with his land-parcels to be sold in America, at his murdered brother-in-law Koslovsky with his sugar mill and his rent-collecting, at the whole Jewish past of moneylending and conniving. "What is the life of the brain-twister, the merchant? I lived it in bitterness! Our Jews lived it in bitterness for centuries! For the best but the worst years of my life, I had to be a merchant, and I say to you that a man cannot be a successful merchant without being a cheat and a thief. I came here and made a new life; even though I was no Gordon with all his philosophies and learning, I have built up this farm, we have a good meshek, and what was it all for? My family, my sons. In this, in the knowledge of the land we were at least one. My beliefs my sons don't follow and our God you don't worship, but in this, that we must restore ourselves to our land, that we must bind ourselves to the soil, in this—"

"But, Tateh," cried Reuven's wife, "who speaks of deserting the land? We need scholars, we need learned men in every field, we need experts—by the time Mati is finished

at the gymnasia, our University will be open in Jerusalem—"

Yes, yes, he knew, he had heard it all, Gidon had even
stood guard with the Brigade at the ceremony when Chaim
Wiezmann had placed there the twelve foundation stones
for the twelve tribes of Israel. Yet some powerful force
within Yankel still cried "No!"

"The Yishuv will need educated men," they were insisting.

"The Yishuv is here! Right here!" he shouted. "I need
him right here!"

Even Schmulik cried out, "What do you want, Tateh, to
make another ox of him, like me?"

At this, Yankel could not bear the torment. The anger,
the Chaimovitch anger, unreasoning, uncontrollable, was
upon him. He leaped up from the table. "The boy stays
here, and an end!" he shouted, and stormed from the
house.

He had not wanted to come to such anger. He had
wanted only to say, "Perhaps after the holidays. Perhaps in
another year." But because it was all of them, all of them
together against him, the anger had broken out . . .

In the barn, Yankel lighted a lamp, tended to the cattle.
Doubtless in the house they were packing the boy's things if
they had not already done so. They would pay no heed to
him. They had decided. Feigel too had let them decide.

Presently he heard Nahum driving away in his carriage.

A plan seized hold of Yankel. It was perhaps foolish,
futile, but he could not keep from doing it. Crawling under
the wagon, he propped up the axles. Laboriously, in the
dark, he took off the wheels, one by one, rolling them into
the kerosene shed, locking it with padlock.

When he lay down in the bed, Feigel did not stir.
"You're asleep?" he asked.

After a moment, she said, "We could get one of the girls
in the village to watch the geese. Even Roitschuler's girl,
Nuta."

Suddenly Yankel found himself saying, half-choked, "I
don't want to see the geese. Let the kvutsa take them all
away and join them to their own flock."

So deeply was he stricken. Feigel let her hand fall over

his, a rare tenderness between them, and he did not move
his hand away.

Then she spoke of one thing that had not come to him.
It was for Leah, she said, that Mati ought to go now. Had
he seen into Leah's eyes, seen her despair? If Mati would
go with her and stay with her for a time—with the yingel,
her spirit always lifted. Otherwise, there was such a darkness in Leah, Feigel feared for her. She couldn't tell what,
but she had a dreadful fear.

"Leah can come home. She can stay here."

"You know she won't do it. No, it would be as if everything was over for her. There, at least, she has the new girls
she brought. And with Mati—" It was Leah after all who
had received him onto her hands when he was born. "It
would be good for her, Yankel. It would help her through
the worst."

Yankel did not reply.

So it must have been for Jacob when his big sons returned from Egypt and declared that his Benjamin, the
child of his heart, his youngest, was demanded.

When he returned from the early Kaddish at the shul,
they were all of them gathered around the propped-up
wagon. His sons and daughters looked at him with such
eyes—as such strangers—was this what his life really deserved of them? The yingel, Mati, even worse, did not look
at him but turned with angry tears in his eyes and ran from
the yard.

No one spoke. Yankel went toward the house. "Yankel—" Feigel was by the pump. "Yankel, you will not
change anything. They will take him in any case. Don't
create hatred in your son."

Never had he felt such a total weeping within him. On
the ledge of the pump, Yankel set down the padlock key.

When they were ready to go, he came out of the house
nevertheless. Mati came over to him and said, "Shalom,
Abba." The boy had such a bright face, it sparkled. The
others were watching as though trying to think of something to say that would make it all easier; Yankel gave the
boy a shoulder-hug and said, "Go with my blessing."

His young daughter-in-law, Gidon's Aviva—from her he
felt the warmest understanding—came over and quietly

kissed him on the forehead. "You'll see, Abba, it will be good."

Then, after a long hugging and snuffling and a last packet of good things to eat from Feigel, Mati got onto the crowded wagon with the rest of them and Gidon drove off.

A saying from the ancient sage, the one called Gamzu, came to Yankel. It was the very saying from which the sage got his name, meaning, "This too." For to everything, even every disaster, the sage was wont to respond, "Gam zu l'tovah"—This too is for the good.

Nu, a saying. Yet who can tell which way is best for a Jew?

ABOUT THE AUTHOR

MEYER LEVIN is a man for whom life and art have never been divided. He has invested the personal experiences of his own life and actual events of contemporary history with meaning and illumination in his writing, always remaining faithful to his own Jewishness and his overriding concern with the Jewish ethos. Chicago, where Meyer Levin was born in 1907, was the scene of his early literary career and provided material for three of his best-known works. *The Old Bunch* (1937) was set in the west side of Chicago, where Meyer Levin was raised, and defined a whole generation's Jewish-American experience during the Depression. *Citizens* (1940) was based on the Chicago "little steel" strike, which he had witnessed. Another sensational Chicago story—the Leopold and Loeb case—suggested the essence of his brilliant psychological novel *Compulsion* (1956). Palestine figured early in Meyer Levin's life and career. As a young man in 1925 he first went to the Holy Land and was struck by the dynamic idealism of the Jewish settlers. Two years later he worked on a kibbutz near Haifa, an experience he later transformed in *Yehuda*, the first novel to describe life on a kibbutz. *The Settlers*, covering the 1907–1920 period of the settlement of Israel owes much of its verisimilitude to these early visits, when tales of pioneer generation were prevalent and many of the legendary figures still alive. *The Harvest*, covering the years 1920 through Israeli independence in 1948, is the continuation of the lives of the characters first seen in *The Settlers*, and it is once again a logical outgrowth of Meyer Levin's interest in and devotion to the new state of Israel.

Meyer Levin turned to writing to synthesize his ideas in an autobiography, *In Search* (1950), where he examines the Jewish psyche in the modern world and defines his own role as a "writer-link" between Israel and the American-Jewish community. In 1956 Levin, his wife Tereska Torres and their two children moved to Israel where he wrote *Eva, The Fanatic, The Stronghold, Gore and Igor, The Settlers* and *The Harvest*. Between novels, Meyer Levin has been a folklorist, playwright, screen writer and contributor to major magazines such as *Esquire, Commentary* and *The New Yorker*. He is also the author of a group of educational books for Jewish youth. Mr. Levin currently divides his time between Israel and New York.

A Special Preview of
the opening pages of the sequel to
THE SETTLERS

THE HARVEST
by
Meyer Levin

"The most impressive book about Jewishness,
Zionism in Israel, America and Europe."
—Irwin Shaw

1

ON THE old docks of Jaffa, exactly where the Chaimovitch family had arrived twenty years back —the extent of Mati's lifetime, since he was already felt in the womb during the drawn-out voyage from Odessa—they were all gathered at summer's end in 1927 to see the lad off to America.

Mati reached the dock early, crowded on the cart seat between his eldest sister, Leah and Giantess, and her life comrade, Natan the Red; although his departure would surely have warranted a special wagon trip, Mati himself had insisted on combining with the morning delivery of carrots, eggplant, and cucumbers from Leah's training farm for girls, at the far edge of Tel Aviv alongside the river Yarkon, to the Carmel market where they would already be almost in Jaffa. For he wanted to arrive early and have plenty of time in case of unforeseen British regulations and procedures, and also he wanted already to be there in case his brother Gidon arrived on the first train from Herzlia. Gidon had so much to do just now, building his house, and with his busy veterinary work in the new town, that Mati had insisted he ought not even come, so at least Gidon shouldn't be left wasting time waiting for them if he arrived early. Though Natan snorted not to worry for Gidon—even in the Jewish Legion, when they had waited months for the British to send them against the Turks, Gidon had never wasted his time—so now if he had arrived ahead of them at the port, Gidon would probably already have found a lame horse to take care of.

The cable from Mati's sponsor, the American scholar Horace Rappaport, at last verifying his tuition grant, had arrived from Chicago only a week ago, at home in Mishkan Yaacov, where Mati had worked all summer every summer during his years at the Herzl Gymnasia in Tel Aviv. With the cable Mati had hurried off to make arrangements for a passport, visas, passage, staying as during his high school days on his sofa at Leah's.

Last night he had said his farewell to his Zippie of the Long Braids, who refused to follow the hair-bob rage from America, not out of conservatism but out of vanity, as she herself put it, with her usual mockery; they had gone strolling on the beach, stopping for kisses, strolling barefoot, in sudden serious talk always punctured by Zippie's humor—ach, after his years in Chicago Mati was certain to return in plus fours chewing a big cigar, married to a Chicago sausage heiress, whom he was bringing for a brief visit to his family, while she herself, having faithfully waited for him, Zippie preposterously proclaimed, would brokenheartedly bow to the will of her Orthodox parents and accept a matchmaker's match with a wealthy Polish land speculator; she would cut off all her hair not for the fashion but for a religious wig, a shaitl, at least a gorgeous high-style one such as you saw on Allenby Road, and she would resign herself to raising a flock of little sons with dangling ear curls! Laughing to tears at the image, Mati suddenly felt sure that Zippie with her humorous mouth was really the One and seized her in their longest, most passionate tongue kiss.

From the Carmel market, Natan turned onto the old road to Jaffa. Ah, where in America would Mati ever see a chain of camels still plodding among the droshkies, or even a droshky among the taxis? And at the bottom of the street Mati had his last look at the Herzl Gymnasia itself, still the most imposing structure of the town, with its castlelike portico where he and his friends had so often lingered, and indeed from which he and his troop of scouts in white Russian blouses had marched to Rothschild Boulevard to the wedding of the visiting American scholar Horace Rappaport, who had carried off their favorite English teacher, Celia, to Chicago, where indeed she and her family had come from in the heyday after the Balfour Declaration.

As they clopped toward Jaffa, Leah could not fail to remark how on her arrival in the land with Reuven, a year ahead of the rest of the family, all this had been empty sand. And as the minaret of Jaffa's Hassan Beq mosque came before them, the same thought lay unspoken among all three—of the sniping from up there during the evil May Day massacre of 1921, when Mati, a schoolboy from the Jordan Valley, had run with a cudgel, when Natan and Gidon had dug out their pistols kept from their years in the Brigade, when Leah had helped carry back the wounded and the dead from this in-between area, laying them out in rows on the assembly hall floor of the Gymnasia. But now all was quiet, the cart passed among the produce-laden donkeys, and Leah called out her cheerful Maasalam now and again to Arab standkeepers; everybody knew and grinned back at Big Leah. Indeed, ever since that raging May Day outburst against the "muscob" with their red-flag parade of Jewish workers, there had been quiet in the land. Partly because of this sense of peace, Mati did not feel so bad about going away to study.

With the ship cost from America, the scholar might not be back for four whole years, not even during summers, so to say farewell to the youngest, the yingel, born a whole generation after Reuven, mother Feigel got her one richly married daughter Shula to poke chubby Nahum awake at dawn so as to drive from Tiberias with the huge American automobile that he had bought for carrying guests from his fancy new hotel to the city's celebrated Hot Springs. The season of the Hot Springs had not yet begun, and besides, Nahum often used his hotel taxi as a Private; he could very well drive the family even all the way to Jaffa today, to see Mati off to America.

Though Nahum with his heavy-lidded round eyes was quick enough once awake, early rising he had long ago given up, along with the practice of accompanying his pious father for the dawn prayer; now that Nahum had the new hotel, his own, he took his time rising. But of all Shula's family it was to young Mati that he sparked; this one was no ox like the next-up brother, Schmulik, who worked their meshek in constant bickering with their aging father, Yankel. Nor would Mati be likely to settle in a kvutsa like their dreamy, idealistic Reuven. This Mati had a different head on him; besides, in the back of his own head Nahum had certain ideas regarding a vast coastal orange grove development to be sold in parcels to American Jewry, and it might prove quite useful to have a family contact, a college student in Chicago; Nahum didn't at all mind rising this day at dawn to drive the lot of them to Jaffa, where he had some Arab landowners to talk to as well.

Indeed, it was Nahum who had to poke Shula and hurry her through her decisions on what to wear for Tel Aviv and how to do her hair, reminding her that it was, after all, not to greet the High Commissioner that they were setting forth and that they still had to stop to pick up Reuven and Elisheva in their kibbutz on the way to Mishkan Yaacov.

At least those two were waiting at their kibbutz gate. Then at the farmstead Mama Feigel had to load in her hampers and her gift parcels to her sister in America—twenty-three years since they had laid eyes on each other, Feigel kept repeating. Schmulik had already departed for Jaffa on his own, for that one on any pretext would zoom off on his motorcycle; his Nussya was staying behind her with babies—true, there was hardly room for her even in the big Buick because on the way through the Vale of Esdraelon Nahum still had to halt to Gilboa to pick up the middle sister, Dvora. Her husband, Menahem, they'd meet in Tel Aviv, for Menahem was again delegated there on some pretext of agricultural planning, as though every British CID man didn't know Menahem sat high up in the Haganah. Divora herself, Nahum respected. In her steadfast, single-minded way she had built up the largest and most modern poultry run in the entire Yishuv, even providing other settlements with her special breed of incubated chicks; indeed, if it was ever imaginable that such a one would leave her kvutsa, Nahum could see himself adding a poultry-raising enterprise to his planned citrus-grove enterprise for investors in the Diaspora.

Dvora was ready, wearing her embroidered Sabbath blouse. Squeezing in between Feigel and Elisheva, she exchanged news about everybody's children—all thriving, Feigel said, thank the Above.

With Natan staying by the cart on the lookout for Gidon, Leah and Mati threaded their way to the harbor edge, where the fishing boats bobbed and the catch was being sorted; from here they saw what was surely Mati's ship, fat and whitish, arriving from her stop in Haifa. Lighters were already being rowed to meet her, but as the steamer dropped anchor, few passengers could be made out descending; these days, because of two years of hard times and unemployment, hardly any immigrants arrived. Still, perhaps some had debarked at Haifa, Leah said hopefully. Gazing at Mati, she joked a bit about last night with his Zippie, trying to get him to tell more. And then Leah sighed about how half of her girls at the training farm had been in love with him; Mati knew what a disappointment it was to Leah that with all the maidens she had put in his way in these years nothing had happened, and he broke into laughter now, and she too, while she admonished, "Aye, Mati! You're just at the age! Be careful there in America; at this age a mistake can ruin whole years of a life!" She was still grinning, but a bit woefully, and Mati knew it was her admission about her ten years lost over her Handsome Moshe, a subject Leah still never touched on and that no one touched on in her presence. This warning was the most intimate she could give him in their parting, and Leah suddenly engulfed him in all her flesh, her baby! Mati flushed as though hearing again her unabashed description of how their mama, Feigel, had given birth to him right into her hands. And they threaded their way back to Natan. Still no sight of Gidon. The train had arrived, as droshkies were now bringing more passengers with their baggage; some were tourists, the last of the season, but also Mati noticed a few families plainly from the Yishuv, a pair with two babies and endless bundles and roped-up valises, all their possessions it seemed, and Leah even believed she recognized them, from Chedera. Ieaving the land. In the last year this had become a common sight; more were leaving, it was whispered, than were entering the Yishuv. Going down from Zion. "Yordim."

A fleck of worry even now came to Mati that he might be mistaken for one such, ready, bag and baggage, to desert. And Leah must have sensed this discomfort in him, for she led the way to a café behind the dock area.

Now, with the ship already sitting out there—though there was still nearly two hours to boarding time—Mati became fidgety; of course, the family could not yet have got here all the way from Tiberias, but where was Gidon? It was Gidon who could give Mati the greatest certainty that he was doing the right thing, to go.

Though Mati had said his farewells a few days before when he had departed from the meshek to get his passport, a father still had to make the journey to see off his yingel, and besides, Yankel knew, Feigel would have inundated him with reproaches or, even worse, taken to her bitter silences had he perhaps suggested staying away from that cursed port of Jaffa, where he had not set foot since their arrival in the land, when the bandit Arab boatmen had stopped their rowing and demanded extra baksheesh, tearing his last coins from his hand, threatening to hurl him and his whole family into the sea, like Jonah before him, only there would be no whale to spit them up! Where indeed had those Moslem bandits learned of Jonah!

Perhaps for four long years he would not see his youngest again, or who even knew when young people went to America whether they would ever return at all to Eretz! Such thoughts, Feigel cried, let them burn like raw vinegar in his entrails!— Giving him one of her looks as for a cockroach. So Yankel had defiantly persisted. And what? In the colleges there in America did not Jewish boys meet shiksehs and marry them? And finish! And an end! Wasn't that how it had been with Yehuda Schneirson's son from Kfar Tabor, who had not needed even to go as far as America, but only to Paris, never to return?

"What do they believe in, your godless children? What would it matter to them, a shikseh or not?" Yankel continued to complain in his usual way. "Unbelievers! Heathens! Apikoirasim!" But inwardly he had long ago lost his bitterness toward their yingel. Despite Yankel's seizure of violence when the youngest had first been taken off to study in Tel Aviv, kidnapped by the older brothers and sisters, Leah and Gidon, the ringleaders of the plot, these years had not proved out Yankel's misgivings. Each summer, just as in these last months, Mati had returned and labored in the meshek like a good settler's son; together with Schmulik, he had extended the groves; a pleasant sight it had been to Yankel, though he would never speak of this to them, to watch them as he wound on his tefillin, while they yoked up the two teams of mules and made off to the fields, leaving him only the smaller tasks around the cattle barn. And in the wheat harvest he and his offspring together, even Gidon coming home to lend a hand, following Reuven sitting high on the huge machine he had brought from his kibbutz for a modest share of the crop. And much as Yankel had protested, this did turn out advantageously in the end. No, nor had his first visceral resistance to the yingel's removal to the city remained in Yankel: his fear of the citified Diaspora luftmensh disease infecting his sons, from the speculators and swindlers permeating that unproductive nothingness built on sand, arriving in the new wave of immigrants from Poland and Rumania. Rumanians especially Yankel had always distrusted, though the group in Mishkan Yaacov had turned out not so bad if you kept your distance from them, even if Schmulik had married among them. Perhaps also Mati had been protected from all such because he lived in Leah's meshek, outside the city itself, though soon enough that pullulating Tel Aviv would smother it, the speculators were already sniffing around, he had heard. Yet a wonder—now Yankel smiled to himself in his beard—a wonder his young Mati hadn't got himself attached to one of Leah's girls there; as Leah said, all the young chalutzoth were crazy for the boy. Oh, his yingel, he would have his time

with the girls! Of all the sons, Yankel had always
secretly felt, though only grunting when his Feigel
declared the same, Mati was the most favored.
And only deep within himself Yankel admitted
there would be now a long-stretching loneliness
as there had been every winter without the boy; the
house was empty now, only himself and his old
woman, even if Schmulik and Nussya lived close
by.

A whole swarm of porters and beggars and vendors had to be dispersed as Nahum's glossy Private,
still shining through the dust of the traversed land,
came to a halt at the port entrance.

Amid the greeting clamors of the assembling
family all of Feigel's parcels and hampers were
handed out, even a specially oilcloth-wrapped huge
round raisin kugel, Mati's favorite delicacy, while
he laughed. "Ima, it's heavy enough to sink the
whole ship!"

Saved up for her mother, Leah had a wonderful
tidbit of family news that she herself had only a
few days ago received from her chaverah Rahel,
the very first person who had greeted her here on
the docks of Jaffa the day she and Reuven had
arrived, young pioneers of the movement. In those
early days it had been the habit of Rahel with her
chaver, Yitzhak, or Avner as he was called by his
underground name, to come to the Jaffa docks to
meet every ship from Odessa on the chance that a
few chalutzim might be landing. Today, of course,
Leah's friends Rahel and Yitzhak Ben-Zvi were
leaders of the Yishuv. Feigel always saw their
names in *Davar*, heads of the workers this and the
the women workers that, of the Jewish Council and
of the Histadrut Labor Federation and of the
Socialist Party, with their chaver David Ben-Gur-
ion, also a close chaver of Leah's from those early
days, a pity he was such a tiny fellow and Leah
a giantess, or something might really have hap-

pened between them! In any case, as Leah now
related, just a few months ago despite the fact that
Zionism was already outlawed by the Soviets—
might they all freeze into icebergs in their own
Siberia where they were sending good Jews—only
a few months ago, despite this ban on Zionism, a
delegation from the Yishuv had been admitted to
the World Agricultural Conference in Moscow,
and from there Rahel as a women's delegate had
brought back a piece of family news for the
Chaimovitches! For around the edges of the conference, Leah related, here and there a Jew, hanging
about, had managed to have a bit of conversation
with one from Eretz, and thus a longtime Zionist from their own town of Cherezinka, a certain
Zalman the Shoemaker—did Feigel remember him?
Indeed, Feigel remembered, for her brother Kalman the Rich, the beet-sugar mill owner, used to
have Zalman make boots for the entire family; with
Zalman's boots there were none to compare! Also,
Leah reminded her mother, it was in the rear of
Zalman's shop that the Young Pioneers of Zion
used to meet. And Leah herself had seen this Zalman when she had gone back eight years ago on
her mission to find the remnants of the Zionist
Youth and bring them to Eretz. Still faithful Zalman
was, a wonder not arrested, except that the com-
missars too coveted his boots. Thus, during the
recent conference he had come to Moscow and approached Rahel and asked for news of Leah and
the other Chaimovitches and sent greetings and
even given news of their relatives still remaining
in Cherezinka. Of Feigel's own family, the Koslov-
skys, there remained only her sister-in-law, the
widow of Kalman, the rich Kalman having been
shot, as they already knew, in the Revolution.
But still alive was his son Tolya, a revolutionist
from boyhood despite his father's riches, the same
Tolya who used to have such arguments with

Reuven about Marxism and Zionism. This very same Tolya was to this day the commissar of Cherezinka, as he had already been at the time of Leah's visit, and only this year, after two sons, a little girl had been born to him. That was the family news. A girl—wait, even her name Rahel had brought back from Zalman—the little girl's name was Tanya.

Indeed, as Leah had sensed it would, this news momentarily lifted Feigel's heaviness over her yingel's departure for so long a time; this family news was indeed something for Mati to carry to America, to bring to Feigel's sister in America, in New Jersey, to his aunt Hannah. A sign of new life in the family, even from the old land now closed off.

And so Mati was admonished by his mother: You hear? Not to forget the baby's name—Tanya. Born to their brother Kalman's son Tolya. With so many messages, Mati had best write it down, Tanya.

Then Menahem was among them. He often had that way of appearing without being noticed, though Mati was sure that Menahem himself always noticed everyone and everything, yet without the piercing eyes or the tense manner that you saw in some of those onetime Shomers. He looked somewhat like a certain math teacher at the Gymnasia, smallish, preoccupied; he even looked something like Eliahu, who everybody knew was the secret head of the Organization—a bit of an office type, a pakid. Menahem exchanged a few words with Dvora, and now with his small smile that always quickly dissolved he took Mati aside: Had he had any further ideas on what he wanted to study? In what to specialize? No special bent had come to Mati; indeed, he did not feel himself exactly a scholar. Maybe that was not a bad thing, said

Menahem, the bit of a smile reappearing and vanishing. Nor, however, did Mati feel a practical call, for engineering or for agricultural studies, such as Reuven had tried to awaken in him. Not in history either, at least not the kind where you had to remember all sorts of dates. Social studies, how things came to change, how governments worked, not so much formal politics, but social ideas, socialism itself, this he had been good at in school. Menahem approved, yes, perhaps politics, he said, political science; the University of Chicago was said to be good for such studies. He even knew a name there, a famous economist, Veblen; Mati must remember. You could trust Menahem to have found out such things. Horace Rappaport might try to direct Mati into theories of education, Menahem said; this was valuable and also highly needed here in the Yishuv, but he didn't believe this was exactly Mati's bent; he grinned, showing a golden tooth. Well, Menahem had no fear but that Mati would find the best field for himself. Perhaps also, an odd thought, but Menahem had picked up the information that in the same University of Chicago there was not only the renowned Professor Breasted, who had carried out the great excavations here in Eretz at Megiddo—wait, he knew Mati was not one to bury himself in the past, even if this meant unburying the past! Mati laughed at this typical touch of Menahem's wittiness, which he showed not in general meetings and such but only to those to whom he was quite close. At this same university there was an outstanding Arabist, Menahem said, and it wouldn't hurt for Mati to study a bit of their history and literature.

Then, as they circled back, for Mati saw a few passengers already handing over their baggage to Arab boatmen, Menahem slipped him a bit of paper containing a name and address in New York. In case. And to let this chaver in New York always know where he could be reached.

There was Gidon arriving, Menahem said. Where? Everyone had expected Gidon to come hurrying from the station, but it had to be Menahem who caught sight of him on his wagon, his little Herzeleh gripping the reins with him, and Aviva with Nurit on her lap—the whole kaboodle had come! The touch of anxiety lifted from Mati; indeed, Gidon was still in good time.

They had come by wagon, Gidon said, so as to pick up some Arab floor tiles, the old-style ones with all the colors, that Aviva perferred for the house. And as Aviva hopped down, Mati flushed at the touch of her fresh lips; she looked and felt so young, as though she were still one of Leah's learning girls.

Though Reuven was the eldest, it was Gidon whom Mati had always felt was the big brother. With Reuven living at his kvutsa, it was Gidon who had set Mati the first time on a horse. And then in the big war, though Reuven too was a sort of soldier, conscripted to labor by the Turks, it was Gidon who had got away to join the British in Egypt, and who had sent letters from the battles in Gallipoli and then from London, and who had been among the first to enroll in the Jewish Brigade, and who had returned with the conquering troops of General Allenby in the very days of the Balfour Declaration for the Jewish homeland!

Though Reuven, the book lover, had also declared that Mati must leave the meshek and study, it was Gidon who had set the wheels back on the wagon after Abba hid them to prevent the boy's departure, and it was Gidon who had brought Mati to the Gymnasia.

Yes, Gidon was telling his Herzeleh, right here on this dock the Turkish police had flung him onto a boat. In the great war. Right here the Turkish police of those days, oh, much fiercer-looking than the British police of today—with bayonets and lashes the Turks had rounded up the Jews of Jaffa and put them on boats and expelled them from the land because, having originally arrived from Russia, they were Russkis, and in the Great War Russkis were the enemies of the Turks. And that had been the beginning of Gidon's wanderings until he returned a victor in the First Jewish Brigade!

And this old tale too gave Mati more heart for his departure; like Gidon who had gone out to the world from here, he would be sure to return.

The hugs, the last admonitions from Ima, Leah, everyone, even Abba embracing him awkwardly with pats on the shoulder and under his breath— as for himself alone—muttering the blessing for the voyage. And Schmulik hitting his back and slipping an extra ten-pound note into his hand, never mind from where, extra money, he had been working outside the farm on the Rutenberg electrification dam on the Jordan. "Take it! Special for some good times!" Schmulik leered. "Girls!" And a last extra hug from Dvora, who was crying. And Mati was climbing into the bobbing vessel, the Arab boatmen this time in great good humor, chanting and laughing, Yallah! Farewell Yahud!

And so continues the mighty saga that follows the fortunes of the Chaimovitch family from 1927 to 1948. Mati, after receiving an education in America returns to help build the state of Israel.

Read the complete Bantam Book, available April 1st, wherever paperbacks are sold.

RELAX!
SIT DOWN
and Catch Up On Your Reading!

Bantam Book Catalog

Here's your up-to-the-minute listing of over 1,400 titles by your favorite authors.

This illustrated, large format catalog gives a description of each title. For your convenience, it is divided into categories in fiction and non-fiction—gothics, science fiction, westerns, mysteries, cookbooks, mysticism and occult, biographies, history, family living, health, psychology, art.

So don't delay—take advantage of this special opportunity to increase your reading pleasure.

Just send us your name and address and 50¢ (to help defray postage and handling costs).

BANTAM BOOKS, INC.
Dept. FC, 414 East Golf Road, Des Plaines, Ill. 60016

Mr./Mrs./Miss_____
                  (please print)

Address_____

City_____State_____Zip_____

Do you know someone who enjoys books? Just give us their names and addresses and we'll send them a catalog too!

Mr./Mrs./Miss_____

Address_____

City_____State_____Zip_____

Mr./Mrs./Miss_____

Address_____

City_____State_____Zip_____

FC—9/76